SWANN'S WAY

Marcel Proust was born in Anteuil in 1871. His father, an eminent Professor of Medicine, was Roman Catholic and his mother was Jewish, factors that were to play an important role in his life and work. He was a brilliant, very literary schoolboy, and later a half-hearted student of law and political science. In his twenties he became an assiduous society figure, frequenting the most fashionable Paris salons of the day. During this period he published a volume of sketches and stories, *Les plaisirs et le jours*, and between 1895 and 1900 wrote a novel, *Jean Santeuil*, which was in many ways a first draft for his masterpiece *A la recherche du temps perdu*. After 1899 his chronic asthma, the death of his parents and his growing impatience with society caused him to lead an increasingly retired life. In the early 1900s he produced celebrated literary pastiches and translations of Ruskin, *The Bible of Amiens* and *Sesame and Lilies* and it was during this period that he wrote *Contre Sainte-Beuve*, although it was not published until 1954. From 1907, he rarely emerged from a sound-proofed room in his apartment on the Boulevard Hausmann in Paris, in order to insulate himself against the distractions of city life as well as the effect of the trees and flowers which he loved but which brought on his attacks of asthma. He slept by day and worked by night, writing letters and devoting himself to the completion of *A la recherche du temps perdu*. He died in 1922 before the publication of the last three books of his great work. With *A la recherche du temps perdu* Proust attempted the perfect rendering of life in art, of the past recreated through memory. It is both a portrait of the artist and a discovery of the aesthetic by which the portrait is painted, and it was to have an immense influence on the literature of the twentieth century.

MARCEL PROUST

Swann's Way

TRANSLATED BY
C. K. Scott Moncrieff

PENGUIN BOOKS

À Monsieur

GASTON CALMETTE

Comme un témoignage de profonde et
affectueuse reconnaissance

MARCEL PROUST

*

PENGUIN BOOKS

Published by the Penguin Group

Penguin Putnam Inc., 375 Hudson Street, New York, New York 10014, U.S.A.

Penguin Books Ltd, 27 Wrights Lane, London W8 5TZ, England

Penguin Books Australia Ltd, Ringwood, Victoria, Australia

Penguin Books Canada Ltd, 10 Alcorn Avenue, Toronto, Ontario, Canada M4V 3B2

Penguin Books (NZ) Ltd, 182–190 Wairau Road, Auckland 10, New Zealand

Penguin Books Ltd, Registered Offices: Harmondsworth, Middlesex, England

First published as *Du côté de chez Swann*

(the first volume of *A la recherche du temps perdu*) 1913

This translation first published 1922

Published in Penguin Books 1957

5 7 9 10 8 6

All rights reserved

ISBN 0 14 11.8058 7

Printed in the United States of America

This edition of *Swann's Way* reprints C. K. Scott Moncrieff's original translation of *Du côté de chez Swann* – the first of the seven volumes of *A la recherche du temps perdu* – which was published seventy-five years ago, in September 1922, two months before Proust died.

At the time of his death Proust left his unfinished novel in an unrevised and partly unpublished state. Successive French editors have corrected the errors and omissions of the early editions and moved towards a definitive text. This progress has been reflected in Terence Kilmartin's revision of Scott Moncrieff's complete translation, published in 1981, and in D. J. Enright's recent further revision (1992).

However, Scott Moncrief has never been replaced, and, as Proust's biographer George Painter remarked, the original *A la recherche* was itself 'a masterly recreation of its original'. Scott Moncrieff introduced the English-speaking world to Proust, and *Swann's Way* introduces Proust's world to us, as well as being in itself a complete and finished work.

Translator's Dedication

To E. J. C.

Here, Summer lingering, loiter I
    When I, with Summer, should be gone ...
Where only London lights the sky
    I go, and with me journeys 'Swann'

Whose pages' dull, laborious woof
    Covers a warp of working-times,
Of firelit nights beneath your roof
    And sunlit days beneath your limes,

While, both at once or each in turn,
    Sharp-tongued but smooth, like buttered knives,
We pared, with studied unconcern,
    The problems of our private lives;

Those tiny problems, dense yet clear,
    Like ivory balls by Chinese craft
Pierced (where each hole absorbed a tear)
    And rounded (where the assembly laughed).

Did all our laughter muffle pain,
    Our candour simulate pretence?
Fear not. I shall not come again
    To tease you with indifference.

Yet I may gaze for Oakham spire
    Where London suns set, watery-pale,
And dream, while tides of crimson fire
    Sweep, smoking, over Catmos vale.

MICHAELMAS, 1921   C. K. S. M.

Contents

*

Overture

For a long time I used to go to bed early. Sometimes, when I had put out my candle, my eyes would close so quickly that I had not even time to say 'I'm going to sleep.' And half an hour later the thought that it was time to go to sleep would awaken me; I would try to put away the book which, I imagined, was still in my hands, and to blow out the light; I had been thinking all the time, while I was asleep, of what I had just been reading, but my thoughts had run into a channel of their own, until I myself seemed actually to have become the subject of my book: a church, a quartet, the rivalry between François I and Charles V. This impression would persist for some moments after I was awake; it did not disturb my mind, but it lay like scales upon my eyes and prevented them from registering the fact that the candle was no longer burning. Then it would begin to seem unintelligible, as the thoughts of a former existence must be to a reincarnate spirit; the subject of my book would separate itself from me, leaving me free to choose whether I would form part of it or no; and at the same time my sight would return and I would be astonished to find myself in a state of darkness, pleasant and restful for the eyes, and even more, perhaps, for my mind, to which it appeared incomprehensible, without a cause, a matter dark indeed.

I would ask myself what o'clock it could be; I could hear the whistling of trains, which, now nearer and now farther off, punctuating the distance like the note of a bird in a forest, showed me in perspective the deserted countryside through which a traveller would be hurrying towards the nearest station: the path that he followed being fixed for ever in his memory by the general excitement due to being in a strange place, to doing unusual things, to the last words of conversation, to farewells exchanged beneath an unfamiliar lamp which echoed still in his ears amid the silence of the night; and to the delightful prospect of being once again at home.

I would lay my cheeks gently against the comfortable cheeks of my pillow, as plump and blooming as the cheeks of babyhood. Or I would strike a match to look at my watch. Nearly midnight. The hour when an invalid, who has been obliged to start on a journey and to sleep in a strange hotel, awakens in a moment of illness and sees with glad relief a streak of daylight showing under his bedroom door. Oh, joy of joys! it is morning. The servants will be about in a minute: he can ring, and someone will come to look after him. The thought of being made comfortable gives him strength to endure his pain. He is certain he heard footsteps: they come nearer, and then die away. The ray of light beneath his door is extinguished. It is midnight; someone has turned out the gas; the last servant has gone to bed, and he must lie all night in agony with no one to bring him any help.

I would fall asleep, and often I would be awake again for short snatches only, just long enough to hear the regular creaking of the wainscot, or to open my eyes to settle the shifting kaleidoscope of the darkness, to savour, in an instantaneous flash of perception, the sleep which lay heavy upon the furniture, the room, the whole surroundings of which I formed but an insignificant part and whose unconsciousness I should very soon return to share. Or, perhaps, while I was asleep I had returned without the least effort to an earlier stage in my life, now for ever outgrown; and had come under the thrall of one of my childish terrors, such as that old terror of my great-uncle's pulling my curls, which was effectually dispelled on the day – the dawn of a new era to me – on which they were finally cropped from my head. I had forgotten that event during my sleep; I remembered it again immediately I had succeeded in making myself wake up to escape my great-uncle's fingers; still, as a measure of precaution, I would bury the whole of my head in the pillow before returning to the world of dreams.

Sometimes, too, just as Eve was created from a rib of Adam, so a woman would come into existence while I was sleeping, conceived from some strain in the position of my limbs. Formed by the appetite that I was on the point of gratifying, she it was, I imagined, who offered me that gratification. My body, conscious that its own warmth was permeating hers, would strive to become one with her, and I would awake. The rest of humanity seemed very remote in comparison with this woman whose company I had left but a moment ago: my cheek was still warm with her kiss, my body bent beneath the weight of hers. If, as would sometimes happen, she had the appearance of some woman whom I had known in waking hours, I would abandon myself altogether to the sole quest of her, like people who set out on a journey to see with their own eyes some city that they have always longed to visit, and imagine that they can taste in reality what has charmed their fancy. And then, gradually, the memory of her would dissolve and vanish, until I had forgotten the maiden of my dream.

When a man is asleep, he has in a circle round him the chain of the hours, the sequence of the years, the order of the heavenly host. Instinctively, when he awakes, he looks to these, and in an instant reads off his own position on the earth's surface and the amount of time that has elapsed during his slumbers; but this ordered procession is apt to grow confused, and to break its ranks. Suppose that, towards morning, after a night of insomnia, sleep descends upon him while he is reading, in quite a different position from that in which he normally goes to sleep, he has only to lift his arm to arrest the sun and turn it back in its course, and, at the moment of waking, he will have no idea of the time, but will conclude that he has just gone to bed. Or suppose that he gets drowsy in some even more abnormal position; sitting in an arm-chair, say, after dinner: then the world will fall topsy-turvy from its orbit, the magic chair will carry him at full speed through time and space, and when he opens his eyes again he will imagine that he went to sleep months earlier and in some far distant country. But for me it was enough if, in my own bed, my sleep was so heavy as completely to relax my consciousness; for then I lost all sense of the place in which I had gone to sleep, and when I awoke at midnight, not knowing where I was, I could not be sure at first who I was; I had only the most rudimentary sense of existence, such as may lurk and flicker in the depths of an animal's consciousness; I was more destitute of human qualities than the cave-dweller; but then the memory, not yet of the place in which I was, but of various other places where I had lived, and might now very possibly be, would come like a rope let down from heaven to draw me up out of the abyss of not-being, from which I could never have escaped by myself: in a flash I would traverse and surmount centuries of civilization, and out of a half-visualized succession of oil-lamps, followed by shirts with turned-down collars, would put together by degrees the component parts of my ego.

Perhaps the immobility of the things that surround us is forced upon them by our conviction that they are themselves, and not anything else, and by the immobility of our conceptions of them. For it always happened that when I awoke like this, and my mind struggled in an unsuccessful attempt to discover where I was, everything would be moving round me through the darkness: things, places, years. My body, still too heavy with sleep to move, would make an effort to construe the form which its tiredness took as an orientation of its various members, so as to induce from that where the wall lay and the furniture stood, to piece together and to give a name to the house in which it must be living. Its memory, the composite memory of its ribs, knees, and shoulder-blades offered it a whole series of rooms in which it had at one time or another slept; while the unseen walls kept changing, adapting themselves to the shape of each successive room that it remembered, whirling madly through the darkness. And even before my brain, lingering in consideration of when things had happened and of what they had looked like, had collected sufficient impressions to enable it to identify the room, it, my body, would recall from each room in succession what the bed was like, where the doors were, how daylight came in at the windows, whether there was a passage outside, what I had had in my mind when I went to sleep, and had found there when I awoke. The stiffened side underneath my body would, for instance, in trying to fix its position, imagine itself to be lying, face to the wall, in a big bed with a canopy; and at once I would say to myself, 'Why, I must have gone to sleep after all, and Mamma never came to say good night!' for I was in the country with my grandfather, who died years ago; and my body, the side upon which I was lying, loyally preserving from the past an impression which my mind should never have forgotten, brought back before my eyes the glimmering flame of the night-light in its bowl of Bohemian glass, shaped like an urn and hung by chains from the ceiling, and the chimney-piece of Sienna marble in my bedroom at Combray, in my great-aunt's house, in those far distant days which, at the moment of waking, seemed present without being clearly defined, but would be-come plainer in a little while when I was properly awake.

Then would come up the memory of a fresh position; the wall slid away in another direction; I was in my room in Mme de Saint-Loup's house in the country: good heavens, it must be ten o'clock, they will have finished dinner! I must have overslept myself, in the little nap which I always take when I come in from my walk with Mme de Saint-Loup, before dressing for the evening. For many years have now elapsed since the Combray days, when, coming in from the longest and latest walks, I would still be in time to see the reflection of the sunset glowing in the panes of my bedroom window. It is a very different kind of existence at Tansonville now with Mme de Saint-Loup, and a different kind of pleasure that I now derive from taking walks only in the evenings, from visiting by moonlight the roads on which I used to play, as a child, in the sunshine; while the bedroom, in which I shall presently fall asleep instead of dressing for dinner, from afar off I can see it, as we return from our walk, with its lamp shining through the window, a solitary beacon in the night.

These shifting and confused gusts of memory never lasted for more than a few seconds; it often happened that, in my spell of uncertainty as to where I was, I did not distinguish the successive theories of which that uncertainty was com-posed any more than, when we watch a horse running, we isolate the successive positions of its body as they appear upon a bioscope. But I had seen first one and then another of the

rooms in which I had slept during my life, and in the end I
would revisit them all in the long course of my waking dream:
rooms in winter, where on going to bed I would at once bury
my head in a nest, built up out of the most diverse materials,
the corner of my pillow, the top of my blankets, a piece of a
shawl, the edge of my bed, and a copy of an evening paper,
all of which things I would contrive, with the infinite patience
of birds building their nests, to cement into one whole;
rooms where, in a keen frost, I would feel the satisfaction of
being shut in from the outer world (like the sea-swallow
which builds at the end of a dark tunnel and is kept warm by
the surrounding earth), and where, the fire keeping in all
night, I would sleep wrapped up, as it were, in a great cloak
of snug and savoury air, shot with the glow of the logs which
would break out again in flame: in a sort of alcove without
walls, a cave of warmth dug out of the heart of the room itself, a zone of heat whose boundaries were constantly shifting
and altering in temperature as gusts of air ran across them to
strike freshly upon my face, from the corners of the room, or
from parts near the window or far from the fireplace which
had therefore remained cold – or rooms in summer, where I
would delight to feel myself a part of the warm evening,
where the moonlight striking upon the half-opened shutters
would throw down to the foot of my bed its enchanted ladder;
where I would fall asleep, as it might be in the open air, like
a titmouse which the breeze keeps poised in the focus of a
sunbeam – or sometimes the Louis XVI room, so cheerful
that I could never feel really unhappy, even on my first night
in it: that room where the slender columns which lightly
supported its ceiling would part, ever so gracefully, to indicate
where the bed was and to keep it separate; sometimes again
that little room with the high ceiling, hollowed in the form of
a pyramid out of two separate storeys, and partly walled with
mahogany, in which from the first moment my mind was
drugged by the unfamiliar scent of flowering grasses, convinced of the hostility of the violet curtains and of the
insolent indifference of a clock that chattered on at the top
of its voice as though I were not there; while a strange and

pitiless mirror with square feet, which stood across one corner of the room, cleared for itself a site I had not looked to find tenanted in the quiet surroundings of my normal field of vision: that room in which my mind, forcing itself for hours on end to leave its moorings, to elongate itself upwards so as to take on the exact shape of the room, and to reach to the summit of that monstrous funnel, had passed so many anxious nights while my body lay stretched out in bed, my eyes staring upwards, my ears straining, my nostrils sniffing uneasily, and my heart beating; until custom had changed the colour of the curtains, made the clock keep quiet, brought an expression of pity to the cruel, slanting face of the glass, disguised or even completely dispelled the scent of flowering grasses, and distinctly reduced the apparent loftiness of the ceiling. Custom! that skilful but unhurrying manager who begins by torturing the mind for weeks on end with her provisional arrangements; whom the mind, for all that, is fortunate in discovering, for without the help of custom it would never contrive, by its own efforts, to make any room seem habitable.

Certainly I was now well awake; my body had turned about for the last time and the good angel of certainty had made all the surrounding objects stand still, had set me down under my bedclothes, in my bedroom, and had fixed, approximately in their right places in the uncertain light, my chest of drawers, my writing-table, my fireplace, the window overlooking the street, and both the doors. But it was no good my knowing that I was not in any of those houses of which, in the stupid moment of waking, if I had not caught sight exactly, I could still believe in their possible presence; for memory was now set in motion; as a rule I did not attempt to go to sleep again at once, but used to spend the greater part of the night recalling our life in the old days at Combray with my great-aunt, at Balbec, Paris, Doncières, Venice, and the rest; remembering again all the places and people that I had known, what I had actually seen of them, and what others had told me.

At Combray, as every afternoon ended, long before the time when I should have to go up to bed, and to lie there, unsleeping, far from my mother and grandmother, my bedroom became the fixed point on which my melancholy and anxious thoughts were centred. Someone had had the happy idea of giving me, to distract me on evenings when I seemed abnormally wretched, a magic lantern, which used to be set on top of my lamp while we waited for dinner-time to come: in the manner of the master-builders and glass-painters of gothic days it substituted for the opaqueness of my walls an impalpable iridescence, supernatural phenomena of many colours, in which legends were depicted, as on a shifting and transitory window. But my sorrows were only increased, because this change of lighting destroyed, as nothing else could have done, the customary impression I had formed of my room, thanks to which the room itself, but for the torture of having to go to bed in it, had become quite endurable. For now I no longer recognized it, and I became uneasy, as though I were in a room in some hotel or furnished lodging, in a place where I had just arrived, by train, for the first time.

Riding at a jerky trot, Golo, his mind filled with an infamous design, issued from the little three-cornered forest which dyed dark green the slope of a convenient hill, and advanced by leaps and bounds towards the castle of poor Geneviève de Brabant. This castle was cut off short by a curved line which was in fact the circumference of one of the transparent ovals in the slides which were pushed into position through a slot in the lantern. It was only the wing of a castle, and in front of it stretched a moor on which Geneviève stood lost in contemplation, wearing a blue girdle. The castle and the moor were yellow, but I could tell their colour without waiting to see them, for before the slides made their appearance the old-gold sonorous name of Brabant had given me an unmistakable clue. Golo stopped for a moment and listened sadly to the little speech read aloud by my great-aunt, which he seemed perfectly to understand, for he modified his attitude with a docility not devoid of a degree of majesty, so as to conform to the indications given in the text; then he rode away at the same jerky trot. And nothing could arrest his slow progress. If the lantern were moved I could still distinguish

Golo's horse advancing across the window-curtains, swelling out with their curves and diving into their folds. The body of Golo himself, being of the same supernatural substance as his steed's, overcame all material obstacles – everything that seemed to bar his way – by taking each as it might be a skeleton and embodying it in himself: the door-handle, for instance, over which, adapting itself at once, would float invincibly his red cloak or his pale face, never losing its nobility or its melancholy, never showing any sign of trouble at such a transubstantiation.

And, indeed, I found plenty of charm in these bright projections, which seemed to have come straight out of a Merovingian past, and to shed around me the reflections of such ancient history. But I cannot express the discomfort I felt at such an intrusion of mystery and beauty into a room which I had succeeded in filling with my own personality until I thought no more of the room than of myself. The anaesthetic effect of custom being destroyed, I would begin to think and to feel very melancholy things. The door-handle of my room, which was different to me from all the other door-handles in the world, inasmuch as it seemed to open of its own accord and without my having to turn it, so unconscious had its manipulation become; lo and behold, it was now an astral body for Golo. And as soon as the dinner-bell rang I would run down to the dining-room, where the big hanging lamp, ignorant of Golo and Bluebeard but well acquainted with my family and the dish of stewed beef, shed the same light as on every other evening; and I would fall into the arms of my mother, whom the misfortunes of Geneviève de Brabant had made all the dearer to me, just as the crimes of Golo had driven me to a more than ordinarily scrupulous examination of my own conscience.

But after dinner, alas, I was soon obliged to leave Mamma, who stayed talking with the others, in the garden if it was fine, or in the little parlour where everyone took shelter when it was wet. Everyone except my grandmother, who held that 'It is a pity to shut oneself indoors in the country,' and used to carry on endless discussions with my father on the very wettest days, because he would send me up to my room with a book instead of letting me stay out of doors. 'That is not the way to make him strong and active,' she would say sadly, 'especially this little man, who needs all the strength and character that he can get.' My father would shrug his shoulders and study the barometer, for he took an interest in meteorology, while my mother, keeping very quiet so as not to disturb him, looked at him with tender respect, but not too hard, not wishing to penetrate the mysteries of his superior mind. But my grandmother, in all weathers, even when the rain was coming down in torrents and Françoise had rushed indoors with the precious wicker arm-chairs, so that they should not get soaked, you would see my grandmother pacing the deserted garden, lashed by the storm, pushing back her grey hair in disorder so that her brows might be more free to imbibe the life-giving draughts of wind and rain. She would say, 'At last one can breathe!' and would run up and down the soaking paths – too straight and symmetrical for her liking, owing to the want of any feeling for nature in the new gardener, whom my father had been asking all morning if the weather were going to improve – with her keen, jerky little step regulated by the various effects wrought upon her soul by the intoxication of the storm, the force of hygiene, the stupidity of my education and of symmetry in gardens, rather than by any anxiety (for that was quite unknown to her) to save her plum-coloured skirt from the spots of mud under which it would gradually disappear to a depth which always provided her maid with a fresh problem and filled her with fresh despair.

When these walks of my grandmother's took place after dinner there was one thing which never failed to bring her back to the house: that was if (at one of those points when the revolutions of her course brought her moth-like, in sight of the lamp in the little parlour where the liqueurs were set out on the card-table) my great-aunt called out to her: 'Bathilde! Come in and stop your husband from drinking brandy!' For, simply to tease her (she had brought so foreign a type of mind into my father's family that everyone made a joke of it), my great-aunt used to make my grandfather, who was forbidden liqueurs, take just a few drops. My poor grandmother would come in and beg and implore her husband not to taste the brandy; and he would become annoyed and swallow his few drops all the same, and she would go out again sad and discouraged, but still smiling, for she was so humble and so sweet that her gentleness towards others, and her continual subordination of herself and of her own troubles, appeared on her face blended in a smile which, unlike those seen on the majority of human faces, had no trace in it of irony, save for herself, while for all of us kisses seemed to spring from her eyes, which could not look upon those she loved without yearning to bestow upon them passionate caresses. The torments inflicted on her by my great-aunt, the sight of my grandmother's vain entreaties, of her in her weakness conquered before she began, but still making the futile endeavour to wean my grandfather from his liqueur-glass – all these were things of the sort to which, in later years, one can grow so well accustomed as to smile at them, to take the tormentor's side with a happy determination which deludes one into the belief that it is not, really, tormenting; but in those days they filled me with such horror that I longed to strike my great-aunt. And yet, as soon as I heard her 'Bathilde! Come in and stop your husband from drinking brandy!' in my cowardice I became at once a man, and did what all we grown men do when face to face with suffering and injustice; I preferred not to see them; I ran up to the top of the house to cry by myself in a little room beside the schoolroom and beneath the roof, which smelt of orrisroot, and was scented also by a wild currant-bush which had climbed up between the stones of the outer wall and thrust a flowering branch in through the half-opened window. Intended for a more special and a baser use, this room, from which, in the daytime, I could see as far as the keep of Roussainville-le-Pin, was for a long time my place of refuge, doubtless because it was the only room whose door I was allowed to lock, whenever my occupation was such as required an inviolable solitude; reading or dreaming, secret tears or paroxysms of desire. Alas! I little knew that my own lack of will-power, my delicate health, and the consequent uncertainty as to my future weighed far more heavily on my grandmother's mind than any little

breach of the rules by her husband, during those endless per-
ambulations, afternoon and evening, in which we used to see
passing up and down, obliquely raised towards the heavens,
her handsome face with its brown and wrinkled cheeks, which
with age had acquired almost the purple hue of tilled fields in
autumn, covered, if she were walking abroad, by a half-lifted
veil, while upon them either the cold or some sad reflection
invariably left the drying traces of an involuntary tear.

My sole consolation when I went upstairs for the night was
that Mamma would come in and kiss me after I was in bed.
But this good night lasted for so short a time: she went down
again so soon that the moment in which I heard her climb the
stairs, and then caught the sound of her garden dress of blue
muslin, from which hung little tassels of plaited straw, rustling
along the double-doored corridor, was for me a moment of
the keenest sorrow. So much did I love that good night that I
reached the stage of hoping that it would come as late as possible, so as to prolong the time of respite during which Mamma
would not yet have appeared. Sometimes when, after kissing
me, she opened the door to go, I longed to call her back, to
say to her 'Kiss me just once again,' but I knew that then she
would at once look displeased, for the concession which she
made to my wretchedness and agitation in coming up to me
with this kiss of peace always annoyed my father, who thought
such ceremonies absurd, and she would have liked to try to
induce me to outgrow the need, the custom of having her
there at all, which was a very different thing from letting the
custom grow up of my asking her for an additional kiss when
she was already crossing the threshold. And to see her look
displeased destroyed all the sense of tranquillity she had
brought me a moment before, when she bent her loving face
down over my bed, and held it out to me like a Host, for an
act of Communion in which my lips might drink deeply the
sense of her real presence, and with it the power to sleep. But
those evenings on which Mamma stayed so short a time in my
room were sweet indeed compared to those on which we had
guests to dinner, and therefore she did not come at all. Our
'guests' were practically limited to M. Swann, who, apart

from a few passing strangers, was almost the only person who
ever came to the house at Combray, sometimes to a neigh-
bourly dinner (but less frequently since his unfortunate marriage, as my family did not care to receive his wife) and sometimes after dinner, uninvited. On those evenings when, as we
sat in front of the house beneath the big chestnut-tree and
round the iron table, we heard, from the far end of the garden,
not the large and noisy rattle which heralded and deafened as
he approached with its ferruginous, interminable, frozen
sound any member of the household who had put it out of
action by coming in 'without ringing', but the double peal –
timid, oval, gilded – of the visitors' bell, everyone would at
once exclaim 'A visitor! Who in the world can it be?' but they
knew quite well that it could only be M. Swann. My great-
aunt, speaking in a loud voice, to set an example, in a tone
which she endeavoured to make sound natural, would tell the
others not to whisper so; that nothing could be more unpleasant for a stranger coming in, who would be led to think
that people were saying things about him which he was not
meant to hear; and then my grandmother would be sent out as
a scout, always happy to find an excuse for an additional turn
in the garden, which she would utilize to remove surrepti-
tiously, as she passed, the stakes of a rose-tree or two, so as to
make the roses look a little more natural, as a mother might
run her hand through her boy's hair, after the barber had
smoothed it down, to make it stick out properly round his
head.

And there we would all stay, hanging on the words which
would fall from my grandmother's lips when she brought us
back her report of the enemy, as though there had been some
uncertainty among a vast number of possible invaders, and
then, soon after, my grandfather would say: 'I can hear
Swann's voice.' And, indeed, one could tell him only by his
voice, for it was difficult to make out his face with its arched
nose and green eyes, under a high forehead fringed with fair,
almost red hair, dressed in the Bressant style, because in the
garden we used as little light as possible, so as not to attract
mosquitoes: and I would slip away as though not going for

anything in particular, to tell them to bring out the syrups; for my grandmother made a great point, thinking it 'nicer', of their not being allowed to seem anything out of the ordinary, which we kept for visitors only. Although a far younger man, M. Swann was very much attached to my grandfather, who had been an intimate friend, in his time, of Swann's father, an excellent but an eccentric man in whom the least little thing would, it seemed, often check the flow of his spirits and divert the current of his thoughts. Several times in the course of a year I would hear my grandfather tell at table the story, which never varied, of the behaviour of M. Swann the elder upon the death of his wife, by whose bedside he had watched day and night. My grandfather, who had not seen him for a long time, hastened to join him at the Swanns' family property on the outskirts of Combray, and managed to entice him for a moment, weeping profusely, out of the death-chamber, so that he should not be present when the body was laid in its coffin. They took a turn or two in the park, where there was a little sunshine. Suddenly M. Swann seized my grandfather by the arm and cried, 'Oh, my dear old friend, how fortunate we are to be walking here together on such a charming day! Don't you see how pretty they are, all these trees – my hawthorns, and my new pond, on which you have never congratulated me? You look as glum as a night-cap. Don't you feel this little breeze? Ah! whatever you may say, it's good to be alive all the same, my dear Amédée!' And then, abruptly, the memory of his dead wife returned to him, and probably thinking it too complicated to inquire into how, at such a time, he could have allowed himself to be carried away by an impulse of happiness, he confined himself to a gesture which he habitually employed whenever any perplexing question came into his mind: that is, he passed his hand across his forehead, dried his eyes, and wiped his glasses. And he could never be consoled for the loss of his wife, but used to say to my grandfather, during the two years for which he survived her, 'It's a funny thing, now; I very often think of my poor wife, but I cannot think of her very much at any one time.' 'Often, but a little at a time, like poor old Swann,' became one of my grandfather's favourite phrases, which he would apply to all kinds of things. And I should have assumed that this father of Swann's had been a monster if my grandfather, whom I regarded as a better judge than myself, and whose word was my law and often led me in the long run to pardon offences which I should have been inclined to condemn, had not gone on to exclaim, 'But, after all, he had a heart of gold.'

For many years, albeit – and especially before his marriage – M. Swann the younger came often to see them at Combray, my great-aunt and grandparents never suspected that he had entirely ceased to live in the kind of society which his family had frequented, or that, under the sort of incognito which the name of Swann gave him among us, they were harbouring – with the complete innocence of a family of honest innkeepers who have in their midst some distinguished highwayman and never know it – one of the smartest members of the Jockey Club, a particular friend of the Comte de Paris and of the Prince of Wales, and one of the men most sought after in the aristocratic world of the Faubourg Saint-Germain.

Our utter ignorance of the brilliant part which Swann was playing in the world of fashion was, of course, due in part to his own reserve and discretion, but also to the fact that middle-class people in those days took what was almost a Hindu view of society, which they held to consist of sharply defined castes, so that everyone at his birth found himself called to that station in life which his parents already occupied, and nothing, except the chance of a brilliant career or of a 'good' marriage, could extract you from that station or admit you to a superior caste. M. Swann, the father, had been a stockbroker; and so 'young Swann' found himself immured for life in a caste where one's fortune, as in a list of taxpayers, varied between such and such limits of income. We knew the people with whom his father had associated, and so we knew his own associates, the people with whom he was 'in a position to mix'. If he knew other people besides, those were youthful acquaintances on whom the old friends of the family, like my relatives, shut their eyes all the more good-naturedly that Swann himself, after he was left an orphan, still came most faithfully to see us; but we

would have been ready to wager that the people outside our
acquaintance whom Swann knew were of the sort to whom he
would not have dared to raise his hat, had he met them while
he was walking with ourselves. Had there been such a thing as
a determination to apply to Swann a social coefficient peculiar
to himself, as distinct from all the other sons of other stockbrokers in his father's position, his coefficient would have
been rather lower than theirs, because, leading a very simple
life, and having always had a craze for 'antiques' and pictures,
he now lived and piled up his collections in an old house which
my grandmother longed to visit, but which stood on the Quai
d'Orléans, a neighbourhood in which my great-aunt thought
it most degrading to be quartered. 'Are you really a connois-
seur, now?' she would say to him; 'I ask for your own sake, as
you are likely to have 'fakes' palmed off on you by the dealers,'
for she did not, in fact, endow him with any critical faculty,
and had no great opinion of the intelligence of a man who, in
conversation, would avoid serious topics and showed a very
dull preciseness, not only when he gave us kitchen recipes,
going into the most minute details, but even when my grandmother's sisters were talking to him about art. When chal-
lenged by them to give an opinion, or to express his admiration
for some picture, he would remain almost impolitely silent,
and would then make amends by furnishing (if he could) some
fact or other about the gallery in which the picture was hung,
or the date at which it had been painted. But as a rule he would
content himself with trying to amuse us by telling us the story
of his latest adventure – and he would have a fresh story for us
on every occasion – with some one whom we ourselves knew,
such as the Combray chemist, or our cook, or our coachman.
These stories certainly used to make my great-aunt laugh, but
she could never tell whether that was on account of the absurd
parts which Swann invariably made himself play in the adventures, or of the wit that he showed in telling us of them. 'It is
easy to see that you are a regular "character", M. Swann!'

As she was the only member of our family who could be
described as a trifle 'common', she would always take care to
remark to strangers, when Swann was mentioned, that he

could easily, if he had wished to, have lived in the Boulevard Haussmann or the Avenue de l'Opéra, and that he was the son of old M. Swann who must have left four or five million francs, but that it was a fad of his. A fad which, moreover, she thought was bound to amuse other people so much that in Paris, when M. Swann called on New Year's Day bringing her a little packet of *marrons glacés*, she never failed, if there were strangers in the room, to say to him: 'Well, M. Swann, and do you still live next door to the Bonded Vaults, so as to be sure of not missing your train when you go to Lyons?' and she would peep out of the corner of her eye, over her glasses, at the other visitors.

But if anyone had suggested to my aunt that this Swann, who, in his capacity as the son of old M. Swann, was 'fully qualified' to be received by any of the 'upper middle class', the most respected barristers and solicitors of Paris (though he was perhaps a trifle inclined to let this hereditary privilege go into abeyance) had another almost secret existence of a wholly different kind: that when he left our house in Paris, saying that he must go home to bed, he would no sooner have turned the corner than he would stop, retrace his steps, and be off to some drawing-room on whose like no stockbroker or associate of stockbrokers had ever set eyes – that would have seemed to my aunt as extraordinary as, to a woman of wider reading, the thought of being herself on terms of intimacy with Aristaeus, of knowing that he would, when he had finished his conversation with her, plunge deep into the realms of Thetis, into an empire veiled from mortal eyes, in which Virgil depicts him as being received with open arms; or – to be content with an image more likely to have occurred to her, for she had seen it painted on the plates we used for biscuits at Combray – as the thought of having had to dinner Ali Baba, who, as soon as he found himself alone and unobserved, would make his way into the cave, resplendent with its unsuspected treasures.

One day when he had come to see us after dinner in Paris, and had begged pardon for being in evening clothes, Françoise, when he had gone, told us that she had got it from his coachman that he had been dining 'with a princess'. 'A pretty sort of princess,' drawled my aunt; 'I know them,' and she shrugged her shoulders without raising her eyes from her knitting, serenely ironical.

Altogether, my aunt used to treat him with scant ceremony. Since she was of the opinion that he ought to feel flattered by our invitations, she thought it only right and proper that he should never come to see us in summer without a basket of peaches or raspberries from his garden, and that from each of his visits to Italy he should bring back some photographs of old masters for me.

It seemed quite natural, therefore, to send to him whenever we wanted a recipe for some special sauce or for a pineapple salad for one of our big dinner-parties, to which he himself would not be invited, not seeming of sufficient importance to be served up to new friends who might be in our house for the first time. If the conversation turned upon the Princes of the House of France, 'Gentlemen you and I will never know, will we, and don't want to, do we?' my great-aunt would say tartly to Swann, who had, perhaps, a letter from Twickenham in his pocket; she would make him play accompaniments and turn over music on evenings when my grandmother's sister sang; manipulating this creature, so rare and refined at other times and in other places, with the rough simplicity of a child who will play with some curio from the cabinet no more carefully than if it were a penny toy. Certainly the Swann who was a familiar figure in all the clubs of those days differed hugely from the Swann created in my great-aunt's mind when, of an evening, in our little garden at Combray, after the two shy peals had sounded from the gate, she would vitalize, by injecting into it everything she had ever heard about the Swann family, the vague and unrecognizable shape which began to appear, with my grandmother in its wake, against a background of shadows, and could at last be identified by the sound of its voice. But then, even in the most insignificant details of our daily life, none of us can be said to constitute a material whole, which is identical for everyone, and need only be turned up like a page in an account-book or the record of a will; our social personality is created by the thoughts of other

people. Even the simple act which we describe as 'seeing someone we know' is, to some extent, an intellectual process. We
pack the physical outline of the creature we see with all the
ideas we have already formed about him, and in the complete
picture of him which we compose in our minds those ideas
have certainly the principal place. In the end they come to fill
out so completely the curve of his cheeks, to follow so exactly
the line of his nose, they blend so harmoniously in the sound of
his voice that these seem to be no more than a transparent
envelope, so that each time we see the face or hear the voice it
is our own ideas of him which we recognize and to which we
listen. And so, no doubt, from the Swann they had built up for
their own purposes my family had left out, in their ignorance,
a whole crowd of the details of his daily life in the world of
fashion, details by means of which other people, when they
met him, saw all the Graces enthroned in his face and stopping
at the line of his arched nose as at a natural frontier; but they
contrived also to put into a face from which its distinction had
been evicted, a face vacant and roomy as an untenanted house,
to plant in the depths of its unvalued eyes a lingering sense,
uncertain but not unpleasing, half-memory and half-oblivion,
of idle hours spent together after our weekly dinners, round
the card-table or in the garden, during our companionable
country life. Our friend's bodily frame had been so well lined
with his sense, and with various earlier memories of his
family, that their own special Swann had become to my people
a complete and living creature; so that even now I have the
feeling of leaving some one I know for another quite different
person when, going back in memory, I pass from the Swann
whom I knew later and more intimately to this early Swann –
this early Swann in whom I can distinguish the charming mistakes of my childhood, and who, incidentally, is less like his
successor than he is like the other people I knew at that time,
as though one's life were a series of galleries in which all the
portraits of any one period had a marked family likeness, the
same (so to speak) tonality – this early Swann abounding in
leisure, fragrant with the scent of the great chestnut-tree, of
baskets of raspberries, and of a sprig of tarragon.

And yet one day, when my grandmother had gone to ask some favour of a lady whom she had known at the Sacré Cœur (and with whom, because of our caste theory, she had not cared to keep up any degree of intimacy in spite of several common interests), the Marquise de Villeparisis, of the famous house of Bouillon, this lady had said to her:

'I think you know M. Swann very well; he is a great friend of my nephews, the des Laumes.'

My grandmother had returned from the call full of praise for the house, which overlooked some gardens, and in which Mme de Villeparisis had advised her to rent a flat; and also for a repairing tailor and his daughter, who kept a little shop in the courtyard, into which she had gone to ask them to put a stitch in her skirt, which she had torn on the staircase. My grandmother had found these people perfectly charming: the girl, she said, was a jewel, and the tailor a most distinguished man, the finest she had ever seen. For in her eyes distinction was a thing wholly independent of social position. She was in ecstasies over some answer the tailor had made, saying to Mamma:

'Sévigné would not have said it better!' and, by way of contrast, of a nephew of Mme de Villeparisis whom she had met at the house:

'My dear, he is so common!'

Now, the effect of that remark about Swann had been, not to raise him in my great-aunt's estimation, but to lower Mme de Villeparisis. It appeared that the deference which, on my grandmother's authority, we owed to Mme de Villeparisis imposed on her the reciprocal obligation to do nothing that would render her less worthy of our regard, and that she had failed in her duty in becoming aware of Swann's existence and in allowing members of her family to associate with him. 'How should she know Swann? A lady who, you always made out, was related to Marshal MacMahon!' This view of Swann's social atmosphere which prevailed in my family seemed to be confirmed later on by his marriage with a woman of the worst class, you might almost say a 'fast' woman, whom, to do him justice, he never attempted to introduce to us, for he continued to come to us alone, though he came more and more seldom; but from whom they thought they could establish, on the assumption that he had found her there, the circle, unknown to them, in which he ordinarily moved.

But on one occasion my grandfather read in a newspaper that M. Swann was one of the most faithful attendants at the Sunday luncheons given by the Duc de X —, whose father and uncle had been among our most prominent statesmen in the reign of Louis Philippe. Now my grandfather was curious to learn all the little details which might help him to take a mental share in the private lives of men like Molé, the Duc Pasquier, or the Duc de Broglie. He was delighted to find that Swann associated with people who had known them. My great-aunt, however, interpreted this piece of news in a sense discreditable to Swann; for anyone who chose his associates outside the caste in which he had been born and bred, outside his 'proper station', was condemned to utter degradation in her eyes. It seemed to her that such a one abdicated all claim to enjoy the fruits of those friendly relations with people of good position which prudent parents cultivate and store up for their children's benefit, for my great aunt had actually ceased to 'see' the son of a lawyer we had known because he had married a 'Highness' and had thereby stepped down – in her eyes – from the respectable position of a lawyer's son to that of those adventurers, upstart footmen, or stable-boys mostly, to whom we read that queens have sometimes shown their favours. She objected, therefore, to my grandfather's plan of questioning Swann, when next he came to dine with us, about these people whose friendship with him we had discovered. On the other hand, my grandmother's two sisters, elderly spinsters who shared her nobility of character but lacked her intelligence, declared that they could not conceive what pleasure their brother-in-law could find in talking about such trifles. They were ladies of lofty ambition, who for that reason were incapable of taking the least interest in what might be called the 'pinchbeck' things of life, even when they had an historic value, or, generally speaking, in anything that was not directly associated with some object aesthetically precious. So complete was their negation of interest in anything which seemed directly or indirectly a part of our everyday life that their sense of hearing – which had gradually come to understand its own futility when the tone of the conversation, at the dinner-table, became frivolous or merely mundane, without the two old ladies' being able to guide it back to the topic dear to themselves – would leave its receptive channels unemployed, so effectively that they were actually becoming atrophied. So that if my grandfather wished to attract the attention of the two sisters, he would have to make use of some such alarm signals as mad-doctors adopt in dealing with their distracted patients; as by beating several times on a glass with the blade of a knife, fixing them at the same time with a sharp word and a compelling glance, violent methods which the said doctors are apt to bring with them into their everyday life among the sane, either from force of professional habit or because they think the whole world a trifle mad.

Their interest grew, however, when, the day before Swann was to dine with us, and when he had made them a special present of a case of Asti, my great-aunt, who had in her hand a copy of the *Figaro* in which to the name of a picture then on view in a Corot exhibition were added the words, 'from the collection of M. Charles Swann,' asked: 'Did you see that Swann is "mentioned" in the *Figaro*?'

'But I have always told you,' said my grandmother, 'that he had plenty of taste.'

'You would, of course,' retorted my great-aunt, 'say anything just to seem different from *us*.' For, knowing that my grandmother never agreed with her, and not being quite confident that it was her own opinion which the rest of us invariably endorsed, she wished to extort from us a wholesale condemnation of my grandmother's views, against which she hoped to force us into solidarity with her own.

But we sat silent. My grandmother's sisters having expressed a desire to mention to Swann this reference to him in the *Figaro*, my great-aunt dissuaded them. Whenever she saw in others an advantage, however trivial, which she herself lacked, she would persuade herself that it was no advantage at all, but a drawback, and would pity so as not to have to envy them.

'I don't think that would please him at all; I know very well, I should hate to see my name printed like that, as large as life, in the paper, and I shouldn't feel at all flattered if anyone spoke to me about it.'

She did not, however, put any great pressure upon my grandmother's sisters, for they, in their horror of vulgarity, had brought to such a fine art the concealment of a personal allusion in a wealth of ingenious circumlocution, that it would often pass unnoticed even by the person to whom it was addressed. As for my mother, her only thought was of managing to induce my father to consent to speak to Swann, not of his wife, but of his daughter, whom he worshipped, and for whose sake it was understood that he had ultimately made his unfortunate marriage.

'You need only say a word; just ask him how she is. It must be so very hard for him.'

My father, however, was annoyed: 'No, no; you have the most absurd ideas. It would be utterly ridiculous.'

But the only one of us in whom the prospect of Swann's arrival gave rise to an unhappy foreboding was myself. And that was because on the evenings when there were visitors, or just M. Swann in the house, Mamma did not come up to my room. I did not, at that time, have dinner with the family: I came out to the garden after dinner, and at nine I said good night and went to bed. But on these evenings I used to dine earlier than the others, and to come in afterwards and sit at table until eight o'clock, when it was understood that I must go upstairs; that frail and precious kiss which Mamma used always to leave upon my lips when I was in bed and just going to sleep I had to take with me from the dining-room to my own, and to keep inviolate all the time that it took me to undress, without letting its sweet charm be broken, without letting its volatile essence diffuse itself and evaporate; and just on those very evenings when I must needs take most pains to receive it with due formality, I had to snatch it, to seize it instantly and in public, without even having the time or being properly free to apply to what I was doing the punctiliousness which madmen use to compel themselves to exclude all other thoughts from their minds while they are shutting a door, so that when the sickness of uncertainty sweeps over them again they can triumphantly face and overcome it with the recollection of the precise moment in which the door was shut.

We were all in the garden when the double peal of the gate-bell sounded shyly. Everyone knew it must be Swann, and yet they looked at one another inquiringly and sent my grandmother scouting.

'See that you thank him intelligibly for the wine,' my grandfather warned his two sisters-in-law; 'you know how good it is, and it is a huge case.'

'Now, don't start whispering!' said my great-aunt. 'How would you like to come into a house and find everyone muttering to themselves?'

'Ah! There's M. Swann,' cried my father. 'Let's ask him if he thinks it will be fine to-morrow.'

My mother fancied that a word from her would wipe out all the unpleasantness which my family had contrived to make Swann feel since his marriage. She found an opportunity to draw him aside for a moment. But I followed her: I could not bring myself to let her go out of reach of me while I felt that in a few minutes I should have to leave her in the dining-room and go up to my bed without the consoling thought, as on ordinary evenings, that she would come up, later, to kiss me.

'Now, M. Swann,' she said, 'do tell me about your daughter; I am sure she shows a taste already for nice things, like her papa.'

'Come along and sit down here with us all on the verandah,' said my grandfather, coming up to him. My mother had to abandon the quest, but managed to extract from the restriction itself a further refinement of thought, as great poets do when the tyranny of rhyme forces them into the discovery of their finest lines.

'We can talk about her again when we are by ourselves,' she said, or rather whispered to Swann. 'It is only a mother who can understand. I am sure that hers would agree with me.'

And so we all sat down round the iron table. I should have liked not to think of the hours of anguish which I should have to spend, that evening, alone in my room, without the possibility of going to sleep: I tried to convince myself that they were of no importance, really, since I should have forgotten them next morning, and to fix my mind on thoughts of the future which would carry me, as on a bridge, across the terrifying abyss that yawned at my feet. But my mind, strained by this foreboding, distended like the look which I shot at my mother, would not allow any other impression to enter. Thoughts did, indeed, enter it, but only on the condition that they left behind them every element of beauty, or even of quaintness, by which I might have been distracted or beguiled. As a surgical patient, by means of a local anaesthetic, can look on with a clear consciousness while an operation is being performed upon him and yet feel nothing, I could repeat to myself some favourite lines, or watch my grandfather attempting to talk to Swann about the Duc d'Audriffet-Pasquier, without being able to kindle any emotion from one or amusement from the other. Hardly had my grandfather begun to question Swann about that orator when one of my grandmother's sisters, in whose ears the question echoed like a solemn but untimely silence which her natural politeness bade her interrupt, addressed the other with:

'Just fancy, Flora, I met a young Swedish governess to-day who told me most interesting things about the cooperative movement in Scandinavia. We really must have her to dine here one evening.'

'To be sure!' said her sister Flora, 'but I haven't wasted my time either. I met such a clever old gentleman at M. Vinteuil's who knows Maubant quite well, and Maubant has told him every little thing about how he gets up his parts. It is the most interesting thing I ever heard. He is a neighbour of M. Vinteuil's, and I never knew; and he is so nice besides.'

'M. Vinteuil is not the only one who has nice neighbours,' cried my aunt Céline in a voice which seemed loud because she was so timid, and seemed forced because she had been planning the little speech for so long; darting, as she spoke, what she called a 'significant glance' at Swann. And my aunt Flora, who realized that this veiled utterance was Céline's way of thanking Swann intelligibly for the Asti, looked at him with a blend of congratulation and irony, either just because she wished to underline her sister's little epigram, or because she envied Swann his having inspired it, or merely because she imagined that he was embarrassed, and could not help having a little fun at his expense.

'I think it would be worth while,' Flora went on, 'to have this old gentleman to dinner. When you get him upon Maubant or Mme Materna he will talk for hours on end.'

'That must be delightful,' sighed my grandfather, in whose mind nature had unfortunately forgotten to include any capacity whatsoever for becoming passionately interested in the cooperative movement among the ladies of Sweden or in the methods employed by Maubant to get up his parts, just as it had forgotten to endow my grandmother's two sisters with a grain of that precious salt which one has oneself to 'add to taste' in order to extract any savour from a narrative of the private life of Molé or of the Comte de Paris.

'I say!' exclaimed Swann to my grandfather, 'what I was going to tell you has more to do than you might think with what you were asking me just now, for in some respects there has been very little change. I came across a passage in Saint-Simon this morning which would have amused you. It is in the volume which covers his mission to Spain; not one of the best, little more in fact than a journal, but at least it is a journal wonderfully well written, which fairly distinguishes it from the devastating journalism that we feel bound to read in these days, morning, noon, and night.'

'I do not agree with you: there are some days when I find reading the papers very pleasant indeed!' my aunt Flora broke in, to show Swann that she had read the note about his Corot in the *Figaro*.

'Yes,' aunt Céline went one better. 'When they write about things or people in whom we are interested.'

'I don't deny it,' answered Swann in some bewilderment. 'The fault I find with our journalism is that it forces us to take an interest in some fresh triviality or other every day, whereas only three or four books in a lifetime give us anything that is of real importance. Suppose that, every morning, when we tore the wrapper off our paper with fevered hands, a transmutation were to take place, and we were to find inside it – oh! I don't know; shall we say Pascal's *Pensées*?' He articulated the title with an ironic emphasis so as not to appear pedantic. 'And then, in the gilt and tooled volumes which we open once in ten years,' he went on, showing that contempt for the things of this world which some men of the world like to affect, 'we should read that the Queen of the Hellenes had arrived at Cannes, or that the Princesse de Léon had given a fancy dress ball. In that way we should arrive at the right proportion between "information" and "publicity". ' But at once regretting that he had allowed himself to speak, even in jest, of serious matters, he added ironically: 'We are having a most entertaining conversation; I cannot think why we climb to these lofty summits,' and then, turning to my grandfather: 'Well, Saint-Simon tells how Maulevrier had had the audacity to offer his hand to his sons. You remember how he says of Maulevrier, "Never did I find in that coarse bottle anything but ill-humour, boorishness, and folly." '

'Coarse or not, I know bottles in which there is something very different!' said Flora briskly, feeling bound to thank Swann as well as her sister, since the present of Asti had been addressed to them both. Céline began to laugh.

Swann was puzzled, but went on: '"I cannot say whether it was his ignorance or a trap," writes Saint-Simon; "he wished to give his hand to my children. I noticed it in time to prevent him." '

My grandfather was already in ecstasies over 'ignorance or a trap', but Miss Céline – the name of Saint-Simon, a 'man of letters', having arrested the complete paralysis of her sense of hearing – had grown angry.

'What! You admire that, do you? Well, it is clever enough! But what is the point of it? Does he mean that one man isn't as good as another? What difference can it make whether he is a duke or a groom so long as he is intelligent and good? He had a fine way of bringing up his children, your Saint-Simon, if he didn't teach them to shake hands with all honest men. Really and truly, it's abominable. And you dare to quote it!'.

And my grandfather, utterly depressed, realizing how futile it would be for him, against this opposition, to attempt to get Swann to tell him the stories which would have amused him, murmured to my mother: 'Just tell me again that line of yours which always comforts me so much on these occasions. Oh, yes:

What virtues, Lord, Thou makest us abhor!

Good, that is, very good.'

I never took my eyes off my mother. I knew that when they were at table I should not be permitted to stay there for the whole of dinner-time, and that Mamma, for fear of annoying my father, would not allow me to give her in public the series of kisses that she would have had in my room. And so I promised to eat and drink and as I felt the hour approach, I would put beforehand into this kiss, which was bound to be so brief and stealthy in execution, everything that my own efforts could put into it: would look out very carefully first the exact spot on her cheek where I would imprint it, and would so prepare my thoughts that I might be able, thanks to these mental preliminaries, to consecrate the whole of the minute Mamma would allow me to the sensation of her cheek against my lips, as a painter who can have his subject for short sittings only prepares his palette, and from what he remembers and from rough notes does in advance everything which he possibly can do in the sitter's absence. But to-night, before the dinner-bell had sounded, my grandfather said with unconscious cruelty: 'The little man looks tired; he'd better go up to bed. Besides we are dining late to-night.'

And my father, who was less scrupulous than my grandmother or mother in observing the letter of a treaty, went on: 'Yes; run along; to bed with you.'

I would have kissed Mamma then and there, but at that moment the dinner-bell rang.

'No, no, leave your mother alone. You've said good night quite enough. These exhibitions are absurd. Go on upstairs.'

And so I must set forth without viaticum; must climb each step of the staircase 'against my heart', as the saying is, climbing in opposition to my heart's desire, which was to return to my mother, since she had not, by her kiss, given my heart leave to accompany me forth. That hateful staircase, up which I always passed with such dismay, gave out a smell of varnish which had to some extent absorbed, made definite and fixed the special quality of sorrow that I felt each evening, and made it perhaps even more cruel to my sensibility because, when it assumed this olfactory guise, my intellect was powerless to resist it. When we have gone to sleep with a maddening toothache and are conscious of it only as a little girl whom we attempt, time after time, to pull out of the water, or as a line of Molière which we repeat incessantly to ourselves, it is a great relief to wake up, so that our intelligence can disentangle the idea of toothache from any artificial semblance of heroism or rhythmic cadence. It was the precise converse of this relief which I felt when my anguish at having to go up to my room invaded my consciousness in a manner infinitely more rapid, instantaneous almost, a manner at once insidious and brutal as I breathed in – a far more poisonous thing than any moral penetration – the peculiar smell of the varnish upon that staircase.

Once in my room I had to stop every loophole, to close the shutters, to dig my own grave as I turned down the bedclothes, to wrap myself in the shroud of my nightshirt. But before burying myself in the iron bed which had been placed there because, on summer nights, I was too hot among the rep curtains of the four-poster, I was stirred to revolt, and attempted the desperate stratagem of a condemned prisoner. I wrote to my mother begging her to come upstairs for an important reason which I could not put in writing. My fear was that Françoise, aunt's cook who used to be put in charge of me when I was at Combray, might refuse to take my note. I had a suspicion that, in her eyes, to carry a message to my mother when there was a stranger in the room would appear flatly inconceivable, just as it would be for the door-keeper of a theatre to hand a letter to an actor upon the stage. For things which might or might not be done possessed a code at once imperious, abundant, subtle, and uncompromising on points themselves imperceptible or irrelevant, which gave it a resemblance to those ancient laws which combine such cruel ordinances as the massacre of infants at the breast with prohibitions, of exaggerated refinement, against 'seething the kid in his mother's milk', or 'eating of the sinew which is upon the hollow of the thigh'. This code, if one could judge it by the sudden obstinacy which she would put into her refusal to carry out certain of our instructions, seemed to have foreseen such social complications and refinements of fashion as nothing in Françoise's surroundings or in her career as a servant in a village household could have put into her head; and we were obliged to assume that there was latent in her some past existence in the ancient history of France, noble and little understood, just as there is in those manufacturing towns where old mansions still testify to their former courtly days, and chemical workers toil among delicately sculptured scenes of the Miracle of Theophilus or the Quatre Fils Aymon.

In this particular instance, the article of her code which made it highly improbable that – barring an outbreak of fire – Françoise would go down and disturb Mamma when M. Swann was there for so unimportant a person as myself was one embodying the respect she showed not only for the family (as for the dead, for the clergy, or for royalty), but also for the stranger within our gates; a respect which I should perhaps have found touching in a book, but which never failed to irritate me on her lips, because of the solemn and gentle tones in which she would utter it, and which irritated me more than usual this evening when the sacred character in which she invested the dinner-party might have the effect of making her decline to disturb its ceremonial. But to give myself one chance of success I lied without hesitation, telling her that it was not in the least myself who had wanted to write to Mamma who, on saying good night to me, had begged me not to forget to send her an answer about something she had asked me to find, and that she would certainly be very angry if this note were not taken to her. I think that Françoise disbelieved me, for, like those primitive men whose senses were so much keener than our own, she could immediately detect, by signs imperceptible by the rest of us, the truth or falsehood of anything that we might wish to conceal from her. She studied the envelope for five minutes as though an examination of the paper itself and the look of my handwriting could enlighten her as to the nature of the contents, or tell her to which article of her code she ought to refer the matter. Then she went out with an air of resignation which seemed to imply; 'What a dreadful thing for parents to have a child like this!'

A moment later she returned to say that they were still at the ice stage and that it was impossible for the butler to deliver the note at once, in front of everybody; but that when the finger-bowls were put round he would find a way of slipping it into Mamma's hand. At once my anxiety subsided; it was now no longer (as it had been a moment ago) until to-morrow that I had lost my mother, for my little line was going – to annoy her, no doubt, and doubly so because this contrivance would make me ridiculous in Swann's eyes – but was going all the same to admit me, invisibly and by stealth, into the same room as herself, was going to whisper from me into her ear; for that forbidden and unfriendly dining-room, where but a moment ago the ice itself – with burned nuts in it – and the finger-bowls seemed to me to be concealing pleasures that were mischievous and of a mortal sadness because Mamma was tasting of them and I was far away, had opened its doors to me and, like a ripe fruit which bursts through its skin, was going to pour out into my intoxicated heart the gushing sweetness of Mamma's attention while she was reading what I had written. Now I was no longer separated from her; the barriers were down; an exquisite thread was binding us. Besides, that was not all, for surely Mamma would come.

As for the agony through which I had just passed, I imagined that Swann would have laughed heartily at it if he had read my letter and had guessed its purpose; whereas, on the contrary, as I was to learn in due course, a similar anguish had been the bane of his life for many years, and no one perhaps could have understood my feelings at that moment so well as himself; to him, that anguish which lies in knowing that the creature one adores is in some place of enjoyment where oneself is not and cannot follow – to him that anguish came through Love, to which it is in a sense predestined, by which it must be equipped and adapted; but when, as had befallen me, such an anguish possesses one's soul before Love has yet entered into one's life, then it must drift, awaiting Love's coming, vague and free, without precise attachment, at the disposal of one sentiment to-day, of another to-morrow, of filial piety or affection for a comrade. And the joy with which I first bound myself apprentice, when Françoise returned to tell me that my letter would be delivered, Swann, too, had known well that false joy which a friend can give us, or some relative of the woman we love, when on his arrival at the house or theatre where she is to be found, for some ball or party or 'first-night' at which he is to meet her, he sees us wandering outside, desperately awaiting some opportunity of communicating with her. He recognizes us, greets us familiarly, and asks what we are doing there. And when we invent a story of having some urgent message to give to his relative or friend, he assures us that nothing could be more simple, takes us in at the door, and promises to send her down to us in five minutes. How much we love him – as at that moment I loved Françoise – the good-natured intermediary who by a single word has made supportable, human, almost propitious the inconceivable, infernal scene of gaiety in the thick of which we had been imagining swarms of enemies, perverse and seductive, beguiling away from us, even making laugh at us, the woman whom we love. If we are to judge of them by him, this relative who has accosted us and who is himself an initiate in those cruel mysteries, then the other guests cannot be so very demoniacal. Those inaccessible and torturing hours into which she had gone to taste of unknown pleasures – behold, a breach in the wall, and we are through it. Behold, one of the moments whose series will go to make up their sum, a moment as genuine as the rest, if not actually more important to ourself because our mistress is more intensely a part of it; we picture it to ourselves, we possess it, we intervene upon it, almost we have

created it: namely, the moment in which he goes to tell her
that we are waiting there below. And very probably the other
moments of the party will not be essentially different, will contain nothing else so exquisite or so well able to make us suffer,
since this kind friend has assured us that 'Of course, she will
be delighted to come down! It will be far more amusing for
her to talk to you than to be bored up there.' Alas! Swann had
learned by experience that the good intentions of a third party
are powerless to control a woman who is annoyed to find herself pursued even into a ball-room by a man whom she does
not love. Too often, the kind friend comes down again alone.

My mother did not appear, but with no attempt to safeguard
my self-respect (which depended upon her keeping up the
fiction that she had asked me to let her know the result of my
search for something or other) made Françoise tell me, in so
many words: 'There is no answer' – words I have so often,
since then, heard the hall-porters in 'mansions' and the
flunkeys in gambling-clubs and the like, repeat to some poor
girl, who replies in bewilderment: 'What! he's said nothing?
It's not possible. You did give him my letter, didn't you? Very
well, I shall wait a little longer.' And just as she invariably
protests that she does not need the extra gas which the porter
offers to light for her, and sits on there, hearing nothing
further, except an occasional remark on the weather which the
porter exchanges with a messenger whom he will send off
suddenly, when he notices the time, to put some customer's
wine on the ice; so, having declined Françoise's offer to make
me some tea or to stay beside me, I let her go off again to the
servants' hall, and lay down and shut my eyes, and tried not to
hear the voices of my family who were drinking their coffee in
the garden.

But after a few seconds I realized that, by writing that line
to Mamma, by approaching – at the risk of making her angry –
so near to her that I felt I could reach out and grasp the moment in which I should see her again, I had cut myself off from
the possibility of going to sleep until I actually had seen her,
and my heart began to beat more and more painfully as I increased my agitation by ordering myself to keep calm and to

acquiesce in my ill-fortune. Then, suddenly, my anxiety subsided, a feeling of intense happiness coursed through me, as when a strong medicine begins to take effect and one's pain vanishes: I had formed a resolution to abandon all attempts to go to sleep without seeing Mamma, and had decided to kiss her at all costs, even with the certainty of being in disgrace with her for long afterwards, when she herself came up to bed. The tranquillity which followed my anguish made me extremely alert, no less than my sense of expectation, my thirst for and my fear of danger.

Noiselessly I opened the window and sat down on the foot of my bed; hardly daring to move in case they should hear me from below. Things outside seemed also fixed in mute expectation, so as not to disturb the moonlight which, duplicating each of them and throwing it back by the extension, forwards, of a shadow denser and more concrete than its substance, had made the whole landscape seem at once thinner and longer, like a map which, after being folded up, is spread out upon the ground. What had to move – a leaf of the chestnut-tree, for instance – moved. But its minute shuddering, complete, finished to the least detail and with the utmost delicacy of gesture, made no discord with the rest of the scene, and yet was not merged in it, remaining clearly outlined. Exposed upon this surface of silence, which absorbed nothing from them, the most distant sounds, those which must have come from gardens at the far end of the town, could be distinguished with such exact 'finish' that the impression they gave of coming from a distance seemed due only to their 'pianissimo' execution, like those movements on muted strings so well performed by the orchestra of the Conservatoire that, although one does not lose a single note, one thinks all the same that they are being played somewhere outside, a long way from the concert hall, so that all the old subscribers, and my grandmother's sisters too, when Swann had given them his seats, used to strain their ears as if they had caught the distant approach of an army on the march, which had not yet rounded the corner of the Rue de Trévise.

I was well aware that I had placed myself in a position than which none could be counted upon to involve me in graver consequences at my parents' hands; consequences far graver, indeed, than a stranger would have imagined, and such as (he would have thought) could follow only some really shameful fault. But in the system of education which they had given me faults were not classified in the same order as in that of other children, and I had been taught to place at the head of the list (doubtless because there was no other class of faults from which I needed to be more carefully protected) those in which I can now distinguish the common feature that one succumbs to them by yielding to a nervous impulse. But such words as these last had never been uttered in my hearing; no one had yet accounted for my temptations in a way which might have led me to believe that there was some excuse for my giving in to them, or that I was actually incapable of holding out against them. Yet I could easily recognize this class of transgressions by the anguish of mind which preceded, as well as by the rigour of the punishment which followed them; and I knew that what I had just done was in the same category as certain other sins for which I had been severely chastised, though infinitely more serious than they. When I went out to meet my mother as she herself came up to bed, and when she saw that I had remained up so as to say good night to her again in the passage, I should not be allowed to stay in the house a day longer, I should be packed off to school next morning; so much was certain. Very good: had I been obliged, the next moment, to hurl myself out of the window, I should still have preferred such a fate. For what I wanted now was Mamma, and to say good night to her. I had gone too far along the road which led to the realization of this desire to be able to retrace my steps.

I could hear my parents' footsteps as they went with Swann; and, when the rattle of the gate assured me that he had really gone, I crept to the window. Mamma was asking my father if he had thought the lobster good, and whether M. Swann had had some more of the coffee-and-pistachio ice. 'I thought it rather so-so,' she was saying; 'next time we shall have to try another flavour.'

'I can't tell you,' said my great-aunt, 'what a change I find in Swann. He is quite antiquated!' She had grown so accustomed to seeing Swann always in the same stage of adolescence that it was a shock to her to find him suddenly less young than the age she still attributed to him. And the others too were beginning to remark in Swann that abnormal, excessive, scandalous senescence, meet only in a celibate, in one of that class for whom it seems that the great day which knows no morrow must be longer than for other men, since for such a one it is void of promise, and from its dawn the moments steadily accumulate without any subsequent partition among his offspring.

'I fancy he has a lot of trouble with that wretched wife of his, who "lives" with a certain Monsieur de Charlus, as all Combray knows. It's the talk of the town.'

My mother observed that, in spite of this, he had looked much less unhappy of late. 'And he doesn't nearly so often do that trick of his, so like his father, of wiping his eyes and passing his hand across his forehead. I think myself that in his heart of hearts he doesn't love his wife any more.'

'Why, of course he doesn't,' answered my grandfather. 'He wrote me a letter about it, ages ago, to which I took care to pay no attention, but it left no doubt as to his feelings, let alone his love for his wife. Hullo! you two; you never thanked him for the Asti!' he went on, turning to his sisters-in-law.

'What! we never thanked him? I think, between you and me, that I put it to him quite neatly,' replied my aunt Flora.

'Yes, you managed it very well; I admired you for it,' said my aunt Céline.

'But you did it very prettily, too.'

'Yes; I liked my expression about "nice neighbours".'

'What! Do you call that thanking him?' shouted my grandfather. 'I heard that all right, but devil take me if I guessed it was meant for Swann. You may be quite sure he never noticed it.'

'Come, come; Swann is not a fool. I am positive he appreciated the compliment. You didn't expect me to tell him the number of bottles, or to guess what he paid for them.'

My father and mother were left alone and sat down for a moment; then my father said: 'Well, shall we go up to bed?'

'As you wish, dear, though I don't feel in the least like sleeping. I don't know why; it can't be the coffee-ice – it wasn't strong enough to keep me awake like this. But I see a light in the servants' hall: poor Françoise has been sitting up for me, so I will get her to unhook me while you go and undress.'

My mother opened the latticed door which led from the hall to the staircase. Presently I heard her coming upstairs to close her window. I went quietly into the passage; my heart was beating so violently that I could hardly move, but at least it was throbbing no longer with anxiety, but with terror and with joy. I saw in the well of the stair a light coming upwards, from Mamma's candle. Then I saw Mamma herself: I threw myself upon her. For an instant she looked at me in astonishment, not realizing what could have happened. Then her face assumed an expression of anger. She said not a single word to me; and, for that matter, I used to go for days on end without being spoken to, for far less offences than this. A single word from Mamma would have been an admission that further intercourse with me was within the bounds of possibility, and that might perhaps have appeared to me more terrible still, as indicating that, with such a punishment as was in store for me, mere silence, and even anger, were relatively puerile.

A word from her then would have implied the false calm in which one converses with a servant to whom one has just decided to give notice; the kiss one bestows on a son who is being packed off to enlist, which would have been denied him for a few days. But she heard my father coming from the dressing-room, where he had gone to take off his clothes, and, to avoid the 'scene' which he would make if he saw me, she said, in a voice half-stifled by her anger: 'Run away at once. Don't let your father see you standing there like a crazy jane!'

But I begged her again to 'Come and say good night to me!' terrified as I saw the light from my father's candle already creeping up the wall, but also making use of his approach as a means of blackmail, in the hope that my mother, not wishing to find me there, as find me he must if she continued to hold out, would give in to me, and say: 'Go back to your room. I will come.'

Too late: my father was upon us. Instinctively I murmured, though no one heard me, 'I am done for!'

I was not, however. My father used constantly to refuse to let me do things which were quite clearly allowed by the more liberal charters granted me by my mother and grandmother, because he paid no heed to 'Principles', and because in his sight there were no such things as 'Rights of Man'. For some quite irrelevant reason, or for no reason at all, he would at the last moment prevent me from taking some particular walk, one so regular and so consecrated to my use that to deprive me of it was a clear breach of faith; or again, as he had done this evening, long before the appointed hour he would snap out: 'Run along up to bed now; no excuses!' But then again, simply because he was devoid of principles (in my grandmother's sense), so he could not, properly speaking, be called inexorable. He looked at me for a moment with an air of annoyance and surprise, and then when Mamma had told him, not without some embarrassment, what had happened, said to her: 'Go along with him, then; you said just now that you didn't feel like sleep, so stay in his room for a little. I don't need anything.'

'But, dear,' my mother answered timidly, 'whether or not I feel like sleep is not the point; we must not make the child accustomed – '

'There's no question of making him accustomed,' said my father, with a shrug of the shoulders; 'you can see quite well that the child is unhappy. After all, we aren't gaolers. You'll end by making him ill, and a lot of good that will do. There are two beds in his room; tell Françoise to make up the big one for you, and stay beside him for the rest of the night. I'm off to bed, anyhow; I'm not nervous like you. Good night.'

It was impossible for me to thank my father; what he called sentimentality would have exasperated him. I stood there, not daring to move; he was still confronting us, an immense figure in his white nightshirt, crowned with the pink and violet scarf of Indian cashmere in which, since he had begun to suffer from neuralgia, he used to tie up his head, standing like Abraham in the engraving after Benozzo Gozzoli which M. Swann had given me, telling Sarah that she must tear herself away from Isaac. Many years have passed since that night. The wall of the staircase, up which I had watched the light of his candle gradually climb, was long ago demolished. And in myself, too, many things have perished which, I imagined, would last for ever, and new structures have arisen, giving birth to new sorrows and new joys which in those days I could not have foreseen, just as now the old are difficult of comprehension. It is a long time, too, since my father has been able to tell Mamma to 'Go with the child.' Never again will such hours be possible for me. But of late I have been increasingly able to catch, if I listen attentively, the sound of the sobs which I had the strength to control in my father's presence, and which broke out only when I found myself alone with Mamma. Actually, their echo has never ceased: it is only because life is now growing more and more quiet round about me that I hear them afresh, like those convent bells which are so effectively drowned during the day by the noises of the streets that one would suppose them to have been stopped for ever, until they sound out again through the silent evening air.

Mamma spent that night in my room: when I had just committed a sin so deadly that I was waiting to be banished from the household, my parents gave me a far greater concession than I should ever have won as the reward of a good action. Even at the moment when it manifested itself in this crowning mercy, my father's conduct towards me was still somewhat arbitrary, and regardless of my deserts, as was characteristic of him and due to the fact that his actions were generally dictated by chance expediencies rather than based on any formal plan. And perhaps even what I called his strictness, when he sent me off to bed, deserved that title less, really, than my mother's or grandmother's attitude, for his nature, which in some respects differed more than theirs from my own, had probably prevented him from guessing, until then, how wretched I was every evening, a thing which my mother and grandmother knew well; but they loved me enough to be unwilling to spare me that suffering, which they hoped to teach me to overcome, so as to reduce my nervous sensibility and to strengthen my will. As for my father, whose affection for me was of another kind, I doubt if he would have shown so much courage, for as soon as he had grasped the fact that I was unhappy he had said to my mother: 'Go and comfort him.'

Mamma stayed all night in my room, and it seemed that she did not wish to mar by recrimination those hours, so different from anything that I had had a right to expect; for when Françoise (who guessed that something extraordinary must have happened when she saw Mamma sitting by my side, holding my hand and letting me cry unchecked) said to her: 'But, Madame, what is little Master crying for?' she replied; 'Why, Françoise, he doesn't know himself: it is his nerves. Make up the big bed for me quickly and then go off to your own.' And thus for the first time my unhappiness was regarded no longer as a fault for which I must be punished but as an involuntary evil which had been officially recognized, a nervous condition for which I was in no way responsible: I had the consolation that I need no longer mingle apprehensive scruples with the bitterness of my tears; I could weep henceforward without sin. I felt no small degree of pride, either, in Françoise's presence at this return to humane conditions which, not an hour after Mamma had refused to come up to my room and had sent the snubbing message that I was to go to sleep, raised me to the dignity of a grown-up person, brought me of a sudden to a sort of puberty of sorrow, to emancipation from tears. I ought then to have been happy; I was not. It struck me that my mother had just made a first concession which must have been painful to her, that it was a first step down from the ideal she had formed for me, and that for the first time she, with all her courage, had to confess herself beaten. It struck me that if I had just scored a victory it was over her; that I had succeeded, as sickness or sorrow or age might have succeeded, in relaxing her will, in altering her judgement; that this evening opened a new era, must remain a black date in the calendar. And if I had dared now, I should have said to Mamma: 'No, I don't want you; you mustn't sleep here.' But I was conscious of the practical wisdom, of what would be called nowadays the realism with which she tempered the ardent idealism of my grandmother's nature, and I knew that now the mischief was done she would prefer to let me enjoy the soothing pleasure of her company, and not to disturb my father again. Certainly my mother's beautiful features seemed to shine again with youth that evening, as she sat gently holding my hands and trying to check my tears; but, just for that reason, it seemed to me that this should not have happened; her anger would have been less difficult to endure than this new kindness which my childhood had not known; I felt that I had with an impious and secret finger traced a first wrinkle upon her soul and made the first white hair show upon her head. This thought redoubled my sobs, and then I saw that Mamma, who had never allowed herself to go to any length of tenderness with me, was suddenly overcome by my tears and had to struggle to keep back her own. Then, as she saw that I had noticed this, she said to me, with a smile: 'Why, my little buttercup, my little canary-boy, he's going to make Mamma as silly as himself if this goes on. Look, since you can't sleep, and Mamma can't either, we mustn't go on in this stupid way; we must do something; I'll get one of your books.' But I had none there. 'Would you like me to get out the books now that your grandmother is going to give you for your birthday? Just think it over first, and don't be disappointed if there is nothing new for you then.'

I was only too delighted, and Mamma went to find a parcel of books in which I could not distinguish, through the paper in which it was wrapped, any more than its squareness and size, but which, even at this first glimpse, brief and obscure as it was, bade fair to eclipse already the paintbox of last New Year's Day and the silkworms of the year before. It contained *La Mare au Diable, Françoise le Champi, La Petite Fadette*, and *Les Maîtres Sonneurs*. My grandmother, as I learned afterwards, had at first chosen Musset's poems, a volume of Rousseau, and *Indiana*; for while she considered light reading as unwholesome as sweets and cakes, she did not reflect that the strong breath of genius must have upon the very soul of a child an influence at once more dangerous and less quickening than those of fresh air and country breezes upon his body. But when my father had seemed almost to regard her as insane on learning the names of the books she proposed to give me, she had journeyed back by herself to Jouy-le-Vicomte to the book-seller's, so that there should be no fear of my not having my present in time (it was a burning hot day, and she had come home so unwell that the doctor had warned my mother not to allow her again to tire herself in that way), and had there fallen back upon the four pastoral novels of George Sand.

'My dear,' she had said to Mamma, 'I could not allow myself to give the child anything that was not well written.'

The truth was that she could never make up her mind to purchase anything from which no intellectual profit was to be derived, and, above all, that profit which good things be-stowed on us by teaching us to seek our pleasures elsewhere than in the barren satisfaction of worldly wealth. Even when she had to make someone a present of the kind called 'use-ful', when she had to give an arm-chair or some table-silver or a walking-stick, she would choose 'antiques', as though their long desuetude had effaced from them any semblance of utility and fitted them rather to instruct us in the lives of the men of other days than to serve the common requirements of our own. She would have liked me to have in my room photographs of ancient buildings or of beautiful places. But at the moment of buying them, and for all that the subject of the picture had an aesthetic value of its own, she would find that vulgarity and utility had too prominent a part in them, through the mechanical nature of their repro-duction by photography. She attempted by a subterfuge, if not to eliminate altogether their commercial banality, at least to minimize it, to substitute for the bulk of it what was art still, to introduce, as it might be, several 'thicknesses' of art; instead of photographs of Chartres Cathedral, of the Fountains of Saint-Cloud, or of Vesuvius she would inquire of Swann whether some great painter had not made pictures of them, and preferred to give me photographs of 'Chartres Cathedral' after Corot, of the 'Fountains of Saint-Cloud' after Hubert Robert, and of 'Vesuvius' after Turner, which were a stage higher in the scale of art. But although the photographer had been prevented from reproducing directly the masterpieces or the beauties of nature, and had there been replaced by a great artist, he resumed his odious position when it came to reproducing the artist's interpretation. Accordingly, having to reckon again with vulgarity, my grandmother would endeavour to postpone the moment of contact still further. She would ask Swann if the picture had not been engraved, preferring, when possible, old engravings with some interest of association apart from themselves, such, for example, as show us a masterpiece in a state in which we can no longer see it to-day, as Morghen's print of the 'Cenacolo' of Leonardo before it was spoiled by restoration. It must be admitted that the results of this method of interpreting the art of making presents were not always happy. The idea which I formed of Venice, from a drawing by Titian which is supposed to have the lagoon in the background, was certainly far less accurate than what I have since derived from ordinary photographs. We could no longer keep count in the family (when my great-aunt tried to frame an indictment of my grandmother) of all the arm-chairs she had presented to married couples, young and old, which on a first attempt to sit down upon them had at once collapsed beneath the weight of their recipient. But my grandmother would have thought it sordid to concern herself too closely with the solidity of any piece of furniture in which could still be discerned a flourish, a smile, a brave conceit of the past. And even what in such pieces supplied a material need, since it did so in a manner to which we are no longer accustomed, was as charming to her as one of those old forms of speech in which we can still see traces of a metaphor whose fine point has been worn away by the rough usage of our modern tongue. In precisely the same way the pastoral novels of George Sand, which she was giving me for my birthday, were regular lumber-rooms of antique furniture, full of expressions that have fallen out of use and returned as imagery, such as one finds now only in country dialects. And my grandmother had bought them in preference to other books, just as she would have preferred to take a house that had a gothic dovecot, or some other such piece of antiquity as would have a pleasant effect on the mind, filling it with a nostalgic longing for impossible journeys through the realms of time.

Mamma sat down by my bed; she had chosen *François le Champi*, whose reddish cover and incomprehensible title gave it a distinct personality in my eyes and a mysterious attraction. I had not then read any real novels. I had heard it said that George Sand was a typical novelist. That prepared me in advance to imagine that *François le Champi* contained something inexpressibly delicious. The course of the narrative, where it tended to arouse curiosity or melt to pity, certain modes of expression which disturb or sadden the reader, and which, with a little experience, he may recognize as 'common form' in novels, seemed to me then distinctive – for to me a new book was not one of a number of similar objects, but was like an individual man, unmatched, and with no cause of existence beyond himself – an intoxicating whiff of the peculiar essence of *François le Champi*. Beneath the everyday incidents, the commonplace thoughts and hackneyed words, I could hear, or overhear, an intonation, a rhythmic utterance fine and strange. The 'action' began: to me it seemed all the more obscure because in those days, when I read to myself, I used often, while I turned the pages, to dream of something quite different. And to the gaps which this habit made in my knowledge of the story more were added by the fact that when it was Mamma who was reading to me aloud she left all the love-scenes out. And so all the odd changes which take place in the relations between the miller's wife and the boy, changes which only the birth and growth of love can explain, seemed to me plunged and steeped in a mystery, the key to which (as I could readily believe) lay in that strange and pleasant-sounding name of *Champi*, which draped the boy who bore it, I knew not why, in its own bright colour, purpurate and charming. If my mother was not a faithful reader, she was none the less admirable when reading a work in which she found the note of true feeling by the respectful

simplicity of her interpretation and by the sound of her
sweet and gentle voice. It was the same in her daily life, when
it was not works of art but men and women whom she was
moved to pity or admire: it was touching to observe with what
deference she would banish from her voice, her gestures, from
her whole conversation, now the note of joy which might
have distressed some mother who had long ago lost a child,
now the recollection of an event or anniversary which might
have reminded some old gentleman of the burden of his years,
now the household topic which might have bored some young
man of letters. And so, when she read aloud the prose of
George Sand, prose which is everywhere redolent of that
generosity and moral distinction which Mamma had learned
from my grandmother to place above all other qualities in life,
and which I was not to teach her until much later to refrain
from placing in the same way, above all other qualities in
literature; taking pains to banish from her voice any weakness
or affectation which might have blocked its channel for that
powerful stream of language, she supplied all the natural
tenderness, all the lavish sweetness which they demanded to
phrases which seemed to have been composed for her voice,
and which were all, so to speak, within her compass. She
came to them with the tone that they required, with the
cordial accent which existed before they were, which dictated
them, but which is not to be found in the words themselves,
and by these means she smoothed away, as she read on, any
harshness there might be or discordance in the tenses of verbs,
endowing the imperfect and the preterite with all the sweetness which there is in generosity, all the melancholy which
there is in love; guided the sentence that was drawing to an
end towards that which was waiting to begin, now hastening,
now slackening the pace of the syllables so as to bring them,
despite their difference of quantity, into a uniform rhythm,
and breathed into this quite ordinary prose a kind of life,
continuous and full of feeling.

My agony was soothed; I let myself be borne upon the
current of this gentle night on which I had my mother by my
side. I knew that such a night could not be repeated; that

the strongest desire I had in the world, namely, to keep my mother in my room through the sad hours of darkness, ran too much counter to general requirements and to the wishes of others for such a concession as had been granted me this evening to be anything but a rare and casual exception. To-morrow night I should again be the victim of anguish and Mamma would not stay by my side. But when these storms of anguish grew calm I could no longer realize their existence; besides, to-morrow evening was still a long way off; I reminded myself that I should still have time to think about things, albeit that remission of time could bring me no access of power, albeit the coming event was in no way dependent upon the exercise of my will, and seemed not quite inevitable only because it was still separated from me by this short interval.

*

And so it was that, for a long time afterwards, when I lay awake at night and revived old memories of Combray, I saw no more of it than this sort of luminous panel, sharply defined against a vague and shadowy background, like the panels which a Bengal fire or some electric sign will illuminate and dissect from the front of a building the other parts of which remain plunged in darkness: broad at its base, the little parlour, the dining-room, the alluring shadows of the path along which would come M. Swann, the unconscious author of my sufferings, the hall through which I would journey to the first step of that staircase, so hard to climb, which constituted, all by itself, the tapering 'elevation' of an irregular pyramid and, at the summit, my bedroom, with the little passage through whose glazed door Mamma would enter; in a word, seen always at the same evening hour, isolated from all its possible surroundings, detached and solitary against its shadowy background, the bare minimum of scenery necessary (like the setting one sees printed at the head of an old play, for its performance in the provinces) to the drama of my undressing, as though all Combray had consisted of but two floors joined by a slender staircase, and as though there had been no time there but seven o'clock at night. I must own that I could have assured any questioner that Combray did include other scenes and did exist at other hours than these. But since the facts which I should then have recalled would have been prompted only by an exercise of the will, by my intellectual memory, and since the pictures which that kind of memory shows us of the past preserve nothing of the past itself, I should never have had any wish to ponder over this residue of Combray. To me it was in reality all dead.

Permanently dead? Very possibly.

There is a large element of hazard in these matters, and a second hazard, that of our own death, often prevents us from awaiting for any length of time the favours of the first.

I feel that there is much to be said for the Celtic belief that the souls of those whom we have lost are held captive in some inferior being, in an animal, in a plant, in some inanimate object, and so effectively lost to us until the day (which to many never comes) when we happen to pass by the tree or to obtain possession of the object which forms their prison. Then they start and tremble, they call us by our name, and as soon as we have recognized their voices the spell is broken. We have delivered them: they have overcome death and return to share our life.

And so it is with our own past. It is a labour in vain to attempt to recapture it: all the efforts of our intellect must prove futile. The past is hidden somewhere outside the realm, beyond the reach of intellect, in some material object (in the sensation which that material object will give us) which we do not suspect. And as for that object, it depends on chance whether we come upon it or not before we ourselves must die.

Many years had elapsed during which nothing of Combray, save what was comprised in the theatre and the drama of my going to bed there, had any existence for me, when one day in winter, as I came home, my mother, seeing that I was cold, offered me some tea, a thing I did not ordinarily take. I declined at first, and then, for no particular reason, changed my mind. She sent out for one of those short, plump little cakes called 'petites madeleines,' which look as though they had been moulded in the fluted scallop of a pilgrim's shell.

And soon, mechanically, weary after a dull day with the prospect of a depressing morrow, I raised to my lips a spoonful of the tea in which I had soaked a morsel of the cake. No sooner had the warm liquid, and the crumbs with it, touched my palate than a shudder ran through my whole body, and I stopped, intent upon the extraordinary changes that were taking place. An exquisite pleasure had invaded my senses, but individual, detached, with no suggestion of its origin. And at once the vicissitudes of life had become indifferent to me, its disasters innocuous, its brevity illusory – this new sensation having had on me the effect which love had of filling me with a precious essence; or rather this essence was not in me, it was myself. I had ceased now to feel mediocre, accidental, mortal. Whence could it have come to me, this all-powerful joy? I was conscious that it was connected with the taste of tea and cake, but that it infinitely transcended those savours, could not, indeed, be of the same nature as theirs. Whence did it come? What did it signify? How could I seize upon and define it?

I drink a second mouthful , in which I find nothing more than in the first, a third, which gives me rather less than the second. It is time to stop; the potion is losing its magic. It is plain that the object of my quest, the truth, lies not in the cup but in myself. The tea has called up in me, but does not itself understand, and can only repeat indefinitely, with a gradual loss of strength, the same testimony; which I, too, cannot interpret, though I hope at least to be able to call upon the tea for it again and to find it there presently, intact and at my disposal, for my final enlightenment. I put down my cup and examine my own mind. It is for it to discover the truth. But how? What an abyss of uncertainty whenever the mind feels that some part of it has strayed beyond its own borders; when it, the seeker, is at once the dark region through which it must go seeking, where all its equipment will avail it nothing. Seek? More than that; create. It is face to face with something which does not so far exist, to which it alone can give reality and substance, which it alone can bring into the light of day.

And I begin again to ask myself what it could have been, this unremembered state which brought with it no logical proof of its existence, but only the sense that it was a happy, that it was a real state in whose presence other states of consciousness melted and vanished. I decided to attempt to make it reappear. I retrace my thoughts to the moment at which I drank the first spoonful of tea. I find again the same state, illuminated by no fresh light. I compel my mind to make one further effort, to follow and recapture once again the fleeting sensation. And that nothing may interrupt it in its course I shut out every obstacle, every extraneous idea, I stop my ears and inhibit all attention to the sounds which come from the next room. And then, feeling that my mind is growing fatigued without having any success to report, I compel it for a change to enjoy that distraction which I have just denied it, to think of other things, to rest and refresh itself before the supreme attempt. And then for the second time I clear an empty space in front of it. I place in position before my mind's eye the still recent taste of that first mouthful, and I feel something start within me, something that leaves its resting-place and attempts to rise, something that has been embedded like an anchor at a great depth; I do not know yet what it is, but I can feel it mounting slowly; I can measure the resistance, I can hear the echo of great spaces traversed.

Undoubtedly what is thus palpitating in the depths of my being must be the image, the visual memory which, being linked to that taste, has tried to follow it into my conscious mind. But its struggles are too far off, too much confused; scarcely can I perceive the colourless reflection in which are blended the uncapturable whirling medley of radiant hues, and I cannot distinguish its form, cannot invite it, as the one possible interpreter, to translate to me the evidence of its contemporary, its inseparable paramour, the taste of cake soaked in tea; cannot ask it to inform me what special circumstance is in question, of what period in my past life.

Will it ultimately reach the clear surface of my consciousness, this memory, this old, dead moment which the magnetism of an identical moment has travelled so far to importune, to disturb, to raise up out of the very depths of my being? I cannot tell. Now that I feel nothing, it has stopped, has perhaps gone down again into its darkness, from which who can say whether it will ever rise? Ten times over I must essay the task, must lean down over the abyss. And each time the natural laziness which deters us from every difficult enterprise, every work of importance, has urged me to leave the thing alone, to drink my tea and to think merely of the worries of to-day and of my hopes for to-morrow, which let themselves be pondered over without effort or distress of mind.

And suddenly the memory returns. The taste was that of the little crumb of madeleine which on Sunday mornings at Combray (because on those mornings I did not go out before church-time), when I went to say good day to her in her bedroom, my aunt Léonie used to give me, dipping it first in her own cup of real or of lime-flower tea. The sight of the little madeleine had recalled nothing to my mind before I tasted it; perhaps because I had so often seen such things in the interval, without tasting them, on the trays in pastry-cooks' windows, that their image had dissociated itself from those Combray days to take its place among others more recent; perhaps because of those memories, so long abandoned and put out of mind, nothing now survived, everything was scattered; the forms of things, including that of the little scallop-shell of pastry, so richly sensual under its severe, religious folds were either obliterated or had been so long dormant as to have lost the power of expansion which would have allowed them to resume their place in my consciousness. But when from a long-distant past nothing subsists, after the people are dead, after the things are broken and scattered, still, alone, more fragile, but with more vitality, more unsubstantial, more persistent, more faithful, the smell and taste of things remain poised a long time, like souls, ready to remind us, waiting and hoping for their moment, amid the ruins of all the rest; and bear unfaltering, in the tiny and almost impalpable drop of their essence, the vast structure of recollection.

And once again I had recognized the taste of the crumb of madeleine soaked in her decoction of lime-flowers which my aunt used to give me (although I did not yet know and must long postpone the discovery of why this memory made me so happy) immediately the old grey house upon the street, where her room was, rose up like the scenery of a theatre to attach itself to the little pavilion, opening on to the garden, which had been built out behind it for my parents (the isolated panel which until that moment had been all that I could see); and with the house the town, from morning to night and in all weathers, the Square where I was sent before luncheon, the streets along which I used to run errands, the country roads we took when it was fine. And just as the Japanese amuse themselves by filling a porcelain bowl with water and steeping in it little crumbs of paper which until then are without character or form, but, the moment they become wet, stretch themselves and bend, take on colour and distinctive shape, become flowers or houses or people, permanent and recognizable, so in that moment all the flowers in our garden and in M. Swann's park, and the water-lilies on the Vivonne and the good folk of the village and their little dwellings and the parish church and the whole of Combray and of its surroundings, taking their proper shapes and growing solid, sprang into being, town and gardens alike, from my cup of tea.

Combray

COMBRAY at a distance, from a twenty-mile radius, as we used to see it from the railway when we arrived there every year in Holy Week, was no more than a church epitomizing the town, representing it, speaking of it and for it to the horizon, and as one drew near, gathering close about its long, dark cloak, sheltering from the wind, on the open plain, as a shepherd gathers his sheep, the woolly grey backs of its flocking houses, which a fragment of its medieval ramparts enclosed, here and there, in an outline as scrupulously circular as that of a little town in a primitive painting. To live in, Combray was a trifle depressing, like its streets, whose houses, built of the blackened stone of the country, fronted with outside steps, capped with gables which projected long shadows downwards, were so dark that one had, as soon as the sun began to go down, to draw back the curtains in the sitting-room windows; streets with the solemn names of Saints, not a few of whom figured in the history of the early lords of Combray, such as the Rue Saint-Hilaire, the Rue Saint-Jacques, in which my aunt's house stood, the Rue Sainte-Hildegarde, which ran past her railings, and the Rue du Saint-Esprit, on to which the little garden gate opened; and these Combray streets exist in so remote a quarter of my memory, painted in colours so different from those in which the world is decked for me to-day, that in fact one and all of them, and the church which towered above them in the Square, seem to me now more unsubstantial than the projections of my magic-lantern; while at times I feel that to be able to cross the Rue Saint-Hilaire again, to engage a room in the Rue de l'Oiseau, in the old hostelry of the Oiseau Flesché, from whose windows in the pavement used to rise a smell of cooking which rises still in my mind, now and then, in the same warm gusts of comfort, would be to secure a contact with the unseen world more marvellously supernatural than it would be to make Golo's acquaintance and to chat with Geneviève de Brabant.

My grandfather's cousin – by courtesy my great-aunt – with whom we used to stay, was the mother of that aunt Léonie who, since her husband's (my uncle Octave's) death, had gradually declined to leave, first Combray, then her house in Combray, then her bedroom, and finally her bed; and who now never 'came down', but lay perpetually in an indefinite condition of grief, physical exhaustion, illness, obsessions, and religious observances. Her own room looked out over the Rue Saint-Jacques, which ran a long way further to end in the Grand-Pré (as distinct from the Petit-Pré, a green space in the centre of the town where three streets met) and which, monotonous and grey, with the three high steps of stone before almost every one of its doors, seemed like a deep furrow cut by some sculptor of gothic images in the very block of stone out of which he had fashioned a Calvary or a Crib. My aunt's life was now practically confined to two adjoining rooms, in one of which she would rest in the afternoon while they aired the other. They were rooms of that country order which (just as in certain climes whole tracts of air or ocean are illuminated or scented by myriads of protozoa which we cannot see) fascinate our sense of smell with the countless odours springing from their own special virtues, wisdom, habits, a whole secret system of life, invisible, superabundant and profoundly moral, which their atmosphere holds in solution; smells natural enough indeed, and coloured by circumstances as are those of the neighbouring countryside, but already humanized, domesticated, confined, an exquisite, skilful, limpid jelly, blending all the fruits of the season which have left the orchard for the store-room, smells changing with the year, but plenishing, domestic smells, which compensate for the sharpness of hoar frost with the sweet savour of warm bread, smells lazy and punctual as a village clock, roving and settled, heedless and provident, linen smells, morning smells, pious smells; rejoicing in a peace which brings only an increase of anxiety, and in a prosiness which serves as a deep source of poetry to the stranger who passes through their midst without having lived amongst them. The air of those rooms was saturated with the fine bouquet of a silence so nourishing, so succulent

61

that I could not enter them without a sort of greedy enjoyment, particularly on those first mornings, chilly still, of the Easter holidays, when I could taste it more fully, because I had just arrived then at Combray: before I went in to wish my aunt good day I would be kept waiting a little time in the outer room, where the sun, a wintry sun still, had crept in to warm itself before the fire, lighted already between its two brick sides and plastering all the room and everything in it with a smell of soot, making the room like one of those great open hearths which one finds in the country, or one of the canopied mantelpieces in old castles under which one sits hoping that in the world outside it is raining or snowing, hoping almost for a catastrophic deluge to add the romance of shelter and security to the comfort of a snug retreat; I would turn to and fro between the prayer-desk and the stamped velvet arm-chairs, each one always draped in its crocheted antimacassar, while the fire, baking like a pie the appetizing smells with which the air of the room was thickly clotted, which the dewy and sunny freshness of the morning had already 'raised' and started to 'set', puffed them and glazed them and fluted them and swelled them into an invisible though not impalpable country cake, an immense puff-pastry, in which, barely waiting to savour the crustier, more delicate, more respectable, but also drier smells of the cupboard, the chest-of-drawers, and the patterned wallpaper I always returned with an unconfessed gluttony to bury myself in the nondescript, resinous, dull, indigestible, and fruity smell of the flowered quilt.

In the next room I could hear my aunt talking quietly to herself. She never spoke save in low tones, because she believed that there was something broken in her head and floating loose there, which she might displace by talking too loud; but she never remained for long, even when alone, without saying something, because she believed that it was good for her throat, and that by keeping the blood there in circulation it would make less frequent the chokings and other pains to which she was liable; besides, in the life of complete inertia which she led she attached to the least of her sensations an extraordinary importance, endowed them with a Protean ubiquity which made it difficult for her to keep them secret, and, failing a confidant to whom she might communicate them, she used to promulgate them to herself in an unceasing monologue which was her sole form of activity. Unfortunately, having formed the habit of thinking aloud, she did not always take care to see that there was no one in the adjoining room, and I would often hear her saying to herself; 'I must not forget that I never slept a wink' – for 'never sleeping a wink' was her great claim to distinction, and one admitted and respected in our household vocabulary; in the morning Françoise would not 'call' her, but would simply 'come to' her; during the day, when my aunt wished to take a nap, we used to say just that she wished to 'be quiet' or to 'rest'; and when in conversation she so far forgot herself as to say 'what made me wake up', or 'I dreamed that', she would flush and at once correct herself.

After waiting a minute, I would go in and kiss her; Françoise would be making her tea; or, if my aunt were feeling 'upset', she would ask instead for her 'tisane', and it would be my duty to shake out of the chemist's little package on to a plate the amount of lime-blossom required for infusion in boiling water. The drying of the stems had twisted them into a fantastic trellis, in whose intervals the pale flowers opened, as though a painter had arranged them there, grouping them in the most decorative poses. The leaves, which had lost their own appearance, assumed those instead of the most incongruous things imaginable, as though the transparent wings of flies or the blank sides of labels or the petals of roses had been collected and pounded, or interwoven as birds weave the material for their nests. A thousand trifling little details – the charming prodigality of the chemist – details which would have been eliminated from an artificial preparation, gave me, like a book in which one is astonished to read the name of a person whom one knows, the pleasure of finding that these were indeed real lime-blossoms, like those I had seen, when coming from the train, in the Avenue de la Gare, altered, but only because they were not imitations but the very same blossoms, which had grown old. And as each new character is merely a metamorphosis from something older, in these little grey balls I recognized green buds plucked before their time; but beyond all else the rosy, moony, tender glow which lit up the blossoms among the frail forest of stems from which they hung like little golden roses – marking, as the radiance upon an old wall still marks the place of a vanished fresco, the difference between those parts of the tree which had and those which had not been 'in bloom' – showed me that these were petals which, before their flowering-time, the chemist's package had embalmed on warm evenings of spring. That rosy candlelight was still their colour, but half-extinguished and deadened in the diminished life which was now theirs, and which may be called the twilight of a flower. Presently my aunt was able to dip in the boiling infusion, in which she would relish the savour of dead or faded blossom, a little madeleine, of which she would hold out a piece to me when it was sufficiently soft.

At one side of her bed stood a big yellow chest-of-drawers of lemon-wood, and a table which served at once as pharmacy and as high altar, on which, beneath a statue of Our Lady and a bottle of Vichy-Célestins, might be found her service-books and her medical prescriptions, everything that she needed for the performance, in bed, of her duties to soul and body, to keep the proper times for pepsin and for vespers. On the other side her bed was bounded by the window: she had the street beneath her eyes, and would read in it from morning to night to divert the tedium of her life, like a Persian prince, the daily but immemorial chronicles of Combray, which she would discuss in detail afterwards with Françoise.

I would not have been five minutes with my aunt before she would send me away in case I made her tired. She would hold out for me to kiss her sad brow, pale and lifeless, on which at this early hour she would not yet have arranged the false hair and through which the bones shone like the points of a crown of thorns or the beads of a rosary, and she would say to me: 'Now, my poor child, you must go away; go and get ready for mass; and if you see Françoise downstairs, tell her not to stay too long amusing herself with you; she must come up soon to see if I want anything.'

Françoise, who had been for many years in my aunt's service and did not at that time suspect that she would one day be transferred entirely to ours, was a little inclined to desert my aunt during the months which we spent in her house. There had been in my infancy, before we first went to Combray, and when my aunt Léonie used to spend the winter in Paris still with her mother, a time when I knew Françoise so little that on New Year's Day, before going into my great-aunt's house, my mother put a five-franc piece in my hand and said: 'Now, be careful. Don't make any mistake. Wait until you hear me say "Good morning, Françoise," and I touch your arm, before you give it to her.' No sooner had we arrived in my aunt's dark hall than we saw in the gloom, beneath the frills of a snowy cap as stiff and fragile as if it had been made of spun sugar, the concentric waves of a smile of anticipatory gratitude. It was Françoise, motionless and erect, framed in the small doorway of the corridor like the statue of a saint in its niche. When we had grown more accustomed to this religious darkness we could discern in her features a disinterested love of all humanity, blended with a tender respect for the 'upper classes' which raised to the most honourable quarter of her heart the hope of receiving her due reward. Mamma pinched my arm sharply and said in a loud voice: 'Good morning, Françoise.' At this signal my fingers parted and I let fall the coin, which found a receptacle in a confused but outstretched hand. But since we had begun to go to Combray there was no one I knew better than Françoise. We were her favourites, and in the first years at least, while she showed the same consideration for us as for my aunt, she enjoyed us with a keener relish, because we had, in addition to our dignity as part of 'the family' (for she had for those invisible bonds by which community of blood unites the members of a family as much respect as any Greek tragedian), the fresh charm of not being her customary employers. And so with what joy would she welcome us, with what sorrow complain that the weather was still so bad for us, on the day of our arrival, just before Easter, when there was often an icy wind;

while Mamma inquired after her daughter and her nephews, and if her grandson was good-looking, and what they were going to make of him, and whether he took after his granny.

Later, when no one else was in the room, Mamma, who knew that Françoise was still mourning for her parents, who had been dead for years, would speak of them kindly, asking her endless little questions about them and their lives.

She had guessed that Françoise was not over-fond of her son-in-law, and that he spoiled the pleasure she found in visiting her daughter, as the two could not talk so freely when he was there. And so one day, when Françoise was going to their house, some miles from Combray, Mamma said to her, with a smile: 'Tell me, Françoise, if Julien has had to go away, and you have Marguerite to yourself all day, you will be very sorry, but you will make the best of it, won't you?'

And Françoise answered, laughing: 'Madame knows everything; Madame is worse than the X-rays' (she pronounced 'x' with an affectation of difficulty and with a smile in deprecation of her, an unlettered woman's daring to employ a scientific term) 'they brought here for Mme Octave, which see what is in your heart' – and she went off, disturbed that anyone should be caring about her, perhaps anxious that we should not see her in tears: Mamma was the first person who had given her the pleasure of feeling that her peasant existence, with its simple joys and sorrows, might offer some interest, might be a source of grief or pleasure to some one other than herself.

My aunt resigned herself to doing without Françoise to some extent during our visits, knowing how much my mother appreciated the services of so active and intelligent a maid, one who looked as smart at five o'clock in the morning in her kitchen, under a cap whose stiff and dazzling frills seemed to be made of porcelain, as when dressed for churchgoing; who did everything in the right way, who toiled like a horse, whether she was well or ill, but without noise, without the appearance of doing anything; the only one of my aunt's maids who when Mamma asked for hot water or black coffee would bring them actually boiling; she was one of those servants who in a household seem least satisfactory, at first, to a stranger, doubtless because they take no pains to make a conquest of him and show him no special attention, knowing very well they have no real need of him, that he will cease to be invited to the house sooner than they will be dismissed from it; who, on the other hand, cling with most fidelity to those masters and mistresses who have tested and proved their real capacity, and do not look for that superficial responsiveness, that slavish affability, which may impress a stranger favourably, but often conceals an utter barrenness of spirit in which no amount of training can produce the least trace of individuality.

When Françoise, having seen that my parents had everything they required, first went upstairs again to give my aunt her pepsin and to find out from her what she would take for luncheon, very few mornings passed but she was called upon to give an opinion, or to furnish an explanation, in regard to some important event.

'Just fancy, Françoise, Mme Goupil went by more than a quarter of an hour late to fetch her sister: if she loses any more time on the way I should not be at all surprised if she got in after the Elevation.'

'Well, there'd be nothing wonderful in that,' would be the answer. Or:

'Françoise, if you had come in five minutes ago, you would have seen Mme Imbert go past with some asparagus twice the size of what mother Callot has: do try to find out from her cook where she got them. You know you've been putting asparagus in all your sauces this spring; you might be able to get some like these for our visitors.'

'I shouldn't be surprised if they came from the Curé's,' Françoise would say, and:

'I'm sure you wouldn't, my poor Françoise,' my aunt would reply, raising her shoulders. 'From the Curé's, indeed! You know quite well that he can never grow anything but wretched little twigs of asparagus, not asparagus at all. I tell you these ones were as thick as my arm. Not your arm, of course, but my poor arm, which has grown so much thinner again this year.' Or:

'Françoise, didn't you hear that bell just now? It split my head.'

'No, Mme Octave.'

'Ah, poor girl, your skull must be very thick; you may thank God for that. It was Maguelone come to fetch Dr Piperaud. He came out with her at once and they went off along the Rue de l'Oiseau. There must be some child ill.'

'Oh dear, dear; the poor little creature!' would come with a sigh from Françoise, who could not hear of any calamity befalling a person unknown to her, even in some distant part of the world, without beginning to lament. Or:

'Françoise, for whom did they toll the passing-bell just now? Oh dear, of course, it would be for Mme Rousseau. And to think that I had forgotten that she passed away the other night. Indeed, it is time the Lord called me home too; I don't know what has become of my head since I lost my poor Octave. But I am wasting your time, my good girl.'

'Indeed no, Mme Octave, my time is not so precious; whoever made our time didn't sell it to us. I am just going to see that my fire hasn't gone out.'

In this way Françoise and my aunt made a critical valuation between them, in the course of the morning sessions, of the earliest happenings of the day. But sometimes these happenings assumed so mysterious or so alarming an air that my aunt felt she could not wait until it was time for Françoise to come upstairs, and then a formidable and quadruple peal would resound through the house.

'But, Mme Octave, it is not time for your pepsin,' Françoise would begin. 'Are you feeling faint?'

'No, thank you, Françoise,' my aunt would reply, 'that is to say, yes; for you know well that there is very seldom a time when I don't feel faint; one day I shall pass away like Mme Rousseau, before I know where I am; but that is not why I rang. Would you believe that I have just seen, as plainly as I see you, Mme Coupil with a little girl I didn't know at all. Run and get a pennyworth of salt from Camus. It's not often that Théodore can't tell you who a person is.'

'But that must be M. Pupin's daughter,' Françoise would

say, preferring to stick to an immediate explanation, since she had been perhaps twice already into Camus's shop that morning.

'M. Pupin's daughter! Oh, that's a likely story, my poor Françoise. Do you think I should not have recognized M. Pupin's daughter!'

'But I don't mean the big one, Mme Octave; I mean the little girl, the one who goes to school at Jouy. I seem to have seen her once already this morning.'

'Oh, if that's what it is!' my aunt would say, 'she must have come over for the holidays. Yes, that is it. No need to ask, she will have come over for the holidays. But then we shall soon see Mme Sazerat come along and ring her sister's door-bell, for her luncheon. That will be it! I saw the boy from Galopin's go by with a tart. You will see that the tart was for Mme Goupil.'

'Once Mme Goupil has anyone in the house, Mme Octave, you won't be long in seeing all her folk going in to their luncheon there, for it's not so early as it was,' would be the answer, for Françoise, who was anxious to retire downstairs to look after our own meal, was not sorry to leave my aunt with the prospect of such a distraction.

'Oh! not before midday!' my aunt would reply in a tone of resignation, darting an uneasy glance at the clock, but stealthily, so as not to let it be seen that she, who had renounced all earthly joys, yet found a keen satisfaction in learning Mme Goupil was expecting company to luncheon, though, alas, she must wait a little more than an hour still before enjoying the spectacle. 'And it will come in the middle of my luncheon!' she would murmur to herself. Her luncheon was such a distraction in itself that she did not like any other to come at the same time. 'At least, you will not forget to give me my creamed eggs on one of the flat plates?' These were the only plates which had pictures on them and my aunt used to amuse herself at every meal by reading the description on whichever might have been sent up to her. She would put on her spectacles and spell out: 'Ali Baba and the Forty Thieves', 'Aladdin, or the Wonderful Lamp', and smile, and say 'Very good indeed.'

'I may as well go across to Camus ...' Françoise would

hazard, seeing that my aunt had no longer any intention of sending her there.

'No, no; it's not worth while now; it's certain to be the Pupin girl. My poor Françoise, I am sorry to have made you come upstairs for nothing.'

But it was not for nothing, as my aunt well knew, that she had rung for Françoise, since at Combray a person whom one 'didn't know at all' was as incredible a being as any mythological deity, and it was apt to be forgotten that after each occasion on which there had appeared in the Rue du Saint-Esprit or in the Square one of these bewildering phenomena, careful and exhaustive researches had invariably reduced the fabulous monster to the proportions of a person whom one 'did know', either personally or in the abstract, in his or her civil status as being more or less closely related to some family in Combray. It would turn out to be Mme Sauton's son discharged from the army, or the Abbé Perdreau's niece come home from her convent, or the Curé's brother, a tax-collector at Châteaudun, who had just retired on a pension or had come to Combray for the holidays. On first noticing them you had been impressed by the thought that there might be in Combray people whom you 'didn't know at all', simply because you had failed to recognize or identify them at once. And yet long beforehand Mme Sauton and the Curé had given warning that they expected their 'strangers'. In the evening, when I came in and went upstairs to tell my aunt the incidents of our walk, if I was rash enough to say to her that we had passed, near the Pont-Vieux, a man whom my grandfather didn't know:

'A man grandfather didn't know at all!' she would exclaim. 'That's a likely story.' None the less, she would be a little disturbed by the news, she would wish to have the details correctly, and so my grandfather would be summoned. 'Who can it have been that you passed near the Pont-Vieux, uncle? A man you didn't know at all?'

'Why, of course I did,' my grandfather would answer; 'it was Prosper, Mme Bouillebœuf's gardener's brother.'

'Ah, well!' my aunt would say, calm again but slightly flushed still; 'and the boy told me that you had passed a man you didn't know at all!' After which I would be warned to be more careful of what I said, and not to upset my aunt so by thoughtless remarks. Everyone was so well known in Combray, animals as well as people, that if my aunt had happened to see a dog go by which she 'didn't know at all' she would think about it incessantly, devoting to the solution of the incomprehensible problem all her inductive talent and her leisure hours.

'That will be Mme Sazerat's dog,' Françoise would suggest, without any real conviction, but in the hope of peace, and so that my aunt should not 'split her head.'

'As if I didn't know Mme Sazerat's dog!' – for my aunt's critical mind would not so easily admit any fresh fact.

'Ah, but that will be the new dog M. Galopin has brought her from Lisieux.'

'Oh, if that's what it is!'

'It seems, it's a most engaging animal,' Françoise would go on, having got the story from Théodore, 'as clever as a Christian, always in a good temper, always friendly, always everything that's nice. It's not often you see an animal so well behaved at that age. Mme Octave, it's high time I left you; I can't afford to stay here amusing myself; look, it's nearly ten o'clock and my fire not lighted yet, and I've still to dress the asparagus.'

'What, Françoise, more asparagus! It's a regular disease of asparagus you have got this year; you will make our Parisians sick of it.'

'No, no, Mme Octave, they like it well enough. They'll be coming back from church soon as hungry as hunters, and they won't eat it out of the back of their spoons, you'll see.'

'Church! why, they must be there now; you'd better not lose any time. Go and look after your luncheon.'

While my aunt gossiped on in this way with Françoise I would have accompanied my parents to mass. How I loved it: how clearly I can see it still, our church at Combray! The old porch by which we went in, black, and full of holes as a colander, was worn out of shape and deeply furrowed at the sides (as also was the holy water stoup to which it led us) just as if the gentle grazing touch of the cloaks of peasant-women going into the church, and of their fingers dipping into the water, had managed by agelong repetition to acquire a destructive force, to impress itself on the stone, to carve ruts in it like those made by cart-wheels upon stone gate-posts against which they are driven every day. Its memorial stones, beneath which the noble dust of the Abbots of Combray, who were buried there, furnished the choir with a sort of spiritual pavement, were themselves no longer hard and lifeless matter, for time had softened and sweetened them, and had made them melt like honey and flow beyond their proper margins, either surging out in a milky, frothing wave, washing from its place a florid gothic capital, drowning the white violets of the marble floor; or else reabsorbed into their limits, contracting still further a crabbed Latin inscription, bringing a fresh touch of fantasy into the arrangement of its curtailed characters, closing together two letters of some word of which the rest were disproportionately scattered. Its windows were never so brilliant as on days when the sun scarcely shone, so that if it was dull outside you might be certain of fine weather in church. One of them was filled from top to bottom by a solitary figure, like the king on a playing-card, who lived up there beneath his canopy of stone, between earth and heaven; and in the blue light of its slanting window, on weekdays sometimes, at noon, when there was no service (at one of those rare moments when the airy, empty church, more human somehow and more luxurious with the sun showing off all its rich furnishings, seemed to have almost a habitable air, like the hall – all sculptured stone and painted glass – of some medieval mansion), you might see Mme Sazerat kneel for an instant, laying down on the chair beside her own a neatly corded parcel of little cakes which she had just bought at the baker's and was taking home for her luncheon. In another, a mountain of rosy snow, at whose foot a battle was being fought, seemed to have frozen the window also, which it swelled and distorted with its cloudy sleet, like a pane to which snowflakes have drifted and clung, but flakes illumined by a sunrise – the same, doubtless, which purpled the reredos of the altar with tints so fresh that they seemed rather to be thrown on it for a moment by a light shining from outside and shortly to be extinguished than painted and permanently fastened on the stone. And all of them were so old that you could see, here and there, their silvery antiquity sparkling with the dust of centuries and showing in its threadbare brilliance the very cords of their lovely tapestry of glass. There was one among them which was a tall panel composed of a hundred little rectangular windows, of blue principally, like a great game of patience of the kind planned to beguile King Charles VI; but, either because a ray of sunlight had gleamed through it or because my own shifting vision had drawn across the window, whose colours died away and were rekindled by turns, a rare and transient fire – the next instant it had taken on all the iridescence of a peacock's tail, then shook and wavered in a flaming and fantastic shower, distilled and dropping from the groin of the dark and rocky vault down the moist walls, as though it were along the bed of some rainbow grotto of sinuous stalactites that I was following my parents, who marched before me, their prayer-books clasped in their hands; a moment later the little lozenge windows had put on the deep transparence, the unbreakable hardness of sapphires clustered on some enormous breastplate; but beyond which could be distinguished, dearer than all such treasures, a fleeting smile from the sun, which could be seen and felt as well here, in the blue and gentle flood in which it washed the masonry, as on the pavement of the Square or the straw of the market-place; and even on our first Sundays, when we came down before Easter, it would console me for the blackness and bareness of the earth outside by making burst into blossom, as in some springtime in old history among the heirs of Saint Louis, this dazzling and gilded carpet of forget-me-nots in glass.

Two tapestries of high warp represented the coronation of Esther (in which tradition would have it that the weaver had given to Ahasuerus the features of one of the kings of France and to Esther those of a lady of Guermantes whose lover he had been); their colours had melted into one another, so as to add expression, relief, light to the pictures. A touch of red over the lips of Esther had strayed beyond their outline; the yellow on her dress was spread with such unctuous plumpness as to

have acquired a kind of solidity, and stood boldly out from the
receding atmosphere; while the green of the trees, which was
still bright in silk and wool among the lower parts of the panel,
but had quite 'gone' at the top, separated in a paler scheme,
above the dark trunks, the yellowing upper branches, tanned
and half-obliterated by the sharp though sidelong rays of an
invisible sun. All these things and, still more than these, the
treasures which had come to the church from personages who
to me were almost legendary figures (such as the golden cross
wrought, it was said, by Saint Éloi and presented by Dagobert,
and the tomb of the sons of Louis the German in porphyry
and enamelled copper), because of which I used to go forward
into the church when we were making our way to our chairs
as into a fairy-haunted valley, where the rustic sees with amazement on a rock, a tree, a marsh, the tangible proofs of the little
people's supernatural passage – all these things made of the
church for me something entirely different from the rest of the
town; a building which occupied, so to speak, four dimensions
of space – the name of the fourth being Time – which had sailed
the centuries with that old nave, where bay after bay, chapel
after chapel, seemed to stretch across and hold down and conquer not merely a few yards of soil, but each successive epoch
from which the whole building had emerged triumphant, hiding the rugged barbarities of the eleventh century in the thick-
ness of its walls, through which nothing could be seen of the
heavy arches, long stopped and blinded with coarse blocks of
ashlar, except where, near the porch, a deep groove was furrowed into one wall by the tower-stair; and even there the bar-
barity was veiled by the graceful gothic arcade which pressed
coquettishly upon it, like a row of grown-up sisters who, to
hide him from the eyes of strangers, arrange themselves smilingly in front of a countrified, unmannerly, and ill-dressed
younger brother; rearing into the sky above the Square a tower which had looked down upon Saint Louis, and seemed to
behold him still; and thrusting down with its crypt into the
blackness of a Merovingian night, through which, guiding us
with groping finger-tips beneath the shadowy vault, ribbed
strongly as an immense bat's wing of stone, Théodore or his

sister would light up for us with a candle the tomb of Sige-
bert's little daughter, in which a deep hole, like the bed of a
fossil, had been bored, or so it was said, 'by a crystal lamp
which, on the night when the Frankish princess was murdered,
had left, of its own accord, the golden chains by which it was
suspended where the apse is to-day and with neither the crystal broken nor the light extinguished had buried itself in the
stone, through which it had gently forced its way.'

And then the apse of Combray; what am I to say of that? It
was so coarse, so devoid of artistic beauty, even of the religious spirit. From outside, since the street crossing which it
commanded was on a lower level, its great wall was thrust upwards from a basement of unfaced ashlar, jagged with flints, in
all of which there was nothing particularly ecclesiastical; the
windows seemed to have been pierced at an abnormal height,
and its whole appearance was that of a prison wall rather than
of a church. And certainly in later years, were I to recall all the
glorious apses that I had seen, it would never enter my mind
to compare with any of them the apse of Combray. Only, one
day, turning out of a little street in some country town, I came
upon three alleyways that converged, and facing them an old
wall, rubbed, worn, crumbling, and unusually high; with windows pierced in it far overhead and the same asymmetrical appearance as the apse of Combray. And at that moment I did
not say to myself, as at Chartres I might have done or at Rheims,
with what strength the religious feeling had been expressed in
its construction, but instinctively I exclaimed 'The Church!'

The church! A dear, familiar friend; close pressed in the
Rue Saint-Hilaire, upon which its north door opened, by its
two neighbours, Mme Loiseau's house and the pharmacy of
M. Rapin, against which its walls rested without interspace; a
simple citizen of Combray, who might have had her number
in the street had the streets of Combray borne numbers, and
at whose door one felt that the postman ought to stop on his
morning rounds, before going into Mme Loiseau's and after
leaving M. Rapin's, there existed, for all that, between the
church and everything in Combray that was not the church a
clear line of demarcation which I have never succeeded in

eliminating from my mind. In vain might Mme Loiseau deck her window-sills with fuchsias, which developed the bad habit of letting their branches trail at all times and in all directions, head downwards, and whose flowers had no more important business, when they were big enough to taste the joys of life, than to go and cool their purple, congested cheeks against the dark front of the church; to me such conduct sanctified the fuchsias not at all; between the flowers and the blackened stones towards which they leaned, if my eyes could discern no interval, my mind preserved the impression of an abyss.

From a long way off one could distinguish and identify the steeple of Saint-Hilaire inscribing its unforgettable form upon a horizon beneath which Combray had not yet appeared; when from the train which brought us down from Paris at Easter-time my father caught sight of it, as it slipped into every fold of the sky in turn, its little iron cock veering continually in all directions, he would say: 'Come, get your wraps together, we are there.' And on one of the longest walks we ever took from Combray there was a spot where the narrow road emerged suddenly on to an immense plain, closed at the horizon by strips of forest over which rose and stood alone the fine point of Saint-Hilaire's steeple, but so sharpened and so pink that it seemed to be no more than sketched on the sky by the finger-nail of a painter anxious to give to such a landscape, to so pure a piece of 'nature', this little sign of art, this single indication of human existence. As one drew near it and could make out the remains of the square tower, half in ruins, which still stood by its side, though without rivalling it in height, one was struck, first of all, by the tone, reddish and sombre, of its stones; and on a misty morning in autumn one would have called it, to see it rising above the violet thunder-cloud of the vineyards, a ruin of purple, almost the colour of the wild vine.

Often in the Square, as we came home, my grandmother would make me stop to look up at it. From the tower win-dows, placed two and two, one pair above another, with that right and original proportion in their spacing to which not only human faces owe their beauty and dignity, it released, it let fall at regular intervals flights of jackdaws which for a little

while would wheel and caw, as though the ancient stones
which allowed them to sport thus and never seemed to see
them, becoming of a sudden uninhabitable and discharging
some infinitely disturbing element, had struck them and driven
them forth. Then after patterning everywhere the violet velvet of the evening air, abruptly soothed, they would return
and be absorbed in the tower, deadly no longer but benignant,
some perching here and there (not seeming to move, but snap-
ping, perhaps, and swallowing some passing insect) on the
points of turrets, as a seagull perches, with an angler's immobility, on the crest of a wave. Without quite knowing why, my
grandmother found in the steeple of Saint-Hilaire that absence
of vulgarity, pretension, and meanness which made her love –
and deem rich in beneficent influences – nature itself, when
the hand of man had not, as did my great-aunt's gardener,
trimmed it, and the works of genius. And certainly every part
one saw of the church served to distinguish the whole from
any other building by a kind of general feeling which pervaded it, but it was in the steeple that the church seemed to display
a consciousness of itself, to affirm its individual and responsible existence. It was the steeple which spoke for the church.
I think, too, that in a confused way my grandmother found in
the steeple of Combray what she prized above anything else in
the world, namely, a natural air and an air of distinction. Ignorant of architecture, she would say:

'My dears, laugh at me if you like; it is not conventionally
beautiful, but there is something in its quaint old face which
pleases me. If it could play the piano, I am sure it would really
play.' And when she gazed on it, when her eyes followed the
gentle tension, the fervent inclination of its stony slopes which
drew together as they rose, like hands joined in prayer, she
would absorb herself so utterly in the outpouring of the spire
that her gaze seemed to leap upwards with it; her lips at the
same time curving in a friendly smile for the worn old stones
of which the setting sun now illumined no more than the topmost pinnacles, which, at the point where they entered that
zone of sunlight and were softened and sweetened by it, seemed to have mounted suddenly far higher, to have become truly

remote, like a song whose singer breaks into falsetto, an octave above the accompanying air.

It was the steeple of Saint-Hilaire which shaped and crowned and consecrated every occupation, every hour of the day, every point of view in the town. From my bedroom window I could discern no more than its base, which had been freshly covered with slates; but when on Sundays I saw these, in the hot light of a summer morning, blaze like a black sun I would say to myself: 'Good heavens! nine o'clock! I must get ready for mass at once if I am to have time to go in and kiss aunt Léonie first,' and I would know exactly what was the colour of the sunlight upon the Square, I could feel the heat and dust of the market, the shade behind the blinds of the shop into which Mamma would perhaps go on her way to mass, penetrating its odour of unbleached calico, to purchase a handkerchief or something, of which the draper himself would let her see what he had, bowing from the waist: who, having made everything ready for shutting up, had just gone into the back shop to put on his Sunday coat and to wash his hands, which it was his habit, every few minutes and even on the saddest occasions, to rub one against the other with an air of enterprise, cunning, and success.

And again, after mass, when we looked in to tell Théodore to bring a larger loaf than usual because our cousins had taken advantage of the fine weather to come over from Thiberzy for luncheon, we had in front of us the steeple, which, baked and brown itself like a larger loaf still of 'holy bread', with flakes and sticky drops on it of sunlight, pricked its sharp point into the blue sky. And in the evening, as I came in from my walk and thought of the approaching moment when I must say good night to my mother and see her no more, the steeple was by contrast so kindly, there at the close of day, that I would imagine it as being laid, like a brown velvet cushion, against – as being thrust into the pallid sky which had yielded beneath its pressure, had sunk slightly so as to make room for it, and had correspondingly risen on either side; while the cries of the birds wheeling to and fro about it seemed to intensify its silence, to elongate its spire still farther, and to invest it with some quality beyond the power of words.

Even when our errands lay in places behind the church, from which it could not be seen, the view seemed always to have been composed with reference to the steeple, which would stand up, now here, now there, among the houses, and was perhaps even more affecting when it appeared thus without the church. And, indeed, there are many others which look best when seen in this way, and I can call to mind vignettes of housetops with surmounting steeples in quite another category of art than those formed by the dreary streets of Combray. I shall never forget, in a quaint Norman town not far from Balbec, two charming eighteenth-century houses, dear to me and venerable for many reasons, between which, when one looks up at them from a fine garden which descends in terraces to the river, the gothic spire of a church (itself hidden by the houses) soars into the sky with the effect of crowning and completing their fronts, but in a material so different, so precious, so beringed, so rosy, so polished, that it is at once seen to be no more a part of them than would be a part of two pretty pebbles lying side by side, between which it had been washed on the beach, the purple, crinkled spire of some sea-shell spun out into a turret and gay with glossy colour. Even in Paris, in one of the ugliest parts of the town, I know a window from which one can see across a first, a second, and even a third layer of jumbled roofs, street beyond street, a violet bell, sometimes ruddy, sometimes too, in the finest 'prints' which the atmosphere makes of it, of an ashy solution of black; which is, in fact, nothing else than the dome of Saint-Augustin, and which imparts to this view of Paris the character of some of the Piranesi views of Rome. But since into none of these little etchings, whatever the taste my memory may have been able to bring to their execution, was it able to contribute an element I have long lost, the feeling which makes us not merely regard a thing as a spectacle, but believe in it as in a creature without parallel, so none of them keeps in dependence on it a whole section of my inmost life as does the memory of those aspects of the steeple of

Combray from the streets behind the church. Whether one saw it at five o'clock when going to call for letters at the post-office, some doors away from one, on the left, raising abruptly with its isolated peak the ridge of housetops; or again, when one had to go in and ask for news of Mme Sazerat, one's eyes followed the line where it ran low again beyond the farther, descending slope, and one knew that it would be the second turning after the steeple; or yet again, if pressing further afield one went to the station, one saw it obliquely, showing in profile fresh angles and surfaces, like a solid body surprised at some unknown point in its revolution; or, from the banks of the Vivonne, the apse, drawn muscularly together and heightened in perspective, seemed to spring upwards with the effort which the steeple made to hurl its spire-point into the heart of heaven: it was always to the steeple that one must return, always it which dominated everything else, summing up the houses with an unexpected pinnacle, raised before me like the Finger of God, whose Body might have been concealed below among the crowd of human bodies without fear of my confounding It, for that reason, with them. And so even to-day in any large provincial town, or in a quarter of Paris which I do not know well, if a passer-by who is 'putting me on the right road' shows me from afar, as a point to aim at, some belfry of a hospital, or a convent steeple lifting the peak of its ecclesiastical cap at the corner of the street which I am to take, my memory need only find in it some dim resemblance to that dear and vanished outline, and the passer-by, should he turn round to make sure that I have not gone astray, would see me, to his astonishment, oblivious of the walk that I had planned to take or the place where I was obliged to call, standing still on the spot, before that steeple, for hours on end, motionless, trying to remember, feeling deep within myself a tract of soil reclaimed from the waters of Lethe slowly drying until the buildings rise on it again; and then no doubt, and then more uneasily than when, just now, I asked him for a direction, I will seek my way again, I will turn a corner ... but ... the goal is in my heart ...

On our way home from mass we would often meet M.

Legrandin, who, detained in Paris by his professional duties as an engineer, could only (except in the regular holiday seasons) visit his home at Combray between Saturday evenings and Monday mornings. He was one of that class of men who, apart from a scientific career in which they may well have proved brilliantly successful, have acquired an entirely different kind of culture, literary or artistic, of which they make no use in the specialized work of their profession, but by which their conversation profits. More 'literary' than many 'men of letters' (we were not aware at this period that M. Legrandin had a distinct reputation as a writer, and so were greatly astonished to find that a well-known composer had set some verses of his to music), endowed with a greater ease in execution than many painters, they imagine that the life they are obliged to lead is not that for which they are really fitted, and they bring to their regular occupations either a fantastic indifference or a sustained and lofty application, scornful, bitter, and conscientious. Tall, with a good figure, a fine, thoughtful face, drooping fair moustache, a look of disillusionment in his blue eyes, an almost exaggerated refinement of courtesy; a talker such as we had never heard; he was in the sight of my family, who never ceased to quote him as an example, the very pattern of a gentleman, who took life in the noblest and most delicate manner. My grandmother alone found fault with him for speaking a little too well, a little too much like a book, for not using a vocabulary as natural as his loosely knotted Lavallière neckties, his short, straight, almost schoolboyish coat. She was astonished, too, at the furious invective which he was always launching at the aristocracy, at fashionable life, and 'snobbishness' – 'undoubtedly,' he would say, 'the sin of which Saint Paul is thinking when he speaks of the sin for which there is no forgiveness.'

Worldly ambition was a thing which my grandmother was so little capable of feeling, or indeed of understanding, that it seemed to her futile to apply so much heat to its condemnation. Besides, she thought it in not very good taste that M. Legrandin, whose sister was married to a country gentleman of Lower Normandy, near Balbec, should deliver himself of such violent attacks upon the nobles, going so far as to blame the Revolution for not having guillotined them all.

'Well met, my friends!' he would say as he came towards us. 'You are lucky to spend so much time here; to-morrow I have to go back to Paris, to squeeze back into my niche.

'Oh, I admit,' he went on, with his own peculiar smile, gently ironical, disillusioned, and vague, 'I have every useless thing in the world in my house there. The only thing wanting is the necessary thing, a great patch of open sky like this. Always try to keep a patch of sky above your life, little boy,' he added, turning to me. 'You have a soul in you of rare quality, an artist's nature; never let it starve for lack of what it needs.'

When, on our reaching the house, my aunt would send to ask us whether Mme Goupil had indeed arrived late for mass, not one of us could inform her. Instead, we increased her anxiety by telling her that there was a painter at work in the church copying the window of Gilbert the Bad. Françoise was at once dispatched to the grocer's, but returned empty-handed owing to the absence of Théodore, whose dual profession of choirman, with a part in the maintenance of the fabric, and of grocer's assistant gave him not only relations with all sections of society, but an encyclopaedic knowledge of their affairs.

'Ah!' my aunt would sigh, 'I wish it were time for Eulalie to come. She is really the only person who will be able to tell me.'

Eulalie was a limping, energetic, deaf spinster who had 'retired' after the death of Mme de la Bretonnerie, with whom she had been in service from her childhood, and had then taken a room beside the church, from which she would incessantly emerge, either to attend some service, or, when there was no service, to say a prayer by herself or to give Théodore a hand; the rest of her time she spent in visiting sick persons like my aunt Léonie, to whom she would relate everything that had occurred at mass or vespers. She was not above adding occasional pocket-money to the little income which was found for her by the family of her old employers by going from time to time to look after the Curé's linen, or that of some other person of note in the clerical world of Combray. Above a mantle of black cloth she wore a little white coif that seemed almost to attach her to some Order, and an infirmity of the skin had stained part of her cheeks and her crooked nose the bright red colour of balsam. Her visits were the one great distraction in the life of my aunt Léonie, who now saw hardly anyone else, except the reverend Curé. My aunt had by degrees erased every other visitor's name from her list, because they all committed the fatal error, in her eyes, of falling into one or other of the two categories of people she most detested. One group, the worse of the two, and the one of which she rid herself first, consisted of those who advised her not to take so much care of herself, and preached (even if only negatively and with no outward signs beyond an occasional disapproving silence or doubting smile) the subversive doctrine that a sharp walk in the sun and a good red beefsteak would do her more good (her, who had had two dreadful sips of Vichy water on her stomach for fourteen hours!) than all her medicine bottles and her bed. The other category was composed of people who appeared to believe that she was more seriously ill than she thought, in fact that she was as seriously ill as she said. And so none of those whom she had allowed upstairs to her room, after considerable hesitation and at Françoise's urgent request, and who in the course of their visit had shown how unworthy they were of the honour which had been done them by venturing a timid: 'Don't you think that if you were just to stir out a little on really fine days . . .?' or who, on the other hand, when she said to them: 'I am very low, very low; nearing the end, dear friends!' had replied: 'Ah, yes, when one has no strength left! Still, you may last a while yet'; each party alike might be certain that her doors would never open to them again. And if Françoise was amused by the look of consternation on my aunt's face whenever she saw, from her bed, any of these people in the Rue du Saint-Esprit, who looked as if they were coming to see her, or heard her own door-bell ring, she would laugh far more heartily, as at a clever trick, at my aunt's devices (which never failed) for having them sent away, and at their look of discomfiture when they had to turn back without having seen her; and would be filled with secret admiration for her mistress, whom she felt to be superior to all these other people, inasmuch as she could and did contrive not to see them. In short, my aunt stipulated, at one and the same time, that whoever came to see her must approve of her way of life, commiserate with her in her sufferings, and assure her of an ultimate recovery.

In all this Eulalie excelled. My aunt might say to her twenty times in a minute: 'The end is come at last, my poor Eulalie!', twenty times Eulalie would retort with: 'Knowing your illness as you do, Mme Octave, you will live to be a hundred, as Mme Sazerin said to me only yesterday.' For one of Eulalie's most rooted beliefs, and one that the formidable list of corrections which her experience must have compiled was powerless to eradicate, was that Mme Sazerat's name was really Mme Sazerin.

'I do not ask to live to a hundred,' my aunt would say, for she preferred to have no definite limit fixed to the number of her days.

And since, besides this, Eulalie knew, as no one else knew, how to distract my aunt without tiring her, her visits, which took place regularly every Sunday, unless something unforeseen occurred to prevent them, were for my aunt a pleasure the prospect of which kept her on those days in a state of expectation, appetizing enough to begin with, but at once changing to the agony of a hunger too long unsatisfied if Eulalie were a minute late in coming. For, if unduly prolonged, the rapture of waiting for Eulalie became a torture, and my aunt would never cease from looking at the time, and yawning, and complaining of each of her symptoms in turn. Eulalie's ring, if it sounded from the front door at the very end of the day, when she was no longer expecting it, would almost make her ill. For the fact was that on Sundays she thought of nothing else than this visit, and the moment that our luncheon was ended Françoise would become impatient for us to leave the dining-room so that she might go upstairs to 'occupy' my aunt. But – and this more than ever from the day on which fine weather definitely set in at Combray – the proud hour of noon, descending from the steeple of Saint-Hilaire which it blazoned for a moment with the twelve points of its sonorous crown, would long have echoed about our table, beside the 'holy bread', which too had come in, after church, in its familiar way; and we would still be found seated in front of our Arabian Nights plates, weighed down by the heat of the day, and even more by our heavy meal. For upon the permanent foundation of eggs, cutlets, potatoes, preserves, and biscuits, whose appearance on the table she no longer announced to us, Françoise would add – as the labour of fields and orchards, the harvest of the tides, the luck of the markets, the kindness of neighbours, and her own genius might provide; and so effectively that our bill of fare, like the quatrefoils that were carved on the porches of cathedrals in the thirteenth century, reflected to some extent the march of the seasons and the incidents of human life – a brill, because the fish-woman had guaranteed its freshness; a turkey, because she had seen a beauty in the market at Roussainville-le-Pin; cardoons with marrow, because she had never done them for us in that way before; a roast leg of mutton, because the fresh air made one hungry and there would be plenty of time for it to 'settle down' in the seven hours before dinner; spinach, by way of a change; apricots, because they were still hard to get; gooseberries, because in another fortnight there would be none left; raspberries, which M. Swann had brought specially; cherries, the first to come from the cherry-tree, which had yielded none for the last two years; a cream cheese, of which in those days I was extremely fond; an almond cake, because she had ordered one the evening before; a fancy loaf, because it was our turn to 'offer' the holy bread. And when all these had been eaten, a work composed expressly for ourselves, but dedicated more particularly to my father, who had a fondness for such things, a cream of chocolate, inspired in the mind, created by the hand of Françoise would be laid before us, light and fleeting as an 'occasional piece' of music, into which she had poured the whole of her talent. Anyone who refused to partake of it, saying: 'No, thank you, I have finished; I am not hungry,' would at once have been lowered to the level of the Philistines who, when an artist makes them a present of one of his works, examine its weight and material, whereas what is of value is the creator's intention and his signature. To have left even the tiniest morsel in the dish would have shown as much discourtesy as to rise and leave a concert hall while the 'piece' was still being played, and under the composer's very eyes.

At length my mother would say to me: 'Now, don't stay here all day; you can go up to your room if you are too hot outside, but get a little fresh air first; don't start reading immediately after your food.'

And I would go and sit down beside the pump and its trough, ornamented here and there, like a gothic font, with a salamander, which modelled upon a background of crumbling stone the quick relief of its slender, allegorical body; on the bench without a back, in the shade of a lilac-tree, in that little corner of the garden which communicated, by a service door, with the Rue du Saint-Esprit, and from whose neglected soil rose, on two steps, an outcrop from the house itself and apparently a separate building, my aunt's back-kitchen. One could see its red-tiled floor gleaming like porphyry. It seemed not so much the cave of Françoise as a little temple of Venus. It would be overflowing with the offerings of the milkman, the fruiterer, the greengrocer, come sometimes from distant villages to dedicate here the first-fruits of their fields. And its roof was always surmounted by the cooing of a dove.

In earlier days I would not have lingered in the sacred grove which surrounded this temple, for, before going upstairs to read, I would steal into the little sitting-room which my uncle Adolphe, a brother of my grandfather and an old soldier who had retired from the service as a major, used to occupy on the ground floor, a room which, even when its opened windows let in the heat, if not actually the rays of the sun which seldom penetrated so far, would never fail to emit that vague and yet fresh odour, suggesting at once an open-air and an old-fashioned kind of existence, which sets and keeps the nostrils dreaming when one goes into a disused gun-room. But for some years now I had not gone into my uncle Adolphe's room, since he no longer came to Combray on account of a quarrel which had arisen between him and my family, by my fault, and in the following circumstances: Once or twice every month, in Paris, I used to be sent to pay him a visit, as he was finishing his luncheon, wearing a plain alpaca coat, and waited upon by his servant in a working-jacket of striped linen, purple and white. He would complain that I had not been to see him for a long time; that he was being neglected; he would offer me a marchpane or a tangerine, and we would cross a room in which no one ever sat, whose fire was never lighted, whose walls were picked out with gilded mouldings, its ceiling painted blue in imitation of the sky, and its furniture uphol-stered in satin, as at my grandparents', only yellow; then we would enter what he called his 'study', a room whose walls were hung with prints which showed, against a dark back-ground, a plump and rosy goddess driving a car, or standing upon a globe, or wearing a star on her brow; pictures which were popular under the Second Empire because there was thought to be something about them that suggested Pompeii, which were then generally despised, and which now people are beginning to collect again for one single and consistent reason (despite any others which they may advance), namely, that they suggest the Second Empire. And there I would stay with my uncle until his man came, with a message from the coachman, to ask him at what time he would like the carriage. My uncle would then be lost in meditation, while his aston-ished servant stood there, not daring to disturb him by the least movement, wondering and waiting for his answer, which never varied. For in the end, after a supreme crisis of hesita-tion, my uncle would utter, infallibly, the words: 'A quarter past two,' which the servant would echo with amazement, but without disputing them: 'A quarter past two! Very good, sir ... I will go and tell him ...'

At this date I was a lover of the theatre: a Platonic lover, of necessity, since my parents had not yet allowed me to enter one, and so incorrect was the picture I drew for myself of the pleasures to be enjoyed there that I almost believed that each of the spectators looked, as into a stereoscope, upon a stage and scenery which existed for himself alone, though closely resembling the thousand other spectacles presented to the rest of the audience individually.

Every morning I would hasten to the Moriss column to see what new plays it announced. Nothing could be more disinterested or happier than the dreams with which these announcements filled my mind, dreams which took their form from the inevitable associations of the words forming the title of the play, and also from the colour of the bills, still damp and wrinkled with paste, on which those words stood out. Nothing unless it were such strange titles as the *Testament de César Girodot*, or *Œdipe-Roi*, inscribed not on the green bills of the Opéra-Comique, but on the wine-coloured bills of the Comédie-Française, nothing seemed to me to differ more profoundly from the sparkling white plume of the *Diamants de la Couronne* than the sleek, mysterious satin of the *Domino Noir*; and since my parents had told me that, for my first visit to the theatre, I should have to choose between these two pieces, I would study exhaustively and in turn the title of one and the title of the other (for those were all that I knew of either), attempting to snatch from each a foretaste of the pleasure which it offered me, and to compare this pleasure with that patent in the other title, until in the end I had shown myself such vivid, such compelling pictures of, on the one hand, a play of dazzling arrogance, and on the other a gentle, velvety play, that I was as little capable of deciding which play I should prefer to see as if, at the dinner-table, they had obliged me to choose between rice *à l'Impératrice* and the famous cream of chocolate.

All my conversations with my playfellows bore upon actors, whose art, although as yet I had no experience of it, was the first of all its numberless forms in which Art itself allowed me to anticipate its enjoyment. Between one actor's tricks of intonation and inflexion and another's, the most trifling differences would strike me as being of an incalculable importance. And from what I had been told of them I would arrange them in the order of their talent in lists which I used to murmur to myself all day long: lists which in the end became petrified in my brain and were a source of annoyance to it, being irremovable.

And later, in my schooldays, whenever I ventured in class,

when the master's head was turned, to communicate with some new friend, I would always begin by asking him whether he had begun yet to go to theatres, and if he agreed that our greatest actor was undoubtedly Got, our second Delaunay, and so on. And if, in his judgement, Febvre came below Thiron, or Delaunay below Coquelin, the sudden volatility which the name of Coquelin, forsaking its stony rigidity, would engender in my mind, in which it moved upwards to the second place, the rich vitality with which the name of Delaunay would suddenly be furnished, to enable it to slip down to fourth, would stimulate and fertilize my brain with a sense of budding and blossoming life.

But if the thought of actors weighed so upon me, if the sight of Maubant, coming out one afternoon from the Théâtre-Français, had plunged me in the throes and sufferings of hopeless love, how much more did the name of a 'star', blazing outside the doors of a theatre, how much more, seen through the window of a brougham which passed me in the street, the hair over her forehead abloom with roses, did the face of a woman who, I would think, was perhaps an actress, leave with me a lasting disturbance, a futile and painful effort to form a picture of her private life.

I classified, in order of talent, the most distinguished: Sarah Bernhardt, Berma, Bartet, Madeleine Brohan, Jeanne Samary; but I was interested in them all. Now my uncle knew many of them personally, and also ladies of another class, not clearly distinguished from actresses in my mind. He used to entertain them at his house. And if we went to see him on certain days only, that was because on the other days ladies might come whom his family could not very well have met. So we at least thought; as for my uncle, his fatal readiness to pay pretty widows (who had perhaps never been married) and countesses (whose high-sounding titles were probably no more than *noms de guerre*) the compliment of presenting them to my grandmother, or even of presenting to them some of our family jewels, had already embroiled him more than once with my grandfather. Often, if the name of some actress were mentioned in conversation, I would hear my father say, with a smile, to my mother: 'One of your uncle's friends,' and I would think of the weary novitiate through which, perhaps for years on end, a grown man, even a man of real importance, might have to pass, waiting on the doorstep of some such lady, while she refused to answer his letters and made her hall-porter drive him away; and imagine that my uncle was able to dispense a little jackanapes like myself from all these sufferings by introducing me in his own home to the actress, unapproachable by all the world, but for him an intimate friend.

And so – on the pretext that some lesson, the hour of which had been altered, now came at such an awkward time that it had already more than once prevented me, and would continue to prevent me, from seeing my uncle – one day, not one of the days which he set apart for our visits, I took advantage of the fact that my parents had had luncheon earlier than usual; I slipped out and, instead of going to read the playbills on their column, for which purpose I was allowed to go out unaccompanied, I ran all the way to his house. I noticed before his door a carriage and pair, with red carnations on the horses' blinkers and in the coachman's buttonhole. As I climbed the staircase I could hear laughter and a woman's voice, and, as soon as I had rung, silence and the sound of shutting doors. The man-servant who let me in appeared embarrassed, and said that my uncle was extremely busy and probably could not see me; he went in, however, to announce my arrival, and the same voice I had heard before said: 'Oh, yes! Do let him come in; just for a moment; it will be so amusing. Is that his photograph there, on your desk? And his mother (your niece, isn't she?) beside it? The image of her, isn't he? I should so like to see the little chap, just for a second.'

I could hear my uncle grumbling and growing angry; finally the man-servant told me to come in.

On the table was the same plate of marchpanes that was always there; my uncle wore the same alpaca coat as on other days; but opposite to him, in a pink silk dress with a great necklace of pearls about her throat, sat a young woman who was just finishing a tangerine. My uncertainty whether I ought to address her as Madame or Mademoiselle made me blush, and not daring to look too much in her direction, in case I should be obliged to speak to her, I hurried across to kiss my uncle. She looked at me and smiled; my uncle said 'My nephew!' without telling her my name or telling me hers, doubtless because, since his difficulties with my grandfather, he had endeavoured as far as possible to avoid any association of his family with this other class of acquaintance.

'How like his mother he is,' said the lady.

'But you have never seen my niece, except in photographs,' my uncle broke in quickly, with a note of anger.

'I beg your pardon, dear friend, I passed her on the staircase last year when you were so ill. It is true I only saw her for a moment, and your staircase is rather dark; but I saw well enough to see how lovely she was. This young gentleman has her beautiful eyes, and also *this*,' she went on, tracing a line with one finger across the lower part of her forehead. 'Tell me,' she asked my uncle, 'is your niece Mme — ; is her name the same as yours?'

'He takes most after his father,' muttered my uncle, who was no more anxious to effect an introduction by proxy, in repeating Mamma's name aloud, than to bring the two together in the flesh. 'He's his father all over, and also like my poor mother.'

'I have not met his father, dear,' said the lady in pink, bowing her head slightly, 'and I never saw your poor mother. You will remember it was just after your great sorrow that we got to know one another.'

I felt somewhat disillusioned, for this young lady was in no way different from other pretty women whom I had seen from time to time at home, especially the daughter of one of our cousins, to whose house I went every New Year's Day. Only better dressed; otherwise my uncle's friend had the same quick and kindly glance, the same frank and friendly manner. I could find no trace in her of the theatrical appearance which I admired in photographs of actresses, nothing of the diabolical expression which would have been in keeping with the life she must lead. I had difficulty in believing that this was one of 'those women', and certainly I should never have believed her one of the 'smart ones' had I not seen the carriage and pair, the pink dress, the pearl necklace, had I not been aware, too, that my uncle knew only the very best of them. But I asked myself how the millionaire who gave her her carriage and her flat and her jewels could find any pleasure in flinging his money away upon a woman who had so simple and respectable an appearance. And yet, when I thought of what her life must be like, its immorality disturbed me more, perhaps, than if it had stood before me in some concrete and recognizable form, by its secrecy and invisibility, like the plot of a novel, the hidden truth of a scandal which had driven out of the home of her middle-class parents and dedicated to the service of all mankind, which had brought to the flowering-point of her beauty, had raised to fame or notoriety this woman, the play of whose features, the intonations of whose voice, like so many others I already knew, made me regard her, in spite of myself, as a young lady of good family, her who was no longer of a family at all.

We had gone by this time into the 'study', and my uncle, who seemed a trifle embarrassed by my presence, offered her a cigarette.

'No, thank you, dear friend,' she said. 'You know I only smoke the ones the Grand Duke sends me. I tell him that they make you jealous.' And she drew from a case cigarettes covered with inscriptions in gold, in a foreign language. 'Why, yes,' she began again suddenly. 'Of course I have met this young man's father with you. Isn't he your nephew? How on earth could I have forgotten? He was so nice, so charming to me,' she went on, modestly and with feeling. But when I thought to myself what must actually have been the rude greeting (which, she made out, had been so charming), I, who knew my father's coldness and reserve, was shocked, as though at some indelicacy on his part, at the contrast between the excessive recognition bestowed on it and his never adequate geniality. It has since struck me as one of the most touching aspects of the part played in life by these idle, painstaking women that they devote all their generosity, all their talent, their transferable dreams of sentimental beauty (for, like all artists, they never seek to realize the value of those dreams, or to enclose them in the four-square frame of everyday life), and their gold, which counts for little, to the fashioning of a fine and precious setting for the rubbed and scratched and ill-polished lives of men. And just as this one filled the smoking-room, where my uncle was entertaining her in his alpaca coat, with her charming person, her dress of pink silk, her pearls, and the refinement suggested by intimacy with a Grand Duke, so, in the same way, she had taken some casual remark by my father, had worked it up delicately, given it a 'turn', a precious title, set in it the gem of a glance from her own eyes, a gem of the first water, blended of humility and gratitude; and so had given it back transformed into a jewel, a work of art, into something altogether charming.

'Look here, my boy, it is time you went away,' said my uncle.

I rose; I could scarcely resist a desire to kiss the hand of the lady in pink, but I felt that to do so would require as much audacity as a forcible abduction of her. My heart beat loud while I counted out to myself 'Shall I do it, shall I not?' and then I ceased to ask myself what I ought to do so as at least to do something. Blindly, hotly, madly, flinging aside all the reasons I had just found to support such action, I seized and raised to my lips the hand she held out to me.

'Isn't he delicious! Quite a ladies' man already; he takes after his uncle. He'll be a perfect "gentleman",' she went on, setting her teeth so as to give the word a kind of English accentuation. 'Couldn't he come to me some day for "a cup of tea", as our friends across the channel say; he need only send me a "blue", in the morning?'

I had not the least idea of what a 'blue' might be. I did not understand half the words which the lady used, but my fear lest there should be concealed in them some question which it would be impolite in me not to answer kept me from withdrawing my close attention from them, and I was beginning to feel extremely tired.

'No, no; it is impossible,' said my uncle, shrugging his shoulders: 'He is kept busy at home all day; he has plenty of work to do. He brings back all the prizes from his school,' he added in a lower tone, so that I should not hear this falsehood and interrupt with a contradiction. 'You can't tell; he may turn out a little Victor Hugo, a kind of Vaulabelle, don't you know.'

'Oh, I love artistic people,' replied the lady in pink; 'there is no one like them for understanding women. Them, and really nice men like yourself. But please forgive my ignorance. Who, what is Vaulabelle? Is it those gilt books in the little glass case in your drawing-room? You know you promised to lend them to me; I will take great care of them.'

My uncle, who hated lending people books, said nothing, and ushered me out into the hall. Madly in love with the lady in pink, I covered my old uncle's tobacco-stained cheeks with passionate kisses, and while he, awkwardly enough, gave me to understand (without actually saying) that he would rather I did not tell my parents about this visit, I assured him, with tears in my eyes, that his kindness had made so strong an impression upon me that some day I would most certainly find a way of expressing my gratitude. So strong an impression had it made upon me that two hours later, after a string of mysterious utterances which did not strike me as giving my parents a sufficiently clear idea of the new importance with which I had been invested, I found it simpler to let them have a full account, omitting no detail, of the visit I had paid that afternoon. In doing this I had no thought of causing my uncle any unpleasantness. How could I have thought such a thing, since I did not wish it? And I could not suppose that my parents would see any harm in a visit in which I myself saw none. Every day of our lives does not some friend or other ask us to make his apologies, without fail, to some woman to whom he has been prevented from writing; and do not we forget to do so, feeling that this woman cannot attach much importance to a silence which has none for ourselves? I imagined, like everyone else, that the brains of other people were lifeless and submissive receptacles with no power of specific reaction to any stimulus which might be applied to them; and I had not the least doubt that when I deposited in the minds of my parents the news of the acquaintance I had made at my uncle's I should

at the same time transmit to them the kindly judgement I myself had based on the introduction. Unfortunately my parents
had recourse to principles entirely different from those which
I suggested they should adopt when they came to form their
estimate of my uncle's conduct. My father and grandfather had
'words' with him of a violent order; as I learned indirectly. A
few days later, passing my uncle in the street as he drove by in
an open carriage, I felt at once all the grief, the gratitude, the
remorse which I should have liked to convey to him. Beside
the immensity of these emotions I considered that merely to
raise my hat to him would be incongruous and petty, and
might make him think that I regarded myself as bound to
show him no more than the commonest form of courtesy. I
decided to abstain from so inadequate a gesture, and turned
my head away. My uncle thought that, in doing so, I was obeying my parents' orders; he never forgave them; and though he
did not die until many years later, not one of us ever set eyes
on him again.

And so I no longer used to go into the little sitting-room
(now kept shut) of my uncle Adolphe; instead, after hanging
about on the outskirts of the back kitchen until Françoise
appeared on its threshold and announced: 'I am going to let
the kitchen-maid serve the coffee and take up the hot water; it
is time I went off to Mme Octave,' I would then decide to go
indoors, and would go straight upstairs to my room to read.
The kitchen-maid was an abstract personality, a permanent
institution to which an invariable set of attributes assured a
sort of fixity and continuity and identity throughout the long
series of transitory human shapes in which that personality
was incarnate; for we never found the same girl there two
years running. In the year in which we ate such quantities of
asparagus, the kitchen-maid whose duty it was to dress them
was a poor sickly creature, some way 'gone' in pregnancy
when we arrived at Combray for Easter, and it was indeed surprising that Françoise allowed her to run so many errands in
the town and to do so much work in the house, for she was
beginning to find a difficulty in bearing before her the mysterious casket, fuller and larger every day, whose splendid outline

could be detected through the folds of her ample smocks.
These last recalled the cloaks in which Giotto shrouds some of
the allegorical figures in his paintings, of which M. Swann had
given me photographs. He it was who pointed out the resemblance, and when he inquired after the kitchen-maid he would
say: 'Well, how goes it with Giotto's Charity?' And indeed
the poor girl, whose pregnancy had swelled and stoutened
every part of her, even to her face, and the vertical, squared
outlines of her cheeks, did distinctly suggest those virgins, so
strong and mannish as to seem matrons rather, in whom the
Virtues are personified in the Arena Chapel. And I can see now
that those Virtues and Vices of Padua resembled her in another
respect as well. For just as the figure of this girl had been
enlarged by the additional symbol which she carried in her
body, without appearing to understand what it meant, without
any rendering in her facial expression of all its beauty and
spiritual significance, but carried as if it were an ordinary and
rather heavy burden, so it is without any apparent suspicion of
what she is about that the powerfully built housewife who is
portrayed in the Arena beneath the label 'Caritas', and a
reproduction of whose portrait hung upon the wall of my
schoolroom at Combray, incarnates that virtue, for it seems
impossible that any thought of charity can ever have found
expression in her vulgar and energetic face. By a fine stroke of
the painter's invention she is tumbling all the treasures of the
earth at her feet, but exactly as if she were treading grapes in a
wine-press to extract their juice, or, still more, as if she had
climbed on a heap of sacks to raise herself higher; and she is
holding out her flaming heart to God, or shall we say 'handing' it to Him, exactly as a cook might hand up a corkscrew
through the skylight of her underground kitchen to some one
who had called down to ask her for it from the ground-level
above. The 'Invidia', again, should have had some look on
her face of envy. But in this fresco, too, the symbol occupies
so large a place and is represented with such realism; the serpent hissing between the lips of Envy is so huge, and so completely fills her wide-opened mouth that the muscles of her
face are strained and contorted, like a child's who is filling a

balloon with his breath, and that Envy, and we ourselves for that matter, when we look at her, since all her attention and ours are concentrated on the action of her lips, have no time, almost, to spare for envious thoughts.

Despite all the admiration that M. Swann might profess for these figures of Giotto, it was a long time before I could find any pleasure in seeing in our schoolroom (where the copies he had brought me were hung) that Charity devoid of charity, that Envy who looked like nothing so much as a plate in some medical book, illustrating the compression of the glottis or uvula by a tumour in the tongue, or by the introduction of the operator's instrument, a Justice whose greyish and meanly regular features were the very same as those which adorned the faces of certain good and pious and slightly withered ladies of Combray whom I used to see at mass, many of whom had long been enrolled in the reserve forces of Injustice. But in later years I understood that the arresting strangeness, the special beauty of these frescoes lay in the great part played in each of them by its symbols, while the fact that these were depicted, not as symbols (for the thought symbolized was no-where expressed), but as real things, actually felt or materially handled, added something more precise and more literal to their meaning, something more concrete and more striking to the lesson they imparted. And even in the case of the poor kitchen-maid, was not our attention incessantly drawn to her belly by the load which filled it; and in the same way, again, are not the thoughts of men and women in the agony of death often turned towards the practical, painful, obscure, internal, intestinal aspect, towards that 'seamy side' of death which is, as it happens, the side that death actually presents to them and forces them to feel, a side which far more closely resembles a crushing burden, a difficulty in breathing, a destroying thirst, than the abstract idea to which we are accustomed to give the name of Death?

There must have been a strong element of reality in those Virtues and Vices of Padua, since they appeared to me to be as much alive as the pregnant servant-girl, while she herself appeared scarcely less allegorical than they. And, quite possibly, this lack (or seeming lack) of participation by a person's soul in the significant marks of its own special virtue has apart from its aesthetic meaning, a reality which, if not strictly psychological, may at least be called physiognomical. Later on, when, in the course of my life, I have had occasion to meet with, in convents for instance, literally saintly examples of practical charity, they have generally had the brisk, decided, undisturbed, and slightly brutal air of a busy surgeon, the face in which one can discern no commiseration, no tenderness at the sight of suffering humanity, and no fear of hurting it, the face devoid of gentleness or sympathy, the sublime face of true goodness.

Then while the kitchen-maid – who, all unawares, made the superior qualities of Françoise shine with added lustre, just as Error, by force of contrast, enhances the triumph of Truth – took in coffee which (according to Mamma) was nothing more than hot water, and then carried up to our rooms hot water which was barely tepid, I would be lying stretched out on my bed, a book in my hand, in my room which trembled with the effort to defend its frail, transparent coolness against the afternoon sun, behind its almost closed shutters through which, however, a reflexion of the sunlight had contrived to slip in on its golden wings, remaining motionless, between glass and woodwork, in a corner, like a butterfly poised upon a flower. It was hardly light enough for me to read, and my feeling of the day's brightness and splendour was derived solely from the blows struck down below, in the Rue de la Cure, by Camus (whom Françoise had assured that my aunt was not 'resting' and that he might therefore make a noise), upon some old packing-cases from which nothing would really be sent flying but the dust, though the din of them, in the resonant atmosphere that accompanies hot weather, seemed to scatter broadcast a rain of blood-red stars; and from the flies who performed for my benefit, in their small concert, as it might be the chamber music of summer; evoking heat and light quite differently from an air of human music which, if you happen to have heard it during a fine summer, will always bring that summer back to your mind, the flies' music is bound to the season by a closer, a more vital tie – born of sunny days, and not to be re-born but with them, containing something of their essential nature, it not merely calls up their image in our memory, but gives us a guarantee that they do really exist, that they are close around us, immediately accessible.

This dim freshness of my room was to the broad daylight of the street what the shadow is to the sunbeam, that is to say, equally luminous, and presented to my imagination the entire panorama of summer, which my senses, if I had been out walking, could have tasted and enjoyed in fragments only; and so was quite in harmony with my state of repose, which (thanks to the adventures related in my books, which had just excited it) bore, like a hand reposing motionless in a stream of running water, the shock and animation of a torrent of activity and life.

But my grandmother, even if the weather, after growing too hot, had broken, and a storm, or just a shower, had burst over us, would come up and beg me to go outside. And as I did not wish to leave off my book, I would go on with it in the garden, under the chestnut-tree, in a little sentry-box of canvas and matting, in the farthest recesses of which I used to sit and feel that I was hidden from the eyes of anyone who might be coming to call upon the family.

And then my thoughts, did not they form a similar sort of hiding-hole, in the depths of which I felt that I could bury myself and remain invisible even when I was looking at what went on outside? When I saw any external object, my consciousness that I was seeing it would remain between me and it, enclosing it in a slender, incorporeal outline which prevented me from ever coming directly in contact with the material form; for it would volatilize itself in some way before I could touch it, just as an incandescent body which is moved towards something wet never actually touches moisture, since it is always preceded, itself, by a zone of evaporation. Upon the sort of screen, patterned with different states and impressions, which my consciousness would quietly unfold while I was reading, and which ranged from the most deeply hidden aspirations of my heart to the wholly external view of the horizon spread out before my eyes at the foot of the garden, what was from the first the most permanent and the most intimate part of me, the lever whose incessant movements controlled all the rest, was my belief in the philosophic richness and beauty of the book I was reading, and my desire to appropriate these to myself, whatever the book might be. For even if I had purchased it at Combray, having seen it outside Borange's, whose grocery lay too far from our house for Françoise to be able to deal there, as she did with Camus, but who enjoyed better custom as a stationer and bookseller; even if I had seen it, tied with string to keep it in its place in the mosaic of monthly parts and pamphlets which adorned either side of his doorway, a doorway more mysterious, more teeming with suggestion than that of a cathedral, I should have noticed and brought it there simply because I had recognized it as a book which had been well spoken of, in my hearing, by the schoolmaster or the school-friend who, at that particular time, seemed to me to be entrusted with the secret of Truth and Beauty, things half-felt by me, half-incomprehensible, the full understanding of which was the vague but permanent object of my thoughts.

Next to this central belief, which, while I was reading, would be constantly in motion from my inner self to the outer world, towards the discovery of Truth, came the emotions aroused in me by the action in which I would be taking part, for these afternoons were crammed with more dramatic and sensational events than occur, often, in a whole lifetime. These were the events which took place in the book I was reading. It is true that the people concerned in them were not what Françoise would have called 'real people'. But none of the feelings which the joys or misfortunes of a 'real' person awaken in us can be awakened except through a mental picture of those joys or misfortunes; and the ingenuity of the first novelist lay in his understanding that, as the picture was the one essential element in the complicated structure of our emotions, so that simplification of it which consisted in the suppression, pure and simple, of 'real' people would be a decided improvement. A 'real' person, profoundly as we may sympathize with him, is in a great measure perceptible only through our senses, that is to say, he remains opaque, offers a dead weight which our sensibilities have not the strength to lift. If some misfortune comes to him, it is only in one small section of the complete idea we have of him that we are capable of feeling any emotion; indeed it is only in one small section of the complete idea he has of himself that he is capable of feeling any emotion either. The novelist's happy discovery was to think of substituting for those opaque sections, impenetrable by the human spirit, their equivalent in immaterial sections, things, that is, which the spirit can assimilate to itself. After which it matters not that the actions, the feelings of this new order of creatures appear to us in the guise of truth, since we have made them our own, since it is in ourselves that they are happening, that they are holding in thrall, while we turn over, feverishly, the pages of the book, our quickened breath and staring eyes. And once the novelist has brought us to that state, in which, as in all purely mental states, every emotion is multiplied tenfold, into which his book comes to disturb us as might a dream, but a dream more lucid, and of a more lasting impression than those which come to us in sleep; why, then, for the space of an hour he sets free within us all the joys and sorrows in the world, a few of which, only, we should have to spend years of our actual life in getting to know, and the keenest, the most intense of which would never have been revealed to us because the slow course of their development stops our perception of them. It is the same in life; the heart changes, and that is our worst misfortune; but we learn of it only from reading or by imagination; for in reality its alteration, like that of certain natural phenomena, is so gradual that, even if we are able to distinguish, successively, each of its different states, we are still spared the actual sensation of change.

Next to, but distinctly less intimate a part of myself than this human element, would come the view, more or less projected before my eyes, of the country in which the action of the story was taking place, which made a far stronger impression on my mind than the other, the actual landscape which would meet my eyes when I raised them from my book. In this way, for two consecutive summers I used to sit in the heat of our

Combray garden, sick with a longing inspired by the book I was then reading for a land of mountains and rivers, where I could see an endless vista of saw-mills, where beneath the limpid currents fragments of wood lay mouldering in beds of watercress; and near by, rambling and clustering along low walls, purple flowers and red. And since there was always lurking in my mind the dream of a woman who would enrich me with her love, that dream in those two summers used to be quickened with the freshness and coolness of running water; and whoever she might be, the woman whose image I called to mind, purple flowers and red would at once spring up on either side of her like complementary colours.

This was not only because an image of which we dream remains for ever distinguished, is adorned and enriched by the association of colours not its own which may happen to surround it in our mental picture; for the scenes in the books I read were to me not merely scenery more vividly portrayed by my imagination than any which Combray could spread before my eyes but otherwise of the same kind. Because of the selection that the author had made of them, because of the spirit of faith in which my mind would exceed and anticipate his printed word, as it might be interpreting a revelation, these scenes used to give me the impression – one which I hardly ever derived from any place in which I might happen to be, and never from our garden, that undistinguished product of the strictly conventional fantasy of the gardener whom my grandmother so despised – of their being actually part of Nature herself, and worthy to be studied and explored.

Had my parents allowed me, when I read a book, to pay a visit to the country it described, I should have felt that I was making an enormous advance towards the ultimate conquest of truth. For even if we have the sensation of being always enveloped in, surrounded by our own soul, still it does not seem a fixed and immovable prison; rather do we seem to be borne away with it, and perpetually struggling to pass beyond it, to break out into the world, with a perpetual discouragement as we hear endlessly, all around us, that unvarying sound which is no echo from without, but the resonance of a vibration from within. We try to discover in things, endeared to us on that account, the spiritual glamour which we ourselves have cast upon them; we are disillusioned, and learn that they are in themselves barren and devoid of the charm which they owed, in our minds, to the association of certain ideas; sometimes we mobilize all our spiritual forces in a glittering array so as to influence and subjugate other human beings who, as we very well know, are situated outside ourselves, where we can never reach them. And so, if I always imagined the woman I loved as in a setting of whatever places I most longed, at the time, to visit; if in my secret longings it was she who attracted me to them, who opened to me the gate of an unknown world, that was not by the mere hazard of a simple association of thoughts; no, it was because my dreams of travel and of love were only moments – which I isolate artificially to-day as though I were cutting sections, at different heights, in a jet of water, rainbow-flashing but seemingly without flow or motion – were only drops in a single, undeviating, irresistible outrush of all the forces of my life.

And then, as I continue to trace the outward course of these impressions from their close-packed intimate source in my consciousness, and before I come to the horizon of reality which envelops them, I discover pleasures of another kind, those of being comfortably seated, of tasting the good scent of the air, of not being disturbed by any visitor; and, when an hour chimed from the steeple of Saint-Hilaire, of watching what was already spent of the afternoon fall drop by drop until I heard the last stroke which enabled me to add up the total sum, after which the silence that followed seemed to herald the beginning, in the blue sky above me, of that long part of the day still allowed me for reading, until the good dinner which Francoise was even now preparing should come to strengthen and refresh me after the strenuous pursuit of its hero through the pages of my book. And, as each hour struck, it would seem to me that a few seconds only had passed since the hour before; the latest would inscribe itself, close to its predecessor, on the sky's surface, and I would be unable to believe that sixty minutes could be squeezed into the tiny arc of blue which was comprised between their two golden figures. Sometimes it would even happen that this precocious hour would sound two strokes more than the last; there must then have been an hour which I had not heard strike; something which had taken place had not taken place for me; the fascination of my book, a magic as potent as the deepest slumber, had stopped my enchanted ears and had obliterated the sound of that golden bell from the azure surface of the enveloping silence. Sweet Sunday afternoons beneath the chestnut-tree in our Combray garden, from which I was careful to eliminate every commonplace incident of my actual life, replacing them by a career of strange adventures and ambitions in a land watered by living streams, you still recall those adventures and ambitions to my mind when I think of you, and you embody and preserve them by virtue of having little by little drawn round and enclosed them (while I went on with my book and the heat of the day declined) in the gradual crystallization, slowly altering in form and dappled with a pattern of chestnut-leaves, of your silent, sonorous, fragrant, limpid hours.

Sometimes I would be torn from my book, in the middle of the afternoon, by the gardener's daughter, who came running like a mad thing, overturning an orange-tree in its tub, cutting a finger, breaking a tooth, and screaming out 'They're coming, they're coming!' so that Françoise and I should run too and not miss anything of the show. That was on days when the cavalry stationed in Combray went out for some military exercise, going as a rule by the Rue Sainte-Hildegarde. While our servants, sitting in a row on their chairs outside the garden railings, stared at the people of Combray taking their Sunday walks and were stared at in return, the gardener's daughter, through the gap which there was between two houses far away in the Avenue de la Gare, would have spied the glitter of helmets. The servants then hurried in with their chairs, for when the troopers filed through the Rue Sainte-Hildegarde they filled it from side to side, and their jostling horses scraped against the walls of the houses, covering and drowning the pavements like banks which present too narrow a channel to a river in flood.

'Poor children,' Françoise would exclaim, in tears almost before she had reached the railings; 'poor boys, to be mown down like grass in a meadow. It's just shocking to think of,' she would go on, laying a hand over her heart, where presumably she had felt the shock.

'A fine sight, isn't it, Mme Françoise, all these young fellows not caring two straws for their lives?' the gardener would ask, just to 'draw' her. And he would not have spoken in vain.

'Not caring for their lives, is it? Why, what in the world is there that we should care for if it's not our lives, the only gift the Lord never offers us a second time? Oh dear, oh dear; you're right all the same; it's quite true, they don't care! I can remember them in '70; in those wretched wars they've no fear of death left in them; they're nothing more nor less than madmen; and then they aren't worth the price of a rope to hang them with; they're not men any more, they're lions.' For by her way of thinking, to compare a man with a lion, which she used to pronounce 'lie-on', was not at all complimentary to the man.

The Rue Sainte-Hildegarde turned too sharply for us to be able to see people approaching at any distance, and it was only through the gap between those two houses in the Avenue de la Gare that we could still make out fresh helmets racing along towards us, and flashing in the sunlight. The gardener wanted to know whether there were still many to come, and he was thirsty besides, with the sun beating down upon his head. So then, suddenly, his daughter would leap out, as though from a beleaguered city, would make a sortie, turn the street corner, and, having risked her life a hundred times over, reappear and bring us, with a jug of liquorice-water, the news that there were still at least a thousand of them, pouring along without a break from the direction of Thiberzy and Méséglise. Françoise and the gardener, having 'made up' their difference, would discuss the line to be followed in case of war.

'Don't you see, Françoise,' he would say, 'Revolution

would be better, because then no one would need to join in unless he liked.'

'Oh, yes, I can see that, certainly; it's more straight-forward.'

The gardener believed that, as soon as war was declared, they would stop all the railways.

'Yes, to be sure; so that we sha'n't get away,' said Françoise. And the gardener would assent, with 'Ay, they're the cunning ones,' for he would not allow that war was anything but a kind of trick which the state attempted to play on the people, or that there was a man in the world who would not run away from it if he had the chance to do so.

But Françoise would hasten back to my aunt, and I would return to my book, and the servants would take their places again outside the gate to watch the dust settle on the pavement, and the excitement caused by the passage of the soldiers subside. Long after order had been restored, an abnormal tide of humanity would continue to darken the streets of Combray. And in front of every house, even of those where it was not, as a rule, 'done', the servants, and sometimes even the masters would sit and stare, festooning their doorsteps with a dark, irregular fringe, like the border of shells and sea-weed which a stronger tide than usual leaves on the beach, as though trimming it with embroidered crape, when the sea itself has retreated.

Except on such days as these, however, I would as a rule be left to read in peace. But the interruption which a visit from Swann once made, and the commentary which he then supplied to the course of my reading, which had brought me to the work of an author quite new to me, called Bergotte, had this definite result that for a long time afterwards it was not against a wall gay with spikes of purple blossom, but on a wholly different background, the porch of a gothic cathedral, that I would see outlined the figure of one of the women of whom I dreamed.

I had heard Bergotte spoken of, for the first time, by a friend older than myself, for whom I had a strong admiration, a precious youth of the name of Bloch. Hearing me confess my love of the *Nuit d'Octobre*, he had burst out in a bray of laughter, like a bugle-call, and told me, by way of warning: 'You must conquer your vile taste for A. de Musset, Esquire. He is a bad egg, one of the very worst, a pretty detestable specimen. I am bound to admit, natheless,' he added graciously, 'that he, and even the man Racine, did, each of them, once in his life, compose a line which is not only fairly rhythmical, but has also what is in my eyes the supreme merit of meaning absolutely nothing. One is

La blanche Oloossone et la blanche Camire,
and the other

La fille de Minos et de Pasiphaë.
They were submitted to my judgement, as evidence for the defence of the two runagates, in an article by my very dear master Father Lecomte, who is found pleasing in the sight of the immortal gods. By which token, here is a book which I have not the time, just now, to read, a book recommended, it would seem, by that colossal fellow. He regards, or so they tell me, its author, one Bergotte, Esquire, as a subtle scribe, more subtle, indeed, than any beast of the field; and, albeit he exhibits on occasion a critical pacificism, a tenderness in suffering fools, for which it is impossible to account, and hard to make allowance, still his word has weight with me as it were the Delphic Oracle. Read you then this lyrical prose, and, if the Titanic master-builder of rhythm who composed *Bhagafat* and the *Lévrier de Magnus* speaks not falsely, then, by Apollo, you may taste, even you, my master, the ambrosial joys of Olympus.' It was in an ostensible vein of sarcasm that he had asked me to call him, and that he himself called me, 'my master'. But, as a matter of fact, we each derived a certain amount of satisfaction from the mannerism, being still at the age in which one believes that one gives a thing real existence by giving it a name.

Unfortunately I was not able to set at rest, by further talks with Bloch, in which I might have insisted upon an explanation, the doubts he had engendered in me when he told me that fine lines of poetry (from which I, if you please, expected nothing less than the revelation of truth itself) were all the finer if they meant absolutely nothing. For, as it happened, Bloch was not invited to the house again. At first, he had been well received there. It is true that my grandfather made out that, whenever I formed a strong attachment to any one of my friends and brought him home with me, that friend was invariably a Jew; to which he would not have objected on principle – indeed his own friend Swann was of Jewish extraction – had he not found that Jews whom I chose as friends were not usually of the best type. And so I was hardly ever able to bring a new friend home without my grandfather's humming the 'O, God of our fathers' from *La Juive*, or else 'Israel, break thy chain', singing the tune alone, of course, to an 'um-ti-tum-ti-tum, tra-la'; but I used to be afraid of my friend's recognizing the sound, and so being able to reconstruct the words.

Before seeing them, merely on hearing their names, about which, as often as not, there was nothing particularly Hebraic, he would divine not only the Jewish origin of such of my friends as might indeed be of the chosen people, but even some dark secret which was hidden in their family.

'And what do they call your friend who is coming this evening?'

'Dumont, grandpapa.'

'Dumont! Oh, I'm frightened of Dumont.'

And he would sing:

> *Archers, be on your guard!*
> *Watch without rest, without sound,*

and then, after a few adroit questions on points of detail, he would call out 'On guard! on guard,' or, if it were the victim himself who had already arrived, and had been obliged, unconsciously, by my grandfather's subtle examination, to admit his origin, then my grandfather, to show us that he had no longer any doubts, would merely look at us, humming almost inaudibly the air of

> *What! do you hither guide the feet*
> *Of this timid Israelite?*

or of

> *Sweet vale of Hebron, dear paternal field,*

or, perhaps, of

Yes, I am of the chosen race.

These little eccentricities on my grandfather's part implied
no ill-will whatsoever towards my friends. But Bloch had displeased my family for other reasons. He had begun by annoying my father, who, seeing him come in with wet clothes, had
asked him with keen interest:

'Why, M. Bloch, is there a change in the weather; has it been
raining? I can't understand it; the barometer has been "set
fair".'

Which drew from Bloch nothing more instructive than 'Sir,
I am absolutely incapable of telling you whether it has rained.
I live so resolutely apart from physical contingencies that my
senses no longer trouble to inform me of them.'

'My poor boy,' said my father after Bloch had gone, 'your
friend is out of his mind. Why, he couldn't even tell me what
the weather was like. As if there could be anything more interesting! He is an imbecile.'

Next, Bloch had displeased my grandmother because, after
luncheon, when she complained of not feeling very well, he
had stifled a sob and wiped the tears from his eyes.

'You cannot imagine that he is sincere,' she observed to me.
'Why, he doesn't know me. Unless he's mad of course.'

And finally he had upset the whole household when he arrived
an hour and a half late for luncheon and covered with mud
from head to foot, and made not the least apology, saying
merely: 'I never allow myself to be influenced in the smallest
degree either by atmospheric disturbances or by the arbitrary
divisions of what is known as Time. I would willingly reintro-
duce to society the opium pipe of China or the Malayan kris,
but I am wholly and entirely without instruction in those infinitely more pernicious (besides being quite bleakly bour-
geois) implements, the umbrella and the watch.'

In spite of all this he would still have been received at Combray. He was, of course, hardly the friend my parents would
have chosen for me; they had, in the end, decided that the tears
which he had shed on hearing of my grandmother's illness
were genuine enough; but they knew, either instinctively or

from their own experience, that our early impulsive emotions have but little influence over our later actions and the conduct of our lives; and that regard for moral obligations, loyalty to our friends, patience in finishing our work, obedience to a rule of life, have a surer foundation in habits solidly formed and blindly followed than in these momentary transports, ardent but sterile. They would have preferred to Bloch, as companions for myself, boys who would have given me no more than it is proper, by all the laws of middle-class morality, for boys to give one another, who would not unexpectedly send me a basket of fruit because they happened, that morning, to have thought of me with affection, but who, since they were incapable of inclining in my favour, by any single impulse of their imagination and emotions, the exact balance of the duties and claims of friendship, were as incapable of loading the scales to my prejudice. Even the injuries we do them will not easily divert from the path of their duty towards us those conventional natures of which my great-aunt furnished a type: who, after quarrelling for years with a niece, to whom she never spoke again, yet made no change in the will in which she had left that niece the whole of her fortune, because she was her next-of-kin, and it was the 'proper thing' to do.

But I was fond of Bloch; my parents wished me to be happy; and the insoluble problems which I set myself on such texts as the 'absolutely meaningless' beauty of *La fille de Minos et de Pasiphaë* tired me more and made me more unwell than I should have been after further talks with him, unwholesome as those talks might seem to my mother's mind. And he would still have been received at Combray but for one thing. That some night, after dinner, having informed me (a piece of news which had a great influence on my later life, making it happier at one time and then more unhappy) that no woman ever thought of anything but love, and that there was not one of them whose resistance a man could not overcome, he had gone on to assure me that he had heard it said on unimpeachable authority that my great-aunt herself had led a 'gay' life in her younger days, and had been notoriously 'kept'. I could not refrain from passing on so important a piece of information to my parents; the next time Bloch called he was not admitted, and afterwards, when I met him in the street, he greeted me with extreme coldness.

But in the matter of Bergotte he had spoken truly.

For the first few days, like a tune which will be running in one's head and maddening one soon enough, but of which one has not for the moment 'got hold', the things I was to love so passionately in Bergotte's style had not yet caught my eye. I could not, it is true, lay down the novel of his which I was reading, but I fancied that I was interested in the story alone, as in the first dawn of love, when we go every day to meet a woman at some party or entertainment by the charm of which we imagine it is that we are attracted. Then I observed the rare, almost archaic phrases which he liked to employ at certain points, where a hidden flow of harmony, a prelude contained and concealed in the work itself would animate and elevate his style; and it was at such points as these, too, that he would begin to speak of the 'vain dream of life', of the 'inexhaustible torrent of fair forms', of the 'sterile, splendid torture of understanding and loving', of the 'moving effigies which ennoble for all time the charming and venerable fronts of our cathedrals'; that he would express a whole system of philosophy, new to me, by the use of marvellous imagery, to the inspiration of which I would naturally have ascribed that sound of harping which began to chime and echo in my ears, an accompaniment to which that imagery added something ethereal and sublime. One of these passages of Bergotte, the third or fourth which I had detached from the rest, filled me with a joy to which the meagre joy I had tasted in the first passage bore no comparison, a joy which I felt myself to have experienced in some innermost chamber of my soul, deep, undivided, vast, from which all obstructions and partitions seemed to have been swept away. For what had happened was that, while I recognized in this passage the same taste for uncommon phrases, the same bursts of music, the same idealist philosophy which had been present in the earlier passages without my having taken them into account as the source of my pleasure, I now no longer had the impression of being confronted by a particular passage in one of Bergotte's works, which traced a purely bi-dimensional figure in outline upon the surface of my mind, but rather of the 'ideal passage' of Bergotte, common to every one of his books, and to which all the earlier, similiar passages, now becoming merged in it, had added a kind of density and volume, by which my own understanding seemed to be enlarged.

I was by no means Bergotte's sole admirer; he was the favourite writer also of a friend of my mother's, a highly literary lady; while Dr du Boulbon had kept all his patients waiting until he finished Bergotte's latest volume; and it was from his consulting room, and from a house in a park near Combray that some of the first seeds were scattered of that taste for Bergotte, a rare growth in those days, but now so universally acclimatized that one finds it flowering everywhere throughout Europe and America, and even in the tiniest villages, rare still in its refinement, but in that alone. What my mother's friend, and, it would seem, what Dr du Boulbon liked above all in the writings of Bergotte was just what I liked, the same flow of melody, the same old-fashioned phrases, and certain others, quite simple and familiar, but so placed by him, in such prominence, as to hint at a particular quality of taste on his part; and also, in the sad parts of his books, a sort of roughness, a tone that was almost harsh. And he himself, no doubt, realized that these were his principal attractions. For in his later books, if he had hit upon some great truth, or upon the name of an historic cathedral, he would break off his narrative, and in an invocation, an apostrophe, a lengthy prayer, would give a free outlet to that effluence which, in the earlier volumes, remained buried beneath the form of his prose, discernible only in a rippling of its surface, and perhaps even more delightful, more harmonious when it was thus veiled from the eye, when the reader could give no precise indication of where the murmur of the current began, or of where it died away. These passages in which he delighted were our favourites also. For my own part I knew all of them by heart. I felt even disappointed when he resumed the thread of his narrative. Whenever he spoke of something whose beauty had until then remained hidden from me, of pine-forests or of hailstorms, of *Notre-Dame de Paris*, of

Athalie, or of *Phèdre*, by some piece of imagery he would make
their beauty explode and drench me with its essence. And so,
dimly realizing that the universe contained innumerable elements which my feeble senses would be powerless to discern,
did he not bring them within my reach, I wished that I might
have his opinion, some metaphor of his, upon everything in
the world, and especially upon such things as I might have an
opportunity, some day, of seeing for myself; and among such
things, more particularly still upon some of the historic buildings of France, upon certain views of the sea, because the emphasis with which, in his books, he referred to these showed
that he regarded them as rich in significance and beauty. But,
alas, upon almost everything in the world his opinion was unknown to me. I had no doubt that it would differ entirely from
my own, since his came down from an unknown sphere towards which I was striving to raise myself; convinced that my
thoughts would have seemed pure foolishness to that perfected
spirit, I had so completely obliterated them all that, if I happened to find in one of his books something which had already occurred to my own mind, my heart would swell with gratitude
and pride as though some deity had, in his infinite bounty, restored it to me, had pronounced it to be beautiful and right. It
happened now and then that a page of Bergotte would express
precisely those ideas which I used often at night, when I was
unable to sleep, to write to my grandmother and mother, and
so concisely and well that his page had the appearance of a collection of mottoes for me to set at the head of my letters. And
so too, in later years, when I began to compose a book of my
own, and the quality of some of my sentences seemed so inadequate that I could not make up my mind to go on with the
undertaking, I would find the equivalent of my sentences in
Bergotte's. But it was only then, when I read them in his pages,
that I could enjoy them; when it was I myself who composed
them, in my anxiety that they should exactly reproduce what I
seemed to have detected in my mind, and in my fear of their not
turning out 'true to life,' I had no time to ask myself whether
what I was writing would be pleasant to read! But indeed
there was no kind of language, no kind of ideas which I really

liked, except these. My feverish and unsatisfactory attempts were themselves a token of my love, a love which brought me no pleasure, but was, for all that, intense and deep. And so, when I came suddenly upon similar phrases in the writings of another, that is to say stripped of their familiar accompaniment of scruples and repressions and self-tormentings, I was free to indulge to the full my own appetite for such things, just as a cook who, once in a while, has no dinner to prepare for other people, can then find time to gormandize himself. And so, when I had found, one day, in a book by Bergotte, some joke about an old family servant, to which his solemn and magnificent style added a great deal of irony, but which was in principle what I had often said to my grandmother about Françoise, and when, another time, I had discovered that he thought not unworthy of reflexion in one of those mirrors of absolute Truth which were his writings, a remark similar to one which I had had occasion to make on our friend M. Legrandin (and, moreover, my remarks on Françoise and M. Legrandin were among those which I would most resolutely have sacrificed for Bergotte's sake, in the belief that he would find them quite without interest); then it was suddenly revealed to me that my own humble existence and the Realms of Truth were less widely separated than I had supposed, that at certain points they were actually in contact; and in my newfound confidence and joy I wept upon his printed page, as in the arms of a long-lost father.

From his books I had formed an impression of Bergotte as a frail and disappointed old man, who had lost his children, and had never found any consolation. And so I would read, or rather sing his sentences in my brain, with rather more *dolce*, rather more *lento* than he himself had, perhaps, intended, and his simplest phrase would strike my ears with something peculiarly gentle and loving in its intonation. More than anything else in the world I cherished his philosophy, and had pledged myself to it in lifelong devotion. It made me impatient to reach the age when I should be eligible to attend the class at school called 'Philosophy'. I did not wish to learn or do anything else there, but simply to exist and be guided entirely by the mind of

Bergotte, and, if I had been told then that the metaphysicians
whom I was actually to follow there resembled him in nothing,
I should have been struck down by the despair a young lover
feels who has sworn lifelong fidelity, when a friend speaks to
him of the other mistresses he will have in time to come.

One Sunday, while I was reading in the garden, I was interrupted by Swann, who had come to call upon my parents.

'What are you reading? May I look? Why, it's Bergotte!
Who has been telling you about him?'

I replied that Bloch was responsible.

'Oh, yes, that boy I saw here once, who looks so like the
Bellini portrait of Mahomet II. It's an astonishing likeness; he
has the same arched eyebrows and hooked nose and prominent
cheekbones. When his beard comes he'll be Mahomet himself.
Anyhow, he has good taste, for Bergotte is a charming creature.' And seeing how much I seemed to admire Bergotte,
Swann, who never spoke at all about the people he knew, made
an exception in my favour and said: 'I know him well; if you
would like him to write a few words on the title-page of your
book I could ask him for you.'

I dared not accept such an offer, but bombarded Swann
with questions about his friend. 'Can you tell me, please, who
is his favourite actor?'

'Actor? No, I can't say. But I do know this: there's not a
man on the stage whom he thinks equal to Berma; he puts her
above everyone. Have you seen her?'

'No, sir, my parents do not allow me to go to the theatre.'

'That is a pity. You should insist. Berma in *Phèdre*, in the
Cid; well, she's only an actress, if you like, but you know that
I don't believe very much in the "hierarchy" of the arts.' As he
spoke I noticed, what had often struck me before in his conversations with my grandmother's sisters, that whenever he
spoke of serious matters, whenever he used an expression
which seemed to imply a definite opinion upon some important subject, he would take care to isolate, to sterilize it by using
a special intonation, mechanical and ironic, as though he had
put the phrase or word between inverted commas, and was
anxious to disclaim any personal responsibility for it; as who

should say 'the "hierarchy", don't you know, as silly people call it.' But then, if it was so absurd, why did he say the 'hierarchy'? A moment later he went on: 'Her acting will give you as noble an inspiration as any masterpiece of art in the world, as – oh, I don't know –' and he began to laugh, 'shall we say the Queens of Chartres?' Until then I had supposed that his horror of having to give a serious opinion was something Parisian and refined, in contrast to the provincial dogmatism of my grandmother's sisters; and I had imagined also that it was characteristic of the mental attitude towards life of the circle in which Swann moved, where, by a natural reaction from the 'lyrical' enthusiams of earlier generations, an excessive importance was given to small and precise facts, formerly regarded as vulgar, and anything in the nature of 'phrase-making' was banned. But now I found myself slightly shocked by this attitude which Swann invariably adopted when face to face with generalities. He appeared unwilling to risk even an opinion, and to be at his ease only when he could furnish, with meticulous accuracy, some precise but unimportant detail. But in so doing he did not take into account that even here he was giving an opinion, holding a brief (as they say) for something, that the accuracy of his details had an importance of its own. I thought again of the dinner that night, when I had been so unhappy because Mamma would not be coming up to my room, and when he had dismissed the balls given by the Princesse de Léon as being of no importance. And yet it was to just that sort of amusement that he was devoting his life. For what other kind of existence did he reserve the duties of saying in all seriousness what he thought about things, of formulating judgements which he would not put between inverted commas; and when would he cease to give himself up to occupations of which at the same time he made out that they were absurd? I noticed, too, in the manner in which Swann spoke to me of Bergotte, something which, to do him justice, was not peculiar to himself, but was shared by all that writer's admirers at that time, at least by my mother's friends and by Dr du Boulbon. Like Swann, they would say of Bergotte: 'He has a charming mind, so individual, he has a way of his own of saying things, which is a little far-fetched, but so pleasant. You never need to look for his name on the title-page, you can tell his work at once.' But none of them had yet gone so far as to say 'He is a great writer, he has great talent.' They did not even credit him with talent at all. They did not speak, because they were not aware of it. We are very slow in recognizing in the peculiar physiognomy of a new writer the type which is labelled 'great talent' in our museum of general ideas. Simply because that physiognomy is new and strange, we can find in it no resemblance to what we are accustomed to call talent. We say rather originality, charm, delicacy, strength; and then one day we add up the sum of these, and find that it amounts simply to talent.

'Are there any books in which Bergotte has written about Berma?' I asked M. Swann.

'I think he has, in that little essay on Racine, but it must be out of print. Still, there has perhaps been a second impression. I will find out. Anyhow, I can ask Bergotte himself all that you want to know next time he comes to dine with us. He never misses a week, from one year's end to another. He is my daughter's greatest friend. They go about together, and look at old towns and cathedrals and castles.'

As I was still completely ignorant of the different grades in the social hierarchy, the fact that my father found it impossible for us to see anything of Swann's wife and daughter had, for a long time, had the contrary effect of making me imagine them as separated from us by an enormous gulf, which greatly enhanced their dignity and importance in my eyes. I was sorry that my mother did not dye her hair and redden her lips as I had heard our neighbour, Mme Sazerat, say that Mme Swann did, to gratify not her husband but M. de Charlus; and I felt that, to her, we must be an object of scorn, which distressed me particularly on account of the daughter, such a pretty little girl, as I had heard, and one of whom I used often to dream, always imagining her with the same features and appearance, which I bestowed upon her quite arbitrarily, but with a charming effect. But from this afternoon, when I had learned that Mlle Swann was a creature living in such rare and fortunate circumstances, bathed, as in her natural element, in such a sea of privilege that, if she should ask her parents whether anyone were coming to dinner, she would be answered in those two syllables, radiant with celestial light, would hear the name of that golden guest who was to her no more than an old friend of her family, Bergotte; that for her the intimate conversation at table, corresponding to what my great-aunt's conversation was for me, would be the words of Bergotte upon all those subjects which he had not been able to take up in his writings, and on which I would fain have heard him utter oracles; and that, above all, when she went to visit other towns, he would be walking by her side, unrecognized and glorious, like the gods who came down, of old, from heaven to dwell among mortal men: then I realized both the rare worth of a creature such as Mlle Swann, and, at the same time, how coarse and ignorant I should appear to her; and I felt so keenly how pleasant and yet how impossible it would be for me to become her friend that I was filled at once with longing and with despair. And usually, from this time forth, when I thought of her, I would see her standing before the porch of a cathedral, explaining to me what each of the statues meant, and, with a smile which was my highest commendation, presenting me, as her friend, to Bergotte. And invariably the charm of all the fancies which the thought of cathedrals used to inspire in me, the charm of the hills and valleys of the Île-de-France and of the plains of Normandy, would radiate brightness and beauty over the picture I had formed in my mind of Mlle Swann; nothing more remained but to know and to love her. Once we believe that a fellow-creature has a share in some unknown existence to which that creature's love for ourselves can win us admission, that is, of all the preliminary conditions which Love exacts, the one to which he attaches most importance, the one which makes him generous or indifferent as to the rest. Even those women who pretend that they judge a man by his exterior only, see in that exterior an emanation from some special way of life. And that is why they fall in love with a soldier or a fireman, whose uniform makes them less particular about his face; they kiss and believe that beneath the crushing breastplate there beats a heart different from the rest, more gallant more adventurous, more tender; and so it is that a young king or a crown prince may travel in foreign countries and make the most gratifying conquests, and yet lack entirely that regular and classic profile which would be indispensable, I dare say, in an outside-broker.

While I was reading in the garden, a thing my great-aunt would never have understood my doing save on a Sunday, that being the day on which it was unlawful to indulge in any serious occupation, and on which she herself would lay aside her sewing (on a week-day she would have said, 'How you can go on amusing yourself with a book; it isn't Sunday, you know!' putting into the word 'amusing' an implication of childishness and waste of time), my aunt Léonie would be gossiping with Françoise until it was time for Eulalie to arrive. She would tell her that she had just seen Mme Goupil go by 'without an umbrella, in the silk dress she had made for her the other day at Châteaudun. If she has far to go before vespers, she may get it properly soaked.'

'Very likely' (which meant also 'very likely not') was the answer, for Françoise did not wish definitely to exclude the possibility of a happier alternative.

'There, now,' went on my aunt, beating her brow, 'that reminds me that I never heard if she got to church this morning before the Elevation. I must remember to ask Eulalie ... Françoise, just look at that black cloud behind the steeple, and how poor the light is on the slates, you may be certain it will rain before the day is out. It couldn't possibly keep on like this, it's been too hot. And the sooner the better, for until the storm breaks my Vichy water won't "go down",' she concluded, since, in her mind, the desire to accelerate the digestion of her Vichy water was of infinitely greater importance than her fear of seeing Mme Goupil's new dress ruined.

'Very likely.'

'And you know that when it rains in the Square there's none too much shelter.' Suddenly my aunt turned pale. 'What, three o'clock!' she exclaimed. 'But vespers will have begun already, and I've forgotten my pepsin! Now I know why that Vichy water has been lying on my stomach.' And falling precipitately upon a prayer-book bound in purple velvet, with gilt clasps, out of which in her haste she let fall a shower of the little pictures, each in a lace fringe of yellowish paper, which she used to mark the places of the greater feasts of the church, my aunt, while she swallowed her drops, began at full speed to mutter the words of the sacred text, its meaning being slightly clouded in her brain by the uncertainty whether the pepsin, when taken so long after the Vichy, would still be able to overtake it and to 'send it down'. 'Three o'clock! It's unbelievable how time flies.'

A little tap at the window, as though some missile had struck it, followed by a plentiful, falling sound, as light, though, as if a shower of sand were being sprinkled from a window overhead; then the fall spread, took on an order, a rhythm, became liquid, loud, drumming, musical, innumerable, universal. It was the rain.

'There, Françoise, what did I tell you? How it's coming down! But I think I heard the bell at the garden gate: go along and see who can be outside in this weather.'

Françoise went and returned. 'It's Mme Amédée' (my grandmother). 'She said she was going for a walk. It's raining hard, all the same.'

'I'm not at all surprised,' said my aunt, looking up towards the sky. 'I've always said that she was not in the least like other people. Well, I'm glad it's she and not myself who's outside in all this.'

'Mme Amédée is always the exact opposite of the rest,' said Françoise, not unkindly, refraining until she should be alone with the other servants from stating her belief that my grandmother was 'a bit off her head'.

'There's Benediction over! Eulalie will never come now,' sighed my aunt. 'It will be the weather that's frightened her away.'

'But it's not five o'clock yet, Mme Octave, it's only half past four.'

'Only half past four! And here am I, obliged to draw back

the small curtains, just to get a tiny streak of daylight. At half past four! Only a week before the Rogation-days. Ah, my poor Françoise, the dear Lord must be sorely vexed with us. The world is going too far in these days. As my poor Octave used to say, we have forgotten God too often, and He is taking vengeance upon us.'

A bright flush animated my aunt's cheeks; it was Eulalie. As ill luck would have it, scarcely had she been admitted to the presence when Françoise reappeared and, with a smile which was meant to indicate her full participation in the pleasure which, she had no doubt, her tidings would give my aunt, articulating each syllable so as to show that, in spite of her having to translate them into indirect speech, she was repeating, as a good servant should, the very words which the new visitor had condescended to use, said: 'His reverence the Curé would be delighted, enchanted, if Mme Octave is not resting just now, and could see him. His reverence does not wish to disturb Mme Octave. His reverence is downstairs; I told him to go into the parlour.'

Had the truth been known, the Curé's visits gave my aunt no such ecstatic pleasure as Françoise supposed, and the air of jubilation with which she felt bound to illuminate her face whenever she had to announce his arrival, did not altogether correspond to what was felt by her invalid. The Curé (an excellent man, with whom I am sorry now that I did not converse more often, for, even if he cared nothing for the arts, he knew a great many etymologies), being in the habit of showing distinguished visitors over his church (he had even planned to compile a history of the Parish of Combray), used to weary her with his endless explanations, which, incidentally, never varied in the least degree. But when his visit synchronized exactly with Eulalie's it became frankly distasteful to my aunt. She would have preferred to make the most of Eulalie, and not to have had the whole of her circle about her at one time. But she dared not send the Curé away, and had to content herself with making a sign to Eulalie not to leave when he did, so that she might have her to herself for a little after he had gone.

'What is this I have been hearing, Father, that a painter has set up his easel in your church, and is copying one of the windows! Old as I am, I can safely say that I have never even heard of such a thing in all my life! What is the world coming to next, I wonder! And the ugliest thing in the whole church, too.'

'I will not go so far as to say that it is quite the ugliest, for, although there are certain things in Saint-Hilaire which are well worth a visit, there are others that are very old now, in my poor basilica, the only one in all the diocese that has never even been restored. The Lord knows, our porch is dirty and out of date; still, it is of a majestic character; take, for instance, the Esther tapestries, though personally I would not give a brass farthing for the pair of them, but experts put them next after the ones at Sens. I can quite see, too, that apart from certain details which are – well, a trifle realistic, they show features which testify to a genuine power of observation. But don't talk to me about the windows. Is it common sense, I ask you, to leave up windows which shut out all the daylight, and even confuse the eyes by throwing patches of colour, to which I should be hard put to it to give a name, on a floor in which there are not two slabs on the same level? And yet they refuse to renew the floor for me because, if you please, those are the tombstones of the Abbots of Combray and the Lords of Guermantes, the old Counts, you know, of Brabant, direct ancestors of the present Duc de Guermantes, and of his Duchesse also, since she was a lady of the Guermantes family, and married her cousin.' (My grandmother, whose steady refusal to take any interest in 'persons' had ended in her confusing all their names and titles, whenever anyone mentioned the Duchesse de Guermantes used to make out that she must be related to Mme de Villeparisis. The whole family would then burst out laughing; and she would attempt to justify herself by harking back to some invitation to a christening or funeral: 'I feel sure that there was a Guermantes in it somewhere.' And for once I would side with the others, and against her, refusing to admit that there could be any connexion between her school-friend and the descendant of Geneviève de Brabant.)

'Look at Roussainville,' the Curé went on. 'It is nothing more nowadays than a parish of farmers, though in olden times the place must have had a considerable importance from its trade in felt hats and clocks. (I am not certain, by the way, of the etymology of Roussainville. I should dearly like to think that the name was originally Rouville, from *Radulfi villa*, analogous, don't you see, to Châteauroux, *Castrum Radulfi*, but we will talk about that some other time.) Very well; the church there has superb windows, almost all quite modern, including that most imposing "Entry of Louis-Philippe into Combray" which would be more in keeping, surely, at Combray itself, and which is every bit as good, I understand, as the famous windows at Chartres. Only yesterday I met Dr Percepied's brother, who goes in for these things, and he told me that he looked upon it as a most beautiful piece of work. But, as I said to this artist, who, by the way, seems to be a most civil fellow, and is a regular virtuoso, it appears, with his brush; what on earth, I said to him, do you find so extraordinary in this window, which is, if anything, a little dingier than the rest?'

'I am sure that if you were to ask his Lordship,' said my aunt in a resigned tone, for she had begun to feel that she was going to be 'tired', 'he would never refuse you a new window.'

'You may depend upon it, Mme Octave,' replied the Curé. 'Why, it was just his Lordship himself who started the outcry about the window, by proving that it represented Gilbert the Bad, a Lord of Guermantes and a direct descendant of Geneviève de Brabant, who was a daughter of the House of Guermantes, receiving absolution from Saint Hilaire.'

'But I don't see where Saint Hilaire comes in.'

'Why yes, have you never noticed, in the corner of the window, a lady in a yellow robe? Very well, that is Saint Hilaire, who is also known, you will remember, in certain parts of the country as Saint Illiers, Saint Hélier, and even, in the Jura, Saint Ylie. But these various corruptions of *Sanctus Hilarius* are by no means the most curious that have occurred in the names of the blessed Saints. Take, for example, my good Eulalie, the case of your own patron, *Sancta Eulalia*; do you know what she has become in Burgundy? Saint Éloi, nothing more or less! The lady has become a gentleman. Do you hear that, Eulalie, after you are dead they will make a man of you!'

'Father will always have his joke.'

'Gilbert's brother, Charles the Stammerer, was a pious prince, but, having early in life lost his father, Pepin the Mad, who died as a result of his mental infirmity, he wielded the supreme power with all the arrogance of a man who has not been subjected to discipline in his youth, so much so that, whenever he saw a man in a town whose face he did not remember, he would massacre the whole place, to the last inhabitant. Gilbert, wishing to be avenged on Charles, caused the church at Combray to be burned down, the original church, that was, which Théodebert, when he and his court left the country residence he had near here, at Thiberzy (which is, of course, *Theodeberiacus*), to go out and fight the Burgundians, had promised to build over the tomb of Saint Hilaire if the Saint brought him victory. Nothing remains of it now but the crypt, into which Théodore has probably taken you, for Gilbert burned all the rest. Finally, he defeated the unlucky Charles with the aid of William' (which the Curé pronounced 'Will'am') 'the Conqueror, which is why so many English still come to visit the place. But he does not appear to have managed to win the affection of the people of Combray, for they fell upon him as he was coming out from mass, and cut off his head. Théodore has a little book, that he lends people, which tells you the whole story.

'But what is unquestionably the most remarkable thing about our church is the view from the belfry, which is full of grandeur. Certainly in your case, since you are not very strong, I should never recommend you to climb our seven and ninety steps, just half the number they have in the famous cathedral at Milan. It is quite tiring enough for the most active person, especially as you have to go on your hands and knees, if you don't wish to crack your skull, and you collect all the cobwebs off the staircase upon your clothes. In any case you should be well wrapped up,' he went on, without noticing my aunt's fury at the mere suggestion that she could ever, possibly, be capable of climbing into his belfry, 'for there's a strong breeze there, once you get to the top. Some people even assure me that they have felt the chill of death up there. No matter, on Sundays there are always clubs and societies, who come, some of them, long distances to admire our beautiful panorama, and they always go home charmed. Wait now, next Sunday, if the weather holds, you will be sure to find a lot of people there, for Rogation-tide. You must admit, certainly, that the view from up there is like a fairy-tale, with what you might call vistas along the plain, which have quite a special charm of their own. On a clear day you can see as far as Verneuil. And then another thing; you can see at the same time places which you are in the habit of seeing one without the other, as, for instance, the course of the Vivonne and the ditches at Saint-Assise-lès-Combray, which are separated, really, by a screen of tall trees; or, to take another example, there are all the canals at Jouy-le-Vicomte, which is *Gaudiacus vicecomitis*, as of course you know. Each time that I have been to Jouy I have seen a bit of a canal in one place, and then I have turned a corner and seen another, but when I saw the second I could no longer see the first. I tried in vain to imagine how they lay by one another; it was no good. But, from the top of Saint-Hilaire, it's quite another matter; the whole countryside is spread out before you like a map. Only, you cannot make out the water; you would say that there were great rifts in the town, slicing it up so neatly that it looks like a loaf of bread which still holds together after it has been cut up. To get it all quite perfect you would have to be in both places at once; up here on the top of Saint-Hilaire and down there at Jouy-le-Vicomte.'

The Curé had so much exhausted my aunt that no sooner had he gone than she was obliged to send away Eulalie also.

'Here, my poor Eulalie,' she said in a feeble voice, drawing a coin from a small purse which lay ready to her hand. 'This is just something so that you shall not forget me in your prayers.'

'Oh, but, Mme Octave, I don't think I ought to; you know very well that I don't come here for that!' So Eulalie would answer, with the same hesitation and the same embarrassment, every Sunday, as though each temptation were the first, and with a look of displeasure which enlivened my aunt and never offended her, for if it so happened that Eulalie, when she took the money, looked a little less sulky than usual, my aunt would remark afterwards, 'I cannot think what has come over Eulalie; I gave her just the trifle I always give, and she did not look at all pleased.'

'I don't think she has very much to complain of, all the same,' Françoise would sigh grimly, for she had a tendency to regard as petty cash all that my aunt might give her for herself or her children, and as treasure riotously squandered on a pampered and ungrateful darling the little coins slipped, Sunday by Sunday, into Eulalie's hand, but so discreetly passed that Françoise never managed to see them. It was not that she wanted to have for herself the money my aunt bestowed on Eulalie. She already enjoyed a sufficiency of all that my aunt possessed, in the knowledge that the wealth of the mistress automatically ennobled and glorified the maid in the eyes of the world; and that she herself was conspicuous and worthy to be praised throughout Combray, Jouy-le-Vicomte, and other cities of men, on account of my aunt's many farms, her frequent and prolonged visits from the Curé, and the astonishing number of bottles of Vichy water which she consumed. Françoise was avaricious only for my aunt; had she had control over my aunt's fortune (which would have more than satisfied her highest ambition) she would have guarded it from the assaults of strangers with a maternal ferocity. She would, however, have seen no great harm in what my aunt, whom she knew to be incurably generous, allowed herself to give away, had she given only to those who were already rich. Perhaps she felt that such persons, not being actually in need of my aunt's presents, could not be suspected of simulating affection for her on that account. Besides, presents offered to

persons of great wealth and position, such as Mme Sazerat,
M. Swann, M. Legrandin, and Mme Goupil, to persons of the
'same class' as my aunt, and who would naturally 'mix with
her', seemed to Françoise to be included among the ornamental customs of that strange and brilliant life led by rich people,
who hunted and shot, gave balls and paid visits, a life which
she would contemplate with an admiring smile. But it was by
no means the same thing if, for this princely exchange of
courtesies, my aunt substituted mere charity, if her beneficia-
ries were of the class which Françoise would label 'people like
myself', or 'people no better than myself', people whom she
despised even more if they did not address her always as 'Mme
Françoise', just to show that they considered themselves to be
'not as good'. And when she saw that, despite all her warn-
ings, my aunt continued to do exactly as she pleased, and to
fling money away with both hands (or so, at least, Françoise
believed) on undeserving objects, she began to find that the
presents she herself received from my aunt were very tiny
compared to the imaginary riches squandered upon Eulalie.
There was not, in the neighbourhood of Combray, a farm of
such prosperity and importance that Françoise doubted
Eulalie's ability to buy it, without thinking twice, out of the
capital which her visits to my aunt had 'brought in'. It must be
added that Eulalie had formed an exactly similar estimate of
the vast and secret hoards of Françoise. So, every Sunday,
after Eulalie had gone, Françoise would mercilessly prophesy
her coming downfall. She hated Eulalie, but was at the same
time afraid of her, and so felt bound, when Eulalie was there,
to 'look pleasant'. But she would make up for that after the
other's departure; never, it is true, alluding to her by name,
but hinting at her in Sibylline oracles, or in utterances of a
comprehensive character, like those of Ecclesiastes, the
Preacher, but so worded that their special application could
not escape my aunt. After peering out at the side of the curtain
to see whether Eulalie had shut the front door behind her;
'Flatterers know how to make themselves welcome, and to
gather up the crumbs; but have patience, have patience; our
God is a jealous God, and one fine day He will be avenged

upon them!' she would declaim, with the sidelong insinuating glance of Joash, thinking of Athaliah alone when he says that the

> *prosperity*
> *Of wicked men runs like a torrent past,*
> *And soon is spent.*

But on this memorable afternoon, when the Curé had come as well, and by his interminable visit had drained my aunt's strength, Françoise followed Eulalie from the room, saying: 'Mme Octave, I will leave you to rest; you look utterly tired out.'

And my aunt answered her not a word, breathing a sigh so faint that it seemed it must prove her last, and lying there with closed eyes, as though already dead. But hardly had Françoise arrived downstairs, when four peals of a bell, pulled with the utmost violence, reverberated through the house, and my aunt, sitting erect upon her bed, called out: 'Has Eulalie gone yet? Would you believe it; I forgot to ask her whether Mme Goupil arrived in church before the Elevation. Run after her, quick!'

But Françoise returned alone, having failed to overtake Eulalie.

'It is most provoking,' said my aunt, shaking her head. 'The one important thing that I had to ask her.'

In this way life went by for my aunt Léonie, always the same, in the gentle uniformity of what she called, with a pretence of deprecation but with a deep tenderness, her 'little jog-trot'. Respected by all and sundry, not merely in her own house, where every one of us, having learned the futility of recommending any healthier mode of life, had become gradually resigned to its observance, but in the village as well, where, three streets away, a tradesman who had to hammer nails into a packing-case would send first to Françoise to make sure that my aunt was not 'resting' – her 'little jog-trot' was, none the less, brutally disturbed on one occasion in this same year. Like a fruit hidden among its leaves, which has grown and ripened unobserved by man, until it falls of its own accord, there came upon us one night the kitchen-maid's confinement. Her pains were unbearable, and, as there was no midwife in Combray, Françoise had to set off before dawn to fetch one from Thiberzy. My aunt was unable to 'rest', owing to the cries of the girl, and as Françoise, though the distance was nothing, was very late in returning, her services were greatly missed. And so, in the course of the morning, my mother said to me: 'Run upstairs, and see if your aunt wants anything.'

I went into the first of her two rooms, and through the open door of the other saw my aunt lying on her side, asleep. I could hear her breathing, in what was almost distinguishable as a snore. I was just going to slip away when something, probably the sound of my entry, interrupted her sleep, and made it 'change speed', as they say of motor-cars nowadays, for the music of her snore broke off for a second and began again on a lower note; then she awoke, and half turned her face, which I could see for the first time; a kind of horror was imprinted on it; plainly she had just escaped from some terrifying dream. She could not see me from where she was lying, and I stood there not knowing whether I ought to go forward or to retire; but all at once she seemed to return to a sense of reality, and to grasp the falsehood of the visions that had terrified her; a smile of joy, a pious act of thanksgiving to God, who is pleased to grant that life shall be less cruel than our dreams, feebly illumined her face, and, with the habit she had formed of speaking to herself, half-aloud, when she thought herself alone, she murmured: 'The Lord be praised! We have nothing to disturb us here but the kitchen-maid's baby. And I've been dreaming that my poor Octave had come back to life, and was trying to make me take a walk every day!' She stretched out a hand towards her rosary, which was lying on the small table, but sleep was once again getting the mastery, and did not leave her the strength to reach it; she fell asleep, calm and contented, and I crept out of the room on tiptoe, without either her or anyone else ever knowing, from that day to this, what I had seen and heard.

When I say that, apart from such rare happenings as this confinement, my aunt's 'little jog-trot' never underwent any variation, I do not include those variations which, repeated at regular intervals and in identical form, did no more, really, than print a sort of uniform pattern upon the greater uniformity of her life. So, for instance, every Saturday, as Françoise had to go in the afternoon to market at Roussainville-le-Pin, the whole household would have to have luncheon an hour earlier. And my aunt had so thoroughly acquired the habit of this weekly exception to her general habits, that she clung to it as much as to the rest. She was so well 'routined' to it, as Françoise would say, that if, on a Saturday, she had had to wait for her luncheon until the regular hour, it would have 'upset' her as much as if she had had, on an ordinary day, to put her luncheon forward to its Saturday time. Incidentally this acceleration of luncheon gave Saturday, for all of us, an individual character, kindly and rather attractive. At the moment when, ordinarily, there was still an hour to be lived through before meal-time sounded, we would all know that in a few seconds we should see the endives make their precocious appearance, followed by the special favour of an omelette, an unmerited steak. The return of this asymmetrical Saturday was one of those petty occurrences, intra-mural, localized, almost civic, which, in uneventful lives and stable orders of society, create a kind of national unity, and become the favourite theme for conversation, for pleasantries, for anecdotes which can be embroidered as the narrator pleases; it would have provided a nucleus, ready-made, for a legendary cycle, if any of us had had the epic mind. At daybreak, before we were dressed, without rhyme or reason, save for the pleasure of proving the strength of our solidarity, we would call to one another good-humouredly, cordially, patriotically, 'Hurry up; there's no time to be lost; don't forget, it's Saturday!' while my aunt, gossiping with Françoise, and reflecting that the day would be even longer than usual, would say, 'You might cook them a nice bit of veal, seeing that it's Saturday.' If, at half past ten, someone absent-mindedly pulled out a watch and said, 'I say, an hour-and-a-half still before luncheon,' everyone else would be in ecstasies over being able to retort at once: 'Why, what are you thinking about? Have you forgotten that it's Saturday?'

And a quarter of an hour later we would still be laughing, and reminding ourselves to go up and tell aunt Léonie about this absurd mistake, to amuse her. The very face of the sky appeared to undergo a change. After luncheon the sun, conscious that it was Saturday, would blaze an hour longer in the zenith, and when someone, thinking that we were late in starting for our walk, said, 'What, only two o'clock!' feeling the heavy throb go by him of the twin strokes from the steeple of Saint-Hilaire (which as a rule passed no one at that hour upon the highways, deserted for the midday meal or for the nap which follows it, or on the banks of the bright and ever-flowing stream, which even the angler had abandoned, and so slipped unaccompanied into the vacant sky, where only a few loitering clouds remained to greet them) the whole family would respond in chorus: 'Why, you're forgetting; we had luncheon an hour earlier; you know very well it's Saturday.'

The surprise of a 'barbarian' (for so we termed everyone who was not acquainted with Saturday's special customs) who had called at eleven o'clock to speak to my father, and had found us at table, was an event which used to cause Françoise as much merriment as, perhaps, anything that had ever happened in her life. And if she found it amusing that the non-plussed visitor should not have known, beforehand, that we had our luncheon an hour earlier on Saturdays, it was still more irresistibly funny that my father himself (fully as she sympathized, from the bottom of her heart, with the rigid chauvinism which prompted him) should never have dreamed that the barbarian could fail to be aware of so simple a matter, and so had replied, with no further enlightenment of the other's surprise at seeing us already in the dining-room: 'You see, it's Saturday.' On reaching this point in the story, Françoise would pause to wipe the tears of merriment from her eyes, and then, to add to her own enjoyment, would prolong the dialogue, inventing a further reply for the visitor to whom the word 'Saturday' had conveyed nothing. And so far from our objecting to these interpolations, we would feel that the story was not yet long enough, and would rally her with:

'Oh, but surely he said something else as well. There was more than that, the first time you told it.'

My great-aunt herself would lay aside her work, and raise her head and look at us over her glasses.

The day had yet another characteristic feature, namely, that during May we used to go out on Saturday evenings after dinner to the 'Month of Mary' devotions.

As we were liable, there, to meet M. Vinteuil, who held very strict views on 'the deplorable untidiness of young people, which seems to be encouraged in these days,' my mother would first see that there was nothing out of order in my appearance, and then we would set out for the church. It was in these 'Month of Mary' services that I can remember having first fallen in love with hawthorn-blossom. The hawthorn was not merely in the church, for there, holy ground as it was, we had all of us a right of entry; but, arranged upon the altar itself, inseparable from the mysteries in whose celebration it was playing a part, it thrust in among the tapers and the sacred vessels its rows of branches, tied to one another horizontally in a stiff, festal scheme of decoration; and they were made more lovely still by the scalloped outline of the dark leaves, over which were scattered in profusion, as over a bridal train, little clusters of buds of a dazzling whiteness. Though I dared not look at them save through my fingers, I could feel that the formal scheme was composed of living things, and that it was Nature herself who, by trimming the shape of the foliage, and by adding the crowning ornament of those snowy buds, had made the decorations worthy of what was at once a public rejoicing and a solemn mystery. Higher up on the altar, a flower had opened here and there with a careless grace, holding so unconcernedly, like a final, almost vaporous bedizening, its bunch of stamens, slender as gossamer, which clouded the flower itself in a white mist, that in following these with my eyes, in trying to imitate, somewhere inside myself, the action of their blossoming, I imagined it as a swift and thoughtless movement of the head with an enticing glance from her contracted pupils, by a young girl in white, careless and alive.

M. Vinteuil had come in with his daughter and had sat down beside us. He belonged to a good family, and had once been music-master to my grandmother's sisters; so that when, after losing his wife and inheriting some property, he had retired to the neighbourhood of Combray, we used often to invite him to our house. But with his intense prudishness he had given up coming, so as not to be obliged to meet Swann, who had made what he called 'a most unsuitable marriage, as seems to be the fashion in these days.' My mother, on hearing that he 'composed', told him by way of a compliment that, when she came to see him, he must play her something of his own. M. Vinteuil would have liked nothing better, but he carried politeness and consideration for others to so fine a point, always putting himself in their place, that he was afraid of boring them, or of appearing egotistical, if he carried out, or even allowed them to suspect, what were his own desires. On the day when my parents had gone to pay him a visit, I had accompanied them, but they had allowed me to remain out-side, and as M. Vinteuil's house, Montjouvain, stood on a site actually hollowed out from a steep hill covered with shrubs, among which I took cover, I had found myself on a level with his drawing-room, upstairs, and only a few feet away from its window. When a servant came in to tell him that my parents had arrived, I had seen M. Vinteuil run to the piano and lay out a sheet of music so as to catch the eye. But as soon as they entered the room he had snatched it away and hidden it in a corner. He was afraid, no doubt, of letting them suppose that he was glad to see them only because it gave him a chance of playing them some of his compositions. And every time that my mother, in the course of her visit, had returned to the sub-ject of his playing, he had hurriedly protested: 'I cannot think who put that on the piano; it is not the proper place for it at all,' and had turned the conversation aside to other topics, simply because those were of less interest to himself.

His one and only passion was for his daughter, and she, with her somewhat boyish appearance, looked so robust that it was hard to restrain a smile when one saw the precautions her father used to take for her health, with spare shawls always in readiness to wrap round her shoulders. My grandmother had drawn our attention to the gentle, delicate, almost timid expression which might often be caught flitting across the face, dusted all over with freckles, of this otherwise stolid child. When she had spoken, she would at once take her own words in the sense in which her audience must have heard them, she would be alarmed at the possibility of a mis-understanding, and one would see, in clear outline, as though in a transparency, beneath the mannish face of the 'good sort' that she was, the finer features of a young woman in tears.

When, before turning to leave the church, I made a genu-flexion before the altar, I felt suddenly, as I rose again, a bitter-sweet fragrance of almonds steal towards me from the hawthorn-blossom, and I then noticed that on the flowers themselves were little spots of a creamier colour, in which I imagined that this fragrance must lie concealed, as the taste of an almond cake lay in the burned parts, or the sweetness of Mlle Vinteuil's cheeks beneath their freckles. Despite the heavy, motionless silence of the hawthorns, these gusts of fragrance came to me like the murmuring of an intense vitality, with which the whole altar was quivering like a roadside hedge explored by living antennae, of which I was reminded by see-ing some stamens, almost red in colour, which seemed to have kept the springtime virulence, the irritant power of stinging insects now transmuted into flowers.

Outside the church we would stand talking for a moment with M. Vinteuil, in the porch. Boys would be chevying one another in the Square, and he would interfere, taking the side of the little ones and lecturing the big. If his daughter said, in her thick, comfortable voice, how glad she had been to see us, immediately it would seem as though some elder and more sensitive sister, latent in her, had blushed at this thoughtless, schoolboyish utterance, which had, perhaps, made us think that she was angling for an invitation to the house. Her father would then arrange a cloak over her shoulders, they would clamber into a little dog-cart which she herself drove, and home they would both go to Montjouvain. As for ourselves, the next day being Sunday, with no need to be up and stirring before high mass, if it was a moonlight night and warm, then, instead of taking us home at once, my father, in his thirst for personal distinction, would lead us on a long walk round by the Calvary, which my mother's utter incapacity for taking her bearings, or even for knowing which road she might be on, made her regard as a triumph of his strategic genius. Sometimes we would go as far as the viaduct, which began to stride on its long legs of stone at the railway station, and to me typified all the wretchedness of exile beyond the last outposts of civilization, because every year, as we came down from Paris, we would be warned to take special care, when we got to Combray, not to miss the station, to be ready before the train stopped, since it would start again in two minutes and proceed across the viaduct, out of the lands of Christendom, of which Combray, to me, represented the farthest limit. We would return by the Boulevard de la Gare, which contained the most attractive villas in the town. In each of their gardens the moonlight, copying the art of Hubert Robert, had scattered its broken staircases of white marble, its fountains of water, and gates temptingly ajar. Its beams had swept away the telegraph office. All that was left of it was a column, half shattered, but preserving the beauty of a ruin which endures for all time. I would by now be dragging my weary limbs, and ready to drop with sleep; the balmy scent of the lime-trees seemed a consolation which I could obtain only at the price of great suffering and exhaustion, and not worthy of the effort. From gates far apart the watchdogs, awakened by our steps in the silence, would set up an antiphonal barking, as I still hear them bark, at times, in the evenings, and it is in their custody (when the public gardens of Combray were constructed on its site) that the Boulevard de la Gare must have taken refuge, for wherever I may be, as soon as they begin their alternate challenge and acceptance, I can see it again with all its lime-trees, and its pavement glistening beneath the moon.

Suddenly my father would bring us to a standstill and ask my mother – 'Where are we?' Utterly worn out by the walk but still proud of her husband, she would lovingly confess that she had not the least idea. He would shrug his shoulders

and laugh. And then, as though it had slipped, with his latch-
key, from his waistcoat pocket, he would point out to us,
where it stood before our eyes, the back-gate of our own
garden, which had come, hand-in-hand with the familiar
corner of the Rue du Saint-Esprit, to await us, to greet us at
the end of our wanderings over paths unknown. My mother
would murmur admiringly 'You really are wonderful!' And
from that instant I had not to take another step; the ground
moved forward under my feet in that garden where, for so
long, my actions had ceased to require any control, or even
attention, from my will. Custom came to take me in her arms,
carried me all the way up to my bed, and laid me down there
like a little child.

Although Saturday, by beginning an hour earlier, and by
depriving her of the services of Françoise, passed more slowly
than other days for my aunt, yet, the moment it was past, and
a new week begun, she would look forward with impatience
to its return, as something that embodied all the novelty and
distraction which her frail and disordered body was still able
to endure. This was not to say, however, that she did not long,
at times, for some even greater variation, that she did not pass
through those abnormal hours in which one thirsts for something different from what one has, when those people who,
through lack of energy or imagination, are unable to generate
any motive power in themselves, cry out, as the clock strikes
or the postman knocks, in their eagerness for news (even if it
be bad news), for some emotion (even that of grief); when the
heartstrings, which prosperity has silenced, like a harp laid by,
yearn to be plucked and sounded again by some hand, even a
brutal hand, even if it shall break them; when the will, which
has with such difficulty brought itself to subdue its impulse, to
renounce its right to abandon itself to its own uncontrolled
desires, and consequent sufferings, would fain cast its guiding
reins into the hands of circumstances, coercive and, it may be,
cruel. Of course, since my aunt's strength, which was completely drained by the slightest exertion, returned but drop by
drop into the pool of her repose, the reservoir was very slow
in filling, and months would go by before she reached that

surplus which other people use up in their daily activities, but
which she had no idea – and could never decide how to employ.
And I have no doubt that then – just as a desire to have her
potatoes served with béchamel sauce, for a change, would be
formed, ultimately, from the pleasure she found in the daily
reappearance of those mashed potatoes of which she was never
'tired' – she would extract from the accumulation of those
monotonous days (on which she so much depended) a keen
expectation of some domestic cataclysm, instantaneous in its
happening, but violent enough to compel her to put into
effect, once for all, one of those changes which she knew
would be beneficial to her health, but to which she could
never make up her mind without some such stimulus. She was
genuinely fond of us; she would have enjoyed the long luxury
of weeping for our untimely decease; coming at a moment
when she felt 'well' and was not in a perspiration, the news
that the house was being destroyed by a fire, in which all the
rest of us had already perished, a fire which, in a little while,
would not leave one stone standing upon another, but from
which she herself would still have plenty of time to escape
without undue haste, provided that she rose at once from her
bed, must often have haunted her dreams, as a prospect which
combined with the two minor advantages of letting her taste
the full savour of her affection for us in long years of mourning, and of causing universal stupefaction in the village when
she should sally forth to conduct our obsequies, crushed but
courageous, moribund but erect, the paramount and priceless
boon of forcing her at the right moment, with no time to be
lost, no room for weakening hesitations, to go off and spend
the summer at her charming farm of Mirougrain, where there
was a waterfall. Inasmuch as nothing of this sort had ever
occurred, though indeed she must often have pondered the
success of such a manoeuvre as she lay alone absorbed in her
interminable games of patience (and though it must have
plunged her in despair from the first moment of its realization,
from the first of those little unforeseen facts, the first word of
calamitous news, whose accents can never afterwards be ex-
punged from the memory, everything that bears upon it the

imprint of actual, physical death, so terribly different from the logical abstraction of its possibility) she would fall back from time to time, to add an interest to her life, upon imagining other, minor catastrophes, which she would follow up with passion. She would beguile herself with a sudden suspicion that Françoise had been robbing her, that she had set a trap to make certain, and had caught her betrayer red-handed; and being in the habit, when she made up a game of cards by herself, of playing her own and her adversary's hands at once, she would first stammer out Françoise's awkward apologies, and then reply to them with such a fiery indignation that any of us who happened to intrude upon her at one of these moments would find her bathed in perspiration, her eyes blazing, her false hair pushed awry and exposing the baldness of her brows. Françoise must often, from the next room, have heard these mordant sarcasms levelled at herself, the mere framing of which in words would not have relieved my aunt's feelings sufficiently, had they been allowed to remain in a purely immaterial form, without the degree of substance and reality which she added to them by murmuring them half-aloud. Sometimes, however, even these counterpane dramas would not satisfy my aunt; she must see her work staged. And so, on a Sunday, with all the doors mysteriously closed, she would confide in Eulalie her doubts of Françoise's integrity and her determination to be rid of her, and on another day she would confide in Françoise her suspicions of the disloyalty of Eulalie, to whom the front-door would very soon be closed for good. A few days more, and, disgusted with her latest confidant, she would again be 'as thick as thieves' with the traitor, while, before the next performance, the two would once more have changed their parts. But the suspicions which Eulalie might occasionally breed in her were no more than a fire of straw, which must soon subside for lack of fuel, since Eulalie was not living with her in the house. It was a very different matter when the suspect was Françoise, of whose presence under the same roof as herself my aunt was perpetually conscious, while for fear of catching cold, were she to leave her bed, she would never dare go downstairs to the kitchen to see for herself whether there was, indeed, any foundation for her suspicions. And so on by degrees, until her mind had no other occupation than to attempt, at every hour of the day, to discover what was being done, what was being concealed from her by Françoise. She would detect the most furtive movement of Françoise's features, something contradictory in what she was saying, some desire which she appeared to be screening. And she would show her that she was unmasked, by a single word, which made Françoise turn pale, and which my aunt seemed to find a cruel satisfaction in driving deep into her unhappy servant's heart. And the very next Sunday a disclosure by Eulalie – like one of those discoveries which suddenly open up an unsuspected field for exploration to some new science which has hitherto followed only the beaten paths – proved to my aunt that her own worst suspicions fell a long way short of the appalling truth. 'But Françoise ought to know that,' said Eulalie, 'now that you have given her a carriage.'

'Now that I have given her a carriage!' gasped my aunt.

'Oh, but I didn't know; I only thought so; I saw her go by yesterday in her open coach, as proud as Artaban, on her way to Roussainville market. I supposed that it must be Mme Octave who had given it to her.'

So on by degrees, until Françoise and my aunt, the quarry and the hunter, could never cease from trying to forestall each other's devices. My mother was afraid lest Françoise should develop a genuine hatred of my aunt, who was doing everything in her power to annoy her. However that might be, Françoise had come, more and more, to pay an infinitely scrupulous attention to my aunt's least word and gesture. When she had to ask for anything she would hesitate, first, for a long time, making up her mind how best to begin. And when she had uttered her request, she would watch my aunt covertly, trying to guess from the expression on her face what she thought of it, and how she would reply. And in this way – whereas an artist who had been reading memoirs of the seventeenth century, and wished to bring himself nearer to the great Louis, would consider that he was making progress in that direction when he constructed a pedigree that traced his own descent from some historic family, or when he engaged in correspondence with one of the reigning sovereigns of Europe, and so would shut his eyes to the mistake he was making in seeking to establish a similarity by an exact and therefore lifeless copy of mere outward forms – a middle-aged lady in a small country town, by doing no more than yield whole-hearted obedience to her own irresistible eccentricities, and to a spirit of mischief engendered by the utter idleness of her existence, could see, without ever having given a thought to Louis XIV, the most trivial occupations of her daily life, her morning toilet, her luncheon, her afternoon nap, by virtue of their despotic singularity, something of the interest that was to be found in what Saint-Simon used to call the 'machinery' of life at Versailles; and was able, too, to persuade herself that her silence, a shade of good humour or of arrogance on her features would provide Françoise with matter for a mental commentary as tense with passion and terror, as did the silence, the good humour, or the arrogance of the King when a courtier, or even his greatest nobles, had presented a petition to him, at the turning of an avenue, at Versailles.

One Sunday, when my aunt had received simultaneous visits from the Curé and from Eulalie, and had been left alone, afterwards, to rest, the whole family went upstairs to bid her good night, and Mamma ventured to condole with her on the unlucky coincidence that always brought both visitors to her door at the same time.

'I hear that things went wrong again to-day, Léonie,' she said kindly, 'you have had all your friends here at once.'

And my great-aunt interrupted with: 'Too many good things . . .' for, since her daughter's illness, she felt herself in duty bound to revive her as far as possible by always drawing her attention to the brightest side of things. But my father had begun to speak.

'I should like to take advantage,' he said, 'of the whole family's being here together, to tell you a story, so as not to have to begin all over again to each of you separately. I am afraid we are in M. Legrandin's bad books; he would hardly say "How d'ye do" to me this morning.'

I did not wait to hear the end of my father's story, for I had been with him myself after mass when we had passed M. Legrandin; instead, I went downstairs to the kitchen to ask for the bill of fare for our dinner, which was of fresh interest to me daily, like the news in a paper, and excited me as might the programme of a coming festivity.

As M. Legrandin had passed close by us on our way from church, walking by the side of a lady, the owner of a country house in the neighbourhood, whom we knew only by sight, my father had saluted him in a manner at once friendly and reserved, without stopping in his walk; M. Legrandin had barely acknowledged the courtesy, and then with an air of surprise, as though he had not recognized us, and with that distant look characteristic of people who do not wish to be agreeable, and who from the suddenly receding depths of their eyes seem to have caught sight of you at the far end of an interminably straight road, and at so great a distance that they content themselves with directing towards you an almost imperceptible movement of the head, in proportion to your doll-like dimensions.

Now, the lady who was walking with Legrandin was a model of virtue, known and highly respected; there could be no question of his being out for amorous adventure, and annoyed at being detected; and my father asked himself how he could possibly have displeased our friend.

'I should be all the more sorry to feel that he was angry with us,' he said, 'because among all those people in their Sunday clothes there is something about him, with his little cut-away coat and his soft neckties, so little "dressed-up", so genuinely simple; an air of innocence, almost, which is really attractive.'

But the vote of the family council was unanimous, that my father had imagined the whole thing, or that Legrandin, at the moment in question, had been preoccupied in thinking about something else. Anyhow, my father's fears were dissipated no later than the following evening. As we returned from a long walk we saw, near the Pont-Vieux, Legrandin himself, who, on account of the holidays, was spending a few days more in Combray. He came up to us with outstretched hand: 'Do you

know, master book-lover,' he asked me, 'this line of Paul Desjardins?

Now are the woods all black, but still the sky is blue.

Is not that a fine rendering of a moment like this? Perhaps you
have never read Paul Desjardins. Read him, my boy, read him;
in these days he is converted, they tell me, into a preaching
friar, but he used to have the most charming water-colour
touch –

Now are the woods all black, but still the sky is blue.

May you always see a blue sky overhead, my young friend;
and then, even when the time comes, which is coming now for
me, when the woods are all black, when night is fast falling,
you will be able to console yourself, as I am doing, by looking
up to the sky.' He took a cigarette from his pocket and stood
for a long time, his eyes fixed on the horizon. 'Good-bye,
friends!' he suddenly exclaimed, and left us.

At the hour when I usually went downstairs to find out
what there was for dinner, its preparation would already have
begun, and Françoise, a colonel with all the forces of nature
for her subalterns, as in the fairy-tales where giants hire themselves out as scullions, would be stirring the coals, putting the
potatoes to steam, and, at the right moment, finishing over the
fire those culinary masterpieces which had been first got ready
in some of the great array of vessels, triumphs of the potter's
craft, which ranged from tubs and boilers and cauldrons and
fish kettles down to jars for game, moulds for pastry, and tiny
pannikins for cream, and included an entire collection of pots
and pans of every shape and size. I would stop by the table,
where the kitchen-maid had shelled them, to inspect the plat-
oons of peas, drawn up in ranks and numbered, like little green
marbles, ready for a game; but what fascinated me would be
the asparagus, tinged with ultramarine and rosy pink which
ran from their heads, finely stippled in mauve and azure,
through a series of imperceptible changes to their white feet,
still stained a little by the soil of their garden-bed: a rainbow-
loveliness that was not of this world. I felt that these celestial
hues indicated the presence of exquisite creatures who had

been pleased to assume vegetable form, who, through the disguise which covered their firm and edible flesh, allowed me to discern in this radiance of earliest dawn, these hinted rainbows, these blue evening shades, that precious quality which I should recognize again when, all night long after a dinner at which I had partaken of them, they played (lyrical and coarse in their jesting as the fairies in Shakespeare's *Dream*) at transforming my humble chamber into a bower of aromatic perfume.

Poor Giotto's Charity, as Swann had named her, charged by Françoise with the task of preparing them for the table, would have them lying beside her in a basket; sitting with a mournful air, as though all the sorrows of the world were heaped upon her; and the light crowns of azure which capped the asparagus shoots above their pink jackets would be finely and separately outlined, star by star, as in Giotto's fresco are the flowers banded about the brows, or patterning the basket of his Virtue at Padua. And, meanwhile, Françoise would be turning on the spit one of those chickens, such as she alone knew how to roast, chickens which had wafted far abroad from Combray the sweet savour of her merits, and which, while she was serving them to us at table, would make the quality of kindness predominate for the moment in my private conception of her character; the aroma of that cooked flesh, which she knew how to make so unctuous and so tender, seeming to me no more than the proper perfume of one of her many virtues.

But the day on which, while my father took counsel with his family upon our strange meeting with Legrandin, I went down to the kitchen, was one of those days when Giotto's Charity, still very weak and ill after her recent confinement, had been unable to rise from her bed; Françoise, being without assistance, had fallen into arrears. When I went in, I saw her in the back kitchen which opened on to the courtyard, in process of killing a chicken; by its desperate and quite natural resistance, which Françoise, beside herself with rage as she attempted to slit its throat beneath the ear, accompanied with shrill cries of 'Filthy creature! Filthy creature!'

it made the saintly kindness and unction of our servant rather
less prominent than it would do, next day at dinner, when it
made its appearance in a skin gold-embroidered like a chasuble,
and its precious juice was poured out drop by drop as from a
pyx. When it was dead Françoise mopped up its streaming
blood, in which, however, she did not let her rancour drown,
for she gave vent to another burst of rage, and, gazing down
at the carcass of her enemy, uttered a final 'Filthy creature!'

I crept out of the kitchen and upstairs, trembling all over;
I could have prayed, then, for the instant dismissal of Françoise. But who would have baked me such hot rolls, boiled
me such fragant coffee, and even – roasted me such chickens?
And, as it happened, everyone else had already had to make
the same cowardly reckoning. For my aunt Léonie knew
(though I was still in ignorance of this) that Françoise, who,
for her own daughter or for her nephews, would have given
her life without a murmur, showed a singular implacability
in her dealings with the rest of the world. In spite of which
my aunt still retained her, for, while conscious of her cruelty,
she could appreciate her services. I began gradually to realize
that Françoise's kindness, her compunction, the sum total of
her virtues concealed many of these back-kitchen tragedies,
just as history reveals to us that the reigns of the kings and
queens who are portrayed as kneeling with clasped hands
in the windows of churches, were stained by oppression and
bloodshed. I had taken note of the fact that, apart from her
own kinsfolk, the sufferings of humanity inspired in her a
pity which increased in direct ratio to the distance separating
the sufferers from herself. The tears which flowed from her
in torrents when she read of the misfortunes of persons
unknown to her, in a newspaper, were quickly stemmed once
she had been able to form a more accurate mental picture of
the victims. One night, shortly after her confinement, the
kitchen-maid was seized with the most appalling pains;
Mamma heard her groans, and rose and awakened Françoise,
who, quite unmoved, declared that all the outcry was mere
malingering, that the girl wanted to 'play the mistress' in
the house. The doctor, who had been afraid of some such

attack, had left a marker in a medical dictionary which we had, at the page on which the symptoms were described, and had told us to turn up this passage, where we would find the measures of 'first aid' to be adopted. My mother sent Françoise to fetch the book, warning her not to let the marker drop out. An hour elapsed, and Françoise had not returned; my mother, supposing that she had gone back to bed, grew vexed, and told me to go myself to the book-case and fetch the volume. I did so, and there found Françoise who, in her curiosity to know what the marker indicated, had begun to read the clinical account of these after-pains, and was violently sobbing, now that it was a question of a type of illness with which she was not familiar. At each painful symptom mentioned by the writer she would exclaim: 'Oh, oh, Holy Virgin, is it possible that God wishes any wretched human creature to suffer so? Oh, the poor girl!'

But when I had called her, and she had returned to the bedside of Giotto's Charity, her tears at once ceased to flow; she could find no stimulus for that pleasant sensation of tenderness and pity which she very well knew, having been moved to it often enough by the perusal of newspapers; nor any other pleasure of the same kind in her sense of weariness and irritation at being pulled out of bed in the middle of the night for the kitchen-maid; so that at the sight of those very sufferings, the printed account of which had moved her to tears, she had nothing to offer but ill-tempered mutterings, mingled with bitter sarcasm, saying, when she thought that we had gone out of earshot: 'Well, she need never have done what she must have done to bring all this about! She found that pleasant enough, I dare say! She had better not put on any airs now. All the same, he must have been a god-forsaken young man to go after *that*. Dear, dear, it's just as they used to say in my poor mother's country:

> *Snaps and snails and puppy-dogs' tails,*
> *And dirty sluts in plenty,*
> *Smell sweeter than roses in young men's noses*
> *When the heart is one-and-twenty.'*

Although, when her grandson had a slight cold in his head, she would set off at night, even if she were ill also, instead of going to bed, to see whether he had everything that he wanted, covering ten miles on foot before daybreak so as to be in time to begin her work, this same love for her own people, and her desire to establish the future greatness of her house on a solid foundation reacted, in her policy with regard to the other servants, in one unvarying maxim, which was never to let any of them set foot in my aunt's room; indeed she showed a sort of pride in not allowing anyone else to come near my aunt, preferring, when she herself was ill, to get out of bed and to administer the Vichy water in person, rather than to concede to the kitchen-maid the right of entry into her mistress's presence. There is a species of hymenoptera, observed by Fabre, the burrowing wasp, which in order to provide a supply of fresh meat for her offspring after her own decease, calls in the science of anatomy to amplify the resources of her instinctive cruelty, and, having made a collection of weevils and spiders, proceeds with marvellous knowledge and skill to pierce the nerve-centre on which their power of locomotion (but none of their other vital functions) depends, so that the paralysed insect, beside which her egg is laid, will furnish the larva, when it is hatched, with a tamed and inoffensive quarry, incapable either of flight or of resistance, but perfectly fresh for the larder: in the same way Françoise had adopted, to minister to her permanent and unfaltering resolution to render the house uninhabitable to any other servant, a series of crafty and pitiless stratagems. Many years later we discovered that, if we had been fed on asparagus day after day throughout that whole season, it was because the smell of the plants gave the poor kitchen-maid, who had to prepare them, such violent attacks of asthma that she was finally obliged to leave my aunt's service.

Alas! we had definitely to alter our opinion of M. Legrandin. On one of the Sundays following our meeting with him on the Pont-Vieux, after which my father had been forced to confess himself mistaken, as mass drew to an end, and, with the sunshine and the noise of the outer world, something else

invaded the church, an atmosphere so far from sacred that
Mme Goupil, Mme Percepied (everyone, in fact, who a
moment ago, when I arrived a little late, had been sitting
motionless, their eyes fixed on their prayer-books; who, I
might even have thought, had not seen me come in, had not
their feet moved slightly to push away the little kneeling-
desk which was preventing me from getting to my chair)
began in loud voices to discuss with us all manner of utterly
mundane topics, as though we were already outside in the
Square, we saw, standing on the sun-baked steps of the
porch, dominating the many-coloured tumult of the market,
Legrandin himself, whom the husband of the lady we had
been with him, on the previous occasion, was just going to
introduce to the wife of another large landed proprietor of
the district. Legrandin's face showed an extraordinary zeal
and animation; he made a profound bow, with a subsidiary
backward movement which brought his spine sharply up
into a position behind its starting-point, a gesture in which he
must have been trained by the husband of his sister, Mme de
Cambremer. This rapid recovery caused a sort of tense
muscular wave to ripple over Legrandin's hips, which I had
not supposed to be so fleshy; I cannot say why, but this
undulation of pure matter, this wholly carnal fluency, with
not the least hint in it of spiritual significance, this wave lashed
to a fury by the wind of an assiduity, an obsequiousness of the
basest sort, awoke my mind suddenly to the possibility of a
Legrandin altogether different from the one whom we knew.
The lady gave him some message for her coachman, and while
he was stepping down to her carriage the impression of joy,
timid and devout, which the introduction had stamped there,
still lingered on his face. Carried away in a sort of dream, he
smiled, then he began to hurry back towards the lady; he
was walking faster than usual, and his shoulders swayed backwards and forwards, right and left, in the most absurd fashion;
altogether he looked, so utterly had he abandoned himself to
it, ignoring all other considerations, as though he were the
lifeless and wire-pulled puppet of his own happiness. Meanwhile we were coming out through the porch; we were

passing close beside him; he was too well bred to turn his head away; but he fixed his eyes, which had suddenly changed to those of a seer, lost in the profundity of his vision, on so distant a point of the horizon that he could not see us, and so had not to acknowledge our presence. His face emerged, still with an air of innocence, from his straight and pliant coat, which looked as though conscious of having been led astray, in spite of itself, and plunged into surroundings of a detested splendour. And a spotted necktie, stirred by the breezes of the Square, continued to float in front of Legrandin, like the standard of his proud isolation, of his noble independence. Just as we reached the house my mother discovered that we had forgotten the 'Saint-Honoré', and asked my father to go back with me and tell them to send it up at once. Near the church we met Legrandin, coming towards us with the same lady, whom he was escorting to her carriage. He brushed past us, and did not interrupt what he was saying to her, but gave us, out of the corner of his blue eye, a little sign, which began and ended, so to speak, inside his eyelids, and as it did not involve the least movement of his facial muscles, managed to pass quite unperceived by the lady; but, striving to compensate by the intensity of his feelings for the somewhere restricted field in which they had to find expression, he made that blue chink, which was set apart for us, sparkle with all the animation of cordiality, which went far beyond mere playfulness, and almost touched the border-line of roguery; he subtilized the refinements of good-fellowship into a wink of connivance, a hint, a hidden meaning, a secret understanding, all the mysteries of complicity in a plot, and finally exalted his assurances of friendship to the level of protestations of affection, even of a declaration of love, lighting up for us, and for us alone, with a secret and languid flame invisible to the great lady upon his other side, an enamoured pupil in a countenance of ice.

Only the day before he had asked my parents to send me to dine with him on this same Sunday evening. 'Come and bear your aged friend company,' he had said to me. 'Like the nosegay which a traveller sends us from some land to which we shall never go again, come and let me breathe from the far country of your adolescence the scent of those flowers of spring among which I also used to wander, many years ago. Come with the primrose, with the canon's beard, with the gold-cup; come with the stone-crop, whereof are posies made, pledges of love, in the Balzacian flora, come with that flower of the Resurrection morning, the Easter daisy, come with the snowballs of the guelder-rose, which begin to embalm with their fragrance the alleys of your great-aunt's garden ere the last snows of Lent are melted from its soil. Come with the glorious silken raiment of the lily, apparel fit for Solomon, and with the many-coloured enamel of the pansies, but come, above all, with the spring breeze, still cooled by the last frosts of winter, wafting apart, for the two butterflies' sake, that have waited outside all morning, the closed portals of the first Jerusalem rose.'

The question was raised at home whether, all things considered, I ought still to be sent to dine with M. Legrandin. But my grandmother refused to believe that he could have been impolite.

'You admit yourself that he appears at church there, quite simply dressed, and all that; he hardly looks like a man of fashion.' She added that, in any event, even if, at the worst, he had been intentionally rude, it was far better for us to pretend that we had noticed nothing. And indeed my father himself, though more annoyed than any of us by the attitude which Legrandin had adopted, may still have held in reserve a final uncertainty as to its true meaning. It was like every attitude or action which reveals a man's deep and hidden character; they bear no relation to what he has previously said, and we cannot confirm our suspicions by the culprit's evidence, for he will admit nothing; we are reduced to the evidence of our own senses, and we ask ourselves, in the face of this detached and incoherent fragment of recollection, whether indeed our senses have not been the victims of a hallucination; with the result that such attitudes, and these alone are of importance in indicating character, are the most apt to leave us in perplexity.

I dined with Legrandin on the terrace of his house, by moonlight. 'There is a charming quality, is there not,' he said to me, 'in this silence; for hearts that are wounded, as mine is, a novelist, whom you will read in time to come, claims that there is no remedy but silence and shadow. And see you this, my boy, there comes in all lives a time, towards which you still have far to go, when the weary eyes can endure but one kind of light, the light which a fine evening like this prepares for us in the stillroom of darkness, when the ears can listen to no music save what the moonlight breathes through the flute of silence.'

I could hear what M. Legrandin was saying; like everything that he said, it sounded attractive; but I was disturbed by the memory of a lady whom I had seen recently for the first time; and thinking, now that I knew that Legrandin was on friendly terms with several of the local aristocracy, that perhaps she also was among his acquaintance, I summoned up all my courage and said to him: 'Tell me, sir, do you, by any chance, know the lady – the ladies of Guermantes?' and I felt glad because, in pronouncing the name, I had secured a sort of power over it, by the mere act of drawing it up out of my dreams and giving it an objective existence in the world of spoken things.

But, at the sound of the word Guermantes, I saw in the middle of each of our friend's blue eyes a little brown dimple appear, as though they had been stabbed by some invisible pin-point, while the rest of his pupils, reacting from the shock, received and secreted the azure overflow. His fringed eyelids darkened, and drooped. His mouth, which had been stiffened and seared with bitter lines, was the first to recover, and smiled, while his eyes still seemed full of pain, like the eyes of a good-looking martyr whose body bristles with arrows.

'No, I do not know them,' he said, but instead of uttering so simple a piece of information, a reply in which there was so little that could astonish me, in the natural and conversational tone which would have befitted it, he recited it with a separate stress upon each word, leaning forward, bowing his head, with at once the vehemence which a man gives, so as to be believed, to a highly improbable statement (as though the fact that he did not know the Guermantes could be due only to some strange accident of fortune) and with the emphasis of a man who, finding himself unable to keep silence about what is to him a painful situation, chooses to proclaim it aloud, so as to convince his hearers that the confession he is making is one that causes him no embarrassment, but is easy, agreeable, spontaneous, that the situation in question, in this case the absence of relations with the Guermantes family, might very well have been not forced upon, but actually designed by Legrandin himself, might arise from some family tradition, some moral principle or mystical vow which expressly forbade his seeking their society.

'No,' he resumed, explaining by his words the tone in which they were uttered. 'No, I do not know them; I have never wished to know them; I have always made a point of preserving complete independence; at heart, as you know, I am a bit of a Radical. People are always coming to me about it, telling me I am mistaken in not going to Guermantes, that I make myself seem ill-bred, uncivilized, an old bear. But that's not the sort of reputation that can frighten me; it's too true! In my heart of hearts I care for nothing in the world now but a few churches, books – two or three pictures – rather more, perhaps, and the light of the moon when the fresh breeze of youth (such as yours) wafts to my nostrils the scent of gardens whose flowers my old eyes are not sharp enough, now, to distinguish.'

I did not understand very clearly why, in order to refrain from going to the houses of people whom one did not know, it should be necessary to cling to one's independence, or how that could give one the appearance of a savage or a bear. But what I did understand was this, that Legrandin was not altogether truthful when he said that he cared only for churches, moonlight, and youth; he cared also, he cared a very great deal for people who lived in country houses, and would be so much afraid, when in their company, of incurring their displeasure that he would never dare to let them see that he numbered, as well, among his friends middle-class people, the families of solicitors and stockbrokers, preferring, if the truth must be known, that it should be revealed in his absence, when he was out of earshot, that judgement should go against him (if so it must) by default: in a word, he was a snob. Of course he would never have admitted all or any of this in the poetical language which my family and I so much admired. And if I asked him, 'Do you know the Guermantes family?' Legrandin the talker would reply, 'No, I have never cared to know them.' But unfortunately the talker was now subordinated to another Legrandin, whom he kept carefully hidden in his breast, whom he would never consciously exhibit, because this other could tell stories about our own Legrandin and about his snobbishness which would have ruined his reputation for ever; and this other Legrandin had replied to me already in that wounded look, that stiffened smile, the undue gravity of his tone in uttering those few words, in the thousand arrows by which our own Legrandin had instantaneously been stabbed and sickened, like a Saint Sebastian of snobbery:

'Oh, how you hurt me! No, I do not know the Guermantes family. Do not remind me of the great sorrow of my life.' And since this other, this irrepressible, dominant, despotic Legrandin, if he lacked our Legrandin's charming vocabulary, showed an infinitely greater promptness in expressing himself, by means of what are called 'reflexes,' it followed that, when Legrandin the talker attempted to silence him, he would already have spoken, and it would be useless for our friend to deplore the bad impression which the revelations of his *alter ego* must have caused, since he could do no more now than endeavour to mitigate them.

This was not to say that M. Legrandin was anything but sincere when he inveighed against snobs. He could not (from his own knowledge, at least) be aware that he was one also, since it is only with the passions of others that we are ever really familiar, and what we come to find out about our own can be no more than what other people have shown us. Upon ourselves they react but indirectly, through our imagination, which substitutes for our actual, primary motives other, secondary motives, less stark and therefore more decent. Never had Legrandin's snobbishness impelled him to make a habit of visiting a duchess as such. Instead, it would set his imagination to make that duchess appear, in Legrandin's eyes, endowed with all the graces. He would be drawn towards the duchess, assuring himself the while that he was yielding to the attractions of her mind, and her other virtues, which the vile race of snobs could never understand. Only his fellow-snobs knew that he was of their number, for, owing to their inability to appreciate the intervening efforts of his imagination, they saw in close juxtaposition the social activities of Legrandin and their primary cause.

At home, meanwhile, we had no longer any illusions as to M. Legrandin, and our relations with him had become much more distant. Mamma would be greatly delighted whenever she caught him red-handed in the sin, which he continued to call the unpardonable sin, of snobbery. As for my father, he found it difficult to take Legrandin's airs in so light, in so detached a spirit; and when there was some talk, one year, of sending me to spend the long summer holidays at Balbec with my grandmother, he said: 'I must, most certainly, tell Legrandin that you are going to Balbec, to see whether he will offer you an introduction to his sister. He probably doesn't remember telling us that she lived within a mile of the place.'

My grandmother, who held that, when one went to the seaside, one ought to be on the beach from morning to night, to taste the salt breezes, and that one should not know anyone in the place, because calls and parties and excursions were so much time stolen from what belonged, by rights, to the sea-air, begged him on no account to speak to Legrandin of our plans; for already, in her mind's eye, she could see his sister, Mme de Cambremer, alighting from her carriage at the door of our hotel just as we were on the point of going out fishing, and obliging us to remain indoors all afternoon to entertain her. But Mamma laughed her fears to scorn, for she herself felt that the danger was not so threatening, and that Legrandin would show no undue anxiety to make us acquainted with his sister. And, as it happened, there was no need for any of us to introduce the subject of Balbec, for it was Legrandin himself who, without the least suspicion that we had ever had any intention of visiting those parts, walked into the trap un-invited one evening, when we met him strolling on the banks of the Vivonne.

'There are tints in the clouds this evening, violets and blues, which are very beautiful, are they not, my friend?' he said to my father, 'especially a blue which is far more floral than atmospheric, a cineraria blue, which it is surprising to see in the sky. And that little pink cloud there, has it not just the tint of some flower, a carnation or hydrangea? Nowhere, perhaps, except on the shores of the English Channel, where Normandy merges into Brittany, have I been able to find such copious examples of what you might call a vegetable kingdom in the clouds. Down there, close to Balbec, among all those places which are still so uncivilized, there is a little bay, charmingly quiet, where the sunsets of the Auge Valley, those red-and-gold sunsets (which, all the same, I am very far from despising) seem commonplace and in-significant; for in that moist and gentle atmosphere these heavenly flower-beds will break into blossom, in a few moments, in the evenings, incomparably lovely, and often lasting for hours before they fade. Others shed their leaves at once, and then it is more beautiful still to see the sky strewn with the scattering of their innumerable petals, sulphurous yellow and rosy red. In that bay, which they call the Opal Bay, the golden sands appear more charming still from being fastened, like fair Andromeda, to those terrible rocks of the surrounding coast, to that funereal shore, famed for the number of its wrecks, where every winter many a brave vessel falls a victim to the perils of the sea. Balbec! the oldest bone in the geological skeleton that underlies our soil, the true Ar-mor, the sea, the land's end, the accursed region which Anatole France – an enchanter whose works our young friend ought to read – has so well depicted, beneath its eternal fogs, as though it were indeed the land of the

Cimmerians in the Odyssey. Balbec; yes, they are building hotels there now, superimposing them upon its ancient and charming soil, which they are powerless to alter; how delightful it is, down there, to be able to step out at once into regions so primitive and so entrancing.'

'Indeed! And do you know anyone at Balbec?' inquired my father. 'This young man is just going to spend a couple of months there with his grandmother, and my wife too, perhaps.'

Legrandin, taken unawares by the question at a moment when he was looking directly at my father, was unable to turn aside his gaze, and so concentrated it with steadily increasing intensity – smiling mournfully the while – upon the eyes of his questioner, with an air of friendliness and frankness and of not being afraid to look him in the face, until he seemed to have penetrated my father's skull, as it had been a ball of glass, and to be seeing, at the moment, a long way beyond and behind it, a brightly coloured cloud, which provided him with a mental alibi, and would enable him to establish the theory that, just when he was being asked whether he knew anyone at Balbec, he had been thinking of something else, and so had not heard the question. As a rule these tactics make the questioner proceed to ask, 'Why, what are you thinking about?' But my father, inquisitive, annoyed, and cruel, repeated: 'Have you friends, then, in that neighbourhood, that you know Balbec so well?'

In a final and desperate effort the smiling gaze of Legrandin struggled to the extreme limits of its tenderness, vagueness, candour, and distraction; then feeling, no doubt, that there was nothing left for it now but to answer, he said to us: 'I have friends all the world over, wherever there are companies of trees, stricken but not defeated, which have come together to offer a common supplication, with pathetic obstinacy, to an inclement sky which has no mercy upon them.'

'That is not quite what I meant,' interrupted my father, obstinate as a tree and merciless as the sky. 'I asked you, in case anything should happen to my mother-in-law and she wanted to feel that she was not all alone down there, at the ends of the earth, whether you knew any of the people.'

'There as elsewhere, I know everyone and I know no one,' replied Legrandin, who was by no means ready yet to surrender; 'places I know well, people very slightly. But, down there, the places themselves seem to me just like people, rare and wonderful people, of a delicate quality which would have been corrupted and ruined by the gift of life. Perhaps it is a castle which you encounter upon the cliff's edge; standing there by the roadside, where it has halted to contemplate its sorrows before an evening sky, still rosy, through which a golden moon is climbing; while the fishing-boats, homeward bound, creasing the watered silk of the Channel, hoist its pennant at their mastheads and carry its colours. Or perhaps it is a simple dwelling-house that stands alone, ugly, if anything, timid-seeming but full of romance, hiding from every eye some imperishable secret of happiness and disenchantment. That land which knows not truth,' he continued with Machiavellian subtlety, 'that land of infinite fiction makes bad reading for any boy; and is certainly not what I should choose or recommend for my young friend here, who is already so much inclined to melancholy, for a heart already predisposed to receive its impressions. Climates that breathe amorous secrets and futile regrets may agree with an old disillusioned man like myself; but they must always prove fatal to a temperament which is still unformed. Believe me,' he went on with emphasis, 'the waters of that bay – more Breton than Norman – may exert a sedative influence, though, even that is of questionable value, upon a heart which, like mine, is no longer unbroken, a heart for whose wounds there is no longer anything to compensate. But at your age, my boy, those waters are contra-indicated ... Good night to you, neighbours,' he added, moving away from us with that evasive abruptness to which we were accustomed; and then, turning towards us, with a physicianly finger raised in warning, he resumed the consultation: 'No Balbec before you are fifty!' he called out to me, 'and even then it must depend on the state of the heart.'

My father spoke to him of it again, as often as we met him, and tortured him with questions, but it was labour in vain: like that scholarly swindler who devoted to the fabrication of forged palimpsests a wealth of skill and knowledge and industry the hundredth part of which would have sufficed to establish him in a more lucrative – but an honourable occupation, M. Legrandin, had we insisted further, would in the end have constructed a whole system of ethics, and a celestial geography of Lower Normandy, sooner than admit to us that, within a mile of Balbec, his own sister was living in her own house; sooner than find himself obliged to offer us a letter of introduction, the prospect of which would never have inspired him with such terror had he been absolutely certain – as, from his knowledge of my grandmother's character, he really ought to have been certain – that in no circumstances whatsoever would we have dreamed of making use of it.

*

We used always to return from our walks in good time to pay aunt Léonie a visit before dinner. In the first weeks of our Combray holidays, when the days ended early, we would still be able to see, as we turned into the Rue du Saint-Esprit, a reflexion of the western sky from the windows of the house and a band of purple at the foot of the Calvary, which was mirrored farther on in the pond; a fiery glow which, accompanied often by a cold that burned and stung, would associate itself in my mind with the glow of the fire over which, at that very moment, was roasting the chicken that was to furnish me, in place of the poetic pleasure I had found in my walk, with the sensual pleasures of good feeding, warmth, and rest. But in summer, when we came back to the house, the sun would not have set; and while we were upstairs paying our visit to aunt Léonie its rays, sinking until they touched and lay along her window-sill, would there be caught and held by the large inner curtains and the bands which tied them back to the wall, and split and scattered and filtered; and then, at last, would fall upon and inlay with tiny flakes of gold the lemon-wood of her chest-of-drawers, illuminating the room in their passage with the same delicate slanting, shadowed beams that fall among the boles of forest trees. But on some days, though very rarely, the chest-of-drawers would long since have shed its momentary adornments, there would no longer, as we turned into the Rue du Saint-Esprit, be any reflexion from the western sky burning along the line of window-panes; the pond beneath the Calvary would have lost its fiery glow, sometimes indeed had changed already to an opalescent pallor, while a long ribbon of moonlight, bent and broken and broadened by every ripple upon the water's surface, would be lying across it, from end to end. Then, as we drew near the house, we would make out a figure standing upon the doorstep, and Mamma would say to me. 'Good heavens! There is Françoise looking out for us; your aunt must be anxious; that means we are late.'

And without wasting time by stopping to take off our 'things' we would fly upstairs to my aunt Léonie's room to reassure her, to prove to her by our bodily presence that all her gloomy imaginings were false, that, on the contrary, nothing had happened to us, but that we had gone the 'Guermantes way,' and, good lord, when one took that walk, my aunt knew well enough that one could never say at what time one would be home.

'There, Françoise,' my aunt would say, 'didn't I tell you that they must have gone the Guermantes way? Good gracious! They must be hungry! And your nice leg of mutton will be quite dried up now, after all the hours it's been waiting. What a time to come in! Well, and so you went the Guermantes way?'

'But, Léonie, I supposed you knew,' Mamma would answer. 'I thought that Françoise had seen us go out by the little gate, through the kitchen-garden.'

For there were, in the environs of Combray, two 'ways' which we used to take for our walks, and so diametrically opposed that we would actually leave the house by a different door, according to the way we had chosen: the way towards Méséglise-la-Vineuse, which we called also 'Swann's way', because, to get there, one had to pass along the boundary of

M. Swann's estate, and the 'Guermantes way'. Of Méséglise-la-Vineuse, to tell the truth, I never knew anything more than the way there, and the strange people who would come over on Sundays to take the air in Combray, people whom, this time, neither my aunt nor any of us would 'know at all', and whom we would therefore assume to be 'people who must have come over from Méséglise.' As for Guermantes, I was to know it well enough one day, but that day had still to come; and, during the whole of my boyhood, if Méséglise was to me something as inaccessible as the horizon, which remained hidden from sight, however far one went, by the folds of a country which no longer bore the least resemblance to the country round Combray; Guermantes, on the other hand, meant no more than the ultimate goal, ideal rather than real, of the 'Guermantes way', a sort of abstract geographical term like the North Pole or the Equator. And so to 'take the Guermantes way' in order to get to Méséglise, or *vice versa*, would have seemed to me as nonsensical a proceeding as to turn to the east in order to reach the west. Since my father used always to speak of the 'Méséglise way' as comprising the finest view of a plain that he knew anywhere, and of the 'Guermantes way' as typical of river scenery, I had invested each of them, by conceiving them in this way as two distinct entities, with that cohesion, that unity which belongs only to the figments of the mind; the smallest detail of either of them appeared to me as a precious thing, which exhibited the special excellence of the whole, while, immediately beside them, in the first stages of our walk, before we had reached the sacred soil of one or the other, the purely material roads, at definite points on which they were set down as the ideal view over a plain and the ideal scenery of a river, were no more worth the trouble of looking at them than, to a keen playgoer and lover of dramatic art, are the little streets which may happen to run past the walls of a theatre. But, above all, I set between them, far more distinctly than the mere distance in miles and yards and inches which separated one from the other, the distance that there was between the two parts of my brain in which I used to think of them, one of those distances of the mind which time serves only to lengthen, which separate things irremediably from one another, keeping them for ever upon different planes. And this distinction was rendered still more absolute because the habit we had of never going both ways on the same day, or in the course of the same walk, but the 'Méséglise way' one time and the 'Guermantes way' another, shut them up, so to speak, far apart and unaware of each other's existence, in the sealed vessels – between which there could be no communication – of separate afternoons.

When we had decided to go the 'Méséglise way' we would start (without undue haste, and even if the sky were clouded over, since the walk was not very long, and did not take us too far from home), as though we were not going anywhere in particular, by the front-door of my aunt's house, which opened on to the Rue du Saint-Esprit. We would be greeted by the gunsmith, we would drop our letters into the box, we would tell Théodore, from Françoise, as we passed, that she had run out of oil or coffee, and we would leave the town by the road which ran along the white fence of M. Swann's park. Before reaching it we would be met on our way by the scent of his lilac-trees, come out to welcome strangers. Out of the fresh little green hearts of their foliage the lilacs raised inquisitively over the fence of the park their plumes of white or purple blossom, which glowed, even in the shade, with the sunlight in which they had been bathed. Some of them, half-concealed by the little tiled house, called the Archers' Lodge, in which Swann's keeper lived, overtopped its gothic gable with their rosy minaret. The nymphs of spring would have seemed coarse and vulgar in comparison with these young houris, who retained, in this French garden, the pure and vivid colouring of a Persian miniature. Despite my desire to throw my arms about their pliant forms and to draw down towards me the starry locks that crowned their fragrant heads, we would pass them by without stopping, for my parents had ceased to visit Tansonville since Swann's marriage, and, so as not to appear to be looking into his park, we would, instead of taking the road which ran beside its boundary and then climbed straight up to the open fields, choose another way, which led in the same direction, but circuitously, and brought us out rather too far from home.

One day my grandfather said to my father: 'Don't you remember Swann's telling us yesterday that his wife and daughter had gone off to Rheims and that he was taking the opportunity of spending a day or two in Paris? We might go along by the park, since the ladies are not at home; that will make it a little shorter.'

We stopped for a moment by the fence. Lilac-time was nearly over; some of the trees still thrust aloft, in tall purple chandeliers, their tiny balls of blossom, but in many places among their foliage where, only a week before, they had still been breaking in waves of fragrant foam, these were now spent and shrivelled and discoloured, a hollow scum, dry and scentless. My grandfather pointed out to my father in what respects the appearance of the place was still the same, and how far it had altered since the walk that he had taken with old M. Swann, on the day of his wife's death; and he seized the opportunity to tell us, once again, the story of that walk.

In front of us a path bordered with nasturtiums rose in the full glare of the sun towards the house. But to our right the park stretched away into the distance, on level ground. Overshadowed by the tall trees which stood close around it, an 'ornamental water' had been constructed by Swann's parents; but, even in his most artificial creations, nature is the material upon which man has to work; certain spots will persist in remaining surrounded by the vassals of their own especial sovereignty, and will raise their immemorial standards among all the 'laid-out' scenery of a park, just as they would have done far from any human interference, in a solitude which must everywhere return to engulf them, springing up out of the necessities of their exposed position, and superimposing itself upon the work of man's hands. And so it was that, at the foot of the path which led down to this artificial lake, there might be seen, in its two tiers woven of trailing forget-me-nots below and of periwinkle flowers above, the natural, delicate, blue garland which binds the luminous, shadowed brows of water-nymphs; while the iris, its swords sweeping

every way in regal profusion, stretched out over agrimony
and water-growing king-cups the lilied sceptres, tattered
glories of yellow and purple, of the kingdom of the lake.

The absence of Mlle Swann, which – since it preserved me
from the terrible risk of seeing her appear on one of the paths,
and of being identified and scorned by this so privileged little
girl who had Bergotte for a friend and used to go with him to
visit cathedrals – made the exploration of Tansonville, now
for the first time permitted me, a matter of indifference to
myself, seemed however to invest the property, in my grandfather's and father's eyes, with a fresh and transient charm, and
(like an entirely cloudless sky when one is going mountain-
eering) to make the day extraordinarily propitious for a walk
in this direction; I should have liked to see their reckoning
proved false, to see, by a miracle, Mlle Swann appear, with her
father, so close to us that we should not have time to escape,
and should therefore be obliged to make her acquaintance.
And so, when I suddenly noticed a straw basket lying forgotten on the grass by the side of a line whose float was bob-
bing in the water, I made a great effort to keep my father and
grandfather looking in another direction, away from this sign
that she might, after all, be in residence. Still, as Swann had
told us that he ought not, really, to go away just then, as he
had some people staying in the house, the line might equally
belong to one of these guests. Not a footstep was to be heard
on any of the paths. Somewhere in one of the tall trees, making
a stage in its height, an invisible bird, desperately attempting
to make the day seem shorter, was exploring with a long, continuous note the solitude that pressed it on every side, but it
received at once so unanimous an answer, so powerful a
repercussion of silence and of immobility that, one would
have said, it had arrested for all eternity the moment which it
had been trying to make pass more quickly. The sunlight fell
so implacably from a fixed sky that one was naturally inclined
to slip away out of the reach of its attentions, and even the
slumbering water, whose repose was perpetually being invaded by the insects that swarmed above its surface, while it
dreamed, no doubt, of some imaginary maelstrom, intensified

the uneasiness which the sight of that floating cork had wrought in me, by appearing to draw it at full speed across the silent reaches of a mirrored firmament; now almost vertical, it seemed on the point of plunging down out of sight, and I had begun to ask myself whether, setting aside the longing and the terror that I had of making her acquaintance, it was not actually my duty to warn Mlle Swann that the fish was biting – when I was obliged to run after my father and grandfather, who were calling me, and were surprised that I had not followed them along the little path, climbing up hill towards the open fields, into which they had already turned. I found the whole path throbbing with the fragrance of hawthorn-blossom. The hedge resembled a series of chapels, whose walls were no longer visible under the mountains of flowers that were heaped upon their altars; while, underneath, the sun cast a square of light upon the ground, as though it had shone in upon them through a window; the scent that swept out over me from them was as rich, and as circumscribed in its range, as though I had been standing before the Lady-altar, and the flowers, themselves adorned also, held out each its little bunch of glittering stamens with an air of inattention, fine, radiating 'nerves' in the flamboyant style of architecture, like those which, in church, framed the stair to the rood-loft or closed the perpendicular tracery of the windows, but here spread out into pools of fleshy white, like strawberry-beds in spring. How simple and rustic, in comparison with these, would seem the dog-roses which, in a few weeks' time, would be climbing the same hillside path in the heat of the sun, dressed in the smooth silk of their blushing pink bodices, which would be undone and scattered by the first breath of wind.

But it was in vain that I lingered before the hawthorns, to breathe in, to marshal before my mind (which knew not what to make of it), to lose in order to rediscover their invisible and unchanging odour, to absorb myself in the rhythm which disposed their flowers here and there with the lightheartedness of youth, and at intervals as unexpected as certain intervals of music; they offered me an indefinite continuation of the same charm, in an inexhaustible profusion, but without letting me delve into it any more deeply, like those melodies which one can play over a hundred times in succession without coming any nearer to their secret. I turned away from them for a moment so as to be able to return to them with renewed strength. My eyes followed up the slope which, outside the hedge, rose steeply to the fields, a poppy that had strayed and been lost by its fellows, or a few cornflowers that had fallen lazily behind, and decorated the ground here and there with their flowers like the border of a tapestry, in which may be seen at intervals hints of the rustic theme which appears triumphant in the panel itself; infrequent still, spaced apart as the scattered houses which warn us that we are approaching a village, they betokened to me the vast expanse of waving corn beneath the fleecy clouds, and the sight of a single poppy hoisting upon its slender rigging and holding against the breeze its scarlet ensign, over the buoy of rich black earth from which it sprang, made my heart beat as does a wayfarer's when he perceives, upon some low-lying ground, an old and broken boat which is being caulked and made sea-worthy, and cries out, although he has not yet caught sight of it, 'The Sea!'

And then I returned to my hawthorns, and stood before them as one stands before those masterpieces of painting which, one imagines, one will be better able to 'take in' when one has looked away, for a moment, at something else; but in vain did I shape my fingers into a frame, so as to have nothing but the hawthorns before my eyes; the sentiment which they aroused in me remained obscure and vague, struggling and failing to free itself, to float across and become one with the flowers. They themselves offered me no enlightenment, and I could not call upon any other flowers to satisfy this mysterious longing. And then, inspiring me with that rapture which we feel on seeing a work by our favourite painter quite different from any of those that we already know, or, better still, when someone has taken us and set us down in front of a picture of which we have hitherto seen no more than a pencilled sketch, or when a piece of music which we have heard played over on the piano bursts out again in our ears with all the splendour and fullness of an orchestra, my grandfather called me to him, and, pointing to the hedge of Tansonville, said: 'You are fond of hawthorns; just look at this pink one; isn't it pretty?'

And it was indeed a hawthorn, but one whose flowers were pink, and lovelier even than the white. It, too, was in holiday attire, for one of those days which are the only true holidays, the holy days of religion, because they are not appointed by any capricious accident, as secular holidays are appointed, upon days which are not specially ordained for such observances, which have nothing about them that is essentially festal – but it was attired even more richly than the rest, for the flowers which clung to its branches, one above another, so thickly as to leave no part of the tree undecorated, like the tassels wreathed about the crook of a rococo shepherdess, were every one of them 'in colour', and consequently of a superior quality, by the aesthetic standards of Combray, to the 'plain', if one was to judge by the scale of prices at the 'stores' in the Square, or at Camus's, where the most expensive biscuits were those whose sugar was pink. And for my own part I set a higher value on cream cheese when it was pink, when I had been allowed to tinge it with crushed strawberries. And these flowers had chosen precisely the colour of some edible and delicious thing, or of some exquisite addition to one's costume for a great festival, which colours, inasmuch as they make plain the reason for their superiority, are those whose beauty is most evident to the eyes of children, and for that reason must always seem more vivid and more natural than any other tints, even after the child's mind has realized that they offer no gratification to the appetite, and have not been selected by the dressmaker. And, indeed, I had felt at once, as I had felt before the white blossom, but now still more marvelling, that it was in no artificial manner, by no device of human construction, that the festal intention of these flowers was revealed, but that it was Nature herself who had spontaneously expressed it (with the simplicity of a woman from a village shop, labouring at the decoration of a street altar for some procession) by burying the bush in these little rosettes, almost too ravishing in colour, this rustic 'pompadour'. High up on the branches, like so many of those tiny rose-trees, their pots concealed in jackets of paper lace, whose slender stems rise in a forest from the altar on the greater festivals, a thousand buds were swelling and opening, paler in colour, but each disclosing as it burst, as at the bottom of a cup of pink marble, its blood-red stain, and suggesting even more strongly than the full-blown flowers the special, irresistible quality of the hawthorn-tree, which, wherever it budded, wherever it was about to blossom, could bud and blossom in pink flowers alone. Taking its place in the hedge, but as different from the rest as a young girl in holiday attire among a crowd of dowdy women in everyday clothes, who are staying at home, equipped and ready for the 'Month of Mary', of which it seemed already to form a part, it shone and smiled in its cool, rosy garments, a Catholic bush indeed, and altogether delightful.

The hedge allowed us a glimpse, inside the park, of an alley bordered with jasmine, pansies, and verbenas, among which the stocks held open their fresh plump purses, of a pink as fragrant and as faded as old Spanish leather, while on the gravel-path a long watering-pipe, painted green, coiling across the ground, poured, where its holes were over the flowers whose perfume those holes inhaled, a vertical and prismatic fan of infinitesimal, rainbow-coloured drops. Suddenly I stood still, unable to move, as happens when something appears that requires not only our eyes to take it in, but involves a deeper kind of perception and takes possession of the whole of our being. A little girl, with fair, reddish hair, who appeared to be returning from a walk, and held a trowel in her hand, was looking at us, raising towards us a face powdered with pinkish freckles. Her black eyes gleamed, and as I did not at that time know, and indeed have never since learned how to reduce to its objective elements any strong impression, since I had not, as they say, enough 'power of observation' to isolate the sense of their colour, for a long time afterwards, whenever I thought of her, the memory of those bright eyes would at once present itself to me as a vivid azure, since her complexion was fair; so much so that, perhaps, if her eyes had not been quite so black – which was what struck one most forcibly on first meeting her – I should not have been, as I was, especially enamoured of their imagined blue.

I gazed at her, at first with that gaze which is not merely a messenger from the eyes, but in whose window all the senses assemble and lean out, petrified and anxious, that gaze which would fain reach, touch, capture, bear off in triumph the body at which it is aimed, and the soul with the body; then (so frightened was I lest at any moment my grandfather and father, catching sight of the girl, might tear me away from her, by making me run on in front of them) with another, an unconsciously appealing look, whose object was to force her to pay attention to me, to see, to know me. She cast a glance forwards and sideways, so as to take stock of my grandfather and father, and doubtless the impression she formed of them was that we were all absurd people, for she turned away with an indifferent and contemptuous air, withdrew herself so as to spare her face the indignity of remaining within their field of vision; and while they, continuing to walk on without noticing her, had overtaken and passed me, she allowed her eyes to wander, over the space that lay between us, in my direction, without any particular expression, without appearing to have seen me, but with an intensity, a half-hidden smile which I was unable to interpret, according to the instruction I had received in the ways of good breeding, save as a mark of infinite disgust; and her hand, at the same time, sketched in the air an indelicate gesture, for which, when it was addressed in public to a person whom one did not know, the little dictionary of manners which I carried in my mind supplied only one meaning, namely, a deliberate insult.

'Gilberte, come along; what are you doing?' called out in a piercing tone of authority a lady in white, whom I had not seen until that moment, while, a little way beyond her, a gentleman in a suit of linen 'ducks', whom I did not know either, stared at me with eyes which seemed to be starting from his head; the little girl's smile abruptly faded, and, seizing her trowel, she made off without turning to look again in my direction, with an air of obedience, inscrutable and sly.

And so was wafted to my ears the name of Gilberte,

bestowed on me like a talisman which might, perhaps, enable me some day to rediscover her whom its syllables had just endowed with a definite personality, whereas, a moment earlier, she had been only something vaguely seen. So it came to me, uttered across the heads of the stocks and jasmines, pungent and cool as the drops which fell from the green watering-pipe; impregnating and irradiating the zone of pure air through which it had passed, which it set apart and isolated from all other air, with the mystery of the life of her whom its syllables designated to the happy creatures that lived and walked and travelled in her company; unfolding through the arch of the pink hawthorn, which opened at the height of my shoulder, the quintessence of their familiarity – so exquisitely painful to myself – with her, and with all that unknown world of her existence, into which I should never penetrate.

For a moment (while we moved away, and my grandfather murmured: 'Poor Swann, what a life they are leading him; fancy sending him away so that she can be left alone with her Charlus – for that was Charlus: I recognized him at once! And the child, too; at her age, to be mixed up in all that!') the impression left on me by the despotic tone in which Gilberte's mother had spoken to her, without her replying, by exhibiting her to me as being obliged to yield obedience to some one else, as not being indeed superior to the whole world, calmed my sufferings somewhat, revived some hope in me, and cooled the ardour of my love. But very soon that love surged up again in me like a reaction by which my humiliated heart was endeavouring to rise to Gilberte's level, or to draw her down to its own. I loved her; I was sorry not to have had the time and the inspiration to insult her, to do her some injury, to force her to keep some memory of me. I knew her to be so beautiful that I should have liked to be able to retrace my steps so as to shake my fist at her and shout, 'I think you are hideous, grotesque; you are utterly disgusting!' However, I walked away, carrying with me, then and for ever afterwards, as the first illustration of a type of happiness rendered inaccessible to a little boy of my kind by certain laws of nature which it was impossible to transgress, the picture of a little girl with reddish hair, and a skin freckled with tiny pink marks, who held a trowel in her hand, and smiled as she directed towards me a long and subtle and inexpressive stare. And already the charm with which her name, like a cloud of incense, had filled that archway in the pink hawthorn through which she and I had, together, heard its sound, was beginning to conquer, to cover, to embalm, to beautify everything with which it had any association: her grandparents, whom my own had been so unspeakably fortunate as to know, the glorious profession of a stockbroker, even the melancholy neighbourhood of the Champs-Élysées, where she lived in Paris.

'Léonie,' said my grandfather on our return, 'I wish we had had you with us this afternoon. You would never have known Tansonville. If I had had the courage I would have cut you a branch of that pink hawthorn you used to like so much.' And so my grandfather told her the story of our walk, either just to amuse her, or perhaps because there was still some hope that she might be stimulated to rise from her bed and to go out of doors. For in earlier days she had been very fond of Tansonville, and, moreover, Swann's visits had been the last that she had continued to receive, at a time when she had already closed her doors to all the world. And just as, when he called, in these later days, to inquire for her (and she was still the only person in our household whom he would ask to see), she would send down to say that she was tired at the moment and resting, but that she would be happy to see him another time, so, this evening, she said to my grandfather, 'Yes, some day when the weather is fine I shall go for a drive as far as the gate of the park.' And in saying this she was quite sincere. She would have liked to see Swann and Tansonville again; but the mere wish to do so sufficed for all that remained of her strength, which its fulfilment would have more than exhausted. Sometimes a spell of fine weather made her a little more energetic, she would rise and put on her clothes; but before she had reached the outer room she would be 'tired' again, and would insist on returning to her bed. The process which had begun in her – and in her a little earlier only than it must come to all of us – was the great and general renunciation

which old age makes in preparation for death, the chrysalis
stage of life, which may be observed wherever life has been
unduly prolonged; even in old lovers who have lived for one
another with the utmost intensity of passion, and in old friends
bound by the closest ties of mental sympathy, who, after a
certain year, cease to make the necessary journey, or even to
cross the street to see one another, cease to correspond, and
know well that they will communicate no more in this world.
My aunt must have been perfectly well aware that she would
not see Swann again, that she would never leave her own
house any more, but this ultimate seclusion seemed to be
accepted by her with all the more readiness for the very reason
which, to our minds, ought to have made it more unbearable;
namely, that such a seclusion was forced upon her by the
gradual and steady diminution in her strength which she was
able to measure daily, which, by making every action, every
movement 'tiring' to her if not actually painful, gave to
inaction, isolation, and silence the blessed, strengthening, and
refreshing charm of repose.

My aunt did not go to see the pink hawthorn in the hedge,
but at all hours of the day I would ask the rest of my family
whether she was not going to go, whether she used not, at one
time, to go often to Tansonville, trying to make them speak of
Mlle Swann's parents and grandparents, who appeared to me
to be as great and glorious as gods. The name, which had for
me become almost mythological, of Swann – when I talked
with my family I would grow sick with longing to hear them
utter it; I dared not pronounce it myself, but I would draw
them into the discussion of matters which led naturally to
Gilberte and her family, in which she was involved, in speaking of which I would feel myself not too remotely banished
from her company; and I would suddenly force my father (by
pretending, for instance, to believe that my grandfather's
business had been in our family before his day, or that the
hedge with the pink hawthorn which my aunt Léonie wished
to visit was on common ground) to correct my statements, to
say, as though in opposition to me and of his own accord:
'No, no, the business belonged to *Swann*'s father, that hedge is

part of *Swann*'s park.' And then I would be obliged to pause
for breath; so stifling was the pressure, upon that part of me
where it was for ever inscribed, of that name which, at the
moment when I heard it, seemed to me fuller, more portentous
than any other name, because it was burdened with the weight
of all the occasions on which I had secretly uttered it in my
mind. It caused me a pleasure which I was ashamed to have
dared to demand from my parents, for so great was it that to
have procured it for me must have involved them in an
immensity of effort, and with no recompense, since for them
there was no pleasure in the sound. And so I would prudently
turn the conversation. And by a scruple of conscience, also.
All the singular seductions which I had stored up in the sound
of that word Swann, I found again as soon as it was uttered.
And then it occurred to me suddenly that my parents could
not fail to experience the same emotions, that they must find
themselves sharing my point of view, that they perceived in
their turn, that they condoned, that they even embraced my
visionary longings, and I was as wretched as though I had
ravished and corrupted the innocence of their hearts.

That year my family fixed the day of their return to Paris
rather earlier than usual. On the morning of our departure I
had had my hair curled, to be ready to face the photographer,
had had a new hat carefully set upon my head, and had been
buttoned into a velvet jacket; a little later my mother, after
searching everywhere for me, found me standing in tears on
that steep little hillside close to Tansonville, bidding a long
farewell to my hawthorns, clasping their sharp branches to my
bosom, and (like a princess in a tragedy, oppressed by the
weight of all her senseless jewellery) with no gratitude towards the officious hand which had, in curling those ringlets,
been at pains to collect all my hair upon my forehead; tramp-
ling underfoot the curl-papers which I had torn from my head,
and my new hat with them. My mother was not at all moved
by my tears, but she could not suppress a cry at the sight of my
battered headgear and my ruined jacket. I did not, however,
hear her. 'Oh, my poor little hawthorns,' I was assuring them
through my sobs, 'it is not you that want to make me

unhappy, to force me to leave you. You, you have never done me any harm. So I shall always love you.' And, drying my eyes, I promised them that, when I grew up, I would never copy the foolish example of other men, but that even in Paris, on fine spring days, instead of paying calls and listening to silly talk, I would make excursions into the country to see the first hawthorn-trees in bloom.

Once in the fields we never left them again during the rest of our Méséglise walk. They were perpetually crossed, as though by invisible streams of traffic, by the wind, which was to me the tutelary genius of Combray. Every year, on the day of our arrival, in order to feel that I really was at Combray, I would climb the hill to find it running again through my clothing, and setting me running in its wake. One always had the wind for companion when one went the 'Méséglise way', on that swelling plain which stretched, mile beyond mile, without any disturbance of its gentle contour. I knew that Mlle Swann used often to go and spend a few days at Laon, and, for all that it was many miles away, the distance was obviated by the absence of any intervening obstacle; when, on hot afternoons, I would see a breath of wind emerge from the farthest horizon, bowing the heads of the corn in distant fields, pouring like a flood over all that vast expanse, and finally settling down, warm and rustling, among the clover and sainfoin at my feet, that plain which was common to us both seemed then to draw us together, to unite us; I would imagine that the same breath had passed by her also, that there was some message from her in what it was whispering to me, without my being able to understand it, and I would catch and kiss it as it passed. On my left was a village called Champieu (*Campus Pagani*, according to the Curé). On my right I could see across the cornfields the two crocketed, rustic spires of Saint-André-des-Champs, themselves as tapering, scaly, plated, honeycombed, yellowed, and roughened as two ears of wheat.

At regular intervals, among the inimitable ornamentation of their leaves, which can be mistaken for those of no other fruit-tree, the apple-trees were exposing their broad petals of white satin, or hanging in shy bunches their unopened, blushing buds. It was while going the 'Méséglise way' that I first noticed the circular shadow which apple-trees cast upon the sunlit ground, and also those impalpable threads of golden silk which the setting sun weaves slantingly downwards from beneath their leaves, and which I would see my father slash through with his stick without ever making them swerve from their straight path.

Sometimes in the afternoon sky a white moon would creep up like a little cloud, furtive, without display, suggesting an actress who does not have to 'come on' for a while, and so goes 'in front' in her ordinary clothes to watch the rest of the company for a moment, but keeps in the background, not wishing to attract attention to herself. I was glad to find her image reproduced in books and paintings, though these works of art were very different – at least in my earlier years, before Bloch had attuned my eyes and mind to more subtle harmonies – from those in which the moon seems fair to me to-day, but in which I should not have recognized her then. It might be, for instance, some novel by Saintine, some landscape by Gleyre, in which she is cut out sharply against the sky, in the form of a silver sickle, some work as unsophisticated and as incomplete as were, at that date, my own impressions, and which it enraged my grandmother's sisters to see me admire. They held that one ought to set before children, and that children showed their own innate good taste in admiring, only such books and pictures as they would continue to admire when their minds were developed and mature. No doubt they regarded aesthetic values as material objects which an unclouded vision could not fail to discern, without needing to have their equivalent in experience of life stored up and slowly ripening in one's heart.

It was along the 'Méséglise way', at Montjouvain, a house built on the edge of a large pond, and overlooked by a steep, shrub-grown hill, that M. Vinteuil lived. And so we used often to meet his daughter driving her dogcart at full speed along the road. After a certain year we never saw her alone, but always accompanied by a friend, a girl older than herself, with an evil reputation in the neighbourhood, who in the end installed herself permanently, one day, at Montjouvain. People said: 'That poor M. Vinteuil must be blinded by love not to see what everyone is talking about, and to let his daughter – a man who is horrified if you use a *word* in the wrong sense – bring a woman like that to live under his roof. He says that she is a most superior woman, with a heart of gold, and that she would have shown extraordinary musical talent if she had only been trained. He may be sure it is not music that she is teaching his daughter.' But M. Vinteuil assured them that it was, and indeed it is remarkable that people never fail to arouse admiration of their moral qualities in the relatives of anyone with whom they are in physical intercourse. Bodily passion, which has been so unjustly decried, compels its victims to display every vestige that is in them of unselfishness and generosity, and so effectively that they shine resplendent in the eyes of all beholders. Dr Percepied, whose loud voice and bushy eyebrows enabled him to play to his heart's content the part of 'double-dealer', a part to which he was not, otherwise, adapted, without in the least degree compromising his unassailable and quite unmerited reputation of being a kind-hearted old curmudgeon, could make the Curé and everyone else laugh until they cried by saying in a harsh voice: 'What d'ye say to this, now? It seems that she plays music with her friend, Mlle Vinteuil. That surprises you, does it? Oh, I know nothing, nothing at all. It was Papa Vinteuil who told me all about it yesterday. After all, she has every right to be fond of music, that girl. I should never dream of thwarting the artistic vocation of a child; nor Vinteuil either, it seems. And then he plays music too, with his daughter's friend. Why, gracious heavens, it must be a regular musical box, that house out there! What are you laughing at? I say they've been playing too much music, those people. I met Papa Vinteuil the other day, by the cemetery. It was all he could do to keep on his feet.'

Anyone who, like ourselves, had seen M. Vinteuil, about this time, avoiding people whom he knew, and turning away as soon as he caught sight of them, changed in a few months into an old man, engulfed in a sea of sorrows, incapable of any effort not directly aimed at promoting his daughter's happiness, spending whole days beside his wife's grave, could hardly have failed to realize that he was gradually dying of a broken heart, could hardly have supposed that he paid no attention to the rumours which were going about. He knew, perhaps he even believed, what his neighbours were saying. There is probably no one, however rigid his virtue, who is not liable to find himself, by the complexity of circumstances, living at close quarters with the very vice which he himself has been most outspoken in condemning, without at first recognizing it beneath the disguise which it assumes on entering his presence, so as to wound him and to make him suffer; the odd words, the unaccountable attitude, one evening, of a person whom he has a thousand reasons for loving. But for a man of M. Vinteuil's sensibility it must have been far more painful than for a hardened man of the world to have to resign himself to one of those situations which are wrongly supposed to occur in Bohemian circles only; for they are produced whenever there needs to establish itself in the security necessary to its development a vice which Nature herself has planted in the soul of a child, perhaps by no more than blending the virtues of its father and mother, as she might blend the colours of their eyes. And yet however much M. Vinteuil may have known of his daughter's conduct it did not follow that his adoration of her grew any less. The facts of life do not penetrate to the sphere in which our beliefs are cherished; as it was not they that engendered those beliefs, so they are powerless to destroy them; they can aim at them continual blows of contradiction and disproof without weakening them; and an avalanche of miseries and maladies coming, one after another, without interruption into the bosom of a family, will not make it lose faith in either the clemency of its God or the capacity of its physician. But when M. Vinteuil regarded his daughter and himself from the point of view of the world, and of their reputation, when he attempted to place himself by her side in the rank which they occupied in the general estimation of their neighbours, then he was bound to give judgement, to utter his own and her social condemnation in precisely the terms which the inhabitant of Combray most hostile to him and his daughter would have employed; he saw himself and her in 'low', in the very 'lowest water', inextricably stranded; and his manners had of late been tinged with that humility, that respect for persons who ranked above him and to whom he must now look up (however far beneath him they might hitherto have been), that tendency to search for some means of rising again to their level, which is an almost mechanical result of any human misfortune.

One day, when we were walking with Swann in one of the streets of Combray, M. Vinteuil, turning out of another street, found himself so suddenly face to face with us all that he had not time to escape; and Swann, with that almost arrogant charity of a man of the world who, amid the dissolution of all his own moral prejudices, finds in another's shame merely a reason for treating him with a friendly benevolence, the outward signs of which serve to enhance and gratify the self-esteem of the bestower because he feels that they are all the more precious to him upon whom they are bestowed, conversed at great length with M. Vinteuil, with whom for a long time he had been barely on speaking terms, and invited him, before leaving us, to send his daughter over, one day, to play at Tansonville. It was an invitation which, two years earlier, would have enraged M. Vinteuil, but which now filled him with so much gratitude that he felt himself obliged to refrain from the indiscretion of accepting. Swann's friendly regard for his daughter seemed to him to be in itself so honourable, so precious a support for his cause that he felt it would perhaps be better to make no use of it, so as to have the wholly Platonic satisfaction of keeping it in reserve.

'What a charming man!' he said to us, after Swann had gone, with the same enthusiasm and veneration which make clever and pretty women of the middle classes fall victims to the physical and intellectual charms of a duchess, even though she be ugly and a fool. 'What a charming man! What a pity that he should have made such a deplorable marriage!'

And then, so strong an element of hypocrisy is there in even the most sincere of men, who cast off, while they are talking to anyone, the opinion they actually hold of him and will express when he is no longer there, my family joined with M. Vinteuil in deploring Swann's marriage, invoking principles and conventions which (all the more because they invoked them in common with him, as though we were all thorough good fellows of the same sort) they appeared to suggest were in no way infringed at Montjouvain. M. Vinteuil did not send his daughter to visit Swann, an omission which Swann was the first to regret. For constantly, after meeting M. Vinteuil, he would remember that he had been meaning for a long time to ask him about someone of the same name as himself, one of his relatives, Swann supposed. And on this occasion he determined that he would not forget what he had to say to him when M. Vinteuil should appear with his daughter at Tansonville.

Since the 'Méséglise way' was the shorter of the two that we used to take for our walks round Combray, and for that reason was reserved for days of uncertain weather, it followed that the climate of Méséglise showed an unduly high rainfall, and we would never lose sight of the fringe of Roussainville wood, so that we could, at any moment, run for shelter beneath its dense thatch of leaves.

Often the sun would disappear behind a cloud, which impinged on its roundness, but whose edge the sun gilded in return. The brightness, though not the light of day, would then be shut off from a landscape in which all life appeared to be suspended, while the little village of Roussainville carved in relief upon the sky the white mass of its gables, with a startling precision of detail. A gust of wind blew from its perch a rook, which floated away and settled in the distance, while beneath a paling sky the woods on the horizon assumed a deeper tone of blue, as though they were painted in one of those cameos which you still find decorating the walls of old houses.

But on other days would begin to fall the rain, of which we had had due warning from the little barometer-figure which the spectacle-maker hung out in his doorway. Its drops, like migrating birds which fly off in a body at a given moment,

would come down out of the sky in close marching order.
They would never drift apart, would make no movement at
random in their rapid course, but each one, keeping in its
place, would draw after it the drop which was following, and
the sky would be as greatly darkened as by the swallows flying
south. We would take refuge among the trees. And when it
seemed that their flight was accomplished, a few last drops,
feebler and slower than the rest, would still come down. But
we would emerge from our shelter, for the rain was playing a
game, now, among the branches, and, even when it was almost
dry again underfoot, a stray drop or two, lingering in the
hollow of a leaf, would run down and hang glistening from
the point of it until suddenly they splashed plump upon our
upturned faces from the whole height of the tree.

Often, too, we would hurry for shelter, tumbling in among
all its stony saints and patriarchs, into the porch of Saint-
André-des-Champs. How typically French that church was!
Over its door the saints, the kings of chivalry with lilies in
their hands, the wedding scenes and funerals were carved as
they might have been in the mind of Françoise. The sculptor
had also recorded certain anecdotes of Aristotle and Virgil,
precisely as Françoise in her kitchen would break into speech
about Saint Louis as though she herself had known him,
generally in order to depreciate, by contrast with him, my
grandparents, whom she considered less 'righteous'. One
could see that the ideas which the medieval artist and the
medieval peasant (who had survived to cook for us in the
nineteenth century) had of classical and of early Christian
history, ideas whose inaccuracy was atoned for by their honest
simplicity, were derived not from books, but from a tradition
at once ancient and direct, unbroken, oral, degraded, unrecognizable, and alive. Another Combray person whom I
could discern also, potential and typified, in the gothic sculptures of Saint-André-des-Champs was young Théodore, the
assistant in Camus's shop. And, indeed, Françoise herself was
well aware that she had in him a countryman and contemporary, for when my aunt was too ill for Françoise to be able,
unaided, to lift her in her bed or to carry her to her chair,

rather than let the kitchen-maid come upstairs and, perhaps, 'make an impression' on my aunt, she would send out for Théodore. And this lad, who was regarded, and quite rightly, in the town as a 'bad character', was so abounding in that spirit which had served to decorate the porch of Saint-André-des-Champs, and particularly in the feelings of respect due, in Françoise's eyes, to all 'poor invalids', and, above all, to her own 'poor mistress', that he had, when he bent down to raise my aunt's head from her pillow, the same air of Pre-Raphaelite simplicity and zeal which the little angels in the bas-reliefs wear, who throng, with tapers in their hands, about the death-bed of Our Lady, as though those carved faces of stone, naked and grey like trees in winter, were, like them, asleep only, storing up life and waiting to flower again in countless plebeian faces, reverend and cunning as the face of Théodore, and glowing with the ruddy brilliance of ripe apples.

There, too, not fastened to the wall like the little angels, but detached from the porch, of more than human stature, erect upon her pedestal as upon a footstool, which had been placed there to save her feet from contact with the wet ground, stood a saint with the full cheeks, the firm breasts which swelled out inside her draperies like a cluster of ripe grapes inside a bag, the narrow forehead, short and stubborn nose, deep-set eyes, and strong, thick-skinned, courageous expression of the country women of those parts. This similarity, which imparted to the statue itself a kindliness that I had not looked to find in it, was corroborated often by the arrival of some girl from the fields, come, like ourselves, for shelter beneath the porch, whose presence there – as when the leaves of a climbing plant have grown up beside leaves carved in stone – seemed intended by fate to allow us, by confronting it with its type in nature, to form a critical estimate of the truth of the work of art. Before our eyes, in the distance, a promised or an accursed land, Roussainville, within whose walls I had never penetrated, Roussainville was now, when the rain had ceased for us, still being chastised, like a village in the Old Testament, by all the innumerable spears and arrows of the storm, which beat down obliquely upon the dwellings of its inhabitants, or else had already received the forgiveness of the Almighty, who had restored to it the light of His sun, which fell upon it in rays of uneven length, like the rays of a monstrance upon an altar.

Sometimes, when the weather had completely broken, we were obliged to go home and to remain shut up indoors. Here and there, in the distance, in a landscape which, what with the failing light and saturated atmosphere, resembled a seascape rather, a few solitary houses clinging to the lower slopes of a hill whose heights were buried in a cloudy darkness shone out like little boats which had folded their sails and would ride at anchor, all night, upon the sea. But what mattered rain or storm? In summer, bad weather is no more than a passing fit of superficial ill-temper expressed by the permanent, under-lying fine weather; a very different thing from the fluid and unstable 'fine weather' of winter, its very opposite, in fact; for has it not (firmly established in the soil, on which it has taken solid form in dense masses of foliage over which the rain may pour in torrents without weakening the resistance offered by their real and lasting happiness) hoisted, to keep them flying throughout the season, in the village streets, on the walls of the houses and in their gardens, its silken banners, violet and white? Sitting in the little parlour, where I would pass the time until dinner with a book, I might hear the water dripping from our chestnut-trees, but I would know that the shower would only glaze and brighten the greenness of their thick, crumpled leaves, and that they themselves had undertaken to remain there, like pledges of summer, all through the rainy night, to assure me of the fine weather's continuing; it might rain as it pleased, but to-morrow, over the white fence of Tansonville, there would surge and flow, numerous as ever, a sea of little heart-shaped leaves; and without the least anxiety I could watch the poplar in the Rue des Perchamps praying for mercy, bowing in desperation before the storm; without the least anxiety I could hear, at the far end of the garden, the last peals of thunder growling among our lilac-trees.

If the weather was bad all morning, my family would abandon the idea of a walk, and I would remain at home. But, later on, I formed the habit of going out by myself on such days, and walking towards Méséglise-la-Vineuse, during that autumn when we had to come to Combray to settle the division of my aunt Léonie's estate; for she had died at last, leaving both parties among her neighbours triumphant in the fact of her demise – those who had insisted that her mode of life was enfeebling and must ultimately kill her, and, equally, those who had always maintained that she suffered from some disease not imaginary, but organic, by the visible proof of which the most sceptical would be obliged to own themselves convinced, once she had succumbed to it; causing no intense grief to any save one of her survivors, but to that one a grief savage in its violence. During the long fortnight of my aunt's last illness Françoise never went out of her room for an instant, never took off her clothes, allowed no one else to do anything for my aunt, and did not leave her body until it was actually in its grave. Then, at last, we understood that the sort of terror in which Françoise had lived of my aunt's harsh words, her suspicions, and her anger, had developed in her a sentiment which we had mistaken for hatred, and which was really veneration and love. Her true mistress, whose decisions it had been impossible to foresee, from whose stratagems it had been so hard to escape, of whose good nature it had been so easy to take advantage, her sovereign, her mysterious and omnipotent monarch was no more. Compared with such a mistress we counted for very little. The time had long passed when, on our first coming to spend our holidays at Combray, we had been of equal importance, in Françoise's eyes, with my aunt.

During that autumn my parents, finding the days so fully occupied with the legal formalities that had to be gone through, and discussions with solicitors and farmers, that they had little time for walks which, as it happened, the weather made precarious, began to let me go, without them, along the 'Méséglise way', wrapped up in a huge Highland plaid which protected me from the rain, and which I was all the more ready to throw over my shoulders because I felt that the stripes of its gaudy tartan scandalized Françoise, whom it was impossible to convince that the colour of one's clothes had nothing whatever to do with one's mourning for the dead, and to whom the grief which we had shown on my aunt's death was wholly unsatisfactory, since we had not entertained the neighbours to a great funeral banquet, and did not adopt a special tone when we spoke of her, while I at times might be heard humming a tune. I am sure that in a book – and to that extent my feelings were closely akin to those of Françoise – such a conception of mourning, in the manner of the *Chanson de Roland* and of the porch of Saint-André-des-Champs, would have seemed most attractive. But the moment that Françoise herself approached, some evil spirit would urge me to attempt to make her angry, and I would avail myself of the slightest pretext to say to her that I regretted my aunt's death because she had been a good woman in spite of her absurdities, but not in the least because she was my aunt; that she might easily have been my aunt and yet have been so odious that her death would not have caused me a moment's sorrow; statements which, in a book, would have struck me as merely fatuous.

And if Françoise then, inspired like a poet with a flood of confused reflections upon bereavements, grief, and family memories, were to plead her inability to rebut my theories, saying: 'I don't know how to *espress* myself' – I would triumph over her with an ironical and brutal common sense worthy of Dr Percepied; and if she went on: 'All the same she was a *geological* relation; there is always the respect due to your *geology*,' I would shrug my shoulders and say: 'It is really very good of me to discuss the matter with an illiterate old woman who cannot speak her own language,' adopting, to deliver judgement on Françoise, the mean and narrow outlook of the pedant, whom those who are most contemptuous of him in the impartiality of their own minds are only too prone to copy when they are obliged to play a part upon the vulgar stage of life.

My walks, that autumn, were all the more delightful because I used to take them after long hours spent over a book. When I was tired of reading, after a whole morning in the house, I would throw my plaid across my shoulders and set out; my body, which in a long spell of enforced immobility had stored up an accumulation of vital energy, was now obliged, like a spinning-top wound and let go, to spend this in every direction. The walls of houses, the Tansonville hedge, the trees of Roussainville wood, the bushes against which Montjouvain leaned its back, all must bear the blows of my walking-stick or umbrella, must hear my shouts of happiness, blows and shouts being indeed no more than expressions of the confused ideas which exhilarated me, and which, not being developed to the point at which they might rest exposed to the light of day, rather than submit to a slow and difficult course of elucidation, found it easier and more pleasant to drift into an immediate outlet. And so it is that the bulk of what appear to be the emotional renderings of our inmost sensations do no more than relieve us of the burden of those sensations by allowing them to escape from us in an indistinct form which does not teach us how it should be interpreted. When I attempt to reckon up all that I owe to the 'Méséglise way', all the humble discoveries of which it was either the accidental setting or the direct inspiration and cause, I am reminded that it was in that same autumn, on one of those walks, near the bushy precipice which guarded Montjouvain from the rear, that I was struck for the first time by this lack of harmony between our impressions and their normal forms of expression. After an hour of rain and wind, against which I had put up a brisk fight, as I came to the edge of the Montjouvain pond, and reached a little hut, roofed with tiles, in which M. Vinteuil's gardener kept his tools, the sun shone out again, and its golden rays, washed clean by the shower, blazed once more in the sky, on the trees, on the wall of the hut, and on the still wet tiles of the roof, which had a chicken perching upon its ridge. The wind pulled out sideways the wild grass that grew in the wall, and the chicken's downy feathers, both of which things let themselves float up on the wind's breath to their full extent, with the unresisting submissiveness of light and lifeless matter. The tiled roof cast up on the pond, whose reflections were now clear again in the sunlight, a square of pink marble, the like of which I had never observed before. And, seeing upon the water, where it reflected the wall, a pallid smile responding to the smiling sky, I cried aloud in my enthusiasm, brandishing my furled umbrella: 'Damn, damn, damn, damn!' But at the same time I felt that I was in duty bound not to content myself with these unilluminating words, but to endeavour to see more clearly into the sources of my enjoyment.

And it was at that moment, too – thanks to a peasant who went past, apparently in a bad enough humour already, but more so when he nearly received my umbrella in his face, and who replied without any cordiality to my 'Fine day, what! good to be out walking!' that I learned that identical emotions do not spring up in the hearts of all men simultaneously, by a pre-established order. Later on I discovered that, whenever I had read for too long and was in a mood for conversation, the friend to whom I would be burning to say something would at that moment have finished indulging himself in the delights of conversation, and wanted nothing now but to be left to read undisturbed. And if I had been thinking with affection of my parents, and forming the most sensible and proper plans for giving them pleasure, they would have been using the same interval of time to discover some misdeed that I had already forgotten, and would begin to scold me severely, just as I flung myself upon them with a kiss.

Sometimes to the exhilaration which I derived from being alone would be added an alternative feeling, so that I could not be clear in my mind to which I should give the casting vote; a feeling stimulated by the desire to see rise up before my eyes a peasant-girl whom I might clasp in my arms. Coming abruptly, and without giving me time to trace it accurately to its source among so many ideas of a very different kind, the pleasure which accompanied this desire seemed only a degree superior to what was given me by my other thoughts. I found an additional merit in everything that was in my mind at the moment, in the pink reflection of the tiled roof, the wild grass in the wall, the village of Roussainville into which I had long desired to penetrate, the trees of its wood and the steeple of its church, created in them by this fresh emotion which made them appear more desirable only because I thought it was they that had provoked it, and which seemed only to wish to bear me more swiftly towards them when it filled my sails with a potent, unknown, and propitious breeze. But if this desire that a woman should appear added for me something more exalting than the charms of nature, they in their turn enlarged what I might, in the woman's charm, have found too much restricted. It seemed to me that the beauty of the trees was hers also, and that, as for the spirit of those horizons, of the village of Roussainville, of the books which I was reading that year, it was her kiss which would make me master of them all; and, my imagination drawing strength from contact with my sensuality, my sensuality expanding through all the realms of my imagination, my desire had no longer any bounds. Moreover – just as in moments of musing contemplation of nature, the normal actions of the mind being suspended, and our abstract ideas of things set on one side, we believe with the profoundest faith in the originality, in the individual existence of the place in which we may happen to be – the passing figure which my desire evoked seemed to be not any one example of the general type of 'woman', but a necessary and natural product of the soil. For at that time everything which was not myself, the earth and the creatures upon it, seemed to me more precious, more important, endowed with a more real existence than they appear to full-grown men. And between the earth and its creatures I made no distinction. I had a desire for a peasant-girl from Méséglise or Roussainville, for a fisher-girl from Balbec, just as I had a desire for Balbec and Méséglise. The pleasure which those girls were empowered to give me would have seemed less genuine, I should have had no faith in it any longer, if I had been at liberty to modify its conditions as I chose. To meet in Paris a fisher-girl from Balbec or a peasant-girl from Méséglise would have been like receiving the present of a shell which I had never seen upon the beach, or of a fern which I had never found among the woods, would have stripped from the pleasure which she was about to give me all those other pleasures in the thick of which my imagination had enwrapped her. But to wander thus among the woods of Roussainville without a peasant-girl to embrace was to see those woods and yet know nothing of their secret treasure, their deep-hidden beauty. That girl whom I never saw save dappled with the shadows of their leaves, was to me herself a plant of local growth, only taller than the rest, and one whose structure would enable me to approach more closely than in them to the intimate savour of the land from which she had sprung. I could believe this all the more readily (and also that the caresses by which she would bring that savour to my senses were themselves of a particular kind, yielding a pleasure which I could never derive from any but herself) since I was still, and must for long remain, in that period of life when one has not yet separated the fact of this sensual pleasure from the various women in whose company one has tasted it, when one has not reduced it to a general idea which makes one regard them thenceforward as the variable instruments of a pleasure that is always the same. Indeed, that pleasure does not exist, isolated and formulated in the consciousness, as the ultimate object with which one seeks a woman's company, or as the cause of the uneasiness which, in anticipation, one then feels. Hardly even does one think of oneself, but only how to escape from oneself. Obscurely awaited, immanent and concealed, it rouses to such a paroxysm, at the moment when at last it makes itself felt, those other pleasures which we find in the tender glance, in the kiss of her who is by our side, that it seems to us, more than anything else, a sort of transport of gratitude for the kindness of heart of our companion and for her touching predilection of ourselves, which we measure by the benefits, by the happiness that she showers upon us.

Alas, it was in vain that I implored the dungeon-keep of Roussainville, that I begged it to send out to meet me some daughter of its village, appealing to it as to the sole confidant to whom I had disclosed my earliest desires when, from the top floor of our house at Combray, from the little room that smelt of orris-root, I had peered out and seen nothing but its tower, framed in the square of the half-opened window, while, with the heroic scruples of a traveller setting forth for unknown climes, or of a desperate wretch hesitating on the verge of self-destruction, faint with emotion, I explored, across the bounds of my own experience, an untrodden path which, I believed, might lead me to my death, even – until passion spent itself and left me shuddering among the sprays of flowering currant which, creeping in through the window, tumbled all about my body. In vain I called upon it now. In vain I compressed the whole landscape into my field of vision, draining it with an exhaustive gaze which sought to extract from it a female creature. I might go alone as far as the porch of Saint-André-des-Champs: never did I find there the girl whom I should inevitably have met, had I been with my grandfather, and so unable to engage her in conversation. I would fix my eyes, without limit of time, upon the trunk of a distant tree, from behind which she must appear and spring towards me; my closest scrutiny left the horizon barren as before; night was falling; without any hope now would I concentrate my attention, as though to force up out of it the creatures which it must conceal, upon that sterile soil, that stale and outworn land; and it was no longer in lightness of heart, but with sullen anger that I aimed blows at the trees of Roussainville wood, from among which no more living creatures made their appearance than if they had been trees painted on the stretched canvas background of a panorama, when, unable to resign myself to having to return home without having held in my arms the woman I so greatly desired, I was yet obliged to retrace my steps towards Combray, and to admit to myself that the chance of her appearing in my path grew smaller every moment. And if she had appeared, would I have dared to speak to her? I felt that she would have regarded me as mad, for I no longer thought of those desires which came to me on my walks, but were never realized, as being shared by others, or as having any existence apart from myself. They seemed nothing more now than the purely subjective, impotent, illusory creatures of my temperament. They were in no way connected now with nature, with the world of real things, which from now onwards lost all its charm and significance, and meant no more to my life than a purely conventional framework, just as the action of a novel is framed in the railway carriage, on a seat of which a traveller is reading it to pass the time.

And it is perhaps from another impression which I received at Montjouvain, some years later, an impression which at that time was without meaning, that there arose, long afterwards, my idea of that cruel side of human passion called 'sadism'. We shall see, in due course, that for quite another reason the memory of this impression was to play an important part in my life. It was during a spell of very hot weather; my parents, who had been obliged to go away for the whole day, had told me that I might stay out as late as I pleased; and having gone as far as the Montjouvain pond, where I enjoyed seeing again the reflection of the tiled roof of the hut, I had lain down in the shade and gone to sleep among the bushes on the steep slope that rose up behind the house, just where I had waited for my parents, years before, one day when they had gone to call on M. Vinteuil. It was almost dark when I awoke, and I wished to rise and go away, but I saw Mlle Vinteuil (or thought, at least, that I recognized her, for I had not seen her often at Combray, and then only when she was still a child, whereas she was now growing into a young woman), who probably had just come in, standing in front of me, and only a few feet away from me, in that room in which her father had entertained mine, and which she had now made into a little sitting-room for herself. The window was partly open; the lamp was lighted; I could watch her every movement without her being able to see me; but, had I gone away, I must have made a rustling sound among the bushes, she would have heard me, and might have thought that I had been hiding there in order to spy upon her.

She was in deep mourning, for her father had but lately died. We had not gone to see her; my mother had not cared to go, on account of that virtue which alone in her fixed any bounds to her benevolence – namely, modesty; but she pitied the girl from the depths of her heart. My mother had not forgotten the sad end of M. Vinteuil's life, his complete absorption, first in having to play both mother and nursery-maid to his daughter, and, later, in the suffering which she had caused him; she could see the tortured expression which was never absent from the old man's face in those terrible last years; she

knew that he had definitely abandoned the task of transcribing
in fair copies the whole of his later work, the poor little
pieces, we imagined, of an old music-master, a retired village
organist, which, we assumed, were of little or no value in
themselves, though we did not despise them, because they
were of such great value to him and had been the chief motive
of his life before he sacrificed them to his daughter; pieces
which, being mostly not even written down, but recorded
only in his memory, while the rest were scribbled on loose
sheets of paper, and quite illegible, must now remain unknown
for ever; my mother thought, also, of that other and still more
cruel renunciation to which M. Vinteuil had been driven, that
of seeing the girl happily settled, with an honest and respectable future; when she called to mind all this utter and crushing
misery that had come upon my aunts' old music-master, she
was moved to very real grief, and shuddered to think of that
other grief, so different in its bitterness, which Mlle Vinteuil
must now be feeling, tinged with remorse at having virtually
killed her father. 'Poor M. Vinteuil,' my mother would say,
'he lived for his daughter, and now he has died for her, without getting his reward. Will he get it now, I wonder, and in
what form? It can only come to him from her.'

At the far end of Mlle Vinteuil's sitting-room, on the
mantelpiece, stood a small photograph of her father which she
went briskly to fetch, just as the sound of carriage wheels was
heard from the road outside, then flung herself down on a sofa
and drew close beside her a little table on which she placed the
photograph, just as, long ago, M. Vinteuil had 'placed' beside
him the piece of music which he would have liked to play over
to my parents. And then her friend came in. Mlle Vinteuil
greeted her without rising, clasping her hands behind her
head, and drew her body to one side of the sofa, as though to
'make room'. But no sooner had she done this than she
appeared to feel that she was perhaps suggesting a particular
position to her friend, with an emphasis which might well be
regarded as importunate. She thought that her friend would
prefer, no doubt, to sit down at some distance from her, upon
a chair; she felt that she had been indiscreet; her sensitive

heart took fright; stretching herself out again over the whole of the sofa, she closed her eyes and began to yawn, so as to indicate that it was a desire to sleep, and that alone, which had made her lie down there. Despite the rude and hectoring familiarity with which she treated her companion I could recognize in her the obsequious and reticent advances, the abrupt scruples and restraints which had characterized her father. Presently she rose and came to the window, where she pretended to be trying to close the shutters and not succeeding.

'Leave them open,' said her friend. 'I am hot.'

'But it's too dreadful! People will see us,' Mlle Vinteuil answered. And then she guessed, probably, that her friend would think that she had uttered these words simply in order to provoke a reply in certain other words, which she seemed, indeed, to wish to hear spoken, but, from prudence, would let her friend be the first to speak. And so, although I could not see her face clearly enough, I am sure that the expression must have appeared on it which my grandmother had once found so delightful, when she hastily went on: 'When I say "see us" I mean, of course, see us reading. It's so dreadful to think that in every trivial little thing you do someone may be overlooking you.'

With the instinctive generosity of her nature, a courtesy beyond her control, she refrained from uttering the studied words which, she had felt, were indispensable from the full realization of her desire. And perpetually, in the depths of her being, a shy and suppliant maiden would kneel before that other element, the old campaigner, battered but triumphant, would intercede with him, and oblige him to retire.

'Oh, yes, it is so extremely likely that people are looking at us at this time of night in this densely populated district!' said her friend, with bitter irony. 'And what if they are?' she went on, feeling bound to annotate with a malicious yet affectionate wink these words which she was repeating, out of good nature, like a lesson prepared beforehand which, she knew, it would please Mlle Vinteuil to hear. 'And what if they are? All the better that they should see us.'

Mlle Vinteuil shuddered and rose to her feet. In her sensitive and scrupulous heart she was ignorant what words ought to flow, spontaneously, from her lips, so as to produce the scene for which her eager senses clamoured. She reached out as far as she could across the limitations of her true character to find the language appropriate to a vicious young woman such as she longed to be thought, but the words which, she imagined, such a young woman might have uttered with sincerity sounded unreal in her own mouth. And what little she allowed herself to say was said in a strained tone, in which her ingrained timidity paralysed her tendency to freedom and audacity of speech; while she kept on interrupting herself with: 'You're sure you aren't cold? You aren't too hot? You don't want to sit and read by yourself? . . .

'Your ladyship's thoughts seem to be rather "warm" this evening,' she concluded, doubtless repeating a phrase which she had heard used, on some earlier occasion, by her friend.

In the V-shaped opening of her crape bodice Mlle Vinteuil felt the sting of her friend's sudden kiss; she gave a little scream and ran away; and then they began to chase one another about the room, scrambling over the furniture, their wide sleeves fluttering like wings, clucking and crowing like a pair of amorous fowls. At last Mlle Vinteuil fell down exhausted upon the sofa, where she was screened from me by the stooping body of her friend. But the latter now had her back turned to the little table on which the old music-master's portrait had been arranged. Mlle Vinteuil realized that her friend would not see it unless her attention were drawn to it, and so exclaimed, as if she herself had just noticed it for the first time: 'Oh! there's my father's picture looking at us; I can't think who can have put it there; I'm sure I've told them twenty times, that is not the proper place for it.'

I remembered the words that M. Vinteuil had used to my parents in apologizing for an obtrusive sheet of music. This photograph was, of course, in common use in their ritual observances, was subjected to daily profanation, for the friend replied in words which were evidently a liturgical response: 'Let him stay there. He can't trouble us any longer. D'you think he'ld start whining, d'you think he'ld pack you out of the house if he could see you now, with the window open, the ugly old monkey?'

To which Mlle Vinteuil replied, 'Oh, please!' – a gentle reproach which testified to the genuine goodness of her nature, not that it was prompted by any resentment at hearing her father spoken of in this fashion (for that was evidently a feeling which she had trained herself, by a long course of sophistries, to keep in close subjection at such moments), but rather because it was the bridle which, so as to avoid all appearance of egotism, she herself used to curb the gratification which her friend was attempting to procure for her. It may well have been, too, that the smiling moderation with which she faced and answered these blasphemies, that this tender and hypocritical rebuke appeared to her frank and generous nature as a particularly shameful and seductive form of that criminal attitude towards life which she was endeavouring to adopt. But she could not resist the attraction of being treated with affection by a woman who had just shown herself so implacable towards the defenceless dead; she sprang on to the knees of her friend and held out a chaste brow to be kissed; precisely as a daughter would have done to her mother, feeling with exquisite joy that they would thus, between them, inflict the last turn of the screw of cruelty, in robbing M. Vinteuil, as though they were actually rifling his tomb, of the sacred rights of fatherhood. Her friend took the girl's head in her hands and placed a kiss on her brow with a docility prompted by the real affection she had for Mlle Vinteuil, as well as by the desire to bring what distraction she could into the dull and melancholy life of an orphan.

'Do you know what I should like to do to that old horror?' she said, taking up the photograph. She murmured in Mlle Vinteuil's ear something that I could not distinguish.

'Oh! You would never dare.'

'Not dare to spit on it? On that?' shouted the friend with deliberate brutality.

I heard no more, for Mlle Vinteuil, who now seemed weary, awkward, preoccupied, sincere, and rather sad, came back to the window and drew the shutters close; but I knew now what was the reward that M. Vinteuil, in return for all the suffering that he had endured in his lifetime, on account of his daughter, had received from her after his death.

And yet I have since reflected that if M. Vinteuil had been able to be present at this scene, he might still, and in spite of everything, have continued to believe in his daughter's sound-ness of heart, and that he might even, in so doing, have been not altogether wrong. It was true that in all Mlle Vinteuil's actions the appearance of evil was so strong and so consistent that it would have been hard to find it exhibited in such com-pleteness save in what is nowadays called a 'sadist'; it is behind the footlights of a Paris theatre, and not under the homely lamp of an actual country house, that one expects to see a girl leading her friend on to spit upon the portrait of a father who has lived and died for nothing and no one but her-self; and when we find in real life a desire for melodramatic effect, it is generally the 'sadic' instinct that is responsible for it. It is possible that, without being in the least inclined towards 'sadism', a girl might have shown the same out-rageous cruelty as Mlle Vinteuil in desecrating the memory and defying the wishes of her dead father, but she would not have given them deliberate expression in an act so crude in its symbolism, so lacking in subtlety; the criminal element in her behaviour would have been less evident to other people, and even to herself, since she would not have admitted to herself that she was doing wrong. But, appearances apart, in Mlle Vinteuil's soul, at least in the earlier stages, the evil element was probably not unmixed. A 'sadist' of her kind is an artist in evil, which a wholly wicked person could not be, for in that case the evil would not have been external, it would have seemed quite natural to her, and would not even have been distinguishable from herself; and as for virtue, respect for the dead, filial obedience, since she would never have practised the cult of these things, she would take no impious delight in their profanation. 'Sadists' of Mlle Vinteuil's sort are creatures so purely sentimental, so virtuous by nature, that even sensual pleasure appears to them as something bad, a privilege reserved for the wicked. And when they allow themselves for a moment to enjoy it they endeavour to impersonate, to assume all the outward appearance of wicked people, for themselves and their partners in guilt, so as to gain the momentary illusion of having escaped beyond the control of their own gentle and scrupulous natures into the inhuman world of pleasure. And I could understand how she must have longed for such an escape when I realized that it was impossible for her to effect it. At the moment when she wished to be thought the very antithesis of her father, what she at once suggested to me were the mannerisms, in thought and speech, of the poor old music-master. Indeed, his photograph was nothing; what she really desecrated, what she corrupted into ministering to her pleasures, but what remained between them and her and prevented her from any direct enjoyment of them, was the likeness between her face and his, his mother's blue eyes which he had handed down to her, like some trinket to be kept in the family, those little friendly movements and inclinations which set up between the viciousness of Mlle Vinteuil and herself a phraseology, a mentality not designed for vice, which made her regard it as not in any way different from the numberless little social duties and courtesies to which she must devote herself every day. It was not evil that gave her the idea of pleasure, that seemed to her attractive; it was pleasure, rather, that seemed evil. And as, every time that she indulged in it, pleasure came to her attended by evil thoughts such as, ordinarily, had no place in her virtuous mind, she came at length to see in pleasure itself something diabolical, to identify it with Evil. Perhaps Mlle Vinteuil felt that at heart her friend was not altogether bad, nor really sincere when she gave vent to those blasphemous utterances. At any rate, she had the pleasure of receiving those kisses on her brow, those smiles, those glances; all feigned, perhaps, but akin in their base and vicious mode of expression to those which would have been discernible on the face of a creature formed not out of kindness and long-suffering, but out of self-indulgence and cruelty. She was able to delude herself for a moment into believing that she was indeed amusing herself in the way in which, with so unnatural an accomplice, a girl might amuse herself who really did experience that savage antipathy towards her father's memory. Perhaps she would not have thought of wickedness as a state so rare, so abnormal, so exotic, one which it was so refreshing to visit, had she been able to distinguish in herself, as in all her fellow men and women, that indifference to the sufferings which they cause which, whatever names else be given it, is the one true, terrible, and lasting form of cruelty.

If the 'Méséglise way' was so easy, it was a very different matter when we took the 'Guermantes way', for that meant a long walk, and we must make sure, first, of the weather. When we seemed to have entered upon a spell of fine days, when Françoise, in desperation that not a drop was falling upon the 'poor crops', gazing up at the sky and seeing there only a little white cloud floating here and there upon its calm, azure surface, groaned aloud and exclaimed: 'You would say they were nothing more or less than a lot of dogfish swimming about and sticking up their snouts! Ah, they never think of making it rain a little for the poor labourers! And then when the corn is all ripe, down it will come, rattling all over the place, and think no more of where it is falling than if it was on the sea!' – when my father's appeals to the gardener had met with the same encouraging answer several times in succession, then someone would say, at dinner: 'To-morrow, if the weather holds, we might go the Guermantes way.' And off we would set, immediately after luncheon, through the little garden gate which dropped us into the Rue des Perchamps, narrow and bent at a sharp angle, dotted with grass-plots over which two or three wasps would spend the day botanizing, a street as quaint as its name, from which its odd characteristics and its personality were, I felt, derived; a street for which one might search in vain through the Combray of to-day, for the public school now rises upon its site. But in my dreams of Combray (like those architects, pupils of Viollet-le-Duc, who, fancying that they can detect, beneath a Renaissance rood-loft and an eighteenth-century altar, traces of a Norman choir, restore the whole church to the state in which it probably was in the twelfth century) I leave not a stone of the modern edifice standing, I pierce through it and 'restore' the Rue des Perchamps. And for such reconstruction memory furnishes me with more detailed guidance than is generally at the disposal of restorers; the pictures which it has preserved – perhaps the last surviving in the world to-day, and soon to follow the rest into oblivion – of what Combray looked like in my childhood's days; pictures which, simply because it was the old Combray that traced their outlines upon my mind before it vanished, are as moving – if I may compare a humble landscape with those glorious works, reproductions of which my grandmother was so fond of bestowing on me – as those old engravings of the 'Cenacolo', or that painting by Gentile Bellini, in which one sees, in a state in which they no longer exist, the masterpiece of Leonardo and the portico of Saint Mark's.

We would pass, in the Rue de l'Oiseau, before the old hostelry of the Oiseau Flesché, into whose great courtyard, once upon a time, would rumble the coaches of the Duchesses de Montpensier, de Guermantes, and de Montmorency, when they had to come down to Combray for some litigation with their farmers, or to receive homage from them. We would come at length to the Mall, among whose tree-tops I could distinguish the steeple of Saint-Hilaire. And I should have liked to be able to sit down and spend the whole day there, reading and listening to the bells, for it was so charming there and so quiet that, when an hour struck, you would have said not that it broke in upon the calm of the day, but that it relieved the day of its superfluity, and that the steeple, with the indolent, painstaking exactitude of a person who has nothing else to do, had simply, in order to squeeze out and let fall the few golden drops which had slowly and naturally accumulated in the hot sunlight, pressed, at a given moment, the distended surface of the silence.

The great charm of the 'Guermantes way' was that we had beside us, almost all the time, the course of the Vivonne. We crossed it first, ten minutes after leaving the house, by a footbridge called the Pont-Vieux. And every year, when we arrived at Combray, on Easter morning, after the sermon, if the weather was fine, I would run there to see (amid all the disorder that prevails on the morning of a great festival, the gorgeous preparations for which make the everyday household utensils that they have not contrived to banish seem more sordid than ever) the river flowing past, sky-blue already between banks still black and bare, its only companions a clump of daffodils, come out before their time, a few primroses, the first in flower, while here and there burned the blue flame of a violet, its stem bent beneath the weight of the drop of perfume stored in its tiny horn. The Pont-Vieux led to a towpath which, at this point, would be overhung in summer by the bluish foliage of a hazel, under which a fisherman in a straw hat seemed to have taken root. At Combray, where I knew everyone, and could always detect the blacksmith or grocer's boy through his disguise of a beadle's uniform or chorister's surplice, this fisherman was the only person whom I was never able to identify. He must have known my family, for he used to raise his hat when we passed; and then I would always be just on the point of asking his name, when someone would make a sign to me to be quiet, or I would frighten the fish. We would follow the tow-path, which ran along the top of a steep bank, several feet above the stream. The ground on the other side was lower, and stretched in a series of broad meadows as far as the village and even to the distant railway station. Over these were strewn the remains, half-buried in the long grass, of the castle of the old Counts of Combray, who, during the Middle Ages, had had on this side the course of the Vivonne as a barrier and defence against attack from the Lords of Guermantes and Abbots of Martinville. Nothing was left now but a few stumps of towers, hummocks upon the broad surface of the fields, hardly visible, broken battlements over which, in their day, the bowmen had hurled down stones, the watchmen had gazed out over Novepont, Clairefontaine, Martinville-le-Sec, Bailleau-l'Exempt, fiefs all of them of Guermantes, a ring in which Combray was locked; but fallen among the grass now, levelled with the ground, climbed and commanded by boys from the Christian Brothers' school, who came there in their playtime, or with lesson-books to be conned; emblems of a past that had sunk down and well-nigh vanished under the earth, that lay by the water's edge now, like an idler taking the air, yet giving me strong food for thought, making the name of Combray connote to me not the little town of to-day only, but an historic city vastly different, seizing and holding my imagination by the remote, incomprehensible features which it half-concealed beneath a spangled veil of buttercups. For the buttercups grew past numbering on this spot which they had chosen for their games among the grass, standing singly, in couples, in whole companies, yellow as the yolk of eggs, and glowing with an added lustre, I felt, because, being powerless to consummate with my palate the pleasure which the sight of them never failed to give me, I would let it accumulate as my eyes ranged over their gilded expanse, until it had acquired the strength to create in my mind a fresh example of absolute, unproductive beauty; and so it had been from my earliest childhood, when from the towpath I had stretched out my arms towards them, before even I could pronounce their charming name – a name fit for the Prince in some French fairy-tale; colonists, perhaps, in some far distant century from Asia, but naturalized now for ever in the village, well satisfied with their modest horizon, rejoicing in the sunshine and the water's edge, faithful to their little glimpse of the railway station; yet keeping, none the less, as do some of our old paintings, in their plebeian simplicity, a poetic scintillation from the golden East.

I would amuse myself by watching the glass jars which the boys used to lower into the Vivonne, to catch minnows, and which, filled by the current of the stream, in which they themselves also were enclosed, at once 'containers' whose transparent sides were like solidified water and 'contents' plunged into a still larger container of liquid, flowing crystal, suggested an image of coolness more delicious and more provoking than the same water in the same jars would have done, standing upon a table laid for dinner, by showing it as perpetually in flight between the impalpable water, in which my hands could not arrest it, and the insoluble glass, in which my palate could not enjoy it. I decided that I would come there again with a line and catch fish; I begged for and obtained a morsel of bread from our luncheon basket; and threw into the Vivonne pellets which had the power, it seemed, to bring about a chemical precipitation, for the water at once grew solid round about them in oval clusters of emaciated tadpoles, which until then it had, no doubt, been holding in solution, invisible, but ready and alert to enter the stage of crystallization.

Presently the course of the Vivonne became choked with water-plants. At first they appeared singly, a lily, for instance, which the current, across whose path it had unfortunately grown, would never leave at rest for a moment, so that, like a ferry-boat mechanically propelled, it would drift over to one bank only to return to the other, eternally repeating its double journey. Thrust towards the bank, its stalk would be straightened out, lengthened, strained almost to breaking-point until the current again caught it, its green moorings swung back over their anchorage and brought the unhappy plant to what might fitly be called its starting-point, since it was fated not to rest there a moment before moving off once again. I would still find it there, on one walk after another, always in the same helpless state, suggesting certain victims of neurasthenia, among whom my grandfather would have included my aunt Léonie, who present without modification, year after year, the spectacle of their odd and unaccountable habits, which they always imagine themselves to be on the point of shaking off, but which they always retain to the end; caught in the treadmill of their own maladies and eccentricities, their futile endeavours to escape serve only to actuate its mechanism, to keep in motion the clockwork of their strange, ineluctable, fatal daily round. Such as these was the water-lily, and also like one of those wretches whose peculiar torments, repeated indefinitely throughout eternity, aroused the curiosity of Dante, who would have inquired of them at greater length and in fuller detail from the victims themselves, had not Virgil, striding on ahead, obliged him to hasten after him at full speed, as I must hasten after my parents.

But farther on the current slackened, where the stream ran through a property thrown open to the public by its owner, who had made a hobby of aquatic gardening, so that the little ponds into which the Vivonne was here diverted were aflower with water-lilies. As the ·banks· at this point were thickly wooded, the heavy shade of the trees gave the water a background which was ordinarily dark green, although sometimes, when we were coming home on a calm evening after a stormy afternoon, I have seen in its depths a clear, crude blue that was almost violet, suggesting a floor of Japanese cloisonné. Here and there, on the surface, floated, blushing like a strawberry, the scarlet heart of a lily set in a ring of white petals.

Beyond these the flowers were more frequent, but paler, less glossy, more thickly seeded, more tightly folded, and disposed, by accident, in festoons so graceful that I would fancy I saw floating upon the stream, as though after the dreary stripping of the decorations used in some Watteau festival, moss-roses in loosened garlands. Elsewhere a corner seemed to be reserved for the commoner kinds of lily; of a neat pink or white like rocket-flowers, washed clean like porcelain, with housewifely care; while, a little farther again, were others, pressed close together in a floating garden-bed, as though pansies had flown out of a garden like butterflies and were hovering with blue and burnished wings over the transparent shadowiness of this watery border; this skiey border also, for it set beneath the flowers a soil of a colour more precious, more moving than their own; and both in the afternoon, when it sparkled beneath the lilies in the kaleidoscope of a happiness silent, restless, and alert, and towards evening, when it was filled like a distant haven with the roseate dreams of the setting sun, incessantly changing and ever remaining in harmony, about the more permanent colour of the flowers themselves, with the utmost profundity, evanescence, and mystery – with a quiet suggestion of infinity; afternoon or evening, it seemed to have set them flowering in the heart of the sky.

After leaving this park the Vivonne began to flow again more swiftly. How often have I watched, and longed to imitate, when I should be free to live as I chose, a rower who had shipped his oars and lay stretched out on his back, his head down, in the bottom of his boat, letting it drift with the current, seeing nothing but the sky which slipped quietly above him, showing upon his features a foretaste of happiness and peace.

We would sit down among the irises at the water's edge. In the holiday sky a lazy cloud streamed out to its full length. Now and then, crushed by the burden of idleness, a carp would heave up out of the water, with an anxious gasp. It was time for us to feed. Before starting homewards we would sit for a long time there, eating fruit and bread and chocolate, on the grass, over which came to our ears, horizontal, faint, but solid still and metallic, the sound of the bells of Saint-Hilaire, which had melted not at all in the atmosphere it was so well accustomed to traverse, but, broken piecemeal by the successive palpitation of all their sonorous strokes, throbbed as it brushed the flowers at our feet.

Sometimes, at the water's edge and embedded in trees, we would come upon a house of the kind called 'pleasure houses', isolated and lost, seeing nothing of the world, save the river which bathed its feet. A young woman, whose pensive face and fashionable veils did not suggest a local origin, and who had doubtless come there, in the popular phrase, 'to bury herself', to taste the bitter sweetness of feeling that her name, and still more the name of him whose heart she had once held, but had been unable to keep, were unknown there, stood framed in a window from which she had no outlook beyond the boat that was moored beside her door. She raised her eyes with an air of distraction when she heard, through the trees that lined the bank, the voices of passers-by of whom, before they came in sight, she might be certain that never had they known, nor would they know, the faithless lover, that nothing in their past lives bore his imprint, which nothing in their future would have occasion to receive. One felt that in her renunciation of life she had willingly abandoned those places in which she would at least have been able to see him whom she loved, for others where he had never trod. And I watched her, as she returned from some walk along a road where she had known that he would not appear, drawing from her submissive fingers long gloves of a precious, useless charm.

Never, in the course of our walks along the 'Guermantes way', might we penetrate as far as the source of the Vivonne, of which I had often thought, which had in my mind so abstract, so ideal an existence, that I had been as much surprised when someone told me that it was actually to be found in the same department, and at a given number of miles from Combray, as I had been on the day when I had learned that there was another fixed point somewhere on the earth's surface, where, according to the ancients, opened the jaws of Hell. Nor could we ever reach that other goal, to which I longed so much to attain, Guermantes itself. I knew that it was the residence of its proprietors, the Duc and Duchesse de Guermantes, I knew that they were real personages who did actually exist, but whenever I thought about them I pictured them to myself either in tapestry, as was the 'Coronation of Esther' which hung in our church, or else in changing, rainbow colours, as was Gilbert the Bad in his window, where he passed from cabbage green, when I was dipping my fingers in the holy water stoup, to plum blue when I had reached our row of chairs, or again altogether impalpable, like the image of Geneviève de Brabant, ancestress of the Guermantes family, which the magic lantern sent wandering over the curtains of my room or flung aloft upon the ceiling – in short, always wrapped in the mystery of the Merovingian age, and bathed, as in a sunset, in the orange light which glowed from the resounding syllable 'antes'. And if, in spite of that, they were for me, in their capacity as a duke and a duchess, real people, though of an unfamiliar kind, this ducal personality was in its turn enormously distended, immaterialized, so as to encircle and contain that Guermantes of which they were duke and duchess, all that sunlit 'Guermantes way' of our walks, the course of the Vivonne, its water-lilies and its overshadowing trees, and an endless series of hot summer afternoons. And I knew that they bore not only the titles of Duc and Duchesse de Guermantes, but that since the fourteenth century, when, after vain attempts to conquer its earlier lords in battle, they had allied themselves by marriage, and so become Counts of Combray, the first citizens, consequently, of the place, and yet the only ones among its citizens who did not reside in it – Comtes de Combray, possessing Combray, threading it on their string of names and titles, absorbing it in their personalities, and illustrating, no doubt, in themselves that strange and pious melancholy which was peculiar to Combray; proprietors of the town, though not of any particular house there; dwelling, presumably, out of doors, in the street, between heaven and earth, like that Gilbert de Guermantes, of whom I could see, in the stained glass of the apse of Saint-Hilaire, only the 'other side' in dull black lacquer, if I raised my eyes to look for him, when I was going to Camus's for a packet of salt.

And then it happened that, going the 'Guermantes way', I passed occasionally by a row of well-watered little gardens, over whose hedges rose clusters of dark blossom. I would stop before them, hoping to gain some precious addition to my experience, for I seemed to have before my eyes a fragment of that riverside country which I had longed so much to see and know since coming upon a description of it by one of my favourite authors. And it was with that story-book land, with its imagined soil intersected by a hundred bubbling watercourses, that Guermantes, changing its form in my mind, became identified, after I heard Dr Percepied speak of the flowers and the charming rivulets and fountains that were to be seen there in the ducal park. I used to dream that Mme de Guermantes, taking a sudden capricious fancy for myself, invited me there, that all day long she stood fishing for trout by my side. And when evening came, holding my hand in her own, as we passed by the little gardens of her vassals, she would point out to me the flowers that leaned their red and purple spikes along the tops of the low walls, and would teach me all their names. She would make me tell her, too, all about the poems that I meant to compose. And these dreams reminded me that, since I wished, some day, to become a writer, it was high time to decide what sort of books I was going to write. But as soon as I asked myself the question, and tried to discover some subject to which I could impart a philosophical significance of infinite value, my mind would stop like a clock, I would see before me vacuity, nothing, would feel either that I was wholly devoid of talent, or that, perhaps, a malady of the brain was hindering its development. Sometimes I would depend upon my father's arranging everything for me. He was so powerful, in such favour with the people who 'really counted', that he made it possible for us to transgress laws which Françoise had taught me to regard as more ineluctable than the laws of life and death, as when we were allowed to postpone for a year the compulsory repointing of the walls of our house, alone among all the houses in that part of Paris, or when he obtained permission from the Minister for Mme Sazerat's son, who had been ordered to some watering-place, to take his degree two months before the proper time, among the candidates whose surnames began with 'A', instead of having to wait his turn as an 'S'. If I had fallen seriously ill, if I had been captured by brigands, convinced that my father's understanding with the supreme powers was too complete, that his letters of introduction to the Almighty were too irresistible for my illness or captivity to turn out anything but vain illusions, in which there was no danger actually threatening me, I should have awaited with perfect composure the inevitable hour of my return to comfortable realities, of my deliverance from bondage or restoration to health. Perhaps this want of talent, this black cavity which gaped in my mind when I ransacked it for the theme of my future writings, was itself no more, either, than an unsubstantial illusion, and would be brought to an end by the intervention of my father, who would arrange with the Government and with Providence that *I* should be the first writer of my day. But at other times, while my parents were growing impatient at seeing me loiter behind instead of following them, my actual life, instead of seeming an artificial creation by my father, and one which he could modify as he chose, appeared, on the contrary, to be comprised in a larger reality which had not been created for my benefit, from whose judgements there was no appeal, in the heart of which I was bound, helpless, without friend or ally, and beyond which no further possibilities lay concealed. It was evident to me then that I existed in the same manner as all other men, that I must grow old, that I must die like them, and that among them I was to be distinguished merely as one of those who have no aptitude for writing. And so, utterly despondent, I renounced literature for ever, despite the encouragements that had been given me by Bloch. This intimate, spontaneous feeling, this sense of the nullity of my intellect, prevailed against all the flattering speeches that might be lavished upon me, as a wicked man, when everyone is loud in the praise of his good deeds, is gnawed by the secret remorse of conscience.

One day my mother said: 'You are always talking about Mme de Guermantes. Well, Dr Percepied did a great deal for her when she was ill, four years ago, and so she is coming to Combray for his daughter's wedding. You will be able to see her in church.' It was from Dr Percepied, as it happened, that I had heard most about Mme de Guermantes, and he had even shown us the number of an illustrated paper in which she was depicted in the costume which she had worn at a fancy dress ball given by the Princesse de Léon.

Suddenly, during the nuptial mass, the beadle, by moving to one side, enabled me to see, sitting in a chapel, a lady with fair hair and a large nose, piercing blue eyes, a billowy scarf of mauve silk, glossy and new and brilliant, and a little spot at the corner of her nose. And because on the surface of her face, which was red, as though she had been very warm, I could make out, diluted and barely perceptible, details which resembled the portrait that had been shown to me; because, more especially, the particular features which I remarked in this lady, if I attempted to catalogue them, formulated themselves in precisely the same terms: *a large nose, blue eyes*, as Dr Percepied had used when describing in my presence the Duchesse de Guermantes, I said to myself: 'This lady is like the Duchesse de Guermantes.' Now the chapel from which she was following the service was that of Gilbert the Bad; beneath its flat tombstones, yellowed and bulging like cells of honey in a comb, rested the bones of the old Counts of Brabant; and I remembered having heard it said that this chapel was reserved for the Guermantes family, whenever any of its members came to attend a ceremony at Combray; there was, indeed, but one woman resembling the portrait of Mme de Guermantes who on that day, the very day on which she was expected to come there, could be sitting in that chapel: it was she! My disappointment was immense. It arose from my not having borne in mind, when I thought of Mme de Guermantes, that I was picturing her to myself in the colours of a tapestry or a painted window, as living in another century, as being of another substance than the rest of the human race. Never had I taken into account that she might have a red face, a mauve scarf like Mme Sazerat; and the oval curve of her cheeks reminded me so strongly of people whom I had seen at home that the suspicion brushed against my mind (though it was immediately banished) that this lady in her creative principle, in the molecules of her physical composition, was perhaps not substantially the Duchesse de Guermantes, but that her body, in ignorance of the name that people had given it, belonged to a certain type of femininity which included, also, the wives of doctors and tradesmen. 'It is, it must be Mme de Guermantes, and no one else!' were the words underlying the attentive and astonished expression with which I was gazing upon this image, which, naturally enough, bore no resemblance to those that had so often, under the same title of 'Mme de Guermantes', appeared to me in dreams, since this one had not been, like the others, formed arbitrarily by myself, but had sprung into sight for the first time, only a moment ago, here in church; an image which was not of the same nature, was not colourable at will, like those others that allowed themselves to imbibe the orange tint of a sonorous syllable, but which was so real that everything, even to the fiery little spot at the corner of her nose, gave an assurance of her subjection to the laws of life, as in a transformation scene on the stage a crease in the dress of a fairy, a quivering of her tiny finger, indicate the material presence of a living actress before our eyes, whereas we were uncertain, till then, whether we were not looking merely at a projection of limelight from a lantern.

Meanwhile I was endeavouring to apply to this image, which the prominent nose, the piercing eyes pinned down and fixed in my field of vision (perhaps because it was they that had first struck it, that had made the first impression on its surface, before I had had time to wonder whether the woman who thus appeared before me might possibly be Mme de Guermantes), to this fresh and unchanging image the idea: 'It is Mme de Guermantes'; but I succeeded only in making the idea pass between me and the image, as though they were two discs moving in separate planes, with a space between. But this Mme de Guermantes of whom I had so often dreamed, now that I could see that she had a real existence independent of myself, acquired a fresh increase of power over my imagination, which, paralysed for a moment by contact with a reality so different from anything that it had expected, began to react and to say within me: 'Great and glorious before the days of Charlemagne, the Guermantes had the right of life and death over their vassals; the Duchesse de Guermantes descends from Geneviève de Brabant. She does not know, nor would she consent to know, any of the people who are here to-day.'

And then – oh, marvellous independence of the human gaze, tied to the human face by a cord so loose, so long, so elastic that it can stray, alone, as far as it may choose – while Mme de Guermantes sat in the chapel above the tombs of her dead ancestors, her gaze lingered here and wandered there, rose to the capitals of the pillars, and even rested upon myself, like a ray of sunlight straying down the nave, but a ray of sunlight which, at the moment when I received its caress, appeared conscious of where it fell. As for Mme de Guermantes herself, since she remained there motionless, sitting like a mother who affects not to notice the rude or awkward conduct of her children who, in the course of their play, are speaking to people whom she does not know, it was impossible for me to determine whether she approved or condemned the vagrancy of her eyes in the careless detachment of her heart.

I felt it to be important that she should not leave the church

before I had been able to look long enough upon her, reminding myself that for years past I had regarded the sight of her as
a thing eminently to be desired, and I kept my eyes fixed on
her, as though by gazing at her I should be able to carry away
and incorporate, to store up, for later reference, in myself the
memory of that prominent nose, those red cheeks, of all those
details which struck me as so much precious, authentic,
unparalleled information with regard to her face. And now
that, whenever I brought my mind to bear upon that face –
and especially, perhaps, in my determination, that form of the
instinct of self-preservation with which we guard everything
that is best in ourselves, not to admit that I had been in any
way deceived – I found only beauty there; setting her once
again (since they were one and the same person, this lady who
sat before me and that Duchesse de Guermantes whom, until
then, I had been used to conjure into an imagined shape) apart
from and above that common run of humanity with which the
sight, pure and simple, of her in the flesh had made me for a
moment confound her, I grew indignant when I heard people
saying, in the congregation round me: 'She is better looking
than Mme Sazerat' or 'than Mlle Vinteuil', as though she had
been in any way comparable with them. And my gaze resting
upon her fair hair, her blue eyes, the lines of her neck, and
overlooking the features which might have reminded me of
the faces of other women, I cried out within myself, as I
admired this deliberately unfinished sketch: 'How lovely she
is! What true nobility! It is indeed a proud Guermantes, the
descendant of Geneviève de Brabant, that I have before me!'
And the care which I took to focus all my attention upon her
face succeeded in isolating it so completely that to-day, when
I call that marriage ceremony to mind, I find it impossible to
visualize any single person who was present except her, and
the beadle who answered me in the affirmative when I inquired whether the lady was, indeed, Mme de Guermantes.
But her, I can see her still quite clearly, especially at the
moment when the procession filed into the sacristy, lighted by
the intermittent, hot sunshine of a windy and rainy day, where
Mme de Guermantes found herself in the midst of all those

Combray people whose names, even, she did not know, but whose inferiority proclaimed her own supremacy so loud that she must, in return, feel for them a genuine, pitying sympathy, and whom she might count on impressing even more forcibly by virtue of her simplicity and natural charm. And then, too, since she could not bring into play the deliberate glances, charged with a definite meaning, which one directs, in a crowd, towards people whom one knows, but must allow her vague thoughts to escape continually from her eyes in a flood of blue light which she was powerless to control, she was anxious not to distress in any way, not to seem to be despising those humbler mortals over whom that current flowed, by whom it was everywhere arrested. I can see again to-day, above her mauve scarf, silky and buoyant, the gentle astonishment in her eyes, to which she had added, without daring to address it to anyone in particular, but so that everyone might enjoy his share of it, the almost timid smile of a sovereign lady who seems to be making an apology for her presence among the vassals whom she loves. This smile rested upon myself, who had never ceased to follow her with my eyes. And I, remembering the glance which she had let fall upon me during the service, blue as a ray of sunlight that had penetrated the window of Gilbert the Bad, said to myself 'Of course, she is thinking about me.' I fancied that I had found favour in her sight, that she would continue to think of me after she had left the church, and would, perhaps, grow pensive again, that evening, at Guermantes, on my account. And at once I fell in love with her, for if it is sometimes enough to make us love a woman that she looks on us with contempt, as I supposed Mlle Swann to have done, while we imagine that she cannot ever be ours, it is enough, also, sometimes that she looks on us kindly, as Mme de Guermantes did then, while we think of her as almost ours already. Her eyes waxed blue as a periwinkle flower, wholly beyond my reach, yet dedicated by her to me; and the sun, bursting out again from behind a threatening cloud and darting the full force of its rays on to the Square and into the sacristy, shed a geranium glow over the red carpet laid down for the wedding, along which Mme de Guermantes smilingly advanced, and covered its woollen texture with a nap of rosy velvet, a bloom of light, giving it that sort of tenderness, of solemn sweetness in the pomp of a joyful celebration, which characterize certain pages of *Lohengrin*, certain paintings by Carpaccio, and make us understand how Baudelaire was able to apply to the sound of the trumpet the epithet 'delicious'.

How often, after that day, in the course of my walks along the 'Guermantes way', and with what an intensified melancholy did I reflect on my lack of qualification for a literary career, and that I must abandon all hope of ever becoming a famous author. The regret that I felt for this, while I lingered alone to dream for a little by myself, made me suffer so acutely that, in order not to feel it, my mind of its own accord, by a sort of inhibition in the instant of pain, ceased entirely to think of verse-making, of fiction, of the poetic future on which my want of talent precluded me from counting. Then, quite apart from all those literary preoccupations, and without definite attachment to anything, suddenly a roof, a gleam of sunlight reflected from a stone, the smell of a road would make me stop still, to enjoy the special pleasure that each of them gave me, and also because they appeared to be concealing, beneath what my eyes could see, something which they invited me to approach and seize from them, but which, despite all my efforts, I never managed to discover. As I felt that the mysterious object was to be found in them, I would stand there in front of them, motionless, gazing, breathing, endeavouring to penetrate with my mind beyond the thing seen or smelt. And if I had then to hasten after my grandfather, to proceed on my way, I would still seek to recover my sense of them by closing my eyes; I would concentrate upon recalling exactly the line of the roof, the colour of the stone, which, without my being able to understand why, had seemed to me to be teeming, ready to open, to yield up to me the secret treasure of which they were themselves no more than the outer coverings. It was certainly not any impression of this kind that could or would restore the hope I had lost of succeeding one day in becoming an author and poet, for each of them was associated with some material object devoid of any intellectual value, and suggesting no abstract truth. But at least they gave me an unreasoning pleasure, the illusion of a sort of fecundity of mind; and in that way distracted me from the tedium, from the sense of my own impotence which I had felt whenever I had sought a philosophic theme for some great literary work. So urgent was the task imposed on my conscience by these impressions of form or perfume or colour – to strive for a perception of what lay hidden beneath them, that I was never long in seeking an excuse which would allow me to relax so strenuous an effort and to spare myself the fatigue that it involved. As good luck would have it, my parents called me; I felt that I had not, for the moment, the calm environment necessary for a success- ful pursuit of my researches, and that it would be better to think no more of the matter until I reached home, and not to exhaust myself in the meantime to no purpose. And so I con- cerned myself no longer with the mystery that lay hidden in a form or a perfume, quite at ease in my mind, since I was taking it home with me, protected by its visible and tangible cover- ing, beneath which I should find it still alive, like the fish which, on days when I had been allowed to go out fishing, I used to carry back in my basket, buried in a couch of grass which kept them cool and fresh. Once in the house again I would begin to think of something else, and so my mind would become littered (as my room was with the flowers that I had gathered on my walks, or the odds and ends that people had given me) with a stone from the surface of which the sun- light was reflected, a roof, the sound of a bell, the smell of fallen leaves, a confused mass of different images, under which must have perished long ago the reality of which I used to have some foreboding, but which I never had the energy to discover and bring to light. Once, however, when we had prolonged our walk far beyond its ordinary limits, and so had been very glad to encounter, half way home, as afternoon darkened into evening, Dr Percepied, who drove past us at full speed in his carriage, saw and recognized us, stopped, and made us jump in beside him, I received an impression of this sort which I did not abandon without having first subjected it to an examination a little more thorough. I had been set on the box beside the coachman, we were going like the wind because the Doctor had still, before returning to Combray, to call at Martinville-le-Sec, at the house of a patient, at whose door he asked us to wait for him. At a bend in the road I experienced, suddenly, that special pleasure, which bore no resemblance to any other, when I caught sight of the twin steeples of Martinville, on which the setting sun was playing, while the movement of the carriage and the windings of the road seemed to keep them continually changing their position; and then of a third steeple, that of Vieuxvicq, which, although separated from them by a hill and a valley, and rising from rather higher ground in the distance, appeared none the less to be standing by their side.

In ascertaining and noting the shape of their spires, the changes of aspect, the sunny warmth of their surfaces, I felt that I was not penetrating to the full depth of my impression, that something more lay behind that mobility, that luminosity, something which they seemed at once to contain and to conceal.

The steeples appeared so distant, and we ourselves seemed to come so little nearer them, that I was astonished when, a few minutes later, we drew up outside the church of Martinville. I did not know the reason for the pleasure which I had found in seeing them upon the horizon, and the business of trying to find out what that reason was seemed to me irksome; I wished only to keep in reserve in my brain those converging lines, moving in the sunshine, and, for the time being, to think of them no more. And it is probable that, had I done so, those two steeples would have vanished for ever, in a great medley of trees and roofs and scents and sounds which I had noticed and set apart on account of the obscure sense of pleasure which they gave me, but without ever exploring them more fully. I got down from the box to talk to my parents while we were waiting for the Doctor to reappear. Then it was time to start; I climbed up again to my place, turning my head to look back, once more, at my steeples, of which, a little later, I caught a farewell glimpse at a turn in the road. The coachman, who seemed little inclined for conversation, having barely acknowledged my remarks, I was obliged, in default of other society, to fall back on my own, and to attempt to recapture the vision of my steeples. And presently their outlines and their sunlit surface, as though they had been a sort of rind, were stripped apart; a little of what they had concealed from me became apparent; an idea came into my mind which had not existed for me a moment earlier, framed itself in words in my head; and the pleasure with which the first sight of them, just now, had filled me was so much enhanced that, overpowered by a sort of intoxication, I could no longer think of anything but them. At this point, although we had now travelled a long way from Martinville, I turned my head and caught sight of them again, quite black this time, for the sun had meanwhile set. Every few minutes a turn in the road would sweep them out of sight; then they showed themseves for the last time, and so I saw them no more.

Without admitting to myself that what lay buried within the steeples of Martinville must be something analogous to a charming phrase, since it was in the form of words which gave me pleasure that it had appeared to me, I borrowed a pencil and some paper from the Doctor, and composed, in spite of the jolting of the carriage, to appease my conscience and to satisfy my enthusiasm, the following little fragment, which I have since discovered, and now reproduce, with only a slight revision here and there.

Alone, rising from the level of the plain, and seemingly lost in that expanse of open country, climbed to the sky the twin steeples of Martinville. Presently we saw three: springing into position, confronting them by a daring volt, a third, a dilatory steeple, that of Vieuxvicq, was come to join them. The minutes passed, we were moving rapidly, and yet the three steeples were always a long way ahead of us, like three birds perched upon the plain, motionless and conspicuous in the sunlight. Then the steeple of Vieuxvicq withdrew, took its proper distance, and the steeples of Martinville remained alone, gilded by the light of the setting sun, which, even at that distance, I could see playing and smiling upon their sloped sides. We had been so long in approaching them that I was thinking of the time that must still elapse before we could reach them when, of a sudden, the carriage, having turned a corner, set us down at their feet; and they had flung themselves so abruptly in our path that we had barely time to stop before being dashed against the porch of the church.

We resumed our course; we had left Martinville some little time, and the village, after accompanying us for a few seconds, had already disappeared, when, lingering alone on the horizon to watch our flight, its steeples and that of Vieuxvicq waved once again, in token of farewell, their sun-bathed pinnacles. Sometimes one would withdraw, so that the other two might watch us for a moment still; then the road changed direction, they veered in the light like three golden pivots, and vanished from my gaze. But, a little later, when we were already close to Combray, the sun having set meanwhile, I caught sight of them for the last time, far away, and seeming no more now than three flowers painted upon the sky above the low line of fields. They made me think, too, of three maidens in a legend, abandoned in a solitary place over which night had begun to fall; and while we drew away from them at a gallop, I could see them timidly seeking their way, and, after some awkward, stumbling movements of their noble silhouettes, drawing close to one another, slipping one behind another, showing nothing more, now, against the still rosy sky than a single dusky form, charming and resigned, and so vanishing in the night.

I never thought again of this page, but at the moment when, on my corner of the box-seat, where the Doctor's coachman was in the habit of placing, in a hamper, the fowls which he had bought at Martinville market, I had finished writing it, I found such a sense of happiness, felt that it had so entirely relieved my mind of the obsession of the steeples, and of the mystery which they concealed, that, as though I myself were a hen and had just laid an egg, I began to sing at the top of my voice.

All day long, during these walks, I had been able to muse upon the pleasure that there would be in the friendship of the Duchesse de Guermantes, in fishing for trout, in drifting by myself in a boat on the Vivonne; and, greedy for happiness, I asked nothing more from life, in such moments, than that it should consist always of a series of joyous afternoons. But when, on our way home, I had caught sight of a farm, on the left of the road, at some distance from two other farms which were themselves close together, and from which, to return to Combray, we need only turn down an avenue of oaks, bordered on one side by a series of orchard-closes, each one planted at regular intervals with apple-trees which cast upon the ground, when they were lighted by the setting sun, the Japanese stencil of their shadows, then, sharply, my heart would begin to beat, I would know that in half an hour we should be at home, and that there, as was the rule on days when we had taken the 'Guermantes way' and dinner was, in consequence, served later than usual, I should be sent to bed as soon as I had swallowed my soup, so that my mother, kept at table, just as though there had been company to dinner, would not come upstairs to say good night to me in bed. The zone of melancholy which I then entered was totally distinct from that other zone, in which I had been bounding for joy a moment earlier, just as sometimes in the sky a band of pink is separated, as though by a line invisibly ruled, from a band of green or black. You may see a bird flying across the pink; it draws near the border-line, touches it, enters and is lost upon the black. The longings by which I had just now been absorbed, to go to Guermantes, to travel, to live a life of happiness – I was now so remote from them that their fulfilment would have afforded me no pleasure. How readily would I have sacrificed them all, just to be able to cry, all night long, in the arms of Mamma! Shuddering with emotion, I could not take my agonized eyes from my mother's face, which was not to appear that evening in the bedroom where I could see myself already lying, in imagination; and wished only that I were lying dead. And this state would persist until the morrow, when, the rays of morning leaning their bars of light, as the gardener might lean his ladder, against the wall overgrown with nasturtiums, which clambered up it as far as my window-sill, I would leap out of bed to run down at once into the garden, with no thought of the fact that evening must return, and with it the hour when I must leave my mother. And so it was from the 'Guermantes way' that I learned to distinguish between these states which reigned alternately in my mind, during certain periods, going so far as to divide every day between them, each one returning to dispossess the other with the regularity of a fever and ague: contiguous, and yet so foreign to one another, so devoid of means of communication, that I could no longer understand, or even picture to myself, in one state what I had desired or dreaded or even done in the other.

So the 'Méséglise way' and the 'Guermantes way' remain for me linked with many of the little incidents of that one of all the divers lives along whose parallel lines we are moved, which is the most abundant in sudden reverses of fortune, the richest in episodes; I mean the life of the mind. Doubtless it makes in us an imperceptible progress, and the truths which have changed for us its meaning and its aspect, which have opened new paths before our feet, we had for long been preparing for their discovery; but that preparation was unconscious; and for us those truths date only from the day, from the minute when they became apparent. The flowers which played then among the grass, the water which rippled past in the sunshine, the whole landscape which served as environment to their apparition lingers around the memory of them still with its unconscious or unheeding air; and, certainly, when they were slowly scrutinized by this humble passer-by, by this dreaming child – as the face of a king is scrutinized by a petitioner lost in the crowd – that scrap of nature, that corner of a garden could never suppose that it would be thanks to him that they would be elected to survive in all their most ephemeral details; and yet the scent of hawthorn which strays plundering along the hedge from which, in a little while, the dog-roses will have banished it, a sound of footsteps followed by no echo, upon a gravel path, a bubble formed at the side of a water-plant by the current, and formed only to burst – my exaltation of mind has borne them with it, and has succeeded in making them traverse all these successive years, while all around them the once-trodden ways have vanished, while those who thronged those ways, and even the memory of those who thronged those trodden ways, are dead. Sometimes the fragment of landscape thus transported into the present will detach itself in such isolation from all associations that it floats uncertainly upon my mind, like a flowering isle of Delos, and I am unable to say from what place, from what time – perhaps, quite simply, from which of my dreams – it comes. But it is pre-eminently as the deepest layer of my mental soil, as firm sites on which I still may build, that I regard the Méséglise and Guermantes 'ways'. It is because I used to think of certain things, of certain people, while I was roaming along them, that the things, the people which they taught me to know, and these alone, I still take seriously, still give me joy. Whether it be that the faith which creates has ceased to exist in me, or that reality will take shape in the memory alone, the flowers that people show me nowadays for the first time never seem to me to be true flowers. The 'Méséglise way' with its lilacs, its hawthorns, its cornflowers, its poppies, its apple trees, the 'Guermantes way' with its river full of tadpoles, its water-lilies, and its buttercups have constituted for me for all time the picture of the land in which I fain would pass my life, in which my only requirements are that I may go out fishing, drift idly in a boat, see the ruins of a gothic fortress in the grass, and find hidden among the cornfields – as Saint-André-des-Champs lay hidden – an old church, monumental, rustic, and yellow like a mill-stone; and the cornflowers, the hawthorns, the apple trees which I may happen, when I go walking, to encounter in the fields, because they are situated at the same depth, on the level of my past life, at once establish contact with my heart. And yet, because there is an element of individuality in places, when I am seized with a desire to see again the 'Guermantes way', it would not be satisfied were I led to the banks of a river in which were lilies as fair, or even fairer than those in the Vivonne, any more than on my return home in the evening, at the hour when there awakened in me that anguish which, later on in life, transfers itself to the passion of love, and may even become its inseparable companion, I should have wished for any strange mother to come in and say good night to me, though she were far more beautiful and more intelligent than my own. No: just as the one thing necessary to send me to sleep contented (in that untroubled peace which no mistress, in later years, has ever been able to give me, since one has doubts of them at the moment when one believes in them, and never can possess their hearts as I used to receive, in her kiss, the heart of my mother, complete, without scruple or reservation, unburdened by any liability save to myself) was that it should be my mother who came, that she should incline towards me that face on which there was, beneath her eye, something that was, it appears, a blemish, and which I loved as much as all the rest – so what I want to see again is the 'Guermantes way' as I knew it, with the farm that stood a little apart from the two neighbouring farms, pressed so close together, at the entrance to the oak avenue; those meadows upon whose surface, when it is polished by the sun to the mirroring radiance of a lake, are outlined the leaves of the apple trees; that whole landscape whose individuality sometimes, at night, in my dreams, binds me with a power that is almost fantastic, of which I can discover no trace when I awake.

No doubt, by virtue of having permanently and indissolubly combined in me groups of different impressions, for no reason save that they had made me feel several separate things at the same time, the Méséglise and Guermantes 'ways' left me exposed, in later life, to much disillusionment, and even to many mistakes. For often I have wished to see a person again without realizing that it was simply because that person recalled to me a hedge of hawthorns in blossom; and I have been led to believe, and to make someone else believe in an aftermath of affection, by what was no more than an inclination to travel. But by the same qualities, and by their persistence in those of my impressions, to-day, to which they can find an attachment, the two 'ways' give to those impressions a foundation, depth, a dimension lacking from the rest. They invest them, too, with a charm, a significance which is for me alone. When, on a summer evening, the resounding sky growls like a tawny lion, and everyone is complaining of the storm, it is along the 'Méséglise way' that my fancy strays alone in ecstasy, inhaling, through the noise of falling rain, the odour of invisible and persistent lilac trees.

*

And so I would often lie until morning, dreaming of the old days at Combray, of my melancholy and wakeful evenings there; of other days besides, the memory of which had been more lately restored to me by the taste – by what would have been called at Combray the 'perfume' – of a cup of tea; and, by an association of memories, of a story which, many years after I had left the little place, had been told me of a love affair in which Swann had been involved before I was born; with that accuracy of detail which it is easier, often, to obtain when we are studying the lives of people who have been dead for centuries than when we are trying to chronicle those of our own most intimate friends, an accuracy which it seems as impossible to attain as it seemed impossible to speak from one town to another, before we learned of the contrivance by which that impossibility has been overcome. All these memories, following one after another, were condensed into a single substance, but had not so far coalesced that I could not discern between the three strata, between my oldest, my instinctive memories, those others, inspired more recently by a taste or 'perfume', and those which were actually the memories of another, from whom I had acquired them at second hand – no fissures, indeed, no geological faults, but at least those veins, those streaks of colour which in certain rocks, in certain marbles, point to differences of origin, age, and formation.

It is true that, when morning drew near, I would long have settled the brief uncertainty of my waking dream, I would know in what room I was actually lying, would have reconstructed it round about me in the darkness, and – fixing my orientation by memory alone, or with the assistance of a feeble glimmer of light at the foot of which I placed the curtains and the window – would have reconstructed it complete and with its furniture, as an architect and an upholsterer might do, working upon an original, discarded plan of the doors and windows; would have replaced the mirrors and set the chest-of-drawers on its accustomed site. But scarcely had daylight itself – and no longer the gleam from a last, dying ember on a brass curtain-rod, which I had mistaken for daylight – traced across the darkness, as with a stroke of chalk across a black-board, its first white correcting ray, when the window, with its curtains, would leave the frame of the doorway, in which I had erroneously placed it, while, to make room for it, the writing-table, which my memory had clumsily fixed where the window ought to be, would hurry off at full speed, thrusting before it the mantelpiece, and sweeping aside the wall of the passage; the well of the courtyard would be enthroned on the spot where, a moment earlier, my dressing-room had lain, and the dwelling-place which I had built up for myself in the dark-ness would have gone to join all those other dwellings of which I had caught glimpses from the whirlpool of awakening; put to flight by that pale sign traced above my window-curtains by the uplifted forefinger of day.

Swann in Love

To admit you to the 'little nucleus', the 'little group', the 'little clan' at the Verdurins', one condition sufficed, but that one was indispensable; you must give tacit adherence to a Creed one of whose articles was that the young pianist, whom Mme Verdurin had taken under her patronage that year, and of whom she said 'Really, it oughtn't to be allowed, to play Wagner as well as that!' left both Planté and Rubinstein 'sitting'; while Dr Cottard was a more brilliant diagnostician than Potain. Each 'new recruit' whom the Verdurins failed to persuade that the evenings spent by other people, in other houses than theirs, were as dull as ditch-water, saw himself banished forthwith. Women being in this respect more rebellious than men, more reluctant to lay aside all worldly curiosity and the desire to find out for themselves whether other drawing-rooms might not sometimes be as entertaining, and the Verdurins feeling, moreover, that this critical spirit and this demon of frivolity might, by their contagion, prove fatal to the orthodoxy of the little church, they had been obliged to expel, one after another, all those of the 'faithful' who were of the female sex.

Apart from the doctor's young wife, they were reduced almost exclusively that season (for all that Mme Verdurin herself was a thoroughly 'good' woman, and came of a respectable middle-class family, excessively rich and wholly undistinguished, with which she had gradually and of her own accord severed all connexion) to a young woman almost of a 'certain class', a Mme de Crécy, whom Mme Verdurin called by her Christian name, Odette, and pronounced a 'love', and to the pianist's aunt, who looked as though she had, at one period, 'answered the bell': ladies quite ignorant of the world, who in their social simplicity were so easily led to believe that the Princesse de Sagan and the Duchesse de Guermantes were obliged to pay large sums of money to other poor wretches, in order to have anyone at their dinner-parties, that if somebody had offered to procure them an invitation to the house of either of those great dames, the old doorkeeper and the woman of 'easy virtue' would have contemptuously declined.

The Verdurins never invited you to dinner; you had your 'place laid' there. There was never any programme for the evening's entertainment. The young pianist would play, but only if he felt inclined, for no one was forced to do anything, and, as M. Verdurin used to say: 'We're all friends here. Liberty Hall, you know!'

If the pianist suggested playing the Ride of the Valkyries, or the Prelude to Tristan, Mme Verdurin would protest, not that the music was displeasing to her, but, on the contrary, that it made too violent an impression. 'Then you want me to have one of my headaches? You know quite well, it's the same every time he plays that. I know what I'm in for. To-morrow, when I want to get up – nothing doing!' If he was not going to play they talked, and one of the friends – usually the painter who was in favour there that year – would 'spin', as M. Verdurin put it, 'a damned funny yarn that made 'em all split with laughter,' and especially Mme Verdurin, for whom – so strong was her habit of taking literally the figurative accounts of her emotions – Dr Cottard, who was then just starting in general practice, would 'really have to come one day and set her jaw, which she had dislocated with laughing too much.'

Evening dress was barred, because you were all 'good pals', and didn't want to look like the 'boring people' who were to be avoided like the plague, and only asked to the big evenings, which were given as seldom as possible, and then only if it would amuse the painter or make the musician better known. The rest of the time you were quite happy playing charades and having supper in fancy dress, and there was no need to mingle any strange element with the little 'clan'.

But just as the 'good pals' came to take a more and more prominent place in Mme Verdurin's life, so the 'bores', the 'nuisances' grew to include everybody and everything that kept her friends away from her, that made them sometimes plead 'previous engagements', the mother of one, the professional duties of another, the 'little place in the country' of a third. If Dr Cottard felt bound to say good night as soon as they rose from table, so as to go back to some patient, who was seriously ill; 'I don't know;' Mme Verdurin would say, 'I'm sure it will do him far more good if you don't go disturbing him again this evening; he will have a good night without you; to-morrow morning you can go round early and you will find him cured.' From the beginning of December it would make her quite ill to think that the 'faithful' might fail her on Christmas and New Year's Days. The pianist's aunt insisted that he must accompany her, on the latter, to a family dinner at her mother's.

'You don't suppose she'll die, your mother,' exclaimed Mme Verdurin bitterly, 'if you don't have dinner with her on New Year's Day, like people in the *provinces*!'

Her uneasiness was kindled again in Holy Week: 'Now you, Doctor, you're a sensible, broad-minded man; you'll come, of course, on Good Friday, just like any other day?' she said to Cottard in the first year of the little 'nucleus', in a loud and confident voice, as though there could be no doubt of his answer. But she trembled as she waited for it, for if he did not come she might find herself condemned to dine alone.

'I shall come on Good Friday – to say good-bye to you, for we are going to spend the holidays in Auvergne.'

'In Auvergne? To be eaten alive by fleas and all sorts of creatures! A fine lot of good that will do you!' And after a solemn pause: 'If you had only told us, we would have tried to get up a party, and all gone there together, comfortably.'

And so, too, if one of the 'faithful' had a friend, or one of the ladies a young man, who was liable, now and then, to make them miss an evening, the Verdurins, who were not in the least afraid of a woman's having a lover, provided that she had him in their company, loved him in their company, and did not prefer him to their company, would say: 'Very well, then, bring your friend along.' And he would be put to the test, to see whether he was willing to have no secrets from Mme Verdurin, whether he was susceptible of being enrolled in the 'little clan'. If he failed to pass, the faithful one who had introduced him would be taken on one side, and would be tactfully assisted to quarrel with the friend or mistress. But if the test proved satisfactory, the newcomer would in turn be numbered among the 'faithful'. And so when, in the course of this same year, the courtesan told M. Verdurin that she had made the acquaintance of such a charming gentleman, M. Swann, and hinted that he would very much like to be allowed to come, M. Verdurin carried the request at once to his wife. He never formed an opinion on any subject until she had formed hers, his special duty being to carry out her wishes and those of the 'faithful' generally, which he did with boundless ingenuity.

'My dear, Mme de Crécy has something to say to you. She would like to bring one of her friends here, a M. Swann. What do you say?'

'Why, as if anybody could refuse anything to a little piece of perfection like that. Be quiet; no one asked your opinion. I tell you that you are a piece of perfection.'

'Just as you like,' replied Odette, in an affected tone, and then went on: 'You know I'm not fishing for compliments.'

'Very well; bring your friend, if he's nice.'

Now there was no connexion whatsoever between the 'little nucleus' and the society which Swann frequented, and a purely worldly man would have thought it hardly worth his while, when occupying so exceptional a position in the world, to seek an introduction to the Verdurins. But Swann was so ardent a lover that, once he had got to know almost all the women of the aristocracy, once they had taught him all that there was to learn, he had ceased to regard those naturalization papers, almost a patent of nobility, which the Faubourg Saint-Germain had bestowed upon him, save as a sort of negotiable bond, a letter of credit with no intrinsic value, which allowed him to improvise a status for himself in some little hole in the country, or in some obscure quarter of Paris, where the good-looking daughter of a local squire or solicitor had taken his fancy. For at such times desire, or love itself, would revive in him a feeling of vanity from which he was now quite free in his everyday life, although it was, no doubt, the same feeling which had originally prompted him towards that career as a man of fashion in which he had squandered his intellectual gifts upon frivolous amusements, and had made use of his erudition in matters of art only to advise society ladies what pictures to buy and how to decorate their houses; and this vanity it was which made him eager to shine, in the sight of any fair unknown who had captivated him for the moment, with a brilliance which the name of Swann by itself did not emit. And he was most eager when the fair unknown was in humble circumstances. Just as it is not by other men of intelligence that an intelligent man is afraid of being thought a fool, so it is not by the great gentleman but by boors and 'bounders' that a man of fashion is afraid of finding his social value underrated. Three-fourths of the mental ingenuity displayed, of the social falsehoods scattered broadcast ever since the world began by people whose importance they have served only to diminish, have been aimed at inferiors. And Swann, who behaved quite simply and was at his ease when with a duchess, would tremble, for fear of being despised, and would instantly begin to pose, were he to meet her grace's maid.

Unlike so many people, who, either from lack of energy or else from a resigned sense of the obligation laid upon them by their social grandeur to remain moored like house-boats to a certain point on the bank of the stream of life, abstain from the pleasures which are offered to them above and below that point, that degree in life in which they will remain fixed until the day of their death, and are content, in the end, to describe as pleasures, for want of any better, those mediocre distractions, that just not intolerable tedium which is enclosed there with them; Swann would endeavour not to find charm and beauty in the women with whom he must pass his time, but to pass his time among women whom he had already found to be beautiful and charming. And these were, as often as not, women whose beauty was of a distinctly 'common' type, for the physical qualities which attracted him instinctively, and without reason, were the direct opposite of those that he admired in the women painted or sculptured by his favourite masters. Depth of character, or a melancholy expression on a woman's face would freeze his senses, which would, however, immediately melt at the sight of healthy, abundant, rosy human flesh.

If on his travels he met a family whom it would have been more correct for him to make no attempt to know, but among whom a woman caught his eye, adorned with a special charm that was new to him, to remain on his 'high horse' and to cheat the desire that she had kindled in him, to substitute a pleasure different from that which he might have tasted in her company by writing to invite one of his former mistresses to come and join him would have seemed to him as cowardly an abdication in the face of life, as stupid a renunciation of a new form of happiness as if, instead of visiting the country where he was, he had shut himself up in his own rooms and looked at 'views' of Paris. He did not immure himself in the solid structure of his social relations, but had made of them, so as to be able to set it up afresh upon new foundations wherever a woman might take his fancy, one of those collapsible tents which explorers carry about with them. Any part of it which was not portable or could not be adapted to some fresh pleasure he would discard as valueless, however enviable it might appear to others. How often had his credit with a duchess, built up of the yearly accumulation of her desire to do him some favour for which she had never found an opportunity, been squandered in a moment by his calling upon her, in an indiscreetly worded message, for a recommendation by telegraph which would put him in touch at once with one of her agents whose daughter he had noticed in the country, just as a starving man might barter a diamond for a crust of bread. Indeed, when it was too late, he would laugh at himself for it, for there was in his nature, redeemed by many rare refinements, an element of clownishness. Then he belonged to that class of intelligent men who have led a life of idleness, and who seek consolation and, perhaps, an excuse in the idea, which their idleness offers to their intelligence, of objects as worthy of their interest as any that could be attained by art or learning, the idea that 'Life' contains situations more interesting and more romantic than all the romances ever written. So, at least, he would assure and had no difficulty in persuading the more subtle among his friends in the fashionable world, notably the Baron de Charlus, whom he liked to amuse with stories of the startling adventures that had befallen him, such as when he had met a woman in the train, and had taken her home with him, before discovering that she was the sister of a reigning monarch, in whose hands were gathered, at that moment, all the threads of European politics, of which he found himself kept informed in the most delightful fashion, or when, in the complexity of circumstances, it depended upon the choice which the Conclave was about to make whether he might or might not become the lover of somebody's cook.

It was not only the brilliant phalanx of virtuous dowagers, generals, and academicians, to whom he was bound by such close ties, that Swann compelled with so much cynicism to serve him as panders. All his friends were accustomed to receive, from time to time, letters which called on them for a word of recommendation or introduction, with a diplomatic adroitness which, persisting throughout all his successive 'affairs' and using different pretexts, revealed more glaringly than the clumsiest indiscretion, a permanent trait in his character and an unvarying quest. I used often to recall to myself when, many years later, I began to take an interest in his character because of the similarities which, in wholly different respects, it offered to my own, how, when he used to write to my grandfather (though not at the time we are now considering, for it was about the date of my own birth that Swann's great 'affair' began, and made a long interruption in his amatory practices) the latter, recognizing his friend's handwriting on the envelope, would exclaim: 'Here is Swann asking for something; on guard!' And, either from distrust or from the unconscious spirit of devilry which urges us to offer a thing only to those who do not want it, my grandparents would meet with an obstinate refusal the most easily satisfied of his prayers, as when he begged them for an introduction to a girl who dined with us every Sunday, and whom they were obliged, whenever Swann mentioned her, to pretend that they no longer saw, although they would be wondering, all through the week, whom they could invite to meet her, and often failed, in the end, to find anyone, sooner than make a sign to him who would so gladly have accepted.

Occasionally a couple of my grandparents' acquaintance, who had been complaining for some time that they never saw Swann now, would announce with satisfaction, and perhaps with a slight inclination to make my grandparents envious of them, that he had suddenly become as charming as he could possibly be, and was never out of their house. My grandfather would not care to shatter their pleasant illusion, but would look at my grandmother, as he hummed the air of:

> *What is this mystery?*
> *I cannot understand it;*

or of:

> *Vision fugitive . . . ,*

or of:

> *In matters such as this*
> *'Tis best to close one's eyes.*

A few months later, if my grandfather asked Swann's new friend 'What about Swann? Do you still see as much of him as ever?' the other's face would lengthen: 'Never mention his name to me again!'

'But I thought that you were such friends . . .'

He had been intimate in this way for several months with some cousins of my grandmother, dining almost every evening at their house. Suddenly, and without any warning, he ceased to appear. They supposed him to be ill, and the lady of the house was going to send to inquire for him when, in her kitchen, she found a letter in his hand, which her cook had left by accident in the housekeeping book. In this he announced that he was leaving Paris and would not be able to come to the house again. The cook had been his mistress, and at the moment of breaking off relations she was the only one of the household whom he had thought it necessary to inform.

But when his mistress for the time being was a woman in society, or at least one whose birth was not so lowly, nor her position so irregular that he was unable to arrange for her reception in 'society', then for her sake he would return to it, but only to the particular orbit in which she moved or into which he had drawn her. 'No good depending on Swann for this evening,' people would say; 'don't you remember, it's his American's night at the Opera?' He would secure invitations for her to the most exclusive drawing-rooms, to those houses where he himself went regularly, for weekly dinners or for poker; every evening, after a slight 'wave' imparted to his stiffly brushed red locks had tempered with a certain softness the ardour of his bold green eyes, he would select a flower for his buttonhole and set out to meet his mistress at the house of one or other of the women of his circle; and then, thinking of the affection and admiration which the fashionable folk, whom he always treated exactly as he pleased, would, when he met them there, lavish upon him in the presence of the woman whom he loved, he would find a fresh charm in that worldly existence of which he had grown weary, but whose substance, pervaded and warmly coloured by the flickering light which he had slipped into its midst, seemed to him beautiful and rare, now that he had incorporated in it a fresh love.

But while each of these attachments, each of these flirtations had been the realization, more or less complete, of a dream born of the sight of a face or a form which Swann had spontaneously, and without effort on his part, found charming, it was quite another matter when, one day at the theatre, he was introduced to Odette de Crécy by an old friend of his own, who had spoken of her to him as a ravishing creature with whom he might very possibly come to an understanding, but had made her out to be harder of conquest than she actually was, so as to appear to be conferring a special favour by the introduction. She had struck Swann not, certainly, as being devoid of beauty, but as endowed with a style of beauty which left him indifferent, which aroused in him no desire, which gave him, indeed, a sort of physical repulsion; as one of those women of whom every man can name some, and each will name different examples, who are the converse of the type which our senses demand. To give him any pleasure her profile was too sharp, her skin too delicate, her cheek-bones too prominent, her features too tightly drawn. Her eyes were fine, but so large that they seemed to be bending beneath their own weight, strained the rest of her face and always made her appear unwell or in an ill humour. Some time after this introduction at the theatre she had written to ask Swann whether she might see his collections, which would interest her so much, she, 'an ignorant woman with a taste for beautiful things', saying that she would know him better when once she had seen him in his 'home', where she imagined him to be 'so comfortable with his tea and his books'; although she had not concealed her surprise at his being in that part of the town, which must be so depressing, and was 'not nearly smart enough for such a very smart man'. And when he allowed her to come she had said to him as she left how sorry she was to have stayed so short a time in a house into which she was so glad to have found her way at last, speaking of him as though he had meant something more to her than the rest of the people she knew, and appearing to unite their two selves with a kind of romantic bond which had made him smile. But at the time of life, tinged already with disenchantment, which Swann was approaching, when a man can content himself with being in love for the pleasure of loving without expecting too much in return, this linking of hearts, if it is no longer, as in early youth, the goal towards which love, of necessity, tends, still is bound to love by so strong an association of ideas that it may well become the cause of love if it presents itself first. In his younger days a man dreams of possessing the heart of the woman whom he loves; later, the feeling that he possesses the heart of a woman may be enough to make him fall in love with her. And so, at an age when it would appear – since one seeks in love before everything else a subjective pleasure – that the taste for feminine beauty must play the larger part in its procreation, love may come into being, love of the most physical order, without any foundation in desire. At this time of life a man has already been wounded more than once by the darts of love; it no longer evolves by itself, obeying its own incomprehensible and fatal laws, before his passive and astonished heart. We come to its aid; we falsify it by memory and by suggestion; recognizing one of its symptoms we recall and recreate the rest. Since we possess its hymn, engraved on our hearts in its entirety, there is no need of any woman to repeat the opening lines, potent with the admiration which her beauty inspires, for us to remember all that follows. And if she begin in the middle, where it sings of our existing, henceforward, for one another only, we are well enough attuned to that music to be able to take it up and follow our partner, without hesitation, at the first pause in her voice.

Odette de Crécy came again to see Swann: her visits grew more frequent, and doubtless each visit revived the sense of disappointment which he felt at the sight of a face whose details he had somewhat forgotten in the interval, not remembering it as either so expressive or, in spite of her youth, so faded; he used to regret, while she was talking to him, that her really considerable beauty was not of the kind which he spontaneously admired. It must be remarked that Odette's face appeared thinner and more prominent than it actually was, because her forehead and the upper part of her cheeks, a single and almost plane surface, were covered by the masses of hair which women wore at that period, drawn forward in a fringe, raised in crimped waves and falling in stray locks over her ears; while as for her figure, and she was admirably built, it was impossible to make out its continuity (on account of the fashion then prevailing, and in spite of her being one of the best-dressed women in Paris) for the corset, jutting forwards in an arch, as though over an imaginary stomach, and ending in a sharp point, beneath which bulged out the balloon of her double skirts, gave a woman, that year, the appearance of being composed of different sections badly fitted together; to such an extent did the frills, the flounces, the inner bodice follow, in complete independence, controlled only by the fancy of their designer or the rigidity of their material, the line which led them to the knots of ribbon, falls of lace, fringes of vertically hanging jet, or carried them along the bust, but nowhere attached themselves to the living creature, who, according as the architecture of their fripperies drew them towards or away from her own, found herself either strait-laced to suffocation or else completely buried.

But, after Odette had left him, Swann would think with a smile of her telling him how the time would drag until he allowed her to come again; he remembered the anxious, timid way in which she had once begged him that it might not be very long, and the way in which she had looked at him then, fixing upon him her fearful and imploring gaze, which gave her a touching air beneath the bunches of artificial pansies fastened in the front of her round bonnet of white straw, tied with strings of black velvet. 'And won't you,' she had ventured, 'come just once and take tea with me?' He had pleaded pressure of work, an essay – which, in reality, he had abandoned years ago – on Vermeer of Delft. 'I know that I am quite useless,' she had replied, 'a little wild thing like me beside a learned great man like you. I should be like the frog in the fable! And yet I should so much like to learn, to know things, to be initiated. What fun it would be to become a regular bookworm, to bury my nose in a lot of old papers!' she had gone on, with that self-satisfied air which a smart woman adopts when she insists that her one desire is to give herself up, without fear of soiling her fingers, to some unclean task, such as cooking the dinner, with her 'hands right in the dish itself'. 'You will only laugh at me, but this painter who stops you from seeing me,' she meant Vermeer, 'I have never even heard of him; is he alive still? Can I see any of his things in Paris, so as to have some idea of what is going on behind that great brow which works so hard, that head which I feel sure is always puzzling away about things; just to be able to say "There, that's what he's thinking about!" What a dream it would be to be able to help you with your work.'

He had sought an excuse in his fear of forming new friend-ships, which he gallantly described as his fear of a hopeless passion. 'You are afraid of falling in love? How funny that is, when I go about seeking nothing else, and would give my soul just to find a little love somewhere!' she had said, so naturally and with such an air of conviction that he had been genuinely touched. 'Some woman must have made you suffer. And you think that the rest are all like her. She can't have understood you: you are so utterly different from ordinary men. That's what I liked about you when I first saw you; I felt at once that you weren't like everybody else.'

'And then, besides, there's yourself — ' he had continued, 'I know what women are; you must have a whole heap of things to do, and never any time to spare.'

'I? Why, I have never anything to do. I am always free, and I always will be free if you want me. At whatever hour of the day or night it may suit you to see me, just send for me, and I shall be only too delighted to come. Will you do that? Do you know what I should really like – to introduce you to Mme Verdurin, where I go every evening. Just fancy my finding you there, and thinking that it was a little for my sake that you had gone.'

No doubt, in thus remembering their conversations, in thinking about her thus when he was alone, he did no more than call her image into being among those of countless other women in his romantic dreams; but if, thanks to some accidental circumstance (or even perhaps without that assistance, for the circumstance which presents itself at the moment when a mental state, hitherto latent, makes itself felt, may well have had no influence whatsoever upon that state), the image of Odette de Crécy came to absorb the whole of his dreams, if from those dreams the memory of her could no longer be eliminated, then her bodily imperfections would no longer be of the least importance, nor would the conformity of her body, more or less than any other, to the requirements of Swann's taste; since, having become the body of her whom he loved, it must henceforth be the only one capable of causing him joy or anguish.

It so happened that my grandfather had known – which was more than could be said of any of their actual acquaintance – the family of these Verdurins. But he had entirely severed his connexion with what he called 'young Verdurin', taking a general view of him as one who had fallen – though without losing hold of his millions – among the riffraff of Bohemia. One day he received a letter from Swann asking whether my grandfather could put him in touch with the Verdurins: 'On guard! on guard!' he exclaimed as he read it, 'I am not at all surprised; Swann was bound to finish up like this. A nice lot of people! I cannot do what he asks, because, in the first place, I no longer know the gentleman in question. Besides, there must be a woman in it somewhere, and I don't mix myself up in such matters. Ah, well, we shall see some fun if Swann begins running after the little Verdurins.'

And on my grandfather's refusal to act as sponsor, it was Odette herself who had taken Swann to the house.

The Verdurins had had dining with them, on the day when Swann made his first appearance, Dr and Mme Cottard, the young pianist and his aunt, and the painter then in favour, while these were joined, in the course of the evening, by several more of the 'faithful'.

Dr Cottard was never quite certain of the tone in which he ought to reply to any observation, or whether the speaker was jesting or in earnest. And so in any event he would embellish all his facial expressions with the offer of a conditional, a provisional smile whose expectant subtlety would exonerate him from the charge of being a simpleton, if the remark addressed to him should turn out to have been facetious. But as he must also be prepared to face the alternative, he never dared to allow this smile a definite expression on his features, and you would see there a perpetually flickering uncertainty, in which you might decipher the question that he never dared to ask: 'Do you really mean that?' He was no more confident of the manner in which he ought to conduct himself in the street, or indeed in life generally, than he was in a drawing-room; and he might be seen greeting passers-by, carriages, and anything that occurred with a malicious smile which absolved his subsequent behaviour of all impropriety, since it proved, if it should turn out unsuited to the occasion, that he was well aware of that, and that if he had assumed a smile, the jest was a secret of his own.

On all those points, however, where a plain question

appeared to him to be permissible, the Doctor was unsparing in his endeavours to cultivate the wilderness of his ignorance and uncertainty and so to complete his education.

So it was that, following the advice given him by a wise mother on his first coming up to the capital from his provincial home, he would never let pass either a figure of speech or a proper name that was new to him without an effort to secure the fullest information upon it.

As regards figures of speech, he was insatiable in his thirst for knowledge, for often imagining them to have a more definite meaning than was actually the case, he would want to know what, exactly, was intended by those which he most frequently heard used: 'devilish pretty', 'blue blood', 'a cat and dog life', 'a day of reckoning', 'a queen of fashion', 'to give a free hand', 'to be at a deadlock', and so forth; and in what particular circumstances he himself might make use of them in conversation. Failing these, he would adorn it with puns and other 'plays upon words' which he had learned by rote. As for the names of strangers which were uttered in his hearing, he used merely to repeat them to himself in a questioning tone, which, he thought, would suffice to furnish him with explanations for which he would not ostensibly seek.

As the critical faculty, on the universal application of which he prided himself, was, in reality, completely lacking, that refinement of good breeding which consists in assuring some one whom you are obliging in any way, without expecting to be believed, that it is really yourself that is obliged to him, was wasted on Cottard, who took everything that he heard in its literal sense. However blind she may have been to his faults, Mme Verdurin was genuinely annoyed, though she still continued to regard him as brilliantly clever, when, after she had invited him to see and hear Sarah Bernhardt from a stage box, and had said politely: 'It is very good of you to have come, Doctor, especially as I'm sure you must often have heard Sarah Bernhardt; and besides, I'm afraid we're rather too near the stage,' the Doctor, who had come into the box with a smile which waited before settling upon or vanishing from his face until some one in authority should enlighten him as to the merits of the spectacle, replied: 'To be sure, we are far too near the stage, and one is getting sick of Sarah Bernhardt. But you expressed a wish that I should come. For me, your wish is a command. I am only too glad to be able to do you this little service. What would one not do to please you, you are so good.' And he went on, 'Sarah Bernhardt; that's what they call the Voice of Gold, ain't it? You see, often, too, that she "sets the boards on fire". That's an odd expression, ain't it?' in the hope of an enlightening commentary, which, however, was not forthcoming.

'D'you know,' Mme Verdurin had said to her husband, 'I believe we are going the wrong way to work when we depreciate anything we offer the Doctor. He is a scientist who lives quite apart from our everyday existence; he knows nothing himself of what things are worth, and he accepts everything that we say as gospel.'

'I never dared to mention it,' M. Verdurin had answered, 'but I've noticed the same thing myself.' And on the following New Year's Day, instead of sending Dr Cottard a ruby that cost three thousand francs, and pretending that it was a mere trifle, M. Verdurin bought an artificial stone for three hundred, and let it be understood that it was something almost impossible to match.

When Mme Verdurin had announced that they were to see M. Swann that evening; 'Swann!' the Doctor had exclaimed in a tone rendered brutal by his astonishment, for the smallest piece of news would always take utterly unawares this man who imagined himself to be perpetually in readiness for anything. And seeing that no one answered him, 'Swann! Who on earth is Swann?' he shouted, in a frenzy of anxiety which subsided as soon as Mme Verdurin had explained, 'Why, Odette's friend, whom she told us about.'

'Ah, good, good; that's all right, then,' answered the Doctor, at once mollified. As for the painter, he was overjoyed at the prospect of Swann's appearing at the Verdurins', because he supposed him to be in love with Odette, and was always ready to assist at lovers' meetings. 'Nothing amuses me more than match-making,' he confided to Cottard; 'I have been tremendously successful, even with women!'

In telling the Verdurins that Swann was extremely 'smart', Odette had alarmed them with the prospect of another 'bore'. When he arrived, however, he made an excellent impression, an indirect cause of which, though they did not know it, was his familiarity with the best society. He had, indeed, one of those advantages which men who have lived and moved in the world enjoy over others, even men of intelligence and refinement, who have never gone into society, namely that they no longer see it transfigured by the longing or repulsion with which it fills the imagination, but regard it as quite unimportant. Their good nature, freed from all taint of snobbishness and from the fear of seeming too friendly, grown independent, in fact, has the ease, the grace of movement of a trained gymnast each of whose supple limbs will carry out precisely the movement that is required without any clumsy participation by the rest of his body. The simple and elementary gestures used by a man of the world when he courteously holds out his hand to the unknown youth who is being introduced to him, and when he bows discreetly before the Ambassador to whom he is being introduced, had gradually pervaded, without his being conscious of it, the whole of Swann's social deportment, so that in the company of people of a lower grade than his own, such as the Verdurins and their friends, he instinctively showed an assiduity, and made overtures with which, by their account, any of their 'bores' would have dispensed. He chilled, though for a moment only, on meeting Dr Cottard; for seeing him close one eye with an ambiguous smile, before they had yet spoken to one another (a grimace which Cottard styled 'letting 'em all come'), Swann supposed that the Doctor recognized him from having met him already somewhere, probably in some house of 'ill-fame', though these he himself very rarely visited, never having made a habit of indulging in the mercenary sort of love. Regarding such an allusion as in bad taste, especially before Odette, whose opinion of himself it might easily alter for the worse, Swann assumed his most icy manner. But when he learned that the lady

next to the Doctor was Mme Cottard, he decided that so young
a husband would not deliberately, in his wife's hearing, have
made any allusion to amusements of that order, and so ceased
to interpret the Doctor's expression in the sense which he had
at first suspected. The painter at once invited Swann to visit
his studio with Odette, and Swann found him very pleasant.
'Perhaps you will be more highly favoured than I have been,'
Mme Verdurin broke in, with mock resentment of the favour,
'perhaps you will be allowed to see Cottard's portrait' (for
which she had given the painter a commission). 'Take care,
Master Biche,' she reminded the painter, whom it was a time-
honoured pleasantry to address as 'Master', 'to catch that nice
look in his eyes, that witty little twinkle. You know, what I
want to have most of all is his smile; that's what I've asked
you to paint – the portrait of his smile.' And since the phrase
struck her as noteworthy, she repeated it very loud, so as to
make sure that as many as possible of her guests should hear it,
and even made use of some indefinite pretext to draw the circle
closer before she uttered it again. Swann begged to be introduced to everyone, even to an old friend of the Verdurins,
called Saniette, whose shyness, simplicity, and good-nature had
deprived him of all the consideration due to his skill in palaeo-
graphy, his large fortune, and the distinguished family to
which he belonged. When he spoke, his words came with a
confusion which was delightful to hear because one felt that it
indicated not so much a defect in his speech as a quality of his
soul, as it were a survival from the age of innocence which he
had never wholly outgrown. All the consonants which he did
not manage to pronounce seemed like harsh utterances of
which his gentle lips were incapable. By asking to be made
known to M. Saniette, Swann made M. Verdurin reverse the
usual form of introduction (saying, in fact, with emphasis on
the distinction: 'M. Swann, pray let me present to you our
friend Saniette') but he aroused in Saniette himself a warmth
of gratitude, which, however, the Verdurins never disclosed
to Swann, since Saniette rather annoyed them, and they did
not feel bound to provide him with friends. On the other hand
the Verdurins were extremely touched by Swann's next

request, for he felt that he must ask to be introduced to the pianist's aunt. She wore a black dress, as was her invariable custom, for she believed that a woman always looked well in black, and that nothing could be more distinguished; but her face was exceedingly red, as it always was for some time after a meal. She bowed to Swann with deference, but drew herself up again with great dignity. As she was entirely uneducated, and was afraid of making mistakes in grammar and pronunciation, she used purposely to speak in an indistinct and garbling manner, thinking that if she should make a slip it would be so buried in the surrounding confusion that no one could be certain whether she had actually made it or not; with the result that her talk was a sort of continuous, blurred expectoration, out of which would emerge, at rare intervals, those sounds and syllables of which she felt positive. Swann supposed himself entitled to poke a little mild fun at her in conversation with M. Verdurin, who, however, was not at all amused.

'She is such an excellent woman!' he rejoined. 'I grant you that she is not exactly brilliant; but I assure you that she can talk most charmingly when you are alone with her.'

'I am sure she can,' Swann hastened to conciliate him. 'All I meant was that she hardly struck me as "distinguished",' he went on, isolating the epithet in the inverted commas of his tone, 'and, after all, that is something of a compliment.'

'Wait a moment,' said M. Verdurin, 'now, this will surprise you; she writes quite delightfully. You have never heard her nephew play? It is admirable; eh, Doctor? Would you like me to ask him to play something, M. Swann?'

'I should count myself most fortunate . . .' Swann was beginning, a trifle pompously, when the Doctor broke in derisively. Having once heard it said, and never having forgotten that in general conversation emphasis and the use of formal expressions were out of date, whenever he heard a solemn word used seriously, as the word 'fortunate' had been used just now by Swann, he at once assumed that the speaker was being deliberately pedantic. And if, moreover, the same word happened to occur, also, in what he called an old 'tag' or 'saw', however common it might still be in current usage, the Doctor jumped to the conclusion that the whole thing was a joke, and interrupted with the remaining words of the quotation, which he seemed to charge the speaker with having intended to introduce at that point, although in reality it had never entered his mind.

'Most fortunate for France!' he recited wickedly, shooting up both arms with great vigour. M. Verdurin could not help laughing.

'What are all those good people laughing at over there? There's no sign of brooding melancholy down in your corner,' shouted Mme Verdurin. 'You don't suppose I find it very amusing to be stuck up here by myself on the stool of repentance,' she went on peevishly, like a spoiled child.

Mme Verdurin was sitting upon a high Swedish chair of waxed pinewood, which a violinist from that country had given her, and which she kept in her drawing-room, although in appearance it suggested a school 'form', and 'swore', as the saying is, at the really good antique furniture which she had besides; but she made a point of keeping on view the presents which her 'faithful' were in the habit of making her from time to time, so that the donors might have the pleasure of seeing them there when they came to the house. She tried to persuade them to confine their tributes to flowers and sweets, which had at least the merit of mortality; but she was never successful, and the house was gradually filled with a collection of foot-warmers, cushions, clocks, screens, barometers, and vases, a constant repetition and a boundless incongruity of useless but indestructible objects.

From this lofty perch she would take her spirited part in the conversation of the 'faithful', and would revel in all their fun; but, since the accident to her jaw, she had abandoned the effort involved in real hilarity, and had substituted a kind of symbolical dumb-show which signified, without endangering or even fatiguing her in any way, that she was 'laughing until she cried'. At the least witticism aimed by any of the circle against a 'bore', or against a former member of the circle who was

now relegated to the limbo of 'bores' – and to the utter despair of M. Verdurin, who had always made out that he was
just as easily amused as his wife, but who, since his laughter
was the 'real thing', was out of breath in a moment, and so
was overtaken and vanquished by her device of a feigned but
continuous hilarity – she would utter a shrill cry, shut tight
her little bird-like eyes, which were beginning to be clouded
over by a cataract, and quickly, as though she had only just
time to avoid some indecent sight or to parry a mortal blow,
burying her face in her hands, which completely engulfed it,
and prevented her from seeing anything at all, she would appear to be struggling to suppress, to eradicate a laugh which,
were she to give way to it, must inevitably leave her inanimate.
So, stupefied with the gaiety of the 'faithful', drunken with
comradeship, scandal, and asseveration, Mme Verdurin,
perched on her high seat like a cage-bird whose biscuit has been
steeped in mulled wine, would sit aloft and sob with fellow-
feeling.

Meanwhile M. Verdurin after first asking Swann's permission to light his pipe ('No ceremony here, you understand,
we're all pals!'), went and begged the young musician to sit
down at the piano.

'Leave him alone; don't bother him; he hasn't come here to
be tormented,' cried Mme Verdurin. 'I won't have him tormented.'

'But why on earth should it bother him?' rejoined M. Verdurin. 'I'm sure M. Swann has never heard the sonata in F
sharp which we discovered; he is going to play us the pianoforte arrangement.'

'No, no, no, not my sonata!' she screamed, 'I don't want to
be made to cry until I get a cold in the head, and neuralgia all
down my face, like last time; thanks very much, I don't intend
to repeat that performance; you are all very kind and consider-
ate; it is easy to see that none of you will have to stay in bed
for a week.'

This little scene, which was re-enacted as often as the young
pianist sat down to play, never failed to delight the audience,
as though each of them were witnessing it for the first time, as

a proof of the seductive originality of the 'Mistress' as she was styled, and of the acute sensitiveness of her musical 'ear'. Those nearest to her would attract the attention of the rest, who were smoking or playing cards at the other end of the room, by their cries of 'Hear, hear!' which, as in Parliamentary debates, showed that something worth listening to was being said. And next day they would commiserate with those who had been prevented from coming that evening, and would assure them that the 'little scene' had never been so amusingly done.

'Well, all right, then,' said M. Verdurin, 'he can play just the *andante*.'

'Just the *andante*! How you do go on,' cried his wife. 'As if it weren't "just the *andante*" that breaks every bone in my body. The "Master" is really too priceless! Just as though, "in the Ninth", he said "we need only have the *finale*", or "just the overture" of the *Meistersingers*.'

The Doctor, however, urged Mme Verdurin to let the pianist play, not because he supposed her to be malingering when she spoke of the distressing effects that music always had upon her, for he recognized the existence of certain neurasthenic states – but from his habit, common to many doctors, of at once relaxing the strict letter of a prescription as soon as it appeared to jeopardize, what seemed to him far more important, the success of some social gathering at which he was present, and of which the patient whom he had urged for once to forget her dyspepsia or headache formed an essential factor.

'You won't be ill this time, you'll find,' he told her, seeking at the same time to subdue her mind by the magnetism of his gaze. 'And, if you are ill, we will cure you.'

'Will you, really?' Mme Verdurin spoke as though, with so great a favour in store for her, there was nothing for it but to capitulate. Perhaps, too, by dint of saying that she was going to be ill, she had worked herself into a state in which she forgot, occasionally, that it was all only a 'little scene', and regarded things, quite sincerely, from an invalid's point of view. For it may often be remarked that invalids grow weary of having the frequency of their attacks depend always on their own prudence in avoiding them, and like to let themselves think that they are free to do everything that they most enjoy doing, although they are always ill after doing it, provided only that they place themselves in the hands of a higher authority which, without putting them to the least inconvenience, can and will, by uttering a word or by administering a tabloid, set them once again upon their feet.

Odette had gone to sit on a tapestry-covered sofa near the piano, saying to Mme Verdurin, 'I have my own little corner, haven't I?'

And Mme Verdurin, seeing Swann by himself upon a chair, made him get up: 'You're not at all comfortable there; go along and sit by Odette; you can make room for M. Swann there, can't you, Odette?'

'What charming Beauvais!' said Swann, stopping to admire the sofa before he sat down on it, and wishing to be polite.

'I am glad you appreciate my sofa,' replied Mme Verdurin, 'and I warn you that if you expect ever to see another like it you may as well abandon the idea at once. They never made any more like it. And these little chairs, too, are perfect marvels. You can look at them in a moment. The emblems in each of the bronze mouldings correspond to the subject of the tapestry on the chair; you know, you combine amusement with instruction when you look at them; – I can promise you a delightful time, I assure you. Just look at the little border round the edges; here, look, the little vine on a red background in this one, the Bear and the Grapes. Isn't it well drawn? What do you say? I think they knew a thing or two about design! Doesn't it make your mouth water, this vine? My husband makes out that I am not fond of fruit, because I eat less than he does. But not a bit of it, I am greedier than any of you, but I have no need to fill my mouth with them when I can feed on them with my eyes. What are you all laughing at now, pray? Ask the Doctor; he will tell you that those grapes act on me like a regular purge. Some people go to Fontainebleau for cures; I take my own little Beauvais cure here. But, M. Swann, you musn't run away without feeling the little bronze mouldings on the backs. Isn't it an exquisite surface? No, no, not with your whole hand like that; feel them properly!'

'If Mme Verdurin is going to start playing about with her bronzes,' said the painter, 'we shan't get any music to-night.'

'Be quiet, you wretch! And yet we poor women,' she went on, 'are forbidden pleasures far less voluptuous than this. There is no flesh in the world as soft as these. None. When M. Verdurin did me the honour of being madly jealous ... come, you might at least be polite. Don't say that you never have been jealous!'

'But, my dear, I have said absolutely nothing. Look here, Doctor, I call you as a witness; did I utter a word?'

Swann had begun, out of politeness, to finger the bronzes, and did not like to stop.

'Come along; you can caress them later; now it is you that are going to be caressed, caressed in the ear; you'll like that, I think. Here's the young gentleman who will take charge of that.'

After the pianist had played, Swann felt and showed more interest in him than in any of the other guests, for the following reason:

The year before, at an evening party, he had heard a piece of music played on the piano and violin. At first he had appreciated only the material quality of the sounds which those instruments secreted. And it had been a source of keen pleasure when, below the narrow ribbon of the violin-part, delicate, unyielding, substantial, and governing the whole, he had suddenly perceived, where it was trying to surge upwards in a flowing tide of sound, the mass of the piano-part, multiform, coherent, level, and breaking everywhere in melody like the deep blue tumult of the sea, silvered and charmed into a minor key by the moonlight. But at a given moment, without being able to distinguish any clear outline, or to give a name to what was pleasing him, suddenly enraptured, he had tried to collect, to treasure in his memory the phrase or harmony – he knew not which – that had just been played, and had opened and expanded his soul, just as the fragrance of certain roses, wafted upon the moist air of evening, has the power of dilating our nostrils. Perhaps it was owing to his own ignorance of music that he had been able to receive so confused an impression, one of those that are, notwithstanding, our only purely musical impressions, limited in their extent, entirely original, and irreducible into any other kind. An impression of this order, vanishing in an instant, is, so to speak, an impression *sine materia*. Presumably the notes which we hear at such moments tend to spread out before our eyes, over surfaces greater or smaller according to their pitch and volume; to trace arabesque designs, to give us the sensation of breadth or tenuity, stability or caprice. But the notes themselves have vanished before these sensations have developed sufficiently to escape submersion under those which the following, or even simultaneous notes have already begun to awaken in us. And this indefinite perception would continue to smother in its molten liquidity the *motifs* which now and then emerge, barely discernible, to plunge again and disappear and drown; recognized only by the particular kind of pleasure which they instil, impossible to describe, to recollect, to name; ineffable; – if our memory, like a labourer who toils at the laying down of firm foundations beneath the tumult of the waves, did not, by fashioning for us facsimiles of those fugitive phrases, enable us to compare and to contrast them with those that follow. And so, hardly had the delicious sensation, which Swann had experienced, died away, before his memory had furnished him with an immediate transcript, summary, it is true, and provisional, but one on which he had kept his eyes fixed while the playing continued, so effectively that, when the same impression suddenly returned, it was no longer uncapturable. He was able to picture to himself its extent, its symmetrical arrangement, its notation, the strength of its expression; he had before him that definite object which was no longer pure music, but rather design, architecture, thought, and which allowed the actual music to be recalled. This time he had distinguished, quite clearly, a phrase which emerged for a few moments from the waves of sound. It had at once held out to him an invitation to partake of intimate pleasures, of whose existence, before hearing it, he had never dreamed, into which he felt that nothing but this phrase could initiate him; and he had been filled with love for it, as with a new and strange desire.

With a slow and rhythmical movement it led him here, there, everywhere, towards a state of happiness noble, unintelligible, yet clearly indicated. And then, suddenly, having reached a certain point from which he was prepared to follow it, after pausing for a moment, abruptly it changed its direction, and in a fresh movement, more rapid, multiform, melancholy, incessant, sweet, it bore him off with it towards a vista of joys unknown. Then it vanished. He hoped, with a passionate longing, that he might find it again, a third time. And reappear it did, though without speaking to him more clearly, bringing him, indeed, a pleasure less profound. But when he was once more at home he needed it, he was like a man into whose life a woman, whom he has seen for a moment passing by, has brought a new form of beauty, which strengthens and enlarges his own power of perception, without his knowing even whether he is ever to see her again whom he loves already, although he knows nothing of her, not even her name.

Indeed this passion for a phrase of music seemed, in the first few months, to be bringing into Swann's life the possibility of a sort of rejuvenation. He had so long since ceased to direct his course towards any ideal goal, and had confined himself to the pursuit of ephemeral satisfactions, that he had come to believe, though without ever formally stating his belief even to himself, that he would remain all his life in that condition, which death alone could alter. More than this, since his mind no longer entertained any lofty ideals, he had ceased to believe in (although he could not have expressly denied) their reality. He had grown also into the habit of taking refuge in trivial considerations, which allowed him to set on one side matters of fundamental importance. Just as he had never stopped to ask himself whether he would not have done better by not going into society, knowing very well that if he had accepted an invitation he must put in an appearance, and that afterwards, if he did not actually call, he must at least leave

cards upon his hostess; so in his conversation he took care
never to express with any warmth a personal opinion about a
thing, but instead would supply facts and details which had a
value of a sort in themselves, and excused him from showing
how much he really knew. He would be extremely precise
about the recipe for a dish, the dates of a painter's birth and
death, and the titles of his works. Sometimes, in spite of himself, he would let himself go so far as to utter a criticism of a
work of art, or of someone's interpretation of life, but then
he would cloak his words in a tone of irony, as though he did
not altogether associate himself with what he was saying. But
now, like a confirmed invalid whom, all of a sudden, a change
of air and surroundings, or a new course of treatment, or, as
sometimes happens, an organic change in himself, spontaneous
and unaccountable, seems to have so far recovered from his
malady that he begins to envisage the possibility, hitherto
beyond all hope, of starting to lead – and better late than never
– a wholly different life, Swann found in himself, in the
memory of the phrase that he had heard, in certain other
sonatas which he had made people play over to him, to see
whether he might not, perhaps, discover his phrase among
them, the presence of one of those invisible realities in which
he had ceased to believe, but to which, as though the music
had had upon the moral barrenness from which he was suffering a sort of recreative influence, he was conscious once again
of a desire, almost, indeed, of the power to consecrate his life.
But, never having managed to find out whose work it was
that he had heard played that evening, he had been unable to
procure a copy, and finally had forgotten the quest. He had
indeed, in the course of the next few days, encountered several
of the people who had been at the party with him, and had
questioned them; but most of them had either arrived after or
left before the piece was played; some had indeed been in the
house, but had gone into another room to talk, and those who
had stayed to listen had no clearer impression than the rest.
As for his hosts, they knew that it was a recently published
work which the musicians whom they had engaged for the
evening had asked to be allowed to play; but, as these last

were now on tour somewhere, Swann could learn nothing further. He had, of course, a number of musical friends, but, vividly as he could recall the exquisite and inexpressible pleasure which the little phrase had given him, and could see, still, before his eyes the forms that it had traced in outline, he was quite incapable of humming over to them the air. And so, at last, he ceased to think of it.

But to-night, at Mme Verdurin's, scarcely had the little pianist begun to play when, suddenly, after a high note held on through two whole bars, Swann saw it approaching, stealing forth from underneath that resonance, which was prolonged and stretched out over it, like a curtain of sound, to veil the mystery of its birth – and recognized, secret, whispering, articulate, the airy and fragrant phrase that he had loved. And it was so peculiarly itself, it had so personal a charm, which nothing else could have replaced, that Swann felt as though he had met, in a friend's drawing-room, a woman whom he had seen and admired, once, in the street, and had despaired of ever seeing again. Finally the phrase withdrew and vanished, pointing, directing, diligent among the wandering currents of its fragrance, leaving upon Swann's features a reflexion of its smile. But now, at last, he could ask the name of his fair unknown (and was told that it was the *andante* movement of Vinteuil's sonata for the piano and violin), he held it safe, could have it again to himself, at home, as often as he would, could study its language and acquire its secret.

And so, when the pianist had finished, Swann crossed the room and thanked him with a vivacity which delighted Mme Verdurin.

'Isn't he charming?' she asked Swann, 'doesn't he just understand it, his sonata, the little wretch? You never dreamed, did you, that a piano could be made to express all that? Upon my word, there's everything in it except the piano! I'm caught out every time I hear it; I think I'm listening to an orchestra. Though it's better, really, than an orchestra, more complete.'

The young pianist bent over her as he answered, smiling

and underlining each of his words as though he were making an epigram: 'You are most generous to me.'

And while Mme Verdurin was saying to her husband, 'Run and fetch him a glass of orangeade; it's well earned!' Swann began to tell Odette how he had fallen in love with that little phrase. When their hostess, who was a little way off, called out, 'Well! It looks to me as though someone was saying nice things to you, Odette!' she replied, 'Yes, very nice,' and he found her simplicity delightful. Then he asked for some information about this Vinteuil; what else he had done, and at what period in his life he had composed the sonata; – what meaning the little phrase could have had for him, that was what Swann wanted most to know.

But none of these people who professed to admire this musician (when Swann had said that the sonata was really charming Mme Verdurin had exclaimed, 'I quite believe it! Charming, indeed! But you don't dare to confess that you don't know Vinteuil's sonata; you have no right not to know it!' – and the painter had gone on with, 'Ah, yes, it's a very fine bit of work, isn't it? Not, of course, if you want something "obvious", something "popular", but, I mean to say, it makes a very great impression on us artists'), none of them seemed ever to have asked himself these questions, for none of them was able to reply.

Even to one or two particular remarks made by Swann on his favourite phrase, 'D'you know, that's a funny thing; I had never noticed it; I may as well tell you that I don't much care about peering at things through a microscope, and pricking myself on pin-points of difference; no; we don't waste time splitting hairs in this house; why not? well, it's not a habit of ours, that's all,' Mme Verdurin replied, while Dr Cottard gazed at her with open-mouthed admiration, and yearned to be able to follow her as she skipped lightly from one stepping-stone to another of her stock of ready-made phrases. Both he, however, and Mme Cottard, with a kind of common sense which is shared by many people of humble origin, would always take care not to express an opinion, or to pretend to admire a piece of music which they would confess to each other, once they were safely at home, that they no more understood than they could understand the art of 'Master' Biche. Inasmuch as the public cannot recognize the charm, the beauty, even the outlines of nature save in the stereotyped impressions of an art which they have gradually assimilated, while an original artist starts by rejecting those impressions, so M. and Mme Cottard, typical, in this respect, of the public, were incapable of finding, either in Vinteuil's sonata or in Biche's portraits, what constituted harmony, for them, in music or beauty in painting. It appeared to them, when the pianist played his sonata, as though he were striking haphazard from the piano a medley of notes which bore no relation to the musical forms to which they themselves were accustomed, and that the painter simply flung the colours haphazard upon his canvas. When, on one of these, they were able to distinguish a human form, they always found it coarsened and vulgarized (that is to say lacking all the elegance of the school of painting through whose spectacles they themselves were in the habit of seeing the people – real, living people, who passed them in the streets) and devoid of truth, as though M. Biche had not known how the human shoulder was constructed, or that a woman's hair was not, ordinarily, purple.

And yet, when the 'faithful' were scattered out of earshot, the Doctor felt that the opportunity was too good to be missed, and so (while Mme Verdurin was adding a final word of commendation of Vinteuil's sonata) like a would-be swimmer who jumps into the water, so as to learn, but chooses a moment when there are not too many people looking on: 'Yes, indeed; he's what they call a musician *di primo cartello!*' he exclaimed, with sudden determination.

Swann discovered no more than that the recent publication of Vinteuil's sonata had caused a great stir among the most advanced school of musicians, but that it was still unknown to the general public.

'I know someone, quite well, called Vinteuil,' said Swann, thinking of the old music-master at Combray who had taught my grandmother's sisters.

'Perhaps that's the man!' cried Mme Verdurin.

'Oh, no!' Swann burst out laughing. 'If you had ever seen him for a moment you wouldn't put the question.'

'Then to put the question is to solve the problem?' the Doctor suggested.

'But it may well be some relative;' Swann went on. 'That would be bad enough; but, after all, there is no reason why a genius shouldn't have a cousin who is a silly old fool. And if that should be so, I swear there's no known or unknown form of torture I wouldn't undergo to get the old fool to introduce me to the man who composed the sonata; starting with the torture of the old fool's company, which would be ghastly.'

The painter understood that Vinteuil was seriously ill at the moment, and that Dr Potain despaired of his life.

'What!' cried Mme Verdurin, 'Do people still call in Potain?'

'Ah! Mme Verdurin,' Cottard simpered, 'you forget that you are speaking of one of my colleagues – I should say, one of my masters.'

The painter had heard, somewhere, that Vinteuil was threatened with the loss of his reason. And he insisted that signs of this could be detected in certain passages in the sonata. This remark did not strike Swann as ridiculous; rather, it puzzled him. For, since a purely musical work contains none of those logical sequences, the interruption or confusion of which, in spoken or written language, is a proof of insanity, so insanity diagnosed in a sonata seemed to him as mysterious a thing as the insanity of a dog or a horse, although instances may be observed of these.

'Don't speak to me about "your masters"; you know ten times as much as he does!' Mme Verdurin answered Dr Cottard, in the tone of a woman who has the courage of her convictions, and is quite ready to stand up to anyone who disagrees with her. 'Anyhow, you don't kill your patients!'

'But, Madame, he is in the Academy.' The Doctor smiled with bitter irony. 'If a sick person prefers to die at the hands of one of the Princes of Science . . . It is far more smart to be able to say, "Yes, I have Potain."'

'Oh, indeed! More smart, is it?' said Mme Verdurin. 'So

there are fashions, nowadays, in illness, are there? I didn't know that ... Oh, you do make me laugh!' she screamed, suddenly, burying her face in her hands. 'And here was I, poor thing, talking quite seriously, and never seeing that you were pulling my leg.'

As for M. Verdurin, finding it rather a strain to start laughing again over so small a matter, he was content with puffing out a cloud of smoke from his pipe, while he reflected sadly that he could never again hope to keep pace with his wife in her Atalanta-flights across the field of mirth.

'D'you know, we like your friend so very much,' said Mme Verdurin, later, when Odette was bidding her good night. 'He is so unaffected, quite charming. If they're all like that, the friends you want to bring here, by all means bring them.'

M. Verdurin remarked that Swann had failed, all the same, to appreciate the pianist's aunt.

'I dare say he felt a little strange, poor man,' suggested Mme Verdurin. 'You can't expect him to catch the tone of the house the first time he comes; like Cottard, who has been one of our little "clan" now for years. The first time doesn't count; it's just for looking round and finding out things. Odette, he understands all right, he's to join us to-morrow at the Châtelet. Perhaps you might call for him and bring him.'

'No, he doesn't want that.'

'Oh, very well; just as you like. Provided he doesn't fail us at the last moment.'

Greatly to Mme Verdurin's surprise, he never failed them. He would go to meet them, no matter where, at restaurants outside Paris (not that they went there much at first, for the season had not yet begun), and more frequently at the play, in which Mme Verdurin delighted. One evening, when they were dining at home, he heard her complain that she had not one of those permits which would save her the trouble of waiting at doors and standing in crowds, and say how useful it would be to them at first nights, and gala performances at the Opera, and what a nuisance it had been, not having one, on the day of Gambetta's funeral. Swann never spoke of his distinguished friends, but only of such as might be regarded as detrimental, whom, therefore, he thought it snobbish, and in not very good taste to conceal; while he frequented the Faubourg Saint-Germain he had come to include, in the latter class, all his friends in the official world of the Third Republic, and so broke in, without thinking: 'I'll see to that, all right. You shall have it in time for the *Danicheff* revival. I shall be lunching with the Prefect of Police to-morrow, as it happens, at the Élysée.'

'What's that? The Élysée?' Dr Cottard roared in a voice of thunder.

'Yes, at M. Grévy's,' replied Swann, feeling a little awkward at the effect which his announcement had produced.

'Are you often taken like that?' the painter asked Cottard, with mock-seriousness.

As a rule, once an explanation had been given, Cottard would say: 'Ah, good, good; that's all right, then,' after which he would show not the least trace of emotion. But this time Swann's last words, instead of the usual calming effect, had that of heating, instantly, to boiling point his astonishment at the discovery that a man with whom he himself was actually sitting at table, a man who had no official position, no honours or distinction of any sort, was on visiting terms with the Head of the State.

'What's that you say? M. Grévy? Do you know M. Grévy?' he demanded of Swann, in the stupid and incredulous tone of a constable on duty at the palace, when a stranger has come up and asked to see the President of the Republic; until, guessing from his words and manner what, as the newspapers say, 'it is a case of', he assures the poor lunatic that he will be admitted at once, and points the way to the reception ward of the police infirmary.

'I know him slightly; we have some friends in common' (Swann dared not add that one of these friends was the Prince of Wales). 'Anyhow, he is very free with his invitations, and, I assure you, his luncheon-parties are not the least bit amusing; they're very simple affairs, too, you know; never more than eight at table,' he went on, trying desperately to cut out everything that seemed to show off his relations with the President in a light too dazzling for the Doctor's eyes.

Whereupon Cottard, at once conforming in his mind to the literal interpretation of what Swann was saying, decided that invitations from M. Grévy were very little sought after, were sent out, in fact, into the highways and hedgerows. And from that moment he never seemed at all surprised to hear that Swann, or anyone else, was 'always at the Élysée'; he even felt a little sorry for a man who had to go to luncheon-parties which, he himself admitted, were a bore.

'Ah, good, good; that's quite all right, then,' he said, in the tone of a customs official who has been suspicious up to now, but, after hearing your explanations, stamps your passport and lets you proceed on your journey without troubling to examine your luggage.

'I can well believe you don't find them amusing, those parties; indeed, it's very good of you to go to them!' said Mme Verdurin, who regarded the President of the Republic only as a 'bore' to be especially dreaded, since he had at his disposal means of seduction, and even of compulsion, which, if employed to captivate her 'faithful', might easily make them 'fail'. 'It seems, he's as deaf as a post; and eats with his fingers.'

'Upon my word! Then it can't be much fun for you, going there.' A note of pity sounded in the Doctor's voice; and then struck by the number – only eight at table – 'Are these luncheons what you would describe as "intimate"?' he inquired briskly, not so much out of idle curiosity as in his linguistic zeal.

But so great and glorious a figure was the President of the French Republic in the eyes of Dr Cottard that neither the modesty of Swann nor the spite of Mme Verdurin could ever wholly efface that first impression, and he never sat down to dinner with the Verdurins without asking anxiously. 'D'you think we shall see M. Swann here this evening? He is a personal friend of M. Grévy's. I suppose that means he's what you'd call a "gentleman"?' He even went to the length of offering Swann a card of invitation to the Dental Exhibition.

'This will let you in, and anyone you take with you,' he explained, 'but dogs are not admitted. I'm just warning you, you understand, because some friends of mine went there once, who hadn't been told, and there was the devil to pay.'

As for M. Verdurin, he did not fail to observe the distressing effect upon his wife of the discovery that Swann had influential friends of whom he had never spoken.

If no arrangements had been made to 'go anywhere', it was at the Verdurins' that Swann would find the 'little nucleus' assembled, but he never appeared there except in the evenings, and would hardly ever accept their invitations to dinner, in spite of Odette's entreaties.

'I could dine with you alone somewhere, if you'd rather,' she suggested.

'But what about Mme Verdurin?'

'Oh, that's quite simple. I need only say that my dress wasn't ready, or that my cab came late. There is always some excuse.'

'How charming of you.'

But Swann said to himself that, if he could make Odette feel (by consenting to meet her only after dinner) that there were other pleasures which he preferred to that of her company, then the desire that she felt for his would be all the longer in reaching the point of satiety. Besides, as he infinitely preferred to Odette's style of beauty that of a little working girl, as fresh and plump as a rose, with whom he happened to be simultaneously in love, he preferred to spend the first part of the evening with her, knowing that he was sure to see Odette later on. For the same reason, he would never allow Odette to call for him at his house, to take him on to the Verdurins'. The little girl used to wait, not far from his door, at a street corner; Rémi, his coachman, knew where to stop; she would jump in beside him, and hold him in her arms until the carriage drew up at the Verdurins'. He would enter the drawing-room; and there, while Mme Verdurin, pointing to the roses which he had sent her that morning, said: 'I am furious with you!' and sent him to the place kept for him, by the side of Odette, the pianist would play to them – for their two selves, and for no one else – that little phrase by Vinteuil which was, so to speak, the national anthem of their love. He began, always, with a sustained *tremolo* from the violin part, which, for several bars, was unaccompanied, and filled all the foreground; until suddenly it seemed to be drawn aside, and – just as in those interiors by Pieter de Hooch, where the subject is set back a long way through the narrow framework of a half-opened door – infinitely remote, in colour quite different, velvety with the radiance of some intervening light, the little phrase appeared, dancing, pastoral, interpolated, episodic, belonging to another world. It passed, with simple and immortal movements, scattering on every side the bounties of its grace, smiling ineffably still; but Swann thought that he could now discern in it some disenchantment. It seemed to be aware how vain, how hollow was the happiness to which it showed the way. In its airy grace there was, indeed, something definitely achieved, and complete in itself, like the mood of philosophic detachment which follows an outburst of vain regret. But little did that matter to him; he looked upon the sonata less in its own light – as what it might express, had, in fact, expressed to a certain musician, ignorant that any Swann or Odette, anywhere in the world, existed, when he composed it, and would express to all those who should hear it played in centuries to come – than as a pledge, a token of his love, which made even the Verdurins and their little pianist think of Odette and, at the same time, of himself – which bound her to him by a lasting tie; and at that point he had (whimsically entreated by Odette) abandoned the idea of getting some 'professional' to play over to him the whole sonata, of which he still knew no more than this one passage. 'Why do you want the rest?' she had asked him, 'Our little bit; that's all we need.' He went farther; agonized by the reflexion, at the moment when it passed by him, so near and yet so infinitely remote, that, while it was addressed to their ears, it knew them not, he would regret, almost, that it had a meaning of its own, an intrinsic and unalterable beauty, foreign to themselves, just as in the jewels given to us, or even in the letters written to us by a woman with whom we are in love, we find fault with the 'water' of a stone, or with the words of a sentence because they are not fashioned exclusively from the spirit of a fleeting intimacy and of a 'lass unparallel'd'.

It would happen, as often as not, that he had stayed so long outside, with his little girl, before going to the Verdurins' that, as soon as the little phrase had been rendered by the pianist, Swann would discover that it was almost time for Odette to go home. He used to take her back as far as the door of her little house in the Rue La Pérouse, behind the Arc de Triomphe. And it was perhaps on this account, and so as not to demand the monopoly of her favours, that he sacrificed the pleasure (not so essential to his well-being) of seeing her earlier in the evening, of arriving with her at the Verdurins', to the exercise of this other privilege, for which she was grateful, of their leaving together; a privilege which he valued all the more because, thanks to it, he had the feeling that no one else would see her, no one would thrust himself between them, no one could prevent him from remaining with her in spirit, after he had left her for the night.

*

And so, night after night, she would be taken home in Swann's carriage; and one night, after she had got down, and while he stood at the gate and murmured 'Till to-morrow, then!' she turned impulsively from him, plucked a last lingering chrysanthemum in the tiny garden which flanked the pathway from the street to her house, and as he went back to his carriage thrust it into his hand. He held it pressed to his lips during the drive home, and when, in due course, the flower withered, locked it away, like something very precious, in a secret drawer of his desk.

He would escort her to her gate, but no farther. Twice only had he gone inside to take part in the ceremony – of such vital importance in her life – of 'afternoon tea'. The loneliness and emptiness of those short streets (consisting, almost entirely, of low-roofed houses, self-contained but not detached, their monotony interrupted here and there by the dark intrusion of some sinister little shop, at once an historical document and a sordid survival from the days when the district was still one of ill repute), the snow which had lain on the garden-beds or clung to the branches of the trees, the careless disarray of the season, the assertion, in this man-made city, of a state of nature, had all combined to add an element of mystery to the warmth, the flowers, the luxury which he had found inside.

Passing by (on his left-hand side, and on what, although raised some way above the street, was the ground floor of the house) Odette's bedroom, which looked out to the back over another little street running parallel with her own, he had climbed a staircase that went straight up between dark painted walls, from which hung Oriental draperies, strings of Turkish beads, and a huge Japanese lantern, suspended by a silken cord from the ceiling (which last, however, so that her visitors should not have to complain of the want of any of the latest comforts of Western civilization, was lighted by a gas-jet inside), to the drawing-rooms, large and small. These were entered through a narrow lobby, the wall of which, chequered with the lozenges of a wooden trellis such as you see on garden walls, only gilded, was lined from end to end by a long rectangular box in which bloomed, as though in a hothouse, a row of large chrysanthemums, at that time still uncommon, though by no means so large as the mammoth blossoms which horticulturists have since succeeded in making grow. Swann was irritated, as a rule, by the sight of these flowers, which had then been 'the rage' in Paris for about a year, but it had pleased him, on this occasion, to see the gloom of the little lobby shot with rays of pink and gold and white by the fragrant petals of these ephemeral stars, which kindle their cold fires in the murky atmosphere of winter afternoons. Odette had received him in a tea-gown of pink silk, which left her neck and arms bare. She had made him sit down beside her in one of the many mysterious little retreats which had been contrived in the various recesses of the room, sheltered by enormous palm-trees growing out of pots of Chinese porcelain, or by screens upon which were fastened photographs and fans and bows of ribbon. She had said at once, 'You're not comfortable there; wait a minute, I'll arrange things for you,' and with a titter of laughter, the complacency of which implied that some little invention of her own was being brought into play, she had installed behind his head and beneath his feet great cushions of Japanese silk, which she pummelled and buffeted as though determined to lavish on him all her riches, and regardless of their value. But when her footman began to come into the room, bringing, one after another, the innumerable lamps which (contained, mostly, in porcelain vases) burned singly or in pairs upon the different pieces of furniture as upon so many altars, rekindling in the twilight, already almost nocturnal, of this winter afternoon, the glow of a sunset more lasting, more roseate, more human – filling, perhaps, with romantic wonder the thoughts of some solitary lover, wandering in the street below and brought to a standstill before the mystery of the human presence which those lighted windows at once revealed and screened from sight – she had kept an eye sharply fixed on the servant, to see whether he set each of the lamps down in the place appointed it. She felt that, if he were to put even one of them where it ought not to be, the general effect of her drawing-room would be destroyed, and that her portrait, which rested upon a sloping easel draped with plush, would not catch the light. And so, with feverish impatience, she followed the man's clumsy movements, scolding him severely when he passed too close to a pair of beaupots, which she made a point of always tidying herself, in case the plants should be knocked over – and went across to them now to make sure that he had not broken off any of the flowers. She found something 'quaint' in the shape of each of her Chinese ornaments, and also in her orchids, the cattleyas especially (these being, with chrysanthemums, her favourite flowers), because they had the supreme merit of not looking in the least like other flowers, but of being made, apparently, out of scraps of silk or satin. 'It looks just as though it had been cut out of the lining of my cloak,' she said to Swann, pointing to an orchid, with a shade of respect in her voice for so 'smart' a flower, for this distinguished, unexpected sister whom nature had suddenly bestowed upon her, so far removed from her in the scale of existence, and yet so delicate, so refined, so much more worthy than many real women of admission to her drawing-room. As she drew his attention, now to the fiery-tongued dragons painted upon a bowl or stitched upon a fire-screen, now to a fleshy cluster of orchids, now to a dromedary of inlaid silver-work with ruby eyes, which kept company, upon her mantelpiece, with a toad carved in jade, she would pretend now to be shrinking from the ferocity of the monsters or laughing at their absurdity, now blushing at the indecency of the flowers, now carried away by an irresistible desire to run across and kiss the toad and dromedary, calling them 'darlings'. And these affectations were in sharp contrast to the sincerity of some of her attitudes, notably her devotion to Our Lady of the Laghetto, who had once, when Odette was living at Nice, cured her of a mortal illness, and whose medal, in gold, she always carried on her person, attributing to it unlimited powers. She poured out Swann's tea, inquired 'Lemon or cream?' and, on his answering 'Cream, please,' went on, smiling, 'A cloud!' And as he pronounced it excellent, 'You see, I know just how you like it.' This tea had indeed seemed to Swann, just as it seemed to her, something precious, and love is so far obliged to find some justification for itself, some guarantee of its duration in pleasures which, on the contrary, would have no existence apart from love and must cease with its passing, that when he left her, at seven o'clock, to go and dress for the evening, all the way home, sitting bolt upright in his brougham, unable to repress the happiness with which the afternoon's adventure had filled him, he kept on repeating to himself: 'What fun it would be to have a little woman like that in a place where one could always be certain of finding, what one never can be certain of finding, a really good cup of tea.' An hour or so later he received a note from Odette, and at once recognized that florid handwriting, in which an affectation of British stiffness imposed an apparent discipline upon its shapeless characters, significant, perhaps, to less intimate eyes than his, of an untidiness of mind, a fragmentary education, a want of sincerity and decision. Swann had left his cigarette-case at her house. 'Why,' she wrote, 'did you not forget your heart also? I should never have let you have that back.'

More important, perhaps, was a second visit which he paid her, a little later. On his way to the house, as always when he knew that they were to meet, he formed a picture of her in his mind; and the necessity, if he was to find any beauty in her face, of fixing his eyes on the fresh and rosy protuberance of her cheekbones, and of shutting out all the rest of those cheeks which were so often languorous and sallow, except when they were punctuated with little fiery spots, plunged him in acute depression, as proving that one's ideal is always unattainable, and one's actual happiness mediocre. He was taking her an engraving which she had asked to see. She was not very well; she received him, wearing a wrapper of mauve *crêpe de Chine*, which draped her bosom, like a mantle, with a richly embroidered web. As she stood there beside him, brushing his cheek with the loosened tresses of her hair, bending one knee in what was almost a dancer's pose, so that she could lean without tiring herself over the picture, at which she was gazing, with bended head, out of those great eyes, which seemed so weary and so sullen when there was nothing to animate her, Swann was struck by her resemblance to the figure of Zipporah, Jethro's Daughter, which is to be seen in one of the Sistine frescoes. He had always found a peculiar fascination in tracing in the paintings of the Old Masters, not merely the general characteristics of the people whom he encountered in his daily life, but rather what seems least susceptible of generalization, the individual features of men and women whom he knew, as, for instance, in a bust of the Doge Loredan by Antonio Rizzo, the prominent cheekbones, the slanting eyebrows, in short, a speaking likeness to his own coachman Rémi; in the colouring of a Ghirlandaio, the nose of M. de Palancy; in a portrait by Tintoretto, the invasion of the plumpness of the cheek by an outcrop of whiskers, the broken nose, the penetrating stare, the swollen eyelids of Dr du Boulbon. Perhaps because he had always regretted, in his heart, that he had confined his attention to the social side of life, had talked, always, rather than acted, he felt that he might find a sort of indulgence bestowed upon him by those great artists, in his perception of the fact that they also had regarded with pleasure and had admitted into the canon of their works such types of physiognomy as give those works the strongest possible certificate of reality and trueness to life; a modern, almost a topical savour; perhaps, also, he had so far succumbed to the prevailing frivolity of the world of fashion that he felt the necessity of finding in an old masterpiece some such obvious and refreshing allusion to a person about whom jokes could be made and repeated and enjoyed to-day. Perhaps, on the other hand, he had retained enough of the artistic temperament to be able to find a genuine satisfaction in watching these individual features take on a more general significance when he saw them, uprooted and disembodied, in the abstract idea of similarity between an historic portrait and a modern original, whom it was not intended to represent. However that might be, and perhaps because the abundance of impressions which he, for some time past, had been receiving – though, indeed, they had come to him rather through the channel of his appreciation of music – had enriched his appetite for painting as well, it was with an unusual intensity of pleasure, a pleasure destined to have a lasting effect upon his character and conduct, that Swann remarked Odette's resemblance to the Zipporah of that Alessandro di Mariano, to whom one shrinks from giving his more popular surname, now that 'Botticelli' suggests not so much the actual work of the Master as that false and banal conception of it which has of late obtained common currency. He no longer based his estimate of the merit of Odette's face on the more or less good quality of her cheeks, and the softness and sweetness – as of carnation-petals – which, he supposed, would greet his lips there, should he ever hazard an embrace, but regarded it rather as a skein of subtle and lovely silken threads, which his gazing eyes collected and wound together, following the

curving line from the skein to the ball, where he mingled the
cadence of her neck with the spring of her hair and the droop
of her eyelids, as though from a portrait of herself, in which
her type was made clearly intelligible.

He stood gazing at her; traces of the old fresco were
apparent in her face and limbs, and these he tried incessantly,
afterwards, to recapture, both when he was with Odette, and
when he was only thinking of her in her absence; and, albeit
his admiration for the Florentine masterpiece was probably
based upon his discovery that it had been reproduced in her,
the similarity enhanced her beauty also, and rendered her
more precious in his sight. Swann reproached himself with
his failure, hitherto, to estimate at her true worth a creature
whom the great Sandro would have adored, and counted himself fortunate that his pleasure in the contemplation of Odette
found a justification in his own system of aesthetic. He told
himself that, in choosing the thought of Odette as the inspiration of his dreams of ideal happiness, he was not, as he had
until then supposed, falling back, merely, upon an expedient
of doubtful and certainly inadequate value, since she contained
in herself what satisfied the utmost refinement of his taste in
art. He failed to observe that this quality would not naturally
avail to bring Odette into the category of women whom he
found desirable, simply because his desires had always run
counter to his aesthetic taste. The words 'Florentine painting'
were invaluable to Swann. They enabled him (gave him, as it
were, a legal title) to introduce the image of Odette into a
world of dreams and fancies which, until then, she had been
debarred from entering, and where she assumed a new and
nobler form. And whereas the mere sight of her in the flesh,
by perpetually reviving his misgivings as to the quality of her
face, her figure, the whole of her beauty, used to cool the
ardour of his love, those misgivings were swept away and that
love confirmed now that he could re-erect his estimate of her
on the sure foundations of his aesthetic principles; while the
kiss, the bodily surrender which would have seemed natural
and but moderately attractive, had they been granted him by a
creature of somewhat withered flesh and sluggish blood,

coming, as now they came, to crown his adoration of a master-piece in a gallery, must, it seemed, prove as exquisite as they would be supernatural.

And when he was tempted to regret that, for months past, he had done nothing but visit Odette, he would assure himself that he was not unreasonable in giving up much of his time to the study of an inestimably precious work of art, cast for once in a new, a different, an especially charming metal, in an unmatched exemplar which he would contemplate at one moment with the humble, spiritual, disinterested mind of an artist, at another with the pride, the selfishness, the sensual thrill of a collector.

On his study table, at which he worked, he had placed, as it were a photograph of Odette, a reproduction of Jethro's Daughter. He would gaze in admiration at the large eyes, the delicate features in which the imperfection of her skin might be surmised, the marvellous locks of hair that fell along her tired cheeks; and, adapting what he had already felt to be beautiful, on aesthetic grounds, to the idea of a living woman, he converted it into a series of physical merits which he con-gratulated himself on finding assembled in the person of one whom he might, ultimately, possess. The vague feeling of sympathy which attracts a spectator to a work of art, now that he knew the type, in warm flesh and blood, of Jethro's Daughter, became a desire which more than compensated, thenceforward, for that with which Odette's physical charms had at first failed to inspire him. When he had sat for a long time gazing at the Botticelli, he would think of his own living Botticelli, who seemed all the livelier in contrast, and as he drew towards him the photograph of Zipporah he would imagine that he was holding Odette against his heart.

It was not only Odette's indifference, however, that he must take pains to circumvent; it was also, not infrequently, his own; feeling that, since Odette had had every facility for seeing him, she seemed no longer to have very much to say to him when they did meet, he was afraid lest the manner – at once trivial, monotous, and seemingly unalterable – which she now adopted when they were together should ultimately destroy in him that romantic hope, that a day might come when she would make avowal of her passion, by which hope alone he had become and would remain her lover. And so to alter, to give a fresh moral aspect to that Odette, of whose unchanging mood he was afraid of growing weary, he wrote, suddenly, a letter full of hinted discoveries and feigned indignation, which he sent off so that it should reach her before dinner-time. He knew that she would be frightened, and that she would reply, and he hoped that, when the fear of losing him clutched at her heart, it would force from her words such as he had never yet heard her utter: and he was right – by repeating this device he had won from her the most affectionate letters that she had, so far, written him, one of them (which she had sent to him at midday by a special messenger from the Maison Dorée – it was the day of the Paris-Murcie Fête given for the victims of the recent floods in Murcia) beginning 'My dear, my hand trembles so that I can scarcely write –'; and these letters he had kept in the same drawer as the withered chrysanthemum. Or else, if she had not had time to write, when he arrived at the Verdurins' she would come running up to him with an 'I've something to say to you!' and he would gaze curiously at the revelation in her face and speech of what she had hitherto kept concealed from him of her heart.

Even as he drew near to the Verdurins' door, and caught sight of the great lamp-lit spaces of the drawing-room windows, whose shutters were never closed, he would begin to melt at the thought of the charming creature whom he would see, as he entered the room, basking in that golden light. Here and there the figures of the guests stood out, sharp and black, between lamp and window, shutting off the light, like those little pictures which one sees sometimes pasted here and there upon a glass screen, whose other panes are mere transparencies. He would try to make out Odette. And then, when he was once inside, without thinking, his eyes sparkled suddenly with such radiant happiness that M. Verdurin said to the painter: 'Hm. Seems to be getting warm.' Indeed, her presence gave the house what none other of the houses that he visited seemed to possess; a sort of tactual sense, a nervous system which ramified into each of its rooms and sent a constant stimulus to his heart.

And so the simple and regular manifestations of a social organism, namely the 'little clan', were transformed for Swann into a series of daily encounters with Odette, and enabled him to feign indifference to the prospect of seeing her, or even a desire not to see her; in doing which he incurred no very great risk since, even although he had written to her during the day, he would of necessity see her in the evening and accompany her home.

But one evening, when, irritated by the thought of that inevitable dark drive together, he had taken his other 'little girl' all the way to the Bois, so as to delay as long as possible the moment of his appearance at the Verdurins', he was so late in reaching them that Odette, supposing that he did not intend to come, had already left. Seeing the room bare of her, Swann felt his heart wrung by sudden anguish; he shook with the sense that he was being deprived of a pleasure whose intensity he began then for the first time to estimate, having always, hitherto, had that certainty of finding it whenever he would, which (as in the case of all our pleasures) reduced, if it did not altogether blind him to its dimensions.

'Did you notice the face he pulled when he saw that she wasn't here?' M. Verdurin asked his wife. 'I think we may say that he's hooked.'

'The face he pulled?' exploded Dr Cottard who, having left the house for a moment to visit a patient, had just returned to fetch his wife and did not know whom they were discussing.

'D'you mean to say you didn't meet him on the doorstep – the loveliest of Swanns?'

'No. M. Swann has been here?'

'Just for a moment. We had a glimpse of a Swann tremendously agitated. In a state of nerves. You see, Odette had left.'

'You mean to say that she has gone the "whole hog" with him; that she has "burned her boats"?' inquired the Doctor cautiously, testing the meaning of his phrases.

'Why, of course not; there's absolutely nothing in it; in fact, between you and me, I think she's making a great mistake, and behaving like a silly little fool, which she is, incidentally.'

'Come, come, come!' said M. Verdurin, 'How on earth do you know that there's "nothing in it"? We haven't been there to see, have we now?'

'She would have told me,' answered Mme Verdurin with dignity. 'I may say that she tells me everything. As she has no one else at present, I told her that she ought to live with him. She makes out that she can't; she admits, she was immensely attracted by him, at first; but he's always shy with her, and that makes her shy with him. Besides, she doesn't care for him in that way, she says; it's an ideal love, "Platonic", you know; she's afraid of rubbing the bloom off – oh, I don't know half the things she says, how should I? And yet he's exactly the sort of man she wants.'

'I beg to differ from you,' M. Verdurin courteously interrupted. 'I am only half satisfied with the gentleman. I feel that he "poses".'

Mme Verdurin's whole body stiffened, her eyes stared blankly as though she had suddenly been turned into a statue; a device by means of which she might be supposed not to have caught the sound of that unutterable word which seemed to imply that it was possible for people to 'pose' in her house, and, therefore, that there were people in the world who 'mattered more' than herself.

'Anyhow, if there is nothing in it, I don't suppose it's because our friend believes in her virtue. And yet, you never know; he seems to believe in her intelligence. I don't know whether you heard the way he lectured her the other evening about Vinteuil's sonata. I am devoted to Odette, but really – to expound theories of aesthetic to her – the man must be a prize idiot.'

'Look here, I won't have you saying nasty things about Odette,' broke in Mme Verdurin in her 'spoiled child' manner. 'She is charming.'

'There's no reason why she shouldn't be charming; we are

not saying anything nasty about her, only that she is not the embodiment of either virtue or intellect. After all,' he turned to the painter, 'does it matter so very much whether she is virtuous or not? You can't tell; she might be a great deal less charming if she were.'

On the landing Swann had run into the Verdurins' butler, who had been somewhere else a moment earlier, when he arrived, and who had been asked by Odette to tell Swann (but that was at least an hour ago) that she would probably stop to drink a cup of chocolate at Prévost's on her way home. Swann set off at once for Prévost's, but every few yards his carriage was held up by others, or by people crossing the street, loathsome obstacles each of which he would gladly have crushed beneath his wheels, were it not that a policeman fumbling with a note-book would delay him even longer than the actual passage of the pedestrian. He counted the minutes feverishly, adding a few seconds to each so as to be quite certain that he had not given himself short measure, and so, possibly, exaggerated whatever chance there might actually be of his arriving at Prévost's in time, and of finding her still there. And then, in a moment of illumination, like a man in a fever who awakes from sleep and is conscious of the absurdity of the dream-shapes among which his mind has been wandering without any clear distinction between himself and them, Swann suddenly perceived how foreign to his nature were the thoughts which he had been revolving in his mind ever since he had heard at the Verdurins' that Odette had left, how novel the heartache from which he was suffering, but of which he was only now conscious, as though he had just woken up. What! all this disturbance simply because he would not see Odette, now, till to-morrow, exactly what he had been hoping, not an hour before, as he drove towards Mme Verdurin's. He was obliged to admit also that now, as he sat in the same carriage and drove to Prévost's, he was no longer the same man, was no longer alone even – but that a new personality was there beside him, adhering to him, amalgamated with him, a creature from whom he might, perhaps, be unable to liberate himself, towards whom he might have to adopt some such stratagem as one uses to outwit a master or a malady. And yet, during this last moment in which he had felt that another, a fresh personality was thus conjoined with his own, life had seemed, somehow, more interesting.

It was in vain that he assured himself that this possible meeting at Prévost's (the tension of waiting for which so ravished, stripped so bare the intervening moments that he could find nothing, not one idea, not one memory in his mind beneath which his troubled spirit might take shelter and repose) would probably, after all, should it take place, be much the same as all their meetings, of no great importance. As on every other evening, once he was in Odette's company, once he had begun to cast furtive glances at her changing countenance, and instantly to withdraw his eyes lest she should read in them the first symbols of desire and believe no more in his indifference, he would cease to be able even to think of her, so busy would he be in the search for pretexts which would enable him not to leave her immediately, and to assure himself, without betraying his concern, that he would find her again, next evening, at the Verdurins'; pretexts, that is to say, which would enable him to prolong for the time being, and to renew for one day more the disappointment, the torturing deception that must always come to him with the vain presence of this woman, whom he might approach, yet never dared embrace.

She was not at Prévost's; he must search for her, then, in every restaurant upon the boulevards. To save time, while he went in one direction, he sent in the other his coachman Rémi (Rizzo's Doge Loredan) for whom he presently – after a fruitless search – found himself waiting at the spot where the carriage was to meet him. It did not appear, and Swann tantalized himself with alternate pictures of the approaching moment, as one in which Rémi would say to him: 'Sir, the lady is there,' or as one in which Rémi would say to him: 'Sir, the lady was not in any of the cafés.' And so he saw himself faced by the close of his evening – a thing uniform, and yet bifurcated by the intervening accident which would either put an end to his agony by discovering Odette, or would oblige him to abandon any hope of finding her that night, to accept the necessity of returning home without having seen her.

The coachman returned; but, as he drew up opposite him, Swann asked, not 'Did you find the lady?' but 'Remind me, to-morrow, to order in some more firewood. I am sure we must be running short.' Perhaps he had persuaded himself that, if Rémi had at last found Odette in some café, where she was waiting for him still, then his night of misery was already obliterated by the realization, begun already in his mind, of a night of joy, and that there was no need for him to hasten towards the attainment of a happiness already captured and held in a safe place, which would not escape his grasp again. But it was also by the force of inertia; there was in his soul that want of adaptability which can be seen in the bodies of certain people who, when the moment comes to avoid a collision, to snatch their clothes out of reach of a flame, or to perform any other such necessary movement, take their time (as the saying is), begin by remaining for a moment in their original position, as though seeking to find in it a starting-point, a source of strength and motion. And probably, if the coachman had interrupted him with, 'I have found the lady,' he would have answered, 'Oh, yes, of course; that's what I told you to do. I had quite forgotten,' and would have continued to discuss his supply of firewood, so as to hide from his servant the emotion that he had felt, and to give himself time to break away from the thraldom of his anxieties and abandon himself to pleasure.

The coachman came back, however, with the report that he could not find her anywhere, and added the advice, as an old and privileged servant, 'I think, sir, that all we can do now is to go home.'

But the air of indifference which Swann could so lightly assume when Rémi uttered his final, unalterable response, fell from him like a cast-off cloak when he saw Rémi attempt to make him abandon hope and retire from the quest.

'Certainly not!' he exclaimed. 'We must find the lady. It is most important. She would be extremely put out –

it's a business matter – and vexed with me if she didn't see me.'

'But I do not see how the lady can be vexed, sir,' answered Rémi, 'since it was she that went away without waiting for you, sir, and said she was going to Prévost's, and then wasn't there.'

Meanwhile the restaurants were closing, and their lights began to go out. Under the trees of the boulevards there were still a few people strolling to and fro, barely distinguishable in the gathering darkness. Now and then the ghost of a woman glided up to Swann, murmured a few words in his ear, asked him to take her home, and left him shuddering. Anxiously he explored every one of these vaguely seen shapes, as though among the phantoms of the dead, in the realms of darkness, he had been searching for a lost Eurydice.

Among all the methods by which love is brought into being, among all the agents which disseminate that blessed bane, there are few so efficacious as the great gust of agitation which, now and then, sweeps over the human spirit. For then the creature in whose company we are seeking amusement at the moment, her lot is cast, her fate and ours decided, that is the creature whom we shall henceforward love. It is not necessary that she should have pleased us, up till then, any more, or even as much as others. All that is necessary is that our taste for her should become exclusive. And that condition is fulfilled so soon as – in the moment when she has failed to meet us – for the pleasure which we were on the point of enjoying in her charming company is abruptly substituted an anxious torturing desire, whose object is the creature herself, an irrational, absurd desire, which the laws of civilized society make it possible to satisfy and difficult to assuage – the insensate, agonizing desire to posses her.

Swann made Rémi drive him to such restaurants as were still open; it was the sole hypothesis, now, of that happiness which he had contemplated so calmly; he no longer concealed his agitation, the price he set upon their meeting, and promised, in case of success, to reward his coachman, as though, by inspiring in him a will to triumph which would reinforce

his own, he could bring it to pass, by a miracle, that Odette –
assuming that she had long since gone home to bed, – might
yet be found seated in some restaurant on the boulevards.
He pursued the quest as far as the Maison Dorée, burst twice
into Tortoni's and, still without catching sight of her, was
emerging from the Café Anglais, striding with haggard gaze
towards his carriage, which was waiting for him at the corner
of the Boulevard des Italiens, when he collided with a person
coming in the opposite direction; it was Odette; she explained,
later, that there had been no room at Prévost's, that she had
gone, instead, to sup at the Maison Dorée, and had been
sitting there in an alcove where he must have overlooked her,
and that she was now looking for her carriage.

She had so little expected to see him that she started back
in alarm. As for him, he had ransacked the streets of Paris,
not that he supposed it possible that he should find her, but
because he would have suffered even more cruelly by aban-
doning the attempt. But now the joy (which, his reason had
never ceased to assure him, was not, that evening at least, to
be realized) was suddenly apparent, and more real than ever
before; for he himself had contributed nothing to it by
anticipating probabilities – it remained integral and external
to himself; there was no need for him to draw on his own
resources to endow it with truth – 'twas from itself that there
emanated, 'twas itself that projected towards him that truth
whose glorious rays melted and scattered like the cloud of a
dream the sense of loneliness which had lowered over him,
that truth upon which he had supported, nay founded, albeit
unconsciously, his vision of bliss. So will a traveller, who has
come down, on a day of glorious weather, to the Mediter-
ranean shore, and is doubtful whether they still exist, those
lands which he has left, let his eyes be dazzled, rather than
cast a backward glance, by the radiance streaming towards
him from the luminous and unfading azure at his feet.

He climbed after her into the carriage which she had kept
waiting, and ordered his own to follow.

She had in her hand a bunch of cattleyas, and Swann could
see, beneath the film of lace that covered her head, more of

the same flowers fastened to a swansdown plume. She was wearing, under her cloak, a flowing gown of black velvet, caught up on one side so as to reveal a large triangular patch of her white silk skirt, with an 'insertion', also of white silk, in the cleft of her low-necked bodice, in which were fastened a few more cattleyas. She had scarcely recovered from the shock which the sight of Swann had given her, when some obstacle made the horse start to one side. They were thrown forward from their seats; she uttered a cry, and fell back quivering and breathless.

'It's all right,' he assured her, 'don't be frightened.' And he slipped his arm round her shoulder, supporting her body against his own; then went on: 'Whatever you do, don't utter a word; just make a sign, yes or no, or you'll be out of breath again. You won't mind if I put the flowers straight on your bodice; the jolt has loosened them. I'm afraid of their dropping out; I'm just going to fasten them a little more securely.'

She was not used to being treated with so much formality by men, and smiled as she answered: 'No, not at all; I don't mind in the least.'

But he, chilled a little by her answer, perhaps, also, to bear out the pretence that he had been sincere in adopting the stratagem, or even because he was already beginning to believe that he had been, exclaimed: 'No, no; you mustn't speak. You will be out of breath again. You can easily answer in signs; I shall understand. Really and truly now, you don't mind my doing this? Look, there is a little – I think it must be pollen, spilt over your dress, – may I brush it off with my hand? That's not too hard; I'm not hurting you, am I? I'm tickling you, perhaps, a little; but I don't want to touch the velvet in case I rub it the wrong way. But, don't you see, I really had to fasten the flowers; they would have fallen out if I hadn't. Like that, now; if I just push them a little farther down ... Seriously, I'm not annoying you, am I? And if I just sniff them to see whether they've really lost all their scent? I don't believe I ever smelt any before; may I? Tell the truth, now.'

Still smiling, she shrugged her shoulders ever so slightly, as who should say, 'You're quite mad; you know very well that I like it.'

He slipped his other hand upwards along Odette's cheek; she fixed her eyes on him with that languishing and solemn air which marks the women of the old Florentine's paintings, in whose faces he had found the type of hers; swimming at the brink of her fringed lids, her brilliant eyes, large and finely drawn as theirs, seemed on the verge of breaking from her face and rolling down her cheeks like two great tears. She bent her neck, as all their necks may be seen to bend, in the pagan scenes as well as in the scriptural. And although her attitude was, doubtless, habitual and instinctive, one which she knew to be appropriate to such moments, and was careful not to forget to assume, she seemed to need all her strength to hold her face back, as though some invisible force were drawing it down towards Swann's. And Swann it was who, before she allowed her face, as though despite her efforts, to fall upon his lips, held it back for a moment longer, at a little distance, between his hands. He had intended to leave time for her mind to overtake her body's movements, to recognize the dream which she had so long cherished and to assist at its realization, like a mother invited as a spectator when a prize is given to the child whom she has reared and loves. Perhaps, moreover, Swann himself was fixing upon these features of an Odette not yet possessed, not even kissed by him, on whom he was looking now for the last time, that comprehensive gaze with which, on the day of his departure, a traveller strives to bear away with him in memory the view of a country to which he may never return.

But he was so shy in approaching her that, after this evening which had begun by his arranging her cattleyas and had ended in her complete surrender, whether from fear of chilling her, or from reluctance to appear, even retrospectively, to have lied, or perhaps because he lacked the audacity to formulate a more urgent requirement than this (which could always be repeated, since it had not annoyed her on the first occasion), he resorted to the same pretext on the following days. If she had any cattleyas pinned to her bodice, he would say: 'It is most unfortunate; the cattleyas don't need tucking in this evening; they've not been disturbed as they were the other night; I think, though, that this one isn't quite straight. May I see if they have more scent than the others?' Or else, if she had none: 'Oh! no cattleyas this evening; then there's nothing for me to arrange.' So that for some time there was no change from the procedure which he had followed on that first evening, when he had started by touching her throat, with his fingers first and then with his lips, but their caresses began invariably with this modest exploration. And long afterwards, when the arrangement (or, rather, the ritual pretence of an arrangement) of her cattleyas had quite fallen into desuetude, the metaphor 'Do a cattleya', transmuted into a simple verb which they would employ without a thought of its original meaning when they wished to refer to the act of physical possession (in which, paradoxically, the possessor possesses nothing), survived to commemorate in their vocabulary the long-forgotten custom from which it sprang. And yet possibly this particular manner of saying 'to make love' had not the precise significance of its synonyms. However disillusioned we may be about women, however we may regard the possession of even the most divergent types as an invariable and monotonous experience, every detail of which is known and can be described in advance, it still becomes a fresh and stimulating pleasure if the women concerned be – or be thought to be – so difficult as to oblige us to base our attack upon some unrehearsed incident in our relations with them, as was originally for Swann the arrangement of the cattleyas. He trembled as he hoped, that evening (but Odette, he told himself, if she were deceived by his stratagem, could not guess his intention), that it was the possession of this woman that would emerge for him from their large and richly coloured petals; and the pleasure which he already felt, and which Odette tolerated, he thought, perhaps only because she was not yet aware of it herself, seemed to him for that reason – as it might have seemed to the first man when he enjoyed it amid the flowers of the earthly paradise – a pleasure which had never before existed, which he was striving now to create, a pleasure – and the special name which he was to give to it preserved its identity – entirely individual and new.

The ice once broken, every evening, when he had taken her home, he must follow her into the house; and often she would come out again in her dressing-gown, and escort him to his carriage, and would kiss him before the eyes of his coachman, saying: 'What on earth does it matter what people see?' And on evenings when he did not go to the Verdurins' (which happened occasionally, now that he had opportunities of meeting Odette elsewhere), when – more and more rarely – he went into society, she would beg him to come to her on his way home, however late he might be. The season was spring, the nights clear and frosty. He would come away from an evening party, jump into his victoria, spread a rug over his knees, tell the friends who were leaving at the same time, and who insisted on his going home with them, that he could not, that he was not going in their direction; then the coachman would start off at a fast trot without further orders, knowing quite well where he had to go. His friends would be left marvelling, and, as a matter of fact, Swann was no longer the same man. No one ever received a letter from him now demanding an introduction to a woman. He had ceased to pay any attention to women, and kept away from the places in which they were ordinarily to be met. In a restaurant, or in the country, his manner was deliberately and directly the opposite of that by which, only a few days earlier, his friends would have recognized him, that manner which had seemed permanently and unalterably his own. To such an extent does passion manifest itself in us as a temporary and distinct character, which not only takes the place of our normal character but actually obliterates the signs by which that character has hitherto been discernible. On the other hand, there was one thing that was, now, invariable, namely that wherever Swann might be spending the evening, he never failed to go on afterwards to Odette. The interval of space separating her from him was one which he

must as inevitably traverse as he must descend, by an irresistible gravitation, the steep slope of life itself. To be frank,
as often as not, when he had stayed late at a party, he would
have preferred to return home at once, without going so far
out of his way, and to postpone their meeting until the
morrow; but the very fact of his putting himself to such inconvenience at an abnormal hour in order to visit her, while
he guessed that his friends, as he left them, were saying to one
another: 'He is tied hand and foot; there must certainly be a
woman somewhere who insists on his going to her at all
hours,' made him feel that he was leading the life of the class of
men whose existence is coloured by a love-affair, and in whom
the perpetual sacrifice which they are making of their comfort
and of their practical interests has engendered a spiritual
charm. Then, though he may not consciously have taken this
into consideration, the certainty that she was waiting for him,
that she was not anywhere or with anyone else, that he would
see her before he went home, drew the sting from that anguish,
forgotten, it is true, but latent and ever ready to be reawakened,
which he had felt on the evening when Odette had left the
Verdurins' before his arrival, an anguish the actual cessation
of which was so agreeable that it might even be called a state
of happiness. Perhaps it was to that hour of anguish that there
must be attributed the importance which Odette had since
assumed in his life. Other people are, as a rule, so immaterial
to us that, when we have entrusted to any one of them the
power to cause so much suffering or happiness to ourselves,
that person seems at once to belong to a different universe, is
surrounded with poetry, makes of our lives a vast expanse,
quick with sensation, on which that person and ourselves are
ever more or less in contact. Swann could not without anxiety
ask himself what Odette would mean to him in the years that
were to come. Sometimes, as he looked up from his victoria
on those fine and frosty nights of early spring, and saw the
dazzling moonbeams fall between his eyes and the deserted
streets, he would think of that other face, gleaming and faintly
roseate like the moon's, which had, one day, risen on the
horizon of his mind, and since then had shed upon the world

that mysterious light in which he saw it bathed. If he arrived after the hour at which Odette sent her servants to bed, before ringing the bell at the gate of her little garden, he would go round first into the other street, over which, at the ground-level, among the windows (all exactly alike, but darkened) of the adjoining houses, shone the solitary lighted window of her room. He would rap upon the pane, and she would hear the signal, and answer, before running to meet him at the gate. He would find, lying open on the piano, some of her favourite music, the *Valse des Roses*, the *Pauvre Fou* of Tagliafico (which, according to the instructions embodied in her will, was to be played at her funeral); but he would ask her, instead, to give him the little phrase from Vinteuil's sonata. It was true that Odette played vilely, but often the fairest impression that remains in our minds of a favourite air is one which has arisen out of a jumble of wrong notes struck by unskilful fingers upon a tuneless piano. The little phrase was associated still, in Swann's mind, with his love for Odette. He felt clearly that this love was something to which there were no correspond-ing external signs, whose meaning could not be proved by any but himself; he realized, too, that Odette's qualities were not such as to justify his setting so high a value on the hours he spent in her company. And often, when the cold government of reason stood unchallenged, he would readily have ceased to sacrifice so many of his intellectual and social interests to this imaginary pleasure. But the little phrase, as soon as it struck his ear, had the power to liberate in him the room that was needed to contain it; the proportions of Swann's soul were altered; a margin was left for a form of enjoyment which cor-responded no more than his love for Odette to any external object, and yet was not, like his enjoyment of that love, purely individual, but assumed for him an objective reality superior to that of other concrete things. This thirst for an untasted charm, the little phrase would stimulate it anew in him, but without bringing him any definite gratification to assuage it. With the result that those parts of Swann's soul in which the little phrase had obliterated all care for material interests, those human considerations which affect all men alike, were left bare by it, blank pages on which he was at liberty to inscribe the name of Odette. Moreover, where Odette's affection might seem ever so little abrupt and disappointing, the little phrase would come to supplement it, to amalgamate with it its own mysterious essence. Watching Swann's face while he listened to the phrase, one would have said that he was inhaling an anaesthetic which allowed him to breathe more deeply. And the pleasure which the music gave him, which was shortly to create in him a real longing, was in fact closely akin, at such moments, to the pleasure which he would have derived from experimenting with perfumes, from entering into contact with a world for which we men were not created, which appears to lack form because our eyes cannot perceive it, to lack significance because it escapes our intelligence, to which we may attain by way of one sense only. Deep repose, mysterious refreshment for Swann, – for him whose eyes, although delicate interpreters of painting, whose mind, although an acute observer of manners, must bear for ever the indelible imprint of the barrenness of his life, – to feel himself transformed into a creature foreign to humanity, blinded, deprived of his logical faculty, almost a fantastic unicorn, a chimera-like creature conscious of the world through his two ears alone. And as, notwithstanding, he sought in the little phrase for a meaning to which his intelligence could not descend, with what a strange frenzy of intoxication must he strip bare his innermost soul of the whole armour of reason, and make it pass, unattended, through the straining vessel, down into the dark filter of sound. He began to reckon up how much that was painful, perhaps even how much secret and unappeased sorrow underlay the sweetness of the phrase; and yet to him it brought no suffering. What matter though the phrase repeated that love is frail and fleeting, when his love was so strong! He played with the melancholy which the phrase diffused, he felt it stealing over him, but like a caress which only deepened and sweetened his sense of his own happiness. He would make Odette play him the phrase again, ten, twenty times on end, insisting that, while she played, she must never cease to kiss him. Every kiss provokes another. Ah, in those earliest days of love how naturally the kisses spring into life. How closely, in their abundance, are they pressed one against another; until lovers would find it as hard to count the kisses exchanged in an hour, as to count the flowers in a meadow in May. Then she would pretend to stop, saying: 'How do you expect me to play when you keep on holding me? I can't do everything at once. Make up your mind what you want; am I to play the phrase or do you want to play with me?' Then he would become annoyed, and she would burst out with a laugh which was transformed, as it left her lips, and descended upon him in a shower of kisses. Or else she would look at him sulkily, and he would see once again a face worthy to figure in Botticelli's 'Life of Moses', he would place it there, giving to Odette's neck the necessary inclination; and when he had finished her portrait in distemper, in the fifteenth century, on the wall of the Sistine, the idea that she was, none the less, in the room with him still, by the piano, at that very moment, ready to be kissed and won, the idea of her material existence, of her being alive, would sweep over him with so violent an intoxication that, with eyes starting from his head and jaws that parted as though to devour her, he would fling himself upon this Botticelli maiden and kiss and bite her cheeks. And then, as soon as he had left the house, not without returning to kiss her once again, because he had forgotten to take away with him, in memory, some detail of her fragrance or of her features, while he drove home in his victoria, blessing the name of Odette who allowed him to pay her these daily visits, which, although they could not, he felt, bring any great happiness to her, still, by keeping him immune from the fever of jealousy – by removing from him every possibility of a fresh outbreak of the heart-sickness which had manifested itself in him that evening, when he had failed to find her at the Verdurins' – might help him to arrive, without any recurrence of those crises, of which the first had been so distressing that it must also be the last, at the termination of this strange series of hours in his life, hours almost enchanted, in the same manner as these other, following hours, in which he drove through a deserted Paris by the light of the moon:

noticing as he drove home that the satellite had now changed
its position, relatively to his own, and was almost touching the
horizon; feeling that his love, also, was obedient to these
immutable laws of nature, he asked himself whether this
period, upon which he had entered, was to last much longer,
whether presently his mind's eye would cease to behold that
dear countenance, save as occupying a distant and diminished
position, and on the verge of ceasing to shed on him the
radiance of its charm. For Swann was finding in things once
more, since he had fallen in love, the charm that he had found
when, in his adolescence, he had fancied himself an artist; with
this difference, that what charm lay in them now was conferred by Odette alone. He could feel reawakening in
himself the inspirations of his boyhood, which had been
dissipated among the frivolities of his later life, but they all
bore, now, the reflexion, the stamp of a particular being;
and during the long hours which he now found a subtle
pleasure in spending at home, alone with his convalescent
spirit, he became gradually himself again, but himself in
thraldom to another.

He went to her only in the evenings, and knew nothing of
how she spent her time during the day, any more than he
knew of her past; so little, indeed, that he had not even the
tiny, initial clue which, by allowing us to imagine what we do
not know, stimulates a desire for knowledge. And so he never
asked himself what she might be doing, or what her life had
been. Only he smiled sometimes at the thought of how, some
years earlier, when he still did not know her, some one had
spoken to him of a woman who, if he remembered rightly,
must certainly have been Odette, as of a 'tart', a 'kept'
woman, one of those women to whom he still attributed
(having lived but little in their company) the entire set of
characteristics, fundamentally perverse, with which they had
been, for many years, endowed by the imagination of certain
novelists. He would say to himself that one has, as often as
not, only to take the exact counterpart of the reputation
created by the world in order to judge a person fairly, when
with such a character he contrasted that of Odette, so good,

so simple, so enthusiastic in the pursuit of ideals, so nearly begged her, so that they might dine together alone, to write to Mme Verdurin, saying that she was unwell, the next day he had seen her, face to face with Mme Verdurin, who asked whether she had recovered, blushing, stammering, and, in spite of herself, revealing in every feature how painful, what a torture it was to her to act a lie; and, while in her answer she multiplied the fictitious details of an imaginary illness, seeming to ask pardon, by her suppliant look and her stricken accents, for the obvious falsehood of her words.

On certain days, however, though these came seldom, she would call upon him in the afternoon, to interrupt his musings or the essay on Vermeer to which he had latterly returned. His servant would come in to say that Mme de Crécy was in the small drawing-room. He would go in search of her, and, when he opened the door, on Odette's blushing countenance, as soon as she caught sight of Swann, would appear – changing the curve of her lips, the look in her eyes, the moulding of her cheeks – an all-absorbing smile. Once he was left alone he would see again that smile, and her smile of the day before, another with which she had greeted him sometime else, the smile which had been her answer, in the carriage that night, when he had asked her whether she objected to his rearranging her cattleyas; and the life of Odette at all other times, since he knew nothing of it, appeared to him upon a neutral and colourless background, like those sheets of sketches by Watteau upon which one sees, here and there, in every corner and in all directions, traced in three colours upon the buff paper, innumerable smiles. But, once in a while, illuminating a chink of that existence which Swann still saw as a complete blank, even if his mind assured him that it was not so, because he was unable to imagine anything that might occupy it, some friend who knew them both, and, suspecting that they were in love, had not dared to tell him anything about her that was of the least importance, would describe Odette's figure, as he had seen her, that very morning, going on foot up the Rue Abbattucci, in a cap trimmed with skunks, wearing a Rembrandt hat, and a bunch of violets in her bosom. This simple outline reduced Swann to utter confusion by enabling him suddenly to perceive that Odette had an existence which was not wholly subordinated to his own; he burned to know whom she had been seeking to fascinate by this costume in which he had never seen her; he registered a vow to insist upon her telling him where she had been going at that intercepted moment, as though, in all the colourless life – a life almost non-existent, since she was then invisible to him – of his mistress, there had been but a single incident apart from all those smiles directed towards himself; namely, her walking abroad beneath a Rembrandt hat, with a bunch of violets in her bosom.

Except when he asked her for Vinteuil's little phrase instead of the *Valse des Roses,* Swann made no effort to induce her to play the things that he himself preferred, or, in literature any more than in music, to correct the manifold errors of her taste. He fully realized that she was not intelligent. When she said how much she would like him to tell her about the great poets, she had imagined that she would suddenly get to know whole pages of romantic and heroic verse, in the style of the Vicomte de Borelli, only even more moving. As for Vermeer of Delft, she asked whether he had been made to suffer by a woman, if it was a woman that had inspired him, and once Swann had told her that no one knew, she had lost all interest in that painter. She would often say: 'I'm sure, poetry; well, of course, there'ld be nothing like it if it was all true, if the poets really believed the things they said. But as often as not you'll find there's no one so mean and calculating as those fellows. I know something about poetry. I had a friend, once, who was in love with a poet of sorts. In his verses he never spoke of anything but love, and heaven, and the stars. Oh! she was properly taken in! He had more than three hundred thousand francs out of her before he'd finished.' If, then, Swann tried to show her in what artistic beauty consisted, how one ought to appreciate poetry or painting, after a minute or two she would cease to listen, saying: 'Yes ... I never thought it would be like that.' And he felt that her disappointment was so great that he preferred to lie to her, assuring her that what he had said was nothing, that he had only touched the surface, that he had not time to go into it all properly, that there was more in it than that. Then she would interrupt with a brisk, 'More in it? What? ... Do tell me!', but he did not tell her, for he realized how petty it would appear to her, and how different from what she had expected, less sensational and less touching; he was afraid, too, lest, disillusioned in the matter of art, she might at the same time be disillusioned in the greater matter of love.

With the result that she found Swann inferior, intellectually, to what she had supposed. 'You're always so reserved; I can't make you out.' She marvelled increasingly at his indifference to money, at his courtesy to everyone alike, at the delicacy of his mind. And indeed it happens, often enough, to a greater man than Swann ever was, to a scientist or artist, when he is not wholly misunderstood by the people among whom he lives, that the feeling in them which proves that they have been convinced of the superiority of his intellect is created not by any admiration for his ideas – for those are entirely beyond them – but by their respect for what they term his good qualities. There was also the respect with which Odette was inspired by the thought of Swann's social position, although she had no desire that he should attempt to secure invitations for herself. Perhaps she felt that such attempts would be bound to fail; perhaps, indeed, she feared lest, merely by speaking of her to his friends, he should provoke disclosures of an unwelcome kind. The fact remains that she had consistently held him to his promise never to mention her name. Her reason for not wishing to go into society was, she had told him, a quarrel which she had had, long ago, with another girl, who had avenged herself by saying nasty things about her. 'But,' Swann objected, 'surely, people don't all know your friend.' 'Yes, don't you see, it's like a spot of oil; people are so horrid.' Swann was unable, frankly, to appreciate this point; on the other hand, he knew that such generalizations as 'People are so horrid', and 'A word of scandal spreads like a spot of oil', were generally accepted as true; there must, therefore, be cases to which they were literally applicable. Could Odette's case be one of these? He teased himself with the

question, though not for long, for he too was subject to that
mental oppression which had so weighed upon his father,
whenever he was faced by a difficult problem. In any event,
that world of society which concealed such terrors for Odette
inspired her, probably, with no very great longing to enter it,
since it was too far removed from the world which she
already knew for her to be able to form any clear conception
of it. At the same time, while in certain respects she had
retained a genuine simplicity (she had, for instance, kept up a
friendship with a little dressmaker, now retired from business,
up whose steep and dark and fetid staircase she clambered
almost every day), she still thirsted to be in the fashion, though
her idea of it was not altogether that held by fashionable
people. For the latter, fashion is a thing that emanates from a
comparatively small number of leaders, who project it to a
considerable distance – with more or less strength according
as one is nearer to or farther from their intimate centre – over
the widening circle of their friends and the friends of their
friends, whose names form a sort of tabulated index. People
'in society' know this index by heart, they are gifted in such
matters with an erudition from which they have extracted a
sort of taste, of tact, so automatic in its operation that Swann,
for example, without needing to draw upon his knowledge of
the world, if he read in a newspaper the names of the people
who had been guests at a dinner, could tell at once how
fashionable the dinner had been, just as a man of letters,
merely by reading a phrase, can estimate exactly the literary
merit of its author. But Odette was one of those persons (an
extremely numerous class, whatever the fashionable world
may think, and to be found in every section of society) who
do not share this knowledge, but imagine fashion to be something of quite another kind, which assumes different aspects
according to the circle to which they themselves belong, but
has the special characteristic – common alike to the fashion of
which Odette used to dream and to that before which Mme
Cottard bowed – of being directly accessible to all. The other
kind, the fashion of 'fashionable people', is, it must be admitted, accessible also; but there are inevitable delays. Odette

would say of someone: 'He never goes to any place that isn't really smart.'

And if Swann were to ask her what she meant by that, she would answer, with a touch of contempt, 'Smart places! Why, good heavens, just fancy, at your age, having to be told what the smart places are in Paris! What do you expect me to say? Well, on Sunday mornings there's the Avenue de l'Impératrice, and round the lake at five o'clock, and on Thursdays the Eden-Théâtre, and the Hippodrome on Fridays; then there are the balls ...'

'What balls?'

'Why, silly, the balls people give in Paris; the smart ones, I mean. Wait now, Herbinger, you know who I mean, the fellow who's in one of the jobbers' offices; yes, of course, you must know him, he's one of the best-known men in Paris, that great big fair-haired boy who wears such swagger clothes; he always has a flower in his buttonhole and a light-coloured overcoat with a fold down the back; he goes about with that old image, takes her to all the first nights. Very well! He gave a ball the other night, and all the smart people in Paris were there. I should have loved to go! but you had to show your invitation at the door, and I couldn't get one anywhere. After all, I'm just as glad, now, that I didn't go; I should have been killed in the crush, and seen nothing. Still, just to be able to say one had been to Herbinger's ball. You know how vain I am! However, you may be quite certain that half the people who tell you they were there are telling stories ... But I am surprised that you weren't there, a regular "tip-topper" like you.'

Swann made no attempt, however, to modify this conception of fashion; feeling that his own came no nearer to the truth, was just as fatuous, devoid of all importance, he saw no advantage to be gained by imparting it to his mistress, with the result that, after a few months, she ceased to take any interest in the people to whose houses he went, except when they were the means of his obtaining tickets for the paddock at race-meetings or first nights at the theatre. She hoped that he would continue to cultivate such profitable acquaintances, but she had come to regard them as less smart since the day when she had passed the Marquise de Villeparisis in the street, wearing a black serge dress and a bonnet with strings.

'But she looks like a pew-opener, like an old charwoman, darling! That a marquise! Goodness knows I'm not a marquise, but you'd have to pay me a lot of money before you'd get me to go about Paris rigged out like that!'

Nor could she understand Swann's continuing to live in his house on the Quai d'Orléans, which, though she dared not tell him so, she considered unworthy of him.

It was true that she claimed to be fond of 'antiques', and used to assume a rapturous and knowing air when she confessed how she loved to spend the whole day 'rummaging' in second-hand shops, hunting for 'bric-à-brac', and things of the 'right date'. Although it was a point of honour, to which she obstinately clung, as though obeying some old family custom, that she should never answer any questions, never give any account of what she did during the daytime, she spoke to Swann once about a friend to whose house she had been invited, and had found that everything in it was 'of the period'. Swann could not get her to tell him what 'period' it was. Only after thinking the matter over she replied that it was 'medieval'; by which she meant that the walls were panelled. Some time later she spoke to him again of her friend, and added, in the hesitating but confident tone in which one refers to a person whom one has met somewhere, at dinner, the night before, of whom one had never heard until then, but whom one's hosts seemed to regard as someone so celebrated and important that one hopes that one's listener will know quite well who is meant, and will be duly impressed: 'Her dining-room . . . is . . . eighteenth-century!' Incidentally, she had thought it hideous, all bare, as though the house were still unfinished; women looked frightful in it, and it would never become the fashion. She mentioned it again, a third time, when she showed Swann a card with the name and address of the man who had designed the dining-room, and whom she wanted to send for, when she had enough money, to see whether he could not do one for her too; not one like that, of course, but one of the sort she used to dream of, one which, unfortunately, her little house would not be large enough to contain, with tall sideboards, Renaissance furniture, and fireplaces like the Château at Blois. It was on this occasion that she let out to Swann what she really thought of his abode on the Quai d'Orléans; he having ventured the criticism that her friend had indulged, not in the Louis XVI style, for, he went on, although that was not, of course, done, still it might be made charming, but in the 'Sham-Antique'.

'You wouldn't have her live, like you, among a lot of broken-down chairs and threadbare carpets!' she exclaimed, the innate respectability of the middle-class housewife rising impulsively to the surface through the acquired dilettantism of the 'light woman'.

People who enjoyed 'picking up' things, who admired poetry, despised sordid calculations of profit and loss, and nourished ideals of honour and love, she placed in a class by themselves, superior to the rest of humanity. There was no need actually to have those tastes, provided one talked enough about them; when a man had told her at dinner that he loved to wander about and get his hands all covered with dust in the old furniture shops, that he would never be really appreciated in this commercial age, since he was not concerned about the things that interested it, and that he belonged to another generation altogether, she would come home saying: 'Why, he's an adorable creature; so sensitive! I had no idea,' and she would conceive for him a strong and sudden friendship. But, on the other hand, men who, like Swann, had these tastes but did not speak of them, left her cold. She was obliged, of course, to admit that Swann was most generous with his money, but she would add, pouting: 'It's not the same thing, you see, with him,' and, as a matter of fact, what appealed to her imagination was not the practice of disinterestedness, but its vocabulary.

Feeling that, often, he could not give her in reality the pleasures of which she dreamed, he tried at least to ensure that she should be happy in his company, tried not to contradict those vulgar ideas, that bad taste which she displayed on every possible occasion, which all the same he loved, as he could not

help loving everything that came from her, which even fascinated him, for were they not so many more of those characteristic features, by virtue of which the essential qualities of the
woman emerged, and were made visible? And so, when she
was in a happy mood because she was going to see the *Reine
Topaze*, or when her eyes grew serious, troubled, petulant, if
she was afraid of missing the flower-show, or merely of not
being in time for tea, with muffins and toast, at the Rue Royale
tea-rooms, where she believed that regular attendance was indispensable, and set the seal upon a woman's certificate of
'smartness', Swann, enraptured, as all of us are, at times, by
the natural behaviour of a child, or by the likeness of a portrait, which appears to be on the point of speaking, would feel
so distinctly the soul of his mistress rising to fill the outlines of
her face that he could not refrain from going across and welcoming it with his lips. 'Oh, then, so little Odette wants us to
take her to the flower-show, does she? she wants to be admired,
does she? very well, we will take her there, we can but obey
her wishes.' As Swann's sight was beginning to fail, he had to
resign himself to a pair of spectacles, which he wore at home,
when working, while to face the world he adopted a single
eyeglass, as being less disfiguring. The first time that she saw
it in his eye, she could not contain herself for joy: 'I really do
think – for a man, that is to say – it is tremendously smart!
How nice you look with it! Every inch a gentleman. All you
want now is a title!' she concluded, with a tinge of regret in
her voice. He liked Odette to say these things, just as, if he had
been in love with a Breton girl, he would have enjoyed seeing
her in her coif and hearing her say that she believed in ghosts.
Always until then, as is comman among men whose taste for
the fine arts develops independently of their sensuality, a grotesque disparity had existed between the satisfactions which
he would accord to either taste simultaneously; yielding to the
seduction of works of art which grew more and more subtle
as the women in whose company he enjoyed them grew more
illiterate and common, he would take a little servant-girl to a
screened box in a theatre where there was some decadent piece
which he had wished to see performed, or to an exhibition of

impressionist painting, with the conviction, moreover, that an educated, 'society' woman would have understood them no better, but would not have managed to keep quiet about them so prettily. But, now that he was in love with Odette, all this was changed; to share her sympathies, to strive to be one with her in spirit was a task so attractive that he tried to find satisfaction in the things that she liked, and did find a pleasure, not only in copying her habits but in adopting her opinions, which was all the deeper because, as those habits and opinions sprang from no roots in her intelligence, they suggested to him nothing except that love, for the sake of which he had preferred them to his own. If he went again to *Serge Panine*, if he looked out for opportunities of going to watch Olivier Métra conducting, it was for the pleasure of being initiated into every one of the ideas in Odette's mind, of feeling that he had an equal share in all her tastes. This charm of drawing him closer to her, which her favourite plays and pictures and places possessed, struck him as being more mysterious than the intrinsic charm of more beautiful things and places, which appealed to him by their beauty, but without recalling her. Besides, having allowed the intellectual beliefs of his youth to grow faint, until his scepticism, as a finished 'man of the world', had gradually penetrated them unawares, he held (or at least he had held for so long that he had fallen into the habit of saying) that the objects which we admire have no absolute value in themselves, that the whole thing is a matter of dates and castes, and consists in a series of fashions, the most vulgar of which are worth just as much as those which are regarded as the most refined. And as he had decided that the importance which Odette attached to receiving cards for a private view was not in itself any more ridiculous than the pleasure which he himself had at one time felt in going to luncheon with the Prince of Wales, so he did not think that the admiration which she professed for Monte-Carlo or for the Righi was any more unreasonable than his own liking for Holland (which she imagined as ugly) and for Versailles (which bored her to tears). And so he denied himself the pleasure of visiting those places, consoling himself with the reflexion that it was for her sake that he wished to feel, to like nothing that was not equally felt and liked by her.

Like everything else that formed part of Odette's environment, and was no more, in a sense, than the means whereby he might see and talk to her more often, he enjoyed the society of the Verdurins. With them, since, at the heart of all their entertainments, dinners, musical evenings, games, suppers in fancy dress, excursions to the country, theatre parties, even the infrequent 'big evenings' when they entertained 'bores', there were the presence of Odette, the sight of Odette, conversation with Odette, an inestimable boon which the Verdurins, by inviting him to their house, bestowed on Swann, he was happier in the little 'nucleus' than anywhere else, and tried to find some genuine merit in each of its members, imagining that his tastes would lead him to frequent their society for the rest of his life. Never daring to whisper to himself, lest he should doubt the truth of the suggestion, that he would always be in love with Odette, at least when he tried to suppose that he would always go to the Verdurins' (a proposition which, *a priori*, raised fewer fundamental objections on the part of his intelligence), he saw himself for the future continuing to meet Odette every evening; that did not, perhaps, come quite to the same thing as his being permanently in love with her, but for the moment, while he was in love with her, to feel that he would not, one day, cease to see her was all that he could ask. 'What a charming atmosphere!' he said to himself. 'How entirely genuine life is to these people! They are far more intelligent, far more artistic, surely, than the people one knows. Mme Verdurin, in spite of a few trifling exaggerations which are rather absurd, has a sincere love of painting and music! What a passion for works of art, what anxiety to give pleasure to artists! Her ideas about some of the people one knows are not quite right, but then their ideas about artistic circles are altogether wrong! Possibly I make no great intellectual demands upon conversation, but I am perfectly happy talking to Cottard, although he does trot out those idiotic puns. And as for the painter, if he is rather unpleasantly affected when he tries to be paradoxical, still he has one of the finest brains that I have ever come across.

Besides, what is most important, one feels quite free there, one does what one likes without constraint or fuss. What a flow of humour there is every day in that drawing-room! Certainly, with a few rare exceptions, I never want to go anywhere else again. It will become more and more of a habit, and I shall spend the rest of my life among them.'

And as the qualities which he supposed to be an intrinsic part of the Verdurin character were no more, really, than their superficial reflexion of the pleasure which had been enjoyed in their society by his love for Odette, those qualities became more serious, more profound, more vital, as that pleasure increased. Since Mme Verdurin gave Swann, now and then, what alone could constitute his happiness; since, on an evening when he felt anxious because Odette had talked rather more to one of the party than to another, and, in a spasm of irritation, would not take the initiative by asking her whether she was coming home, Mme Verdurin brought peace and joy to his troubled spirit by the spontaneous exclamation: 'Odette! You'll see M. Swann home, won't you?'; since, when the summer holidays came, and after he had asked himself uneasily whether Odette might not leave Paris without him, whether he would still be able to see her every day, Mme Verdurin was going to invite them both to spend the summer with her in the country; Swann, unconsciously allowing gratitude and self-interest to filter into his intelligence and to influence his ideas, went so far as to proclaim that Mme Verdurin was 'a great and noble soul'. Should any of his fellow-pupils in the Louvre school of painting speak to him of some rare or eminent artist, 'I'ld a hundred times rather,' he would reply, 'have the Verdurins.' And, with a solemnity of diction which was new in him: 'They are magnanimous creatures, and magnanimity is, after all, the one thing that matters, the one thing that gives us distinction here on earth. Look you, there are only two classes of men, the magnanimous, and the rest; and I have reached an age when one has to take sides, to decide once and for all whom one is going to like and dislike, to stick to the people one likes, and, to make up for the time one has wasted with the others, never to leave them again as long as one lives. Very well!' he went on, with the slight emotion which a man feels when, even without being fully aware of what he is doing, he says something, not because it is true but because he enjoys saying it, and listens to his own voice uttering the words as though they came from someone else, 'the die is now cast; I have elected to love none but magnanimous souls, and to live in an atmosphere of magnanimity. You ask me whether Mme Verdurin is really intelligent. I can assure you that she has given me proofs of a nobility of heart, of a loftiness of soul, to which no one could possibly attain – how could they? – without a corresponding loftiness of mind. Without question, she has a profound understanding of art. But it is not, perhaps, in that that she is most admirable; every little action, ingeniously, exquisitely kind, which she has performed for my sake, every friendly attention, simple little things, quite domestic and yet quite sublime, reveal a more profound comprehension of existence than all your text-books of philosophy.'

*

He might have reminded himself, all the same, that there were various old friends of his family who were just as simple as the Verdurins, companions of his early days who were just as fond of art, that he knew other 'great-hearted creatures', and that, nevertheless, since he had cast his vote in favour of simplicity, the arts, and magnanimity, he had entirely ceased to see them. But these people did not know Odette, and, if they had known her, would never have thought of introducing her to him.

And so there was probably not, in the whole of the Verdurin circle, a single one of the 'faithful' who loved them, or believed that he loved them as dearly as did Swann. And yet, when M. Verdurin said that he was not satisfied with Swann, he had not only expressed his own sentiments, he had unwittingly discovered his wife's. Doubtless Swann had too particular an affection for Odette, as to which he had failed to take Mme Verdurin daily into his confidence; doubtless the very discretion with which he availed himself of the Verdurins' hospitality, refraining, often, from coming to dine with them for a reason which they never suspected, and in place of which they saw only an anxiety on his part not to have to decline an invitation to the house of some 'bore' or other; doubtless, also, and despite all the precautions which he had taken to keep it from them, the gradual discovery which they were making of his brilliant position in society – doubtless all these things contributed to their general annoyance with Swann. But the real, the fundamental reason was quite different. What had happened was that they had at once discovered in him a locked door, a reserved, impenetrable chamber in which he still professed silently to himself that the Princesse de Sagan was not grotesque, and that Cottard's jokes were not amusing; in a word (and for all that he never once abandoned his friendly attitude towards them all, or revolted from their dogmas), they had discovered an impossibility of imposing those dogmas upon him, of entirely converting him to their faith, the like of which they had never come across in anyone before. They would have forgiven his going to the houses of 'bores' (to whom, as it happened, in his heart of hearts he infinitely preferred the Verdurins and all their little 'nucleus') had he consented to set a good example by openly renouncing those 'bores' in the presence of the 'faithful'. But that was an abjuration which, as they well knew, they were powerless to extort.

What a difference was there in a 'newcomer' whom Odette had asked them to invite, although she herself had met him only a few times, and on whom they were building great hopes – the Comte de Forcheville! (It turned out that he was nothing more or less than the brother-in-law of Saniette, a discovery which filled all the 'faithful' with amazement: the manners of the old palaeographer were so humble that they had always supposed him to be of a class inferior, socially, to their own, and had never expected to learn that he came of a rich and relatively aristocratic family.) Of course, Forcheville was enormously the 'swell', which Swann was not or had quite ceased to be; of course he would never dream of placing, as Swann now placed, the Verdurin circle above any other. But he lacked that natural refinement which prevented Swann from associating himself with the criticisms (too obviously false to be worth his notice) that Mme Verdurin levelled at people whom he knew. As for the vulgar and affected tirades in which the painter sometimes indulged, the bagman's pleasantries which Cottard used to hazard – whereas Swann, who liked both men sincerely, could easily find excuses for these without having either the courage or the hypocrisy to applaud them, Forcheville, on the other hand, was on an intellectual level which permitted him to be stupefied, amazed by the invective (without in the least understanding what it was all about), and to be frankly delighted by the wit. And the very first dinner at the Verdurin's at which Forcheville was present threw a glaring light upon all the differences between them, made his qualities start into prominence and precipitated the disgrace of Swann.

There was, at this dinner, besides the usual party, a professor from the Sorbonne, one Brichot, who had met M. and Mme Verdurin at a watering-place somewhere, and, if his duties at the university and his other works of scholarship had not left him with very little time to spare, would gladly have come to them more often. For he had that curiosity, that superstitious outlook on life, which, combined with a certain amount of scepticism with regard to the object of their studies, earn for men of intelligence, whatever their profession, for doctors who do not believe in medicine, for schoolmasters who do not believe in Latin exercises, the reputation of having broad, brilliant, and indeed superior minds. He affected, when at Mme Verdurin's, to choose his illustrations from among the most topical subjects of the day, when he spoke of philosophy or history, principally because he regarded those sciences as no more, really, than a preparation for life itself, and imagined that he was seeing put into practice by the 'little clan' what hitherto he had known only from books; and also, perhaps, because, having had drilled into him as a boy, and having unconsciously preserved a feeling of reverence for certain subjects, he thought that he was casting aside the scholar's gown when he ventured to treat those subjects with a conversational licence, which seemed so to him only because the folds of the gown still clung.

Early in the course of the dinner, when M. de Forcheville,

seated on the right of Mme Verdurin, who, in the 'new-comer's' honour, had taken great pains with her toilet, observed to her: 'Quite original, that white dress,' the Doctor, who had never taken his eyes off him, so curious was he to learn the nature and attributes of what he called a 'de', and was on the look-out for an opportunity of attracting his attention, so as to come into closer contact with him, caught in its flight the adjective '*blanche*' and, his eyes still glued to his plate, snapped out, '*Blanche?* Blanche of Castile?' then, without moving his head, shot a furtive glance to right and left of him, doubtful, but happy on the whole. While Swann, by the painful and futile effort which he made to smile, testified that he thought the pun absurd, Forcheville had shown at once that he could appreciate its subtlety, and that he was a man of the world, by keeping within its proper limits a mirth the spontaneity of which had charmed Mme Verdurin.

'What are you to say of a scientist like that?' she asked Forcheville. 'You can't talk seriously to him for two minutes on end. Is that the sort of thing you tell them at your hospital?' she went on, turning to the Doctor. 'They must have some pretty lively times there, if that's the case. I can see that I shall have to get taken in as a patient!'

'I think I heard the Doctor speak of that wicked old humbug, Blanche of Castile, if I may so express myself. Am I not right, Madame?' Brichot appealed to Mme Verdurin, who, swooning with merriment, her eyes tightly closed, had buried her face in her two hands, from between which, now and then, escaped a muffled scream.

'Good gracious, Madame, I would not dream of shocking the reverent-minded, if there are any such around this table, *sub rosa* ... I recognize, moreover, that our ineffable and Athenian – oh, how infinitely Athenian – Republic is capable of honouring, in the person of that obscurantist old she-Capet, the first of our chiefs of police. Yes, indeed, my dear host, yes, indeed!' he repeated in his ringing voice, which sounded a separate note for each syllable, in reply to a protest by M. Verdurin. 'The Chronicle of Saint Denis, and the authenticity of its information is beyond question, leaves us no room for doubt on that point. No one could be more fitly chosen as Patron by a secularizing proletariat than that mother of a Saint, who let him see some pretty fishy saints besides, as Sugar says, and other great St Bernards of the sort; for with her it was a case of taking just what you pleased.'

'Who is that gentleman?' Forcheville asked Mme Verdurin. 'He seems to speak with great authority.'

'What! Do you mean to say you don't know the famous Brichot? Why, he's celebrated all over Europe.'

'Oh, that's Bréchot, is it?' exclaimed Forcheville, who had not quite caught the name. 'You must tell me all about him'; he went on, fastening a pair of goggle eyes on the celebrity. 'It's always interesting to meet well-known people at dinner. But, I say, you ask us to very select parties here. No dull evenings in this house, I'm sure.'

'Well, you know what it is really,' said Mme Verdurin modestly. 'They feel safe here. They can talk about whatever they like, and the conversation goes off like fireworks. Now Brichot, this evening, is nothing. I've seen him, don't you know, when he's been with me, simply dazzling; you'ld want to go on your knees to him. Well, with anyone else he's not the same man, he's not in the least witty, you have to drag the words out of him, he's even boring.'

'That's strange,' remarked Forcheville with fitting astonishment.

A sort of wit like Brichot's would have been regarded as out-and-out stupidity by the people among whom Swann had spent his early life, for all that it is quite compatible with real intelligence. And the intelligence of the Professor's vigorous and well-nourished brain might easily have been envied by many of the people in society who seemed witty enough to Swann. But these last had so thoroughly inculcated into him their likes and dislikes, at least in everything that pertained to their ordinary social existence, including that annex to social existence which belongs, strictly speaking, to the domain of intelligence, namely, conversation, that Swann could not see anything in Brichot's pleasantries; to him they were merely pedantic, vulgar, and disgustingly coarse. He was shocked, too, being accustomed to good manners, by the rude, almost barrack-room tone which this student-in-arms adopted, no matter to whom he was speaking. Finally, perhaps, he had lost all patience that evening as he watched Mme Verdurin welcoming, with such unnecessary warmth, this Forcheville fellow, whom it had been Odette's unaccountable idea to bring to the house. Feeling a little awkward, with Swann there also, she had asked him on her arrival: 'What do you think of my guest?'

And he, suddenly realizing for the first time that Forcheville, whom he had known for years, could actually attract a woman, and was quite a good specimen of a man, had retorted: 'Beastly!' He had, certainly, no idea of being jealous of Odette, but did not feel quite so happy as usual, and when Brichot, having begun to tell them the story of Blanche of Castile's mother, who, according to him, 'had been with Henry Plantagenet for years before they were married,' tried to prompt Swann to beg him to continue the story, by interjecting 'Isn't that so, M. Swann?' in the martial accents which one uses in order to get down to the level of an unintelligent rustic or to put the 'fear of God' into a trooper, Swann cut his story short, to the intense fury of their hostess, by begging to be excused for taking so little interest in Blanche of Castile, as he had something that he wished to ask the painter. He, it appeared, had been that afternoon to an exhibition of the work of another artist, also a friend of Mme Verdurin, who had recently died, and Swann wished to find out from him (for he valued his discrimination) whether there had really been anything more in this later work than the virtuosity which had struck people so forcibly in his earlier exhibitions.

'From that point of view it was extraordinary, but it did not seem to me to be a form of art which you could call "elevated",' said Swann with a smile.

'Elevated . . . to the height of an Institute!' interrupted Cottard, raising his arms with mock solemnity. The whole table burst out laughing.

'What did I tell you?' said Mme Verdurin to Forcheville.

'It's simply impossible to be serious with him. When you least expect it, out he comes with a joke.'

But she observed that Swann, and Swann alone, had not unbent. For one thing he was none too well pleased with Cottard for having secured a laugh at his expense in front of Forcheville. But the painter, instead of replying in a way that might have interested Swann, as he would probably have done had they been alone together, preferred to win the easy admiration of the rest by exercising his wit upon the talent of their dead friend.

'I went up to one of them,' he began, 'just to see how it was done; I stuck my nose into it. Yes, I don't think! Impossible to say whether it was done with glue, with soap, with sealing-wax, with sunshine, with leaven, with excrem . . .'

'And one make twelve!' shouted the Doctor, wittily, but just too late, for no one saw the point of his interruption.

'It looks as though it were done with nothing at all', resumed the painter. 'No more chance of discovering the trick than there is in the "Night Watch", or the "Regents", and it's even bigger work than either Rembrandt or Hals ever did. It's all there, – and yet, no, I'll take my oath it isn't.'

Then, just as singers who have reached the highest note in their compass proceed to hum the rest of the air in falsetto, he had to be satisfied with murmuring, smiling the while, as if, after all, there had been something irresistibly amusing in the sheer beauty of the painting: 'It smells all right; it makes your head go round; it catches your breath; you feel ticklish all over – and not the faintest clue to how it's done. The man's a sorcerer; the thing's a conjuring-trick, it's a miracle,' bursting outright into laughter, 'it's dishonest!' Then stopping, solemnly raising his head, pitching his voice on a double-bass note which he struggled to bring into harmony, he concluded, 'And it's so loyal!'

Except at the moment when he had called it 'bigger than the "Night Watch"', a blasphemy which had called forth an instant protest from Mme Verdurin, who regarded the 'Night Watch' as the supreme masterpiece of the universe (conjointly with the 'Ninth' and the 'Samothrace'), and at

the word 'excrement', which had made Forcheville throw a
sweeping glance round the table to see whether it was 'all
right', before he allowed his lips to curve in a prudish and
conciliatory smile, all the party (save Swann) had kept their
fascinated and adoring eyes fixed upon the painter.

'I do so love him when he goes up in the air like that!'
cried Mme Verdurin, the moment that he had finished, enraptured that the table-talk should have proved so entertaining on the very night that Forcheville was dining with
them for the first time. 'Hallo, you!' she turned to her
husband, 'What's the matter with you, sitting there gaping
like a great animal? You know, though, don't you,' she
apologized for him to the painter, 'that he can talk quite well
when he chooses; anybody would think it was the first time
he had ever listened to you. If you had only seen him while
you were speaking; he was just drinking it all in. And to-
morrow he will tell us everything you said, without missing
a word.'

'No, really, I'm not joking!' protested the painter, enchanted by the success of his speech. 'You all look as if you
thought I was pulling your legs, that it was just a trick. I'll
take you to see the show, and then you can say whether I've
been exaggerating; I'll bet you anything you like, you'll come
away more "up in the air" than I am!'

'But we don't suppose for a moment that you're exaggerating; we only want you to go on with your dinner, and
my husband too. Give M. Biche some more sole, can't you
see his has got cold? We're not in any hurry; you're dashing
round as if the house was on fire. Wait a little; don't serve
the salad just yet.'

Mme Cottard, who was a shy woman and spoke but seldom,
was not lacking, for all that, in self-assurance when a happy
inspiration put the right word in her mouth. She felt that it
would be well received; the thought gave her confidence, and
what she was doing was done with the object not so much of
shining herself, as of helping her husband on in his career.
And so she did not allow the word 'salad', which Mme
Verdurin had just uttered, to pass unchallenged.

'It's not a Japanese salad, is it?' she whispered, turning towards Odette.

And then, in her joy and confusion at the combination of neatness and daring which there had been in making so discreet and yet so unmistakable an allusion to the new and brilliantly successful play by Dumas, she broke down in a charming, girlish laugh, not very loud, but so irresistible that it was some time before she could control it.

'Who is that lady? She seems devilish clever,' said Forcheville.

'No, it is not. But we will have one for you if you will all come to dinner on Friday.'

'You will think me dreadfully provincial, sir,' said Mme Cottard to Swann, 'but, do you know, I haven't been yet to this famous *Francillon* that everybody's talking about. The Doctor has been (I remember now, he told me what a very great pleasure it had been to him to spend the evening with you there) and I must confess, I don't see much sense in spending money on seats for him to take me, when he's seen the play already. Of course an evening at the Théâtre-Français is never wasted, really; the acting's so good there always; but we have some very nice friends,' (Mme Cottard would hardly ever utter a proper name, but restricted herself to 'some friends of ours' or 'one of my friends', as being more 'distinguished', speaking in an affected tone and with all the importance of a person who need give names only when she chooses) 'who often have a box, and are kind enough to take us to all the new pieces that are worth going to, and so I'm certain to see this *Francillon* sooner or later, and then I shall know what to think. But I do feel such a fool about it, I must confess, for, whenever I pay a call anywhere, I find everybody talking – it's only natural – about that wretched Japanese salad. Really and truly, one's beginning to get just a little tired of hearing about it,' she went on, seeing that Swann seemed less interested than she had hoped in so burning a topic. 'I must admit, though, that it's sometimes quite amusing, the way they joke about it: I've got a friend, now, who is most original, though she's really a beautiful woman, most popular in society, goes everywhere, and she tells me that she got her cook to make one of these Japanese salads, putting in everything that young M. Dumas says you're to put in, in the play. Then she asked just a few friends to come and taste it. I was not among the favoured few, I'm sorry to say. But she told us all about it on her next "day"; it seems it was quite horrible, she made us all laugh till we cried. I don't know; perhaps it was the way she told it.' Mme Cottard added doubtfully, seeing that Swann still looked grave.

And, imagining that it was, perhaps, because he had not been amused by *Francillon*; 'Well, I daresay I shall be disappointed with it, after all. I don't suppose it's as good as the piece Mme de Crécy worships, *Serge Panine*. There's a play, if you like; so deep, makes you think! But just fancy giving a receipt for a salad on the stage of the Théâtre-Français! Now *Serge Panine* – ! But then, it's like everything that comes from the pen of M. Georges Ohnet, it's so well written. I wonder if you know the *Maître des Forges*, which I like even better than *Serge Panine*.'

'Pardon me,' said Swann with polite irony, 'but I can assure you that my want of admiration is almost equally divided between those masterpieces.'

'Really, now; that's very interesting. And what don't you like about them? Won't you ever change your mind? Perhaps you think he's a little too sad. Well, well, what I always say is, one should never argue about plays or novels. Everyone has his own way of looking at things, and what may be horrible to you is, perhaps, just what I like best.'

She was interrupted by Forcheville's addressing Swann. What had happened was that, while Mme Cottard was discussing *Francillon*, Forcheville had been expressing to Mme Verdurin his admiration for what he called the 'little speech' of the painter. 'Your friend has such a flow of language, such a memory!' he had said to her when the painter had come to a standstill, 'I've seldom seen anything like it. He'd make a first-rate preacher. By Jove, I wish I was like that. What with him and M. Bréchot you've drawn two lucky numbers tonight; though I'm not so sure that, simply as a speaker, this one doesn't knock spots off the Professor. It comes more naturally with him, less like reading from a book. Of course, the way he goes on, he does use some words that are a bit realistic, and all that; but that's quite the thing nowadays; anyhow, it's not often I've seen a man hold the floor as cleverly as that, "hold the spittoon", as we used to say in the regiment, where, by the way, we had a man he rather reminds me of. You could take anything you liked – I don't know what – this glass, say; and he'd talk away about it for hours; no, not this glass; that's a silly thing to say, I'm sorry; but something a little bigger, like the battle of Waterloo, or anything of that sort, he'd tell you things you simply wouldn't believe. Why, Swann was in the regiment then; he must have known him.'

'Do you see much of M. Swann?' asked Mme Verdurin.

'Oh dear, no!' he answered, and then, thinking that if he made himself pleasant to Swann he might find favour with Odette, he decided to take this opportunity of flattering him by speaking of his fashionable friends, but speaking as a man of the world himself, in a tone of good-natured criticism, and not as though he were congratulating Swann upon some undeserved good fortune: 'Isn't that so, Swann? I never see anything of you, do I? – But then, where on earth is one to see him? The creature spends all his time shut up with the La Trémoïlles, with the Laumes and all that lot!' The imputation would have been false at any time, and was all the more so, now that for at least a year Swann had given up going to almost any house but the Verdurins'. But the mere names of families whom the Verdurins did not know were received by them in a reproachful silence. M. Verdurin, dreading the painful impression which the mention of these 'bores', especially when flung at her in this tactless fashion, and in front of all the 'faithful,' was bound to make on his wife, cast a covert glance at her, instinct with anxious solicitude. He saw then that in her fixed resolution to take no notice, to have escaped contact, altogether, with the news which had just been addressed to her, not merely to remain dumb but to have been deaf as well, as we pretend to be when a friend

who has been in the wrong attempts to slip into his conversation some excuse which we should appear to be accepting, should we appear to have heard it without protesting, or
when someone utters the name of an enemy, the very mention
of whom in our presence is forbidden; Mme Verdurin, so
that her silence should have the appearance, not of consent
but of the unconscious silence which inanimate objects preserve, had suddenly emptied her face of all life, of all mobility;
her rounded forehead was nothing, now, but an exquisite
study in high relief, which the name of those La Trémoïlles,
with whom Swann was always 'shut up', had failed to penetrate; her nose, just perceptibly wrinkled in a frown, exposed
to view two dark cavities that were, surely, modelled from
life. You would have said that her half-opened lips were just
about to speak. It was all no more, however, than a wax cast,
a mask in plaster, the sculptor's design for a monument, a
bust to be exhibited in the Palace of Industry, where the public
would most certainly gather in front of it and marvel to see
how the sculptor, in expressing the unchallengeable dignity
of the Verdurins, as opposed to that of the La Trémoïlles or
Laumes, whose equals (if not, indeed, their betters) they were,
and the equals and betters of all other 'bores' upon the face
of the earth, had managed to invest with a majesty that was
almost Papal the whiteness and rigidity of his stone. But the
marble at last grew animated and let it be understood that
it didn't do to be at all squeamish if one went to that house,
since the woman was always tipsy and her husband so uneducated that he called a corridor a 'collidor'!

'You'd need to pay me a lot of money before I'd let any
of that lot set foot inside my house,' Mme Verdurin concluded,
gazing imperially down on Swann.

She could scarcely have expected him to capitulate so completely as to echo the holy simplicity of the pianist's aunt, who
at once exclaimed: 'To think of that, now! What surprises me
is that they can get anybody to go near them; I'm sure I should
be afraid; one can't be too careful. How can people be so common as to go running after them?'

But he might, at least, have replied, like Forcheville: 'Gad, she's a duchess; there are still plenty of people who are impressed by that sort of thing,' which would at least have permitted Mme Verdurin the final retort, 'And a lot of good may it do them!' Instead of which, Swann merely smiled, in a manner which showed, quite clearly, that he could not, of course, take such an absurd suggestion seriously. M. Verdurin, who was still casting furtive and intermittent glances at his wife, could see with regret, and could understand only too well that she was now inflamed with the passion of a Grand Inquisitor who cannot succeed in stamping out a heresy; and so, in the hope of bringing Swann round to a retraction (for the courage of one's opinions is always a form of calculating cowardice in the eyes of the 'other side'), he broke in:

'Tell us frankly, now, what you think of them yourself. We shan't repeat it to them, you may be sure.'

To which Swann answered: 'Why, I'm not in the least afraid of the Duchess (if it is of the La Trémoïlles that you're speaking). I can assure you that everyone likes going to see her. I don't go so far as to say that she's at all "deep" ' – he pronounced the word as if it meant something ridiculous, for his speech kept the traces of certain mental habits which the recent change in his life, a rejuvenation illustrated by his passion for music, had inclined him temporarily to discard, so that at times he would actually state his views with considerable warmth – 'but I am quite sincere when I say that she is intelligent, while her husband is positively a bookworm. They are charming people.'

His explanation was terribly effective; Mme Verdurin now realized that this one state of unbelief would prevent her 'little nucleus' from ever attaining to complete unanimity, and was unable to restrain herself, in her fury at the obstinacy of this wretch who could not see what anguish his words were causing her, but cried aloud, from the depths of her tortured heart, 'You may think so if you wish, but at least you need not say so to us.'

'It all depends upon what you call intelligence.' Forcheville felt that it was his turn to be brilliant. 'Come now, Swann, tell us what you mean by intelligence.'

'There,' cried Odette, 'that's one of the big things I beg him to tell me about, and he never will.'

'Oh, but . . .' protested Swann.

'Oh, but nonsense!' said Odette.

'A water-butt?' asked the Doctor.

'To you,' pursued Forcheville, 'does intelligence mean what they call clever talk; you know, the sort of people who worm their way into society?'

'Finish your sweet, so that they can take your plate away!' said Mme Verdurin sourly to Saniette, who was lost in thought and had stopped eating. And then, perhaps a little ashamed of her rudeness, 'It doesn't matter; take your time about it; there's no hurry; I only reminded you because of the others, you know; it keeps the servants back.'

'There is,' began Brichot, with a resonant smack upon every syllable, 'a rather curious definition of intelligence by that pleasing old anarchist Fénelon . . .'

'Just listen to this!' Mme Verdurin rallied Forcheville and the Doctor. 'He's going to give us Fénelon's definition of intelligence. That's interesting. It's not often you get a chance of hearing that!'

But Brichot was keeping Fénelon's definition until Swann should have given his own. Swann remained silent, and, by this fresh act of recreancy, spoiled the brilliant tournament of dialectic which Mme Verdurin was rejoicing at being able to offer to Forcheville.

'You see, it's just the same as with me!' Odette was peevish. 'I'm not at all sorry to see that I'm not the only one he doesn't find quite up to his level.'

'These de La Trémouailles whom Mme Verdurin has exhibited to us as so little to be desired,' inquired Brichot, articulating vigorously, 'are they, by any chance, descended from the couple whom that worthy old snob, Sévigné, said she was delighted to know, because it was so good for her peasants? True, the Marquise had another reason, which in her case probably came first, for she was a thorough journalist at heart, and always on the look-out for "copy". And, in the journal which she used to send regularly to her daughter, it was Mme de La Trémouaille, kept well-informed through all her grand connexions, who supplied the foreign politics.'

'Oh dear, no. I'm quite sure they aren't the same family,' said Mme Verdurin desperately.

Saniette who, ever since he had surrendered his untouched plate to the butler, had been plunged once more in silent meditation, emerged finally to tell them, with a nervous laugh, a story of how he had once dined with the Duc de La Trémoïlle; the point of which was that the Duke did not know that George Sand was the pseudonym of a woman. Swann, who really liked Saniette, felt bound to supply him with a few facts illustrative of the Duke's culture, which would prove that such ignorance on his part was literally impossible; but suddenly he stopped short; he had realized, as he was speaking, that Saniette needed no proof, but knew already that the story was untrue for the simple reason that he had at that moment invented it. The worthy man suffered acutely from the Ver- durins' always finding him so dull; and as he was conscious of having been more than ordinarily morose this evening, he had made up his mind that he would succeed in being amusing, at least once, before the end of dinner. He surrendered so quickly, looked so wretched at the sight of his castle in ruins, and replied in so craven a tone to Swann, appealing to him not to persist in a refutation which was already superfluous, 'All right; all right; anyhow, even if I have made a mistake that's not a crime, I hope,' that Swann longed to be able to console him by insisting that the story was indubitably true and exquisitely funny. The Doctor, who had been listening, had an idea that it was the right moment to interject '*Se non è vero*,' but he was not quite certain of the words, and was afraid of being caught out.

After dinner, Forcheville went up to the Doctor. 'She can't have been at all bad looking, Mme Verdurin; anyhow, she's a woman you can really talk to; that's all I want. Of course she's getting a bit broad in the beam. But Mme de Crécy! There's a little woman who knows what's what, all right. Upon my word and soul, you can see at a glance she's got the American eye, that girl has. We are speaking of Mme de Crécy', he explained, as M. Verdurin joined them, his pipe in his mouth. 'I should say that, as a specimen of the female form –'

'I'ld rather have it in my bed than a clap of thunder!' the words came tumbling from Cottard, who had for some time been waiting in vain until Forcheville should pause for breath, so that he might get in this hoary old joke, a chance for which might not, he feared, come again, if the conversation should take a different turn; and he produced it now with that excessive spontaneity and confidence which may often be noticed attempting to cover up the coldness, and the slight flutter of emotion, inseparable from a prepared recitation. Forcheville knew and saw the joke, and was thoroughly amused. As for M. Verdurin, he was unsparing of his merriment, having recently discovered a way of expressing it by a symbol, different from his wife's, but equally simple and obvious. Scarcely had he begun the movement of head and shoulders of a man who was 'shaking with laughter' than he would begin also to cough, as though, in laughing too violently, he had swallowed a mouthful of smoke from his pipe. And by keeping the pipe firmly in his mouth he could prolong indefinitely the dumb-show of suffocation and hilarity. So he and Mme Verdurin (who, at the other side of the room, where the painter was telling her a story, was shutting her eyes preparatory to flinging her face into her hands) resembled two masks in a theatre, each representing Comedy, but in a different way.

M. Verdurin had been wiser than he knew in not taking his pipe out of his mouth, for Cottard, having occasion to leave the room for a moment, murmured a witty euphemism which he had recently acquired and repeated now whenever he had to go to the place in question: 'I must just go and see the Duc d'Aumale for a minute,' so drolly, that M. Verdurin's cough began all over again.

'Now, then, take your pipe out of your mouth; can't you see, you'll choke if you try to bottle up your laughter like that,' counselled Mme Verdurin, as she came round with a tray of liqueurs.

'What a delightful man your husband is; he has the wit of a dozen!' declared Forcheville to Mme Cottard. 'Thank you, thank you, an old soldier like me can never say "No" to a drink.'

'M. de Forcheville thinks Odette charming,' M. Verdurin told his wife.

'Why, do you know, she wants so much to meet you again some day at luncheon. We must arrange it, but don't on any account let Swann hear about it. He spoils everything, don't you know. I don't mean to say that you're not to come to dinner too, of course; we hope to see you very often. Now that the warm weather's coming, we're going to have dinner out of doors whenever we can. That won't bore you, will it, a quiet little dinner, now and then, in the Bois? Splendid, splendid, that will be quite delightful ...

'Aren't you going to do any work this evening, I say?' she screamed suddenly to the little pianist, seeing an opportunity for displaying, before a 'newcomer' of Forcheville's importance, at once her unfailing wit and her despotic power over the 'faithful'.

'M. de Forcheville was just going to say something dreadful about you,' Mme Cottard warned her husband as he reappeared in the room. And he, still following up the idea of Forcheville's noble birth, which had obsessed him all through dinner, began again with: 'I am treating a Baroness just now, Baroness Putbus; weren't there some Putbuses in the Crusades? Anyhow they've got a lake in Pomerania that's ten times the size of the Place de la Concorde. I am treating her for dry arthritis; she's a charming woman. Mme Verdurin knows her too, I believe.'

Which enabled Forcheville, a moment later, finding himself alone with Mme Cottard, to complete his favourable verdict on her husband with: 'He's an interesting man, too; you can see that he knows some good people. Gad! but they get to know a lot of things, those doctors.'

'D'you want me to play the phrase from the sonata for M. Swann?' asked the pianist.

'What the devil's that? Not the sonata-snake, I hope!' shouted M. de Forcheville, hoping to create an effect. But Dr Cottard, who had never heard this pun, missed the point of it, and imagined that M. de Forcheville had made a mistake. He dashed in boldly to correct it: 'No, no. The word isn't *serpent-à-sonates*, it's *serpent-à-sonnettes*!' he explained in a tone at once zealous, impatient, and triumphant.

Forcheville explained the joke to him. The Doctor blushed.

'You'll admit it's not bad, eh, Doctor?'

'Oh! I've known it for ages.'

Then they were silenced; heralded by the waving *tremolo* of the violin-part, which formed a bristling bodyguard of sound two octaves above it – and as in a mountainous country, against the seeming immobility of a vertically falling torrent, one may distinguish, two hundred feet below, the tiny form of a woman walking in the valley — the little phrase had just appeared, distant but graceful, protected by the long, gradual unfurling of its transparent, incessant, and sonorous curtain. And Swann, in his heart of hearts, turned to it, spoke to it as to a confidant in the secret of his love, as to a friend of Odette who would assure him that he need pay no attention to this Forcheville.

'Ah! you've come too late!' Mme Verdurin greeted one of the 'faithful', whose invitation had been only to 'look in after dinner', 'we've been having a simply incomparable Brichot! You never heard such eloquence! But he's gone. Isn't that so, M. Swann? I believe it's the first time you've met him,' she went on, to emphasize the fact that it was to her that Swann owed the introduction. 'Isn't that so; wasn't he delicious, our Brichot?'

Swann bowed politely.

'No? You weren't interested?' she asked dryly.

'Oh, but I assure you, I was quite enthralled. He is perhaps a little too peremptory, a little too jovial for my taste. I should like to see him a little less confident at times, a little more tolerant, but one feels that he knows a great deal, and on the whole he seems a very sound fellow.'

The party broke up very late. Cottard's first words to his wife were: 'I have rarely seen Mme Verdurin in such form as she was to-night.'

'What exactly is your Mme Verdurin? A bit of a bad hat,

eh?' said Forcheville to the painter, to whom he had offered a 'lift.' Odette watched his departure with regret; she dared not refuse to let Swann take her home, but she was moody and irritable in the carriage, and, when he asked whether he might come in, replied, 'I suppose so,' with an impatient shrug of her shoulders. When they had all gone, Mme Verdurin said to her husband: 'Did you notice the way Swann laughed, such an idiotic laugh, when we spoke about Mme La Trémoïlle?'

She had remarked, more than once, how Swann and Forcheville suppressed the particle 'de' before that lady's name. Never doubting that it was done on purpose to show that they were not afraid of a title, she had made up her mind to imitate their arrogance, but had not quite grasped what grammatical form it ought to take. Moreover, the natural corruptness of her speech overcoming her implacable republicanism, she still said instinctively 'the de La Trémoïlles,' or, rather (by an abbreviation sanctified by the usage of music-hall singers and the writers of the 'captions' beneath caricatures, who elide the 'de'), 'the d'La Trémoïlles,' but she corrected herself at once to 'Madame La Trémoïlle. – The *Duchess*, as Swann calls her,' she added ironically, with a smile which proved that she was merely quoting, and would not, herself, accept the least responsibility for a classification so puerile and absurd.

'I don't mind saying that I thought him extremely stupid.' M. Verdurin took it up. 'He's not sincere. He's a crafty customer, always hovering between one side and the other. He's always trying to run with the hare and hunt with the hounds. What a difference between him and Forcheville. There, at least, you have a man who tells you straight out what he thinks. Either you agree with him or you don't. Not like the other fellow, who's never definitely fish or fowl. Did you notice, by the way, that Odette seemed all out for Forcheville, and I don't blame her, either. And then, after all, if Swann tries to come the man of fashion over us, the champion of distressed Duchesses, at any rate the other man has got a title; he's always Comte de Forcheville!' he let the words slip delicately from his lips, as though, familiar with every page of the history of that dignity, he were making a scrupulously exact estimate of its value, in relation to others of the sort.

'I don't mind saying,' Mme Verdurin went on, 'that he saw fit to utter some most venomous, and quite absurd insinuations against Brichot. Naturally, once he saw that Brichot was popular in this house, it was a way of hitting back at us, of spoiling our party. I know his sort, the dear, good friend of the family, who pulls you all to pieces on the stairs as he's going away.'

'Didn't I say so?' retorted her husband. 'He's simply a failure; a poor little wretch who goes through life mad with jealousy of anything that's at all big.'

Had the truth been known, there was not one of the 'faithful' who was not infinitely more malicious than Swann; but the others would all take the precaution of tempering their malice with obvious pleasantries, with little sparks of emotion and cordiality; while the least indication of reserve on Swann's part, undraped in any such conventional formula as 'Of course, I don't want to say anything – ' to which he would have scorned to descend, appeared to them a deliberate act of treachery. There are certain original and distinguished authors in whom the least 'freedom of speech' is thought revolting because they have not begun by flattering the public taste, and serving up to it the commonplace expressions to which it is used; it was by the same process that Swann infuriated M. Verdurin. In his case as in theirs it was the novelty of his language which led his audience to suspect the blackness of his designs.

Swann was still unconscious of the disgrace that threatened him at the Verdurins', and continued to regard all their absurdities in the most rosy light, through the admiring eyes of love.

As a rule he made no appointments with Odette except for the evenings; he was afraid of her growing tired of him if he visited her during the day as well; at the same time he was reluctant to forfeit, even for an hour, the place that he held in her thoughts, and so was constantly looking out for an opportunity of claiming her attention, in any way that would not be displeasing to her. If, in a florist's or a jeweller's window, a plant or an ornament caught his eye, he would at once think of sending them to Odette, imagining that the pleasure which the casual sight of them had given him would instinctively be felt, also, by her, and would increase her affection for himself; and he would order them to be taken at once to the Rue La Pérouse, so as to accelerate the moment in which, as she received an offering from him, he might feel himself, in a sense, transported into her presence. He was particularly anxious, always, that she should receive these presents before she went out for the evening, so that her sense of gratitude towards him might give additional tenderness to her welcome when he arrived at the Verdurins', might even – for all he knew – if the shopkeeper made haste, bring him a letter from her before dinner, or herself, in person, upon his doorstep, come on a little extraordinary visit of thanks. As in an earlier phase, when he had experimented with the reflex action of anger and contempt upon her character, he sought now by that of gratification to elicit from her fresh particles of her intimate feelings, which she had never yet revealed.

Often she was embarrassed by lack of money, and under pressure from a creditor would come to him for assistance. He enjoyed this, as he enjoyed everything which could impress Odette with his love for herself, or merely with his influence, with the extent of the use that she might make of him. Probably if anyone had said to him, at the beginning, 'It's your position that attracts her,' or at this stage, 'It's your money that she's really in love with,' he would not have believed the suggestion, nor would he have been greatly distressed by the thought that people supposed her to be attached to him, that people felt them to be united by any ties so binding as those of snobbishness or wealth. But even if he had accepted the possibility, it might not have caused him any suffering to discover that Odette's love for him was based on a foundation more lasting than mere affection, or any attractive qualities which she might have found in him; on a sound, commercial interest; an interest which would postpone for ever the fatal day on which she might be tempted to bring their relations to an end. For the moment, while he lavished presents upon her, and performed all manner of services, he could rely on advantages not contained in his person, or in his intellect, could forgo the endless, killing effort to make himself attractive. And this delight in being a lover, in living by love alone, of the reality of which he was inclined to be doubtful, the price which, in the long run, he must pay for it, as a dilettante in immaterial sensations, enhanced its value in his eyes – as one sees people who are doubtful whether the sight of the sea and the sound of its waves are really enjoyable, become convinced that they are, as also of the rare quality and absolute detachment of their own taste, when they have agreed to pay several pounds a day for a room in an hotel, from which that sight and that sound may be enjoyed.

One day, when reflexions of this order had brought him once again to the memory of the time when someone had spoken to him of Odette as of a 'kept' woman, and when, once again, he had amused himself with contrasting that strange personification, the 'kept' woman – an iridescent mixture of unknown and demoniacal qualities, embroidered, as in some fantasy of Gustave Moreau, with poison-dripping flowers, interwoven with precious jewels – with that Odette upon whose face he had watched the passage of the same expressions of pity for a sufferer, resentment of an act of injustice, gratitude for an act of kindness, which he had seen, in earlier days, on his own mother's face, and on the faces of friends; that Odette, whose conversation had so frequently turned on the things that he himself knew better than anyone, his collections, his room, his old servant, his banker, who kept all his title-deeds and bonds; – the thought of the banker reminded him that he must call on him shortly, to draw some money. And indeed, if, during the current month, he were to come less liberally to the aid of Odette in her financial difficulties than in the month before, when he had given her five thousand francs, if he refrained from offering her a diamond necklace for which she longed, he would be allowing her admiration for his generosity to decline, that gratitude which had made him so happy, and would even be running the risk of her imagining that his love for her (as she saw its visible manifestations grow fewer) had itself diminished. And then, suddenly, he asked himself whether that was not precisely what was implied by 'keeping' a woman (as if, in fact, that idea of 'keeping' could be derived from elements not at all mysterious or perverse, but belonging to the intimate routine of his daily life, such as that thousand-franc note, a familiar and domestic object, torn in places and mended with gummed paper, which his valet, after paying the household accounts and the rent, had locked up in a drawer in the old writing-desk whence he had extracted it to send it, with four others, to Odette) and whether it was not possible to apply to Odette, since he had known her (for he never imagined for a moment that she could ever have taken a penny from someone else, before), that title, which he had believed so wholly inapplicable to her, of 'kept' woman. He could not explore the idea farther, for a sudden access of that mental lethargy which was, with him, congenital, intermittent, and providential, happened, at that moment, to extinguish every particle of light in his brain, as instantaneously as, at a later period, when electric lighting had been everywhere installed, it became possible, merely by fingering a switch, to cut off all the supply of light from a house. His mind fumbled, for a moment, in the darkness, he took off his spectacles, wiped the glasses, passed his hands over his eyes, but saw no light until he found himself face to face with a wholly different idea, the realization that he must endeavour, in the coming month, to send Odette six or seven thousand-franc notes instead of five, simply as a surprise for her and to give her pleasure.

In the evening, when he did not stay at home until it was time to meet Odette at the Verdurins', or rather at one of the open-air restaurants which they liked to frequent in the Bois and especially at Saint-Cloud, he would go to dine in one of those fashionable houses in which, at one time, he had been a constant guest. He did not wish to lose touch with people who, for all that he knew, might be of use, some day, to Odette, and thanks to whom he was often, in the meantime, able to procure for her some privilege or pleasure. Besides, he had been used for so long to the refinement and comfort of good society that, side by side with his contempt, there had grown up also a desperate need for it, with the result that, when he had reached the point after which the humblest lodgings appeared to him as precisely on a par with the most princely mansions, his senses were so thoroughly accustomed to the latter that he could not enter the former without a feeling of acute discomfort. He had the same regard – to a degree of identity which they would never have suspected – for the little families with small incomes who asked him to dances in their flats ('straight upstairs to the fifth floor, and the door on the left') as for the Princesse de Parme, who gave the most splendid parties in Paris; but he had not the feeling of being actually 'at the ball' when he found himself herded with the fathers of families in the bedroom of the lady of the house, while the spectacle of wash-hand-stands covered over with towels, and of beds converted into cloak-rooms, with a mass of hats and greatcoats sprawling over their counterpanes, gave him the same stifling sensation that, nowadays, people who have been used for half a lifetime to electric light derive from a smoking lamp or a candle that needs to be snuffed. If he were dining out, he would order his carriage for half past seven; while he changed his clothes, he would be wondering, all the time, about Odette, and in this way was never alone, for the constant thought of Odette gave to the moments in which he was separated from her the same peculiar charm as to those in which she was at his side. He would get into his carriage and drive off, but he knew that this thought had jumped in after him and had settled down upon his knee, like a pet animal which he might take everywhere, and would keep with him at the dinner-table, unobserved by his fellow-guests. He would stroke and fondle it, warm himself with it, and, as a feeling of languor swept over him, would give way to a slight shuddering movement which contracted his throat and nostrils – a new experience, this, – as he fastened the bunch of columbines in his buttonhole. He had for some time been feeling neither well nor happy, especially since Odette had brought Forcheville to the Verdurins', and he would have liked to go away for a while to rest in the country. But he could never summon up courage to leave Paris, even for a day, while Odette was there. The weather was warm; it was the finest part of the spring. And for all that he was driving through a city of stone to immure himself in a house without grass or garden, what was incessantly before his eyes was a park which he owned, near Combray, where, at four in the afternoon, before coming to the asparagus-bed, thanks to the breeze that was wafted across the fields from Méséglise, he could enjoy the fragrant coolness of the air as well beneath an arbour of hornbeams in the garden as by the bank of the pond, fringed with forget-me-not and iris; and where, when he sat down to dinner, trained and twined by the gardener's skilful hand, there ran all about his table currant-bush and rose.

After dinner, if he had an early appointment in the Bois or at Saint-Cloud, he would rise from table and leave the house so abruptly – especially if it threatened to rain, and so to scatter the 'faithful' before their normal time – that on one occasion the Princesse des Laumes (at whose house dinner had been so late that Swann had left before the coffee came in, to join the Verdurins on the Island in the Bois) observed:

'Really, if Swann were thirty years older, and had diabetes, there might be some excuse for his running away like that. He seems to look upon us all as a joke.'

He persuaded himself that the spring-time charm, which he could not go down to Combray to enjoy, he would find at least on the Île des Cygnes or at Saint-Cloud. But as he could think only of Odette, he would return home not knowing even if he had tasted the fragrance of the young leaves, or if the moon had been shining. He would be welcomed by the little phrase from the sonata, played in the garden on the restaurant piano. If there was none in the garden, the Verdurins would have taken immense pains to have a piano brought out either from a private room or from the restaurant itself; not because Swann was now restored to favour; far from it. But the idea of arranging an ingenious form of entertainment for someone, even for someone whom they disliked, would stimulate them, during the time spent in its preparation, to a momentary sense of cordiality and affection. Now and then he would remind himself that another fine spring evening was drawing to a close, and would force himself to notice the trees and the sky. But the state of excitement into which Odette's presence never failed to throw him, added to a feverish ailment which, for some time now, had scarcely left him, robbed him of that sense of quiet and comfort which is an indispensable background to the impressions that we derive from nature.

One evening, when Swann had consented to dine with the Verdurins, and had mentioned during dinner that he had to attend, next day, the annual banquet of an old comrades' association, Odette had at once exclaimed across the table, in front of everyone, in front of Forcheville, who was now one of the 'faithful', in front of the painter, in front of Cottard:

'Yes, I know, you have your banquet to-morrow; I shan't see you, then, till I get home; don't be too late.'

And although Swann had never yet taken offence, at all seriously, at Odette's demonstrations of friendship for one or other of the 'faithful', he felt an exquisite pleasure on hearing her thus avow, before them all, with that calm immodesty, the fact that they saw each other regularly every evening, his privileged position in her house, and her own preference for him which it implied. It was true that Swann had often reflected that Odette was in no way a remarkable woman; and in the supremacy which he wielded over a creature so distinctly inferior to himself there was nothing that especially flattered him when he heard it proclaimed to all the 'faithful'; but since he had observed that, to several other men than himself, Odette seemed a fascinating and desirable woman, the attraction which her body held for him had aroused a painful longing to secure the absolute mastery of even the tiniest particles of her heart. And he had begun to attach an incalculable value to those moments passed in her house in the evenings, when he held her upon his knee, made her tell him what she thought about this or that, and counted over that treasure to which, alone of all his earthly possessions, he still clung. And so, after this dinner, drawing her aside, he took care to thank her effusively, seeking to indicate to her by the extent of his gratitude the corresponding intensity of the pleasures which it was in her power to bestow on him, the supreme pleasure being to guarantee him immunity, for so long as his love should last and he remain vulnerable, from the assaults of jealousy.

When he came away from his banquet, the next evening, it was pouring with rain, and he had nothing but his victoria. A friend offered to take him home in a closed carriage, and as Odette, by the fact of her having invited him to come, had given him an assurance that she was expecting no one else, he could, with a quiet mind and an untroubled heart, rather than set off thus in the rain, have gone home and to bed. But perhaps, if she saw that he seemed not to adhere to his resolution to end every evening, without exception, in her company, she might grow careless, and fail to keep free for him just the one evening on which he particularly desired it.

It was after eleven when he reached her door, and as he made his apology for having been unable to come away earlier, she complained that it was indeed very late; the storm had made her unwell, her head ached, and she warned him that she would not let him stay longer than half an hour, that at midnight she would send him away; a little while later she felt tired and wished to sleep.

'No cattleya, then, to-night?' he asked, 'and I've been looking forward so to a nice little cattleya.'

But she was irresponsive; saying nervously: 'No, dear, no cattleya to-night. Can't you see, I'm not well?'

'It might have done you good, but I won't bother you.'

She begged him to put out the light before he went; he drew the curtains close round her bed and left her. But, when he was in his own house again, the idea suddenly struck him that, perhaps, Odette was expecting someone else that evening, that she had merely pretended to be tired, that she had asked him to put the light out only so that he should suppose that she was going to sleep, that the moment he had left the house she lighted it again, and had reopened her door to the stranger who was to be her guest for the night. He looked at his watch. It was about an hour and a half since he had left her; he went out, took a cab, and stopped it close to her house, in a little street running at right angles to that other street, which lay at the back of her house, and along which he used to go, sometimes, to tap upon her bedroom window, for her to let him in. He left his cab; the streets were all deserted and dark; he walked a few yards and came out almost opposite her house. Amid the glimmering blackness of all the row of windows, the lights in which had long since been put out, he saw one, and only one, from which overflowed, between the slats of its shutters, closed like a wine-press over its mysterious golden juice, the light that filled the room within, a light which on so many evenings, as soon as he saw it, far off, as he turned into the street, had rejoiced his heart with its message; 'She is there – expecting you,' and now tortured him with; 'She is there with the man she was expecting.' He must know who; he tiptoed along by the wall until he reached the window, but between the slanting bars of the shutters he could see nothing; he could hear, only, in the silence of the night, the murmur of conversation. What agony he suffered as he watched that light, in whose golden atmosphere were moving, behind the closed sash, the unseen and detested pair, as he listened to that murmur which revealed the presence of the man who had crept in after his own departure, the perfidy of Odette, and the pleasures which she was at that moment tasting with the stranger.

And yet he was not sorry that he had come; the torment which had forced him to leave his own house had lost its sharpness when it lost its uncertainty, now that Odette's other life, of which he had had, at that first moment, a sudden helpless suspicion, was definitely there, almost within his grasp, before his eyes, in the full glare of the lamp-light, caught and kept there, an unwitting prisoner, in that room into which, when he would, he might force his way to surprise and seize it; or rather he would tap upon the shutters, as he had often done when he had come there very late, and by that signal Odette would at least learn that he knew, that he had seen the light and had heard the voices; while he himself, who a moment ago had been picturing her as laughing at him, as sharing with that other the knowledge of how effectively he had been tricked, now it was he that saw them, confident and persistent in their error, tricked and trapped by none other than himself, whom they believed to be a mile away, but who was there, in person, there with a plan, there with the knowledge that he was going, in another minute, to tap upon the shutter. And, perhaps, what he felt (almost an agreeable feeling) at that moment was something more than relief at the solution of doubt, at the soothing of a pain; was an intellectual pleasure. If, since he had fallen in love, things had recovered a little of the delicate attraction that they had had for him long ago – though only when a light was shed upon them by a thought, a memory of Odette – now it was another of the faculties, prominent in the studious days of his youth, that Odette had quickened with new life, the passion for truth, but for a truth which, too, was interposed between himself and his mistress, receiving its light from her alone, a private and personal truth the sole object of which (an infinitely precious object, and one almost impersonal in its absolute beauty) was Odette – Odette in her activities, her environment, her projects, and her past. At every other period in his life, the little everyday words and actions of another person had always seemed wholly valueless to Swann; if gossip about such things were repeated to him, he would dismiss it as insignificant, and while he listened it was only the lowest, the most commonplace part of his mind that was interested; at such moments he felt utterly dull and uninspired. But in this strange phase of love the personality of another person becomes so enlarged, so deepened, that the curiosity which he could now feel aroused in himself, to know the least details of a woman's daily occupation, was the same thirst for knowledge with which he had once studied history. And all manner of actions, from which, until now, he would have recoiled in shame, such as spying, to-night, outside a window, to-morrow, for all he knew, putting adroitly provocative questions to casual witnesses, bribing servants, listening at doors, seemed to him, now, to be precisely on a level with the deciphering of manuscripts, the weighing of evidence, the interpretation of old monuments, that was to say, so many different methods of scientific investigation, each one having a definite intellectual value and being legitimately employable in the search for truth.

As his hand stole out towards the shutters he felt a pang of shame at the thought that Odette would now know that he had suspected her, that he had returned, that he had posted himself outside her window. She had often told him what a horror she had of jealous men, of lovers who spied. What he was going to do would be extremely awkward, and she would detest him for ever after, whereas now, for the moment, for so long as he refrained from knocking, perhaps even in the act of infidelity, she loved him still. How often is not the prospect of future happiness thus sacrificed to one's impatient insistence upon an immediate gratification. But his desire to know the truth was stronger, and seemed to him nobler than his desire for her. He knew that the true story of certain events, which he would have given his life to be able to reconstruct accurately and in full, was to be read within that window, streaked with bars of light, as within the illuminated, golden boards of one of those precious manuscripts, by whose wealth of artistic treasures the scholar who consults them cannot remain unmoved. He yearned for the satisfaction of knowing the truth which so impassioned him in that brief, fleeting, precious transcript, on that translucent page, so warm, so beautiful. And besides, the advantage which he felt – which he so desperately wanted to feel – that he had over them, lay perhaps not so much in knowing as in being able to show them that he knew. He drew himself up on tiptoe. He knocked. They had not heard; he knocked again; louder; their conversation ceased. A man's voice – he strained his ears to distinguish whose, among such of Odette's friends as he knew, the voice could be – asked:

'Who's that?'

He could not be certain of the voice. He knocked once again. The window first, then the shutters were thrown open. It was too late, now, to retire, and since she must know

all, so as not to seem too contemptible, too jealous and inquisitive, he called out in a careless, hearty, welcoming tone:
'Please don't bother: I just happened to be passing, and
saw the light. I wanted to know if you were feeling better.'

He looked up. Two old gentlemen stood facing him, in
the window, one of them with a lamp in his hand; and
beyond them he could see into the room, a room that he
had never seen before. Having fallen into the habit, when
he came late to Odette, of identifying her window by the fact
that it was the only one still lighted in a row of windows
otherwise all alike, he had been misled, this time, by the light,
and had knocked at the window beyond hers, in the adjoining
house. He made what apology he could and hurried home,
overjoyed that the satisfaction of his curiosity had preserved
their love intact, and that, having feigned for so long, when
in Odette's company, a sort of indifference, he had not now,
by a demonstration of jealousy, given her that proof of the
excess of his own passion which, in a pair of lovers, fully and
finally dispenses the recipient from the obligation to love the
other enough. He never spoke to her of this misadventure,
he ceased even to think of it himself. But now and then his
thoughts in their wandering course would come upon this
memory where it lay unobserved, would startle it into life,
thrust it more deeply down into his consciousness, and leave
him aching with a sharp, far-rooted pain. As though this had
been a bodily pain, Swann's mind was powerless to alleviate
it; in the case of bodily pain, however, since it is independent
of the mind, the mind can dwell upon it, can note that it has
diminished, that it has momentarily ceased. But with this
mental pain, the mind, merely by recalling it, created it
afresh. To determine not to think of it was but to think of it
still, to suffer from it still. And when, in conversation with
his friends, he forgot his sufferings, suddenly a word casually
uttered would make him change countenance as a wounded
man does when a clumsy hand has touched his aching limb.
When he came away from Odette, he was happy, he felt calm,
he recalled the smile with which, in gentle mockery, she had
spoken to him of this man or of that, a smile which was all

tenderness for himself; he recalled the gravity of her head which she seemed to have lifted from its axis to let it droop and fall, as though against her will, upon his lips, as she had done on that first evening in the carriage; her languishing gaze at him while she lay nestling in his arms, her bended head seeming to recede between her shoulders, as though shrinking from the cold.

But then, at once, his jealousy, as it had been the shadow of his love, presented him with the complement, with the converse of that new smile with which she had greeted him that very evening, – with which, now, perversely, she was mocking Swann while she tendered her love to another – of that lowering of her head, but lowered now to fall on other lips, and (but bestowed upon a stranger) of all the marks of affection that she had shown to him. And all these voluptuous memories which he bore away from her house were, as one might say, but so many sketches, rough plans, like the schemes of decoration which a designer submits to one in outline, enabling Swann to form an idea of the various attitudes, aflame or faint with passion, which she was capable of adopting for others. With the result that he came to regret every pleasure that he tasted in her company, every new caress that he invented (and had been so imprudent as to point out to her how delightful it was) every fresh charm that he found in her, for he knew that, a moment later, they would go to enrich the collection of instruments in his secret torture-chamber.

A fresh turn was given to the screw when Swann recalled a sudden expression which he had intercepted, a few days earlier, and for the first time, in Odette's eyes. It was after dinner at the Verdurins'. Whether it was because Forcheville, aware that Saniette, his brother-in-law, was not in favour with them, had decided to make a butt of him, and to shine at his expense, or because he had been annoyed by some awkward remark which Saniette had made to him, although it had passed unnoticed by the rest of the party who knew nothing of whatever tactless allusion it might conceal, or possibly because he had been for some time looking out for an opportunity of securing the expulsion from the house of a fellow-guest who knew rather too much about him, and whom he knew to be so nice-minded that he himself could not help feeling embarrassed at times merely by his presence in the room, Forcheville replied to Saniette's tactless utterance with such a volley of abuse, going out of his way to insult him, emboldened, the louder he shouted, by the fear, the pain, the entreaties of his victim, that the poor creature, after asking Mme Verdurin whether he should stay and receiving no answer, had left the house in stammering confusion and with tears in his eyes. Odette had looked on, impassive, at this scene; but when the door had closed behind Saniette, she had forced the normal expression of her face down, as the saying is, by several pegs, so as to bring herself on to the same level of vulgarity as Forcheville; her eyes had sparkled with a malicious smile of congratulation upon his audacity, of ironical pity for the poor wretch who had been its victim; she had darted at him a look of complicity in the crime which so clearly implied: 'That's finished him off, or I'm very much mistaken. Did you see what a fool he looked? He was actually crying!' that Forcheville, when his eyes met hers, sobered in a moment from the anger, or pretended anger with which he was still flushed, smiled as he explained: 'He need only have made himself pleasant and he'd have been here still; a good scolding does a man no harm, at any time.'

One day when Swann had gone out early in the afternoon to pay a call, and had failed to find the person at home whom he wished to see, it occurred to him to go, instead, to Odette, at an hour when, although he never went to her house then as a rule, he knew that she was always at home, resting or writing letters until tea-time, and would enjoy seeing her for a moment, if it did not disturb her. The porter told him that he believed Odette to be in; Swann rang the bell, thought that he heard a sound, that he heard footsteps, but no one came to the door. Anxious and annoyed, he went round to the other little street, at the back of her house, and stood beneath her bedroom window; the curtains were drawn and he could see

nothing; he knocked loudly upon the pane, he shouted; still
no one came. He could see that the neighbours were staring at
him. He turned away, thinking that, after all, he had perhaps
been mistaken in believing that he heard footsteps; but he
remained so preoccupied with the suspicion that he could turn
his mind to nothing else. After waiting for an hour, he returned. He found her at home; she told him that she had been
in the house when he rang, but had been asleep; the bell had
awakened her; she had guessed that it must be Swann, and
had run out to meet him, but he had already gone. She had, of
course, heard him knocking at the window. Swann could at
once detect in this story one of those fragments of literal truth
which liars, when taken by surprise, console themselves by
introducing into the composition of the falsehood which they
have to invent, thinking that it can be safely incorporated, and
will lend the whole story an air of verisimilitude. It was true
that, when Odette had just done something which she did not
wish to disclose, she would take pains to conceal it in a secret
place in her heart. But as soon as she found herself face to face
with the man to whom she was obliged to lie, she became
uneasy, all her ideas melted like wax before a flame, her in-
ventive and her reasoning faculties were paralysed, she might
ransack her brain but would find only a void; still, she must
say something, and there lay within her reach precisely the fact
which she had wished to conceal, which, being the truth, was
the one thing that had remained. She broke off from it a tiny
fragment, of no importance in itself, assuring herself that,
after all, it was the best thing to do, since it was a detail of the
truth, and less dangerous, therefore, than a falsehood. 'At any
rate, this is true;' she said to herself; 'that's always something
to the good; he may make inquiries; he will see that this is true;
it won't be this, anyhow, that will give me away.' But she was
wrong; it was what gave her away; she had not taken into
account that this fragmentary detail of the truth had sharp
edges which could not be made to fit in, except to those contiguous fragments of the truth from which she had arbitrarily
detached it, edges which, whatever the fictitious details in
which she might embed it, would continue to show, by their

overlapping angles and by the gaps which she had forgotten to fill, that its proper place was elsewhere.

'She admits that she heard me ring, and then knock, that she knew it was myself, that she wanted to see me,' Swann thought to himself. 'But that doesn't correspond with the fact that she did not let me in.'

He did not, however, draw her attention to this inconsistency, for he thought that, if left to herself, Odette might perhaps produce some falsehood which would give him a faint indication of the truth; she spoke; he did not interrupt her, he gathered up, with an eager and sorrowful piety, the words that fell from her lips, feeling (and rightly feeling, since she was hiding the truth behind them as she spoke) that, like the veil of a sanctuary, they kept a vague imprint, traced a faint outline of that infinitely precious and, alas, undiscoverable truth; – what she had been doing, that afternoon, at three o'clock, when he had called, – a truth of which he would never possess any more than these falsifications, illegible and divine traces, a truth which would exist henceforward only in the secretive memory of this creature, who could contemplate it in utter ignorance of its value, but would never yield it up to him. It was true that he had, now and then, a strong suspicion that Odette's daily activities were not in themselves passionately interesting, and that such relations as she might have with other men did not exhale, naturally, in a universal sense, or for every rational being, a spirit of morbid gloom capable of infecting with fever or of inciting to suicide. He realized, at such moments, that that interest, that gloom, existed in him only as a malady might exist, and that, once he was cured of the malady, the actions of Odette, the kisses that she might have bestowed, would become once again as innocuous as those of countless other women. But the consciousness that the painful curiosity with which Swann now studied them had its origin only in himself was not enough to make him decide that it was unreasonable to regard that curiosity as important, and to take every possible step to satisfy it. Swann had, in fact, reached an age the philosophy of which – supported, in his case, by the current philosophy of the day, as well as by that of the circle in which he had spent most of his life, the group that surrounded the Princesse des Laumes, in which one's intelligence was understood to increase with the strength of one's disbelief in everything, and nothing real and incontestable was to be discovered, except the individual tastes of each of its members – is no longer that of youth, but a positive, almost a medical philosophy, the philosophy of men who, instead of fixing their aspirations upon external objects, endeavour to separate from the accumulation of the years already spent a definite residue of habits and passions which they can regard as characteristic and permanent, and with which they will deliberately arrange, before anything else, that the kind of existence which they choose to adopt shall not prove inharmonious. Swann deemed it wise to make allowance in his life for the suffering which he derived from not knowing what Odette had done, just as he made allowance for the impetus which a damp climate always gave to his eczema; to anticipate in his budget the expenditure of a considerable sum on procuring, with regard to the daily occupations of Odette, information the lack of which would make him unhappy, just as he reserved a margin for the gratification of other tastes from which he knew that pleasure was to be expected (at least, before he had fallen in love) such as his taste for collecting things, or for good cooking.

When he proposed to take leave of Odette, and to return home, she begged him to stay a little longer, and even detained him forcibly, seizing him by the arm as he was opening the door to go. But he gave no thought to that, for, among the crowd of gestures and speeches and other little incidents which go to make up a conversation, it is inevitable that we should pass (without noticing anything that arouses our interest) by those that hide a truth for which our suspicions are blindly searching, whereas we stop to examine others beneath which nothing lies concealed. She kept on saying: 'What a dreadful pity; you never by any chance come in the afternoon, and the one time you do come then I miss you.' He knew very well that she was not sufficiently in love with him to be so keenly distressed merely at having missed his

visit, but as she was a good-natured woman, anxious to give
him pleasure, and often sorry when she had done anything
that annoyed him, he found it quite natural that she should be
sorry, on this occasion, that she had deprived him of that
pleasure of spending an hour in her company, which was so
very great a pleasure, if not to herself, at any rate to him.
All the same, it was a matter of so little importance that her
air of unrelieved sorrow began at length to bewilder him.
She reminded him, even more than was usual, of the faces of
some of the women created by the painter of the 'Primavera'.
She had, at that moment, their downcast, heartbroken expression, which seems ready to succumb beneath the burden
of a grief too heavy to be borne, when they are merely allowing
the Infant Jesus to play with a pomegranate, or watching
Moses pour water into a trough. He had seen the same sorrow
once before on her face, but when, he could no longer say.
Then suddenly, he remembered; it was when Odette had lied,
in apologizing to Mme Verdurin on the evening after the
dinner from which she had stayed away on a pretext of illness,
but really so that she might be alone with Swann. Surely,
even had she been the most scrupulous of women, she could
hardly have felt remorse for so innocent a lie. But the lies
which Odette ordinarily told were less innocent, and served
to prevent discoveries which might have involved her in the
most terrible difficulties with one or another of her friends.
And so, when she lied, smitten with fear, feeling herself to be
but feebly armed for her defence, unconfident of success, she
was inclined to weep from sheer exhaustion, as children weep
sometimes when they have not slept. She knew, also, that her
lie, as a rule, was doing a serious injury to the man to whom
she was telling it, and that she might find herself at his mercy
if she told it badly. Therefore she felt at once humble and
culpable in his presence. And when she had to tell an insignificant, social lie its hazardous associations, and the memories which it recalled, would leave her weak with a sense of
exhaustion and penitent with a consciousness of wrongdoing.

What depressing lie was she now concocting for Swann's
benefit, to give her that pained expression, that plaintive

voice, which seemed to falter beneath the effort that she was forcing herself to make, and to plead for pardon? He had an idea that it was not merely the truth about what had occurred that afternoon that she was endeavouring to hide from him, but something more immediate, something, possibly, which had not yet happened, but might happen now at any time, and, when it did, would throw a light upon that earlier event. At that moment, he heard the front-door bell ring. Odette never stopped speaking, but her words dwindled into an inarticulate moan. Her regret at not having seen Swann that afternoon, at not having opened the door to him, had melted into a universal despair.

He could hear the gate being closed, and the sound of a carriage, as though someone were going away – probably the person whom Swann must on no account meet – after being told that Odette was not at home. And then, when he reflected that, merely by coming at an hour when he was not in the habit of coming, he had managed to disturb so many arrangements of which she did not wish him to know, he had a feeling of discouragement that amounted, almost, to distress. But since he was in love with Odette, since he was in the habit of turning all his thoughts towards her, the pity with which he might have been inspired for himself he felt for her only, and murmured: 'Poor darling!' When finally he left her, she took up several letters which were lying on the table, and asked him if he would be so good as to post them for her. He walked along to the post-office, took the letters from his pocket, and, before dropping each of them into the box, scanned its address. They were all to tradesmen, except the last, which was to Forcheville. He kept it in his hand. 'If I saw what was in this,' he argued, 'I should know what she calls him, what she says to him, whether there really is anything between them. Perhaps, if I don't look inside, I shall be lacking in delicacy towards Odette, since in this way alone I can rid myself of a suspicion which is, perhaps, a calumny on her, which must, in any case, cause her suffering, and which can never possibly be set at rest, once the letter is posted.'

He left the post-office and went home, but he had kept the

last letter in his pocket. He lighted a candle, and held up close to its flame the envelope which he had not dared to open. At first he could distinguish nothing, but the envelope was thin, and by pressing it down on to the stiff card which it enclosed he was able, through the transparent paper, to read the concluding words. They were a coldly formal signature. If, instead of its being himself who was looking at a letter addressed to Forcheville, it had been Forcheville who had read a letter addressed to Swann, he might have found words in it of another, a far more tender kind! He took a firm hold of the card, which was sliding to and fro, the envelope being too large for it, and then, by moving it with his finger and thumb, brought one line after another beneath the part of the envelope where the paper was not doubled, through which alone it was possible to read.

In spite of all these manoeuvres he could not make it out clearly. Not that it mattered, for he had seen enough to assure himself that the letter was about some trifling incident of no importance, and had nothing at all to do with love; it was something to do with Odette's uncle. Swann had read quite plainly at the beginning of the line 'I was right', but did not understand what Odette had been right in doing, until suddenly a word which he had not been able, at first, to decipher, came to light and made the whole sentence intelligible: 'I was right to open the door; it was my uncle.' To open the door! Then Forcheville had been there when Swann rang the bell, and she had sent him away, hence the sound that Swann had heard.

After that he read the whole letter; at the end she apologized for having treated Forcheville with so little ceremony, and reminded him that he had left his cigarette-case at her house, precisely what she had written to Swann after one of his first visits. But to Swann she had added: 'Why did you not forget your heart also? I should never have let you have that back.' To Forcheville nothing of that sort; no allusion that could suggest any intrigue between them. And, really, he was obliged to admit that in all this business Forcheville had been worse treated than himself, since Odette was writing to him to make him believe that her visitor had been an uncle. From which it followed that he, Swann, was the man to whom she attached importance, and for whose sake she had sent the other away. And yet, if there had been nothing between Odette and Forcheville, why not have opened the door at once, why have said, 'I was right to open the door; it was my uncle.' Right? if she was doing nothing wrong at that moment how could Forcheville possibly have accounted for her not opening the door? For a time Swann stood still there, heartbroken, bewildered, and yet happy; gazing at this envelope which Odette had handed to him without a scruple, so absolute was her trust in his honour; through its transparent window there had been disclosed to him, with the secret history of an incident which he had despaired of ever being able to learn, a fragment of the life of Odette, seen as through a narrow, luminous incision, cut into its surface without her knowledge. Then his jealousy rejoiced at the discovery, as though that jealousy had had an independent existence, fiercely egotistical, gluttonous of everything that would feed its vitality, even at the expense of Swann himself. Now it had food in store, and Swann could begin to grow uneasy afresh every evening, over the visits that Odette had received about five o'clock, and could seek to discover where Forcheville had been at that hour. For Swann's affection for Odette still preserved the form which had been imposed on it, from the beginning, by his ignorance of the occupations in which she passed her days, as well as by the mental lethargy which prevented him from supplementing that ignorance by imagination. He was not jealous, at first, of the whole of Odette's life, but of those moments only in which an incident, which he had perhaps misinterpreted, had led him to suppose that Odette might have played him false. His jealousy, like an octopus which throws out a first, then a second, and finally a third tentacle, fastened itself irremovably first to that moment, five o'clock in the afternoon, then to another, then to another again. But Swann was incapable of inventing his sufferings. They were only the memory, the perpetuation of a suffering that had come to him from without.

From without, however, everything brought him fresh suffering. He decided to separate Odette from Forcheville, by taking her away for a few days to the south. But he imagined that she was coveted by every male person in the hotel, and that she coveted them in return. And so he, who, in old days, when he travelled, used always to seek out new people and crowded places, might now be seen fleeing savagely from human society as if it had cruelly injured him. And how could he not have turned misanthrope, when in every man he saw a potential lover for Odette? Thus his jealousy did even more than the happy, passionate desire which he had originally felt for Odette had done to alter Swann's character, completely changing, in the eyes of the world, even the outward signs by which that character had been intelligible.

A month after the evening on which he had intercepted and read Odette's letter to Forcheville, Swann went to a dinner which the Verdurins were giving in the Bois. As the party was breaking up he noticed a series of whispered discussions between Mme Verdurin and several of her guests, and thought that he heard the pianist being reminded to come next day to a party at Chatou; now he, Swann, had not been invited to any party.

The Verdurins had spoken only in whispers, and in vague terms, but the painter, perhaps without thinking, shouted out: 'There must be no lights of any sort, and he must play the Moonlight Sonata in the dark, for us to see by.'

Mme Verdurin, seeing that Swann was within earshot, assumed that expression in which the two fold desire to make the speaker be quiet and to preserve, oneself, an appearance of guilelessness in the eyes of the listener, is neutralized in an intense vacuity; in which the unflinching signs of intelligent complicity are overlaid by the smiles of innocence, an expression invariably adopted by anyone who has noticed a blunder, the enormity of which is thereby at once revealed if not to those who have made it, at any rate to him in whose hearing it ought not to have been made. Odette seemed suddenly to be in despair, as though she had decided not to struggle any longer against the crushing difficulties of life, and Swann was anxiously counting the minutes that still separated him from the point at which, after leaving the restaurant, while he drove her home, he would be able to ask for an explanation, to make her promise, either that she would not go to Chatou next day, or that she would procure an invitation for him also, and to lull to rest in her arms the anguish that still tormented him. At last the carriages were ordered. Mme Verdurin said to Swann:

'Good-bye, then. We shall see you soon, I hope,' trying by the friendliness of her manner and the constraint of her smile, to prevent him from noticing that she was not saying, as she would always have until then:

'To-morrow, then, at Chatou, and at my house the day after.'

M. and Mme Verdurin made Forcheville get into their carriage; Swann's was drawn up behind it, and he waited for theirs to start before helping Odette into his own.

'Odette, we'll take you,' said Mme Verdurin, 'we've kept a little corner specially for you, beside M. de Forcheville.'

'Yes, Mme Verdurin,' said Odette meekly.

'What! I thought I was to take you home,' cried Swann, flinging discretion to the winds, for the carriage-door hung open, time was precious, and he could not, in his present state, go home without her.

'But Mme Verdurin has asked me . . .'

'That's all right, you can quite well go home alone; we've left you like this dozens of times,' said Mme Verdurin.

'But I had something important to tell Mme de Crécy.'

'Very well, you can write it to her instead.'

'Good-bye,' said Odette, holding out her hand.

He tried hard to smile, but could only succeed in looking utterly dejected.

'What do you think of the airs that Swann is pleased to put on with us?' Mme Verdurin asked her husband when they had reached home. 'I was afraid he was going to eat me, simply because we offered to take Odette back. It really is too bad, that sort of thing. Why doesn't he say, straight out, that we keep a disorderly house? I can't conceive how Odette can stand such manners. He positively seems to be saying, all the time, "You belong to me!" I shall tell Odette exactly what I think about it all, and I hope she will have the sense to understand me.' A moment later she added, inarticulate with rage: 'No, but, don't you see, the filthy creature . . .' using unconsciously, and perhaps in satisfaction of the same obscure need to justify herself – like Françoise at Combray when the chicken refused to die – the very words which the last convulsions of an inoffensive animal in its death agony wring from the peasant who is engaged in taking its life. And when Mme Verdurin's carriage had moved on, and Swann's took its place, his coachman, catching sight of his face, asked whether he was unwell, or had heard bad news.

Swann sent him away; he preferred to walk, and it was on foot, through the Bois, that he came home. He talked to himself, aloud, and in the same slightly affected tone which he had been used to adopt when describing the charms of the 'little nucleus' and extolling the magnanimity of the Verdurins. But just as the conversation, the smiles, the kisses of Odette became as odious to him as he had once found them charming, if they were diverted to others than himself, so the Verdurins' drawing-room, which, not an hour before, had still seemed to him amusing, inspired with a genuine feeling for art and even with a sort of moral aristocracy, now that it was another than himself whom Odette was going to meet there, to love there without restraint, laid bare to him all its absurdities, its stupidity, its shame.

He drew a fanciful picture, at which he shuddered in disgust, of the party next evening at Chatou. 'Imagine going to Chatou, of all places! Like a lot of drapers after closing time! Upon my word, these people are sublime in their smugness; they can't really exist; they must all have come out of one of Labiche's plays!' The Cottards would be there; possibly Brichot. 'Could anything be more grotesque than the lives of these little creatures, hanging on to one another like that. They'ld imagine they were utterly lost, upon my soul they would, if they didn't all meet again to-morrow at *Chatou*!' Alas! there would be the painter there also, the painter who enjoyed match-making, who would invite Forcheville to come with Odette to his studio. He could see Odette, in a dress far too smart for the country, 'for she is so vulgar in that way, and, poor little thing, she is such a fool!'

He could hear the jokes that Mme Verdurin would make after dinner, jokes which, whoever the 'bore' might be at whom they were aimed, had always amused him because he could watch Odette laughing at them, laughing with him, her laughter almost a part of his. Now he felt that it was possibly at him that they would make Odette laugh. 'What a fetid form of humour!' he exclaimed, twisting his mouth into an expression of disgust so violent that he could feel the muscles of his throat stiffen against his collar. 'How, in God's name, can a creature made in His image find anything to laugh at in those nauseating witticisms? The least sensitive nose must be driven away in horror from such stale exhalations. It is really impossible to believe that any human being is incapable of understanding that, in allowing herself merely to smile at the expense of a fellow-creature who has loyally held out his hand to her, she is casting herself into a mire from which it will be impossible, with the best will in the world, ever to rescue her. I dwell so many miles above the puddles in which these filthy little vermin sprawl and crawl and bawl their cheap obscenities, that I cannot possibly be spattered by the witticisms of a Verdurin!' he cried, tossing up his head and arrogantly straightening his body. 'God knows that I have honestly attempted to pull Odette out of that sewer, and to teach her to breathe a nobler and a purer air. But human patience has its limits, and mine is at an end,' he concluded, as though this sacred mission to tear Odette away from an atmosphere of sarcasms dated from longer than a few minutes ago, as though he had not undertaken it only since it had occurred to him that those sarcasms might, perchance, be directed at himself, and might have the effect of detaching Odette from him.

He could see the pianist sitting down to play the Moonlight Sonata, and the grimaces of Mme Verdurin, in terrified anticipation of the wrecking of her nerves by Beethoven's music.

'Idiot, liar!' he shouted, 'and a creature like that imagines that she's fond of *Art*!' She would say to Odette, after deftly insinuating a few words of praise for Forcheville, as she had so often done for himself: 'You can make room for M. de Forcheville there, can't you, Odette?' ... '"In the dark!" Codfish! Pander!' ... 'Pander' was the name he applied also to the music which would invite them to sit in silence, to dream together, to gaze in each other's eyes, to feel for each other's hands. He felt that there was much to be said, after all, for a sternly censorious attitude towards the arts, such as Plato adopted, and Bossuet, and the old school of education in France.

In a word, the life which they led at the Verdurins', which he had so often described as 'genuine', seemed to him now the worst possible form of life, and their 'little nucleus' the most degraded class of society. 'It really is,' he repeated, 'beneath the lowest rung of the social ladder, the nethermost circle of Dante. Beyond a doubt, the august words of the Florentine refer to the Verdurins! When one comes to think of it, surely people "in society" (and, though one may find fault with them now and then, still, after all they are a very different matter from that gang of blackmailers) show a profound sagacity in refusing to know them, or even to dirty the tips of their fingers with them. What a sound intuition there is in that "*Noli me tangere*" motto of the Faubourg Saint-Germain.'

He had long since emerged from the paths and avenues of the Bois, he had almost reached his own house, and still, for he had not yet thrown off the intoxication of grief, or his whim of insincerity, but was ever more and more exhilarated by the false intonation, the artificial sonority of his own voice, he continued to perorate aloud in the silence of the night: 'People "in society" have their failings, as no one knows better than I; but, after all, they are people to whom some things, at least, are impossible. So-and-so' (a fashionable woman whom he had known) 'was far from being perfect, but, after all, one did find in her a fundamental delicacy, a loyalty in her conduct which made her, whatever happened, incapable of a felony, which fixes a vast gulf between her and an old hag like Verdurin. Verdurin! What a name! Oh, there's something complete about them, something almost fine in their trueness to type; they're the most perfect specimens of their disgusting class! Thank God, it was high time that I stopped condescending to promiscuous intercourse with such infamy, such dung.'

But, just as the virtues which he had still attributed, an hour or so earlier, to the Verdurins, would not have sufficed, even although the Verdurins had actually possessed them, if they had not also favoured and protected his love, to excite Swann to that state of intoxication in which he waxed tender over their magnanimity, an intoxication which, even when disseminated through the medium of other persons, could have come to him from Odette alone; – so the immorality (had it really existed) which he now found in the Verdurins would have been powerless, if they had not invited Odette with Forcheville and without him, to unstop the vials of his wrath and to make him scarify their 'infamy'. Doubtless Swann's voice showed a finer perspicacity than his own when it refused to utter those words full of disgust at the Verdurins and their circle, and of joy at his having shaken himself free of it, save in an artificial and rhetorical tone, and as though his words had been chosen rather to appease his anger than to express his thoughts. The latter, in fact, while he abandoned himself to invective, were probably, though he did not know it, occupied with a wholly different matter, for once he had reached his house, no sooner had he closed the front door behind him than he suddenly struck his forehead, and, making his servant open the door again, dashed out into the street shouting, in a voice which, this time, was quite natural: 'I believe I have found a way of getting invited to the dinner at Chatou to-morrow!' But it must have been a bad way, for M. Swann was not invited; Dr Cottard, who, having been summoned to attend a serious case in the country, had not seen the Verdurins for some days, and had been prevented from appearing at Chatou, said, on the evening after this dinner, as he sat down to table at their house:

'Why, aren't we going to see M. Swann this evening? He is quite what you might call a personal friend of ...'

'I sincerely trust that we shan't!' cried Mme Verdurin. 'Heaven preserve us from him; he's too deadly for words, a stupid, ill-bred boor.'

On hearing these words Cottard exhibited an intense astonishment blended with entire submission, as though in the face of a scientific truth which contradicted everything that he had previously believed, but was supported by an irresistible weight of evidence; with timorous emotion he bowed his head over his plate, and merely replied: 'Oh – oh – oh – oh – oh!' traversing, in an orderly retirement of his forces, into the depths of his being, along a descending scale, the whole compass of his voice. After which there was no more talk of Swann at the Verdurins'.

And so that drawing-room which had brought Swann and Odette together became an obstacle in the way of their meeting. She no longer said to him, as she had said in the early days of their love: 'We shall meet, anyhow, to-morrow evening; there's a supper-party at the Verdurins,' but 'We shan't be able to meet to-morrow evening, there's a supper-party at the Verdurins.' Or else the Verdurins were taking her to the Opéra-Comique, to see *Une Nuit de Cléopâtre*, and Swann could read in her eyes that terror lest he should ask her not to go, which, but a little time before, he could not have restrained from greeting with a kiss as it flitted across the face of his mistress, but which now exasperated him. 'Yet I'm not really angry,' he assured himself, 'when I see how she longs to run away and scratch for maggots in that dunghill of cacophony. I'm disappointed; not for myself, but for her; disappointed to find that, after living for more than six months in daily contact with myself, she has not been capable of improving her mind even to the point of spontaneously eradicating from it a taste for Victor Massé! More than that, to find that she has not arrived at the stage of understanding that there are evenings on which anyone with the least shade of refinement of feeling should be willing to forgo an amusement when she is asked to do so. She ought to have the sense to say: "I shall not go," if it were only from policy, since it is by what she answers now that the quality of her soul will be determined once and for all.' And having persuaded himself that it was solely, after all, in order that he might arrive at a favourable estimate of Odette's spiritual worth that he wished her to stay at home with him that evening instead of going to the Opéra-Comique, he adopted the same line of reasoning with her, with the same degree of insincerity as he had used with himself, or even with a degree more, for in her case he was yielding also to the desire to capture her by her own self-esteem.

'I swear to you,' he told her, shortly before she was to leave for the theatre, 'that, in asking you not to go, I should hope, were I a selfish man, for nothing so much as that you should refuse, for I have a thousand other things to do this evening, and I shall feel that I have been tricked and trapped myself, and shall be thoroughly annoyed, if, after all, you tell me that you are not going. But my occupations, my pleasures are not everything; I must think of you also. A day may come when, seeing me irrevocably sundered from you, you will be entitled to reproach me with not having warned you at the decisive hour in which I felt that I was going to pass judgement on you, one of those stern judgements which love cannot long resist. You see, your *Nuit de Cléopâtre* (what a title!) has no bearing on the point. What I must know is whether you are indeed one of those creatures in the lowest grade of mentality and even of charm, one of those contemptible creatures who are incapable of forgoing a pleasure. For if you are such, how could anyone love you, for you are not even a person, a definite, imperfect, but at least perceptible entity. You are a formless water that will trickle down any slope that it may come upon, a fish devoid of memory, incapable of thought, which all its life long in its aquarium will continue to dash itself, a hundred times a day, against a wall of glass, always mistaking it for water. Do you realize that your answer will have the effect – I do not say of making me cease from that moment to love you, that goes without saying, but of making you less attractive to my eyes when I realize that you are not a person, that you are beneath everything in the world and have

not the intelligence to raise yourself one inch higher. Obviously,
I should have preferred to ask you, as though it had been a
matter of little or no importance, to give up your *Nuit de
Cléopâtre* (since you compel me to sully my lips with so abject
a name), in the hope that you would go to it none the less. But,
since I had resolved to weigh you in the balance, to make so
grave an issue depend upon your answer, I considered it more
honourable to give you due warning.'

Meanwhile, Odette had shown signs of increasing emotion
and uncertainty. Although the meaning of his tirade was
beyond her, she grasped that it was to be included among the
scenes of reproach or supplication, scenes which her familiarity
with the ways of men enabled her, without paying any heed
to the words that were uttered, to conclude that men would
not make unless they were in love; that, from the moment
when they were in love, it was superfluous to obey them,
since they would only be more in love later on. And so, she
would have heard Swann out with the utmost tranquillity
had she not noticed that it was growing late, and that if he
went on speaking for any length of time she would 'never'
as she told him with a fond smile, obstinate but slightly
abashed, 'get there in time for the Overture'.

On other occasions he had assured himself that the one
thing which, more than anything else, would make him cease
to love her, would be her refusal to abandon the habit of lying.
'Even from the point of view of coquetry, pure and simple,'
he had told her, 'can't you see how much of your attraction
you throw away when you stoop to lying? By a frank admission – how many faults you might redeem! Really, you are far
less intelligent than I supposed!' In vain, however, did Swann
expound to her thus all the reasons that she had for not lying;
they might have succeeded in overthrowing any universal
system of mendacity, but Odette had no such system; she contented herself, merely, whenever she wished Swann to remain
in ignorance of anything that she had done, with not telling
him of it. So that a lie was, to her, something to be used only
as a special expedient; and the one thing that could make her
decide whether she should avail herself of a lie or not was a

reason which, too, was of a special and contingent order, namely the risk of Swann's discovering that she had not told him the truth.

Physically, she was passing through an unfortunate phase; she was growing stouter, and the expressive, sorrowful charm, the surprised, wistful expressions which she had formerly had, seemed to have vanished with her first youth, with the result that she became most precious to Swann at the very moment when he found her distinctly less good-looking. He would gaze at her for hours on end, trying to recapture the charm which he had once seen in her and could not find again. And yet the knowledge that, within this new and strange chrysalis, it was still Odette that lurked, still the same volatile temperament, artful and evasive, was enough to keep Swann seeking, with as much passion as ever, to captivate her. Then he would look at photographs of her, taken two years before, and would remember how exquisite she had been. And that would console him, a little, for all the sufferings that he voluntarily endured on her account.

When the Verdurins took her off to Saint-Germain, or to Chatou, or to Meulan, as often as not, if the weather was fine, they would propose to remain there for the night, and not to go home until next day. Mme Verdurin would endeavour to set at rest the scruples of the pianist, whose aunt had remained in Paris: 'She will be only too glad to be rid of you for a day. How on earth could she be anxious, when she knows you're with us? Anyhow, I'll take you all under my wing; she can put the blame on me.'

If this attempt failed, M. Verdurin would set off across country until he came to a telegraph office or some other kind of messenger, after first finding out which of the 'faithful' had anyone whom they must warn. But Odette would thank him, and assure him that she had no message for anyone, for she had told Swann, once and for all, that she could not possibly send messages to him, before all those people, without compromising herself. Sometimes she would be absent for several days on end, when the Verdurins took her to see the tombs at Dreux, or to Compiègne, on the painter's advice, to watch the sun setting through the forest – after which they went on to the Château of Pierrefonds.

'To think that she could visit really historic buildings with me, who have spent ten years in the study of architecture, who am constantly bombarded, by people who really count, to take them over Beauvais or Saint-Loup-de-Naud, and refuse to take anyone but her; and instead of that she trundles off with the lowest, the most brutally degraded of creatures, to go into ecstasies over the petrified excretions of Louis-Philippe and Viollet-le-Duc! One hardly needs much knowledge of art, I should say, to do that; though, surely, even without any particularly refined sense of smell, one would not deliberately choose to spend a holiday in the latrines, so as to be within range of their fragrant exhalations.'

But when she had set off for Dreux or Pierrefonds – alas, without allowing him to appear there, as though by accident, at her side, for, as she said, that would 'create a dreadful impression', – he would plunge into the most intoxicating romance in the lover's library, the railway time-table, from which he learned the ways of joining her there in the afternoon, in the evening, even in the morning. The ways? More than that, the authority, the right to join her. For, after all, the time-table, and the trains themselves, were not meant for dogs. If the public were carefully informed, by means of printed advertisements, that at eight o'clock in the morning a train started for Pierrefonds which arrived there at ten, that could only be because going to Pierrefonds was a lawful act, for which permission from Odette would be superfluous; an act, moreover, which might be performed from a motive altogether different from the desire to see Odette, since persons who had never even heard of her performed it daily, and in such numbers as justified the labour and expense of stoking the engines.

So it came to this; that she could not prevent him from going to Pierrefonds if he chose to do so. Now that was precisely what he found that he did choose to do, and would at that moment be doing were he, like the travelling public, not acquainted with Odette. For a long time past he had

wanted to form a more definite impression of Viollet-le-Duc's
work as a restorer. And the weather being what it was, he
felt an overwhelming desire to spend the day roaming in the
forest of Compiègne.

It was, indeed, a piece of bad luck that she had forbidden
him access to the one spot that tempted him to-day. To-day!
Why, if he went down there, in defiance of her prohibition,
he would be able to see her that very day! But then, whereas,
if she had met, at Pierrefonds, some one who did not matter,
she would have hailed him with obvious pleasure: 'What,
you here?' and would have invited him to come and see her
at the hotel where she was staying with the Verdurins; if,
on the other hand, it was himself, Swann, that she encountered
there, she would be annoyed, would complain that she was
being followed, would love him less in consequence, might
even turn away in anger when she caught sight of him. 'So,
then, I am not to be allowed to go away for a day anywhere!'
she would reproach him on her return, whereas in fact it was
he himself who was not allowed to go.

He had had the sudden idea, so as to contrive to visit
Compiègne and Pierrefonds without letting it be supposed
that his object was to meet Odette, of securing an invitation
from one of his friends, the Marquis de Forestelle, who had a
country house in that neighbourhood. This friend, to whom
Swann suggested the plan without disclosing its ulterior
purpose, was beside himself with joy; he did not conceal his
astonishment at Swann's consenting at last, after fifteen years,
to come down and visit his property, and since he did not
(he told him) wish to stay there, promised to spend some
days, at least, in taking him for walks and excursions in
the district. Swann imagined himself down there already with
M. de Forestelle. Even before he saw Odette, even if he did
not succeed in seeing her there, what a joy it would be to set
foot on that soil where, not knowing the exact spot in which,
at any moment, she was to be found, he would feel all around
him the thrilling possibility of her suddenly appearing: in
the courtyard of the Château, now beautiful in his eyes since
it was on her account that he had gone to visit it; in all the

streets of the town, which struck him as romantic; down every ride of the forest, roseate with the deep and tender glow of sunset; – innumerable and alternative hiding-places, to which would fly simultaneously for refuge, in the uncertain ubiquity of his hopes, his happy, vagabond, and divided heart. 'We mustn't, on any account,' he would warn M. de Forestelle, 'run across Odette and the Verdurins. I have just heard that they are at Pierrefonds, of all places, to-day. One has plenty of time to see them in Paris; it would hardly be worth while coming down here if one couldn't go a yard without meeting them.' And his host would fail to understand why, once they had reached the place, Swann would change his plans twenty times in an hour, inspect the dining-rooms of all the hotels in Compiègne without being able to make up his mind to settle down in any of them, although he had found no trace anywhere of the Verdurins, seeming to be in search of what he had claimed to be most anxious to avoid, and would in fact avoid, the moment he found it, for if he had come upon the little 'group' he would have hastened away at once with studied indifference, satisfied that he had seen Odette and she him, especially that she had seen him when he was not, apparently, thinking about her. But no; she would guess at once that it was for her sake that he had come there. And when M. de Forestelle came to fetch him, and it was time to start, he excused himself: 'No, I'm afraid not; I can't go to Pierrefonds to-day. You see, Odette is there.' And Swann was happy in spite of everything in feeling that if he, alone among mortals, had not the right to go to Pierrefonds that day, it was because he was in fact, for Odette, someone who differed from all other mortals, her lover; and because that restriction which for him alone was set upon the universal right to travel freely where one would, was but one of the many forms of that slavery, that love which was so dear to him. Decidedly, it was better not to risk a quarrel with her, to be patient, to wait for her return. He spent his days in poring over a map of the forest of Compiègne, as though it had been that of the 'Pays du Tendre'; he surrounded himself with photographs of the Château of Pierrefonds. When the day dawned on which it was possible that she might return, he opened the time-table again, calculated what train she must have taken, and, should she have postponed her departure, what trains were still left for her to take. He did not leave the house, for fear of missing a telegram, he did not go to bed, in case, having come by the last train, she decided to surprise him with a midnight visit. Yes! The front door bell rang. There seemed some delay in opening the door, he wanted to awaken the porter, he leaned out of the window to shout to Odette, if it was Odette, for in spite of the orders which he had gone downstairs a dozen times to deliver in person, they were quite capable of telling her that he was not at home. It was only a servant coming in. He noticed the incessant rumble of passing carriages, to which he had never before paid any attention. He could hear them, one after another, a long way off, coming nearer, passing his door without stopping, and bearing away into the distance a message which was not for him. He waited all night, to no purpose, for the Verdurins had returned unexpectedly, and Odette had been in Paris since midday; it had not occurred to her to tell him; not knowing what to do with herself she had spent the evening alone at a theatre, had long since gone home to bed, and was peacefully asleep.

As a matter of fact, she had never given him a thought. And such moments as these, in which she forgot Swann's very existence, were of more value to Odette, did more to attach him to her, than all her infidelities. For in this way Swann was kept in that state of painful agitation which had once before been effective in making his interest blossom into love, on the night when he had failed to find Odette at the Verdurins' and had hunted for her all evening. And he did not have (as I had, afterwards, at Combray in my childhood) happy days in which to forget the sufferings that would return with the night. For his days, Swann must pass them without Odette; and as he told himself, now and then, to allow so pretty a woman to go out by herself in Paris was just as rash as to leave a case filled with jewels in the middle of the street. In this mood he would scowl furiously at the passers-by, as though they were so many pickpockets. But their faces – a collective and formless mass – escaped the grasp of his imagination, and so failed to feed the flame of his jealousy. The effort exhausted Swann's brain, until, passing his hand over his eyes, he cried out: 'Heaven help me!' as people, after lashing themselves into an intellectual frenzy in their endeavours to master the problems of the reality of the external world, or that of the immortality of the soul, afford relief to their weary brains by an unreasoning act of faith. But the thought of his absent mistress was incessantly, indissolubly blended with all the simplest actions of Swann's daily life – when he took his meals, opened his letters, went for a walk or to bed – by the fact of his regret at having to perform those actions without her; like those initials of Philibert the Fair which, in the church of Brou, because of her grief, her longing for him, Margaret of Austria intertwined everywhere with her own. On some days, instead of staying at home, he would go for luncheon to a restaurant not far off, to which he had been attracted, some time before, by the excellence of its cookery, but to which he now went only for one of those reasons, at once mystical and absurd, which people call 'romantic'; because this restaurant (which, by the way, still exists) bore the same name as the street in which Odette lived: the Lapérouse. Sometimes, when she had been away on a short visit somewhere, several days would elapse before she thought of letting him know that she had returned to Paris. And then she would say quite simply, without taking (as she would once have taken) the precaution of covering herself, at all costs, with a little fragment borrowed from the truth, that she had just, at that very moment, arrived by the morning train. What she said was a falsehood; at least for Odette it was a falsehood, inconsistent, lacking (what it would have had, if true) the support of her memory of her actual arrival at the station; she was even prevented from forming a mental picture of what she was saying, while she said it, by the contradictory picture, in her mind, of whatever quite different thing she had indeed been doing at the moment when she pretended to have been alighting from the train. In Swann's mind, however, these words, meeting no opposition, settled and hardened until they assumed the indestructibility of a truth so indubitable that, if some friend happened to tell him that he had come by the same train and had not seen Odette, Swann would have been convinced that it was his friend who had made a mistake as to the day or hour, since his version did not agree with the words uttered by Odette. These words had never appeared to him false except when, before hearing them, he had suspected that they were going to be. For him to believe that she was lying, an anticipatory suspicion was indispensable. It was also, however, sufficient. Given that, everything that Odette might say appeared to him suspect. Did she mention a name; it was obviously that of one of her lovers; once this supposition had taken shape, he would spend weeks in tormenting himself; on one occasion he even approached a firm of 'inquiry agents' to find out the address and the occupation of the unknown rival who would give him no peace until he could be proved to have gone abroad, and who (he ultimately learned) was an uncle of Odette, and had been dead for twenty years.

Although she would not allow him, as a rule, to meet her at public gatherings, saying that people would talk, it happened occasionally that, at an evening party to which he and she had each been invited – at Forchevilles', at the painter's, or at a charity ball given in one of the Ministries – he found himself in the same room with her. He could see her, but dared not remain for fear of annoying her by seeming to be spying upon the pleasures which she tasted in other company, pleasures which – while he drove home in utter loneliness, and went to bed, as anxiously as I myself was to go to bed, some years later, on the evenings when he came to dine with us at Combray – seemed illimitable to him since he had not been able to see their end. And, once or twice, he derived from such evenings that kind of happiness which one would be inclined (did it not originate in so violent a reaction from an anxiety abruptly terminated) to call peaceful, since it consists in a pacifying of the mind: he had looked in for a moment at a revel in the painter's studio, and was getting ready to go home; he was leaving behind him Odette, transformed into a brilliant stranger, surrounded by men to whom her glances and her gaiety, which were not for him, seemed to hint at some voluptuous pleasure to be enjoyed there or elsewhere (possibly at the Bal des Incohérents, to which he trembled to think that she might be going on afterwards) which made Swann more jealous than the thought of their actual physical union, since it was more difficult to imagine; he was opening the door to go, when he heard himself called back in these words (which, by cutting off from the party that possible ending which had so appalled him, made the party itself seem innocent in retrospect, made Odette's return home a thing no longer inconceivable and terrible, but tender and familiar, a thing that kept close to his side, like a part of his own daily life, in his carriage; a thing that stripped Odette herself of the excess of brilliance and gaiety in her appearance, showed that it was only a disguise which she had assumed for a moment, for his sake and not in view of any mysterious pleasures, a disguise of which she had already wearied) – in these words, which Odette flung out after him as he was crossing the threshold: 'Can't you wait a minute for me? I'm just going; we'll drive back together and you can drop me.' It was true that on one occasion Forcheville had asked to be driven home at the same time, but when, on reaching Odette's gate, he had begged to be allowed to come in too, she had replied, with a finger pointed at Swann: 'Ah! That depends on this gentleman. You must ask him. Very well, you may come in, just for a minute, if you insist, but you mustn't stay long, for, I warn you, he likes to sit and talk quietly with me, and he's not at all pleased if I have visitors when he's here. Oh, if you only knew the creature as I know him; isn't that so, my love, there's no one that really knows you, is there, except me?'

And Swann was, perhaps, even more touched by the spectacle of her addressing him thus, in front of Forcheville, not only in these tender words of predilection, but also with certain criticisms, such as: 'I feel sure you haven't written yet to your friends, about dining with them on Sunday. You needn't go if you don't want to, but you might at least be polite,' or, 'Now, have you left your essay on Vermeer here, so that you can do a little more to it to-morrow? What a lazy-bones! I'm going to make you work, I can tell you,' which proved that Odette kept herself in touch with his social engagements and his literary work, that they had indeed a life in common. And as she spoke she bestowed on him a smile which he interpreted as meaning that she was entirely his.

And then, while she was making them some orangeade, suddenly, just as when the reflector of a lamp that is badly fitted begins by casting all round an object, on the wall beyond it, huge and fantastic shadows which, in time, contract and are lost in the shadow of the object itself, all the terrible and disturbing ideas which he had formed of Odette melted away and vanished in the charming creature who stood there before his eyes. He had the sudden suspicion that this hour spent in Odette's house, in the lamp-light, was, perhaps, after all, not an artificial hour, invented for his special use (with the object of concealing that frightening and delicious thing which was incessantly in his thoughts without his ever being able to form a satisfactory impression of it, an hour of Odette's real life, of her life when he was not there, looking on) with theatrical properties and pasteboard fruits, but was perhaps a genuine hour of Odette's life; that, if he himself had not been there, she would have pulled forward the same arm-chair for Forcheville, would have poured out for him, not any unknown brew, but precisely that orangeade which she was now offering to them both; that the world inhabited by Odette was not that other world, fearful and supernatural, in which he spent his time in placing her – and which existed, perhaps, only in his imagination, but the real universe, exhaling no special atmosphere of gloom, comprising that table at which he might sit down, presently, and write, and this drink which he was being permitted, now, to taste; all the objects which he contemplated with as much curiosity and admiration as gratitude, for if, in absorbing his dreams, they had delivered him from an obsession, they themselves were, in turn, enriched by the absorption; they showed him the palpable realization of his fancies, and they interested his mind; they took shape and grew solid before his eyes, and at the same time they soothed his troubled heart. Ah! had fate but allowed him to share a single dwelling with Odette, so that in her house he should be in his own; if, when asking his servant what there would be for luncheon, it had been Odette's bill of fare that he had learned from the reply; if, when Odette wished to go for a walk, in the morning, along the Avenue du Bois-de-Boulogne, his duty as a good husband had obliged him, though he had no desire to go out, to accompany her, carrying her cloak when she was too warm; and in the evening, after dinner, if she wished to stay at home, and not to dress, if he had been forced to stay beside her, to do what she asked; then how completely would all the trivial details of Swann's life, which seemed to him now so gloomy, simply because they would, at the same time, have formed part of the life of Odette, have taken on – like that lamp, that orangeade, that arm-chair, which had absorbed so much of his dreams, which materialized so much of his longing, – a sort of superabundant sweetness and a mysterious solidity.

And yet he was inclined to suspect that the state for which he so much longed was a calm, a peace, which would not have created an atmosphere favourable to his love. When Odette ceased to be for him a creature always absent, regretted, imagined; when the feeling that he had for her was no longer the same mysterious disturbance that was wrought in him by the phrase from the sonata, but constant affection and grati- tude, when those normal relations were established between them which would put an end to his melancholy madness; then, no doubt, the actions of Odette's daily life would appear to him as being of but little intrinsic interest – as he had several times, already, felt that they might be, on the day, for instance, when he had read, through its envelope, her letter to Forcheville. Examining his complaint with as much scientific detachment as if he had inoculated himself with it in order to study its effects, he told himself that, when he was cured of it, what Odette might or might not do would be indifferent to him. But in his morbid state, to tell the truth, he feared death itself no more than such a recovery, which would, in fact, amount to the death of all that he then was.

After these quiet evenings, Swann's suspicions would be temporarily lulled; he would bless the name of Odette, and next day, in the morning, would order the most attractive jewels to be sent to her, because her kindness to him overnight had excited either his gratitude, or the desire to see them repeated, or a paroxysm of love for her which had need of such outlet.

But at other times, grief would again take hold of him; he would imagine that Odette was Forcheville's mistress, and that, when they had both sat watching him from the depths of the Verdurins' landau, in the Bois, on the evening before the party at Chatou to which he had not been invited, while he implored her in vain, with that look of despair on his face which even his coachman had noticed, to come home with him, and then turned away, solitary, crushed, – she must have employed, to draw Forcheville's attention to him, while she murmured; 'Do look at him, storming!' the same glance, brilliant, malicious, sidelong, cunning, as on the evening when Forcheville had driven Saniette from the Verdurins'.

At such times Swann detested her. 'But I've been a fool, too,' he would argue. 'I'm paying for other men's pleasures with my money. All the same, she'd better take care, and not pull the string too often, for I might very well stop giving her anything at all. At any rate, we'd better knock off supplementary favours for the time being. To think that, only yesterday, when she said she would like to go to Bayreuth for the season, I was such an ass as to offer to take one of those jolly little places the King of Bavaria has there, for the two of us. However she didn't seem particularly keen; she hasn't said yes or no yet. Let's hope that she'll refuse. Good God! Think of listening to Wagner for a fortnight on end with her, who takes about as much interest in music as a fish does in little apples; it will be fun!' And his hatred, like his love, needing to manifest itself in action, he amused himself with urging his evil imaginings further and further, because, thanks to the perfidies with which he charged Odette,

he detested her still more, and would be able, if it turned out –
as he tried to convince himself – that she was indeed guilty of
them, to take the opportunity of punishing her, emptying upon
her the overflowing vials of his wrath. In this way, he went
so far as to suppose that he was going to receive a letter from
her, in which she would ask him for money to take the house
at Bayreuth, but with the warning that he was not to come
there himself, as she had promised Forcheville and the Verdurins to invite them. Oh, how he would have loved it, had
it been conceivable that she would have the audacity. What
joy he would have in refusing, in drawing up that vindictive
reply, the terms of which he amused himself by selecting and
declaiming aloud, as though he had actually received her letter.

The very next day, her letter came. She wrote that the
Verdurins and their friends had expressed a desire to be
present at these performances of Wagner, and that, if he
would be so good as to send her the money, she would be
able at last, after going so often to their house, to have the
pleasure of entertaining the Verdurins in hers. Of him she
said not a word; it was to be taken for granted that their
presence at Bayreuth would be a bar to his.

Then that annihilating answer, every word of which he
had carefully rehearsed overnight, without venturing to hope
that it could ever be used, he had the satisfaction of having
it conveyed to her. Alas! he felt only too certain that with the
money which she had, or could easily procure, she would be
able, all the same, to take a house at Bayreuth, since she wished
to do so, she who was incapable of distinguishing between
Bach and Clapisson. Let her take it, then; she would have to
live in it more frugally, that was all. No means (as there would
have been if he had replied by sending her several thousand-
franc notes) of organizing, each evening, in her hired castle,
those exquisite little suppers, after which she might perhaps be
seized by the whim (which, it was possible, had never yet
seized her) of falling into the arms of Forcheville. At any rate,
this loathsome expedition, it would not be Swann who had to
pay for it. Ah! if he could only manage to prevent it, if she
could sprain her ankle before starting, if the driver of the

carriage which was to take her to the station would consent
(no matter how great the bribe) to smuggle her to some place
where she could be kept for a time in seclusion, that perfidious
woman, her eyes tinselled with a smile of complicity for
Forcheville, which was what Odette had become for Swann
in the last forty-eight hours.

But she was never that for very long; after a few days the
shining, crafty eyes lost their brightness and their duplicity,
that picture of an execrable Odette saying to Forcheville:
'Look at him storming!' began to grow pale and to dissolve. Then gradually reappeared and rose before him, softly
radiant, the face of the other Odette, of that Odette who also
turned with a smile to Forcheville, but with a smile in which
there was nothing but affection for Swann, when she said:
'You mustn't stay long, for this gentleman doesn't much
like my having visitors when he's here. Oh! if you only
knew the creature as I know him!' that same smile with
which she used to thank Swann for some instance of his
courtesy which she prized so highly, for some advice for which
she had asked him in one of those grave crises in her life,
when she could turn to him alone.

Then, to this other Odette, he would ask himself what
could have induced him to write that outrageous letter, of
which, probably, until then, she had never supposed him
capable, a letter which must have lowered him from the high,
from the supreme place which, by his generosity, by his
loyalty, he had won for himself in her esteem. He would
become less dear to her, since it was for those qualities, which
she found neither in Forcheville nor in any other, that she
loved him. It was for them that Odette so often showed him
a reciprocal kindness, which counted for less than nothing in
his moments of jealousy, because it was not a sign of reciprocal
desire, was indeed a proof rather of affection than of love, but
the importance of which he began once more to feel in
proportion as the spontaneous relaxation of his suspicions,
often accelerated by the distraction brought to him by reading
about art or by the conversation of a friend, rendered his
passion less exacting of reciprocities.

Now that, after this swing of the pendulum, Odette had naturally returned to the place from which Swann's jealousy had for the moment driven her, in the angle in which he found her charming, he pictured her to himself as full of tenderness, with a look of consent in her eyes, and so beautiful that he could not refrain from moving his lips towards her, as though she had actually been in the room for him to kiss; and he preserved a sense of gratitude to her for that bewitching kindly glance, as strong as though she had really looked thus at him, and it had not been merely his imagination that had portrayed it in order to satisfy his desire.

What distress he must have caused her! Certainly he found adequate reasons for his resentment, but they would not have been sufficient to make him feel that resentment, if he had not so passionately loved her. Had he not nourished grievances, just as serious, against other women, to whom he would, none the less, render willing service to-day, feeling no anger towards them because he no longer loved them? If the day ever came when he would find himself in the same state of indifference with regard to Odette, he would then understand that it was his jealousy alone which had led him to find something atrocious, unpardonable, in this desire ·(after all, so natural a desire, springing from a childlike ingenuousness and also from a certain delicacy in her nature) to be able, in her turn, when an occasion offered, to repay the Verdurins for their hospitality, and to play the hostess in a house of her own.

He returned to the other point of view – opposite to that of his love and of his jealousy, to which he resorted at times by a sort of mental equity, and in order to make allowance for different eventualities – from which he tried to form a fresh judgement of Odette, based on the supposition that he had never been in love with her, that she was to him just a woman like other women, that her life had not been (whenever he himself was not present) different, a texture woven in secret apart from him, and warped against him.

Wherefore believe that she would enjoy down there with Forcheville or with other men intoxicating pleasures which she had never known with him, and which his jealousy alone had fabricated in all their elements? At Bayreuth, as in Paris, if it should happen that Forcheville thought of him at all, it would only be as of someone who counted for a great deal in the life of Odette, someone for whom he was obliged to make way, when they met in her house. If Forcheville and she scored a triumph by being down there together in spite of him, it was he who had engineered that triumph by striving in vain to prevent her from going there, whereas if he had approved of her plan, which for that matter was quite defensible, she would have had the appearance of being there by his counsel, she would have felt herself sent there, housed there by him, and for the pleasure which she derived from entertaining those people who had so often entertained her, it was to him that she would have had to acknowledge her indebtedness.

And if – instead of letting her go off thus, at cross-purposes with him, without having seen him again – he were to send her this money, if he were to encourage her to take this journey, and to go out of his way to make it comfortable and pleasant for her, she would come running to him, happy, grateful, and he would have the joy – the sight of her face – which he had not known for nearly a week, a joy which none other could replace. For, the moment that Swann was able to form a picture of her without revulsion, that he could see once again the friendliness in her smile, and that the desire to tear her away from every rival was no longer imposed by his jealousy upon his love, that love once again became, more than anything, a taste for the sensations which Odette's person gave him, for the pleasure which he found in admiring, as one might a spectacle, or in questioning, as one might a phenomenon, the birth of one of her glances, the formation of one of her smiles, the utterance of an intonation of her voice. And this pleasure, different from every other, had in the end created in him a need of her, which she alone, by her presence or by her letters, could assuage, almost as disinterested, almost as artistic, as perverse as another need which characterized this new period in Swann's life, when the sereness, the depression of the preceding years had been followed by a sort of spiritual superabundance, without his knowing to what he owed this unlooked-for enrichment of his life, any more than a person in delicate health who from a certain moment grows stronger, puts on flesh, and seems for a time to be on the road to a complete recovery: – this other need, which, too, developed in him independently of the visible, material world, was the need to listen to music and to learn to know it.

And so, by the chemical process of his malady, after he had created jealousy out of his love, he began again to generate tenderness, pity for Odette. She had become once more the old Odette, charming and kind. He was full of remorse for having treated her harshly. He wished her to come to him, and, before she came, he wished to have already procured for her some pleasure, so as to watch her gratitude taking shape in her face and moulding her smile.

So, too, Odette, certain of seeing him come to her in a few days, as tender and submissive as before, and plead with her for a reconciliation, became inured, was no longer afraid of displeasing him, or even of making him angry, and refused him, whenever it suited her, the favours by which he set most store.

Perhaps she did not realize how sincere he had been with her during their quarrel, when he had told her that he would not send her any money, but would do what he could to hurt her. Perhaps she did not realize, either, how sincere he still was, if not with her, at any rate with himself, on other occasions when, for the sake of their future relations, to show Odette that he was capable of doing without her, that a rupture was still possible between them, he decided to wait some time before going to see her again.

Sometimes several days had elapsed, during which she had caused him no fresh anxiety; and as, from the next few visits which he would pay her, he knew that he was likely to derive not any great pleasure, but, more probably, some annoyance which would put an end to the state of calm in which he found himself, he wrote to her that he was very busy, and would not be able to see her on any of the days that he had suggested. Meanwhile, a letter from her, crossing his, asked him to postpone one of those very meetings. He asked himself, why; his suspicions, his grief, again took hold of him. He could no longer abide, in the new state of agitation into which he found himself plunged, by the arrangements which he had made in his preceding state of comparative calm; he would run to find her, and would insist upon seeing her on each of the following days. And even if she had not written first, if she merely acknowledged his letter, it was enough to make him unable to rest without seeing her. For, upsetting all Swann's calculations, Odette's acceptance had entirely changed his attitude. Like everyone who possesses something precious, so as to know what would happen if he ceased for a moment to possess it, he had detached the precious object from his mind, leaving, as he thought, everything else in the same state as when it was there. But the absence of one part from a whole is not only that, it is not simply a partial omission, it is a disturbance of all the other parts, a new state which it was impossible to foresee from the old.

But at other times – when Odette was on the point of going away for a holiday – it was after some trifling quarrel for which he had chosen the pretext, that he decided not to write to her and not to see until her return, giving the appearance (and expecting the reward) of a serious rupture, which she would perhaps regard as final, to a separation, the greater part of which was inevitable, since she was going away, which, in fact, he was merely allowing to start a little sooner than it must. At once he could imagine Odette, puzzled, anxious, distressed at having received neither visit nor letter from him, and this picture of her, by calming his jealousy, made it easy for him to break himself of the habit of seeing her. At odd moments, no doubt, in the furthest recesses of his brain, where his determination had thrust it away, and thanks to the length of the interval, the three weeks' separation to which he had agreed, it was with pleasure that he would consider the idea that he would see Odette again on her return; but it was also with so little impatience that he began to ask himself whether he would not readily consent to the doubling of the period of so easy an abstinence. It had lasted, so far, but three days, a much shorter time than he had often, before, passed without seeing Odette, and without having, as on this occasion he had, premeditated a separation. And yet, there and then, some tiny trace of contrariety in his mind, or of weakness in his body, – by inciting him to regard the present as an exceptional moment, one not to be governed by the rules, one in which prudence itself would allow him to take advantage of the soothing effects of a pleasure and to give his will (until the time should come when its efforts might serve any purpose) a holiday – suspended the action of his will, which ceased to exert its inhibitive control; or, without that even, the thought of some information for which he had forgotten to ask Odette, such as if she had decided in what colour she would have her carriage repainted, or, with regard to some investment, whether they were 'ordinary' or 'preference' shares that she wished him to buy (for it was all very well to show her that he could live without seeing her, but if, after that, the carriage had to be painted over again, if the shares produced no dividend, a fine lot of good he would have done), – and suddenly, like a stretched piece of elastic which is let go, or the air in a pneumatic machine which is ripped open, the idea of seeing her again, from the remote point in time to which it had been attached, sprang back into the field of the present and of immediate possibilities.

It sprang back thus without meeting any further resistance, so irresistible, in fact, that Swann had been far less unhappy in watching the end gradually approaching, day by day, of the fortnight which he must spend apart from Odette, than he was when kept waiting for ten minutes while his coachman brought round the carriage which was to take him to her, minutes which he passed in transports of impatience and joy, in which he recaptured a thousand times over, to lavish on it all the wealth of his affection, that idea of his meeting with Odette, which, by so abrupt a repercussion, at a moment when he supposed it so remote, was once more present and on the very surface of his consciousness. The fact was that this idea no longer found, as an obstacle in its course, the desire to contrive without further delay to resist its coming, which had ceased to have

any place in Swann's mind since, having proved to himself –
or so, at least, he believed – that he was so easily capable of
resisting it, he no longer saw any inconvenience in postponing
a plan of separation which he was now certain of being able to
put into operation whenever he would. Furthermore, this idea
of seeing her again came back to him adorned with a novelty,
a seductiveness, armed with a virulence, all of which long
habit had enfeebled, but which had acquired new vigour during this privation, not of three days but of a fortnight (for a
period of abstinence may be calculated, by anticipation, as
having lasted already until the final date assigned to it) and
had converted what had been, until then, a pleasure in store,
which could easily be sacrificed, into an unlooked-for happiness which he was powerless to resist. Finally, the idea returned
to him with its beauty enhanced by his own ignorance of
what Odette might have thought, might, perhaps, have done
on finding that he showed no sign of life, with the result that
what he was going now to meet was the entrancing revelation
of an Odette almost unknown.

But she, just as she had supposed that his refusal to send her
money was only a feint, saw nothing but a pretext in the question which he came, now, to ask her, about the repainting of
her carriage, or the purchase of stock. For she could not reconstruct the several phases of these crises through which he
passed, and in the general idea which she formed of them she
made no attempt to understand their mechanism, looking only
to what she knew beforehand, their necessary, never-failing
and always identical termination. An imperfect idea (though
possibly all the more profound in consequence), if one were to
judge from the point of view of Swann, who would doubtless
have considered that Odette failed to understand him, just as a
morphinomaniac or a consumptive, each persuaded that he
has been thrown back, one by some outside event, at the moment when he was just going to shake himself free from his
inveterate habit, the other by an accidental indisposition at the
moment when he was just going to be finally cured, feels himself to be misunderstood by the doctor who does not attach
the same importance to these pretended contingencies, mere

disguises, according to him, assumed, so as to be perceptible by his patients, by the vice of one and the morbid state of the other, which in reality have never ceased to weigh heavily and incurably upon them while they were nursing their dreams of normality and health. And, as a matter of fact, Swann's love had reached that stage at which the physician and (in the case of certain affections) the boldest of surgeons ask themselves whether to deprive a patient of his vice or to rid him of his malady is still reasonable, or indeed possible.

Certainly, of the extent of this love Swann had no direct knowledge. When he sought to measure it, it happened sometimes that he found it diminished, shrunken almost to nothing; for instance, the very moderate liking, amounting almost to dislike, which, in the days before he was in love with Odette, he had felt for her expressive features, her faded complexion, returned on certain days. 'Really, I am making distinct headway,' he would tell himself on the morrow, 'when I come to think it over carefully, I find that I got hardly any pleasure, last night, out of being in bed with her; it's an odd thing, but I actually thought her ugly.' And certainly he was sincere, but his love extended a long way beyond the province of physical desire. Odette's person, indeed, no longer held any great place in it. When his eyes fell upon the photograph of Odette on his table, or when she came to see him, he had difficulty in identifying her face, either in the flesh or on the pasteboard, with the painful and continuous anxiety which dwelt in his mind. He would say to himself, almost with astonishment, 'It is she!' as when suddenly someone shows us in a detached, externalized form one of our own maladies, and we find in it no resemblance to what we are suffering. 'She?' – he tried to ask himself what that meant; for it is something like love, like death (rather than like those vague conceptions of maladies), a thing which one repeatedly calls in question, in order to make oneself probe further into it, in the fear that the question will find no answer, that the substance will escape our grasp – the mystery of personality. And this malady, which was Swann's love, had so far multiplied, was so closely interwoven with all his habits, with all his actions, with his thoughts, his health, his sleep, his life, even with what he hoped for after his death, was so entirely one with him that it would have been impossible to wrest it away without almost entirely destroying him; as surgeons say, his case was past operation.

By this love Swann had been so far detached from all other interests that when by chance he reappeared in the world of fashion, reminding himself that his social relations, like a beautifully wrought setting (although she would not have been able to form any very exact estimate of its worth), might, still, add a little to his own value in Odette's eyes (as indeed they might have done had they not been cheapened by his love itself, which for Odette depreciated everything that it touched by seeming to denounce such things as less precious than itself), he would feel there, simultaneously with his distress at being in places and among people that she did not know, the same detached sense of pleasure as he would have derived from a novel or a painting in which were depicted the amusements of a leisured class; just as, at home, he used to enjoy the thought of the smooth efficiency of his household, the smartness of his own wardrobe and of his servants' liveries, the soundness of his investments, with the same relish as when he read in Saint-Simon, who was one of his favourite authors, of the machinery of daily life at Versailles, what Mme de Maintenon ate and drank, or the shrewd avarice and great pomp of Lulli. And in the small extent to which this detachment was not absolute, the reason for this new pleasure which Swann was tasting was that he could emigrate for a moment into those few and distant parts of himself which had remained almost foreign to his love and to his pain. In this respect the personality, with which my great-aunt endowed him, of 'young Swann', as distinct from the more individual personality of Charles Swann, was that in which he now most delighted. Once when, because it was the birthday of the Princesse de Parme (and because she could often be of use, indirectly, to Odette, by letting her have seats for galas and jubilees and all that sort of thing), he had decided to send her a basket of fruit, and was not quite sure where or how to order it, he had entrusted the task to a cousin of his mother who, delighted to be doing a commission for him, had written to him, laying stress on the fact that she had not chosen all the fruit at the same place, but the grapes from Crapote, whose speciality they were, the strawberries from Jauret, the pears from Chevet, who always had the best, and so on, 'every fruit visited and examined, one by one, by myself.' And in the sequel, by the cordiality with which the Princess thanked him, he had been able to judge of the flavour of the strawberries and of the ripeness of the pears. But, most of all, that 'every fruit visited and examined, one by one, by myself' had brought balm to his sufferings by carrying his mind off to a region which he rarely visited, although it was his by right, as the heir of a rich and respectable middle-class family in which had been handed from generation to generation the knowledge of the 'right places' and the art of ordering things from shops.

Of a truth, he had too long forgotten that he was 'young Swann' not to feel, when he assumed that part again for a moment, a keener pleasure than he was capable of feeling at other times – when, indeed, he was grown sick of pleasure; and if the friendliness of the middle-class people, for whom he had never been anything else than 'young Swann', was less animated than that of the aristocrats (though more flattering, for all that, since in the middle-class mind friendship is inseparable from respect), no letter from a Royal Personage, offering him some princely entertainment, could ever be so attractive to Swann as the letter which asked him to be a witness, or merely to be present at a wedding in the family of some old friends of his parents; some of whom had 'kept up' with him, like my grandfather, who, the year before these events, had invited him to my mother's wedding, while others barely knew him by sight, but were, they thought, in duty bound to show civility to the son, to the worthy successor of the late M. Swann.

But, by virtue of his intimacy, already time-honoured, with so many of them, the people of fashion, in a certain sense, were also a part of his house, his service, and his family. He felt, when his mind dwelt upon his brilliant connexions, the same external support, the same solid comfort as when he looked at the fine estate, the fine silver, the fine table-linen which had come down to him from his forebears. And the thought that, if he were seized by a sudden illness and confined to the house, the people whom his valet would instinctively run to find would be the Duc de Chartres, the Prince de Reuss, the Duc de Luxembourg, and the Baron de Charlus, brought him the same consolation as our old Françoise derived from the knowledge that she would, one day, be buried in her own fine cloths, marked with her name, not darned at all (or so exquisitely darned that it merely enhanced one's idea of the skill and patience of the seamstress), a shroud from the constant image of which in her mind's eye she drew a certain satisfactory sense, if not actually of wealth and prosperity, at any rate of self-esteem. But most of all, – since in every one of his actions and thoughts which had reference to Odette, Swann was constantly subdued and swayed by the unconfessed feeling that he was, perhaps not less dear, but at least less welcome to her than anyone, even the most wearisome of the Verdurins' 'faithful', – when he betook himself to a world in which he was the paramount example of taste, a man whom no pains were spared to attract, whom people were genuinely sorry not to see, he began once again to believe in the existence of a happier life, almost to feel an appetite for it, as an invalid may feel who has been in bed for months and on a strict diet, when he picks up a newspaper and reads the account of an official banquet or the advertisement of a cruise round Sicily.

If he was obliged to make excuses to his fashionable friends for not paying them visits, it was precisely for the visits that he did pay her that he sought to excuse himself to Odette. He still paid them (asking himself at the end of each month whether, seeing that he had perhaps exhausted her patience, and had certainly gone rather often to see her, it would be enough if he sent her four thousand francs), and for each visit he found a pretext, a present that he had to bring her, some information which she required, M. de Charlus, whom he had met actually going to her house, and who had insisted upon Swann's accompanying him. And, failing any excuse, he would beg M. de Charlus to go to her at once, and to tell her, as though spontaneously, in the course of conversation, that he had just remembered something that he had to say to Swann, and would she please send a message to Swann's house asking him to come to her then and there; but as a rule Swann waited at home in vain, and M. de Charlus informed him, later in the evening, that his device had not proved successful. With the result that, if she was now frequently away from Paris, even when she was there he scarcely saw her; that she who, when she was in love with him, used to say, 'I am always free' and 'What can it matter to me, what other people think?' now, whenever he wanted to see her, appealed to the proprieties or pleaded some engagement. When he spoke of going to a charity entertainment, or a private view, or a first night at which she was to be present, she would expostulate that he wished to advertise their relations in public, that he was treating her like a woman off the streets. Things came to such a pitch that, in an effort to save himself from being altogether forbidden to meet her anywhere, Swann, remembering that she knew and was deeply attached to my great-uncle Adolphe, whose friend he himself also had been, went one day to see him in his little flat in the Rue de Bellechasse, to ask him to use his influence with Odette. As it happened, she invariably adopted, when she spoke to Swann about my uncle, a poetical tone, saying: 'Ah, he! He is not in the least like you; it is an exquisite thing, a great, a beautiful thing, his friendship for me. He's not the sort of man who would have so little consideration for me as to let himself be seen with me everywhere in public.' This was embarrassing for Swann, who did not know quite to what rhetorical pitch he should screw himself up in speaking of Odette to my uncle. He began by alluding to her excellence, *a priori*, the axiom of her seraphic superhumanity, the revelation of her inexpressible virtues, no conception of which could possibly be formed. 'I should like to speak to you about her,' he went on, 'you, who know what a woman supreme above all women, what an adorable being, what an angel Odette is. But you know, also, what life is in Paris. Everyone doesn't see Odette in the light in which you and I have been privileged to see her. And so there are people who think that I am behaving rather foolishly; she won't even allow me to meet her out of doors, at the theatre. Now you, in whom she has such enormous confidence, couldn't you say a few words for me to her, just to assure her that she exaggerates the harm which my bowing to her in the street might do her?'

My uncle advised Swann not to see Odette for some days, after which she would love him all the more; he advised Odette to let Swann meet her everywhere, and as often as he pleased. A few days later Odette told Swann that she had just had a rude awakening; she had discovered that my uncle was the same as other men; he had tried to take her by assault. She calmed Swann, who, at first, was for rushing out to challenge my uncle to a duel, but he refused to shake hands with him when they met again. He regretted this rupture all the more because he had hoped, if he had met my uncle Adolphe again sometimes and had contrived to talk things over with him in strict confidence, to be able to get him to throw a light on certain rumours with regard to the life that Odette had led, in the old days, at Nice. For my uncle Adolphe used to spend the winter there, and Swann thought that it might indeed have been there, perhaps, that he had first known Odette. The few words which someone had let fall, in his hearing, about a man who, it appeared, had been Odette's lover, had left Swann dumbfounded. But the very things which he would, before knowing them, have regarded as the most terrible to learn and the most impossible to believe, were, once he knew them, incorporated for all time in the general mass of his sorrow; he admitted them, he could no longer have understood their not existing. Only, each one of them in its passage traced an indelible line, altering the picture that he had formed of his mistress. At one time indeed he felt that he could understand that this moral 'lightness', of which he would never have suspected Odette, was perfectly well known, and that at Baden or Nice, when she had gone, in the past, to spend several months in one or the other place, she had enjoyed a sort of amorous notoriety. He attempted, in order to question them, to get into touch again with certain men of that stamp; but these were aware that he knew Odette, and, besides, he was afraid of putting the thought of her into their heads, of setting them once more upon her track. But he, to whom, up till then, nothing could have seemed so tedious as was all that pertained to the cosmopolitan life of Baden or of Nice, now that he learned that Odette had, perhaps, led a 'gay' life once in those pleasure-cities, although he could never find out whether it had been solely to satisfy a want of money which, thanks to himself, she no longer felt, or from some capricious instinct which might, at any moment, revive in her, he would lean, in impotent anguish, blinded and dizzy, over the bottomless abyss into which had passed, in which had been engulfed those years of his own, early in MacMahon's *Septennat*, in which one spent the winter on the Promenade des Anglais, the summer beneath the limes of Baden, and would find in those years a sad but splendid profundity, such as a poet might have lent to them; and he would have devoted to the reconstruction of all the insignificant details that made up the daily round on the Côte d'Azur in those days, if it could have helped him to understand something that still baffled him in the smile or in the eyes of Odette, more enthusiasm than does the aesthete who ransacks the extant documents of fifteenth-century Florence, so as to try to penetrate farther into the soul of the Primavera, the fair Vanna, or the Venus of Botticelli. He would sit, often, without saying a word to her, only gazing at her and dreaming; and she would comment: 'You do look sad!' It was not very long since, from the idea that she was an excellent creature, comparable to the best woman that he had known, he had passed to that of her being 'kept'; and yet already, by an inverse process, he had returned from the Odette de Crécy, perhaps too well known to the holiday-makers, to the 'ladies' men' of Nice and Baden, to this face, the expression on which was often so gentle, to this nature so eminently human. He would ask himself: 'What does it mean, after all, to say that everyone at Nice knows who Odette de Crécy is? Reputations of that sort, even when they're true, are always based upon other people's ideas'; he would reflect that this legend – even if it were authentic – was something external to Odette, was not inherent in her like a mischievous and ineradicable personality; that the creature who might have been led astray was a woman with frank eyes, a heart full of pity for the sufferings of others, a docile body which he had pressed tightly in his arms and explored with his fingers, a woman of whom he might one day come into absolute possession if he succeeded in making himself indispensable to her. There she was, often tired, her face left blank for the nonce by that eager, feverish preoccupation with the unknown things which made Swann suffer; she would push back her hair with both hands; her forehead, her whole face would seem to grow larger; then, suddenly, some ordinary human thought, some worthy sentiment such as are to be found in all creatures when, in a moment of rest or meditation, they are free to express themselves, would flash out from her eyes like a ray of gold. And immediately the whole of her face would light up like a grey landscape, swathed in clouds which, suddenly, are swept away and the dull scene transfigured, at the moment of the sun's setting. The life which occupied Odette at such times, even the future which she seemed to be dreamily regarding, Swann could have shared with her. No evil disturbance seemed to have left any effect on them. Rare as they became, those moments did not occur in vain. By the process of memory, Swann joined the fragments together, abolished the intervals between them, cast, as in molten gold, the image of an Odette compact of kindness and tranquillity, for whom he was to make, later on (as we shall see in the second part of this story) sacrifices which the other Odette would never have won from him. But how rare those moments were, and how seldom he now saw her! Even in regard to their evening meetings, she would never tell him until the last minute whether she would be able to see him, for, reckoning on his being always free, she wished first to be certain that no one else would offer to come to her. She would plead that she was obliged to wait for an answer which was of the very greatest importance, and if, even after she had made Swann come to her house, any of her friends asked her, half-way through the evening, to join them at some theatre, or at supper afterwards, she would jump for joy and dress herself with all speed. As her toilet progressed, every movement that she made brought Swann nearer to the moment when he would have to part from her, when she would fly off with irresistible force; and when at length she was ready, and, plunging into her mirror a last glance strained and brightened by her anxiety to look well, smeared a little salve on her lips, fixed a stray lock of hair over her brow, and called for her cloak of sky-blue silk with golden tassels, Swann would be looking so wretched that she would be unable to restrain a gesture of impatience as she flung at him: 'So that is how you thank me for keeping you here till the last minute! And I thought I was being so nice to you. Well, I shall know better another time!' Sometimes, at the risk of annoying her, he made up his mind that he would find out where she had gone, and even dreamed of a defensive alliance with Forcheville, who might perhaps have been able to tell him. But anyhow, when he knew with whom she was spending the evening, it was very seldom that he could not discover, among all his innumerable acquaintance, someone who knew – if only indirectly – the man with whom she had gone out, and could easily obtain this or that piece of information about him. And while he was writing to one of his friends, asking him to try to get a little light thrown upon some point or other, he would feel a sense of relief on ceasing to vex himself with questions to which there was no answer and transferring to someone else the strain of interrogation. It is true that Swann was little the wiser for such information as he did receive. To know a thing does not enable us, always, to prevent its happening, but after all the things that we know we do hold, if not in our hands, at any rate in our minds, where we can dispose of them as we choose, which gives us the illusion of a sort of power to control them. He was quite happy whenever M. de Charlus was with Odette. He knew that between M. de Charlus and her nothing untoward could ever happen, that when M. de Charlus went anywhere with her, it was out of friendship for himself, and that he would make no difficulty about telling him everything that she had done. Sometimes she had declared so emphatically to Swann that it was impossible for him to see her on a particular evening, she seemed to be looking forward so keenly to some outing, that Swann attached a very real importance to the fact that M. de Charlus was free to accompany her. Next day, without daring to put many questions to M. de Charlus, he would force him, by appearing not quite to understand his first answers, to give him more, after each of which he would feel himself increasingly relieved, for he very soon learned that Odette had spent her evening in the most innocent of dissipations.

'But what do you mean, my dear Mémé, I don't quite understand . . . You didn't go straight from her house to the Musée Grévin? Surely you went somewhere else first? No? That is very odd! You don't know how amusing you are, my dear Mémé. But what an odd idea of hers to go on to the Chat Noir afterwards; it was her idea, I suppose? No? Yours? That's strange. After all, it wasn't a bad idea; she must have known dozens of people there? No? She never spoke to a soul? How extraordinary! Then you sat there like that, just you and she, all by yourselves? I can picture you, sitting there! You are a worthy fellow, my dear Mémé; I'm exceedingly fond of you.'

Swann was now quite at ease. To him, who had so often happened, when talking to friends who knew nothing of his love, friends to whom he hardly listened, to hear certain detached sentences (as, for instance, 'I saw Mme de Crécy yesterday; she was with a man I didn't know'), sentences which dropped into his heart and passed at once into a solid state, grew hard as stalagmites, and seared and tore him as they lay there irremovable, – how charming, by way of contrast, were the words: 'She didn't know a soul; she never spoke to a soul.' How freely they coursed through him, how fluid they were, how vaporous, how easy to breathe! And yet, a moment later, he was telling himself that Odette must find him very dull if those were the pleasures that she preferred to his company. And their very insignificance, though it reassured him, pained him as if her enjoyment of them had been an act of treachery.

Even when he could not discover where she had gone, it would have sufficed to alleviate the anguish that he then felt, for which Odette's presence, the charm of her company, was the sole specific (a specific which in the long run served, like many other remedies, to aggravate the disease, but at least brought temporary relief to his sufferings), it would have sufficed, had Odette only permitted him to remain in her house while she was out, to wait there until that hour of her return, into whose stillness and peace would flow, to be mingled and lost there, all memory of those intervening hours which some sorcery, some cursed spell had made him imagine as, somehow, different from the rest. But she would not; he must return home; he forced himself, on the way, to form various plans, ceased to think of Odette; he even reached the stage, while he undressed, of turning over all sorts of happy ideas in his mind; it was with a light heart, buoyed with the anticipation of going to see some favourite work of art on the morrow, that he jumped into bed and turned out the light; but no sooner had he made himself ready to sleep, relaxing a self-control of which he was not even conscious, so habitual had it become, than an icy shudder convulsed his body and he burst into sobs. He did not wish to know why, but dried his eyes, saying with a smile: 'This is delightful; I'm becoming neurasthenic.' After which he could not save himself from utter exhaustion at the thought that, next day, he must begin afresh his attempts to find out what Odette had been doing, must use all his influence to contrive to see her. This compulsion to an activity without respite, without variety, without result, was so cruel a scourge that one day, noticing a swelling over his stomach, he felt an actual joy in the idea that he had, perhaps, a tumour which would prove fatal, that he need not concern himself with anything further, that it was his malady which was going to govern his life, to make a plaything of him, until the not-distant end. If indeed, at this period, it often happened that, though without admitting it even to himself, he longed for death, it was in order to escape not so much from the keenness of his sufferings as from the monotony of his struggle.

And yet he would have wished to live until the time came when he no longer loved her, when she would have no reason for lying to him, when at length he might learn from her whether, on the day when he had gone to see her in the afternoon, she had or had not been in the arms of Forcheville. Often for several days on end the suspicion that she was in love with someone else would distract his mind from the question of Forcheville, making it almost immaterial to him, like those new developments of a continuous state of ill-health which seem for a little time to have delivered us from their predecessors. There were even days when he was not tormented by any suspicion. He fancied that he was cured. But next morning, when he awoke, he felt in the same place the same pain, a sensation which, the day before, he had, as it were, diluted in the torrent of different impressions. But it had not stirred from its place. Indeed, it was the sharpness of this pain that had awakened him.

Since Odette never gave him any information as to those vastly important matters which took up so much of her time every day (albeit he had lived long enough in the world to know that such matters are never anything else than pleasures) he could not sustain for any length of time the effort to imagine them; his brain would become a void; then he would pass a finger over his tired eyelids, in the same way as he might have wiped his eyeglass, and would cease altogether to think. There emerged, however, from this unexplored tract, certain occupations which reappeared from time to time, vaguely connected by Odette with some obligation towards distant relatives or old friends who, inasmuch as they were the only people whom she was in the habit of mentioning as preventing her from seeing him, seemed to Swann to compose the necessary, unalterable setting of her life. Because of the tone in which she referred, from time to time, to 'the day when I go with my friend to the Hippodrome', if, when he felt unwell and had thought, 'Perhaps Odette would be kind and come to see me,' he remembered, suddenly, that it was one of those very days, he would correct himself with an 'Oh, no! It's not worth while asking her to come; I should have thought of it before, this is the day when she goes with her friend to the Hippodrome. We must confine ourselves to what is possible; no use wasting our time in proposing things that can't be accepted and are declined in advance.' And this duty that was incumbent upon Odette, of going to the Hippodrome, to which Swann thus gave way, seemed to him to be not merely ineluctable in itself; but the mark of necessity which stamped it seemed to make plausible and legitimate everything that was even remotely connected with it. If, when Odette, in the street, had acknowledged the salute of a passer-by, which had aroused Swann's jealousy, she replied to his questions by associating the stranger with any of the two or three paramount duties of which she had often spoken to him; if, for instance, she said: 'That's a gentlemen who was in my friend's box the other day; the one I go to the Hippodrome with,' that explanation would set Swann's suspicions at rest; it was, after all, inevitable that this friend should have other guests than Odette in her box at the Hippodrome, but he had never sought to form or succeeded in forming any coherent impression of them. Oh! how he would have loved to know her, that friend who went to the Hippodrome, how he would have loved her to invite him there with Odette. How readily he would have sacrificed all his acquaintance for no matter what person who was in the habit of seeing Odette, were she but a manicurist or a girl out of a shop. He would have taken more trouble, incurred more expense for them than for queens. Would they not have supplied him, out of what was contained in their knowledge of the life of Odette, with the one potent anodyne for his pain? With what joy would he have hastened to spend his days with one or other of those humble folk with whom Odette kept up friendly relations, either with some ulterior motive or from genuine simplicity of nature. How willingly would he have fixed his abode for ever in the attics of some sordid but enviable house, where Odette went but never took him, and where, if he had lived with the little retired dressmaker, whose lover he would readily have pretended to be, he would have been visited by Odette almost daily. In those regions, that were almost slums, what a modest existence, abject, if you please, but delightful, nourished by tranquillity and happiness, he would have consented to lead indefinitely.

It sometimes happened, again, that, when, after meeting Swann, she saw some man approaching, whom he did not know, he could distinguish upon Odette's face that look of sorrow which she had worn on the day when he had come to her while Forcheville was there. But this was rare; for, on the days when, in spite of all that she had to do, and of her dread of what people would think, she did actually manage to see Swann, the predominant quality in her attitude, now, was self-assurance; a striking contrast, perhaps an unconscious revenge for, perhaps a natural reaction from the timorous emotion which, in the early days of their friendship, she had felt in his presence, and even in his absence, when she began a letter to him with the words: 'My dear, my hand trembles so that I can scarcely write.' (So, at least, she pretended, and a little of that emotion must have been sincere, or she would not have been anxious to enlarge and emphasize it.) So Swann had been pleasing to her then. Our hands do not tremble except for ourselves, or for those whom we love. When they have ceased to control our happiness how peaceful, how easy, how bold do we become in their presence! In speaking to him, in writing to him now, she no longer employed those words by which she had sought to give herself the illusion that he belonged to her, creating opportunities for saying 'my' and 'mine' when she referred to him: 'You are all that I have in the world; it is the perfume of our friendship, I shall keep it,' nor spoke to him of the future, of death itself, as of a single adventure which they would have to share. In those early days, whatever he might say to her, she would answer admiringly: 'You know, you will never be like other people!' – she would gaze at his long, slightly bald head, of which people who knew only of his successes used to think: 'He's not regularly good-looking, if you like, but he is smart; that tuft, that eyeglass, that smile!' and, with more curiosity perhaps to know him as he really was than desire to become his mistress, she would sigh:

'I do wish I could find out what there is in that head of yours!'

But now, whatever he might say, she would answer, in a

tone sometimes of irritation, sometimes indulgent: 'Ah! so
you never will be like other people!'

She would gaze at his head, which was hardly aged at all
by his recent anxieties (though people now thought of it, by
the same mental process which enables one to discover the
meaning of a piece of symphonic music of which one has read
the programme, or the 'likenesses' in a child whose family
one has known: 'He's not positively ugly, if you like, but he
is really rather absurd; that eyeglass, that tuft, that smile!'
realizing in their imagination, fed by suggestion, the invisible
boundary which divides, at a few months' interval, the head
of an ardent lover from a cuckold's), and would say:

'Oh, I do wish I could change you; put some sense into
that head of yours.'

Always ready to believe in the truth of what he hoped, if it
was only Odette's way of behaving to him that left room for
doubt, he would fling himself greedily upon her words: 'You
can if you like,' he would tell her.

And he tried to explain to her that to comfort him, to control him, to make him work would be a noble task, to which
numbers of other women asked for nothing better than to be
allowed to devote themselves, though it is only fair to add
that in those other women's hands the noble task would have
seemed to Swann nothing more than an indiscreet and
intolerable usurpation of his freedom of action. 'If she
didn't love me, just a little,' he told himself, 'she would not
wish to have me altered. To alter me, she will have to see
me more often.' And so he was able to trace, in these faults
which she found in him, a proof at least of her interest,
perhaps even of her love; and, in fact, she gave him so little,
now, of the last, that he was obliged to regard as proofs of her
interest in him the various things which, every now and then,
she forbade him to do. One day she announced that she did
not care for his coachman, who, she thought, was perhaps
setting Swann against her, and, anyhow, did not show that
promptness and deference to Swann's orders which she would
have liked to see. She felt that he wanted to hear her say:
'Don't have him again when you come to me,' just as he

might have wanted her to kiss him. So, being in a good temper, she said it; and he was deeply moved. That evening, when talking to M. de Charlus, with whom he had the satisfaction of being able to speak of her openly (for the most trivial remarks that he uttered now, even to people who had never heard of her, had always some sort of reference to Odette), he said to him:

'I believe, all the same, that she loves me; she is so nice to me now, and she certainly takes an interest in what I do.'

And if, when he was starting off for her house, getting into his carriage with a friend whom he was to drop somewhere on the way, his friend said: 'Hullo! that isn't Loredan on the box?' with what melancholy joy would Swann answer him:

'Oh! Good heavens, no! I can tell you, I daren't take Loredan when I go to the Rue La Pérouse; Odette doesn't like me to have Loredan, she thinks he doesn't suit me. What on earth is one to do? Women, you know, women. My dear fellow, she would be furious. Oh, lord, yes; I've only to take Rémi there; I should never hear the last of it!'

These new manners, indifferent, listless, irritable, which Odette now adopted with Swann, undoubtedly made him suffer; but he did not realize how much he suffered; since it had been with a regular progression, day after day, that Odette had chilled towards him, it was only by directly contrasting what she was to-day with what she had been at first that he could have measured the extent of the change that had taken place. Now this change was his deep, his secret wound, which pained him day and night, and whenever he felt that his thoughts were straying too near it, he would quickly turn them into another channel for fear of being made to suffer too keenly. He might say to himself in a vague way: 'There was a time when Odette loved me more,' but he never formed any definite picture of that time. Just as he had in his study a cupboard at which he contrived never to look, which he turned aside to avoid passing whenever he entered or left the room, because in one of its drawers he had locked away the chrysanthemum which she had given him on one of those first evenings when he had taken her home in his carriage, and the letters in which she said: 'Why did you not forget your heart also? I should never have let you have that back,' and 'At whatever hour of the day or night you may need me, just send me a word, and dispose of me as you please,' so there was a place in his heart to which he would never allow his thoughts to trespass too near, forcing them, if need be, to evade it by a long course of reasoning so that they should not have to pass within reach of it; the place in which lingered his memories of happy days.

But his so meticulous prudence was defeated one evening when he had gone out to a party.

It was at the Marquise de Saint-Euverte's, on the last, for that season, of the evenings on which she invited people to listen to the musicians who would serve, later on, for her charity concerts. Swann, who had intended to go to each of the previous evenings in turn, but had never been able to make up his mind, received, while he was dressing for this party, a visit from the Baron de Charlus, who came with an offer to go with him to the Marquise's, if his company could be of any use in helping Swann not to feel quite so bored when he got there, to be a little less unhappy. But Swann had thanked him with:

'You can't conceive how glad I should be of your company. But the greatest pleasure that you can give me will be if you will go instead to see Odette. You know what a splendid influence you have over her. I don't suppose she'll be going anywhere this evening, unless she goes to see her old dressmaker, and I'm sure she would be delighted if you went with her there. In any case, you'll find her at home before then. Try to keep her amused, and also to give her a little sound advice. If you could arrange something for to-morrow which would please her, something that we could all three do together. Try to put out a feeler, too, for the summer; see if there's anything she wants to do, a cruise that we might all three take; anything you can think of. I don't count upon seeing her to-night, myself; still if she would like me to come, or if you find a loophole, you've only to send me a line at Mme de Saint-Euverte's up till midnight; after that I shall be here. Ever so many thanks for all you are doing for me – you know what I feel about you!'

His friend promised to go and do as Swann wished as soon as he had deposited him at the door of the Saint-Euverte house, where he arrived soothed by the thought that M. de Charlus would be spending the evening in the Rue La Pérouse, but in a state of melancholy indifference to everything that did not involve Odette, and in particular to the details of fashionable life, a state which invested them with the charm that is to be found in anything which, being no longer an object of our desire, appears to us in its own guise. On alighting from his carriage, in the foreground of that fictitious summary of their domestic existence which hostesses are pleased to offer to the guests on ceremonial occasions, and in which they show a great regard for accuracy of costume and setting, Swann was amused to discover the heirs and successors of Balzac's 'tigers' – now 'grooms' – who normally followed their mistress when she walked abroad, but now, hatted and booted, were posted out of doors, in front of the house on the gravelled drive, or outside the stables, as gardeners might be drawn up for inspection at the ends of their several flower-beds. The peculiar tendency which he had always had to look for analogies between living people and the portraits in galleries reasserted itself here, but in a more positive and more general form; it was society as a whole, now that he was detached from it, which presented itself to him in a series of pictures. In the cloak-room, into which, in the old days, when he was still a man of fashion, he would have gone in his overcoat, to emerge from it in evening dress, but without any impression of what had occurred there, his mind having been, during the minute or two that he had spent in it, either still at the party which he had just left, or already at the party into which he was just about to be ushered, he now noticed, for the first time, roused by the unexpected arrival of so belated a guest, the scattered pack of splendid effortless animals, the enormous footmen who were drowsing here and there upon benches and chests, until, pointing their noble greyhound profiles, they towered upon their feet and gathered in a circle round about him.

One of them, of a particularly ferocious aspect, and not unlike the headsman in certain Renaissance pictures which represent executions, tortures, and the like, advanced upon him with an implacable air to take his 'things'. But the harshness of his steely glare was compensated by the softness of his cotton gloves, so effectively that, as he approached Swann, he seemed to be exhibiting at once an utter contempt for his person and the most tender regard for his hat. He took it with care to which the precision of his movements imparted something that was almost over-fastidious, and with a delicacy that was rendered almost touching by the evidence of his splendid strength. Then he passed it to one of his satellites, a novice and timid, who was expressing the panic that overpowered him by casting furious glances in every direction, and displayed all the dumb agitation of a wild animal in the first hours of its captivity.

A few feet away, a strapping great lad in livery stood musing, motionless, statuesque, useless, like that purely decorative warrior whom one sees in the most tumultuous of Mantegna's paintings, lost in dreams, leaning upon his shield, while all around him are fighting and bloodshed and death; detached from the group of his companions who were thronging about Swann, he seemed as determined to remain unconcerned in the scene, which he followed vaguely with his cruel, greenish eyes, as if it had been the Massacre of the Innocents or the Martyrdom of Saint James. He seemed precisely to have sprung from that vanished race – if, indeed, it ever existed, save in the reredos of San Zeno and the frescoes of the Eremitani, where Swann had come in contact with it, and where it still dreams – fruit of the impregnation of a classical statue by some one of the Master's Paduan models, or of Albrecht Dürer's Saxons. And the locks of his reddish hair, crinkled by nature, but glued to his head by brilliantine, were treated broadly as they are in that Greek sculpture which the Mantuan painter never ceased to study, and which, if in its creator's purpose it represents but man, manages at least to extract from man's simple outlines such a variety of richness, borrowed, as it were, from the whole of animated nature, that a head of hair, by the glossy undulation and beak-like points of its curls, or in the overlaying of the florid triple diadem of its brushed tresses, can suggest at once a bunch of seaweed, a brood of fledgling doves, a bed of hyacinths, and a serpent's writhing back. Others again, no less colossal, were disposed upon the steps of a monumental staircase which, by their decorative presence and marmorean immobility, was made worthy to be named, like that god-crowned ascent in the Palace of the Doges, the 'Staircase of the Giants', and on which Swann now set foot, saddened by the thought that Odette had never climbed it. Ah, with what joy would he, on the other hand, have raced up the dark, evil-smelling, breakneck flights to the little dressmaker's, in whose attic he would so gladly have paid the price of a weekly stage-box at the Opera for the right to spend the evening there when Odette came, and other days too, for the privilege of talking about her, of living among people whom she was in the habit of seeing when he was not there, and who, on that account, seemed to keep secret among themselves some part of the life of his mistress more real, more inaccessible, and more mysterious than anything that he knew. Whereas upon that pestilential, enviable staircase to the old dressmaker's, since there was no other, no service stair in the building, one saw in the evening outside every door an empty, unwashed milk-can set out, in readiness for the morning round, upon the door-mat; on the despicable, enormous staircase which Swann was at the moment climbing, on either side of him, at different levels, before each anfractuosity made in its walls by the window of the porter's lodge or the entrance to a set of rooms, representing the departments of indoor service which they controlled, and doing homage for them to the guests, a gate-keeper, a major-domo, a steward (worthy men who spent the rest of the week in semi-independence in their own domains, dined there by themselves like small shop-keepers, and might to-morrow lapse to the plebeian service of some successful doctor or industrial magnate), scrupulous in carrying out to the letter all the instructions that had been heaped upon them before they were allowed to don the brilliant livery which they wore only at long intervals, and in which they did not feel altogether at their ease, stood each in the arcade of his doorway, their splendid pomp tempered by a democratic good-fellowship, like saints in their niches, and a gigantic usher, dressed Swiss Guard fashion, like the beadle in a church, struck the pavement with his staff as each fresh arrival passed him. Coming to the top of the staircase, up which he had been followed by a servant with a pallid countenance and a small pigtail clubbed at the back of his head, like one of Goya's sacristans or a tabellion in an old play, Swann passed by an office in which the lackeys, seated like notaries before their massive registers, rose solemnly to their feet and inscribed his name. He next crossed a little hall which – just as certain rooms are arranged by their owners to serve as the setting for a single work of art (from which they take their name), and, in their studied bareness, contain nothing else besides – displayed to him as he entered it, like some priceless effigy by Benvenuto Cellini of an armed watchman, a young footman, his body slightly bent forward, rearing above his crimson gorget an even more crimson face, from which seemed to burst forth torrents of fire, timidity, and zeal, who, as he pierced the Aubusson tapestries that screened the door of the room in which the music was being given with his impetuous, vigilant, desperate gaze, appeared, with a soldierly impassibility or a supernatural faith – an allegory of alarums, incarnation of alertness, commemoration of a riot – to be looking out, angel or sentinel, from the tower of dungeon or cathedral, for the approach of the enemy or for the hour of Judgement. Swann had now only to enter the concert-room, the doors of which were thrown open to him by an usher loaded with chains, who bowed low before him as though tendering to him the keys of a conquered city. But he thought of the house in which at that very moment he might have been, if Odette had but permitted, and the remembered glimpse of an empty milk-can upon a door-mat wrung his heart.

He speedily recovered his sense of the general ugliness of the human male when, on the other side of the tapestry curtain, the spectacle of the servants gave place to that of the guests. But even this ugliness of faces, which of course were mostly familiar to him, seemed something new and uncanny, now that their features, – instead of being to him symbols of practical utility in the identification of this or that man, who until then had represented merely so many pleasures to be sought-after, boredoms to be avoided, or courtesies to be acknowledged – were at rest, measurable by aesthetic coordinates alone, in the autonomy of their curves and angles. And in these men, in the thick of whom Swann now found himself packed, there was nothing (even to the monocle which many of them wore, and which, previously, would, at the most, have enabled Swann to say that so-and-so wore a monocle) which, no longer restricted to the general connotation of a habit, the same in all of them, did not now strike him with a sense of individuality in each. Perhaps because he did not regard General de Froberville and the Marquis de Bréauté, who were talking together just inside the door, as anything more than two figures in a picture, whereas they were the old and useful friends who had put him up for the Jockey Club and had supported him in duels, the General's monocle, stuck like a shell-splinter in his common, scarred, victorious, over-bearing face, in the middle of a forehead which it left half-blinded, like the single-eyed flashing front of the Cyclops, appeared to Swann as a monstrous wound which it might have been glorious to receive but which it was certainly not decent to expose, while that which M. de Bréauté wore, as a festive badge, with his pearl-grey gloves, his crush hat and white tie, substituting it for the familiar pair of glasses (as Swann himself did) when he went out to places, bore, glued to its other side, like a specimen prepared on a slide for the microscope, an infinitesimal gaze that swarmed with friendly feeling and never ceased to twinkle at the loftiness of ceilings, the delightfulness of parties, the interestingness of programmes, and the excellence of refreshments.

'Hallo! you here! why, it's ages since I've seen you,' the

General greeted Swann and, noticing the look of strain on his face and concluding that it was perhaps a serious illness that had kept him away, went on, 'You're looking well, old man!' while M. de Bréauté turned with, 'My dear fellow, what on earth are you doing here?' to a 'society novelist' who had just fitted into the angle of eyebrow and cheek his own monocle, the sole instrument that he used in his psychological investigations and remorseless analyses of character, and who now replied, with an air of mystery and importance, rolling the 'r': – 'I am observing!'

The Marquis de Forestelle's monocle was minute and rimless, and, by enforcing an incessant and painful contraction of the eye over which it was incrusted like a superfluous cartilage, the presence of which there was inexplicable and its substance unimaginable, it gave to his face a melancholy refinement, and led women to suppose him capable of suffering terribly when in love. But that of M. de Saint-Candé, girdled, like Saturn, with an enormous ring, was the centre of gravity of a face which composed itself afresh every moment in relation to the glass, while his thrusting red nose and swollen sarcastic lips endeavoured by their grimaces to rise to the level of the steady flame of wit that sparkled in the polished disc, and saw itself preferred to the most ravishing eyes in the world by the smart, depraved young women whom it set dreaming of artificial charms and a refinement of sensual bliss; and then, behind him, M. de Palancy, who with his huge carp's head and goggling eyes moved slowly up and down the stream of festive gatherings, unlocking his great mandibles at every moment as though in search of his orientation, had the air of carrying about upon his person only an accidental and perhaps purely symbolical fragment of the glass wall of his aquarium, a part intended to suggest the whole which recalled to Swann, a fervent admirer of Giotto's Vices and Virtues at Padua, that Injustice by whose side a leafy bough evokes the idea of the forests that enshroud his secret lair.

Swann had gone forward into the room, under pressure from Mme de Saint-Euverte and in order to listen to an aria from *Orfeo* which was being rendered on the flute, and had taken up a position in a corner from which, unfortunately, his horizon was bounded by two ladies of 'uncertain' age, seated side by side, the Marquise de Cambremer and the Vicomtesse de Franquetot, who, because they were cousins, used to spend their time at parties in wandering through the rooms, each clutching her bag and followed by her daughter, hunting for one another like people at a railway station, and could never be at rest until they had reserved, by marking them with their fans or handkerchiefs, two adjacent chairs; Mme de Cambremer, since she knew scarcely anyone, being all the more glad of a companion, while Mme de Franquetot, who, on the contrary, was extremely popular, thought it effective and original to show all her fine friends that she preferred to their company that of an obscure country cousin with whom she had childish memories in common. Filled with ironical melancholy, Swann watched them as they listened to the pianoforte intermezzo (Liszt's 'Saint Francis preaching to the birds') which came after the flute, and followed the virtuoso in his dizzy flight; Mme de Franquetot anxiously, her eyes starting from her head, as though the keys over which his fingers skipped with such agility were a series of trapezes, from any one of which he might come crashing, a hundred feet, to the ground, stealing now and then a glance of astonishment and unbelief at her companion, as who should say: 'It isn't possible, I would never have believed that a human being could do all that!'; Mme de Cambremer, as a woman who had received a sound musical education, beating time with her head – transformed for the nonce into the pendulum of a metronome, the sweep and rapidity of whose movements from one shoulder to the other (performed with that look of wild abandonment in her eye which a sufferer shows who is no longer able to analyse his pain, or anxious to master it, and says merely 'I can't help it') so increased that at every moment her diamond ear-rings caught in the trimming of her bodice, and she was obliged to put straight the bunch of black grapes which she had in her hair, though without any interruption of her constantly accelerated motion. On the other side (and a little way in front) of Mme de Franquetot, was the Marquise de Gallardon, absorbed in her favourite meditation, namely upon her own kinship with the Guermantes family, from which she derived both publicly and in private a good deal of glory not unmingled with shame, the most brilliant ornaments of that house remaining somewhat aloof from her, perhaps because she was just a tiresome old woman, or because she was a scandalous old woman, or because she came of an inferior branch of the family, or very possibly for no reason at all. When she found herself seated next to someone whom she did not know, as she was at this moment next to Mme de Franquetot, she suffered acutely from the feeling that her own consciousness of her Guermantes connexion could not be made externally manifest in visible characters, like those which, in the mosaics in Byzantine churches, placed one beneath another, inscribe in a vertical column by the side of some Sacred Personage the words which he is supposed to be uttering. At this moment she was pondering the fact that she had never received an invitation, or even a call, from her young cousin the Princesse des Laumes, during the six years that had already elapsed since the latter's marriage. The thought filled her with anger – and with pride; for, by virtue of having told everyone who expressed surprise at never seeing her at Mme des Laumes's, that it was because of the risk of meeting the Princesse Mathilde there – a degradation which her own family, the truest and bluest of Legitimists, would never have forgiven her, she had come gradually to believe that this actually was the reason for her not visiting her young cousin. She remembered, it is true, that she had several times inquired of Mme des Laumes how they might contrive to meet, but she remembered it only in a confused way, and besides did more than neutralize this slightly humiliating reminiscence by murmuring, 'After all, it isn't for me to take the first step; I am at least twenty years older than she is.' And fortified by these unspoken words she flung her shoulders proudly back until they seemed to part company with her bust, while her head, which lay almost horizontally upon them, made one think of the 'stuck-on' head of a pheasant which is brought to the table regally adorned with its feathers. Not that she in the least degree resembled a pheasant, having been endowed by nature with a short and squat and masculine figure; but successive mortifications had given her a backward tilt, such as one may observe in trees which have taken root on the very edge of a precipice and are forced to grow backwards to preserve their balance. Since she was obliged, in order to console herself for not being quite on a level with the rest of the Guermantes, to repeat to herself incessantly that it was owing to the uncompromising rigidity of her principles and pride that she saw so little of them, the constant iteration had gradually remoulded her body, and had given her a sort of 'bearing' which was accepted by the plebeian as a sign of breeding, and even kindled, at times, a momentary spark in the jaded eyes of old gentlemen in clubs. Had anyone subjected Mme de Gallardon's conversation to that form of analysis which by noting the relative frequency of its several terms would furnish him with the key to a ciphered message, he would at once have remarked that no expression, not even the commonest forms of speech, occurred in it nearly so often as 'at my cousins the Guermantes'', 'at my aunt Guermantes's', 'Elzéar de Guermantes's health', 'my cousin Guermantes's box'. If anyone spoke to her of a distinguished personage, she would reply that, although she was not personally acquainted with him, she had seen him hundreds of times at her aunt Guermantes's, but she would utter this reply in so icy a tone, with such a hollow sound, that it was at once quite clear that if she did not know the celebrity personally that was because of all the obstinate, ineradicable principles against which her arching shoulders were stretched back to rest, as on one of those ladders on which gymnastic instructors make us 'extend' so as to develop the expansion of our chests.

At this moment the Princesse des Laumes, who had not been expected to appear at Mme de Saint-Euverte's that evening, did in fact arrive. To show that she did not wish any special attention, in a house to which she had come by an act of condescension, to be paid to her superior rank, she had entered the room with her arms pressed close to her sides, even when there was no crowd to be squeezed through, no one attempting to get past her; staying purposely at the back, with the air of being in her proper place, like a king who stands in the waiting procession at the doors of a theatre where the management have not been warned of his coming; and strictly limiting her field of vision – so as not to seem to be advertising her presence and claiming the consideration that was her due – to the study of a pattern in the carpet or of her own skirt, she stood there on the spot which had struck her as the most modest (and from which, as she very well knew, a cry of rapture from Mme de Saint-Euverte would extricate her as soon as her presence there was noticed), next to Mme de Cambremer, whom, however, she did not know. She observed the dumb-show by which her neighbour was expressing her passion for music, but she refrained from copying it. This was not to say that, for once that she had consented to spend a few minutes in Mme de Saint-Euverte's house, the Princesse des Laumes would not have wished (so that the act of politeness to her hostess which she had performed by coming might, so to speak, 'count double') to show herself as friendly and obliging as possible. But she had a natural horror of what she called 'exaggerating', and always made a point of letting people see that she 'simply must not' indulge in any display of emotion that was not in keeping with the tone of the circle in which she moved, although such displays never failed to make an impression upon her, by virtue of that spirit of imitation, akin to timidity, which is developed in the most self-confident persons, by contact with an unfamiliar environment, even though it be inferior to their own. She began to ask herself whether these gesticulations might not, perhaps, be a necessary concomitant of the piece of music that was being played, a piece which, it might be, was in a different category from all the music that she had ever heard before; and whether to abstain from them was not a sign of her own inability to understand the music, and of discourtesy towards the lady of the house; with the result that, in order to express by a compromise both of her contradictory inclinations in turn, at one moment she would merely straighten her shoulder-straps or feel in her golden hair for the little balls of coral or of pink enamel, frosted with tiny diamonds, which formed its simple but effective ornament, studying, with a cold interest, her impassioned neighbour, while at another she would beat time for a few bars with her fan, but, so as not to forfeit her independence, she would beat a different time from the pianist's. When he had finished the Liszt Intermezzo and had begun a Prelude by Chopin, Mme de Cambremer turned to Mme de Franquetot with a tender smile, full of intimate reminiscence, as well as of satisfaction (that of a competent judge) with the performance. She had been taught in her girlhood to fondle and cherish those long-necked, sinuous creatures, the phrases of Chopin, so free, so flexible, so tactile, which begin by seeking their ultimate resting-place somewhere beyond and far wide of the direction in which they started, the point which one might have expected them to reach, phrases which divert themselves in those fantastic bypaths only to return more deliberately – with a more premeditated reaction, with more precision, as on a crystal bowl which, if you strike it, will ring and throb until you cry aloud in anguish – to clutch at one's heart.

Brought up in a provincial household with few friends or visitors, hardly ever invited to a ball, she had fuddled her mind, in the solitude of her old manor-house, over setting the pace, now crawling-slow, now passionate, whirling, breathless, for all those imaginary waltzing couples, gathering them like flowers, leaving the ballroom for a moment to listen, where the wind sighed among the pine-trees, on the shore of the lake, and seeing of a sudden advancing towards her, more different from anything one had ever dreamed of than earthly lovers are, a slender young man, whose voice was resonant and strange and false, in white gloves. But nowadays the old-fashioned beauty of this music seemed to have become a trifle stale. Having forfeited, some years back, the esteem of 'really musical' people, it had lost its distinction and its charm, and even those whose taste was frankly bad had ceased to find in it more than a moderate pleasure to which they hardly liked to confess. Mme de Cambremer cast a furtive glance behind her. She knew that her young daughter-in-law (full of respect for her new and noble family, except in such matters as related to the intellect, upon which, having 'got as far' as Harmony and the Greek alphabet, she was specially enlightened) despised Chopin, and felt quite ill when she heard him played. But finding herself free from the scrutiny of this Wagnerian, who was sitting, at some distance, in a group of her own contemporaries, Mme de Cambremer let herself drift upon a stream of exquisite memories and sensations. The Princesse des Laumes was touched also. Though without any natural gift for music, she had received, some fifteen years earlier, the instruction which a music-mistress of the Faubourg Saint-Germain, a woman of genius who had been, towards the end of her life, reduced to penury, had started, at seventy, to give to the daughters and granddaughters of her old pupils. This lady was now dead. But her method, an echo of her charming touch, came to life now and then in the fingers of her pupils, even of those who had been in other respects quite mediocre, had given up music, and hardly ever opened a piano. And so Mme des Laumes could let her head sway to and fro, fully aware of the cause, with a perfect appreciation of the manner in which the pianist was rendering this Prelude, since she knew it by heart. The closing notes of the phrase that he had begun sounded already on her lips. And she murmured 'How charming it is!' with a stress on the opening consonants of the adjective, a token of her refinement by which she felt her lips so romantically compressed, like the petals of a beautiful, budding flower, that she instinctively brought her eyes into harmony, illuminating them for a moment with a vague and sentimental gaze. Meanwhile Mme de Gallardon had arrived at the point of saying to herself how annoying it was that she had so few opportunities of meeting the Princesse des Laumes, for she meant to teach her a lesson by not acknowledging her bow. She did not know that her cousin was in the room. A movement of Mme Franquetot's head disclosed the Princess. At once Mme de Gallardon dashed towards her, upsetting all her neighbours; although determined to preserve a distant and glacial manner which should remind everyone present that she had no desire to remain on friendly

terms with a person in whose house one might find oneself,
any day, cheek by jowl with the Princesse Mathilde, and to
whom it was not her duty to make advances since she was not
'of her generation', she felt bound to modify this air of dignity
and reserve by some non-committal remark which would
justify her overture and would force the Princess to engage in
conversation; and so, when she reached her cousin, Mme de
Gallardon, with a stern countenance and one hand thrust out
as though she were trying to 'force' a card, began with: 'How
is your husband?' in the same anxious tone that she would
have used if the Prince had been seriously ill. The Princess,
breaking into a laugh which was one of her characteristics,
and was intended at once to show the rest of an assembly that
she was making fun of someone and also to enhance her own
beauty by concentrating her features around her animated lips
and sparkling eyes, answered: 'Why, he's never been better in
his life!' And she went on laughing.

Mme de Gallardon then drew herself up and, chilling her
expression still further, perhaps because she was still uneasy
about the Prince's health, said to her cousin:

'Oriane,' (at once Mme des Laumes looked with amused
astonishment towards an invisible third, whom she seemed to
call to witness that she had never authorized Mme de Gallardon to use her Christian name) 'I should be so pleased if you
would look in, just for a minute, to-morrow evening, to hear
a quintet, with the clarinet, by Mozart. I should like to have
your opinion of it.'

She seemed not so much to be issuing an invitation as to be
asking a favour, and to want the Princess's opinion of the
Mozart quintet just as though it had been a dish invented by a
new cook, whose talent it was most important that an epicure
should come to judge.

'But I know that quintet quite well. I can tell you now –
that I adore it.'

'You know, my husband isn't at all well; it's his liver.
He would like so much to see you,' Mme de Gallardon re-
sumed, making it now a corporal work of charity for the
Princess to appear at her party.

The Princess never liked to tell people that she would not go to their houses. Every day she would write to express her regret at having been kept away – by the sudden arrival of her husband's mother, by an invitation from his brother, by the Opera, by some excursion to the country – from some party to which she had never for a moment dreamed of going. In this way she gave many people the satisfaction of feeling that she was on intimate terms with them, that she would gladly have come to their houses, and that she had been prevented from doing so only by some princely occurrence which they were flattered to find competing with their own humble entertainment. And then, as she belonged to that witty 'Guermantes set' – in which there survived something of the alert mentality, stripped of all commonplace phrases and conventional sentiments, which dated from Mérimée, and found its final expression in the plays of Meilhac and Halévy – she adapted its formula so as to suit even her social engagements, transposed it into the courtesy which was always struggling to be positive and precise, to approximate itself to the plain truth. She would never develop at any length to a hostess the expression of her anxiety to be present at her party; she found it more pleasant to disclose to her all the various little incidents on which it would depend whether it was or was not possible for her to come.

'Listen, and I'll explain;' she began to Mme Gallardon. 'To-morrow evening I must go to a friend of mine, who has been pestering me to fix a day for ages. If she takes us to the theatre afterwards, then I can't possibly come to you, much as I should love to; but if we just stay in the house, I know there won't be anyone else there, so I can slip away.'

'Tell me, have you seen your friend M. Swann?'

'No! my precious Charles! I never knew he was here. Where is he? I must catch his eye.'

'It's a funny thing that he should come to old Saint-Euverte's,' Mme de Gallardon went on. 'Oh, I know he's very clever,' meaning by that 'very cunning', 'but that makes no difference; fancy a Jew here, and she the sister and sister-in-law of two Archbishops.'

'I am ashamed to confess that I am not in the least shocked,' said the Princesse des Laumes.

'I know he's a converted Jew, and all that, and his parents and grandparents before him. But they do say that the converted ones are worse about their religion than the practising ones, that it's all just a pretence; is that true, d'you think?'

'I can throw no light at all on the matter.'

The pianist, who was 'down' to play two pieces by Chopin, after finishing the Prelude had at once attacked a Polonaise. But once Mme de Gallardon had informed her cousin that Swann was in the room, Chopin himself might have risen from the grave and played all his works in turn without Mme des Laumes's paying him the slightest attention. She belonged to that one of the two divisions of the human race in which the untiring curiosity which the other half feels about the people whom it does not know is replaced by an unfailing interest in the people whom it does. As with many women of the Faubourg Saint-Germain, the presence, in any room in which she might find herself, of another member of her set, even although she had nothing in particular to say to him, would occupy her mind to the exclusion of every other consideration. From that moment, in the hope that Swann would catch sight of her, the Princess could do nothing but (like a tame white mouse when a lump of sugar is put down before its nose and then taken away) turn her face, in which were crowded a thousand signs of intimate connivance, none of them with the least relevance to the sentiment underlying Chopin's music, in the direction where Swann was, and, if he moved, divert accordingly the course of her magnetic smile.

'Oriane, don't be angry with me,' resumed Mme de Gallardon, who could never restrain herself from sacrificing her highest social ambitions, and the hope that she might one day emerge into a light that would dazzle the world, to the immediate and secret satisfaction of saying something disagreeable, 'people do say about your M. Swann that he's the sort of man one can't have in the house; is that true?'

'Why, you, of all people, ought to know that it's true,' replied the Princesse des Laumes, 'for you must have asked him a hundred times, and he's never been to your house once.'

And leaving her cousin mortified afresh, she broke out again into a laugh which scandalized everyone who was trying to listen to the music, but attracted the attention of Mme de Saint-Euverte, who had stayed, out of politeness, near the piano, and caught sight of the Princess now for the first time. Mme de Saint-Euverte was all the more delighted to see Mme des Laumes, as she imagined her to be still at Guermantes, looking after her father-in-law, who was ill.

'My dear Princess, you here?'

'Yes, I tucked myself away in a corner, and I've been hearing such lovely things.'

'What, you've been in the room quite a time?'

'Oh, yes, quite a long time, which seemed very short; it was only long because I couldn't see you.'

Mme de Saint-Euverte offered her own chair to the Princess, who declined it with:

'Oh, please, no! Why should you? It doesn't matter in the least where I sit.' And deliberately picking out, so as the better to display the simplicity of a really great lady, a low seat without a back: 'There now, that hassock, that's all I want. It will make me keep my back straight. Oh! Good heavens, I'm making a noise again; they'll be telling you to have me "chucked out".'

Meanwhile, the pianist having doubled his speed, the emotion of the music-lovers was reaching its climax, a servant was handing refreshments about on a salver, and was making the spoons rattle, and, as on every other 'party-night', Mme de Saint-Euverte was making signs to him, which he never saw, to leave the room. A recent bride, who had been told that a young woman ought never to appear bored, was smiling vigorously, trying to catch her hostess's eye so as to flash a token of her gratitude for the other's having 'thought of her' in connexion with so delightful an entertainment. And yet, although she remained more calm than Mme de Franquetot, it was not without some uneasiness that she followed the flying fingers; what alarmed her being not the pianist's fate but the piano's, on which a lighted candle, jumping at each *fortissimo*, threatened, if not to set its shade on fire, at least to spill wax upon the ebony. At last she could contain herself no longer, and, running up the two steps of the platform on which the piano stood, flung herself on the candle to adjust its sconce. But scarcely had her hand come within reach of it when, on a final chord, the piece finished, and the pianist rose to his feet. Nevertheless, the bold initiative shown by this young woman and the moment of blushing confusion between her and the pianist which resulted from it, produced an impression that was favourable on the whole.

'Did you see what that girl did just now, Princess?' asked General de Froberville, who had come up to Mme des Laumes as her hostess left her for a moment. 'Odd, wasn't it? Is she one of the performers?'

'No, she's a little Mme de Cambremer,' replied the Princess carelessly, and then, with more animation: 'I am only repeating what I heard just now, myself; I haven't the faintest notion who said it, it was someone behind me who said that they were neighbours of Mme de Saint-Euverte in the country, but I don't believe anyone knows them, really. They must be "country cousins"! By the way, I don't know whether you're particularly "well up" in the brilliant society which we see before us, because I've no idea who all these astonishing people can be. What do you suppose they do with themselves when they're not at Mme de Saint-Euverte's parties? She must have ordered them in with the musicians and the chairs and the food. "Universal providers", you know. You must admit, they're rather splendid, General. But can she really have the courage to hire the same "supers" every week? It isn't possible!'

'Oh, but Cambremer is quite a good name; old, too,' protested the General.

'I see no objection to its being old,' the Princess answered dryly, 'but whatever else it is it's not euphonious,' she went on, isolating the word euphonious as though between inverted commas, a little affectation to which the Guermantes set were addicted.

'You think not, eh! She's a regular little peach, though,' said the General, whose eyes never strayed from Mme de Cambremer. 'Don't you agree with me, Princess?'

'She thrusts herself forward too much; I think, in so young a woman, that's not very nice – for I don't suppose she's my generation,' replied Mme des Laumes (the last word being common, it appeared, to Gallardon and Guermantes). And then, seeing that M. de Froberville was still gazing at Mme de Cambremer, she added, half out of malice towards the lady, half wishing to oblige the General: 'Not very nice . . . for her husband! I am sorry that I do not know her, since she seems to attract you so much; I might have introduced you to her,' said the Princess, who, if she had known the young woman, would most probably have done nothing of the sort. 'And now I must say good night, because one of my friends is having a birthday party, and I must go and wish her many happy returns,' she explained, modestly and with truth, reducing the fashionable gathering to which she was going to the simple proportions of a ceremony which would be boring in the extreme, but at which she was obliged to be present, and there would be something touching about her appearance. 'Besides, I must pick up Basin. While I've been here, he's gone to see those friends of his – you know them too, I'm sure, – who are called after a bridge – oh, yes, the Iénas.'

'It was a battle before it was a bridge, Princess; it was a victory!' said the General. 'I mean to say, to an old soldier like me,' he went on, wiping his monocle and replacing it, as though he were laying a fresh dressing on the raw wound underneath, while the Princess instinctively looked away, 'that Empire nobility, well, of course, it's not the same thing, but, after all, taking it as it is, it's very fine of its kind; they were people who really did fight like heroes.'

'But I have the deepest respect for heroes,' the Princess assented, though with a faint trace of irony. 'If I don't go with Basin to see this Princesse d'Iéna, it isn't for that, at all; it's simply because I don't know them. Basin knows them; he worships them. Oh, no, it's not what you think; he's not in love with her. I've nothing to set my face against! Besides, what good has it ever done when I have set my face against them?' she queried sadly, for the whole world knew that, ever since the day upon which the Prince des Laumes had married his fascinating cousin, he had been consistently unfaithful to her. 'Anyhow, it isn't that at all. They're people he has known for ever so long, they do him very well, and that suits me down to the ground. But I must tell you what he's told me about their house; it's quite enough. Can you imagine it, all their furniture is "Empire"!'

'But, my dear Princess, that's only natural; it belonged to their grandparents.'

'I don't say it didn't, but that doesn't make it any less ugly. I quite understand that people can't always have nice things, but at least they needn't have things that are merely grotesque. What do you say? I can think of nothing more devastating, more utterly smug than that hideous style – cabinets covered all over with swans' heads, like bath-taps!'

'But I believe, all the same, that they've got some lovely things; why, they must have that famous mosaic table on which the Treaty of . . .'

'Oh, I don't deny, they may have things that are interesting enough from the historic point of view. But things like that can't, ever, be beautiful . . . because they're simply horrible! I've got things like that myself, that came to Basin from the Montesquious. Only, they're up in the attics at Guermantes, where nobody ever sees them. But, after all, that's not the point, I would fly to see them, with Basin; I would even go to see them among all their sphinxes and brasses, if I knew them, but – I don't know them! D'you know, I was always taught, when I was a little girl, that it was not polite to call on people one didn't know.' She assumed a tone of childish gravity. 'And so I am just doing what I was taught to do. Can't you see those good people, with a totally strange woman bursting into their house? Why, I might get a most hostile reception.'

And she coquettishly enhanced the charm of the smile which the idea had brought to her lips, by giving to her blue eyes, which were fixed on the General, a gentle, dreamy expression.

'My dear Princess, you know that they'ld be simply wild with joy.'

'No, why?' she inquired, with the utmost vivacity, either so as to seem unaware that it would be because she was one of the first ladies in France, or so as to have the pleasure of hearing the General tell her so. 'Why? How can you tell? Perhaps they would think it the most unpleasant thing that could possibly happen. I know nothing about them, but if they're anything like me, I find it quite boring enough to see the people I do know; I'm sure if I had to see people I didn't know as well, even if they had "fought like heroes", I should go stark mad. Besides, except when it's an old friend like you, whom one knows quite apart from that, I'm not sure that "heroism" takes one very far in society. It's often quite boring enough to have to give a dinner-party, but if one had to offer one's arm to Spartacus, to let him take one down . . . ! Really, no; it would never be Vercingetorix I should send for, to make a fourteenth. I feel sure, I should keep him for really big "crushes". And as I never give any . . .'

'Ah! Princess, it's easy to see you're not a Guermantes for nothing. You have your share of it, all right, the "wit of the Guermantes"!'

'But people always talk about the wit of *the* Guermantes; I never could make out why. Do you really know any *others* who have it?' she rallied him, with a rippling flow of laughter, her features concentrated, yoked to the service of her animation, her eyes sparkling, blazing with a radiant sunshine of gaiety which could be kindled only by such speeches – even if the Princess had to make them herself – as were in praise of her wit or of her beauty. 'Look, there's Swann talking to your Cambremer woman; over there, beside old Saint-Euverte, don't you see him? Ask him to introduce you. But hurry up, he seems to be just going!'

'Did you notice how dreadfully ill he's looking?' asked the General.

'My precious Charles? Ah, he's coming at last; I was beginning to think he didn't want to see me!'

Swann was extremely fond of the Princesse des Laumes,

and the sight of her recalled to him Guermantes, a property close to Combray, and all that country which he so dearly loved and had ceased to visit, so as not to be separated from Odette. Slipping into the manner, half-artistic, half-amorous – with which he could always manage to amuse the Princess – a manner which came to him quite naturally whenever he dipped for a moment into the old social atmosphere, and wishing also to express in words, for his own satisfaction, the longing that he felt for the country:

'Ah!' he exclaimed, or rather intoned, in such a way as to be audible at once to Mme de Saint-Euverte, to whom he spoke, and to Mme des Laumes, for whom he was speaking, 'Behold our charming Princess! See, she has come up on purpose from Guermantes to hear Saint Francis preach to the birds, and has only just had time, like a dear little tit-mouse, to go and pick a few little hips and haws and put them in her hair; there are even some drops of dew upon them still, a little of the hoar-frost which must be making the Duchess, down there, shiver. It is very pretty indeed, my dear Princess.'

'What! The Princess came up on purpose from Guermantes? But that's too wonderful! I never knew; I'm quite bewildered,' Mme de Saint-Euverte protested with quaint simplicity, being but little accustomed to Swann's way of speaking. And then, examining the Princess's head-dress, 'Why, you're quite right; it is copied from . . . what shall I say, not chestnuts, no, – oh, it's a delightful idea, but how can the Princess have known what was going to be on my programme? The musicians didn't tell me, even.'

Swann, who was accustomed, when he was with a woman whom he had kept up the habit of addressing in terms of gallantry, to pay her delicate compliments which most other people would not and need not understand, did not condescend to explain to Mme de Saint-Euverte that he had been speaking metaphorically. As for the Princess, she was in fits of laughter, both because Swann's wit was highly appreciated by her set, and because she could never hear a compliment addressed to herself without finding it exquisitely subtle and irresistibly amusing.

'Indeed! I'm delighted, Charles, if my little hips and haws meet with your approval. But tell me, why did you bow to that Cambremer person, are you also her neighbour in the country?'

Mme de Saint-Euverte, seeing that the Princess seemed quite happy talking to Swann, had drifted away.

'But you are, yourself, Princess!'

'I! Why, they must have "countries" everywhere, those creatures! Don't I wish I had!'

'No, not the Cambremers; her own people. She was a Legrandin, and used to come to Combray. I don't know whether you are aware that you are Comtesse de Combray, and that the Chapter owes you a due.'

'I don't know what the Chapter owes me, but I do know that I'm "touched" for a hundred francs, every year, by the Curé, which is a due that I could very well do without. But surely these Cambremers have rather a startling name. It ends just in time, but it ends badly!' she said with a laugh.

'It begins no better.' Swann took the point.

'Yes; that double abbreviation!'

'Someone very angry and very proper who didn't dare to finish the first word.'

'But since he couldn't stop himself beginning the second, he'ld have done better to finish the first and be done with it. We are indulging in the most refined form of humour, my dear Charles, in the very best of taste – but how tiresome it is that I never see you now,' she went on in a coaxing tone, 'I do so love talking to you. Just imagine, I could not make that idiot Froberville see that there was anything funny about the name Cambremer. Do agree that life is a dreadful business. It's only when I see you that I stop feeling bored.'

Which was probably not true. But Swann and the Princess had the same way of looking at the little things of life – the effect, if not the cause of which was a close analogy between their modes of expression and even of pronunciation. This similarity was not striking because no two things could have been more unlike than their voices. But if one took the trouble to imagine Swann's utterances divested of the sonority that enwrapped them, of the moustache from under which they emerged, one found that they were the same phrases, the same inflexions, that they had the 'tone' of the Guermantes set. On important matters, Swann and the Princess had not an idea in common. But since Swann had become so melancholy, and was always in that trembling condition which precedes a flood of tears, he had the same need to speak about his grief that a murderer has to tell someone about his crime. And when he heard the Princess say that life was a dreadful business, he felt as much comforted as if she had spoken to him of Odette.

'Yes, life is a dreadful business! We must meet more often, my dear friend. What is so nice about you is that you are not cheerful. We could spend a most pleasant evening together.'

'I'm sure we could; why not come down to Guermantes? My mother-in-law would be wild with joy. It's supposed to be very ugly down there, but I must say, I find the neighbourhood not at all unattractive; I have a horror of "picturesque spots".'

'I know it well, it's delightful!' replied Swann. 'It's almost too beautiful, too much alive for me just at present; it's a country to be happy in. It's perhaps because I have lived there, but things there speak to me so. As soon as a breath of wind gets up, and the cornfields begin to stir, I feel that someone is going to appear suddenly, that I am going to hear some news; and those little houses by the water's edge ... I should be quite wretched!'

'Oh! my dearest Charles, do take care; there's that appalling Rampillon woman; she's seen me; hide me somewhere, do tell me again, quickly, what it was that happened to her; I get so mixed up; she's just married off her daughter, or her lover, (I never can remember) – perhaps both – to each other! Oh, no, I remember now, she's been dropped by her Prince ... Pretend to be talking, so that the poor old Berenice shan't come and invite me to dinner. Anyhow, I'm going. Listen, my dearest Charles, now that I have seen you, once in a blue moon, won't you let me carry you off and take you to the Princesse de Parme's, who would be so pleased to see you (you know), and Basin too, for that matter; he's meeting me

there. If one didn't get news of you, sometimes, from Mémé
... Remember, I never see you at all now!'

Swann declined. Having told M. de Charlus that, on leaving
Mme de Saint-Euverte's, he would go straight home, he did
not care to run the risk, by going now to the Princesse de
Parme's, of missing a message which he had, all the time, been
hoping to see brought in to him by one of the footmen, during
the party, and which he was perhaps going to find left with his
own porter, at home.

'Poor Swann,' said Mme des Laumes that night to her
husband; 'he is always charming, but he does look so dreadfully unhappy. You will see for yourself, for he has promised to
dine with us one of these days. I do feel that it's really absurd
that a man of his intelligence should let himself be made to
suffer by a creature of that kind, who isn't even interesting,
for they tell me, she's an absolute idiot!' she concluded with
the wisdom invariably shown by people who, not being in
love themselves, feel that a clever man ought to be unhappy
only about such persons as are worth his while; which is
rather like being astonished that anyone should condescend to
die of cholera at the bidding of so insignificant a creature as
the comma bacillus.

Swann now wished to go home, but, just as he was making
his escape, General de Froberville caught him and asked for
an introduction to Mme de Cambremer, and he was obliged
to go back into the room to look for her.

'I say, Swann, I'ld rather be married to that little woman
than killed by savages, what do you say?'

The words 'killed by savages' pierced Swann's aching
heart; and at once he felt the need of continuing the conversation. 'Ah!' he began, 'some fine lives have been lost in that
way ... There was, you remember, that explorer whose
remains Dumont d'Urville brought back, La Pérouse ...'
(and he was at once happy again, as though he had named
Odette). 'He was a fine character, and interests me very much,
does La Pérouse,' he ended sadly.

'Oh, yes, of course, La Pérouse,' said the General. 'It's
quite a well-known name. There's a street called that.'

'Do you know anyone in the Rue La Pérouse?' asked Swann excitedly.

'Only Mme de Chanlivault, the sister of that good fellow Chaussepierre. She gave a most amusing theatre-party the other evening. That's a house that will be really smart some day, you'll see!'

'Oh, so she lives in the Rue La Pérouse. It's attractive; I like that street; it's so sombre.'

'Indeed it isn't. You can't have been in it for a long time; it's not at all sombre now; they're beginning to build all round there.'

When Swann did finally introduce M. de Froberville to the young Mme de Cambremer, since it was the first time that she had heard the General's name, she hastily outlined upon her lips the smile of joy and surprise with which she would have greeted him if she had never, in the whole of her life, heard anything else; for, as she did not yet know all the friends of her new family, whenever anyone was presented to her, she assumed that he must be one of them, and thinking that she would show her tact by appearing to have heard 'such a lot about him' since her marriage, she would hold out her hand with an air of hesitation which was meant as a proof at once of the inculcated reserve which she had to overcome and of the spontaneous friendliness which successfully overcame it. And so her parents-in-law, whom she still regarded as the most eminent pair in France, declared that she was an angel; all the more that they preferred to appear, in marrying her to their son, to have yielded to the attraction rather of her natural charm than of her considerable fortune.

'It's easy to see that you're a musician heart and soul, Madame,' said the General, alluding to the incident of the candle.

Meanwhile the concert had begun again, and Swann saw that he could not now go before the end of the new number. He suffered greatly from being shut up among all these people whose stupidity and absurdities wounded him all the more cruelly since, being ignorant of his love, incapable, had they known of it, of taking any interest, or of doing more than smile at it as at some childish joke, or deplore it as an act of insanity, they made it appear to him in the aspect of a subjective state which existed for himself alone, whose reality there was nothing external to confirm; he suffered overwhelmingly, to the point at which even the sound of the instruments made him want to cry, from having to prolong his exile in this place to which Odette would never come, in which no one, nothing was aware of her existence, from which she was entirely absent.

But suddenly it was as though she had entered, and this apparition tore him with such anguish that his hand rose impulsively to his heart. What had happened was that the violin had risen to a series of high notes, on which it rested as though expecting something, an expectancy which it prolonged without ceasing to hold on to the notes, in the exaltation with which it already saw the expected object approaching, and with a desperate effort to continue until its arrival, to welcome it before itself expired, to keep the way open for a moment longer, with all its remaining strength, that the stranger might enter in, as one holds a door open that would otherwise automatically close. And before Swann had had time to understand what was happening, to think: 'It is the little phrase from Vinteuil's sonata. I mustn't listen!', all his memories of the days when Odette had been in love with him, which he had succeeded, up till that evening, in keeping invisible in the depths of his being, deceived by this sudden reflection of a season of love, whose sun, they supposed, had dawned again, had awakened from their slumber, had taken wing and risen to sing maddeningly in his ears, without pity for his present desolation, the forgotten strains of happiness.

In place of the abstract expressions 'the time when I was happy', 'the time when I was loved', which he had often used until then, and without much suffering, for his intelligence had not embodied in them anything of the past save fictitious extracts which preserved none of the reality, he now recovered everything that had fixed unalterably the peculiar, volatile essence of that lost happiness; he could see it all; the snowy, curled petals of the chrysanthemum which she had tossed after him into his carriage, which he had kept pressed to his lips – the address 'Maison Dorée', embossed on the note-paper on which he had read 'My hand trembles so as I write to you', the frowning contraction of her eyebrows when she said pleadingly: 'You won't let it be very long before you send for me?'; he could smell the heated iron of the barber whom he used to have in to singe his hair while Loredan went to fetch the little working girl; could feel the torrents of rain which fell so often that spring, the ice-cold homeward drive in his victoria, by moonlight; all the network of mental habits, of seasonable impressions, of sensory reactions, which had extended over a series of weeks its uniform meshes, by which his body now found itself inextricably held. At that time he had been satisfying a sensual curiosity to know what were the pleasures of those people who lived for love alone. He had supposed that he could stop there, that he would not be obliged to learn their sorrows also; how small a thing the actual charm of Odette was now in comparison with that formidable terror which extended it like a cloudy halo all around her, that enormous anguish of not knowing at every hour of the day and night what she had been doing, of not possessing her wholly, at all times and in all places! Alas, he recalled the accents in which she had exclaimed: 'But I can see you at any time; I am always free!' – she, who was never free now; the interest, the curiosity that she had shown in his life, her passionate desire that he should do her the favour – of which it was he who, then, had felt suspicious, as of a possibly tedious waste of his time and disturbance of his arrangements – of granting her access to his study; how she had been obliged to beg that he would let her take him to the Verdurins'; and, when he did allow her to come to him once a month, how she had first, before he would let himself be swayed, had to repeat what a joy it would be to her, that custom of their seeing each other daily, for which she had longed at a time when to him it had seemed only a tiresome distraction, for which, since that time, she had conceived a distaste and had definitely broken herself of it, while it had

become for him so insatiable, so dolorous a need. Little had
he suspected how truly he spoke when, on their third meeting,
as she repeated: 'But why don't you let me come to you
oftener?' he had told her, laughing, and in a vein of gallantry,
that it was for fear of forming a hopeless passion. Now, alas,
it still happened at times that she wrote to him from a restaurant or hotel, on paper which bore a printed address, but
printed in letters of fire that seared his heart. 'Written from
the Hôtel Vouillemont. What on earth can she have gone
there for? With whom? What happened there?' He remembered the gas-jets that were being extinguished along the
Boulevard des Italiens when he had met her, when all hope
was gone, among the errant shades upon that night which had
seemed to him almost supernatural and which now (that night
of a period when he had not even to ask himself whether he
would be annoying her by looking for her and by finding her,
so certain was he that she knew no greater happiness than to
see him and to let him take her home) belonged indeed to a
mysterious world to which one never may return again once
its doors are closed. And Swann could distinguish, standing,
motionless, before that scene of happiness in which it lived
again, a wretched figure which filled him with such pity,
because he did not at first recognize who it was, that he must
lower his head, lest anyone should observe that his eyes were
filled with tears. It was himself.

When he had realized this, his pity ceased; he was jealous,
now, of that other self whom she had loved, he was jealous
of those men of whom he had so often said, without much
suffering: 'Perhaps she's in love with them,' now that he had
exchanged the vague idea of loving, in which there is no love,
for the petals of the chrysanthemum and the 'letter-heading'
of the Maison d'Or; for they were full of love. And then, his
anguish becoming too keen, he passed his hand over his
forehead, let the monocle drop from his eye, and wiped its
glass. And doubtless, if he had caught sight of himself at that
moment, he would have added to the collection of the
monocles which he had already identified, this one which he
removed, like an importunate, worrying thought, from his

head, while from its misty surface, with his handkerchief, he sought to obliterate his cares.

There are in the music of the violin – if one does not see the instrument itself, and so cannot relate what one hears to its form, which modifies the fullness of the sound – accents which are so closely akin to those of certain contralto voices, that one has the illusion that a singer has taken her place amid the orchestra. One raises one's eyes; one sees only the wooden case, magical as a Chinese box; but, at moments, one is still tricked by the deceiving appeal of the Siren; at times, too, one believes that one is listening to a captive spirit, struggling in the darkness of its masterful box, a box quivering with enchantment, like a devil immersed in a stoup of holy water; sometimes, again, it is in the air, at large, like a pure and supernatural creature that reveals to the ear, as it passes, its invisible message.

As though the musicians were not nearly so much playing the little phrase as performing the rites on which it insisted before it would consent to appear, as proceeding to utter the incantations necessary to procure, and to prolong for a few moments, the miracle of its apparition, Swann, who was no more able now to see it than if it had belonged to a world of ultra-violet light, who experienced something like the refreshing sense of a metamorphosis in the momentary blindness with which he had been struck as he approached it, Swann felt that it was present, like a protective goddess, a confidant of his love, who, so as to be able to come to him through the crowd, and to draw him aside to speak to him, had disguised herself in this sweeping cloak of sound. And as she passed him, light, soothing, as softly murmured as the perfume of a flower, telling him what she had to say, every word of which he closely scanned, sorry to see them fly away so fast, he made involuntarily with his lips the motion of kissing, as it went by him, the harmonious, fleeting form.

He felt that he was no longer in exile and alone since she, who addressed herself to him, spoke to him in a whisper of Odette. For he had no longer, as of old, the impression that Odette and he were not known to the little phrase. Had it not often been the witness of their joys? True that, as often, it had warned him of their frailty. And indeed, whereas, in that distant time, he had divined an element of suffering in its smile, in its limpid and disillusioned intonation, to-night he found there rather the charm of a resignation that was almost gay. Of those sorrows, of which the little phrase had spoken to him then, which he had seen it – without his being touched by them himself – carry past him, smiling, on its sinuous and rapid course, of those sorrows which were now become his own, without his having any hope of being, ever, delivered from them, it seemed to say to him, as once it had said of his happiness: 'What does all that matter; it is all nothing.' And Swann's thoughts were borne for the first time on a wave of pity and tenderness towards that Vinteuil, towards that unknown, exalted brother who also must have suffered so greatly; what could his life have been? From the depths of what well of sorrow could he have drawn that god-like strength, that unlimited power of creation?

When it was the little phrase that spoke to him of the vanity of his sufferings, Swann found a sweetness in that very wisdom which, but a little while back, had seemed to him intolerable when he thought that he could read it on the faces of indifferent strangers, who would regard his love as a digression that was without importance. 'Twas because the little phrase, unlike them, whatever opinion it might hold on the short duration of these states of the soul, saw in them something not, as everyone else saw, less serious than the events of everyday life, but, on the contrary, so far superior to everyday life as to be alone worthy of the trouble of expressing it. Those graces of an intimate sorrow, 'twas them that the phrase endeavoured to imitate, to create anew; and even their essence, for all that it consists in being incommunicable and in appearing trivial to everyone save him who has experience of them, the little phrase had captured, had rendered visible. So much so that it made their value be confessed, their divine sweetness be tasted by all those same onlookers – provided only that they were in any sense musical – who, the next moment, would ignore, would disown them in real life, in every individual love that came into being beneath their eyes. Doubtless the form in which it had codified those graces could not be analysed into any logical elements. But ever since, more than a year before, discovering to him many of the riches of his own soul, the love of music had been born and for a time at least had dwelt in him, Swann had regarded musical *motifs* as actual ideas, of another world, of another order, ideas veiled in shadows, unknown, impenetrable by the human mind, which none the less were perfectly distinct one from another, unequal among themselves in value and in significance. When, after that first evening at the Verdurins', he had had the little phrase played over to him again, and had sought to disentangle from his confused impressions how it was that, like a perfume or a caress, it swept over and enveloped him, he had observed that it was to the closeness of the intervals between the five notes which composed it and to the constant repetition of two of them that was due that impression of a frigid, a contracted sweetness; but in reality he knew that he was basing this conclusion not upon the phrase itself, but merely upon certain equivalents, substituted (for his mind's convenience) for the mysterious entity of which he had become aware, before ever he knew the Verdurins, at that earlier party, when for the first time he had heard the sonata played. He knew that his memory of the piano falsified still further the perspective in which he saw the music, that the field open to the musician is not a miserable stave of seven notes, but an immeasurable keyboard (still, almost all of it, unknown), on which, here and there only, separated by the gross darkness of its unexplored tracts, some few among the millions of keys, keys of tenderness, of passion, of courage, of serenity, which compose it, each one differing from all the rest as one universe differs from another, have been discovered by certain great artists who do us the service, when they awaken in us the emotion corresponding to the theme which they have found, of showing us what richness, what variety lies hidden, unknown to us, in that great black impenetrable night, discouraging exploration, of our soul, which we have been content to regard as valueless and waste and void. Vinteuil had been one of those musicians. In his little phrase, albeit it presented to the mind's eye a clouded surface, there was contained, one felt, a matter so consistent, so explicit, to which the phrase gave so new, so original a force, that those who had once heard it preserved the memory of it in the treasure-chamber of their minds. Swann would repair to it as to a conception of love and happiness, of which at once he knew as well in what respects it was peculiar as he would know of the *Princesse de Clèves*, or of *René*, should either of those titles occur to him. Even when he was not thinking of the little phrase, it existed, latent, in his mind, in the same way as certain other conceptions without material equivalent, such as our notions of light, of sound, of perspective, of bodily desire, the rich possessions wherewith our inner temple is diversified and adorned. Perhaps we shall lose them, perhaps they will be obliterated, if we return to nothing in the dust. But so long as we are alive, we can no more bring ourselves to a state in which we shall not have known them than we can with regard to any material object, than we can, for example, doubt the luminosity of a lamp that has just been lighted, in view of the changed aspect of everything in the room, from which has vanished even the memory of the darkness. In that way Vinteuil's phrase, like some theme, say, in *Tristan*, which represents to us also a certain acquisition of sentiment, had espoused our mortal state, had endued a vesture of humanity that was affecting enough. Its destiny was linked, for the future, with that of the human soul, of which it was one of the special, the most distinctive ornaments. Perhaps it is not-being that is the true state, and all our dream of life is without existence; but, if so, we feel that it must be that these phrases of music, these conceptions which exist in relation to our dream, are nothing either. We shall perish, but we have for our hostages these divine captives who shall follow and share our fate. And death in their company is something less bitter, less inglorious, perhaps even less certain.

So Swann was not mistaken in believing that the phrase of the sonata did, really, exist. Human as it was from this point of view, it belonged, none the less, to an order of supernatural creatures whom we have never seen, but whom, in spite of that, we recognize and acclaim with rapture when some explorer of the unseen contrives to coax one forth, to bring it down from that divine world to which he has access to shine for a brief moment in the firmament of ours. This was what Vinteuil had done for the little phrase. Swann felt that the composer had been content (with the musical instruments at his disposal) to draw aside its veil, to make it visible, following and respecting its outlines with a hand so loving, so prudent, so delicate, and so sure, that the sound altered at every moment, blunting itself to indicate a shadow, springing back into life when it must follow the curve of some more bold projection. And one proof that Swann was not mistaken when he believed in the real existence of this phrase, was that anyone with an ear at all delicate for music would at once have detected the imposture had Vinteuil, endowed with less power to see and to render its forms, sought to dissemble (by adding a line, here and there, of his own invention) the dimness of his vision or the feebleness of his hand.

The phrase had disappeared. Swann knew that it would come again at the end of the last movement, after a long passage which Mme Verdurin's pianist always 'skipped'. There were in this passage some admirable ideas which Swann had not distinguished on first hearing the sonata, and which he now perceived, as if they had, in the cloak-room of his memory, divested themselves of their uniform disguise of novelty. Swann listened to all the scattered themes which entered into the composition of the phrase, as its premisses enter into the inevitable conclusion of a syllogism; he was assisting at the mystery of its birth. 'Audacity,' he exclaimed to himself, 'as inspired, perhaps, as a Lavoisier's or an Ampère's, the audacity of a Vinteuil making experiment, discovering the secret laws that govern an unknown force, driving across a region unexplored towards the one possible goal the invisible team in which he has placed his trust and which he never may discern!' How charming the dialogue which Swann now heard between piano and violin, at the beginning of the last passage. The suppression of human speech, so far from letting fancy reign there uncontrolled (as one might have thought), had eliminated it altogether. Never was spoken language of such inflexible necessity, never had it known questions so pertinent, such obvious replies. At first the piano complained alone, like a bird deserted by its mate; the violin heard and answered it, as from a neighbouring tree. It was as at the first beginning of the world, as if there were not yet but these twain upon the earth, or rather in this world closed against all the rest, so fashioned by the logic of its creator that in it there should never be any but themselves; the world of this sonata. Was it a bird, was it the soul, not yet made perfect, of the little phrase, was it a fairy, invisibly somewhere lamenting, whose plaint the piano heard and tenderly repeated? Its cries were so sudden that the violinist must snatch up his bow and race to catch them as they came. Marvellous bird! The violinist seemed to wish to charm, to tame, to woo, to win it. Already it had passed into his soul, already the little phrase which it evoked shook like a medium's the body of the violinist, 'possessed' indeed. Swann knew that the phrase was going to speak to him once again. And his personality was now so divided that the strain of waiting for the imminent moment when he would find himself face to face, once more, with the phrase, convulsed him in one of those sobs which a fine line of poetry or a piece of alarming news will wring from us, not when we are alone, but when we repeat one or the other to a friend, in whom we see ourselves reflected, like a third person, whose probable emotion softens him. It reappeared, but this time to remain poised in the air, and to sport there for a moment only, as though immobile, and shortly to expire. And so Swann lost nothing of the precious time for which it lingered. It was still there, like an iridescent bubble that floats for a while unbroken. As a rainbow, when its brightness fades, seems to subside, then soar again and, before it is extinguished, is glorified with greater splendour than it has ever shown; so to the two colours which the phrase had hitherto allowed to appear it added others now, chords shot with every hue in the prism, and made them sing. Swann dared not move, and would have liked to compel all the other people in the room to remain still also, as if the slightest movement might embarrass the magic presence, supernatural, delicious, frail, that would so easily vanish. But no one, as it happened, dreamed of speaking. The ineffable utterance of one solitary man, absent, perhaps dead (Swann did not know whether Vinteuil were still alive), breathed out above the rites of those two hierophants, sufficed to arrest the attention of three hundred minds, and made of that stage on which a soul was thus called into being one of the noblest altars on which a supernatural ceremony could be performed. It followed that, when the phrase at last was finished, and only its fragmentary echoes floated among the subsequent themes which had already taken its place, if Swann at first was annoyed to see the Comtesse de Monteriender, famed for her imbecilities, lean over towards him to confide in him her impressions, before even the sonata had come to an end; he could not refrain from smiling, and perhaps also found an underlying sense, which she was incapable of perceiving, in the words that she used. Dazzled by the virtuosity of the performers, the Comtesse exclaimed to Swann: 'It's astonishing! I have never seen anything to beat it...' But a scrupulous regard for accuracy making her correct her first assertion, she added the reservation... 'anything to beat it... since the table-turning!'

From that evening, Swann understood that the feeling which Odette had once had for him would never revive, that his hopes of happiness would not be realized now. And the days on which, by a lucky chance, she had once more shown herself kind and loving to him, or if she had paid him any attention, he recorded those apparent and misleading signs of a slight movement on her part towards him with the same tender and sceptical solicitude, the desperate joy that people reveal who, when they are nursing a friend in the last days of an incurable malady, relate, as significant facts of infinite value: 'Yesterday he went through his accounts himself, and actually corrected a mistake that we had made in adding them up; he ate an egg to-day and seemed quite to enjoy it, if he digests it properly we shall try him with a cutlet to-morrow,' – although they themselves know that these things are meaningless on the eve of an inevitable death. No doubt Swann was assured that if he had now been living at a distance from Odette he would gradually have lost all interest in her, so that he would have been glad to learn that she was leaving Paris for ever; he would have had the courage to remain there; but he had not the courage to go.

He had often thought of going. Now that he was once again at work upon his essay on Vermeer, he wanted to return, for a few days at least, to The Hague, to Dresden, to Brunswick. He was certain that a 'Toilet of Diana' which had been acquired by the Mauritshuis at the Goldschmidt sale as a Nicholas Maes was in reality a Vermeer. And he would have liked to be able to examine the picture on the spot, so as to strengthen his conviction. But to leave Paris while Odette was there, and even when she was not there – for in strange places where our sensations have not been numbed by habit, we refresh, we revive an old pain – was for him so cruel a project that he felt himself to be capable of entertaining it incessantly in his mind only because he knew himself to be resolute in his determination never to put it into effect. But it would happen that, while he was asleep, the intention to travel would reawaken in him (without his remembering that this particular tour was impossible) and would be realized. One night he dreamed that he was going away for a year; leaning from the window of the train towards a young man on the platform who wept as he bade him farewell, he was seeking to persuade this young man to come away also. The train began to move; he awoke in alarm, and remembered that he was not going away, that he would see Odette that evening, and next day and almost every day. And then, being still deeply moved by his dream, he would thank heaven for those special circumstances which made him independent, thanks to which he could remain in Odette's vicinity, and could even succeed in making her allow him to see her sometimes; and, counting over the list of his advantages: his social position – his fortune, from which she stood too often in need of assistance not to shrink from the prospect of a definite rupture (having even, so people said, an ulterior plan of getting him to marry her) – his friendship with M. de Charlus, which, it must be confessed, had never won him any very great favour from Odette, but which gave him the pleasant feeling that she was always hearing complimentary things said about him by this common friend for whom she had so great an esteem – and even his own intelligence, the whole of which he employed in weaving, every day, a fresh plot which would make his presence, if not agreeable, at any rate necessary to Odette – he thought of what might have happened to him if all these advantages had been lacking, he thought that, if he had been, like so many other men, poor and humble, without resources, forced to undertake any task that might be offered to him, or tied down by parents or by a wife, he might have been obliged to part from Odette, that that dream, the terror of which was still so recent, might well have been true; and he said to himself: 'People don't know when they are happy. They're never so unhappy as they think they are.' But he reflected that this existence had lasted already for several years, that all that he could now hope for was that it should last for ever, that he would sacrifice his work, his pleasures, his friends, in fact the whole of his life to the daily expectation of a meeting which, when it occurred, would bring him no happiness; and he asked himself whether he was not mistaken, whether the circumstances that had favoured their relations and had prevented a final rupture had not done a disservice to his career, whether the outcome to be desired was not that as to which he rejoiced that it happened only in dreams – his own departure; and he said to himself that people did not know when they were unhappy, that they were never so happy as they supposed.

Sometimes he hoped that she would die, painlessly, in some accident, she who was out of doors, in the streets, crossing busy thoroughfares, from morning to night. And as she always returned safe and sound, he marvelled at the strength, at the suppleness of the human body, which was able continually to hold in check, to outwit all the perils that environed it (which to Swann seemed innumerable, since his own secret desire had strewn them in her path), and so allowed its occupant, the soul, to abandon itself, day after day, and almost with impunity, to its career of mendacity, to the pursuit of pleasure. And Swann felt a very cordial sympathy with that Mahomet II whose portrait by Bellini he admired, who, on finding that he had fallen madly in love with one of his wives, stabbed her, in order, as his Venetian biographer artlessly relates, to recover his spiritual freedom. Then he would be ashamed of thinking thus only of himself, and his own sufferings would seem to deserve no pity now that he himself was disposing so cheaply of Odette's very life.

Since he was unable to separate himself from her without a subsequent return, if at least he had seen her continuously and without separations his grief would ultimately have been assuaged, and his love would, perhaps, have died. And from the moment when she did not wish to leave Paris for ever he had hoped that she would never go. As he knew that her one prolonged absence, every year, was in August and September, he had abundant opportunity, several months in advance, to dissociate from it the grim picture of her absence throughout Eternity which was lodged in him by anticipation, and which, consisting of days closely akin to the days through which he was then passing, floated in a cold transparency in his mind, which it saddened and depressed, though without causing him any intolerable pain. But that conception of the future, that flowing stream, colourless and unconfined, a single word from Odette sufficed to penetrate through all Swann's defences, and like a block of ice immobilized it, congealed its fluidity, made it freeze altogether; and Swann felt himself suddenly filled with an enormous and unbreakable mass which pressed on the inner walls of his consciousness until he was fain to burst asunder; for Odette had said casually, watching him with a malicious smile: 'Forcheville is going for a fine trip at Whitsuntide. He's going to Egypt!' and Swann had at once understood that this meant: 'I am going to Egypt at Whitsuntide with Forcheville.' And, in fact, if, a few days later, Swann began: 'About that trip that you told me you were going to take with Forcheville,' she would answer carelessly: 'Yes, my dear boy, we're starting on the 19th; we'll send you a "view" of the Pyramids.' Then he was determined to know whether she was Forcheville's mistress, to ask her point-blank, to insist upon her telling him. He knew that there were some perjuries which, being so superstitious, she would not commit, and besides, the fear, which had hitherto restrained his curiosity, of making Odette angry if he questioned her, of making himself odious, had ceased to exist now that he had lost all hope of ever being loved by her.

One day he received an anonymous letter which told him that Odette had been the mistress of countless men (several of whom it named, among them Forcheville, M. de Bréauté, and the painter) and women, and that she frequented houses of ill-fame. He was tormented by the discovery that there was to be numbered among his friends a creature capable of sending him such a letter (for certain details betrayed in the writer a familiarity with his private life). He wondered who it could be. But he had never had any suspicion with regard to the unknown actions of other people, those which had no visible connexion with what they said. And when he wanted to know whether it was rather beneath the apparent character of M. de Charlus, or of M. des Laumes, or of M. d'Orsan that he must place the untravelled region in which this ignoble action might have had its birth; as none of these men had ever, in conversation with Swann, suggested that he approved of anonymous letters, and as everything that they had ever said to him implied that they strongly disapproved, he saw no further reason for associating this infamy with the character of any one of them more than with the rest. M. de Charlus was somewhat inclined to eccentricity, but he was fundamentally good and kind; M. des Laumes was a trifle dry, but wholesome and straight. As for M. d'Orsan, Swann had never met anyone who, even in the most depressing circumstances, would come to him with a more heartfelt utterance, would act more properly or with more discretion. So much so that he was unable to understand the rather indelicate part commonly attributed to M. d'Orsan in his relations with a certain wealthy woman, and that whenever he thought of him he was obliged to set that evil reputation on one side, as irreconcilable with so many unmistakable proofs of his genuine sincerity and refinement. For a moment Swann felt that his mind was becoming clouded, and he thought of something else so as to recover a little light; until he had the courage to return to those other reflections. But then, after not having been able to suspect anyone, he was forced to suspect everyone that he knew. After all, M. de Charlus might be most fond of him, might be most good-natured; but he was a neuropath; to-morrow, perhaps, he would burst into tears on hearing that Swann was ill; and to-day, from jealousy, or in anger, or carried away by some sudden idea, he might have wished to do him a deliberate injury. Really, that kind of man was the worst of all. The Prince des Laumes was, certainly, far less devoted to Swann than was M. de Charlus. But for that very reason he had not the same susceptibility with regard to him; and besides, his was a nature which, though, no doubt, it was cold, was as incapable of a base as of a magnanimous action. Swann regretted that he had formed no attachments in his life except to such people. Then he reflected that what prevents men from doing harm to their neighbours is fellow-feeling, that he could not, in the last resort, answer for any but men whose natures were analogous to his own, as was, so far as the heart went, that of M. de Charlus. The mere thought of causing Swann so much distress would have been revolting to him. But with a man who was insensible, of another order of humanity, as was the Prince des Laumes, how was one to foresee the actions to which he might be led by the promptings of a different nature? To have a good heart was everything and M. de Charlus had one. But M. d'Orsan was not lacking in that either, and his relations with Swann – cordial, but scarcely intimate, arising from the pleasure which, as they held the same views about everything, they found in talking together – were more quiescent than the enthusiastic affection of M. de Charlus, who was apt to be led into passionate activity, good or evil. If there was anyone by whom Swann felt that he had always been understood, and (with delicacy) loved, it was M. d'Orsan. Yes, but the life he led; it could hardly be called honourable. Swann regretted that he had never taken any notice of those rumours, that he himself had admitted, jestingly, that he had never felt so keen a sense of sympathy, or of respect, as when he was in thoroughly 'detrimental' society. 'It is not for nothing,' he now assured himself, 'that when people pass judgement upon their neighbour, their finding is based upon his actions. It is those alone that are significant, and not at all what we say or what we think. Charlus and des Laumes may have this or that fault, but they are men of honour. Orsan, perhaps, has not the same faults, but he is not a man of honour. He may have acted dishonourably once again.' Then he suspected Rémi, who, it was true, could only have inspired the letter, but he now felt himself, for a moment, to be on the right track. To begin with, Loredan had his own reasons for wishing harm to Odette. And then, how were we not to suppose that our servants, living in a situation inferior to our own, adding to our fortunes and to our frailties imaginary riches and vices for which they at once envied and despised us, should not find themselves led by fate to act in a manner abhorrent to people of our own class? He also suspected my grandfather. On every occasion when Swann had asked him to do him any service, had he not invariably declined? Besides, with his ideas of middle-class respectability, he might have thought that he was acting for Swann's good. He suspected, in turn, Bergotte, the painter, the Verdurins; paused for a moment to admire once again the wisdom of people in society, who refused to mix in the artistic circles in which such things were possible, were, perhaps, even openly avowed, as excellent jokes; but then he recalled the marks of honesty that were to be observed in those Bohemians, and contrasted them with the life of expedients, often bordering on fraudulence, to which the want of money, the craving for luxury, the corrupting influence of their pleasures often drove members of the aristocracy. In a word, this anonymous letter proved that he himself knew a human being capable of the most infamous conduct, but he could see no reason

why that infamy should lurk in the depths – which no strange
eye might explore of the warm heart rather than the cold,
the artist's rather than the business-man's, the noble's rather
than the flunkey's. What criterion ought one to adopt, in
order to judge one's fellows? After all, there was not a single
one of the people whom he knew who might not, in certain
circumstances, prove capable of a shameful action. Must he
then cease to see them all? His mind grew clouded; he passed
his hands two or three times across his brow, wiped his
glasses with his handkerchief, and remembering that, after
all, men who were as good as himself frequented the society
of M. de Charlus, the Prince des Laumes, and the rest, he
persuaded himself that this meant, if not that they were
incapable of shameful actions, at least that it was a necessity in
human life, to which everyone must submit, to frequent the
society of people who were, perhaps, not incapable of such
actions. And he continued to shake hands with all the friends
whom he had suspected, with the purely formal reservation
that each one of them had, possibly, been seeking to drive
him to despair. As for the actual contents of the letter, they
did not disturb him; for in not one of the charges which it
formulated against Odette could he see the least vestige of
fact. Like many other men, Swann had a naturally lazy mind,
and was slow in invention. He knew quite well as a general
truth, that human life is full of contrasts, but in the case of
any one human being he imagined all that part of his or her
life with which he was not familiar as being identical with the
part with which he was. He imagined what was kept secret
from him in the light of what was revealed. At such times as
he spent with Odette, if their conversation turned upon an
indelicate act committed, or an indelicate sentiment expressed
by some third person, she would ruthlessly condemn the culprit by virtue of the same moral principles which Swann had
always heard expressed by his own parents, and to which he
himself had remained loyal; and then, she would arrange her
flowers, would sip her tea, would show an interest in his work.
So Swann extended those habits to fill the rest of her life, he
reconstructed those actions when he wished to form a picture

of the moments in which he and she were apart. If anyone had portrayed her to him as she was, or rather as she had been for so long with himself, but had substituted some other man, he would have been distressed, for such a portrait would have struck him as lifelike. But to suppose that she went to bad houses, that she abandoned herself to orgies with other women, that she led the crapulous existence of the most abject, the most contemptible of mortals – would be an insane wandering of the mind, for the realization of which, thank heaven, the chrysanthemums that he could imagine, the daily cups of tea, the virtuous indignation left neither time nor place. Only, now and again, he gave Odette to understand that people maliciously kept him informed of everything that she did; and making opportune use of some detail – insignicant but true – which he had accidentally learned, as though it were the sole fragment which he would allow, in spite of himself, to pass his lips, out of the numberless other fragments of that complete reconstruction of her daily life which he carried secretly in his mind, he led her to suppose that he was perfectly informed upon matters, which, in reality, he neither knew nor suspected, for if he often adjured Odette never to swerve from or make alteration of the truth, that was only, whether he realized it or no, in order that Odette should tell him everything that she did. No doubt, as he used to assure Odette, he loved sincerity, but only as he might love a pander who could keep him in touch with the daily life of his mistress. Moreover, his love of sincerity, not being disinterested, had not improved his character. The truth which he cherished was that which Odette would tell him; but he himself, in order to extract that truth from her, was not afraid to have recourse to falsehood, that very falsehood which he never ceased to depict to Odette as leading every human creature down to utter degradation. In a word, he lied as much as did Odette, because, while more unhappy than she, he was no less egotistical. And she, when she heard him repeating thus to her the things that she had done, would stare at him with a look of distrust and, at all hazards, of indignation, so as not to appear to be humiliated, and to be blushing for her actions.

One day, after the longest period of calm through which he had yet been able to exist without being overtaken by an attack of jealousy, he had accepted an invitation to spend the evening at the theatre with the Princesse des Laumes. Having opened his newspaper to find out what was being played, the sight of the title – *Les Filles de Marbre*, by Théodore Barrière – struck him so cruel a blow that he recoiled instinctively from it and turned his head away. Illuminated, as though by a row of footlights, in the new surroundings in which it now appeared, that word 'marble', which he had lost the power to distinguish, so often had it passed, in print, beneath his eyes, had suddenly become visible once again, and had at once brought back to his mind the story which Odette had told him, long ago, of a visit which she had paid to the Salon at the Palais d'Industrie with Mme Verdurin, who had said to her, 'Take care, now! I know how to melt you, all right. You're not made of marble.' Odette had assured him that it was only a joke, and he had not attached any importance to it at the time. But he had had more confidence in her then than he had now. And the anonymous letter referred explicitly to relations of that sort. Without daring to lift his eyes to the newspaper, he opened it, turned the page so as not to see again the words, *Filles de Marbre*, and began to read mechanically the news from the provinces. There had been a storm in the Channel, and damage was reported from Dieppe, Cabourg, Beuzeval . . . Suddenly he recoiled again in horror.

The name of Beuzeval had suggested to him that of another place in the same district, Beuzeville, which carried also, bound to it by a hyphen, a second name, to wit Bréauté, which he had often seen on maps, but without ever previously remarking that it was the same name as that borne by his friend M. de Bréauté, whom the anonymous letter accused of having been Odette's lover. After all, when it came to M. de Bréauté, there was nothing improbable in the charge; but so far as Mme Verdurin was concerned, it was a sheer impossibility. From the fact that Odette did occasionally tell a lie, it was not fair to conclude that she never, by any chance, told the truth, and in these bantering conversations with Mme

Verdurin which she herself had repeated to Swann, he could recognize those meaningless and dangerous pleasantries which, in their inexperience of life and ignorance of vice, women often utter (thereby certifying their own innocence), who – as, for instance, Odette – would be the last people in the world to feel any undue affection for one another. Whereas, on the other hand, the indignation with which she had scattered the suspicions which she had unintentionally brought into being, for a moment, in his mind by her story, fitted in with everything that he knew of the tastes, the temperament of his mistress. But at that moment, by an inspiration of jealousy, analogous to the inspiration which reveals to a poet or a philosopher, who has nothing, so far, but an odd pair of rhymes or a detached observation, the idea or the natural law which will give power, mastery to his work, Swann recalled for the first time a remark which Odette had made to him, at least two years before: 'Oh, Mme Verdurin, she won't hear of anything just now but me. I'm a 'love', if you please, and she kisses me, and wants me to go with her everywhere, and call her by her Christian name.' So far from seeing in these expressions any connexion with the absurd insinuations, intended to create an atmosphere of vice, which Odette had since repeated to him, he had welcomed them as a proof of Mme Verdurin's warm-hearted and generous friendship. But now this old memory of her affection for Odette had coalesced suddenly with his more recent memory of her unseemly conversation. He could no longer separate them in his mind, and he saw them blended in reality, the affection imparting a certain seriousness and importance to the pleasantries which, in return, spoiled the affection of its innocence. He went to see Odette. He sat down, keeping at a distance from her. He did not dare to embrace her, not knowing whether in her, in himself, it would be affection or anger that a kiss would provoke. He sat there silent, watching their love expire. Suddenly he made up his mind.

'Odette, my darling,' he began, 'I know, I am being simply odious, but I must ask you a few questions. You remember what I once thought about you and Mme Verdurin?

Tell me, was it true? Have you, with her or anyone else, ever?'

She shook her head, pursing her lips together; a sign which people commonly employ to signify that they are not going, because it would bore them to go, when someone has asked, 'Are you coming to watch the procession go by?', or 'Will you be at the review?'. But this shake of the head, which is thus commonly used to decline participation in an event that has yet to come, imparts for that reason an element of uncertainty to the denial of participation in an event that is past. Furthermore, it suggests reasons of personal convenience, rather than any definite repudiation, any moral impossibility. When he saw Odette thus make him a sign that the insinuation was false, he realized that it was quite possibly true.

'I have told you, I never did; you know quite well,' she added, seeming angry and uncomfortable.

'Yes, I know all that; but are you quite sure? Don't say to me, "You know quite well"; say, "I have never done anything of that sort with any woman".'

She repeated his words like a lesson learned by rote, and as though she hoped, thereby, to be rid of him: 'I have never done anything of that sort with any woman.'

'Can you swear it to me on your Laghetto medal?'

Swann knew that Odette would never perjure herself on that.

'Oh, you do make me so miserable,' she cried, with a jerk of her body as though to shake herself free of the constraint of his question. 'Have you nearly done? What is the matter with you to-day? You seem to have made up your mind that I am to be forced to hate you, to curse you! Look, I was anxious to be friends with you again, for us to have a nice time together, like the old days; and this is all the thanks I get!'

However, he would not let her go, but sat there like a surgeon who waits for a spasm to subside that has interrupted his operation but need not make him abandon it.

'You are quite wrong in supposing that I bear you the

least ill-will in the world, Odette,' he began with a persuasive and deceitful gentleness. 'I never speak to you except of what I already know, and I always know a great deal more than I say. But you alone can mollify by your confession what makes me hate you so long as it has been reported to me only by other people. My anger with you is never due to your actions; I can and do forgive you everything because I love you; but to your untruthfulness, the ridiculous untruthfulness which makes you persist in denying things which I know to be true. How can you expect that I shall continue to love you, when I see you maintain, when I hear you swear to me a thing which I know to be false? Odette, do not prolong this moment which is torturing us both. If you are willing to end it at once, you shall be free of it for ever. Tell me, upon your medal, yes or no, whether you have ever done those things.'

'How on earth can I tell?' she was furious. 'Perhaps I have, ever so long ago, when I didn't know what I was doing, perhaps two or three times.'

Swann had prepared himself for all possibilities. Reality must, therefore, be something which bears no relation to possibilities, any more than the stab of a knife in one's body bears to the gradual movement of the clouds overhead, since those words 'two or three times' carved, as it were, a cross upon the living tissues of his heart. A strange thing, indeed, that those words, 'two or three times', nothing more than a few words, words uttered in the air, at a distance, could so lacerate a man's heart, as if they had actually pierced it, could sicken a man, like a poison that he had drunk. Instinctively Swann thought of the remark that he had heard at Mme de Saint-Euverte's: 'I have never seen anything to beat it since the table-turning.' The agony that he now suffered in no way resembled what he had supposed. Not only because, in the hours when he most entirely mistrusted her, he had rarely imagined such a culmination of evil, but because, even when he did imagine that offence, it remained vague, uncertain, was not clothed in the particular horror which had escaped with the words 'perhaps two or three times', was not armed with that specific cruelty, as different from anything that he had known as a new malady by which one is attacked for the first time. And yet this Odette, from whom all this evil sprang, was no less dear to him, was, on the contrary, more precious, as if, in proportion as his sufferings increased, there increased at the same time the price of the sedative, of the antidote which this woman alone possessed. He wished to pay her more attention, as one attends to a disease which one discovers, suddenly, to have grown more serious. He wished that the horrible thing which, she had told him, she had done 'two or three times' might be prevented from occurring again. To ensure that, he must watch over Odette. People often say that, by pointing out to a man the faults of his mistress, you succeed only in strengthening his attachment to her, because he does not believe you; yet how much more so if he does! But, Swann asked himself, how could he manage to protect her? He might perhaps be able to preserve her from the contamination of any one woman, but there were hundreds of other women; and he realized how insane had been his ambition when he had begun (on the evening when he had failed to find Odette at the Verdurins') to desire the possession – as if that were ever possible – of another person. Happily for Swann, beneath the mass of suffering which had invaded his soul like a conquering horde of barbarians, there lay a natural foundation, older, more placid, and silently laborious, like the cells of an injured organ which at once set to work to repair the damaged tissues, or the muscles of a paralysed limb which tend to recover their former movements. These older, these autochthonous indwellers in his soul absorbed all Swann's strength, for a while, in that obscure task of reparation which gives one an illusory sense of repose during convalescence, or after an operation. This time it was not so much – as it ordinarily was – in Swann's brain that the slackening of tension due to exhaustion took effect, it was rather in his heart. But all the things in life that have once existed tend to recur, and, like a dying animal that is once more stirred by the throes of a convulsion which was, apparently, ended, upon Swann's heart, spared for a moment only, the same agony returned of its own accord to trace the same cross again.

He remembered those moonlit evenings, when, leaning back in the victoria that was taking him to the Rue La Pérouse, he would cultivate with voluptuous enjoyment the emotions of a man in love, ignorant of the poisoned fruit that such emotions must inevitably bear. But all those thoughts lasted for no more than a second, the time that it took him to raise his hand to his heart, to draw breath again, and to contrive to smile, so as to dissemble his torment. Already he had begun to put further questions. For his jealousy, which had taken an amount of trouble, such as no enemy would have incurred, to strike him this mortal blow, to make him forcibly acquainted with the most cruel pain that he had ever known, his jealousy was not satisfied that he had yet suffered enough, and sought to expose his bosom to an even deeper wound. Like an evil deity, his jealousy was inspiring Swann, was thrusting him on towards destruction. It was not his fault, but Odette's alone, if at first his punishment was not more severe.

'My darling,' he began again, 'it's all over now; was it with anyone I know?'

'No, I swear it wasn't; besides, I think I exaggerated, I never really went as far as that.'

He smiled, and resumed with: 'Just as you like. It doesn't really matter, but it's unfortunate that you can't give me any name. If I were able to form an idea of the person that would prevent my ever thinking of her again. I say it for your own sake, because then I shouldn't bother you any more about it. It's so soothing to be able to form a clear picture of things in one's mind. What is really terrible is what one cannot imagine. But you've been so sweet to me; I don't want to tire you. I so thank you, with all my heart, for all the good that you have done me. I've quite finished now. Only one word more: how many times?'

'Oh, Charles! can't you see, you're killing me? It's all ever so long ago. I've never given it a thought. Anyone would say that you were positively trying to put those ideas into my head again. And then you'd be a lot better off!' she concluded, with unconscious stupidity but with intentional malice.

'I only wished to know whether it had been since I knew
you. It's only natural. Did it happen here, ever? You can't
give me any particular evening, so that I can remind myself
what I was doing at the time? You understand, surely, that
it's not possible that you don't remember with whom, Odette,
my love.'

'But I don't know; really, I don't. I think it was in the
Bois, one evening when you came to meet us on the Island.
You had been dining with the Princesse des Laumes,' she
added, happy to be able to furnish him with an exact detail,
which testified to her veracity. 'At the next table there was
a woman whom I hadn't seen for ever so long. She said
to me, "Come along round behind the rock, there, and look
at the moonlight on the water!" At first I just yawned, and
said, "No, I'm too tired, and I'm quite happy where I am,
thank you." She swore there'd never been anything like it
in the way of moonlight. "I've heard that tale before," I said
to her; you see, I knew quite well what she was after.' Odette
narrated this episode almost as if it were a joke, either because
it appeared to her to be quite natural, or because she thought
that she was thereby minimizing its importance, or else so as
not to appear ashamed. But, catching sight of Swann's face,
she changed her tone, and:

'You are a fiend!' she flung at him, 'you enjoy tormenting
me, making me tell you lies, just so that you'll leave me in
peace.'

This second blow struck at Swann was even more ex-
cruciating than the first. Never had he supposed it to have
been so recent an affair, hidden from his eyes that had been
too innocent to discern it, not in a past which he had never
known, but in evenings which he so well remembered, which
he had lived through with Odette, of which he had supposed
himself to have such an intimate, such an exhaustive knowledge, and which now assumed, retrospectively, an aspect of
cunning and deceit and cruelty. In the midst of them parted,
suddenly, a gaping chasm, that moment on the Island in the
Bois de Boulogne. Without being intelligent, Odette had the
charm of being natural. She had recounted, she had acted the

little scene with so much simplicity that Swann, as he gasped
for breath, could vividly see it: Odette yawning, the 'rock,
there', . . . He could hear her answer – alas, how lightheartedly – 'I've heard that tale before!' He felt that she would tell
him nothing more that evening, that no further revelation was
to be expected for the present. He was silent for a time, then
said to her:

'My poor darling, you must forgive me; I know, I am
hurting you dreadfully, but it's all over now; I shall never
think of it again.'

But she saw that his eyes remained fixed upon the things
that he did not know, and on that past era of their love,
monotonous and soothing in his memory because it was vague,
and now rent, as with a sword-wound, by the news of that
minute on the Island in the Bois, by moonlight, while he
was dining with the Princesse des Laumes. But he had so
far acquired the habit of finding life interesting – of marvelling
at the strange discoveries that there were to be made in it –
that even while he was suffering so acutely that he did not
believe it possible to endure such agony for any length of time,
he was saying to himself: 'Life is indeed astonishing, and
holds some fine surprises; it appears that vice is far more
common than one has been led to believe. Here is a woman
in whom I had absolute confidence, who looks so simple,
so honest, who, in any case, even allowing that her morals
are not strict, seemed quite normal and healthy in her taste
and inclinations. I receive a most improbable accusation, I
question her, and the little that she admits reveals far more
than I could ever have suspected.' But he could not confine
himself to these detached observations. He sought to form
an exact estimate of the importance of what she had just told
him, so as to know whether he might conclude that she had
done these things often, and was likely to do them again. He
repeated her words to himself: 'I knew quite well what she
was after.' 'Two or three times.' 'I've heard that tale before.'
But they did not reappear in his memory unarmed; each of
them held a knife with which it stabbed him afresh. For a
long time, like a sick man who cannot restrain himself from

attempting, every minute, to make the movement that, he knows, will hurt him, he kept on murmuring to himself: 'I'm quite happy where I am, thank you', 'I've heard that tale before'. But the pain was so intense that he was obliged to stop. He was amazed to find that actions which he had always, hitherto, judged so lightly, had dismissed, indeed, with a laugh, should have become as serious to him as a disease which might easily prove fatal. He knew any number of women whom he could ask to keep an eye on Odette, but how was he to expect them to adjust themselves to his new point of view, and not to remain at that which for so long had been his own, which had always guided him in his voluptuous existence; not to say to him with a smile: 'You jealous monster, wanting to rob other people of their pleasure!' By what trap-door, suddenly lowered, had he (who had never found, in the old days, in his love for Odette, any but the most refined of pleasures) been precipitated into this new circle of hell from which he could not see how he was ever to escape. Poor Odette! He wished her no harm. She was but half to blame. Had he not been told that it was her own mother who had sold her, when she was still little more than a child, at Nice, to a wealthy Englishman. But what an agonizing truth was now contained for him in those lines of Alfred de Vigny's *Journal d'un Poète* which he had previously read without emotion: 'When one feels oneself smitten by love for a woman, one ought to say to oneself, "What are her surroundings? What has been her life?" All one's future happiness lies in the answer.' Swann was astonished that such simple phrases, spelt over in his mind, as, 'I've heard that tale before', or 'I knew quite well what she was after', could cause him so much pain. But he realized that what he had mistaken for simple phrases were indeed parts of the panoply which held and could inflict on him the anguish that he had felt while Odette was telling her story. For it was the same anguish that he was now feeling afresh. It was no good, his knowing now, – indeed, it was no good, as time went on, his having partly forgotten and altogether forgiven the offence – whenever he repeated her words his old anguish refashioned him as he had been before Odette began to speak: ignorant, trustful; his merciless jealousy placed him once again, so that he might be effectively wounded by Odette's admission, in the position of a man who does not yet know the truth; and after several months this old story would still dumbfound him, like a sudden revelation. He marvelled at the terrible recreative power of his memory. It was only by the weakening of that generative force, whose fecundity diminishes as age creeps over one, that he could hope for a relaxation of his torments. But, as soon as the power that any one of Odette's sentences had to make Swann suffer seemed to be nearly exhausted, lo and behold another, one of those to which he had hitherto paid least attention, almost a new sentence, came to relieve the first, and to strike at him with undiminished force. The memory of the evening on which he had dined with the Princesse des Laumes was painful to him, but it was no more than the centre, the core of his pain. That radiated vaguely round about it, overflowing into all the preceding and following days. And on whatever point in it he might intend his memory to rest, it was the whole of that season, during which the Verdurins had so often gone to dine upon the Island in the Bois, that sprang back to hurt him. So violently, that by slow degrees the curiosity which his jealousy was ever exciting in him was neutralized by his fear of the fresh tortures which he would be inflicting upon himself were he to satisfy it. He recognized that all the period of Odette's life which had elapsed before she first met him, a period of which he had never sought to form any picture in his mind, was not the featureless abstraction which he could vaguely see, but had consisted of so many definite, dated years, each crowded with concrete incidents. But were he to learn more of them, he feared lest her past, now colourless, fluid, and supportable, might assume a tangible, an obscene form, with individual and diabolical features. And he continued to refrain from seeking a conception of it, not any longer now from laziness of mind, but from fear of suffering. He hoped that, some day, he might be able to hear the Island in the Bois, or the Princesse des Laumes mentioned without feeling any twinge of that old rending pain; meanwhile he thought it imprudent to provoke Odette into furnishing him with fresh sentences, with the names of more places and people and of different events, which, when his malady was still scarcely healed, would make it break out again in another form.

But, often enough, the things that he did not know, that he dreaded, now, to learn, it was Odette herself who, spontaneously and without thought of what she did, revealed them to him; for the gap which her vices made between her actual life and the comparatively innocent life which Swann had believed, and often still believed his mistress to lead, was far wider than she knew. A vicious person, always affecting the same air of virtue before people whom he is anxious to keep from having any suspicion of his vices, has no register, no gauge at hand from which he may ascertain how far those vices (their continuous growth being imperceptible by himself) have gradually segregated him from the normal ways of life. In the course of their cohabitation, in Odette's mind, with the memory of those of her actions which she concealed from Swann, her other, her innocuous actions were gradually coloured, infected by these, without her being able to detect anything strange in them, without their causing any explosion in the particular region of herself in which she made them live, but when she related them to Swann, he was overwhelmed by the revelation of the duplicity to which they pointed. One day, he was trying – without hurting Odette – to discover from her whether she had ever had any dealings with procuresses. He was, as a matter of fact, convinced that she had not; the anonymous letter had put the idea into his mind, but in a purely mechanical way; it had been received there with no credulity, but it had, for all that, remained there, and Swann, wishing to be rid of the burden – a dead weight, but none the less disturbing – of this suspicion, hoped that Odette would now extirpate it for ever.

'Oh dear, no! Not that they don't simply persecute me to go to them,' she added, her smile revealing a gratified vanity which she no longer saw that it was impossible should appear legitimate to Swann. 'There was one of them waited more than two hours for me yesterday, said she would give me any money I asked. It seems, there's an Ambassador who said to her, "I'll kill myself if you don't bring her to me" – meaning me! They told her I'd gone out, but she waited and waited, and in the end I had to go myself and speak to her, before she'ld go away. I do wish you could have seen the way I tackled her; my maid was in the next room, listening, and told me I shouted fit to bring the house down: – "But when you hear me say that I don't want to! The idea of such a thing, I don't like it at all! I should hope I'm still free to do as I please and when I please and where I please! If I needed the money, I could understand . . ." The porter has orders not to let her in again; he will tell her that I am out of town. Oh, I do wish I could have had you hidden somewhere in the room while I was talking to her. I know, you'ld have been pleased, my dear. There's some good in your little Odette, you see, after all, though people do say such dreadful things about her.'

Besides, her very admissions – when she made any – of faults which she supposed him to have discovered, rather served Swann as a starting-point for fresh doubts than they put an end to the old. For her admissions never exactly coincided with his doubts. In vain might Odette expurgate her confession of all its essential parts, there would remain in the accessories something which Swann had never yet imagined, which crushed him anew, and was to enable him to alter the terms of the problem of his jealousy. And these admissions he could never forget. His spirit carried them along, cast them aside, then cradled them again in its bosom, like corpses in a river. And they poisoned it.

She spoke to him once of a visit that Forcheville had paid her on the day of the Paris-Murcie Fête. 'What! you knew him as long ago as that? Oh, yes, of course you did,' he corrected himself, so as not to show that he had been ignorant of the fact. And suddenly he began to tremble at the thought that, on the day of the Paris-Murcie Fête, when he had received that letter which he had so carefully preserved, she had been having luncheon, perhaps, with Forcheville at the Maison d'Or. She swore that she had not. 'Still, the Maison d'Or reminds me of something or other which, I knew at the time, wasn't true,' he pursued, hoping to frighten her. 'Yes, that I hadn't been there at all that evening when I told you I had just come from there, and you had been looking for me at Prévost's,' she replied (judging by his manner that he knew) with a firmness that was based not so much upon cynicism as upon timidity, a fear of crossing Swann, which her own self-respect made her anxious to conceal, and a desire to show him that she could be perfectly frank if she chose. And so she struck him with all the sharpness and force of a headsman wielding his axe, and yet could not be charged with cruelty, since she was quite unconscious of hurting him; she even began to laugh, though this may perhaps, it is true, have been chiefly to keep him from thinking that she was ashamed, at all, or confused. 'It's quite true, I hadn't been to the Maison Dorée. I was coming away from Forcheville's. I had, really, been to Prévost's – that wasn't a story – and he met me there and asked me to come in and look at his prints. But someone else came to see him. I told you that I was coming from the Maison d'Or because I was afraid you might be angry with me. It was rather nice of me, really, don't you see? I admit, I did wrong, but at least I'm telling you all about it now, a'n't I? What have I to gain by not telling you, straight, that I lunched with him on the day of the Paris-Murcie Fête, if it were true? Especially as at that time we didn't know one another quite so well as we do now, did we, dear?'

He smiled back at her with the sudden, craven weakness of the utterly spiritless creature which these crushing words had made of him. And so, even in the months of which he had never dared to think again, because they had been too happy, in those months when she had loved him, she was already lying to him! Besides that moment (that first evening on which they had 'done a cattleya') when she had told him that she was coming from the Maison Dorée, how many others must there have been, each of them covering a falsehood of which Swann had had no suspicion. He recalled how she had said to him once: 'I need only tell Mme Verdurin that my dress wasn't ready, or that my cab came late. There is always some excuse.' From himself too, probably, many times when she had glibly uttered such words as explain a delay or justify an alteration of the hour fixed for a meeting, those moments must have hidden, without his having the least inkling of it at the time, an engagement that she had had with some other man, some man to whom she had said: 'I need only tell Swann that my dress wasn't ready, or that my cab came late. There is always some excuse.' And beneath all his most pleasant memories, beneath the simplest words that Odette had ever spoken to him in those old days, words which he had believed as though they were the words of a Gospel, beneath her daily actions which she had recounted to him, beneath the most ordinary places, her dressmaker's flat, the Avenue du Bois, the Hippo-drome, he could feel (dissembled there, by virtue of that temporal superfluity which, after the most detailed account of how a day has been spent, always leaves something over, that may serve as a hiding-place for certain unconfessed actions), he could feel the insinuation of a possible under-current of falsehood which debased for him all that had remained most precious, his happiest evenings, the Rue La Pérouse itself, which Odette must constantly have been leav-ing at other hours than those of which she told him; extending the power of the dark horror that had gripped him when he had heard her admission with regard to the Maison Dorée, and, like the obscene creatures in the 'Desolation of Nineveh', shattering, stone by stone, the whole edifice of his past . . . If, now, he turned aside whenever his memory repeated the cruel name of the Maison Dorée, it was because that name recalled to him, no longer, as, such a little time since, at Mme de Saint-Euverte's party, the good fortune which he long had lost, but a misfortune of which he was now first aware. Then it befell the Maison Dorée, as it had befallen the Island in the Bois, that gradually its name ceased to trouble him. For what we suppose to be our love, our jealousy are, neither of them, single, continuous, and individual passions. They are com-posed of an infinity of successive loves, of different jealousies, each of which is ephemeral, although by their uninterrupted multitude they give us the impression of continuity, the illusion of unity. The life of Swann's love, the fidelity of his jealousy, were formed out of death, of infidelity, of innumerable desires, innumerable doubts, all of which had Odette for their object. If he had remained for any length of time without seeing her, those that died would not have been replaced by others. But the presence of Odette continued to sow in Swann's heart alternate seeds of love and suspicion.

On certain evenings she would suddenly resume towards him a kindness of which she would warn him sternly that he must take immediate advantage, under penalty of not seeing it repeated for years to come; he must instantly accompany her home, to 'do a cattleya', and the desire which she pretended to have for him was so sudden, so inexplicable, so imperious, the kisses which she lavished on him were so demonstrative and so unfamiliar, that this brutal and unnatural fondness made Swann just as unhappy as any lie or unkind action. One evening when he had thus, in obedience to her command, gone home with her, and while she was interspersing her kisses with passionate words, in strange contrast to her habitual coldness, he thought suddenly that he heard a sound; he rose, searched everywhere and found nobody, but he had not the courage to return to his place by her side; whereupon she, in a towering rage, broke a vase with 'I never can do anything right with you, you impossible person!' And he was left uncertain whether she had not actually had some man concealed in the room, whose jealousy she had wished to wound, or else to inflame his senses.

Sometimes he repaired to 'gay' houses, hoping to learn something about Odette, although he dared not mention her name. 'I have a little thing here, you're sure to like,' the 'manageress' would greet him, and he would stay for an hour or so, talking dolefully to some poor girl who sat there astonished that he went no further. One of them, who was still quite young and attractive, said to him once, 'Of course, what I should like would be to find a real friend, then he might be quite certain, I should never go with any other men again.'

'Indeed, do you think it possible for a woman really to be touched by a man's being in love with her, and never to be unfaithful to him?' asked Swann anxiously. 'Why, surely! It all depends on their characters!' Swann could not help making the same remarks to these girls as would have delighted the Princesse des Laumes. To the one who was in search of a friend he said, with a smile: 'But how nice of you, you've put on blue eyes, to go with your sash.' 'And you too, you've got blue cuffs on.' 'What a charming conversation we are having, for a place of this sort! I'm not boring you, am I; or keeping you?' 'No, I've nothing to do, thank you. If you bored me I should say so. But I love hearing you talk.' 'I am highly flattered ... Aren't we behaving prettily?' he asked the 'manageress', who had just looked in. 'Why, yes, that's just what I was saying to myself, how sensibly they're behaving! But that's how it is! People come to my house now, just to talk. The Prince was telling me, only the other day, that he's far more comfortable here than with his wife. It seems that, nowadays, all the society ladies are like that; a perfect scandal, I call it. But I'll leave you in peace now, I know when I'm not wanted,' she ended discreetly, and left Swann with the girl who had the blue eyes. But presently he rose and said good-bye to her. She had ceased to interest him. She did not know Odette.

The painter having been ill, Dr Cottard recommended a sea-voyage; several of the 'faithful' spoke of accompanying him; the Verdurins could not face the prospect of being left alone in Paris, so first of all hired, and finally purchased a yacht; thus Odette was constantly going on a cruise. Whenever she had been away for any length of time, Swann would feel that he was beginning to detach himself from her, but, as though this moral distance were proportionate to the physical distance between them, whenever he heard that Odette had returned to Paris, he could not rest without seeing her. Once, when they had gone away, as everyone thought, for a month only, either they succumbed to a series of temptations, or else M. Verdurin had cunningly arranged everything beforehand, to please his wife, and disclosed his plans to the 'faithful' only as time went on; anyhow, from Algiers they flitted to Tunis; then to Italy, Greece, Constantinople, Asia Minor. They had been absent for nearly a year, and Swann felt perfectly at ease and almost happy. Albeit M. Verdurin had endeavoured to persuade the pianist and Dr Cottard that their respective aunt and patients had no need of them, and that in any event, it was most rash to allow Mme Cottard to return to Paris, where, Mme Verdurin assured him, a revolution had just broken out, he was obliged to grant them their liberty at Constantinople. And the painter came home with them. One day, shortly after the return of these four travellers, Swann, seeing an omnibus approach him, labelled 'Luxembourg', and having some business there, had jumped on to it and had found himself sitting opposite Mme Cottard, who was paying a round of visits to people whose 'day' it was, in full review order, with a plume in her hat, a silk dress, a muff, an umbrella (which would do for a parasol if the rain kept off), a card-case, and a pair of white gloves fresh from the cleaners. Wearing these badges of rank, she would, in fine weather, go on foot from one house to another in the same neighbourhood, but when she had to proceed to another district, would make use of a transfer-ticket on the omnibus. For the first minute or two, until the natural courtesy of the woman broke through the starched surface of the doctor's wife, not being certain, either, whether she ought to mention the Verdurins before Swann, she produced, quite naturally, in her slow and awkward, but not unattractive voice, which, every now and then, was completely drowned by the rattling of the omnibus, topics selected from those which she had picked up and would repeat in each of the score of houses up the stairs of which she clambered in the course of an afternoon.

'I needn't ask you, M. Swann, whether a man so much in the movement as yourself has been to the Mirlitons, to see the portrait by Machard that the whole of Paris is running after. Well, and what do you think of it? Whose camp are you in, those who bless or those who curse? It's the same in every house in Paris now, no one will speak of anything else but Machard's portrait; you aren't smart, you aren't really cultured, you aren't up-to-date unless you give an opinion on Machard's portrait.'

Swann having replied that he had not seen this portrait, Mme Cottard was afraid that she might have hurt his feelings by obliging him to confess the omission.

'Oh, that's quite all right! At least you have the courage to be quite frank about it. You don't consider yourself disgraced because you haven't seen Machard's portrait. I do think that so nice of you. Well now, I have seen it; opinion is divided, you know, there are some people who find it rather laboured, like whipped cream, they say; but I think it's just ideal. Of course, she's not a bit like the blue and yellow ladies that our friend Biche paints. That's quite clear. But I must tell you, perfectly frankly (you'll think me dreadfully old-fashioned, but I always say just what I think), that I don't understand his work. I can quite see the good points there are in his portrait of my husband; oh, dear me, yes; and it's certainly less odd than most of what he does, but even then he had to give the poor man a blue moustache! But Machard! Just listen to this now, the husband of my friend, I am on my way to see at this very moment (which has given me the very great pleasure of your company), has promised her that, if he is elected to the Academy (he is one of the Doctor's colleagues), he will get Machard to paint her portrait. So she's got something to look forward to! I have another friend who insists that she'd rather have Leloir. I'm only a wretched Philistine, and I've no doubt Leloir has perhaps more knowledge of painting even than Machard. But I do think that the most important thing about a portrait, especially when it's going to cost ten thousand francs, is that it should be like, and a pleasant likeness, if you know what I mean.'

Having exhausted this topic, to which she had been inspired by the loftiness of her plume, the monogram on her card-case, the little number inked inside each of her gloves by the cleaner, and the difficulty of speaking to Swann about the Verdurins, Mme Cottard, seeing that they had still a long way to go before they would reach the corner of the Rue Bona-parte, where the conductor was to set her down, listened to the promptings of her heart, which counselled other words than these.

'Your ears must have been burning,' she ventured, 'while we were on the yacht with Mme Verdurin. We were talking about you all the time.'

Swann was genuinely astonished, for he supposed that his name was never uttered in the Verdurins' presence.

'You see,' Mme Cottard went on, 'Mme de Crécy was there; need I say more? When Odette is anywhere it's never long before she begins talking about you. And you know quite well, it isn't nasty things she says. What! you don't believe me!' she went on, noticing that Swann looked sceptical. And, carried away by the sincerity of her conviction, without putting any evil meaning into the word, which she used purely in the sense in which one employs it to speak of the affection that unites a pair of friends; 'Why, she *adores* you! No, indeed; I'm sure it would never do to say anything against you when she was about; one would soon be taught one's place! Whatever we might be doing, if we were looking at a picture, for instance, she would say, "If only we had him here, he's the man who could tell us whether it's genuine or not. There's no one like him for that." And all day long she would be saying, "What can he be doing just now? I do hope he's doing a little work! It's too dreadful that a fellow with such gifts as he has should be so lazy." (Forgive me, won't you.) "I can see him this very moment; he's thinking of us, he's wondering where we are." Indeed, she used an expression which I thought very pretty at the time. M. Verdurin asked her, "How in the world can you see what he's doing, when he's a thousand miles away?" And Odette answered, "Nothing is impossible to the eye of a friend."

'No, I assure you, I'm not saying it just to flatter you; you have a true friend in her, such as one doesn't often find. I can tell you, besides, in case you don't know it, that you're the only one. Mme Verdurin told me as much herself on our last day with them (one talks more freely, don't you know, before a parting), "I don't say that Odette isn't fond of us, but anything that we may say to her counts for very little beside what

Swann might say." Oh, mercy, there's the conductor stopping for me; here have I been chatting away to you, and would have gone right past the Rue Bonaparte, and never noticed ... Will you be so very kind as to tell me whether my plume is straight?'

And Mme Cottard withdrew from her muff, to offer it to Swann, a white-gloved hand from which there floated, with a transfer-ticket, an atmosphere of fashionable life that pervaded the omnibus, blended with the harsher fragrance of newly cleaned kid. And Swann felt himself overflowing with gratitude to her, as well as to Mme Verdurin (and almost to Odette, for the feeling that he now entertained for her was no longer tinged with pain, was scarcely even to be described, now, as love), while from the platform of the omnibus he followed her with loving eyes, as she gallantly threaded her way along the Rue Bonaparte, her plume erect, her skirt held up in one hand, while in the other she clasped her umbrella and her card-case, so that its monogram could be seen, her muff dancing in the air before her as she went.

To compete with and so to stimulate the moribund feelings that Swann had for Odette, Mme Cottard, a wiser physician, in this case, than ever her husband would have been, had grafted among them others more normal, feelings of gratitude, of friendship, which in Swann's mind were to make Odette seem again more human (more like other women, since other women could inspire the same feelings in him), were to hasten her final transformation back into that Odette, loved with an undisturbed affection, who had taken him home one evening after a revel at the painter's, to drink orangeade with Forcheville, that Odette with whom Swann had calculated that he might live in happiness.

In former times, having often thought with terror that a day must come when he would cease to be in love with Odette, he had determined to keep a sharp look-out, and as soon as he felt that love was beginning to escape him, to cling tightly to it and to hold it back. But now, to the faintness of his love there corresponded a simultaneous faintness in his desire to remain her lover. For a man cannot change, that is to say become another person, while he continues to obey the dictates of the self which he has ceased to be. Occasionally the name, if it caught his eye in a newspaper, of one of the men whom he supposed to have been Odette's lovers, reawakened his jealousy. But it was very slight, and, inasmuch as it proved to him that he had not completely emerged from that period in which he had so keenly suffered – though in it he had also known a way of feeling so intensely happy – and that the accidents of his course might still enable him to catch an occasional glimpse, stealthily and at a distance, of its beauties, this jealousy gave him, if anything, an agreeable thrill, as to the sad Parisian, when he has left Venice behind him and must return to France, a last mosquito proves that Italy and summer are still not too remote. But, as a rule, with this particular period of his life from which he was emerging, when he made an effort, if not to remain in it, at least to obtain, while still he might, an uninterrupted view of it, he discovered that already it was too late; he would have looked back to distinguish, as it might be a landscape that was about to disappear, that love from which he had departed; but it is so difficult to enter into a state of complete duality and to present to oneself the lifelike spectacle of a feeling which one has ceased to possess, that very soon, the clouds gathering in his brain, he could see nothing, he would abandon the attempt, would take the glasses from his nose and wipe them; and he told himself that he would do better to rest for a little, that there would be time enough later on, and settled back into his corner with as little curiosity, with as much torpor as the drowsy traveller who pulls his cap down over his eyes so as to get some sleep in the railway-carriage that is drawing him, he feels, faster and faster, out of the country in which he has lived for so long, and which he vowed that he would not allow to slip away from him without looking out to bid it a last farewell. Indeed, like the same traveller, if he does not awake until he has crossed the frontier and is again in France, when Swann happened to alight, close at hand, upon something which proved that Forcheville had been Odette's lover, he discovered that it caused him no pain, that love was now utterly remote, and he regretted that he had had no warning of the moment in which he had emerged from it for ever. And just as, before kissing Odette for the first time, he had sought to imprint upon his memory the face that for so long had been familiar, before it was altered by the additional memory of their kiss, so he could have wished – in thought at least – to have been in a position to bid farewell, while she still existed, to that Odette who had inspired love in him and jealousy, to that Odette who had caused him so to suffer, and whom now he would never see again. He was mistaken. He was destined to see her once again, a few weeks later. It was while he was asleep, in the twilight of a dream. He was walking with Mme Verdurin, Dr Cottard, a young man in a fez whom he failed to identify, the painter, Odette, Napoleon III, and my grandfather, along a path which followed the line of the coast, and overhung the sea, now at a great height, now by a few feet only, so that they were continually going up and down; those of the party who had reached the downward slope were no longer visible to those who were still climbing; what little daylight yet remained was failing, and it seemed as though a black night was immediately to fall on them. Now and then the waves dashed against the cliff, and Swann could feel on his cheek a shower of freezing spray. Odette told him to wipe this off, but he could not, and felt confused and helpless in her company, as well as because he was in his nightshirt. He hoped that, in the darkness, this might pass unnoticed; Mme Verdurin, however, fixed her astonished gaze upon him for an endless moment, in which he saw her face change its shape, her nose grow longer, while beneath it there sprouted a heavy moustache. He turned away to examine Odette; her cheeks were pale, with little fiery spots, her features drawn and ringed with shadows; but she looked back at him with eyes welling with affection, ready to detach themselves like tears and to fall upon his face, and he felt that he loved her so much that he would have liked to carry her off with him at once. Suddenly Odette turned her wrist, glanced at a tiny watch, and said: 'I must go.' She took leave of everyone, in the same formal manner, without taking

Swann aside, without telling him where they were to meet that evening, or next day. He dared not ask, he would have liked to follow her, he was obliged, without turning back in her direction, to answer with a smile some question by Mme Verdurin; but his heart was frantically beating, he felt that he now hated Odette, he would gladly have crushed those eyes which, a moment ago, he had loved so dearly, have torn the blood into those lifeless cheeks. He continued to climb with Mme Verdurin, that is to say that each step took him farther from Odette, who was going downhill, and in the other direction. A second passed and it was many hours since she had left him. The painter remarked to Swann that Napoleon III had eclipsed himself immediately after Odette. 'They had obviously arranged it between them,' he added; 'they must have agreed to meet at the foot of the cliff, but they wouldn't say good-bye together; it might have looked odd. She is his mistress.' The strange young man burst into tears. Swann endeavoured to console him. 'After all, she is quite right,' he said to the young man, drying his eyes for him and taking off the fez to make him feel more at ease. 'I've advised her to do that, myself, a dozen times. Why be so distressed? He was obviously the man to understand her.' So Swann reasoned with himself, for the young man whom he had failed, at first, to identify, was himself also; like certain novelists, he had distributed his own personality between two characters, him who was the 'first person' in the dream, and another whom he saw before him, capped with a fez.

As for Napoleon III, it was to Forcheville that some vague association of ideas, then a certain modification of the Baron's usual physiognomy, and lastly the broad ribbon of the Legion of Honour across his breast, had made Swann give that name; but actually, and in everything that the person who appeared in his dream represented and recalled to him, it was indeed Forcheville. For, from an incomplete and changing set of images, Swann in his sleep drew false deductions, enjoying, at the same time, such creative power that he was able to reproduce himself by a simple act of division, like certain lower organisms; with the warmth that he felt in his own palm he modelled the hollow of a strange hand which he thought that he was clasping, and out of feelings and impressions of which he was not yet conscious, he brought about sudden vicissitudes which, by a chain of logical sequences, would produce, at definite points in his dream, the person required to receive his love or to startle him awake. In an instant night grew black about him; an alarum rang, the inhabitants ran past him, escaping from their blazing houses; he could hear the thunder of the surging waves, and also of his own heart, which, with equal violence, was anxiously beating in his breast. Suddenly the speed of these palpitations redoubled, he felt a pain, a nausea that were inexplicable; a peasant, dreadfully burned, flung at him as he passed: 'Come and ask Charlus where Odette spent the night with her friend. He used to go about with her, and she tells him everything. It was they that started the fire.' It was his valet, come to awaken him, and saying:

'Sir, it is eight o'clock, and the barber is here. I have told him to call again in an hour.'

But these words, as they dived down through the waves of sleep in which Swann was submerged, did not reach his consciousness without undergoing that refraction which turns a ray of light, at the bottom of a bowl of water, into another sun; just as, a moment earlier, the sound of the door-bell, swelling in the depths of his abyss of sleep into the clangour of an alarum, had engendered the episode of the fire. Meanwhile the scenery of his dream-stage scattered in dust, he opened his eyes, heard for the last time the boom of a wave in the sea, grown very distant. He touched his cheek. It was dry. And yet he could feel the sting of the cold spray, and the taste of salt on his lips. He rose, and dressed himself. He had made the barber come early because he had written, the day before, to my grandfather, to say that he was going, that afternoon, to Combray, having learned that Mme de Cambremer – Mlle Legrandin that had been – was spending a few days there. The association in his memory of her young and charming face with a place in the country which he had not visited for so long, offered him a combined attraction which had made him decide at last to leave Paris for a while. As the different changes and chances that bring us into the company of certain other people in this life do not coincide with the periods in which we are in love with those people, but, overlapping them, may occur before love has begun, and may be repeated after love is ended, the earliest appearances, in our life, of a creature who is destined to afford us pleasure later on, assume retrospectively in our eyes a certain value as an indication, a warning, a presage. It was in this fashion that Swann had often carried back his mind to the image of Odette, encountered in the theatre, on that first evening when he had no thought of ever seeing her again – and that he now recalled the party at Mme de Saint-Euverte's, at which he had introduced General de Froberville to Mme de Cambremer. So manifold are our interests in life that it is not uncommon that, on a single occasion, the foundations of a happiness which does not yet exist are laid down simultaneously with aggravations of a grief from which we are still suffering. And, no doubt, that might have occurred to Swann elsewhere than at Mme de Saint-Euverte's. Who, indeed, can say whether, in the event of his having gone, that evening, somewhere else, other happinesses, other griefs would not have come to him, which, later, would have appeared to have been inevitable? But what did seem to him to have been inevitable was what had indeed taken place, and he was not far short of seeing something providential in the fact that he had at last decided to go to Mme de Saint-Euverte's that evening, because his mind, anxious to admire the richness of invention that life shows, and incapable of facing a difficult problem for any length of time, such as to discover what, actually, had been most to be wished for, came to the conclusion that the sufferings through which he had passed that evening, and the pleasures, at that time unsuspected, which were already being brought to birth – the exact balance between which was too difficult to establish – were linked by a sort of concatenation of necessity.

But while, an hour after his awakening, he was giving instructions to the barber, so that his stiffly brushed hair should not become disarranged on the journey, he thought once again of his dream; he saw once again, as he had felt them close beside him, Odette's pallid complexion, her too thin cheeks, her drawn features, her tired eyes, all the things which – in the course of those successive bursts of affection which had made of his enduring love for Odette a long oblivion of the first impression that he had formed of her – he had ceased to observe after the first few days of their intimacy, days to which, doubtless, while he slept, his memory had returned to seek the exact sensation of those things. And with that old, intermittent fatuity, which reappeared in him now that he was no longer unhappy, and lowered, at the same time, the average level of his morality, he cried out in his heart: 'To think that I have wasted years of my life, that I have longed for death, that the greatest love that I have ever known has been for a woman who did not please me, who was not in my style!'

Place-names: The Name

A mong the rooms which used most commonly to take
shape in my mind during my long nights of sleeplessness,
there was none that differed more utterly from the rooms at
Combray, thickly powdered with the motes of an atmosphere
granular, pollenous, edible, and instinct with piety, than my
room in the Grand Hôtel de la Plage, at Balbec, the walls of
which, washed with ripolin, contained, like the polished sides
of a basin in which the water glows with a blue, lurking fire,
a finer air, pure, azure-tinted, saline. The Bavarian upholsterer
who had been entrusted with the furnishing of this hotel had
varied his scheme of decoration in different rooms, and in that
which I found myself occupying had set against the walls,
on three sides of it, a series of low book-cases with glass
fronts, in which, according to where they stood, by a law of
nature which he had, perhaps, forgotten to take into account,
was reflected this or that section of the ever-changing view
of the sea, so that the walls were lined with a frieze of sea-
scapes, interrupted only by the polished mahogany of the
actual shelves. And so effective was this that the whole room
had the appearance of one of those model bedrooms which
you see nowadays in Housing Exhibitions, decorated with
works of art which are calculated by their designer to refresh the
eyes of whoever may ultimately have to sleep in the rooms, the
subjects being kept in some degree of harmony with the locality
and surroundings of the houses for which the rooms are planned.

And yet nothing could have differed more utterly, either,
from the real Balbec than that other Balbec of which I had
often dreamed, on stormy days, when the wind was so strong
that Françoise, as she took me to the Champs-Élysées, would
warn me not to walk too near the side of the street, or I might
have my head knocked off by a falling slate, and would recount
to me, with many lamentations, the terrible disasters and
shipwrecks that were reported in the newspaper. I longed for
nothing more than to behold a storm at sea, less as a mighty

447

spectacle than as a momentary revelation of the true life of nature; or rather there were for me no mighty spectacles save those which I knew to be not artificially composed for my entertainment, but necessary and unalterable – the beauty of landscapes or of great works of art. I was not curious, I did not thirst to know anything save what I believed to be more genuine than myself, what had for me the supreme merit of showing me a fragment of the mind of a great genius, or of the force or the grace of nature as she appeared when left entirely to herself, without human interference. Just as the lovely sound of her voice, reproduced, all by itself, upon the phonograph, could never console a man for the loss of his mother, so a mechanical imitation of a storm would have left me as cold as did the illuminated fountains at the Exhibition. I required also, if the storm was to be absolutely genuine, that the shore from which I watched it should be a natural shore, not an embankment recently constructed by a municipality. Besides, nature, by all the feelings that she aroused in me, seemed to me the most opposite thing in the world to the mechanical inventions of mankind. The less she bore their imprint, the more room she offered for the expansion of my heart. And, as it happened, I had preserved the name of Balbec, which Legrandin had cited to us, as that of a sea-side place in the very midst of 'that funereal coast, famed for the number of its wrecks, swathed, for six months in the year, in a shroud of fog and flying foam from the waves.

'You feel, there, below your feet still,' he had told me, 'far more even than at Finistère (and even though hotels are now being superimposed upon it, without power, however, to modify that oldest bone in the earth's skeleton) you feel there that you are actually at the land's end of France, of Europe, of the Old World. And it is the ultimate encampment of the fishermen, precisely like the fishermen who have lived since the world's beginning, facing the everlasting kingdom of the sea-fogs and shadows of the night.' One day when, at Combray, I had spoken of this coast, this Balbec, before M. Swann, hoping to learn from him whether it was the best point to select for seeing the most violent storms, he had replied: 'I should think I did know Balbec! The church at Balbec, built in the twelfth and thirteenth centuries, and still half romanesque, is perhaps the most curious example to be found of our Norman gothic, and so exceptional that one is tempted to describe it as Persian in its inspiration.' And that region, which, until then, had seemed to me to be nothing else than a part of immemorial nature, that had remained contemporaneous with the great phenomena of geology – and as remote from human history as the Ocean itself, or the Great Bear, with its wild race of fishermen for whom, no more than for their whales, had there been any Middle Ages – it had been a great joy to me to see it suddenly take its place in the order of the centuries, with a stored consciousness of the romanesque epoch, and to know that the gothic trefoil had come to diversify those wild rocks also, at the appointed hour, like those frail but hardy plants which, in the Polar regions, when the spring returns, scatter their stars about the eternal snows. And if gothic art brought to those places and people a classification which, otherwise, they lacked, they too conferred one upon it in return. I tried to form a picture in my mind of how those fishermen had lived, the timid and unsuspected essay towards social intercourse which they had attempted there, clustered upon a promontory of the shores of Hell, at the foot of the cliffs of death; and gothic art seemed to me a more living thing now that, detaching it from the towns in which, until then, I had always imagined it, I could see how, in a particular instance, upon a reef of savage rocks, it had taken root and grown until it flowered in a tapering spire. I was taken to see reproductions of the most famous of the statues at Balbec – shaggy, blunt-faced Apostles, the Virgin from the porch – and I could scarcely breathe for joy at the thought that I might myself, one day, see them take a solid form against their eternal background of salt fog. Thereafter, on dear, tempestuous February nights, the wind – breathing into my heart, which it shook no less violently than the chimney of my bedroom, the project of a visit to Balbec – blended in me the desire for gothic architecture with that for a storm upon the sea.

I should have liked to take, the very next day, the good, the

generous train at one twenty-two, of which never without a
palpitating heart could I read, in the railway company's bills
or in advertisements of circular tours, the hour of departure:
it seemed to me to cut, at a precise point in every afternoon, a
most fascinating groove, a mysterious mark, from which the
diverted hours still led one on, of course, towards evening,
towards to-morrow morning, but to an evening and morning
which one would behold, not in Paris but in one of those
towns through which the train passed and among which it
allowed one to choose; for it stopped at Bayeux, at Coutances,
at Vitré, at Questambert, at Pontorson, at Balbec, at Lannion,
at Lamballe, at Benodet, at Pont-Aven, at Quimperlé, and
progressed magnificently surcharged with names which it
offered me, so that, among them all, I did not know which to
choose, so impossible was it to sacrifice any. But even without
waiting for the train next day, I could, by rising and dressing
myself with all speed, leave Paris that very evening, should
my parents permit, and arrive at Balbec as dawn spread west-
ward over the raging sea, from whose driven foam I would
seek shelter in that church in the Persian manner. But at the
approach of the Easter holidays, when my parents had
promised to let me spend them, for once, in the North of
Italy, lo! in place of those dreams of tempests, by which I had
been entirely possessed, not wishing to see anything but
waves dashing in from all sides, mounting always higher
upon the wildest of coasts, beside churches as rugged and
precipitous as cliffs, in whose towers the sea-birds would be
wailing; suddenly, effacing them, taking away all their charm,
excluding them because they were its opposite and could only
have weakened its effect, was substituted in me the converse
dream of the most variegated of springs, not the spring of
Combray, still pricking with all the needle-points of the
winter's frost, but that which already covered with lilies and
anemones the meadows of Fiesole, and gave Florence a dazzling golden background, like those in Fra Angelico's pictures. From that moment, only sunlight, perfumes, colours,
seemed to me to have any value; for this alternation of images
had effected a change of front in my desire, and – as abrupt as

those that occur sometimes in music – a complete change of tone in my sensibility. Thus it came about that a mere atmospheric variation would be sufficient to provoke in me that modulation, without there being any need for me to await the return of a season. For often we find a day, in one, that has strayed from another season, and makes us live in that other, summons at once into our presence and makes us long for its peculiar pleasures, and interrupts the dreams that we were in process of weaving, by inserting, out of its turn, too early or too late, this leaf, torn from another chapter, in the interpolated calendar of Happiness. But soon it happened that, like those natural phenomena from which our comfort or our health can derive but an accidental and all too modest benefit, until the day when science takes control of them, and, producing them at will, places in our hands the power to order their appearance, withdrawn from the tutelage and independent of the consent of chance, similarly the production of these dreams of the Atlantic and of Italy ceased to depend entirely upon the changes of the seasons and of the weather. I need only, to make them reappear, pronounce the names: Balbec, Venice, Florence, within whose syllables had gradually accumulated all the longing inspired in me by the places for which they stood. Even in spring, to come in a book upon the name of Balbec sufficed to awaken in me the desire for storms at sea and for the Norman gothic; even on a stormy day the name of Florence or of Venice would awaken the desire for sunshine, for lilies, for the Palace of the Doges and for Santa Maria del Fiore.

But if their names thus permanently absorbed the image that I had formed of these towns, it was only by transforming that image, by subordinating its reappearance in me to their own special laws; and in consequence of this they made it more beautiful, but at the same time more different from anything that the towns of Normandy or Tuscany could in reality be, and, by increasing the arbitrary delights of my imagination, aggravated the disenchantment that was in store for me when I set out upon my travels. They magnified the idea that I formed of certain points on the earth's surface, making them more special, and in consequence more real. I did not then represent to myself towns, landscapes, historic buildings, as pictures more or less attractive, cut out here and there of a substance that was common to them all, but looked on each of them as on an unknown thing, different from all the rest, a thing for which my soul was athirst, by the knowledge of which it would benefit. How much more individual still was the character that they assumed from being designated by names, names that were only for themselves, proper names such as people have. Words present to us little pictures of things, lucid and normal, like the pictures that are hung on the walls of schoolrooms to give children an illustration of what is meant by a carpenter's bench, a bird, an anthill; things chosen as typical of everything else of the same sort. But names present to us – of persons and of towns which they accustom us to regard as individual, as unique, like persons – a confused picture, which draws from the names, from the brightness or darkness of their sound, the colour in which it is uniformly painted, like one of those posters, entirely blue or entirely red, in which, on account of the limitations imposed by the process used in their reproduction, or by a whim on the designer's part, are blue or red not only the sky and the sea, but the ships and the church and the people in the streets. The name of Parma, one of the towns that I most longed to visit, after reading the *Chartreuse*, seeming to me compact and glossy, violet-tinted, soft; if anyone were to speak of such or such a house in Parma, in which I should be lodged, he would give me the pleasure of thinking that I was to inhabit a dwelling that was compact and glossy, violet-tinted, soft, and that bore no relation to the houses in any other town in Italy, since I could imagine it only by the aid of that heavy syllable of the name of Parma, in which no breath of air stirred, and of all that I had made it assume of Stendhalian sweetness and the reflected hue of violets. And when I thought of Florence, it was of a town miraculously embalmed, and flower-like, since it was called the City of the Lilies, and its Cathedral, Our Lady of the Flower. As for Balbec, it was one of those names in which, as on an old piece of Norman pottery that still keeps the colour of the earth from which it was fashioned, one sees depicted still the representation of some long-abolished custom, of some feudal right, of the former condition of some place, of an obsolete way of pronouncing the language, which had shaped and welded its incongruous syllables and which I never doubted that I should find spoken there at once, even by the inn-keeper who would pour me out coffee and milk on my arrival, taking me down to watch the turbulent sea, unchained, before the church; to whom I lent the aspect, disputatious, solemn, and medieval, of some character in one of the old romances.

Had my health definitely improved, had my parents allowed me, if not actually to go down to stay at Balbec, at least to take, just once, so as to become acquainted with the architecture and landscapes of Normandy or of Brittany, that one twenty-two train into which I had so often clambered in imagination, I should have preferred to stop, and to alight from it, at the most beautiful of its towns; but in vain might I compare and contrast them; how was one to choose, any more than between individual people, who are not interchangeable, between Bayeux, so lofty in its noble coronet of rusty lace, whose highest point caught the light of the old gold of its second syllable; Vitré, whose acute accent barred its ancient glass with wooden lozenges; gentle Lamballe, whose whiteness ranged from egg-shell yellow to a pearly grey; Coutances, a Norman Cathedral, which its final consonants, rich and yellowing, crowned with a tower of butter; Lannion with the rumble and buzz, in the silence of its village street, of the fly on the wheel of the coach; Questambert, Pontorson, ridiculously silly and simple, white feathers and yellow beaks strewn along the road to those well-watered and poetic spots; Benodet, a name scarcely moored that seemed to be striving to draw the river down into the tangle of its seaweeds; Pont-Aven, the snowy, rosy flight of the wing of a lightly poised coif, tremulously reflected in the greenish waters of a canal; Quimperlé, more firmly attached, this, and since the Middle Ages, among the rivulets with which it babbled, threading their pearls upon a grey background, like the pattern made, through the cobwebs upon a window, by rays of sunlight changed into blunt points of tarnished silver?

These images were false for another reason also; namely, that they were necessarily much simplified; doubtless the object to which my imagination aspired, which my senses took in but incompletely and without any immediate pleasure, I had committed to the safe custody of names; doubtless because I had accumulated there a store of dreams, those names now magnetized my desires; but names themselves are not very comprehensive; the most that I could do was to include in each of them two or three of the principal curiosities of the town, which would lie there side by side, without interval or partition; in the name of Balbec, as in the magnifying glasses set in those penholders which one buys at sea-side places, I could distinguish waves surging round a church built in the Persian manner. Perhaps, indeed, the enforced simplicity of these images was one of the reasons for the hold that they had over me. When my father had decided, one year, that we should go for the Easter holidays to Florence and Venice, not finding room to introduce into the name of Florence the elements that ordinarily constitute a town, I was obliged to let a supernatural city emerge from the impregnation by certain vernal scents of what I supposed to be, in its essentials, the genius of Giotto. All the more – and because one cannot make a name extend much further in time than in space – like some of Giotto's paintings themselves which show us at two separate moments the same person engaged in different actions, here lying on his bed, there just about to mount his horse, the name of Florence was divided into two compartments. In one, beneath an architectural dais, I gazed upon a fresco over which was partly drawn a curtain of morning sunlight, dusty, aslant, and gradually spreading; in the other (for, since I thought of names not as an inaccessible ideal but as a real and enveloping substance into which I was about to plunge, the life not yet lived, the life intact and pure which I enclosed in them, gave to the most material pleasures, to the simplest scenes, the same attraction that they have in the works of the Primitives), I moved swiftly – so as to arrive, as soon as might be, at the table that was spread for me, with fruit and a flask of Chianti – across a Ponte Vecchio heaped with jonquils, narcissi, and anemones. That (for all that I was still in Paris) was what I saw, and not what was actually round about me. Even from the simplest, the most realistic point of view, the countries for which we long occupy, at any given moment, a far larger place in our true life than the country in which we may happen to be. Doubtless, if, at that time, I had paid more attention to what was in my mind when I pronounced the words 'going to Florence, to Parma, to Pisa, to Venice', I should have realized that what I saw was in no sense a town, but something as different from anything that I knew, something as delicious as might be for a human race whose whole existence had passed in a series of late winter afternoons, that inconceivable marvel, a morning in spring. These images, unreal, fixed, always alike, filling all my nights and days, differentiated this period in my life from those which had gone before it (and might easily have been confused with it by an observer who saw things only from without, that is to say, who saw nothing), as in an opera a fresh melody introduces a novel atmosphere which one could never have suspected if one had done no more than read the libretto, still less if one had remained outside the theatre, counting only the minutes as they passed. And besides, even from the point of view of mere quantity, in our life the days are not all equal. To reach the end of a day, natures that are slightly nervous, as mine was, make use, like motor-cars, of different 'speeds'. There are mountainous uncomfortable days, up which one takes an infinite time to pass, and days downward sloping, through which one can go at full tilt, singing as one goes. During this month – in which I went laboriously over, as over a tune, though never to my satisfaction, these visions of Florence, Venice, Pisa, from which the desire that they excited in me drew and kept something as profoundly personal as if it had been love, love for another person – I never ceased to believe that they corresponded to a reality independent of myself, and they made me conscious of as glorious a hope as could have been cherished by a Christian in the primitive age of faith, on the eve of his entry into Paradise. Moreover, without my paying any heed to

the contradiction that there was in my wishing to look at and
to touch with my organs of sense what had been elaborated by
the spell of my dreams and not perceived by my senses at all –
though all the more tempting to them, in consequence, more
different from anything that they knew – it was that which recalled to me the reality of these visions, which inflamed my
desire all the more by seeming to hint a promise that my desire
should be satisfied. And for all that the motive force of my
exaltation was a longing for aesthetic enjoyments, the guide-
books ministered even more to it than books on aesthetics,
and, more again than the guide-books, the railway time-tables.
What moved me was the thought that this Florence which I
could see, so near and yet inaccessible, in my imagination, if the tract which separated it from me, in myself, was
not one that I might cross, could yet be reached by a circuit,
by a digression, were I to take the plain, terrestrial path. When
I repeated to myself, giving thus a special value to what I was
going to see, that Venice was the 'School of Giorgione, the
home of Titian, the most complete museum of the domestic
architecture of the MiddleAges,' I felt happy indeed. As I was
even more when, on one of my walks, as I stepped out briskly
on account of the weather, which, after several days of a precocious spring, had relapsed into winter (like the weather that
we had invariable found awaiting us at Combray, in Holy
Week), – seeing upon the boulevards that the chestnut-trees,
though plunged in a glacial atmosphere that soaked through
them like a stream of water, were none the less beginning,
punctual guests, arrayed already for the party, and admitting
no discouragement, to shape and chisel and carve in its frozen
lumps the irrepressible verdure whose steady growth the
abortive power of the cold might hinder but could not succeed
in restraining – I reflected that already the Ponte Vecchio was
heaped high with an abundance of hyacinths and anemones,
and that the spring sunshine was already tinging the waves of
the Grand Canal with so dusky an azure, with emeralds so
splendid that when they washed and were broken against the
foot of one of Titian's paintings they could vie with it in the
richness of their colouring. I could no longer contain my joy

when my father, in the intervals of tapping the barometer and complaining of the cold, began to look out which were the best trains, and when I understood that by making one's way, after luncheon, into the coal-grimed laboratory, the wizard's cell that undertook to contrive a complete transmutation of its surroundings, one could awaken, next morning, in the city of marble and gold, in which 'the building of the wall was of jasper and the foundation of the wall an emerald.' So that it and the City of the Lilies were not just artificial scenes which I could set up at my pleasure in front of my imagination, but did actually exist at a certain distance from Paris which must inevitably be traversed if I wished to see them, at their appointed place on the earth's surface, and at no other; in a word they were entirely real. They became even more real to me when my father, by saying: 'Well, you can stay in Venice from the 20th to the 29th, and reach Florence on Easter morning,' made them both emerge, no longer only from the abstraction of Space, but from that imaginary Time in which we place not one, merely, but several of our travels at once, which do not greatly tax us since they are but possibilities, – that Time which reconstructs itself so effectively that one can spend it again in one town after one has already spent it in another – and consecrated to them some of those actual, calendar days which are certificates of the genuineness of what one does on them, for those unique days are consumed by being used, they do not return, one cannot live them again here when one has lived them elsewhere; I felt that it was towards the week that would begin with the Monday on which the laundress was to bring back the white waistcoat that I had stained with ink, that they were hastening to busy themselves with the duty of emerging from that ideal Time in which they did not, as yet, exist, those two Queen Cities of which I was soon to be able, by the most absorbing kind of geometry, to inscribe the domes and towers on a page of my own life. But I was still on the way, only, to the supreme pinnacle of happiness; I reached it finally (for not until then did the revelation burst upon me that on the clattering streets, reddened by the light reflected from Giorgione's frescoes, it was not, as I had, despite so many promptings, continued to imagine, the men 'majestic and terrible as the sea, bearing armour that gleamed with bronze beneath the folds of their blood-red cloaks', who would be walking in Venice next week, on the Easter vigil; but that I myself might be the minute personage whom, in an enlarged photograph of St Mark's that had been lent to me, the operator had portrayed, in a bowler hat, in front of the portico), when I heard my father say: 'It must be pretty cold, still, on the Grand Canal; whatever you do, don't forget to pack your winter greatcoat and your thick suit.' At these words I was raised to a sort of ecstasy; a thing that I had until then deemed impossible, I felt myself to be penetrating indeed between those 'rocks of amethyst, like a reef in the Indian Ocean'; by a supreme muscular effort, a long way in excess of my real strength, stripping myself, as of a shell that served no purpose, of the air in my own room which surrounded me, I replaced it by an equal quantity of Venetian air, that marine atmosphere, indescribable and peculiar as the atmosphere of the dreams which my imagination had secreted in the name of Venice; I could feel at work within me a miraculous disincarnation; it was at once accompanied by that vague desire to vomit which one feels when one has a very sore throat; and they had to put me to bed with a fever so persistent that the Doctor not only assured my parents that a visit, that spring, to Florence and Venice was absolutely out of the question, but warned them that, even when I should have completely recovered, I must, for at least a year, give up all idea of travelling, and be kept from anything that was liable to excite me.

And, alas, he forbade also, most categorically, my being allowed to go to the theatre, to hear Berma; the sublime artist, whose genius Bergotte had proclaimed, might, by introducing me to something else that was, perhaps, as important and as beautiful, have consoled me for not having been to Florence and Venice, for not going to Balbec. My parents had to be content with sending me, every day, to the Champs-Élysées, in the custody of a person who would see that I did not tire myself; this person was none other than Françoise, who had entered our service after the death of my aunt Léonie. Going to the Champs-Élysées I found unendurable. If only Bergotte had described the place in one of his books, I should, no doubt, have longed to see and to know it, like so many things else of which a simulacrum had first found its way into my imagination. That kept things warm, made them live, gave them personality, and I sought then to find their counterpart in reality, but in this public garden there was nothing that attached itself to my dreams.

*

One day, as I was weary of our usual place, beside the wooden horses, Françoise had taken me for an excursion – across the frontier guarded at regular intervals by the little bastions of the barley-sugar women – into those neighbouring but foreign regions, where the faces of the passers-by were strange, where the goat-carriage went past; then she had gone to lay down her things on a chair that stood with its back to a shrubbery of laurels; while I waited for her I was pacing the broad lawn, of meagre close-cropped grass already faded by the sun, dominated, at its far end, by a statue rising from a fountain, in front of which a little girl with reddish hair was playing with a shuttlecock; when, from the path, another little girl, who was putting on her cloak and covering up her battledore, called out sharply: 'Good-bye, Gilberte, I'm going home now; don't forget, we're coming to you this evening, after dinner.' The name Gilberte passed close by me, evoking all the more forcibly her whom it labelled in that it did not merely refer to her, as one speaks of a man in his absence, but was directly addressed to her; it passed thus close by me, in action, so to speak, with a force that increased with the curve of its trajectory and as it drew near to its target; – carrying in its wake, I could feel, the knowledge, the impression of her to whom it was addressed that belonged not to me but to the friend who called to her, everything that, while she uttered the words, she more or less vividly reviewed, possessed in her memory, of their daily intimacy, of the visits that they paid to each other, of that unknown existence which was all the more inaccessible, all the more painful to me from being, conversely, so familiar so tractable to this happy girl who let her message brush past me without my being able to penetrate its surface, who flung it on the air with a light-hearted cry: letting float in the atmosphere the delicious attar which that message had distilled, by touching them with precision, from certain invisible points in Mlle Swann's life, from the evening to come, as it would be, after dinner, at her home, – forming, on its celestial passage through the midst of the children and their nursemaids, a little cloud, exquisitely coloured, like the cloud that, curling over one of Poussin's gardens, reflects minutely, like a cloud in the ópera, teeming with chariots and horses, some apparition of the life of the gods; casting, finally, on that ragged grass, at the spot on which she stood (at once a scrap of withered lawn and a moment in the afternoon of the fair player, who continued to beat up and catch her shuttle-cock until a governess, with a blue feather in her hat, had called her away) a marvellous little band of light, of the colour of heliotrope, spread over the lawn like a carpet on which I could not tire of treading to and fro with lingering feet, nostalgic and profane, while Françoise shouted: 'Come on, button up your coat, look, and let's get away!' and I remarked for the first time how common her speech was, and that she had, alas, no blue feather in her hat.

Only, would *she* come again to the Champs-Élysées? Next day she was not there; but I saw her on the following days; I spent all my time revolving round the spot where she was at play with her friends, to such effect that once, when, they found, they were not enough to make up a prisoner's base, she sent one of them to ask me if I cared to complete their side, and from that day I played with her whenever she came. But this did not happen every day; there were days when she had been prevented from coming by her lessons, by her catechism, by a luncheon-party, by the whole of that life, separated from my own, which twice only, condensed into the name of Gilberte, I had felt pass so painfully close to me, in the hawthorn lane near Combray and on the grass of the Champs-Élysées. On such days she would have told us beforehand that we should not see her; if it were because of her lessons, she would say: 'It is too tiresome, I shan't be able to come to-morrow; you will all be enjoying yourselves here without me,' with an air of regret which to some extent consoled me; if, on the other hand, she had been invited to a party, and I, not knowing this, asked her whether she was coming to play with us, she would reply: 'Indeed I hope not! Indeed I hope Mamma will let me go to my friend's.' But on these days I did at least know that I should not see her, whereas on others, without any warning, her mother would take her for a drive, or some such thing, and next day she would say: 'Oh, yes! I went out with Mamma,' as though it had been the most natural thing in the world, and not the greatest possible misfortune for someone else. There were also the days of bad weather on which her governess, afraid, on her own account, of the rain, would not bring Gilberte to the Champs-Élysées.

And so, if the heavens were doubtful, from early morning I would not cease to interrogate them, observing all the omens. If I saw the lady opposite, just inside her window, putting on her hat, I would say to myself: 'That lady is going out; it must, therefore, be weather in which one can go out. Why should not Gilberte do the same as that lady?' But the day grew dark. My mother said that it might clear again, that one burst of sunshine would be enough, but that more probably it would rain; and if it rained, of what use would it be to go to the Champs-Élysées? And so, from breakfast-time, my anxious eyes never left the uncertain, clouded sky. It remained dark. Outside the window, the balcony was grey. Suddenly, on its sullen stone, I did not indeed see a less negative colour, but I felt as it were an effort towards a less negative colour, the pulsation of a hesitating ray that struggled to discharge its light. A moment later the balcony was as pale and luminous as a standing water at dawn, and a thousand shadows from the iron-work of its balustrade had come to rest on it. A breath of wind dispersed them; the stone grew dark again, but, like tamed creatures, they returned; they began, imperceptibly, to grow lighter, and by one of those continuous crescendos, such as, in music, at the

end of an overture, carry a single note to the extreme fortissimo, making it pass rapidly through all the intermediate
stages, I saw it attain to that fixed, unalterable gold of fine
days, on which the sharply cut shadows of the wrought iron
of the balustrade were outlined in black like a capricious
vegetation, with a fineness in the delineation of their smallest
details which seemed to indicate a deliberate application, an
artist's satisfaction, and with so much relief, so velvety a
bloom in the restfulness of their sombre and happy mass that
in truth those large and leafy shadows which lay reflected
on that lake of sunshine seemed aware that they were pledges
of happiness and peace of mind.

Brief, fading ivy, climbing, fugitive flora, the most colourless, the most depressing, to many minds, of all that creep on
walls or decorate windows; to me the dearest of them all,
from the day when it appeared upon our balcony, like the
very shadow of the presence of Gilberte, who was perhaps
already in the Champs-Élysées, and as soon as I arrived there
would greet me with: 'Let's begin at once. You are on my
side.' Frail, swept away by a breath, but at the same time
in harmony, not with the season, with the hour; promise of
that immediate pleasure which the day will deny or fulfil, and
thereby of the one paramount immediate pleasure, the pleasure
of loving and of being loved; more soft, more warm upon the
stone than even moss is; alive, a ray of sunshine sufficing for
its birth, and for the birth of joy, even in the heart of winter.

And on those days when all other vegetation had disappeared, when the fine jerkins of green leather which covered
the trunks of the old trees were hidden beneath the snow;
after the snow had ceased to fall, but when the sky was still
too much overcast for me to hope that Gilberte would
venture out, then suddenly – inspiring my mother to say:
'Look, it's quite fine now; I think you might perhaps try
going to the Champs-Élysées after all,' – on the mantle of
snow that swathed the balcony, the sun had appeared and was
stitching seams of gold, with embroidered patches of dark
shadow. That day we found no one there, or else a solitary
girl, on the point of departure, who assured me that Gilberte

was not coming. The chairs, deserted by the imposing but uninspiring company of governesses, stood empty. Only, near the grass, was sitting a lady of uncertain age who came in all weathers, dressed always in an identical style, splendid and sombre, to make whose acquaintance I would have, at that period, sacrificed, had it lain in my power, all the greatest opportunities in my life to come. For Gilberte went up every day to speak to her: she used to ask Gilberte for news of her 'dearest mother' and it struck me that, if I had known her, I should have been for Gilberte someone wholly different, someone who knew people in her parents' world. While her grandchildren played together at a little distance, she would sit and read the *Débats*, which she called 'My old *Débats*!' as, with an aristocratic familiarity, she would say, speaking of the police-sergeant or the woman who let the chairs, 'My old friend the police-sergeant,' or 'The chair-keeper and I, who are old friends.'

Françoise found it too cold to stand about, so we walked to the Pont de la Concorde to see the Seine frozen over, on to which everyone, even children, walked fearlessly, as though upon an enormous whale, stranded, defenceless, and about to be cut up. We returned to the Champs-Élysées: I was growing sick with misery between the motionless wooden horses and the white lawn, caught in a net of black paths from which the snow had been cleared, while the statue that surmounted it held in its hand a long pendant icicle which seemed to explain its gesture. The old lady herself, having folded up her *Débats*, asked a passing nursemaid the time, thanking her with, 'How very good of you!' then begged the road-sweeper to tell her grandchildren to come, as she felt cold, adding, 'A thousand thanks. I am sorry to give you so much trouble!' Suddenly the sky was rent in two: between the punch-and-judy and the horses, against the opening horizon, I had just seen, like a miraculous sign, Mademoiselle's blue feather. And now Gilberte was running at full speed towards me, sparkling and rosy beneath a cap trimmed with fur, enlivened by the cold, by being late, by her anxiety for a game; shortly before she reached me, she slipped on a piece of ice and, either to regain her

balance, or because it appeared to her graceful, or else pretending that she was on skates, it was with outstretched arms that
she smilingly advanced, as though to embrace me. 'Bravo!
bravo! that's splendid; "topping", I should say, like you –
"sporting," I suppose I ought to say, only I'm a hundred-and-
one, a woman of the old school,' exclaimed the lady, uttering,
on behalf of the voiceless Champs-Élysées, their thanks to
Gilberte for having come, without letting herself be frightened
away by the weather. 'You are like me, faithful at all costs
to our old Champs-Élysées; we are two brave souls! You
wouldn't believe me, I dare say, if I told you that I love them,
even like this. This snow (I know, you'll laugh at me), it
makes me think of ermine!' And the old lady began to laugh
herself.

The first of these days – to which the snow, a symbol of the
powers that were able to deprive me of the sight of Gilberte,
imparted the sadness of a day of separation, almost the aspect
of a day of departure, because it changed the outward form
and almost forbade the use of the customary scene of our only
encounters, now altered, covered, as it were, in dust-sheets –
that day, none the less, marked a stage in the progress of my
love, for it was, in a sense, the first sorrow that she was to
share with me. There were only our two selves of our little
company, and to be thus alone with her was not merely like
a beginning of intimacy, but also on her part – as though she
had come there solely to please me, and in such weather – it
seemed to me as touching as if, on one of those days on which
she had been invited to a party, she had given it up in order
to come to me in the Champs-Élysées; I acquired more
confidence in the vitality, in the future of a friendship which
could remain so much alive amid the torpor, the solitude, the
decay of our surroundings; and while she dropped pellets
of snow down my neck, I smiled lovingly at what seemed to
me at once a predilection that she showed for me in thus
tolerating me as her travelling companion in this new, this
wintry land, and a sort of loyalty to me which she preserved
through evil times. Presently, one after another, like shyly
hopping sparrows, her friends arrived, black against the snow.

We got ready to play and, since this day which had begun so sadly was destined to end in joy, as I went up, before the game started, to the friend with the sharp voice whom I had heard, that first day, calling Gilberte by name, she said to me: 'No, no, I'm sure you'ld much rather be in Gilberte's camp; besides, look, she's signalling to you.' She was in fact summoning me to cross the snowy lawn to her camp, to 'take the field', which the sun, by casting over it a rosy gleam, the metallic lustre of old and worn brocades, had turned into a Field of the Cloth of Gold.

This day, which I had begun with so many misgivings, was, as it happened, one of the few on which I was not unduly wretched.

For, although I no longer thought, now, of anything save not to let a single day pass without seeing Gilberte (so much so that once, when my grandmother had not come home by dinner-time, I could not resist the instinctive reflection that, if she had been run over in the street and killed, I should not for some time be allowed to play in the Champs-Élysées; when one is in love one has no love left for anyone), yet those moments which I spent in her company, for which I had waited with so much impatience all night and morning, for which I had quivered with excitement, to which I would have sacrificed everything else in the world, were by no means happy moments; well did I know it, for they were the only moments in my life on which I concentrated a scrupulous, undistracted attention, and yet I could not discover in them one atom of pleasure. All the time that I was away from Gilberte, I wanted to see her, because, having incessantly sought to form a mental picture of her, I was unable, in the end, to do so, and did not know exactly to what my love corresponded. Besides, she had never yet told me that she loved me. Far from it, she had often boasted that she knew other little boys whom she preferred to myself, that I was a good companion, with whom she was always willing to play, although I was too absent-minded, not attentive enough to the game. Moreover, she had often shown signs of apparent coldness towards me, which might have shaken my faith that

I was for her a creature different from the rest, had that faith been founded upon a love that Gilberte had felt for me, and not, as was the case, upon the love that I felt for her, which strengthened its resistance to the assaults of doubt by making it depend entirely upon the manner in which I was obliged, by an internal compulsion, to think of Gilberte. But my feelings with regard to her I had never yet ventured to express to her in words. Of course, on every page of my exercise-books, I wrote out, in endless repetition, her name and address, but at the sight of those vague lines which I might trace, without her having to think, on that account, of me, I felt discouraged, because they spoke to me, not of Gilberte, who would never so much as see them, but of my own desire, which they seemed to show me in its true colours, as something purely personal, unreal, tedious, and ineffective. The most important thing was that we should see each other, Gilberte and I, and should have an opportunity of making a mutual confession of our love which, until then, would not officially (so to speak) have begun. Doubtless the various reasons which made me so impatient to see her would have appeared less urgent to a grown man. As life goes on, we acquire such adroitness in the culture of our pleasures, that we content ourselves with that which we derive from thinking of a woman, as I was thinking of Gilberte, without troubling ourselves to ascertain whether the image corresponds to the reality, – and with the pleasure of loving her, without needing to be sure, also, that she loves us; or again that we renounce the pleasure of confessing our passion for her, so as to preserve and enhance the passion that she has for us, like those Japanese gardeners who, to obtain one perfect blossom, will sacrifice the rest. But at the period when I was in love with Gilberte, I still believed that Love did really exist, apart from ourselves; that, allowing us, at the most, to surmount the obstacles in our way, it offered us its blessings in an order in which we were not free to make the least alteration; it seemed to me that if I had, on my own initiative, substituted for the sweetness of a confession a pretence of indifference, I should not only have been depriving myself of one of the joys of which I had most often dreamed, I should have been fabricating, of my own free will, a love that was artificial and without value, that bore no relation to the truth, whose mysterious and fore-ordained ways I should thus have been declining to follow.

But when I arrived at the Champs-Élysées – and, as at first sight it appeared, was in a position to confront my love, so as to make it undergo the necessary modifications, with its living and independent cause – as soon as I was in the presence of that Gilberte Swann on the sight of whom I had counted to revive the images that my tired memory had lost and could not find again, of that Gilberte Swann with whom I had been playing the day before, and whom I had just been prompted to greet, and then to recognize, by a blind instinct like that which, when we are walking, sets one foot before the other, without giving us time to think what we are doing, then at once it became as though she and the little girl who had inspired my dreams had been two different people. If, for instance, I had retained in my memory overnight two fiery eyes above plump and rosy cheeks, Gilberte's face would now offer me (and with emphasis) something that I distinctly had not remembered, a certain sharpening and prolongation of the nose which, instantaneously associating itself with certain others of her features, assumed the importance of those characteristics which, in natural history, are used to define a species, and transformed her into a little girl of the kind that have sharpened profiles. While I was making my-self ready to take advantage of this long-expected moment, and to surrender myself to the impression of Gilberte which I had prepared beforehand but could no longer find in my head, to an extent which would enable me, during the long hours which I must spend alone, to be certain that it was indeed herself whom I had in mind, that it was indeed my love for her that I was gradually making grow, as a book grows when one is writing it, she threw me a ball; and, like the idealist philosopher whose body takes account of the external world in the reality of which his intellect declines to believe, the same self which had made me salute her before I had identified her now urged me to catch the ball that she tossed to me (as though she had been a companion, with whom I had come to play, and not a sister-soul with whom my soul had come to be united), made me, out of politeness, until the time came when she had to go, address a thousand polite and trivial remarks to her, and so prevented me both from keeping a silence in which I might at last have laid my hand upon the indispensable, escaped idea, and from uttering the words which might have made that definite progress in the course of our love on which I was always obliged to count only for the following afternoon. There was, however, an occasional development. One day, we had gone with Gilberte to the stall of our own special vendor, who was always particularly nice to us, since it was to her that M. Swann used to send for his gingerbread, of which, for reasons of health (he suffered from a racial eczema, and from the constipation of the prophets) he consumed a great quantity, – Gilberte pointed out to me with a laugh two little boys who were like the little artist and the little naturalist in the children's story-books. For one of them would not have a red stick of rock because he preferred the purple, while the other, with tears in his eyes, refused a plum which his nurse was buying for him, because, as he finally explained in passionate tones: 'I want the other plum; it's got a worm in it!' I purchased two ha'penny marbles. With admiring eyes I saw, luminous and imprisoned in a bowl by themselves, the agate marbles which seemed precious to me because they were as fair and smiling as little girls, and because they cost fivepence each. Gilberte, who was given a great deal more pocket money than I ever had, asked me which I thought the prettiest. They were as transparent, as liquid-seeming as life itself. I would not have had her sacrifice a single one of them. I should have liked her to be able to buy them, to liberate them all. Still, I pointed out one that had the same colour as her eyes. Gilberte took it, turned it about until it shone with a ray of gold, fondled it, paid its ransom, but at once handed me her captive, saying: 'Take it; it is for you, I give it to you, keep it to remind yourself of me.'

Another time, being still obsessed by the desire to hear

Berma in classic drama, I had asked her whether she had not
a copy of a pamphlet in which Bergotte spoke of Racine, and
which was now out of print. She had told me to let her know
the exact title of it, and that evening I had sent her a little
telegram, writing on its envelope the name, Gilberte Swann,
which I had so often traced in my exercise books. Next day
she brought me in a parcel tied with pink bows and sealed
with white wax, the pamphlet, a copy of which she had
managed to find. 'You see, it is what you asked me for,' she
said, taking from her muff the telegram that I had sent her.
But in the address on the pneumatic message – which, only
yesterday, was nothing, was merely a 'little blue' that I had
written, and, after a messenger had delivered it to Gilberte's
porter and a servant had taken it to her in her room, had
become a thing without value or distinction, one of the
'little blues' that she had received in the course of the day –
I had difficulty in recognizing the futile, straggling lines of
my own handwriting beneath the circles stamped on it at
the post-office, the inscriptions added in pencil by a postman,
signs of effectual realization, seals of the external world,
violet bands symbolical of life itself, which for the first
time came to espouse, to maintain, to raise, to rejoice my
dream.

And there was another day on which she said to me:
'You know, you may call me "Gilberte"; in any case, I'm
going to call you by your first name. It's too silly not to.'
Yet she continued for a while to address me by the more
formal '*vous*', and, when I drew her attention to this, smiled,
and composing, constructing a phrase like those that are put
into the grammar books of foreign languages with no other
object than to teach us to make use of a new word, ended it
with my Christian name. And when I recalled, later, what
I had felt at the time, I could distinguish the impression of
having been held, for a moment, in her mouth, myself, naked,
without, any longer, any of the social qualifications which
belonged equally to her other companions and, when she used
my surname, to my parents, accessories of which her lips – by
the effort that she made, a little after her father's manner, to

articulate the words to which she wished to give a special value – had the air of stripping, of divesting me, as one peels the skin from a fruit of which one is going to put only the pulp into one's mouth, while her glance, adapting itself to the same new degree of intimacy as her speech, fell on me also more directly, not without testifying to the consciousness, the pleasure, even the gratitude that it felt, accompanying itself with a smile.

But at that actual moment, I was not able to appreciate the worth of these new pleasures. They were given, not by the little girl whom I loved, to me who loved her, but by the other, her with whom I used to play, to my other self, who possessed neither the memory of the true Gilberte, nor the fixed heart which alone could have known the value of a happiness for which it alone had longed. Even after I had returned home I did not taste them, since, every day, the necessity which made me hope that on the morrow I should arrive at the clear, calm, happy contemplation of Gilberte, that she would at last confess her love for me, explaining to me the reasons by which she had been obliged, hitherto, to conceal it, that same necessity forced me to regard the past as of no account, to look ahead of me only, to consider the little advantages that she had given me not in themselves and as if they were self-sufficient, but like fresh rungs of the ladder on which I might set my feet, which were going to allow me to advance a step further and finally to attain the happiness which I had not yet encountered.

If, at times, she showed me these marks of her affection, she troubled me also by seeming not to be pleased to see me, and this happened often on the very days on which I had most counted for the realization of my hopes. I was sure that Gilberte was coming to the Champs-Élysées, and I felt an elation which seemed merely the anticipation of a great happiness when – going into the drawing-room in the morning to kiss Mamma, who was already dressed to go out, the coils of her black hair elaborately built up, and her beautiful hands, plump and white, fragrant still with soap – I had been apprised, by seeing a column of dust standing by itself in the air above the piano, and by hearing a barrel-organ playing, beneath the window, *En revenant de la revue*, that the winter had received, until nightfall, an unexpected, radiant visit from a day of spring. While we sat at luncheon, by opening her window, the lady opposite had sent packing, in the twinkling of an eye, from beside my chair – to sweep in a single stride over the whole width of our dining-room – a sunbeam which had lain down there for its midday rest and returned to continue it there a moment later. At school, during the one o'clock lesson, the sun made me sick with impatience and boredom as it let fall a golden stream that crept to the edge of my desk, like an invitation to the feast at which I could not myself arrive before three o'clock, until the moment when Françoise came to fetch me at the school gate, and we made our way towards the Champs-Élysées through streets decorated with sunlight, dense with people, over which the balconies, detached by the sun and made vaporous, seemed to float in front of the houses like clouds of gold. Alas! in the Champs-Élysées I found no Gilberte; she had not yet arrived. Motionless, on the lawn nurtured by the invisible sun which, here and there, kindled to a flame the point of a blade of grass, while the pigeons that had alighted upon it had the appearance of ancient sculptures which the gardener's pick had heaved to the surface of a hallowed soil, I stood with my eyes fixed on the horizon, expecting at every moment to see appear the form of Gilberte following that of her governess, behind the statue that seemed to be holding out the child, which it had in its arms, and which glistened in the stream of light, to receive benediction from the sun. The old lady who read the *Débats* was sitting on her chair, in her invariable place, and had just accosted a park-keeper, with a friendly wave of her hand towards him as she exclaimed 'What a lovely day!' And when the chair-woman came up to collect her penny, with an infinity of smirks and affectations she folded the ticket away inside her glove, as though it had been a posy of flowers, for which she had sought, in gratitude to the donor, the most becoming place upon her person. When she had found it, she performed a circular movement with her neck, straightened her boa, and fastened upon the collector, as she showed her the end of yellow paper that stuck out over her bare wrist, the bewitching smile with which a woman says to a young man, pointing to her bosom: 'You see, I'm wearing your roses!'

I dragged Françoise, on the way towards Gilberte, as far as the Arc de Triomphe; we did not meet her, and I was returning towards the lawn convinced, now, that she was not coming, when, in front of the wooden horses, the little girl with the sharp voice flung herself upon me: 'Quick, quick, Gilberte's been here a quarter of an hour. She's just going. We've been waiting for you, to make up a prisoner's base.'

While I had been going up the Avenue des Champs-Élysées, Gilberte had arrived by the Rue Boissy-d'Anglas, Mademoiselle having taken advantage of the fine weather to go on some errand of her own; and M. Swann was coming to fetch his daughter. And so it was my fault; I ought not to have strayed from the lawn; for one never knew for certain from what direction Gilberte would appear, whether she would be early or late, and this perpetual tension succeeded in making more impressive not only the Champs-Élysées in their entirety, and the whole span of the afternoon, like a vast expanse of space and time, on every point and at every moment of which it was possible that the form of Gilberte might appear, but also that form itself, since behind its appearance I felt that there lay concealed the reason for which it had shot its arrow into my heart at four o'clock instead of at half past two; crowned with a smart hat, for paying calls, instead of the plain cap, for games; in front of the Ambassadeurs and not between the two puppet-shows; I divined one of those occupations in which I might not follow Gilberte, occupations that forced her to go out or to stay at home, I was in contact with the mystery of her unknown life. It was this mystery, too, which troubled me when, running at the sharp-voiced girl's bidding, so as to begin our game without more delay, I saw Gilberte, so quick and informal with us, make a ceremonious bow to the old lady with the *Débats* (who acknowledged it with 'What a lovely sun! You'd think there was a fire burning') speaking to her with

a shy smile, with an air of constraint which called to my mind
the other little girl that Gilberte must be when at home with
her parents, or with friends of her parents, paying visits, in
all the rest, that escaped me, of her existence. But of that
existence no one gave me so strong an impression as did
M. Swann, who came a little later to fetch his daughter.
That was because he and Mme Swann – inasmuch as their
daughter lived with them, as her lessons, her games, her
friendships depended upon them – contained for me, like
Gilberte, perhaps even more than Gilberte, as befitted subjects that had an all-powerful control over her in whom it
must have had its source, an undefined, an inaccessible quality
of melancholy charm. Everything that concerned them was
on my part the object of so constant a preoccupation that the
days on which, as on this day, M. Swann (whom I had seen
so often, long ago, without his having aroused my curiosity,
when he was still on good terms with my parents) came for
Gilberte to the Champs-Élysées, once the pulsations to which
my heart had been excited by the appearance of his grey hat
and hooded cape had subsided, the sight of him still impressed
me as might that of an historic personage, upon whom one had
just been studying a series of books, and the smallest details
of whose life one learned with enthusiasm. His relations with
the Comte de Paris, which, when I heard them discussed at
Combray, seemed to me unimportant, became now in my
eyes something marvellous, as if no one else had ever known
the House of Orleans; they set him in vivid detachment
against the vulgar background of pedestrians of different
classes who encumbered that particular path in the Champs-
Élysées, in the midst of whom I admired his condescending
to figure without claiming any special deference, which as
it happened none of them dreamed of paying him, so profound was the incognito in which he was wrapped.

He responded politely to the salutations of Gilberte's companions, even to mine, for all that he was no longer on good
terms with my family, but without appearing to know who
I was. (This reminded me that he had constantly seen me in
the country; a memory which I had retained, but kept out

of sight, because, since I had seen Gilberte again, Swann had become to me pre-eminently her father, and no longer the Combray Swann; as the ideas which, nowadays, I made his name connote were different from the ideas in the system of which it was formerly comprised, which I utilized not at all now when I had occasion to think of him, he had become a new, another person; still I attached him by an artificial thread, secondary and transversal, to our former guest; and as nothing had any longer any value for me save in the extent to which my love might profit by it, it was with spasm of shame and of regret at not being able to erase them from my memory that I recaptured the years in which, in the eyes of this same Swann who was at this moment before me in the Champs-Élysées, and to whom, fortunately, Gilberte had perhaps not mentioned my name, I had so often, in the evenings, made myself ridiculous by sending to ask Mamma to come upstairs to my room to say good-night to me, while she was drinking coffee with him and my father and my grand-parents at the table in the garden.) He told Gilberte that she might play one game; he could wait for a quarter of an hour; and, sitting down, just like anyone else, on an iron chair, paid for his ticket with that hand which Philippe VII had so often held in his own, while we began our game upon the lawn, scattering the pigeons, whose beautiful, iridescent bodies (shaped like hearts and, surely, the lilacs of the feathered kingdom) took refuge as in so many sanctuaries, one on the great basin of stone, on which its beak, as it disappeared below the rim, conferred the part, assigned the purpose of offering to the bird in abundance the fruit or grain at which it appeared to be pecking, another on the head of the statue, which it seemed to crown with one of those enamelled objects whose polychrome varies in certain classical works the monotony of the stone, and with an attribute which, when the goddess bears it, entitles her to a particular epithet and makes of her, as a different Christian name makes of a mortal, a fresh divinity.

On one of these sunny days which had not realized my hopes, I had not the courage to conceal my disappointment from Gilberte.

'I had ever so many things to ask you,' I said to her; 'I thought that to-day was going to mean so much in our friendship. And no sooner have you come than you go away! Try to come early to-morrow, so that I can talk to you.'

Her face lighted up and she jumped for joy as she answered: 'To-morrow, you may make up your mind, my dear friend, I shan't come! First of all I've a big luncheon-party; then in the afternoon I am going to a friend's house to see King Theodosius arrive from her windows; won't that be splendid? – and then, next day, I'm going to *Michel Strogoff*, and after that it will soon be Christmas, and the New Year holidays! Perhaps they'll take me south, to the Riviera; won't that be nice? Though I should miss the Christmas-tree here; anyhow, if I do stay in Paris, I shan't be coming here, because I shall be out paying calls with Mamma. Good-bye – there's Papa calling me.'

I returned home with Françoise through streets that were still gay with sunshine, as on the evening of a holiday when the merriment is over. I could scarcely drag my legs along.

'I'm not surprised', said Françoise, 'it's not the right weather for the time of year; it's much too warm. Oh dear, oh dear, to think of all the poor sick people there must be everywhere; you would think that up there, too, everything's got out of order.'

I repeated to myself, stifling my sobs, the words in which Gilberte had given utterance to her joy at the prospect of not coming back, for a long time, to the Champs-Élysées. But already the charm with which, by the mere act of thinking, my mind was filled as soon as it thought of her, the privileged position, unique even if it were painful, in which I was inevitably placed in relation to Gilberte by the contraction of a scar in my mind, had begun to add to that very mark of her indifference something romantic, and in the midst of my tears my lips would shape themselves in a smile which was indeed the timid outline of a kiss. And when the time came for the postman I said to myself, that evening as on every other: 'I am going to have a letter from Gilberte, she is going to tell me, at last, that she has never ceased to love me, and to explain to me the mysterious reason by which she has been forced to conceal her love from me until now, to put on the appearance of being able to be happy without seeing me; the reason for which she has assumed the form of the other Gilberte, who is simply a companion.'

Every evening I would beguile myself into imagining this letter, believing that I was actually reading it, reciting each of its sentences in turn. Suddenly I would stop, in alarm. I had realized that, if I was to receive a letter from Gilberte, it could not, in any case, be this letter, since it was I myself who had just composed it. And from that moment I would strive to keep my thoughts clear of the words which I should have liked her to write to me, from fear lest, by first selecting them myself, I should be excluding just those identical words – the dearest, the most desired – from the field of possible events. Even if, by an almost impossible coincidence, it had been precisely the letter of my invention that Gilberte had addressed to me of her own accord, recognizing my own work in it I should not have had the impression that I was receiving something that had not originated in myself, something real, something new, a happiness external to my mind, independent of my will, a gift indeed from love.

While I waited I read over again a page which, although it had not been written to me by Gilberte, came to me, none the less, from her, that page by Bergotte upon the beauty of the old myths from which Racine drew his inspiration, which (with the agate marble) I always kept within reach. I was touched by my friend's kindness in having procured the book for me; and as everyone is obliged to find some reason for his passion, so much so that he is glad to find in the creature whom he loves qualities which (he has learned by reading or in conversation) are worthy to excite a man's love, that he assimilates them by imitation and makes out of them fresh reasons for his love, even although these qualities be diametrically opposed to those for which his love would have sought, so long as it was spontaneous – as Swann, before my day, had sought to establish the aesthetic basis of Odette's beauty – I, who had at first

loved Gilberte, in Combray days, on account of all the unknown element in her life into which I would fain have
plunged headlong, have undergone reincarnation, discarding
my own separate existence as a thing that no longer mattered, I
thought now, as of an inestimable advantage, that of this, my
own, my too familiar, my contemptible existence Gilberte
might one day become the humble servant, the kindly, the
comforting collaborator, who in the evenings, helping me in
my work, would collate for me the texts of rare pamphlets. As
for Bergotte, that infinitely wise, almost divine old man, because of whom I had first, before I had even seen her, loved
Gilberte, now it was for Gilberte's sake that, chiefly, I loved
him. With as much pleasure as the pages that he had written
about Racine, I studied the wrapper, folded under great seals
of white wax and tied with billows of pink ribbon, in which
she had brought those pages to me. I kissed the agate marble,
which was the better part of my love's heart, the part that was
not frivolous but faithful, and, for all that it was adorned with
the mysterious charm of Gilberte's life, dwelt close beside me,
inhabited my chamber, shared my bed. But the beauty of that
stone, and the beauty also of those pages of Bergotte which I
was glad to associate with the idea of my love for Gilberte, as
if, in the moments when my love seemed no longer to have any
existence, they gave it a kind of consistency, were, I perceived,
anterior to that love, which they in no way resembled; their
elements had been determined by the writer's talent, or by
geological laws, before ever Gilberte had known me, nothing
in book or stone would have been different if Gilberte had not
loved me, and there was nothing, consequently, that authorized
me to read in them a message of happiness. And while my love,
incessantly waiting for the morrow to bring a confession of
Gilberte's love for me, destroyed, unravelled every evening,
the ill-done work of the day, in some shadowed part of my
being was an unknown weaver who would not leave where
they lay the severed threads, but collected and rearranged them
without any thought of pleasing me, or of toiling for my advantage, in the different order which she gave to all her handi-
work. Without any special interest in my love, not beginning

by deciding that I was loved, she placed, side by side, those of Gilberte's actions that had seemed to me inexplicable and her faults which I had excused. Then, one with another, they took on a meaning. It seemed to tell me, this new arrangement, that when I saw Gilberte, instead of coming to me in the Champs-Élysées, going to a party, or on errands with her governess, when I saw her prepared for an absence that would extend over the New Year holidays, I was wrong in thinking, in saying: 'It is because she is frivolous,' or 'easily led'. For she would have ceased to be either if she had loved me, and if she had been forced to obey it would have been with the same despair in her heart that I felt on the days when I did not see her. It showed me further, this new arrangement, that I ought, after all, to know what it was to love, since I loved Gilberte; it drew my attention to the constant anxiety that I had to 'show off' before her, by reason of which I tried to persuade my mother to get for Françoise a waterproof coat and a hat with a blue feather, or, better still, to stop sending with me to the Champs-Élysées an attendant with whom I blushed to be seen (to all of which my mother replied that I was not fair to Françoise, that she was an excellent woman and devoted to us all) and also that sole, exclusive need to see Gilberte, the result of which was that, months in advance, I could think of nothing but how to find out at what date she would be leaving Paris and where she was going, feeling that the most attractive country in the world would be but a place of exile if she were not to be there, and asking only to be allowed to stay for ever in Paris, so long as I might see her in the Champs-Élysées; and it had little difficulty in making me see that neither my anxiety nor my need could be justified by anything in Gilberte's conduct. She, on the contrary, was genuinely fond of her governess, without troubling herself over what I might choose to think about it. It seemed quite natural to her not to come to the Champs-Élysées if she had to go shopping with Mademoiselle, delightful if she had to go out somewhere with her mother. And even supposing that she would ever have allowed me to spend my holidays in the same place as herself, when it came to choosing that place she considered her parents' wishes, a thousand different amusements of which she had been told, and not at all that it should be the place to which my family were proposing to send me. When she assured me (as sometimes happened) that she liked me less than some other of her friends, less than she had liked me the day before, because by my clumsiness I had made her side lose a game, I would beg her pardon, I would beg her to tell me what I must do in order that she should begin again to like me as much as, or more than the rest; I hoped to hear her say that that was already my position; I besought her, as though she had been able to modify her affection for me as she or I chose, to give me pleasure, merely by the words that she would utter, as my good or bad conduct should deserve. Was I, then, not yet aware that what I felt, myself, for her, depended neither upon her actions nor upon my desires?

It showed me finally, the new arrangement planned by my unseen weaver, that, if we find ourselves hoping that the actions of a person who has hitherto caused us anxiety may prove not to have been sincere, they shed in their wake a light which our hopes are powerless to extinguish, a light to which, rather than to our hopes, we must put the question, what will be that person's actions on the morrow.

These new counsels, my love listened and heard them; they persuaded it that the morrow would not be different from all the days that had gone before; that Gilberte's feeling for me, too long established now to be capable of alteration, was indifference; that in my friendship with Gilberte, it was I alone who loved. 'That is true,' my love responded, 'there is nothing more to be made of that friendship. It will not alter now.' And so the very next day (unless I were to wait for a public holiday, if there was one approaching, some anniversary, the New Year, perhaps, one of those days which are not like other days, on which time starts afresh, casting aside the heritage of the past, declining its legacy of sorrows) I would appeal to Gilberte to terminate our old and to join me in laying the foundations of a new friendship.

*

479

I had always, within reach, a plan of Paris, which, because I could see drawn on it the street in which M. and Mme Swann lived, seemed to me to contain a secret treasure. And to please myself, as well as by a sort of chivalrous loyalty, in any connexion or with no relevance at all, I would repeat the name of that street until my father, not being, like my mother and grandmother, in the secret of my love, would ask: 'But why are you always talking about that street? There's nothing wonderful about it. It is an admirable street to live in because it's only a few minutes' walk from the Bois, but there are a dozen other streets just the same.'

I made every effort to introduce the name of Swann into my conversation with my parents; in my own mind, of course, I never ceased to murmur it; but I needed also to hear its exquisite sound, and to make myself play that chord, the voiceless rendering of which did not suffice me. Moreover, that name of Swann, with which I had for so long been familiar, was to me now (as happens at times to people suffering from aphasia, in the case of the most ordinary words) the name of something new. It was for ever present in my mind, which could not, however, grow accustomed to it. I analysed it, I spelt it; its orthography came to me as a surprise. And with its familiarity it had simultaneously lost its innocence. The pleasure that I derived from the sound of it I felt to be so guilty, that it seemed to me as though the others must read my thoughts, and would change the conversation if I endeavoured to guide it in that direction. I fell back upon subjects which still brought me into touch with Gilberte, I eternally repeated the same words, and it was no use my knowing that they were but words – words uttered in her absence, which she could not hear, words without virtue in themselves, repeating what were, indeed, facts, but powerless to modify them – for still it seemed to me that by dint of handling, of stirring in this way everything that had reference to Gilberte, I might perhaps make emerge from it something that would bring me happiness. I told my parents again that Gilberte was very fond of her governess, as if the statement, when repeated for the hundredth time, would at last have the effect of making Gilberte suddenly burst into the room, come to live with us for ever. I had already sung the praises of the old lady who read the *Débats* (I had hinted to my parents that she must at least be an Ambassador's widow, if not actually a Highness) and I continued to descant on her beauty, her splendour, her nobility, until the day on which I mentioned that, by what I had heard Gilberte call her, she appeared to be a Mme Blatin.

'Oh, now I know whom you mean,' cried my mother, while I felt myself grow red all over with shame. 'On guard! on guard! – as your grandfather says. And so it's she that you think so wonderful? Why, she's perfectly horrible, and always has been. She's the widow of a bailiff. You can't remember, when you were little, all the trouble I used to have to avoid her at your gymnastic lessons, where she was always trying to get hold of me – I didn't know the woman, of course – to tell me that you were "much too nice-looking for a boy". She has always had an insane desire to get to know people, and she must be quite insane, as I have always thought, if she really does know Mme Swann. For even if she does come of very common people, I have never heard anything said against her character. But she must always be forcing herself upon strangers. She is, really, a horrible woman, frightfully vulgar, and besides, she is always creating awkward situations.'

As for Swann, in my attempts to resemble him, I spent the whole time, when I was at table, in drawing my finger along my nose and in rubbing my eyes. My father would exclaim: 'The child's a perfect idiot, he's becoming quite impossible.' More than all else I should have liked to be as bald as Swann. He appeared to me to be a creature so extraordinary that I found it impossible to believe that people whom I knew and often saw knew him also, and that in the course of the day anyone might run against him. And once my mother, while she was telling us, as she did every evening at dinner, where she had been and what she had done that afternoon, merely by the words: 'By the way, guess whom I saw at the Trois Quartiers – at the umbrella counter – Swann!' caused to burst open in the midst of her narrative (an arid desert to me) a mystic blossom. What a melancholy satisfaction to learn that, that very afternoon, threading through the crowd his supernatural form, Swann had gone to buy an umbrella. Among the events of the day, great and small, but all equally unimportant, that one alone aroused in me those peculiar vibrations by which my love for Gilberte was invariably stirred. My father complained that I took no interest in anything, because I did not listen while he was speaking of the political developments that might follow the visit of King Theodosius, at that moment in France as the nation's guest and (it was hinted) ally. And yet how intensely interested I was to know whether Swann had been wearing his hooded cape!

'Did you speak to him?' I asked.

'Why, of course I did,' answered my mother, who always seemed afraid lest, were she to admit that we were not on the warmest of terms with Swann, people would seek to reconcile us more than she cared for, in view of the existence of Mme Swann, whom she did not wish to know. 'It was he who came up and spoke to me. I hadn't seen him.'

'Then you haven't quarrelled?'

'Quarrelled? What on earth made you think that we had quarrelled?' she briskly parried, as though I had cast doubt on the fiction of her friendly relations with Swann, and was planning an attempt to 'bring them together'.

'He might be cross with you for never asking him here.'

'One isn't obliged to ask everyone to one's house, you know; has he ever asked me to his? I don't know his wife.'

'But he used often to come, at Combray.'

'I should think he did! He used to come at Combray, and now, in Paris, he has something better to do, and so have I. But I can promise you, we didn't look in the least like people who had quarrelled. We were kept waiting there for some time, while they brought him his parcel. He asked after you; he told me you had been playing with his daughter –' my mother went on, amazing me with the portentous revelation of my own existence in Swann's mind; far more than that, of my existence in so complete, so material a form that when I stood before him, trembling with love, in the Champs-Élysées, he had known my name, and who my mother was, and had been able to blend with my quality as his daughter's playmate certain facts with regard to my grandparents and their connexions, the place in which we lived, certain details of our past life, all of which I myself perhaps did not know. But my mother did not seem to have noticed anything particularly attractive in that counter at the Trois Quartiers where she had represented to Swann, at that moment in which he caught sight of her, a definite person with whom he had sufficient memories in common to impel him to come up to her and to speak.

Nor did either she or my father seem to find any occasion now to mention Swann's family, the grandparents of Gilberte, or to use the title of stockbroker, topics as which nothing else gave me so keen a pleasure. My imagination had isolated and consecrated in the social Paris a certain family, just as it had set apart in the structural Paris a certain house, on whose porch it had fashioned sculptures and made its windows precious. But these ornaments I alone had eyes to see. Just as my father and mother looked upon the house in which Swann lived as one that closely resembled the other houses built at the same period in the neighbourhood of the Bois, so Swann's family seemed to them to be in the same category as many other families of stockbrokers. Their judgement was more or less favourable according to the extent to which the family in question shared in merits that were common to the rest of the universe, and there was about it nothing that they could call unique. What, on the other hand, they did appreciate in the Swanns they found in equal, if not in greater measure elsewhere. And so, after admitting that the house was in a good position, they would go on to speak of some other house that was in a better, but had nothing to do with Gilberte, or of financiers on a larger scale than her grandfather had been; and if they had appeared, for a moment, to be of my opinion, that was a mistake which was very soon corrected. For in order to distinguish in all Gilberte's surroundings, an indefinable quality analogous, in the scale of emotions, to what in the scale of colours is called infra-red, a supplementary sense of perception was required, with which love, for the time being, had endowed me; and this my parents lacked.

On the days when Gilberte had warned me that she would not be coming to the Champs-Élysées, I would try to arrange my walks so that I should be brought into some kind of contact with her. Sometimes I would lead Françoise on a pilgrimage to the house in which the Swanns lived, making her repeat to me unendingly all that she had learned from the governess with regard to Mme Swann. 'It seems, she puts great faith in medals. She would never think of starting on a journey if she had heard an owl hoot, or the death-watch in the wall, or if she had seen a cat at midnight, or if the furniture had creaked. Oh yes! she's a most religious lady, she is!' I was so madly in love with Gilberte that if, on our way, I caught sight of their old butler taking the dog out, my emotion would bring me to a standstill, I would fasten on his white whiskers eyes that melted with passion. And Françoise would rouse me with: 'What's wrong with you now, child?' and we would continue on our way until we reached their gate, where a porter, different from every other porter in the world, and saturated, even to the braid on his livery, with the same melancholy charm that I had felt to be latent in the name of Gilberte, looked at me as though he knew that I was one of those whose natural unworthiness would for ever prevent them from penetrating into the mysteries of the life inside, which it was his duty to guard, and over which the ground-floor windows appeared conscious of being protectingly closed, with far less resemblance, between the nobly sweeping arches of their muslin curtains, to any other windows in the world than to Gilberte's glancing eyes. On other days we would go along the boulevards, and I would post myself at the corner of the Rue Duphot; I had heard that Swann was often to be seen passing there, on his way to the dentist's; and my imagination so far differentiated Gilberte's father from the rest of humanity, his presence in the midst of a crowd of real people introduced among them so miraculous an element, that even before we reached the Madeleine I would be trembling with emotion at the thought that I was approaching a street from which that supernatural apparition might at any moment burst upon me unawares.

But most often of all, on days when I was not to see Gilberte, as I had heard that Mme Swann walked almost every day along the Allée des Acacias, round the big lake, and in the Allée de la Reine Marguerite, I would guide Françoise in the direction of the Bois de Boulogne. It was to me like one of those zoological gardens in which one sees assembled together a variety of flora, and contrasted effects in landscape; where from a hill one passes to a grotto, a meadow, rocks, a stream, a trench, another hill, a marsh, but knows that they are there only to enable the hippopotamus, zebra, crocodile, rabbit, bear, and heron to disport themselves in a natural or a picturesque setting; this, the Bois, equally complex, uniting a multitude of little worlds, distinct and separate – placing a stage set with red trees, American oaks, like an experimental forest in Virginia, next to a fir-wood by the edge of the lake, or to a forest grove from which would suddenly emerge, in her lissom covering of furs, with the large, appealing eyes of a dumb animal, a hastening walker – was the Garden of Woman; and like the myrtle-alley in the Aeneid, planted for their delight with trees of one kind only, the Allée des Acacias was thronged by the famous Beauties of the day. As, from a long way off, the sight of the jutting crag from which it dives into the pool thrills with joy the children who know that they are going to behold the seal, long before I reached the acacia-alley, their fragrance, scattered abroad, would make me feel that I was approaching the incomparable presence of a vegetable personality, strong and tender; then, as I drew near, the sight of their topmost branches, their lightly tossing foliage, in its easy grace, its coquettish outline, its delicate fabric, over which hundreds of flowers were laid, like winged and throbbing colonies of precious insects; and finally their name itself, feminine, indolent, and seductive, made my heart beat, but with a social longing, like those waltzes which remind us only of the names of the fair dancers, called aloud as they entered the ball-room. I had been told that I should see in the alley certain women of fashion, who, in spite of their not all having

485

husbands, were constantly mentioned in conjunction with Mme Swann, but most often by their professional names; – their new names, when they had any, being but a sort of incognito, a veil which those who would speak of them were careful to draw aside, so as to make themselves understood. Thinking that Beauty – in the order of feminine elegance – was governed by occult laws into the knowledge of which they had been initiated, and that they had the power to realize it, I accepted before seeing them, like the truth of a coming revelation, the appearance of their clothes, of their carriages and horses, of a thousand details among which I placed my faith as in an inner soul which gave the cohesion of a work of art to that ephemeral and changing pageant. But it was Mme Swann whom I wished to see, and I waited for her to go past, as deeply moved as though she were Gilberte, whose parents, saturated, like everything in her environment, with her own special charm, excited in me as keen a passion as she did herself, indeed a still more painful disturbance (since their point of contact with her was that intimate, that internal part of her life which was hidden from me) and furthermore, for I very soon learned, as we shall see in due course, that they did not like my playing with her, that feeling of veneration which we always have for those who hold, and exercise without restraint, the power to do us an injury.

I assigned the first place, in the order of aesthetic merit and of social grandeur, to simplicity, when I saw Mme Swann on foot, in a 'polonaise' of plain cloth, a little toque on her head trimmed with a pheasant's wing, a bunch of violets in her bosom, hastening along the Allée des Acacias as if it had been merely the shortest way back to her own house, and acknowledging with a rapid glance the courtesy of the gentlemen in carriages, who, recognizing her figure at a distance, were raising their hats to her and saying to one another that there was never anyone so well turned out as she. But instead of simplicity it was to ostentation that I must assign the first place if, after I had compelled Françoise, who could hold out no longer, and complained that her legs were 'giving'

beneath her, to stroll up and down with me for another hour,
I saw at length, emerging from the Porte Dauphine, figuring
for me a royal dignity, the passage of a sovereign, an impression such as no real Queen has ever since been able to give
me, because my notion of their power has been less vague, and
more founded upon experience – borne along by the flight of
a pair of fiery horses, slender and shapely as one sees them in
the drawings of Constantin Guys, carrying on its box an
enormous coachman, furred like a cossack, and by his side a
diminutive groom, like Toby, 'the late Beaudenord's tiger,' I
saw – or rather I felt its outlines engraved upon my heart by a
clean and killing stab – a matchless victoria, built rather high,
and hinting, through the extreme modernity of its appointments, at the forms of an earlier day, deep down in which lay
negligently back Mme Swann, her hair, now quite pale with
one grey lock, girt with a narrow band of flowers, usually
violets, from which floated down long veils, a lilac parasol in
her hand, on her lips an ambiguous smile in which I read only
the benign condescension of Majesty, though it was pre-
eminently the enticing smile of the courtesan, which she
graciously bestowed upon the men who bowed to her. That
smile was, in reality, saying to one: 'Oh yes, I do remember
quite well; it was wonderful!' to another: 'How I should
have loved to! We were unfortunate!', to a third: 'Yes, if you
like! I must just keep in the line for a minute, then as soon as
I can I will break away.' When strangers passed she still
allowed to linger about her lips a lazy smile, as though she
expected or remembered some friend, which made them say:
'What a lovely woman!' And for certain men only she had a
sour, strained, shy, cold smile which meant: 'Yes, you old
goat, I know that you've got a tongue like a viper, that you
can't keep quiet for a moment. But do you suppose that I care
what you say?' Coquelin passed, talking, in a group of listening friends, and with a sweeping wave of his hand bade a
theatrical good day to the people in the carriages. But I
thought only of Mme Swann, and pretended to have not yet
seen her, for I knew that, when she reached the pigeon-
shooting ground, she would tell her coachman to 'break

away' and to stop the carriage, so that she might come back on foot. And on days when I felt that I had the courage to pass close by her I would drag Françoise off in that direction; until the moment came when I saw Mme Swann, letting trail behind her the long train of her lilac skirt, dressed, as the populace imagine queens to be dressed, in rich attire such as no other woman might wear, lowering her eyes now and then to study the handle of her parasol, paying scant attention to the passers-by, as though the important thing for her, her one object in being there was to take exercise, without thinking that she was seen, and that every head was turned towards her. Sometimes, however, when she had looked back to call her dog to her, she would cast, almost imperceptibly, a sweeping glance round about.

Those even who did not know her were warned by something exceptional, something beyond the normal in her – or perhaps by a telepathic suggestion such as would move an ignorant audience to a frenzy of applause when Berma was 'sublime' – that she must be someone well known. They would ask one another, 'Who is she?', or sometimes would interrogate a passing stranger, or would make a mental note of how she was dressed so as to fix her identity, later, in the mind of a friend better informed than themselves, who would at once enlighten them. Another pair, half-stopping in their walk, would exchange:

'You know who that is? Mme Swann! That conveys nothing to you? Odette de Crécy, then?'

'Odette de Crécy! Why, I thought as much. Those great, sad eyes ... But I say, you know, she can't be as young as she was once, eh? I remember, I had her on the day that MacMahon went.'

'I shouldn't remind her of it, if I were you. She is now Mme Swann, the wife of a gentleman in the Jockey Club, a friend of the Prince of Wales. Apart from that, though, she is wonderful still.'

'Oh, but you ought to have known her then; Gad, she was lovely! She lived in a very odd little house with a lot of Chinese stuff. I remember, we were bothered all the time by the newsboys, shouting outside; in the end she made me get up and go.'

Without listening to these memories, I could feel all about her the indistinct murmur of fame. My heart leaped with impatience when I thought that a few seconds must still elapse before all these people, among whom I was dismayed not to find a certain mulatto banker who (or so I felt) had a contempt for me, were to see the unknown youth, to whom they had not, so far, been paying the slightest attention, salute (without knowing her, it was true, but I thought that I had sufficient authority since my parents knew her husband and I was her daughter's playmate) this woman whose reputation for beauty, for misconduct, and for elegance was universal. But I was now close to Mme Swann; I pulled off my hat with so lavish, so prolonged a gesture that she could not repress a smile. People laughed. As for her, she had never seen me with Gilberte, she did not know my name, but I was for her – like one of the keepers in the Bois, like the boatman, or the ducks on the lake, to which she threw scraps of bread – one of the minor personages, familiar, nameless, as devoid of individual character as a stage hand in a theatre, of her daily walks abroad.

On certain days when I had missed her in the Allée des Acacias I would be so fortunate as to meet her in the Allée de la Reine Marguerite, where women went who wished to be alone, or to appear to be wishing to be alone; she would not be alone for long, being soon overtaken by some man or other, often in a grey 'tile' hat, whom I did not know, and who would talk to her for some time, while their two carriages crawled behind.

*

That sense of the complexity of the Bois de Boulogne which made it an artificial place and, in the zoological or mythological sense of the word, a Garden, I captured again, this year, as I crossed it on my way to Trianon, on one of those mornings, early in November, when in Paris, if we stay indoors, being so near and yet prevented from witnessing the transformation scene of autumn, which is drawing so rapidly to a close without our assistance, we feel a regret for the fallen leaves that becomes a fever, and may even keep us awake at night. Into my closed room they had been drifting already for a month, summoned there by my desire to see them, slipping between my thoughts and the object, whatever it might be, upon which I was trying to concentrate them, whirling in front of me like those brown spots that sometimes, whatever we may be looking at, will seem to be dancing or swimming before our eyes. And on that morning, not hearing the splash of the rain as on the previous days, seeing the smile of fine weather at the corners of my drawn curtains, as from the corners of closed lips may escape the secret of their happiness, I had felt that I could actually see those yellow leaves, with the light shining through them, in their supreme beauty; and being no more able to restrain myself from going to look at the trees than, in my childhood's days, when the wind howled in the chimney, I had been able to resist the longing to visit the sea, I had risen and left the house to go to Trianon, passing through the Bois de Boulogne. It was the hour and the season in which the Bois seems, perhaps, most multiform, not only because it is then most divided, but because it is divided in a different way. Even in the unwooded parts, where the horizon is large, here and there against the background of a dark and distant mass of trees, now leafless or still keeping their summer foliage unchanged, a double row of orange-red chestnuts seemed, as in a picture just begun, to be the only thing painted, so far, by an artist who had not yet laid any colour on the rest, and to be offering their cloister, in full daylight, for the casual exercise of the human figures that would be added to the picture later on.

Farther off, at a place where the trees were still all green, one alone, small, stunted, lopped, but stubborn in its resistance, was tossing in the breeze an ugly mane of red. Elsewhere, again, might be seen the first awakening of this Maytime of the leaves, and those of an ampelopsis, a smiling miracle, like a red hawthorn flowering in winter, had that very morning all 'come out', so to speak, in blossom. And the Bois had the temporary, unfinished, artificial look of a nursery garden or a park in which, either for some botanic purpose or in preparation for a festival, there have been embedded among the trees of commoner growth, which have not yet been uprooted and transplanted elsewhere, a few rare specimens, with fantastic foliage, which seem to be clearing all round themselves an empty space, making room, giving air, diffusing light. Thus it was the time of year at which the Bois de Boulogne displays more separate characteristics, assembles more distinct elements in a composite whole than at any other. It was also the time of day. In places where the trees still kept their leaves, they seemed to have undergone an alteration of their substance from the point at which they were touched by the sun's light, still, at this hour in the morning, almost horizontal, as it would be again, a few hours later, at the moment when, just as dusk began, it would flame up like a lamp, project afar over the leaves a warm and artificial glow, and set ablaze the few topmost boughs of a tree that would itself remain unchanged, a sombre incombustible candelabrum beneath its flaming crest. At one spot the light grew solid as a brick wall, and like a piece of yellow Persian masonry, patterned in blue, daubed coarsely upon the sky the leaves of the chestnuts; at another, it cut them off from the sky towards which they stretched out their curling, golden fingers. Half-way up the trunk of a tree draped with wild vine, the light had grafted and brought to blossom, too dazzling to be clearly distinguished, an enormous posy, of red flowers apparently, perhaps of a new variety of carnation. The different parts of the Bois, so easily confounded in summer in the density and monotony of their universal green, were now clearly divided. A patch of brightness indicated the approach to almost every one of them, or else a splendid mass of foliage stood out before it like an oriflamme. I could make out, as on a coloured map, Armenonville, the Pré Catalan, Madrid, the Race-course, and the shore of the lake. Here and there would appear some meaningless erection, a sham grotto, a mill, for which the trees made room by drawing away from it, or which was borne upon the soft green platform of a grassy lawn. I could feel that the Bois was not really a wood,

that it existed for a purpose alien to the life of its trees; my
sense of exaltation was due not only to admiration of the
autumn tints but to a bodily desire. Ample source of a joy
which the heart feels at first without being conscious of its
cause, without understanding that it results from no external
impulse! Thus I gazed at the trees with an unsatisfied longing
which went beyond them and, without my knowledge,
directed itself towards that masterpiece of beautiful strolling
women which the trees enframed for a few hours every day.
I walked towards the Allée des Acacias. I passed through
forest groves in which the morning light, breaking them into
new sections, lopped and trimmed the trees, united different
trunks in marriage, made nosegays of their branches. It would
skilfully draw towards it a pair of trees; making deft use of
the sharp chisel of light and shade, it would cut away from
each of them half of its trunk and branches, and, weaving
together the two halves that remained, would make of them
either a single pillar of shade, defined by the surrounding
light, or a single luminous phantom whose artificial, quivering contour was encompassed in a network of inky shadows.
When a ray of sunshine gilded the highest branches, they
seemed, soaked and still dripping with a sparkling moisture,
to have emerged alone from the liquid, emerald-green atmosphere in which the whole grove was plunged as though
beneath the sea. For the trees continued to live by their own
vitality, and when they had no longer any leaves, that vitality
gleamed more brightly still from the nap of green velvet that
carpeted their trunks, or in the white enamel of the globes of
mistletoe that were scattered all the way up to the topmost
branches of the poplars, rounded as are the sun and moon in
Michelangelo's 'Creation'. But, forced for so many years
now, by a sort of grafting process, to share the life of feminine
humanity, they called to my mind the figure of the dryad,
the fair worldling, swiftly walking, brightly coloured, whom
they sheltered with their branches as she passed beneath them,
and obliged to acknowledge, as they themselves acknowledged, the power of the season; they recalled to me the happy
days when I was young and had faith, when I would hasten

eagerly to the spots where masterpieces of female elegance would be incarnate for a few moments beneath the unconscious, accommodating boughs. But the beauty for which the firs and acacias of the Bois de Boulogne made me long, more disquieting in that respect than the chestnuts and lilacs of Trianon which I was going to see, was not fixed somewhere outside myself in the relics of an historical period, in works of art, in a little temple of love at whose door was piled an oblation of autumn leaves ribbed with gold. I reached the shore of the lake; I walked on as far as the pigeon-shooting ground. The idea of perfection which I had within me I had bestowed, in that other time, upon the height of a victoria, upon the raking thinness of those horses, frenzied and light as wasps upon the wing, with bloodshot eyes like the cruel steeds of Diomed, which now, smitten by a desire to see again what I had once loved, as ardent as the desire that had driven me, many years before, along the same paths, I wished to see renewed before my eyes at the moment when Mme Swann's enormous coachman, supervised by a groom no bigger than his fist, and as infantile as Saint George in the picture, endeavoured to curb the ardour of the flying, steel tipped pinions with which they thundered along the ground. Alas! there was nothing now but motor-cars driven each by a moustached mechanic, with a tall footman towering by his side. I wished to hold before my bodily eyes, that I might know whether they were indeed as charming as they appeared to the eyes of memory, little hats, so low-crowned as to seem no more than garlands about the brows of women. All the hats now were immense, covered with fruits and flowers and all manner of birds. In place of the lovely gowns in which Mme Swann walked like a Queen, appeared Greco-Saxon tunics, with Tanagra folds, or sometimes, in the Directoire style, 'Liberty chiffons' sprinkled with flowers like sheets of wallpaper. On the heads of the gentlemen who might have been eligible to stroll with Mme Swann in the Allée de la Reine Marguerite, I found not the grey 'tile' hats of old, nor any other kind. They walked the Bois bare-headed. And seeing all these new elements of the spectacle, I had no longer the faith which, applied to them, would have given them consistency, unity, life; they passed in a scattered sequence before me, at random, without reality, containing in themselves no beauty that my eyes might have endeavoured, as in the old days, to extract from them and to compose in a picture. They were just women, in whose elegance I had no belief, and whose clothes seemed to me unimportant. But when a belief vanishes, there survives it – more and more ardently, so as to cloak the absence of the power, now lost to us, of imparting reality to new phenomena – an idolatrous attachment to the old things which our belief in them did once animate, as if it was in that belief and not in ourselves that the divine spark resided, and as if our present incredulity had a contingent cause – the death of the gods.

'Oh, horrible!' I exclaimed to myself. 'Does anyone really imagine that these motor-cars are as smart as the old carriage-and-pair? I dare say, I am too old now – but I was not intended for a world in which women shackle themselves in garments that are not even made of cloth. To what purpose shall I walk among these trees if there is nothing left now of the assembly that used to meet beneath the delicate tracery of reddening leaves, if vulgarity and fatuity have supplanted the exquisite thing that once their branches framed? Oh, horrible! My consolation is to think of the women whom I have known, in the past, now that there is no standard left of elegance. But how can the people who watch these dreadful creatures hobble by, beneath hats on which have been heaped the spoils of aviary or garden-bed – how can they imagine the charm that there was in the sight of Mme Swann, crowned with a close-fitting lilac bonnet, or with a tiny hat from which rose stiffly above her head a single iris?' Could I ever have made them understand the emotion that I used to feel on winter mornings, when I met Mme Swann on foot, in an otter-skin coat, with a woollen cap from which stuck out two blade-like partridge-feathers, but enveloped also in the deliberate, artificial warmth of her own house, which was suggested by nothing more than the bunch of violets crushed into her bosom, whose flowering, vivid and blue against the grey sky, the freezing air, the naked boughs, had the same charming effect of using the season and the weather merely as a setting, and of living actually in a human atmosphere, in the atmosphere of this woman, as had in the vases and beaupots of her drawing-room, beside the blazing fire, in front of the silk-covered sofa, the flowers that looked out through closed windows at the falling snow? But it would not have sufficed me that the costumes alone should still have been the same as in those distant years. Because of the solidarity that binds together the different parts of a general impression, parts that our memory keeps in a balanced whole, of which we are not permitted to subtract or to decline any fraction, I should have liked to be able to pass the rest of the day with one of those women, over a cup of tea, in a little house with dark-painted walls (as Mme Swann's were still in the year after that in which the first part of this story ends) against which would glow the orange flame, the red combustion, the pink and white flickering of her chrysanthemums in the twilight of a November evening, in moments similar to those in which (as we shall see) I had not managed to discover the pleasures for which I longed. But now, albeit they had led to nothing, those moments struck me as having been charming enough in themselves. I sought to find them again as I remembered them. Alas! there was nothing now but flats decorated in the Louis XVI style, all white paint, with hortensias in blue enamel. Moreover, people did not return to Paris, now, until much later. Mme Swann would have written to me, from a country house, that she would not be in town before February, had I asked her to reconstruct for me the elements of that memory which I felt to belong to a distant era, to a date in time towards which it was forbidden me to ascend again the fatal slope, the elements of that longing which had become, itself, as inaccessible as the pleasure that it had once vainly pursued. And I should have required also that they were the same women, those whose costume interested me because, at a time when I still had faith, my imagination had individualized them and had provided each of them with a legend. Alas! in the acacia-avenue – the myrtle-alley

- I did see some of them again, grown old, no more now than grim spectres of what once they had been, wandering to and fro, in desperate search of heaven knew what, through the Virgilian groves. They had long fled, and still I stood vainly questioning the deserted paths. The sun's face was hidden. Nature began again to reign over the Bois, from which had vanished all trace of the idea that it was the Elysian Garden of Woman; above the gimcrack windmill the real sky was grey; the wind wrinkled the surface of the Grand Lac in little wavelets, like a real lake; large birds passed swiftly over the Bois, as over a real wood, and with shrill cries perched, one after another, on the great oaks which, beneath their Druidical crown, and with Dodonaic majesty, seemed to proclaim the unpeopled vacancy of this estranged forest, and helped me to understand how paradoxical it is to seek in reality for the pictures that are stored in one's memory, which must inevitably lose the charm that comes to them from memory itself and from their not being apprehended by the senses. The reality that I had known no longer existed. It sufficed that Mme Swann did not appear, in the same attire and at the same moment, for the whole avenue to be altered. The places that we have known belong now only to the little world of space on which we map them for our own convenience. None of them was ever more than a thin slice, held between the contiguous impressions that composed our life at that time; remembrance of a particular form is but regret for a particular moment; and houses, roads, avenues are as fugitive, alas, as the years.